SEATTLE

*Bodies Are Mended and Hearts Healed
in Four Complete Novels of Romance*

Colleen L. Reece

BARBOUR BOOKS

An Imprint of Barbour Publishing, Inc.

Lamp in Darkness ©1994 by Connie Loraine
Flickering Flames ©1995 by Connie Loraine
A Kindled Spark ©1996 by Colleen L. Reece
Hearth of Fire ©1998 by Barbour Publishing

Cover photo: © Corbis

ISBN 1-58660-551-8

All Scripture quotations, unless otherwise noted, are taken from the King James Version of the Bible.

Scripture taken from the HOLY BIBLE, NEW INTERNATIONAL VERSION®. NIV®. copyright © 1973, 1978, 1984 by International Bible Society. Used by permission of Zondervan Publishing House. All rights reserved.

Published by Barbour Books, an imprint of Barbour Publishing, Inc., P.O. Box 719, Uhrichsville, Ohio 44683, www.barbourbooks.com.

 Member of the
Evangelical Christian
Publishers Association

Printed in the United States of America.
5 4 3 2

COLLEEN L. REECE

Colleen learned to read beneath the rays of a kerosene lamp. The kitchen, dining room, and her bedroom in her home near the small logging town of Darrington, Washington, were once a one-room schoolhouse where her mother taught all eight grades!

An abundance of love for God and each other outweighed the lack of electricity or running water and provided the basis for many of Colleen's 135 books. Her rigid "refuse to compromise" stance has helped sell more than 3 million copies that spread the good news of repentance, forgiveness, and salvation through Christ.

Colleen helped launch Barbour Publishing's Romance Reader flip books and the American Adventure series and had her own Juli Scott Super Sleuth Christian teen mystery series. Colleen is most well-known for helping to launch **Heartsong Presents** in 1992, for which she has been awarded Favorite Author in numerous Reader's Polls. In 1998, Colleen was inducted into the Heartsong Hall of Fame in recognition for her contribution to Heartsong's success.

The first two titles in this series of "Seattle" stories was first written for **Heartsong Presents** under Colleen's pen name of Connie Loraine.

Her personal creed: simply to help make the world a better place because she lived.

You may write to Colleen c/o Barbour Publishing, Inc., P.O. Box 719, Uhrichsville, Ohio 44683.

LAMP IN DARKNESS

Prologue

S eattle fog curled into the city's streets like a kitten twined around a beloved owner's legs. Wisps and drifts softened streetlights and muted brilliant neat piles of autumn leaves waiting to be gathered and recycled. The mournful howl of a Puget Sound ferry coming in from Bainbridge Island added an eerie touch and reminded Seattle's inhabitants that Halloween lurked just a few days away.

Nicholas Fairchild stood at the window of his clifftop mansion and surveyed the scene. Some of the night's loneliness crept into his soul. Sixty-five, still vigorous and one of the wealthiest men in Washington State, his mood matched the fog, despite a softly lit, luxurious room and the cheerful flames of a gas log fireplace. His lips twisted. Pollution alerts had banned the use of wood fires. How he missed seeing great logs burning in the huge fireplace, their sweet-smelling smoke scenting his home. Progress to many people and the need for clean air meant sacrificing some things for the good of many.

Nicholas turned from the window and sharply closed the custom draperies, but he could not shut out the feeling of desolation he carried or his own personal ghosts. Always one to go to the crux of a problem, he sat down in a leather chair, stared into the small fire and into himself. "God, I've spent all my life amassing a fortune. I'm respected for working hard, being honest, and refusing to take advantage of others. Am I feeling this way just because of the fog? Or are You trying to tell me something?" He shifted his weight, reached for a switch, and noiselessly shut off all the lights. A rosy glow from the fire painted his gray hair auburn and showed the planes and hollows of his not handsome, yet interesting, face with its changing expressions.

Perhaps if he had married—Nicholas shook his head. The only woman he had ever cared for had died before they could share their dreams. His sensitive mouth compressed into a grim line. Did all men who reached the top find it this lonely? How many years lay ahead and what would he do with them?

Nicholas turned to his unfailing source of strength. "If there is something You want me to do, Lord, more than what I already am, please guide me. In Jesus' name, amen."

After a long moment he stood and slowly trod the thick carpeting to his bedroom. His gaze turned to the bookcase that covered an entire wall and provided an alternative to sleepless nights. He hesitated, then selected Catherine Marshall's tribute to her husband, who had been chaplain of the United States Senate in the late '40s, as well as a preacher like few others. *The Best of Peter Marshall*'s pages fell open to a story Nicholas had read and pondered many times: "By Invitation of Jesus."

Nicholas showered, made ready for bed, and began to read, feeling he had unexpectedly paid a visit to old friends.

How alike he was to that fictional man in the other Washington, sitting in his comfortable home with a rising wind! How similar their social positions, their desire to live godly lives, their realization that life should be more than money, power, or prestige. Nicholas caught his breath as if he had never heard the story. He followed the account of the other man feeling a presence come into the room; he had realized how far short his banquets and dinners fell from the one described in Luke 14, the one where Jesus told His hearers to call to a feast the poor, maimed, lame, and blind, not those who could repay the giver. His heart again thrilled to the invitation of the man in the story, the bidding that began, *JESUS OF NAZARETH requests the honor of your presence. . . .*

Nicholas closed the book, needing no more reading to refresh his memory of a story he knew by heart. The Washington man had literally followed Jesus' command. He had filled his mansion with those of the streets, those who needed him—and Christ—most.

A familiar stirring quickened the troubled man's weary mind and swept boredom and sadness from his heart. He rose and crossed to the window, expecting to find the fog had lifted. It had not. Thick and gray, it blanketed the city except for the spire of a large cathedral not far from the Fairchild mansion. Skillfully lighted, it pointed the way to heaven for those who took the time to look up and beyond earth and its woes.

Nicholas watched the spire until fatigue sent him to bed and sleep. Did the fog, the story, and the spire combine with his prayer for guidance, his longing to make the latter years even more of a witness to his risen Lord than his earlier days? He never knew. He only knew that in his dreams he wandered fogged-in Seattle streets until he reached the stone steps of the nearby cathedral. Figures, huddled and erect, proud and beaten, grouped on the steps and clutched at his clothing as he struggled up through the crowd trying to ascend the eternal staircase. His dream shifted. The steeple vanished, but the stairway went on. He recognized many who also toiled upwards. Sometimes they slipped and fell. "Oh, help them!" he wanted to cry, but no words came. He stooped, took a downtrodden soul by the arm, and encouraged him to climb. The friendly support made all the difference. Around him, others followed Nicholas' example. Person began to help person until many were lifted from their places and brought higher.

The fog faded. Nicholas opened his blue eyes to a new day and skies that smiled. Where were the ennui and dread that had accompanied his recent wakings? Where was the desire to turn over, drown himself in sleep, and escape facing another monotonous repeat of the days before?

"Thank You, God." He stretched and threw wide the curtains of his soul. "I still don't know exactly what You want of me, but whatever it is, I'm ready."

During the early winter months, Nicholas Fairchild sought his Lord in mighty prayer. He studied the Bible, especially the passages where Jesus gave admonition and instruction. He also realized one day that most of his studies had narrowed to the Book of Luke, the great physician. An idea whose magnitude and daring would call forth every ounce of energy, all the resources Nicholas could muster, seeded itself in his brain and heart. He spoke of it to no one except God, as was his custom when contemplating a new venture.

A week before Christmas he felt the time had come. Like Peter Marshall's rich man, Nicholas chuckled at the expression on his associates' faces when they read what he asked to be sent to a hundred leading men and women in the city of Seattle. First came shock. Next, disbelief. Then, a quick look at their employer. Finally, the unswerving loyalty of employees to employer who long had made them feel they worked *with* Fairchild, not just for him.

Two days later, his missives hit like hailstones. One hundred recipients of hand-delivered messages gaped when they read the words, patterned after those in "By Invitation of Jesus."

> *JESUS CHRIST invites you to a meeting of*
> *great importance on Christmas Eve,*
> *8:00 P.M. at the residence of Nicholas Fairchild.*
> *RSVP*

"Christmas Eve!" Physicians and architects, attorneys and contractors, bankers and ministers groaned in protest. Had Fairchild gone mad, calling a meeting at such a time? Rumor buzzed like saws in a lumber mill, yet affirmative responses poured in. With the exception of a few renowned medical personnel with critical cases, all who were summoned came.

Nicholas welcomed them on a rainy Christmas Eve that contrasted sharply with the light and warmth inside his home. His servants had arranged space by throwing wide the enormous doors between library, living and drawing rooms. Comfortable chairs welcomed the curious, half-resentful guests. One, more familiar with the host than most, voiced their unanimous unspoken question, "Why have you summoned us and in such a strange manner?"

"Fellow citizens, I have decided to build a hospital and I need your help."

Mouths dropped open and a dozen voices cried, "A hospital? Seattle has a multitude of hospitals, many known worldwide. Fred Hutchinson Cancer Research Center, Children's, Harborview, Providence, Swedish, the University of Washington's Medical Center, and a dozen more."

Nicholas straightened his spare frame. "I know. But I have to build a hospital." He saw scorn and skepticism in their faces. "All those you mentioned and others are matchless and I hope my new venture will be affiliated with them and use their services often. But this one will be like no other—anywhere."

"Why?" someone asked after a few seconds of stunned silence.

He braced against their inevitable reaction. "First, no patient will ever be refused care, no matter how long term or extensive, on the basis of ability to pay."

He ignored the shocked ripple of sound and plunged on.

"Second, the finest medical personnel only will be considered and salaries will be above the norm." He drew a deep breath. "There will, however, be one qualification every person from head surgeon to janitor must meet and that is to be an active, practicing Christian who combines humankind's best skills with intense prayer."

"You can't make that stick," a deep voice criticized. "The government won't stand for that kind of discrimination."

Nicholas smiled a curious smile. He had anticipated every objection. "This hospital will in no way be connected with the government. Neither will it receive grants. To do so would open it up to legal restrictions and defeat its purpose."

"It will take millions!"

"I have them." Nicholas quietly surveyed the watching faces.

Some looked mildly interested. Others raised their eyebrows and exchanged glances. A few faces showed recognition of what such a place could mean to those persons Nicholas spoke of.

"Think of it. A hospital whose portals are carved with scriptural promises. A place that is less an institution and more a haven. A staff who begins each shift fresh from a prayer service where each patient is brought before the throne of God. A group of individuals bound together and to their work by One Chief." The memory of his dream and subsequent searching filled his voice with pleading and he spread wide his hands. "I believe it can be done. No, I believe it will be done. You can help if you choose, but with or without you, this hospital is going to be built."

For a minute his sincerity echoed from the walls and hushed even the most disbelieving, but not for long.

"Fairchild, you can't even get land in Seattle for a hospital," a certain developer declared as he waved his arms.

"That's right," a city planner added. "Even if you could, you'll be stopped dead in the water by zoning laws, not to mention environmental impact statements and a dozen other things."

Again came the curious smile and glint in their host's eyes that boded inside knowledge. Nicholas walked to a nearby table, picked up a worn Bible that lay open and prepared.

"Matthew 6:33–34: 'But seek ye first the kingdom of God, and his righteousness; and all these things shall be added unto you. Take therefore no thought for the morrow: for the morrow shall take thought for the things of itself. Sufficient unto the day is the evil thereof.' Could anything be nearer the kingdom of God and His righteousness than a temple of prayer and medicine whose doors beckon all who need to come unto them—and to Him?"

"You actually expect *God* to provide the land, waive all the regulations, and pave the way for you to build this charity hospital?" the developer demanded. "Fairchild, I didn't think any grown man in today's world could be that naive."

Strangely, no one laughed—except Nicholas, who held up the Bible.

"We're also told to become little children, trusting and expectant," he said to his fascinated audience who had forgotten it was Christmas Eve in the bizarre twist the meeting had taken. "I tell you, if this plan is of God— and I will stake my reputation and everything I own that it is—no power can prevent its completion."

"I'll lay ten to one odds that your Nicholas Fairchild Hospital will never be built," challenged a TV reporter, who had suspected something unusual would take place at Fairchild's and slipped in uninvited with the guests.

"I'll lay you a million to one odds it won't," Nicholas fired back, to the consternation of the crowd, who, in spite of themselves, showed a growing belief the thing was possible, although not probable.

"What is this, a hoax?" The reporter didn't give an inch. Disgust dripped from her sharp tongue. "Nice thing, bring all these people here on Christ's birthday just to preach at them, then back down."

The commanding presence that had taken Nicholas from humble beginnings to his current position made him loom taller and more formidable than ever.

"Madam, you said the Nicholas Fairchild Hospital will never be built. I only agreed. Do you think I would demean myself to name a place such as I have described after me or any other man or woman?" His blue eyes darkened with righteous indignation. "Must I remind you that while I will serve to the best of my ability in an advisory capacity, I will never be the chief?"

The woman clutched her purse with tense fingers, but her training and experience in ferreting out stories served her well.

"Then what is this—fantasy—to be called?"

A smile that erased everything but a humbleness not always found in influential leaders made Nicholas's craggy face almost handsome.

"It will be known as the Shepherd of Love Hospital, and engraved beside each door will be words taken from the Twenty-third Psalm, 'The Lord is my shepherd. . . . Though I walk through the valley of the shadow of death, I will fear no evil.' "

Even the wave of approval that swept the assembly could not still the avid reporter who anticipated a pay raise for this story.

"Isn't that misleading? You aren't going to guarantee that every patient will be cured, are you?" She paused, then added, "Why, if you do, the other hospitals might as well close down immediately."

"The Shepherd of Love Hospital will not claim the power of life or death. It ultimately rests with the Chief." Nicholas's lips trembled at the significance of the simple statement. "Yet I do expect a high success rate. Any of the leading physicians who are here tonight can tell you a patient's mental attitude plays a far greater part in the healing process than most people realize. By talking with patients, reassuring them and praying with them as they permit, our staff will be going far beyond the usual means to help prepare patients for what lies ahead."

Several leading doctors nodded.

"You said *they permit.*" The reporter stuck as close to every word as a bloodhound to a trail. "This implies you expect to serve other than just Christian patients."

Nicholas astounded her and the others with a ringing laugh. "Sinners, saints, and all in-between will be welcomed," he solemnly replied, although his eyes twinkled in their bright blueness. "Didn't our Master invite all to come to Him? The only requirement will be that those who do come need help—physical, emotional, mental, or spiritual."

When eyebrows raised, he added, "Oh, yes, we will have chaplains and counselors for those who are hurting other than in their bodies."

He waited for more questions. When none came, he quietly told his guests, "I know you feel I may be straying from my senses. I'm not. I intend to go into this project the same way I have done with other projects all my life. Perhaps I have only really come to my senses and to a realization of the need Seattle has for the Shepherd of Love Hospital."

They left in little groups, to homes and belated Christmas Eve celebrations to spread the word and muse over what they had heard. In closing Nicholas had assured them they would never be asked for money, only for goodwill and prayers. If some chose to contribute time or finances, it must be as a result of their own beliefs in the project and its underlying principles. Caught between this man's record of success in all he did and their own doubts it could ever happen, those who had attended the meeting passed on their differing views to others.

Seattle rocked when the TV reporter's version burst into the homes of the city's residents. She scrupulously stuck to the facts but couldn't help ending with an editorial comment, "Such a vision as the one presented may appear believable in this season of goodwill and peace on earth. In reality, it will in all probability become known as Nicholas Fairchild's one great folly. Good night and happy holidays."

"Fairchild's Folly" stuck as a nickname. Yet when weeks ran into months, Seattle marveled. A recluse who owned a huge chunk of property on a wooded hill overlooking the Sound emerged from the carved woodwork of his library. To the dismay of his expectant heirs, he deeded the entire property to Nicholas with the stipulation it be used for the unusual hospital he had read about. He further astounded the city by turning over most of his vast fortune to the future hospital, reserving only enough to keep him comfortably in a private retirement home until the Shepherd of Love was completed, at which time he would take up permanent residence in a quiet wing he insisted be added for "old codgers" like him.

Amazement turned to wonder when Nicholas and the small but dedicated corps of those who prayed and accepted the work as God's will breezed through the formalities of legal work.

One year from the first meeting, a grateful Nicholas turned over the first shovelful of earth, with reporters stumbling over themselves for pictures. Word had spread throughout the country about the aim, purpose, and determination of "Fairchild's Folly." When unasked-for checks poured in, foundations became fact, and a bevy of electricians, plumbers, and builders haunted the site from dawn to dusk, Seattle awakened from its derision and believed.

By the second Christmas Eve, the hospital's long, low buildings spread across the donated land. Winter sunlight turned the white stone walls to cream and glinted off windows that sparkled with loving care. Sixty-seven, and younger in mind and spirit than he had been for years, Nicholas took a final, solitary trek from one building to another, each building joined to the others by covered passages. Shining steel instruments were sterilized and waiting for surgeons' hands that would be used with full realization of the One who guided them. Pastel-painted rooms with empty beds and attractive curtains stood in cleanliness. At Nicholas's insistence, no part of the hospital stood more than two stories high. Now he admired the gleaming corridors as he walked them. A lump rose in his throat. Tomorrow in a public, well-attended ceremony, the Shepherd of Love Hospital would be dedicated and the Chief recognized. Tonight Nicholas felt the Presence of that Chief. Not a single decision had been made without seeking God in prayer. Surely a hospital so conceived, so carried out, would fulfill its dual purpose: to heal the sick and to bring souls to a knowledge of the living Christ.

And God saw that it was good.

Nicholas knelt in the empty hallway, filled with gratitude and deep humility. "Oh, Lord, I know how You felt when You created heaven and earth. Please, help me and those who come here, whether to heal or to be healed, to always remember this work is not of our making but a gift from You. We are Your tools, God. Keep us polished, bright and worthy. I ask these things in Jesus' name, amen."

On Christmas Day, the Shepherd of Love Hospital opened its doors to a crowd of curious Seattleites who swarmed through the new building, peered into its every corner, and ran exploring fingers over the Bible verses carved here and there, impressive in their simplicity.

Three years later, Jonica Carr came to the hospital.

Chapter 1

Thy word is a lamp unto my feet,
and a light unto my path.
PSALM 119:105

What a strange inscription to grace the door of a hospital director's office! Jonica Carr thought. She paused, took a deep breath, and chastised herself. Now that the moment she had waited ten years for had arrived, why should she tremble? What did it matter that although she vaguely recognized the quotation, she couldn't reconcile it with the medical field?

She rubbed damp hands together and dried them with a tissue from her carelessly worn shoulder bag. The action brought a vision of herself at fifteen, nervously perspiring and waiting for the first and only boy who had ever asked her out.

Anguish rolled over her as if it were yesterday. The shy boy's arrival. Her father's rage. Subsequent days, weeks, and years of high school walled off from classmates by pride that permitted no pity, only hatred for her strong, five-foot-ten-inch, 150-pound body.

Did the timid teenager she thought she'd left behind still live inside? Jonica brushed aside the thought and squared her shoulders under the soft blue blazer that matched both her eyes and the pleated skirt of her suit. She no longer walked stooped over, ashamed of her body. Superb health and determination born of desperation had brought her far from that long-ago night when she vowed to become someone, to escape her abusive home and make it on her own. She remembered the envious looks of classmates when her top grades won her a full scholarship in nursing, her chosen field. Jonica had breezed through the four-year university course with honors, although some of her fellow graduates opted for the two-year LPN course, rather than studying for BS degrees and RN status.

Still hesitating outside the director's office, Jonica rapidly reviewed her upward climb. She'd been unwilling to become lost in the shuffle of an enormous hospital so she had accepted a position in a small Tacoma hospital that recognized hard work and skill. Her big break came—literally—during Jonica's third year when the night shift charge nurse was suddenly called away because her father was injured in a fall.

"Put Carr in charge," the charge nurse told the powers-that-be. "I'll only be gone a week and it isn't worth getting someone in who isn't used to how we do things. Besides, except for emergencies, how many surgeries are scheduled between eleven and seven?" In that week, followed by another when the charge nurse's father became worse, Jonica ran things so smoothly the surgical department manager saw her potential and promptly ordered that she be considered for training for a charge nurse's duties. Months later, the charge nurse position became vacant. The ambitious second-in-command relished the dilemma the hospital faced, with the entire surgical department clamoring for her to get the job while administration openly doubted that any twenty-four year old could handle such a responsible position. They compromised by assigning her the duties and the title for a probationary period of six months—and fell over themselves at the end of her trial months with praise and admiration for her calm, unruffled demeanor that reassured patients and staff alike. Jonica overheard the chief of staff comment that he'd never seen "such a cool cucumber as Carr in emergencies."

"May I help you?"

A deep masculine voice jerked her back to the present. She whipped around. A tallish, slim man with white streaks in his hair and eyes as blue as her own stood smiling at her.

"I—was just going in." She put her hand to the doorknob and couldn't help adding, "I'm Jonica Carr, the new night charge nurse in surgery."

An odd expression crossed the older man's face. "It's a pleasure to meet you. Welcome to Shepherd of Love."

"Thank you." She noticed how young and alive he looked when his smile broadened. "Do you work here?"

He nodded and gallantly swung the door inward for her. "I'll be seeing you again, Miss Carr. Or is it Mrs.? Or Ms.?"

She glanced both ways and whispered, "Miss, but I like Jonica best." He bowed and swung off down the highly polished corridor, stopping now and then to admire the continuing mural of sea, forest, and mountains that brightened the walls.

"He loves this place," she murmured. It seemed a good omen, as had the friendliness of the staff when she had applied for her new job just a few weeks earlier, not expecting to get it but confident she could do it well if chosen. She knocked on the closed door.

"Come in, Miss Carr." The hospital director rose from behind his practical desk, a style in keeping with the paneled walls and muted carpeting. An open window with a view of an early-summer Puget Sound brought a fresh breeze and cooled Jonica's flushed face. "We feel fortunate to have you join us." When she couldn't hide her surprise, he smiled. She liked his keen eyes, modest dress, and obvious efficiency tempered by caring. "Oh, yes, I make it a point to know each of the staff personally. If there is ever anything you need, do not hesitate to come to me. You'll notice I prefer to be personally available rather than use a secretary as a buffer. Now." He changed to brisk business. "We chose you despite your youth and limited charge nurse experience because of several factors. First, your record is impeccable. Even more important, your deportment at your personal interview showed clearly your ability to maintain your composure under trying circumstances." He smiled again. "Interviewing for a position, even at Shepherd of Love, or perhaps I should say especially at Shepherd of Love, can be trying." He shuffled papers and paused. "Only one question on your application had a rather sketchy answer, but I'm sure that's due to our short-sightedness in not leaving enough room to write everything you'd like."

Her heart plummeted. She knew what question this observing man meant. It had taken her longer to respond to the simple query, *Are you a Christian?* than to fill in the rest of the lengthy form. Hadn't her penned words, *Yes. I was baptized as a teenager and have been faithful in attending church except when on duty,* been enough? If not, why had they waited until now to question her on it? Surely she wouldn't be disqualified now that official notice of her appointment had come and she'd served her thirty-day notice in Tacoma!

"You are a Christian, aren't you?" the kindly director prodded.

"Of course." She certainly wasn't a heathen. She believed in God and accepted Jesus as His Son. If sometimes she felt God was some faraway Power who had little interest in her, she need not confess it.

Her quick reply appeared to settle any doubts the director might harbor. He rose, shook hands, then asked, "Did you tour the hospital when you were here before?"

"Oh, yes!" She knew eagerness sent a glow to her face. "It's perfect—large enough to have the best equipment yet small enough to feel almost like a family home." Wistfulness crept into her voice.

"Do you think you can be happy with us?"

She sobered. "I know I can." She blinked and scoffed at the instant moisture crowding her eyes. She never cried, hadn't since she ran away from home all those years ago, from the stepfather she hated, the pretty but weak mother whose only defense against him was a threat to leave if he ever touched Jonica in any way. In rapid-fire order a series of temporary dwelling places flashed through her mind: shelters, when available; doorways when shelters weren't; studying at libraries and working in fast-food restaurants; her first rented room—in a miserable dump just one step above the street. How she had begrudged the time work took from school and studying! A less determined person would have given up and dropped out. She did neither. She also learned to thank whatever God there might be for her height and weight. Twice they had helped her out of danger when men approached her.

"I–I never really had a home until I went to college," she said.

"You have one now, Miss Carr." He walked into the hall with her and again she wanted to cry. "Are you settled into your quarters?"

She nodded, not trusting herself to speak.

He patted her shoulder as he would have done had she been a favorite daughter. She did not shrink from his touch, as she'd learned to do when some colleagues acted too friendly. Unless she were totally mistaken about people—and her years of fighting for survival in a hostile world had developed inner awareness beyond the ordinary—only goodness filled her new boss.

Did he divine her thoughts? "Remember, Miss Carr, I'm only the hospital director. God is our Chief." He smiled again and vanished inside his office, leaving the door standing open. She had the feeling it normally stayed open; perhaps it had blown shut today before she came.

Fifteen minutes later she luxuriated in a warm shower. She had settled into the charming combination bed/sitting room with kitchenette and bath attached to the hospital and offered at nominal cost to those employees who wished to live on the grounds. The small suites were located in a separate building at the farthest point from the ambulance entry where a stand of giant trees and colorful flowerbeds muted the noise. Acoustical tile ensured additional quiet.

Jonica's particular suite sported off-white walls, a deep blue rug, and matching draperies. She had chosen it over a counterpart done in yellows and gratefully rejoiced the rooms were tastefully furnished. Her struggle to succeed had left little time to accumulate furniture, even if she'd had a place to keep it. An end unit, her suite faced north, with a view of more trees and gardens from the bed/sitting room at one end. A large window at the west showed white-capped Puget Sound. The kitchenette and bath each had a small window, screened for safety, that overlooked more of the well-tended grounds.

"And he wondered if I could be happy here!" Jonica repeated while she toweled her thick, medium brown hair, then coaxed it into the simple, pulled-back style that suited her so well, with a slight turn under at her nape. She added a touch of lipstick, the only makeup she ever wore, and deliberately surveyed her image—not pretty or glamorous, but clean and fresh-looking with lovely, clear skin untouched by beauty aids. Donning an aqua skirt and blouse outfit, she suddenly grinned. "Not bad at all." She blew a kiss at her reflection, slipped into white sandals, reached for a matching purse, and headed toward the small private dining room where she had eaten the day she was interviewed. Enjoying the day, she soaked in the sunshine and the laughter that came from a group of off-duty nurses grouped in comfortable chairs outside the staff quarters.

"Come join us," one called. "You're Jonica Carr, aren't you? If you're half the wonder woman rumor has it, Shepherd of Love's really blessed to get you!"

Jonica searched the greeting for a sting and found none. She found herself eager to get off to the right start with these women, some of whom could be in her charge.

"I can see my press agent's been here doing a good job," she said lightly and felt delighted at the laughs it brought.

The friendly nurses evidently found her acceptable. A strange pang went through the newcomer. All through college and training, even at Tacoma, she'd been too busy getting ahead to make many close friends. One of the nicest things about working at Shepherd of Love might be having that opportunity. She sat down beside a dark-skinned nurse whose twinkly dark eyes laughed even when her lips remained straight. She looked about Jonica's age.

"Nancy Galbraith. We're glad to have you here." Warmth radiated from her simple greeting. "Pediatrics."

"Patty Thompson, Outpatient," said the blond who had first spoken.

"Shina Ito, Obstetrics." The tiny Japanese girl pronounced it *sheena*.

"What an unusual name. I like it," Jonica said impulsively.

"It means good, virtuous," Patty put in. "She's too modest to say so."

"You could take a lesson from her," the final member of the group heckled.

"I am modest. Shina's just modester—oh dear, there's no such word, is there?" Patty pretended embarrassment but Jonica saw how her eyes twinkled. "At least I introduced myself."

"I'm Lindsey Best," the freckled, redhead said with a wide grin. "I don't have to say anything more with that name, right?"

Jonica felt as if she'd had a second warm shower. "Right. Where do you work?"

The irrepressible Lindsey who rivaled Patty in clowning (but turned out to be an excellent nurse) put on a fake drawl and opened her green eyes wide. "Why, I'm a little ol' surg'cal nurse, Boss. Ah goes to work at 'leven an' gets off at seven—sometimes." A smirk accompanied her final words, "Anyone'll tell you, ah'm the Best."

Patty made a strangling sound, glanced at her watch, and leaped up. "Steak for supper, people. Let's go." One by one the others stood, with the graceful Nancy lingering to walk beside Jonica while the others linked arms and started toward the dining room.

"Don't let Lindsey's joking fool you. She's a crack nurse and will back you up completely. Underneath that red hair is a dedicated Christian and a real professional."

"How old is she?" Jonica asked.

"They're all about twenty-three, just long enough out of training to remember all of what they have learned with some experience. They all did some affiliation work here and couldn't wait to apply for jobs when they became accredited." A little frown brought her silky eyebrows together. "We have a high turnover on the nursing staff, unfortunately."

Jonica stopped short and stared at her companion. She brushed away an overly friendly bee who headed for the nearest rosebush.

"I'd have thought you wouldn't have much turnover at all. Who in their right mind would want to leave all this?"

"Don't sound so disappointed." Nancy's gaze followed Jonica's around their beautiful surroundings. "It's just that we get such high quality nurses and doctors, they often end up married and deciding to go into the mission field!" Laughter filled her dark eyes. "It's a professional hazard."

Jonica bit her tongue to keep from blurting out, "Have you found it so?" but something in Nancy's natural dignity prevented it. Instead she said, "I'll have to watch my step."

"Why?" Nancy looked honestly surprised. "Believe me, if you fall in love at Shepherd of Love Hospital you know you'll have a head start on beating the divorce statistics."

"It almost sounds as if everyone here is an angel or something."

"No, Jonica. We're all sinners, but we've been saved by the grace of our Lord Jesus Christ." Nancy turned and gazed over the blue, blue Sound. "We make mistakes but we know we are forgiven so we pick ourselves up and go on. With Jesus as a Best Friend, how wrong can we get, as long as we cling close to Him and follow the path He laid out by walking it before us?"

Jonica didn't answer the rhetorical question, but something inside her quivered. She'd never heard anyone talk like this, not even the ministers in the rather formal church she had made a point of attending. Her baptism had been a meaningless rite, performed because other members of her class were going to join the church and she'd hoped it might make a difference. At thirteen she'd also hoped to be one of the group by conforming. Neither thing had happened but she had noticed the only really happy couples she knew were those at church. Her young heart, so deprived of love, warmth, and respect at home, silently reached out and she promised herself that one day she would find love. In a childish prayer she told God, although He had not come closer when the drops of water fell on her head, "Please, help me someday find the kindest man in the whole world, someone who will be good to me—always."

Later, she added the fruits of her observations and reached two conclusions: If she were ever to have what she called a "happily-ever-after," a carryover from fairy-tale days, she must (1) find a Christian and (2) marry a professional person so her home would not be the battlefield over money her childhood home had been, with its endless wrong-side-of-the-street arguments that still assaulted her ears.

The day after the almost-date fiasco, fifteen-year-old Jonica slipped away from the world she hated, willing to endure whatever it took to achieve her goals and find joy. She coolly chose nursing not from any desire to help others, although it did come later, but as an entrance into respectability and professionalism. She ignored statistics that the chance of a nurse marrying a doctor was greatly exaggerated in novels.

She would make herself so indispensable that some doctor or administrator could not help seeing her value. Unaware how deeply the fantasy had ingrained itself into her, Jonica did realize her shining knight did not ride horseback, but instead wore a stethoscope in many of her dreams.

While working in the Tacoma hospital, she had achieved the respect she sought. There had even been interns and residents who invited her out, never suspecting her outward sophistication masked insecurity and a lack of social ease. Jonica tired of them when they expected a return on their invitations at the end of the evening and so she earned a reputation for coldness. Now Nancy's blunt admission that Christians struggled but could overcome through Christ interested her. She opened her mouth to ask more, but hastily snapped it shut. As a professed Christian, she was expected to know this. She could not betray how shallow her Christianity really was and risk losing her job and the chance to live in this new world.

All through the years, Jonica had held fast to the belief that those who kept quiet and observed could learn what was necessary in almost every case. She would do the same now.

Patty, Shina, and Lindsey had already entered the dining room and taken a table when Nancy and Jonica arrived. The new nurse liked the way tables for eight stood scattered throughout the relaxing green-painted room with soft white curtains blowing in the summer breeze. "Over here," the pert blond called and Nancy led the way, explaining no special seating arrangements prevailed.

"You'll see the hospital director eating with the ward clerks, the chaplain sitting with the cleaning crew," she explained. Two young doctors proved the point by dropping into chairs at the nurses' table, then an older man approached them. "May I sit with you?"

"Of course." The table's occupants welcomed the older man with cries of delight. Jonica looked into his blue eyes and smiled. "As you said, we did meet again."

"Oh, you already know Mr. Fairchild?" Lindsey asked.

He appeared not to hear and asked one of the doctors to offer a blessing for their table. It gave the usually unshakable Jonica a chance to control herself. She barely heard the words of the blessing. If anyone had told her she would eat her first on-the-job supper at the same table with a living legend, she'd have considered that person crazy.

Chapter 2

Jonica ate her delicious steak, tossed green salad, and baked potato, her attention fixed on Nicholas Fairchild. How could such a great man look so humble? With a flash of insight she decided, *That's why he is so great. He sees himself as a tool in the hands of the Great Physician, of no more use on his own than a shining steel scalpel before a skilled surgeon picks it up.*

Despite her lack of intimacy with a God who guided people, Jonica had been tremendously impressed by Fairchild's story, learned first from newscasts and the papers while she was still in training. Along with the rest of Seattle she had curiously watched "Fairchild's Folly" become reality and secretly rejoiced when it happened. Watching any person do what others said couldn't be done inspired her to believe her own dreams could one day come true if she only worked hard enough.

"Mr. Fairchild." She spoke into a small pool of silence that had fallen while hungry nurses and doctors devoured the excellent meal. "Did you ever once doubt?" She thought of times when even her strongest faith faltered.

Nicholas laid down his fork and a faint flush dyed his youthful-looking skin, lightly tanned and healthy.

"I can honestly say I never doubted the existence of Shepherd of Love Hospital. Perhaps because again and again legalities and stumbling blocks disappeared." His blue eyes darkened and Jonica saw the loving way his glance traveled around the pleasant room, resting for a moment on each table filled with laughing, chatting staff members. "On the other hand, I many times wondered why God had so graciously chosen me to help accomplish what we have here today."

Jonica felt her throat constrict. Longing surged through her. How wonderful it would be to have the tranquillity she saw stamped on this man's humble face. Well, she could think of no other place on earth more inclined to foster such peace and faith than Shepherd of Love. Just a few hours at the hospital complex had clearly shown an availability of spiritual strength as well as physical healing. Such an atmosphere offered the hope that one day her own deep scars would truly mend, not just be covered up by the determination to forget.

"There's Dr. Hamilton."

Caught by a note of awe in Patty's voice that hadn't been there even for Nicholas Fairchild, Jonica amusedly looked at the blond nurse. Hero worship and deep respect shone in her eyes. Jonica suddenly felt years older than Patty or Lindsey, although so few years separated them in age. Not so with Nancy. A slight sadness when her lovely dark face wasn't smiling betrayed maturity and an evident overcoming of whatever life had handed out. And Shina remained an unknown personality.

For the second time, Patty interrupted her musings. She tackled her strawberry shortcake and laughingly confessed, "I've never wanted to work anywhere except Outpatient, but if anything could lure me away, it would be that man."

"Don't talk with your mouth full," Lindsey told her.

"Yes, Mama." Patty wrinkled her tip-tilted nose and swallowed before she continued. "Every single woman here admires him." She smirked at Lindsey. "Of course, since you work with him all the time you have the *best* chance. Get it?"

A mutual groan swept around the table. "Shhh," Patty warned. "He's coming over here. He probably saw Jonica."

The new nurse refused to turn and satisfy her curiosity, even when a pleasant voice spoke from behind her. "Good evening. Is this Miss Carr? Jonica?"

"Indeed it is," Mr. Fairchild said heartily. "I'd like you to meet Dr. Paul Hamilton, Miss Carr. He's our chief surgeon."

The new arrival stepped into view and held out a beautifully shaped hand. Jonica noted the long, surgeon's fingers first, then her gaze traveled past sharply creased gray slacks trimly belted, an open-necked white sport shirt, and strong shoulders to a face neither pretty boy nor hunk—just masculine and attractive. Eyes as dark as his crow black short hair smiled, as did firm lips. *Thirty-two, perhaps, about six foot, two inches, two hundred pounds with not an ounce of fat,* Jonica decided. She liked his firm handshake.

"May I?" He didn't wait for an answer but took an empty chair from a nearby table and pushed it in-between Jonica and Nancy.

"Have you had your supper, Paul?" Nicholas asked, eyes bright with approval of his chief surgeon. "He lives with his father a short distance from here," the hospital founder explained for Jonica's benefit.

"I ate with Dad but it's been all of an hour ago and we didn't have strawberry shortcake." He eyed Patty's rapidly dwindling dessert then pushed back and strode toward the kitchen. "Hope they have some left." A few moments later he returned, triumphantly smiling and carrying a huge wedge of shortcake. Jonica thought he looked like an eager boy when he dived into it. Conversation flowed around her and she relaxed. With Patty and Lindsey heckling each other and the two young doctors vying for their attention, she could relax and listen.

"Just because she's my roommate Lindsey thinks she can oversee my life." Patty gave a mock groan, then ruined the effect by adding, "I'll have to admit she does a pretty good job!"

Everyone roared, but redheaded Lindsey merely raised one eyebrow and superciliously announced, "I'm at least a month older than Patty and the Bible says we're to respect our elders."

Jonica couldn't help seeing how much Mr. Fairchild liked the good-natured ribbing. His blue eyes twinkled, and when he at last rose to go, he seemed reluctant but said he had a meeting. "I'll see you in our little prayer service before you go on duty," he told Jonica and walked away, spare frame erect.

"It's hard to believe he's seventy." Nancy Galbraith had remained quiet during the roommates' sham squabble, as had Shina, who softly put in, "He's really ageless."

The doctors also excused themselves and Paul Hamilton said, "Thanks for the good company. Sorry I wasn't here the day you interviewed, Miss Carr, but I've read your credentials and I know you'll be a tremendous asset to our surgical staff." He strode off in a long lope.

"Wow!" Patty stared after him. "I never knew him to say anything like that before."

"You mean he doesn't compliment people?" Jonica felt torn between pride and apprehension. Was the chief surgeon hard to work with?

"Sure he does." Lindsey scowled at her best friend. "He just usually doesn't make it quite so strong." A smile of pure mischief turned her freckles to tiny copper pennies. "Looks like someone has finally made an impression on our good doctor."

"It's about time," Patty began, but Lindsey and Shina shushed her, and the five nurses left the dining hall, saying, "Come on, Jonica—we can call you that, can't we? Last names are so impersonal." Jonica nodded and Patty said, "We'll show you our rooms. Shina lives with her family and drives in, though."

She led the way to the T-shaped building that housed staff. Jonica admired its efficiency. Two stories high, the covered passageway that protected staff from bad weather opened into the middle of the lower floor in the center of the T's cross bar, a lovely living room that could have done credit to any nice home.

The east end of the cross bar held filled bookshelves that made Jonica, an avid reader, long to drop into a comfortable chair and take time to indulge herself.

"There's a library of medical books in the hospital itself," Lindsey explained. "These are the best of the current Christian and secular books available, everything from novels to Bible studies, plus a whole lot more."

"The planners deliberately put the library on this side of the living room so it would be quiet," Shina said. "There's a recreation room with TV, piano, tape players, pingpong table, and games on the west side, with a small laundry room on the end, although the hospital laundry will do our uniforms."

Jonica already knew the upright of the T contained eleven rooms downstairs, eleven up: five on each side of the hall and one longer, narrower at the end.

"Men upstairs, women down," Nancy explained. "I'm right next to you." She flung open the door of a charming suite done in rose and white. "Patty and Lindsey's is a double and bigger, two doors down."

Jonica admired the soft greens but privately considered her room the prettiest. She flushed and asked, "I have a better view—why didn't one of you take that room when it became available?"

"We all live in the ones we have since first coming to Shepherd of Love," Patty explained, suddenly serious. "The personnel division asked if we wished to change and we said no. So did the other women." She smiled a singularly sweet smile. "Besides, we heard you were coming so we saved the room for you. We're hoping you'll want to stay a long time."

A rush of emotion threatened to swamp Jonica. She had never lived with a group of women who saved the best for a stranger. On the contrary, through college and afterwards, she as well as her colleagues went for what they wanted. *I'm going to have a lot to learn in order to fit in,* she realized. "How many other staff members live here?"

"It varies," Shina said. "If my family didn't want me to stay at home so badly I'd love to live here. I'm working on it. My favorite is the yellow room you could have chosen, right down here next to all of you. I think I'm making progress, too. Father said the other day he didn't like seeing me so tired from commuting and driving after dark when I have evening or night shifts." Her charming slanted eyes sparkled. "Maybe soon you'll have another occupant."

"All the other rooms are filled," Patty informed them. "And sometimes there's a waiting list, so if you want that room, Shina, you'd better say so quick."

The doll-like nurse smiled. "That decides it. I'll talk with Father and Mother tonight." She glanced at her watch. "Oh-oh, we'd better let Jonica finish getting settled before she goes on duty."

"You know you report a half hour early, don't you?" Nancy reminded. "Each shift starts with a short staff prayer service and reports from the previous shift."

"I won't be late."

"If you want to catch a nap, I'll rap on the door when it's fifteen minutes before you have to leave," Nancy promised.

"I don't think I'll sleep. I'm too excited."

Lindsey fired a parting shot. She drew her lanky body up to full height, perhaps an inch shorter than Jonica but slimmer.

"Nurse Carr, I must remind you that charge nurses must never get excited. They are to remain in control at all times so their subordinates, meaning slaves like me, can have a good example set before them and—" She dropped her lecturing pretense and promised to wait for her new supervisor. Again Jonica marveled at the camaraderie between employees. No abominable caste system here that distanced floor nurse from charge nurse from nurse manager.

Her attractive rooms held out welcoming arms when she stepped into her suite. Earlier she had gone out and locked the door leading outdoors. This time she came in from the long corridor, wondering about the other residents. If the nurses she had met so far were representative, living conditions couldn't help but be ideal. She dropped lightly to the comfortable couch provided as part of the furnishings. No need to open the bed in the opposite corner.

Bits and pieces flashed through her overactive mind, feelings and comments, personalities and questions. Then her training stepped forward at her command. Jonica shut off everything, blanked her mind, took deep and relaxing breaths, and slept until tapping at the door and Nancy's soft "Fifteen minute warning" brought her awake and refreshed.

By the time Jonica had slid into the pantsuit uniform she'd chosen for her first shift, Lindsey appeared wearing a similar outfit.

"I crawl into my surgical blues once on duty," she said. "But I like to have something else with me. If it isn't too rough a night, I can change there for breakfast. If it is—it's back here for a shower before I show up in the staff dining room." A lovely pink crept into her freckled cheeks. "No use looking like a drab."

Jonica suspected one of the young doctors who had joined them for supper might have something to do with Lindsey's elaborate explanation, but she said nothing. Not until a firmer foundation had been established would she make observations that could be construed as prying. She changed the subject.

"Have you had a lot of rough nights lately?"

"No, but it's just when things are going well that something can happen. Pray God it doesn't." She sobered and a look of pain came into her brown eyes. "One of the nurses I trained with works at Harborview. I admire her but I couldn't handle her job. Harborview has a terrific trauma unit and gets some horrendous cases—bad burns flown in by helicopter, victims of gang fights; that kind of thing. We send our most critically injured to them. Shepherd of Love is a wonderful hospital, but it can't be all things to all people so we work closely with the other Seattle hospitals."

"Is there any problem of feeling too proud to ask for help?"

Lindsey's eyes rounded. "Of course not. We want the very best for every single person who walks or is carried in our doors. When we can't give it, we send patients to someone who can—although it's really Someone with a capital S who holds the ultimate outcome in His hands."

"You're very sure of that, aren't you." A statement, not a question, yet Jonica held her breath waiting for the reply.

"If I weren't, I wouldn't be here," Lindsey said simply. "Neither would any of the others. Take Dr. Hamilton, for example. He could work at any hospital in Seattle, but he believes healing comes from God working with and through His servants so he stays here at Shepherd of Love. Although I heard a rumor—" She knitted her brows and broke off. They'd reached the end of the long covered passage and the doors to the main hospital building. "Enough gossip. We have a job to do."

Jonica knew from the time she gathered with her night shift staff in the little prayer meeting, everything in life before had pointed her to this moment. She had felt it just before entering the hospital director's office earlier that day. The feeling had intensified with her fellow nurses' friendliness. Now, while one of the chaplains conducted a very brief service in which critically ill and recuperating patients alike were brought before the Lord to receive the blessing they most needed, Jonica let the wonder sink into her soul. She rose with the rest, strengthened and ready.

Yet she lingered a moment to shyly ask the chaplain, "Do the patients know we pray for them?"

"Yes, Miss Carr. And the amazing thing is, even those who profess to have no belief in God never object. I've heard self-proclaimed atheists mutter, 'Can't do no harm,' and go under the anesthetic far more relaxed than they realize."

Jonica slipped away, still marveling.

Once she met the rest of her night shift, any remaining qualm about efficiency died forever. She also learned that her department did not begin and end with the arrival and departure of patients, but carried over into other parts of the hospital. When sent to ICU, they still continued as part of the surgical team's concern. They remained on Surgery's prayer list while in the wards and until released from the hospital or into the Heavenly Father's justice and mercy. So did their loved ones who experienced a different type of pain, often even deeper than the patient's.

The night passed quietly. The sterile instruments and gleaming life-giving machines remained in waiting, ready when needed. Halfway through the shift, Jonica put Emily, a fiftyish surgical nurse with the most seniority, in charge while she took a break. When Lindsey had first introduced Emily, the new charge nurse looked at her keenly, wondering if there would be any resentment from having to take orders from someone not even half her age. One look into the steady gray eyes dispelled that fear. So did Emily's comment, "Dr. Hamilton's already told me how blessed we are to have you here."

Pleasure sent a little red flag of color to Jonica's face. "That will give me something to live up to, Emily."

"Don't worry about it. No one here has. God's not about to send some flibbertigibbet after all the praying we did for just the right person." She smiled and motioned her supervisor away. "We'll page you if you're needed. Take your break." The telephone rang. Jonica paused. Emily answered, quickly handing it to her.

"Emergency. We're sending up a male Caucasian. . . ." In staccato sentences, the ER gave the vital statistics. Jonica repeated them for Emily and Lindsey's benefit, pen racing. Before she completed the call, her trustworthy two had flown to scrub.

"Who's on call?" Jonica desperately wished she knew every surgeon personally. What appeared to be a ruptured appendix would require skill, speed, and teamwork.

"Dr. Hamilton." Lindsey continued to scrub hands and arms while she answered. "Will you assist?"

"Yes." Jonica hurried to get scrubbed. "Emily, circulate. Lindsey, double-check the instrument table."

Even before the patient appeared, Dr. Hamilton loped in, glanced at the meticulous arrangements and nodded approval. "Glad to have you aboard, Jonica. Emily, Lindsey, this is old stuff for us." Gowned, masked, and ready, they nodded. The surgeon scrubbed and stood alert. "Good thing I dropped in to see how one of my patients was making it," he said from behind his sterile mask. He sighed and Jonica saw the brooding look in his dark eyes above the gauze.

"ER filled me in a bit more. Man had been having pains all day, thought he had a virus. Took antacid and it didn't help. Temperature rose and scared his wife. Patient didn't want to come because it had stopped hurting. He's probably filled with infection. Let's pray before he gets here."

Never had Jonica experienced anything stranger than standing in that operating room ready to assist with surgery and listening to the surgeon pray for the patient, the staff, and himself.

The same skill that earned her the job bonded her into the surgical team. She slapped instruments into Paul Hamilton's hand as if they had worked together for years, anticipating his needs. Only once did he have to ask for a particular instrument. Like a miracle of life, the pallid face of the patient tinged with color and Jonica rejoiced. She also remembered to whisper a prayer of thanks, although her lips twisted wryly and she wondered if she did it because, like the atheist said, "It can't do no harm," or if she really believed God, not Dr. Paul Hamilton, had saved the man.

"If antibiotics do their job, he should live for many years," the doctor announced when they had finished and were cleaning up. "Thanks, team." He smiled at each in exactly the same way, from the hastily summoned anesthetist to the cleaning crew waiting to restore the operating room to sterility and perfect order, then walked out with a spring in his step.

"Does he always walk that way?" Jonica didn't realize she'd spoken aloud until Lindsey soberly said, "Only when he feels the patient will recover." She dried her hands, grimaced, and added, "I want a shower before breakfast, but you have to give your report to the day shift so I'll see you in a bit." A brilliant smile tilted her mobile lips upward. "You did great, Boss." She disappeared out the door, but her warm approval stayed behind like a summer day's lingering warmth after the sun set over Puget Sound.

Chapter 3

D r. Paul Hamilton flicked the remote control. The garage door of the home he'd lived in as long as he could remember slid open. He drove his Honda Accord in, shut off the motor, and got out, pausing to listen to the singing of a bird choir in a nearby maple. Exhilarated by the way the surgery had gone, he smiled at the dawning sky and said, "Thank You, Lord," before closing the garage door and fitting his key into the kitchen door lock.

"It's unlocked, Son," a resonant voice called.

Paul pushed the door wide. "Dad, how many times have I told you not to wait up for me?"

"I didn't." Innocence wreathed the lean face that resembled Paul's, except prematurely snow-white hair crowned Peter Hamilton's young-looking face. "I heard you leave and decided it was a good time for prayer."

A look of warm understanding and mutual respect flowed between them and Paul flinched, wondering how Dad would react if one day his only son decided to follow his heart. He quickly clamped down on the thought. Right now, his future remained nebulous and certain dreams unpredictable. He sniffed. "Bacon and eggs?"

"Plus orange juice, hot muffins, and jam in ten minutes; just enough time for you to change." Peter slipped the pan of muffins into the conventional oven, scorning the microwave Paul favored when he infrequently cooked.

"How do you always know the exact time to have meals ready?" Paul demanded.

"The Lord works in mysterious ways." The older man expertly turned the bacon and turned the burner to low.

Paul chuckled all the way to the shower off his bedroom. Leave it to Dad to come up with that kind of answer! Yet, was it so strange? From the day Dr. Peter Hamilton gathered his small son close in his arms and said, "Mother's gone to live with Jesus, Son, but we have each other. It's going to be lonely and we'll miss her, but she won't have to be sick ever again. Someday, after we've done the work here on earth God has for us to accomplish, we'll go live with her forever," a far closer bond than father-son existed between the two.

They kept their wife and mother alive through photos and memories, and always the hope for a glorious tomorrow.

As Paul grew and made childhood friends, then older companions, no one ever replaced his father as number one. All the old-fashioned words that described such a friendship as theirs—buddy or pal—fell short. Yet Dr. Peter, as his colleagues knew him, refrained from telling his son what to do. When Paul brought his troubles and choices to him, Peter wisely discussed all the options and their possible results, then trusted the solid foundation he had built in the boy's life for the right decision. A few times Paul chose less than best but with his clear vision and prompted by, "What would Dad and Mom and God want me to do?" he soon corrected things.

Now Paul toweled himself vigorously, donned casual clothes, and brushed his short, wet hair. He thought of the moment he'd told Dad he planned to follow in his steps. For only the second time in his life, Paul saw his father cry. Only this time the tears signified joy, not the loss of a beloved, faithful wife.

Sudden depression blighted Paul's mood. Perhaps the stirrings inside him, the discontent, meant he simply needed a vacation. Somehow, there never seemed to be a good time. Always a special patient—and every patient became special to him—needed his skill. He wasn't arrogant enough to believe no one else could care for those persons; he simply grew into the lives of all who sought him and humbly gave his best.

"Wonder how Dad would like to go fishing?" he mused, then headed for the kitchen and breakfast.

How many times had he and Dad sat at the small table next to the bay window overlooking Mount Rainier, sharing ideas and cases and the goodness of their Master? Simple white curtains, a replica of those that had hung there before Mrs. Hamilton died, were pulled back and framed a magnificent view of the still-snowcapped peak.

After the blessing, Paul loaded his plate with everything in sight. Peter stuck with the muffins and juice. Since his mild stroke that necessitated an extended leave of absence from his practice, he faithfully avoided cholesterol-high foods. So did Paul, for the most part. His father had become an excellent cook and planned healthful, attractive meals. Only occasionally did he serve bacon or eggs.

Pride rested in his black eyes and he abruptly said, "You know, Son, all these years of living together we've only had one serious disagreement. I call that remarkable."

His comment followed so closely along the lines Paul had been thinking that he laid down his fork. "Lacy."

"Yes." Dr. Peter cocked one eyebrow in the same mannerism he so often used. "She's back in Seattle."

"Really? I couldn't care less." Paul resumed eating and his heart didn't skip a single beat.

"There was a time. . ."

Paul grimly supplied the missing words. "When I was a total fool. Thank God I didn't wreck my life and that He showed me her false nature before we married."

Dr. Peter's face wore a troubled expression. "She's getting a divorce." He hesitated. "Now that you've earned status as a surgeon, Mrs. Jones-Duncan, as I understand she wishes to be known, may find you—attractive."

Paul set down his juice glass. "I hope she doesn't. I have absolutely no feelings for Lacy, not even anger." He tilted his chair back, folded his hands behind his head, and stared unseeingly at Mount Rainier, which had turned strawberry-ice-cream pink from the rising sun.

"Psychologists say people always remember their first loves. I guess puppy love describes my experience, or infatuation. A seventeen-year-old boy is dazzled by a tiny, blond cheerleader. They pledge mutual love and think it will last forever. Graduation means a step closer to marriage to her, a step closer to becoming a doctor to the boy who is leaving childhood behind and becoming a man. Bitter arguments and tears follow, accusations that he doesn't love her or he wouldn't forget her while preparing for a profession that takes forever. An older, richer fish swims into her social pool. Girl leaves boy, marries for money. Boy grieves. God opens his eyes and the day comes when the boy, a man now, forgives her and finds in doing so, he is free."

"Well said, Son." Dr. Peter sounded relieved. "I appreciate your opening your heart. You're right—no one can ever be a truly free person until he forgives those who have wronged him."

Paul put his chair back on all four legs and picked up his fork again.

"You always knew how shallow Lacy really was, didn't you? I know you kept still when I raved about her, but I could tell you didn't agree with my estimate, especially when I considered her an angel sent from heaven just for me. Funny how we twist what we want into believing it's what God wants for us. You're right, though. Lacy is about the only thing we've disagreed on."

"The New Testament Peter and Paul had their differences, too," Dr.

Peter reminded his son and they both laughed. Paul had known from baby-hood that his mother chose the name Paul after the grand old warhorse in the Bible who carried the gospel to many in his lifetime and to countless millions after his death through his epistles. Small he might have been, but tall he stood in the history of the earth. A name to be proud of, one that needed his namesake's best.

Filled with good food, that namesake yawned and stretched. "I'm hitting the sack. I'm scheduled for gallbladder surgery at two. Oh, Dad, the new night charge nurse came and she's a wonder. Never saw anyone better at anticipating what I needed and getting it to me." Admiration gave way to a frown. "I think we need to keep her in our prayers, though."

"Why?" Dr. Peter leaned forward, interested and ready.

"I don't exactly know. Something in her eyes. I got the feeling she hasn't had the happiest life in the world. She has blue eyes but at times they darken until they almost look black."

"You noticed all that during surgery? My, you are observant," Dr. Peter said mildly.

Paul laughed, yawned again. "I met her at supper. We were too busy cleaning up a ruptured appendix later to get much of a look."

"What's she like? I had a chat with Nicholas Fairchild after Miss—Carr, isn't it—interviewed. He said if her recommendations are to be believed, she's a whiz; his word, not mine. It's probably out of date now."

"Maybe, but it describes her." Weariness forgotten for a moment, Paul added, "I'll admit I wondered how any woman that young could be a charge nurse, even on night shift. Her records half-convinced me and tonight's performance won me completely. She's going to be one of the best things that's happened to Shepherd of Love for a long time, although all our staff is top-notch." He stood, stretched until his fingertips grazed the ceiling, and headed toward the hall that led to the bedroom area. "What's she like? Tall, I'd guess about five foot, ten inches. Strong—145 pounds, maybe more, but perfectly proportioned. Surprisingly slim hands. Carries her head up, her shoulders back. Eyes front like a soldier facing a hostile area. Plain brown hair and no makeup I could see except lipstick. Not a bit pretty, but an interesting face with smooth skin."

If Dr. Peter secretly wondered at the detailed description of the newcomer, he kept it to himself. "Doesn't sound much like Lacy."

Paul laughed until the house filled with his mirth. "Wait until you see Jonica and you'll see how right you are!"

"She's a Christian, of course, or she wouldn't be working at Shepherd of Love." Dr. Peter stacked the dishes.

"You said it." This time the yawn threatened to dislocate Paul's jaw. "Call me at twelve-thirty, Dad." He whistled a few bars of "Surely Goodness and Mercy" and went to a well-deserved, much-needed rest.

The inner alarm that seldom failed him roused Paul from a deep sleep just five minutes before it was time to be called. Before Dr. Peter knocked on his door, he was up and dressed, his mind busy with the upcoming surgery. In spite of the enormous early breakfast, he did full justice to lunch: homemade vegetable soup with good bread and a vegetable and fresh fruit tray. He also discussed the surgery just ahead and the two doctors joined in prayer.

The short drive to the hospital offered summer at its best. The fragrance of freshly mowed lawns, nodding roses, and a tang of salt from the Sound came through the open car window. A verse from James Russell Lowell's poem "June" from *The Vision of Sir Launfal,* learned at his father's knee, came to mind and Paul softly quoted:

> *And what is so rare as a day in June?*
> *Then, if ever, come perfect days;*
> *Then Heaven tries earth if it be in tune,*
> *And over it softly her warm ear lays;*
> *Whether we look, or whether we listen,*
> *We hear life murmur, or see it glisten.*

Nothing could be more true in Seattle. Spring rains gave way to days like this and made them even more appreciated than they are in places that boast continuous sunshine and flowers. Once at the hospital, Paul parked and walked inside, only then remembering he'd forgotten to ask Dad about going fishing. He shrugged. Time enough for that once he finished his day's work.

The gallbladder removal went even better than the early morning surgery, yet Paul noticed a difference. His assisting doctor and nurse, anesthetist, and others were just as competent, yet he vaguely missed Jonica Carr's deft skill, her confident selection of the instruments he would need next. The male nurse who performed today's work did a fine job but not quite so rapidly. He waited to be asked rather than intuitively sensing the surgeon's needs.

"Go ahead and close," Paul told his assistant surgeon, then stepped back and observed. Any time he felt comfortable doing so, he allowed his assistant to gain valuable experience. Unlike some surgeons, however, he never left the operating room until the final suture had been set and the bandaging done. It had nothing to do with trust. He would gladly go under the knife of any surgeon who practiced at Shepherd of Love. He simply always remembered his father's advice, "Never leave any task until it is completed," and lived by that rule except in the rare instances when summoned to the second operating room in case of emergency.

Paul decided to use the free time period following surgery to catch up on some reading. A stack of new medical journals in the doctors' lounge offered interesting developments. He considered it part of his stewardship to keep informed. Science and medicine continued to make such giant strides that no physician or surgeon dared to stop studying. In addition, the comfortable room held easy chairs, and off-duty personnel frequented it.

Today it lay empty with sunlight streaming through the natural woven blinds, which were lowered to filter the light because of the western exposure. Paul idly scanned article titles, dipping into those that interested him most. He sighed when he heard himself paged. "Dr. Hamilton, please report to the central waiting area." Long strides took him down the corridor past Radiology and the Lab, the Surgicenter suite, and ICU. He turned sharply and reached the open area in the center of the lower floor, with its airy feeling enhanced by a large skylight and off-white tile. Attractive couches and chairs flanked magazine stands. An information desk stood at one side, but before he reached it, a petite blond whirlwind met him.

"Hello, Paul."

For a fraction of a second he was seventeen again, swelling with pride that his girl was the prettiest girl in school. A heartbeat later he rejoiced. Not a flutter of pulse accompanied his first look into Lacy Jones-Duncan's pert face after thirteen years, only sadness when his sharp gaze picked out tiny lines beneath the carefully applied makeup, a quickly hidden tightening of her thin lips. She didn't look thirty-two; neither was she the high school cheerleader he'd fallen for like a load of rock being dumped, in spite of her unchanged figure. "Hello, Lacy. Dad said he heard you were back."

She offered her hand. He took it, uncomfortable when the small, soft fingers curled around his and she said in a husky voice, "You haven't changed, except now you're a man."

He shook off her clinging grip, seated her on a couch, and took the chair at the end, despite her motioning for him to sit next to her. Her next words shocked him.

"Have you changed, Paul? Inside, I mean? I know you never married. It's one of the reasons I—" She looked down then swept him an upward glance. He recognized it as the same appeal for sympathy she used to win from his boyish heart—the determination to protect and fight for her long after the days of chivalry ended.

How could he ever have been deceived? Paul crossed his arms and looked straight into her brimming blue eyes from which not a single tear fell to mar her makeup. "I am sorry to hear you are leaving your husband, Lacy."

"Are you?" She clasped her hands as if in prayer. Disappointment filled her face. "If you only knew how much I regretted my marriage. I was selfish and wanted my own way. Before I'd been married six months, I knew what an awful thing it was to marry a man I didn't love, could never love. All these years, I can't tell you what it's been like. I stayed with him but I never forgot you. Darling, have you forgiven me?"

"Long ago, Lacy," he told her honestly.

"Then everything will be all right." She held out a white hand free of rings. "We can pick up right where we left off when I insanely listened to—"

Paul got up and stared at her. "Never."

She also rose. "But you said you'd forgiven me."

Aware of curious stares from various staff members and visitors, Paul lowered his voice. "I have absolutely no feelings for you, angry or otherwise. I'm sorry you aren't happy but it has nothing to do with me."

"It has everything to do with you. I left my husband for you and told him so." Her face hardened, then melted.

He couldn't believe the rage that filled him. To keep from saying things that would dishonor his Lord, Paul chilled his voice and merely stated, "That is highly unfortunate, Mrs. Duncan, but I am not responsible for your actions."

He loped off, feeling her angry gaze boring into his back. Unable to get the disturbing scene out of his mind, he went back and checked the surgical schedule. Nothing for him until the next morning and another surgeon on call. Good. He needed to get away—from the hospital, from anything that would remind him of Lacy Jones-Duncan standing in the central waiting area and calmly disclosing she had left her husband—for him! Could anything be more grotesque? He felt unclean from the encounter. He, who hated divorce, although realized it was necessary in rare cases. He, who had kept himself physically, morally, and mentally free of temptation. His close relationship with God permitted no dallying with impure thoughts that could lead to sin. If ever he married, he would bring to his bride a clean slate and expect to receive the same. He despised the current trend of labeling immorality "natural," to be indulged in at will. His Bible told him differently. While he did not condemn those who slipped, and repeatedly told them God offered forgiveness for all sin, he shrank from becoming even temporarily separated from God by his own actions.

"Now is a good time to go fishing," he murmured. "We can head out right away, get in a few hours, and have time to talk. Doesn't matter if we catch anything or not."

* * *

Dr. Peter agreed and they headed for a stream east of Bellevue, far enough off the beaten path that it hadn't been infested with fishermen. It required a three-mile climb to reach it, and by the time they got there, much of Paul's disgust had been worked out in the steep terrain. In addition, his father's quiet, "Leave it in God's hands," had stilled the tumult, as it always did. They caught no fish, but neither cared.

"No man ever had a better dad," Paul said on the way home, hands steady on the wheel. "I noticed you did splendidly on the hike, too. Before long you'll be back practicing."

"I can hardly wait." Dr. Peter stared at the darkening evening. "But you'll lose a mighty fine cook." His voice sounded husky. "Paul, if your mother knows how you turned out, and I can't help believing she does, I know she's just as proud as I am."

"Thanks, Dad." He cleared his throat of the sudden obstruction that rose at the tribute and they finished the rest of the drive in the silence of companionship that has no need for words.

Chapter 4

Jonica slept deeply and dreamlessly after her first night on duty at Shepherd of Love. When she awakened in mid-afternoon, she decided to put her kitchenette to use and prepared a light meal, just enough to keep her going until supper. Several in-between hours loomed before she had to go on duty again, so she decided to wander through the hospital complex and familiarize herself with the location of the various departments. The day she had interviewed, the relaxed but efficient atmosphere had made a good impression, but she had been mainly concerned with how her interview went. She also had to hurry back to Tacoma and her next shift. Now she could take the time to simply prowl and observe.

A curving staircase rose from the central waiting area to the second floor. Jonica admired the skylighted area and contrasted it with some of the stuffy waiting rooms she had seen. Her sharp gaze noted the abundance of books and magazines provided and the high percentage of Christian reading material and Bibles. Already she felt part of the hospital team and she made a point of smiling at staff, patients, and visitors.

The Family Center, which included Parenting Education, Labor and Delivery, Recovery, Pediatrics, and Children's Therapy, occupied one entire side of the second story. Nancy Galbraith, busy with her small charges in Pediatrics, waved and called, "Feel free," then gestured around the colorfully decorated ward and semiprivate rooms. Jonica caught a glimpse of doll-like Shina Ito hurrying toward a delivery room. Neither nurse wore traditional white. Nancy explained Nicholas Fairchild felt pastel uniforms offered brightness to sick children's lives, and the nurses were only too glad to choose pink, blue, green, yellow, or peach in place of stark white.

The opposite side of the building housed Oncology and Occupational and Physical Therapy. Through shining windows she glimpsed the single story Retirement Center, reached by a covered passage but partially screened off by trees to give residents the same privacy the staff enjoyed in their quarters.

Not an inch of space had been wasted in the designing of the complex, yet a feeling of spaciousness pervaded. Linen and storage closets filled nooks between departments. Adequate lounges offered the staff a comfortable place to rest. A solarium tucked away at one end hosted disabled patients and a multitude of green growing things, as well as fresh air and sunlight.

Jonica marveled at the completeness of the small hospital. She slowly retraced her steps to the staircase leading down to the central waiting area and descended. Halfway down she stopped abruptly. For the moment, she had the stairway to herself, but below her and a little to one side Dr. Paul Hamilton stood talking with a petite blond woman. Caught in the uncomfortable position of eavesdropper to the conversation that rose with the small woman's voice, Jonica hesitated. If she turned and went back upstairs, surely the two would see her. She could avert her gaze and go down, yet that meant they would also know she had heard their conversation. She stood quietly, wishing herself anywhere but there, while the woman in the too-young outfit brazenly proclaimed an undying love for the stern-faced doctor who stood staring at her. Several staff members and visitors had come into the open space and Jonica caught their curious glances.

Couldn't the woman see them? Or didn't she care? Her angry voice floated up to where Jonica tried to make herself inconspicuous, despising the stranger for the humiliation she was obviously causing Jonica's new boss.

"I left my husband for you and told him so." The blond made no effort to lower her voice.

Paul Hamilton's reply came as clear as if produced in a sound chamber.

"That is highly unfortunate, Mrs. Duncan, but I am not responsible for your actions."

Bravo! Jonica inwardly shouted and a little smile played on her lips. Dr. Hamilton's abrupt departure released the new nurse from her unwilling role as listener. She took a few steps downward but stopped again at the look that filled the woman's face. The blond's features contorted in a combination of chagrin, anger, and spite until Jonica shivered. All the expensive garb in the world—and the blond wore as costly an outfit as Jonica had ever seen—didn't hide the same look of vindictiveness Jonica had faced a thousand times before: from her stepfather and from all those who live to get even with someone for an insult real or imagined.

She couldn't tear her gaze away from the woman. Perhaps the visitor felt it. She glanced up. Blue eyes colder than surgical steel swept Jonica's tall frame. She marched toward the stairway and rudely demanded, "Just why are you staring at me?"

Feeling as put down as she had all through high school when her strong build contrasted with the tiny girls, who scooped up the boys' hearts and all the honors except those Jonica claimed, the dignity of her profession braced Jonica. She didn't reply. Instead, she simply walked down to the central waiting area, brushed past the woman as if she didn't exist, and walked away, head high. Yet she couldn't help wondering how this unpleasant person had touched Dr. Hamilton's life. Obviously there had once been something between them.

"Psst. Jonica." A flushed face and beckoning hand motioned her from behind a screen of living green that partitioned off a small space. "Mercy, did you get a load of Her Nibs?" Patty Thompson's innocent blue eyes had rounded to saucer-like proportions.

"How could I help it? Her voice certainly carried." Jonica let out an exasperated breath. "Who is she, anyway?"

"The Queen of Sheba. Well, almost." Patty giggled but fierce resentment showed in her pretty face, and the newcomer again felt the bonds of loyalty that existed at Shepherd of Love for one of its own against anyone who dared attack a staff member, verbally or otherwise.

"About a million years ago, right out of high school, Lacy Jones, Jones-Duncan now, pressed for Dr. Hamilton to marry her."

"They were sweethearts?" Jonica found the idea distasteful.

"High school stuff. You know, cheerleader dazzlement," Patty grimaced. "That's probably not a word but it describes it." She rushed on. "He said no way, according to rumor. She married pots of money and now she's back." Shrewd knowledge of human nature touched Patty's face. "He's big game, now. She's already got the money but Duncan's a jerk, drinks a lot." She shrugged and looked ashamed. "Guess I shouldn't judge. If I had to be married to someone like her, I might not be any better."

"So here she is trying to rekindle an old flame."

"She won't." Patty drew herself up to her full five-foot-five-inch height, a small mother hen ready to do battle for Dr. Hamilton, who resembled a frail chick less than anyone in the world.

Patty glanced at her watch. "Uh-oh, I have to go. Break's over." She started off in the rapid nurse's walk that covered ground but didn't alarm patients or visitors. Then she turned. "Jonica, if I were you I'd run like crazy if I saw Ms. Lacy Jones-Duncan coming my way. When you didn't answer her question and went past her, something in her eyes. . ." Patty didn't finish. "I'm not a scaredy cat but the way she looked sent ice cubes down my spine." She walked on down the hall toward the corner that led to Outpatient, leaving

Jonica standing there torn between her new friend's concern and the desire to laugh. Little likelihood existed that she'd have any dealings with the blond bombshell who wanted an old love back.

Again the corners of her lips went up. If the chill in his voice represented his true feelings, the chief surgeon at Shepherd of Love wasn't about to fall like a ripe peach at his former lady-love's feet.

Jonica's smile died. She blinked and wondered why a sudden depression had fallen like a blight over her excitement and newfound joy. Patty's warning certainly wasn't responsible. Could it be that seeing the tiny blond and learning she had once attracted the tall Dr. Hamilton brought back all her dislike of her own sturdy body? "Don't be a fool," she muttered to herself once she got outside and a little breeze off the Sound cooled her flaming cheeks. "You're here to work, not to find a man." She ignored the mocking little voice inside that taunted, *Is that so?*, and kept walking. Yet her honest heart admitted that when she did find someone to love, she hoped he'd be tall, strong, and caring like her new boss.

Day by day her new job absorbed her attention until the scene in the central waiting area took on a dreamlike quality. A few times she caught glimpses of Lacy Jones-Duncan pattering here and there in the hospital on ridiculously spiked heels, usually with face tilted admiringly at a tall specialist or resident—but never at Dr. Hamilton. An unspoken sympathy for the man obviously being stalked ran in currents throughout Shepherd of Love, and many a ploy protected the chief surgeon from Lacy's continuous presence. When she had him paged, someone else appeared with the information that he wasn't available.

"He isn't, to her." Red-haired, freckled Lindsey deftly set controls on the sterilizer. Little gold specks danced in her brown eyes.

"He never will be," gray-eyed Emily crisply added. "The sooner that one knows it, the better." She sighed. "It's not in Dr. Hamilton to be downright rude, but I'm beginning to think that's what he will have to do to 'get shut of her,' as my grandma used to say."

Suddenly Lacy no longer haunted the hospital halls. No one knew why but Emily's eyes gleamed. Perhaps she had talked with the tall doctor. In any event, the Surgicenter breathed more easily than it had in weeks, until a rainy summer night when screaming ambulances showed the toll the weather had exacted. "During dry spells road oil films the highways," Emily said. "Until enough rain falls to wash it away, it's like a coating of ice and most drivers don't recognize it. The man and woman being sent up now were traveling far too fast for the condition of the road and now they are paying for it."

The door burst open. Paul Hamilton charged in, face white.

"What is it?" Lindsey demanded.

He pressed his lips in a straight line. "Mrs. Duncan is being brought in for immediate surgery." He strode to a sink and began to scrub. "So is her husband. He's the most critical so I'll take him. Another surgeon's been called in to care for Lacy. She has deep gashes on her legs and arms but will be all right."

"I thought they were divorced," Emily put in.

"I did, too." He broke off. "Poor guy, I'd send him to Harborview if I dared, but his wife—if she still is that—absolutely insisted he be cared for here. It's going to be a long, hard surgery. Jonica, you'll assist me?"

"Of course." Yet in spite of her experience she had to breathe deeply when she saw their patient. She had never seen such an extensive head wound. Only God could save this man. All through the long hours, she prayed and slapped instruments into Paul's capable hands. She marveled at the way his steady fingers probed, at how his quiet voice gave instructions.

Suddenly the anesthetist barked, "Blood pressure dropping. We're losing him!"

"Steady." Dr. Hamilton's eyes glowed above his mask. "God, help us according to Your will." A succession of maneuvers followed, a trained team doing everything possible to extend life—to no avail. Duncan refused to respond to treatment. He died on the operating table despite heroic efforts on the part of the dedicated staff.

Brain dull with fatigue, Jonica stumbled out. In a few moments, she would issue orders for cleaning up, although the crew knew all too well how urgent such work was on a night that could produce many other demands for the operating theatres. Dr. Hamilton stood with shoulders slumped, staring at the wall. He turned when she came up to him. "We did our best."

"Yes." Jonica choked over the word. How futile it seemed when their best wasn't good enough. A new thought entered her weary mind. "I wonder how Mrs.—his wife—is and how she will take it."

"God help us all when we tell her." Paul's dark eyes filled with trouble. "No one on earth can predict how Lacy will react." He looked down at his stained hand and clothing. "I'd better get cleaned up, just in case."

Compassion caused Jonica to reach out a detaining hand and impulsively lay it on his sleeve. "Everyone in the OR knows how hard you tried."

Slowly some of the strain left his lean face. "Thank you." A look of gratitude and something Jonica could not interpret lighted his face. He touched her hand lightly then wheeled and went to get cleaned up.

Surprisingly, no more cases came up from the Emergency Room. "ER does a great job," Emily told the younger nurses. "Good thing, too. I have a feeling we'll have our hands full with the patient we have and she isn't even hurt badly."

The prediction proved all too accurate. Jonica had accompanied Lacy to a recovery room and lingered while a special hovered over her. Before the patient would consent to being treated, she had demanded full anesthesia and round-the-clock specials. Lindsey and Emily were too valuable to tie up in maintenance care, so a part-time special came in.

"Let me know the minute she's conscious," Jonica directed. "She has to be told about her husband."

"Better let Dr. Hamilton do that," the special suggested. "She's not likely to take the news well from a nurse."

Jonica didn't know what to expect. Lacy obviously hadn't loved Duncan, but her unpredictable nature could erupt in a dozen different ways. Because of this, Jonica sent the special on break and remained out of Lacy's sight when Dr. Hamilton came in, compassion in his face.

"Lacy, I have bad news for you. We did everything we possibly could, but your hus—Duncan didn't make it through surgery. Even if he had, his brain was so damaged he could never have been completely normal again."

The blue eyes showed she understood, but Lacy said nothing. Jonica held her breath and waited. Dr. Hamilton stood rigid by the bed. "Do you understand what I'm saying?"

"Yes. I needn't have divorced him."

Paul straightened as if he'd been hit.

"Don't look so shocked." Lacy stretched out a hand toward him. "He wouldn't have wanted to live if he—" For the first time she seemed to think of her own injuries. "Am I going to be scarred?"

"Plastic surgery will erase almost every trace, in time." Jonica sensed cold anger beneath the commonplace words.

Lacy closed her eyes. When she opened them again she whispered, "I should never have gone with him tonight, but he pleaded and I do like the Space Needle. Paul." A little color came into her face. "It's all for the best, Fate, maybe. I know you hate divorce but now we won't have to worry about it, will we?" She licked dry lips and it reminded Jonica of a sleek cat getting into cream.

"You don't know what you're saying, Mrs. Duncan. Now I suggest that you rest." He turned to go.

"I do know what I'm saying, Paul Hamilton. You're mine. You've always been mine and always will be."

"Nurse?" He turned toward Jonica, who hastily prepared a hypodermic and stepped toward the ranting woman. "Lacy, we're going to give you something to make you sleep."

She turned her gaze from him to Jonica and screamed, "Get that cow out of here. Help, someone. She's trying to kill me! I saw her watching me." She aimed her rage at Jonica.

The special bustled back in through the open door. "What's going on in here?"

"That nurse is going to kill me," Lacy panted and strained away, eyes glazed with fear.

"Give her the hypodermic," Paul ordered.

An impulse she didn't understand caused Jonica to thrust the syringe into the special's hand. "You do it. I'm upsetting her."

The capable special seized the syringe, administered the dosage, and ignored Lacy's shrieks that died as the medicine took effect. "Don't pay any attention to all her yelling," she said comfortingly. "Anesthesia does strange things to people." She shooed Jonica and Dr. Hamilton out. "Just leave her to me. Tomorrow she'll feel a lot differently."

Shaken, Jonica doubted it. When she finally got off duty and staggered to her room, she knew she'd never be able to sleep. Lacy's tantrum was especially out of place because of the loving aura that surrounded Shepherd of Love Hospital. The ugly taunts and unjust accusations hung in the air like a poison, marring the tranquillity that had come to mean so much even in the few short weeks Jonica had been there. She tossed and turned, snatching a little sleep but not enough.

A heavy feeling shrouded her spirit and when a knock came at her door in mid-afternoon, it didn't suprise her. She slipped into a robe and answered.

"Jonica, the hospital director has asked to see us." Dr. Hamilton stood in the hall, dark eyes brooding and sad.

"About last night?"

"I assume so. I'm sorry you have to be mixed up in all this." His honest face underscored just how much he regretted it. "Although it will probably turn out to be no more than a squall, it's never pleasant to have lies told about us." He sighed and cocked one eyebrow, then grinned. "Jesus told us to pray for those who despitefully use us. Well, I guess He also meant those who *spitefully* accuse us, with no justification whatsoever." The grin faded, leaving his face bleak. "What I don't understand is why she has it in for you."

"I overheard your conversation, that time she talked with you in the central waiting area when she said—you said. . ." She couldn't bring herself to repeat it.

"I see. Too bad I didn't see a long, long time ago. I suppose you've heard of my puppy love." His sense of humor evidently conquered his fore-boding for he added, "Thank God He didn't allow it to become a dog's life." As if noticing for the first time she still wore a robe, he added, "I'll wait in the hall," and closed her door.

Jonica hastily donned a simple skirt and blouse, thrust her bare feet into sandals, brushed her teeth and hair and swiped a dash of lipstick on her trembling lips. She accompanied Dr. Hamilton to the director's office, matching her long, free stride to his. Her heart sank at the look in the hospital director's eyes, the gravity in Nicholas Fairchild's, but the director's opening words set her at ease.

"Before I tell you why I've called you here, I want to reassure both of you—" He stressed the word *both*. "Nicholas and I have the fullest confidence in you."

Jonica wanted to thank him but couldn't. Fear such as she hadn't ex-perienced since leaving high school assailed her and her heart thudded to the soles of her feet when the kindly, troubled man went on.

"Mrs. Duncan has made some very serious charges against you. Ridiculous as they are, we have to face them. Jonica, she is charging you with an attempt to do her physical harm by giving her an injection."

"That is the most outrageous thing I've ever heard!" Paul Hamilton gritted his teeth. "What's she charging me with, aiding and abetting?"

"Far worse, Paul." Nicholas Fairchild looked older than Jonica had ever seen him. "She is threatening to sue you and the hospital for malpractice."

"For heaven's sake, why? I didn't even treat her!"

The director's words fell like sharp stones on a smooth surface. "Not her. Mrs. Duncan accuses you of the wrongful death of her husband."

Chapter 5

Jonica didn't realize she had bitten her lip until she tasted sweet-sickish blood. She blindly reached for a tissue in her pocket and pressed it to her mouth. Unbelievable. Was this all a nightmare that would end soon? If not, could it be a figment of her imagination? She removed the tissue. A small red stain brought her back to reality.

"It's bad enough accusing me—and I didn't even give her the injection," she fiercely stated. "But to charge Dr. Hamilton with such an obscene accusation is incredible! Every one of us in surgery knew it would take a miracle to save Mr. Duncan. Long after he was gone Dr. Hamilton and the others continued to work, trying every method to revive him." Angry tears threatened as she swallowed and regained her control. "Anyone who says anything different is a despicable liar."

Paul looked a bit taken aback at her warm defense, then the same odd look that had filled his eyes after surgery the night before crept into them. "Thank you, Jonica." He turned to the two men. "What do we do now? Shall I try and talk with her?"

"Absolutely not," the director ordered. "That's evidently what she wants and she will construe it as a pacifying move."

"Can she actually get a lawyer who will represent her?" Jonica wondered aloud.

"Unfortunately, yes. There are always those notoriety-seeking attorneys who will take chances just for the publicity. However, we have one of the finest legal minds in the city available to us as well as the counsel of our heavenly Father," Nicholas interjected. He smiled at Jonica.

"I wouldn't worry too much over this. It isn't the first and won't be the last time Shepherd of Love has faced persecution. We have always been guided and blessed."

The meeting ended with the promise they would get together again when the attorney could meet with them. Dr. Hamilton walked out with Jonica. "I wouldn't blame you if you picked up your belongings and fled, after this. Or at least, never wanted to see me again." He hesitated. "I was wondering, though: Would you consider going out to dinner with me tonight? It would get our minds off this mess."

"Why, I. . ."

"If it would make you feel more comfortable, we'll invite Emily and eat at my home," he told her. "She and Dad are old friends and I'd like for you to know my father." He eyed her. "Dad's a great cook."

"It sounds wonderful." Jonica silently ordered herself to settle down and read nothing more into the invitation than what was absolutely fact. Dr. Hamilton obviously felt sorry for her and hoped to soften Lacy's vindictiveness.

"I'll see that you and Emily get back in plenty of time for your shift," Paul promised and Jonica thought what a considerate person he was and such a good Christian. If there were more persons who believed and lived their faith as did Paul, probably a whole lot of people wouldn't be turned off by those who professed to be Christian. A little bell rang inside. Wasn't that what she did? She refused to let the bell clang. The prospect of a sort of date with her boss left no room for a psychological inquisition as to her motives.

Jonica's fatigue miraculously dwindled with a warm shower and the ritual of dressing. Her mint green summery dress, white sandals and purse were perfect. She snatched a lightweight sweater when Emily knocked. Seattle summer evenings cooled off.

"You certainly look nice," Emily told her.

"So do you. That soft pink shirtwaist style does things for your gray hair and eyes," Jonica responded honestly. The prospect of dinner with good friends brightened her face and raised her spirits. "Emily, you aren't trying to impress Mr. Hamilton, are you?"

Her right-hand nurse grunted but the pink in her cheeks deepened. "Would if I could," she said forthrightly. "Dr. Hamilton's a fine man. We're good friends, no more. I doubt that he will ever remarry. He had the best the first time around."

Jonica hugged the shorter woman. "I suppose you've been asked this a hundred times, but. . ." She broke off.

"You want to know why I haven't married." Emily's mischievous grin made her look like a pixie. "So do I." She ignored Jonica's peal of laughter and added, "I figured out that when I admired someone, he liked someone else. By the time several of them got around to noticing me, I had forgotten what it was I admired in them!" She laughed and her eyes twinkled. "Besides, I'd never marry anyone unless I believed with all my heart God wanted him in my life." She cast a shrewd glance at her tall supervisor. "I know He led me into nursing and to Shepherd of Love. If God ever wants me to marry, I'll know it. Not bad advice for some of you younger women, either."

"Not bad at all," Jonica soberly agreed, wondering why the thought that God might care enough about His followers' daily lives to actually help them choose a life's companion wisely should send such a surge of longing through her—not for that companion, but for the relationship she sensed Emily shared with her Master.

Before she could examine the thought, Dr. Hamilton came loping down the hall toward them looking unnecessarily trim and attractive in well-creased slacks and a pale yellow shirt. "Ready, girls?" He made a face. "Uh, hope that doesn't offend you." Teasing anxiety lighted his dark eyes. "Today's women don't like to be called 'girls,' do they?"

"I do," Emily sturdily retorted. "Always will, too." An affectionate look softened her face into a broad smile. "At the risk of sounding over-eager, are you going to stand here all day or can we go eat?"

In the wave of laughter that followed, Jonica escaped having to express her opinion on the girls-versus-women subject. Not that it mattered. She had a sneaking hunch it wouldn't matter what Dr. Paul Hamilton called her if he wore that relaxed, admiring smile that did tribute to the all-rightness of her ensemble.

The short drive from the hospital gave Jonica a chance to observe Paul. She'd insisted that Emily take the front passenger's seat and sat directly behind her. What a strong jaw and firm lips the doctor had. She liked the easy way his capable hands rested on the wheel, ready for whatever the other drivers might do. Once he swung sharply to miss a small cat who unwisely darted across the street.

Paul pulled into the driveway of his home and Jonica lingered outside for a moment after he courteously opened her door. "It's charming." Her curious gaze noted the sheltering maple filled with birds singing evening praise and the way the simple ranch-style home clung to the ground amid shrubs and colorful flowers. Inside proved to be even more satisfying. The view of Mount Rainier framed by white curtains in the dining room bay window awed her.

"You like our home." Peter Hamilton's observation jerked Jonica's fascinated gaze from the mountain.

"I love it." A gleam in the senior doctor's black eyes at their guest's fervent reply was reflected in his son's across the room.

"We've kept it the way it was originally furnished," Paul said, as they sat down to their meal.

Dr. Peter offered prayer, then the conversation continued.

"You're smart," Emily asserted. She cut another bite of the delicious Swiss steak on her plate. "Too many people are going in for uncomfortable furniture just because it's stylish. Never could see why. If a person can't be comfortable in her own home, why have one?"

"So that's why you live in a staff suite," Paul teased.

Emily shrugged. "I might just surprise you and up and get married one of these days. Right, Jonica?"

Startled, Jonica snapped to attention from observing the muted tones of rug and slip covers, the spotlessness that would do credit to an operating room, and the feeling of peace that pervaded this home. "Sorry, I missed what you said." She laid down her fork and looked at Paul. "Now I know why you always look so calm. It's your home."

"It's mostly Dad and, even more, our heavenly Father."

She picked up her fork again and took a bite of crisp, icy salad. "You don't know how lucky you are." She sensed a rush of emotion and quickly changed the subject. "What kind of roses are they, Dr. Hamilton?" She sniffed the fragrance that vied with that of the excellent food and concentrated on the low centerpiece of cream roses with their rosy fuchsia edges.

"Double Delight and they are." He smiled appreciatively. "But why not call me Peter, as Emily does? Or Dr. Peter, if you prefer?"

I wish I could have had a father like him, thought Jonica. The longing to know a true father's love almost overwhelmed her. She contrasted this godly man with her abusive stepfather and barely controlled a shudder. It was hard to believe both men were supposedly created in the image of God—the one who called on Him profanely; the other whose face showed that he daily strove to become a reflection of their common Father.

The evening passed in a blur of laughter and warmth, one of the happiest Jonica had spent in years. She reluctantly told Dr. Peter good-bye when the time came for Paul to drive her and Emily back to the hospital. "I can't tell you how much it's meant," she said in a low voice.

"Come back any time, my dear." Dr. Peter's keen black eyes smiled as well as his mobile mouth. He pressed her hand. "I'm here most of the time, at least for awhile longer. Don't wait for a formal invitation. I really mean that."

She knew he did. She also had a feeling that if she were ever in real trouble, her new friend would back her to whatever limits necessary.

On the short ride to Shepherd of Love, Jonica suddenly realized something. "Why, we didn't talk about Mrs. Jones-Duncan at all."

"On purpose." Paul's eyes, so like his father's, filled with mischief. She could see them in the corner of the rearview mirror. "Dad and I have a standing rule not to ruin good food with problems we can't solve. Time enough later to discuss them." He shrugged his wide shoulders. "God will have to take care of it, probably using our hospital attorney on call."

"I dread going back on duty tonight," Jonica whispered.

"Don't. Lacy asked for and received a transfer to a private center that caters to the elite, although she could just as well have gone home and returned to Outpatient for change of dressings."

"Good thing she didn't." Emily bounced a little in spite of her seat belt. "Patty Thompson works there and she is not a fan of Lacy Jones-Duncan in the least."

Jonica hid a grin, remembering Patty's mother hen act and her identifying the troublemaker as Her Nibs and the Queen of Sheba. Just knowing she wouldn't have to contend with Lacy made going on duty a pleasure.

One of the things the night charge nurse liked best about Shepherd of Love Hospital was the lack of kowtowing to the rich or treating nonpaying patients as unworthy. Each patient received the same quality care, compassion, and interest. Shortly after Jonica arrived, she overheard a new nurse speak angrily to a patient. Three days later the nurse was dismissed. "She lost the whole point of our service," Nancy Galbraith said at the supper table that night. At the other end of the spectrum, the former recluse who had given land for the hospital ended up in a ward when he came over from the Retirement Center for observation. Semiprivate rooms were filled and the hospital didn't move one patient to make room for another except in critical cases.

The generous donor's comment, "Treats 'em all alike," plus his added, "Good," swept through the hospital grapevine.

———◆•※•◆———

A few dark clouds loomed on the fair skies of Jonica's new world. Lacy Jones-Duncan persisted in her hate suit, although rumor had it a dozen lawyers turned her down before she hired a tacky attorney who advertised on TV and billboards. He agreed to take her case on a 40 percent contingency basis—a hefty chunk if she won her five-million-dollar civil suit. He immediately filed the complaint against Dr. Paul Hamilton and Shepherd of Love Hospital.

"Why the hospital?" Jonica wondered.

"She knows Paul doesn't have the money," their attorney explained. "In legal terms, the hospital is the 'deep pocket,' or the source of funds."

"What happens now?"

"Her counsel has walked the complaint into court and we've received copies; a court date will be put on the docket." He smiled. "It doesn't mean a thing. They need a prima facie case to win—that means self-evident, valid—which they don't have. You'll also note that no mention is made of the earlier accusations toward Miss Carr. A fisherman like this one doesn't bother with sardines when he's out for whales."

"Thank God for that," Paul put in.

Their keen-eyed lawyer continued, "My office will begin the discovery process, which is to gather medical records including the autopsy and depositions, statements from witnesses, and so on. We then prepare and file a motion for summary judgment that shows Mrs. Jones-Duncan's claim is without merit. Copies go to her attorney. Time is allowed for a response and claims or counterclaims, if any. The judge will call in counsel for both parties and, unless I'm grossly mistaken, will rule that the allegations are totally unfounded and end the whole thing." His eyes twinkled.

"Then I won't even have to appear?" Paul asked.

"Not unless the judge denies my motion for summary judgment, and he won't." Confidence underscored every word of the prediction.

A few weeks later Jonica and Paul were again summoned to the lawyer's office. "Good news," he announced. "The judge really let the plaintiff's attorney have it." He leaned back in his chair and laughed broadly. "Told him the case was ludicrous, then went a step farther and fined the attorney. He will be required to pay all defense attorney's fees."

"What?" Jonica stared. "How could he do that?"

"There's a rule that states lawyers may not file cases that have no justification. It's designed to prevent unscrupulous lawyers from clogging the courts with such cases." He rose, shook hands with each of them, and advised, "I'd forget the whole thing if I were you."

The letdown left Jonica feeling a bit shaky. When they went outside, Paul smiled at her. "All right?"

"I think so. I'm just glad it's all over. How could you be so calm all through this?"

"Dad and I prepared with prayer."

Tapping heels on the sidewalk announced Lacy Jones-Duncan's arrival.

"Oh, Paul," she cried. "That awful lawyer insisted I sue you."

"Strange that an attorney hires a client. If you'll excuse us, we have things to do," Paul disdainfully told her.

Lacy turned toward Jonica. "This is all your fault," she furiously accused the nurse who had unwillingly witnessed her double humiliation. "Don't think he will ever fall for you."

Her brittle laugh could have shattered fine crystal.

"Remember this. I keep what's mine even if I no longer want it, and Paul Hamilton has been my property since the day I turned sixteen." She turned and ran down the sidewalk.

"Too bad to waste such a dramatic exit on such a small audience," Paul observed, although Jonica noticed how a little twitch in his cheek showed anger. "She's wrong, you know. My only interest in her is the concern I have for anyone who flouts God and His laws." His eyes glowed and he suddenly laughed. "She's also wrong about something else. I not only could be interested in someone like you, I am. Very interested." With a squeeze of her hand that sent stars shooting into her brain, he smiled and turned away when the hospital attorney called him.

Jonica floated through the next few weeks. Never had an autumn been more beautiful. Maple yellow and sumac red painted the hills around Seattle. Late roses nodded, bloomed, and nodded again. Dahlias and goldenrod added their color, and crispy nights cooled the city, but no frost came. A time of transition, she thought one afternoon when she and Lindsey finished a strenuous workout on the hospital tennis courts. A period of quiet in between the past and the future, one to be enjoyed for itself. On days like this, filled with activity and the challenge of her night work, Jonica felt herself unwinding. Lindsey and her other nurse friends who clustered at one end of the staff quarters provided diversion, while Paul—she didn't finish her musing.

"Did you hear the latest?" Lindsey flung her racket on the grass and herself into a lawn chaise.

Jonica followed suit. "What latest?"

"Our late but not missed patient Ms. Lacy Jones-Duncan is back."

"Back? I didn't know she'd gone away."

"Oh, my, yes." Lindsey rolled her eyes. "Didn't you see the big news splash that 'the grieving widow of one of our illustrious citizens, whose untimely death left her prostrated, observed a period of mourning aboard a private yacht, but has bravely returned to her lovely Seattle home that holds so many precious memories'? A lot of hooey, if you ask me." She brushed away a drop of perspiration from her freckled nose and cocked a reddish eyebrow. "Hope she doesn't try to get her painted claws into Doc Hamilton." A wide grin spread and she stretched. "I actually don't think it's possible, what with him spending every spare minute escorting a certain night charge nurse about."

Jonica glanced down but couldn't help the smile that curved her lips. "That has to be his decision."

"Oh?"

Jonica mimicked her friend to perfection. "I don't see any signs of warfare concerning the young doctor who hangs over your shoulder whenever he can."

"Hey, that's different." Lindsey sat up straight and smoothed her rumpled red curly hair before admitting, "I guess I'm just talking. If I have to snare a guy, I don't want him."

She leaned forward and her mischief died. "Jonica, Dr. Paul's a great man and a wonderful Christian. I think he's learning to care for you and I don't blame him a bit. The rest of us hero worship him but you're different, more mature. You have our collective blessing. You're a grand person." She cleared her voice of huskiness and seriousness at the same time and the brown eyes glinted gold. "Not a bad boss, either."

The two headed for showers arm in arm and laughing, but a little gray cloud persisted. Could she ever be good enough for Paul?

Shina Ito had moved into the pretty yellow suite shortly after Jonica arrived. She had also invited her special friends home with her for authentic Japanese cuisine. The nurses enjoyed the food and cordial welcome, although as Patty said afterwards, "I can see why it took you so long to convince your parents you should live at Shepherd of Love."

Shina smiled. "My parents are very traditional except they are Christian. I am so glad." Her move gave Jonica time to know the small nurse better and she liked what she saw.

"Funny how you and I, Patty and Lindsey, Shina and Emily kind of hang together," she told Nancy Galbraith one day when she followed up a surgical case to Pediatrics, where her little patient recuperated.

"We all live at the one end of the hall," Nancy told her practically. "The nurses at the other end do the same, except more of them come and go while we're permanent."

For the second time Jonica found questions trembling on her lips.

Nancy never referred to her past, never mentioned plans for the future. Friendly and extremely efficient, she joined in with the younger nurses yet didn't chatter or share as they did. Jonica respected her privacy, yet couldn't help wondering why such a beautiful person wasn't sought after. Once she noticed a soft look in the shining dark eyes and face when Dr. Damon Barton, an on-call children's specialist from private practice, came in for a consultation. Tall and well built, Dr. Barton's warm dark skin and flashing eyes commanded attention. Nancy's expression changed immediately—yet Jonica still wondered.

Chapter 6

Jonica Carr is the most restful woman I have ever known." Paul Hamilton's remark fell into the companionable silence he and his father often shared, especially when the autumn evenings grew chill and they set the small gas fireplace glowing.

"She has changed immeasurably since the first time she came here," Peter commented. "I sensed tension in her and conflict; not all because of Lacy Duncan's persecution, either. Now, there is peace. I believe God is working in her life."

Doubt crept into the younger doctor's voice. "She said she was a Christian on her application."

"Not all Christians have the peace of God in their souls." His father sighed. "I don't mean to pry, but do you care for Jonica?"

"I admire and respect her. I like the way she stands up to life. I appreciate her strength, even when I catch sight of a lost little girl lurking in her eyes at times." Paul stared into the flames. "At those times I long to put my arms around her and offer my protection for always. Yes, Dad, I care for her."

"Have you told her?"

"Not in words. I have a feeling she can't be rushed." He suddenly laughed. "To think I ever considered marrying Lacy when a woman such as Jonica exists. It hardly seems possible."

"She reminds me of your mother in some ways." Shadows hid Peter's face.

"You still miss her, after all these years." Not a question, but a statement.

"Yes. I always will."

The simple words brought mist to Paul's eyes. "Dad, have you ever considered remarrying?"

"Yes. How would you feel about it?"

Paul had the feeling a great deal rested on his response. He considered for a long moment before saying, "Until I met Jonica I think I would have resented it."

"And now?"

Again that sense of urgency came. "Someday I'll marry and establish a home of my own. I hate to think of you being alone. I think Mother would feel the same."

Peter stretched his hand out to his son, who clasped it in a hard shake. "There's something I need to share with you. No woman can ever fill your mother's place. Yet in the past months I've looked ahead. Paul, do you know one of the saddest things about being alone, especially after the death of a beloved companion? It isn't what most people think—the loss of intimacy; it's knowing you don't have someone to grow old with. God willing, I can look forward to many years ahead, busy years now that I'm physically better. As you say, one day you will be gone. That's as it should be. Lately I've felt the need to make room in my heart not for a replacement love, but for an additional love; new feelings, shared interest, but I. . ."

"Didn't know how I'd feel." Paul supplied the missing words. The phrase "knowing you don't have someone to grow old with" had struck deep. "Dad, is it Emily Davis?"

"It might be." The dark eyes flashed. "If she'll have an old codger like me. Our friendship goes back to the time of your mother. Of course, the real test is whether we both feel God is directing us."

"I know what you mean. I'm still working on that about Jonica," his son said. "Dad, thanks." He didn't add, *Thanks for sharing your holy of holies with me.* Dad would know. He always did.

By Thanksgiving Paul knew he loved Jonica with the deep devotion of marriage. He suspected his father knew it as well. Peter confirmed it by asking, "What are you waiting for?" outright on Thanksgiving evening when Emily and Jonica had gone after sharing the Hamiltons' day.

"There's something I have to settle in my own mind first." Why hadn't he told Dad weeks before? Paul chastised himself.

His mouth dropped open when Peter quietly said, "You're going to leave Shepherd of Love."

"How did you know?"

His father's dark eyes flashed. "A good father knows a lot about his son. That's why God knew Jesus would carry out His mission on earth." He paused. "Where is it you are being called?"

"To a new ministry." Spoken aloud, the feelings he had dealt with for months took on reality. "Dad, I've given all I have to medicine. I've loved it, but it isn't enough. Six months or so ago I happened to drive through a downtown area I hadn't seen for ages. Hurting people, some vacant-faced, others empty-eyed, lined the streets. Girls barely into their teens turned tricks. Men, women, and children slept in doorways because the overflowing shelters ran out of space.

"Such things ought not to be!" Paul fired to the subject, stood, and paced the room. "These are children of God, too, or could be if more persons cared. The various organizations such as the Union Gospel Mission and Salvation Army perform miracles, yet they can't do everything."

"What is God asking you to do?"

Paul had the curious feeling his entire life had pointed to this moment. "I believe I am to set up a combination clinic, with Shepherd of Love standards that allow treatment for all whether or not they can pay. A clinic that requires Christian personnel and offers shelter to the needy until a place can be found for them elsewhere." He took a deep breath and added, "I also believe I must study in my off-hours until I can be a lay preacher as well as a doctor. I need to know Scripture backward and forward so when the medical skills fail, God can use me as a bedside pastor."

Peter didn't speak for a long time. When he did, Paul heard excitement and hesitancy in his father's voice. "And Jonica?"

Some of his enthusiasm trickled away. "If she truly loves me, she will follow. If not—" He spread his hands. "I have to take orders from my Chief."

A quick intake of breath betrayed the older doctor's emotion.

"Son, for the past several weeks I've known I'm ready to go back to work but have held off. I haven't known why, yet have rather dreaded it." His face shone. "Can you use some help at your clinic and shelter? I wouldn't mind selling my practice and changing to a new and exciting ministry." He drummed his fingers on the arm of his chair. "I think we need to go see Nicholas Fairchild. He had a dream given by God and carried it out. He can give us a lot of good advice."

Seventy-one-year-old Nicholas looked younger than he had at sixty-five when father and son presented their dream to him. His blue eyes glistened with renewed vigor. "Now that the hospital is doing well, paying its own way, why, I'd like to invest in your plan," he enthused. "Why not make it an offshoot and call it Shepherd of Love Sanctuary? That implies rescue and help, the things Jesus taught in His ministry."

Paul felt so overwhelmed after the initial meeting with Nicholas that he told his father on the way home, "I can't believe how smoothly it went. It's as if God had prepared him to receive the idea before we ever walked into his house."

"Who's to say He didn't?" Peter chuckled. "Remember how Nicholas sprang the original hospital idea on a skeptical Seattle, only to discover God had gone ahead of him in every aspect? Paul, when people discover God's will and prepare to do it, He unties knots we don't even know exist. One thing, though." He cleared his throat. "You and I had best be talking things over with Jonica and Emily or if I know Nicholas Fairchild—and I do—the Shepherd of Love Sanctuary will be built and in operation before we can say thanks!"

———◆◆◆———

Jonica turned from her phone, well pleased. "Wonder why Paul sounded so excited?" she murmured. Her heart leaped. When had she known Dr. Hamilton was the man she had dreamed of for years? The first night she came to the hospital? The first time he performed surgery and she assisted? In the stuffy hospital room where Lacy Jones-Duncan maintained he belonged to her? Or had she come to love him gradually, the way a rosebud slowly opens to light and rain and sunshine, unfolding in beauty and fragrance?

A light knock at the door summoned her. Emily Davis stood there. "I just received the strangest call from Peter Hamilton," she said and came inside. "I've never heard him sound so—so officious. He almost ordered me to be ready to be picked up in thirty minutes." She dropped into a chair, indignation spoiled by a rather pleased smile.

"That's odd. I got the same kind of call from Paul," Jonica told her. "What could be up? You've been seeing a lot of Dr. Peter, haven't you?"

"Yes, and I intend to go on doing the same," the peppery nurse stated. "Jonica, I believe he is going to ask me to marry him and don't think I'll hesitate before saying yes."

"You said once you'd have to know God wanted you to marry."

"I do." Happiness filled Emily's countenance and an assurance the younger nurse envied. "This is one of the finest gifts God has given me. Peter will never love me as he did Paul's mother. I know that and don't care. He will love me in a different manner, one all my own and special. There are many kinds of love and ours will be blessed by God." Her kind eyes looked straight into Jonica's. "So will yours and Paul's, if you accept him."

"He's never said he loved me." Jonica turned her back, unwilling to hope for something when she felt so unworthy.

"Wrong. He has silently shouted it in a dozen ways," Emily contradicted. "Don't be surprised if I become your, uh, would it be stepmother-in-law?"

"You're incorrigible!" Jonica whipped around and giggled.

"I know, but I'm nice. Smug, too." Emily ducked out the door, slammed it behind her, and left Jonica to get ready for Paul.

When Paul arrived, the look in his eyes set Jonica's heart racing the way it had a few weeks earlier when he kissed her for the first time. Yet more than physical attraction, the sense of having come home filled her—the feeling nothing on earth would ever hurt her again as long as Dr. Hamilton stayed near. Now the wild-rose slacks and jacket outfit she wore paled by comparison with her burning face. She tried to hide it by casually remarking, "Emily said your father called her."

"Yes." Paul laughed in sheer exuberance. "We're going our separate ways, however." He ushered her out, put her into his car as if she were something inestimably precious, then climbed behind the wheel and started the motor.

Heavy traffic required his attention and Jonica sat beside him, content just to be with him. He reached I-5, headed south, and cut off on I-405, working his way south and east. A succession of smaller roads brought them to a forested area that overlooked Mount Rainier, a peaceful valley, and a shining river. Paul pulled into a roadside area.

"Come, Jonica."

He bounded out of the car, opened her door, and took her hand. A short climb led to a bench placed to make the most of the view. Paul put his arm around her shoulders and for a long moment they watched afternoon shadows gather.

She shivered, more with excitement than from the cold, although the late November sun's rays held little warmth.

Again Paul said, "Come." He led her back to the car. Once inside he quietly told her, "Jonica, I love you. I always will. If you will marry me, we can make life all it should be, serving together and honoring our God."

Roman candles of joy shot through her. She opened her mouth to speak, but Paul lightly placed a hand over her lips.

"Before you say anything, I must tell you some news. First, do you love me?"

She could only nod speechlessly.

"Then perhaps it will be all right." He took his hand away and smiled. "I still want to explain before you make promises you might regret."

Her heart beat painfully. It couldn't be that this fine man meant to confess an unholy past, something to do with Lacy Jones-Duncan, could it? Where had that poisonous thought come from? She would stake her life on Paul's honor.

"It wouldn't be fair to ask you to marry me when I'm chief surgeon at Shepherd of Love, then spring my news on you," Paul said. His dark eyes looked troubled, not shining and happy as they had a few moments earlier. "I'm leaving the hospital."

An involuntary gasp escaped her lips. She stared at him. What on earth. . . ? Her world rocked.

"For months, even before you came, restlessness inside me and a feeling of urgency has let me know God wanted something more than I've been doing." Paul spread his hands wide. An excited gleam replaced some of the shadow in his dark eyes. "I told Dad and he confirmed the rightness of my decision—he's been ready to get back to practicing medicine but holding off for the same reason: the feeling his practice isn't where he needs to be." Paul looked like a boy with a new kite, all enthusiasm and expectations.

Jonica longed to assure him it didn't matter where he went, she'd trail along. She couldn't get the words out. What kind of man was this, who calmly walked away from a prestigious position where he was loved and respected because he felt God wanted him to do another job? *I really don't know him at all*, she thought, fingers tightly clutched. *I knew he trusted his Master, but this is incredible. I'll never understand his trust and obedience to God, but how I wish I could.*

She finally found her voice. "Where are you going?" It came out as a whisper, sounding strained and fearful.

Paul glanced out the window, back in the direction they had come. "To the highways and byways."

All the insecurity Jonica had fought for years rushed over her. They increased when Paul continued.

"Dad and I, under Nicholas Fairchild's sponsorship, are going to establish a Shepherd of Love Sanctuary in the hard-core area of Seattle to bring healing and salvation to those who need it most."

She shrank back from him until her shoulders pushed hard against the car door. "No, oh, no!" She blindly held her hands out, pushing away the poverty, misery, and abuse she had run away from ten years earlier. A feeling of revulsion washed through her.

"Jonica, what is it?" Face colorless, Paul took her cold, shaking hands in his warm ones. The concern in his voice proved too much. Tearing sobs shattered the peacefulness in the car.

"I can't go back. I can't. Oh, Paul don't make me go back!"

A river of hot tears pressed behind her eyelids. If they once fell, she could never stop crying. Jonica freed her hands and groped in her purse for a tissue, pressing it against her burning eyes.

Paul sat stone-still, asking no questions. Through her own agony, she could see his suffering and tried to explain. "I came from such an area. I vowed I'd never go back. My stepfather. . ." She shuddered.

"Did he hurt you?" Steel laced his voice.

"Only by making our home miserable and wearing my mother down with his drinking and cursing. I can't remember a time they weren't fighting over something, usually money."

"You wouldn't have to work at the Sanctuary," Paul said in an even voice that held not the slightest hint of condemnation.

Jonica could sense his bitter disappointment. He had come to her with bright hopes of their working side by side under the command of God. She had destroyed his dreams, able only to offer a half loaf. Paul needed a wife who would share and support him, not one who hated his work and resented it. Even if she kept on at Shepherd of Love and they lived far from the new ministry, its shadow couldn't help reaching out toward them and eventually swallowing her up. *Why, God?* her heart desperately asked, knowing Paul had irrevocably set his face in the way he believed he must go. With or without her, Dr. Paul Hamilton would follow wherever his Master led. If his heart ached for a woman who would not, no, could not, join him, his patients would never suspect.

And what of her? Now that her long-held dream had come so close to being realized, then was snatched from her by some capricious quirk, must she slink away to lick her wounds, hoping to heal but knowing herself prey to bitterness beyond anything she had ever known? The prospect appalled her. "Paul." Her voice shook. "Are you certain?"

He stared at her. Compassion filled his eyes but his face went haggard. "Yes, Jonica, I am. I know this is a shock. Couldn't you think about it?" A note of hope persisted through his despair.

Eager to postpone a jagged break that would leave her bleeding inside, she assented. "Yes." She snatched the reprieve as a condemned prisoner grabs a pardon. Would even sharing Paul with down-and-outers be worse than losing his love forever? Her confused heart and mind clung to the question, for which she had no answer—yet.

Paul didn't push it. Instead, he tenderly kissed her lips and started the motor. If Jonica lived to be a hundred, she would never forget the love, resignation, and sadness in his face during the long drive home. When he left her at her door, he kissed her again and told her, "I'll be praying for you."

Even through her abstraction, she noticed he hadn't said for us. Had he subconsciously accepted her protest as final? She stood in a warm shower for what felt like ages, willing the water to scrub away her doubts and uncertainties. Why couldn't she be like that biblical woman—Ruth, wasn't it? The one who said whither thou goest. The thought haunted her, and after she dried and slipped into a warm gown, she crawled into bed and opened her Bible. Thank God she had the night off. Her lip curled. Why should she thank God for such a trivial thing when He had just taken Paul from her? She remembered a sermon in which the pastor had said God was a jealous God. Perhaps He didn't want Paul getting entangled with a person like her who had never really come to know Him.

She sighed, found the Book of Ruth, and read the age-old love story. The oft-quoted words of the heart of it shimmered behind a fine mist.

Intreat me not to leave thee, or to return from following after thee: for whither thou goest, I will go; and where thou lodgest, I will lodge: thy people shall be my people, and thy God my God—Ruth 1:16.

The Bible slid from her weak fingers to the coverlet. Jonica closed her eyes against the beauty of the promise and the pain that assailed her. Ruth had given her vow to a mother-in-law. Why, then, couldn't a modern Ruth do the same for the man she loved with all the pent-up feelings of years that longed to pour themselves out?

She tried to pray. "Lord, if it were anywhere except. . ." The words died on her lips. She thought of Ruth again, her love for her mother-in-law. It paled in comparison with the love Jonica felt for Peter Hamilton. She had come to look on him as the father she always wanted and she knew he returned her love. How would he react when he learned she had rejected his son because she would not follow him to the Sanctuary?

A picture of him came to mind. His steady eyes held regret but not an ounce of condemnation, just as his son's eyes had done earlier.

"God, why can't You be as loving and understanding as Peter is?" she cried. "He would never let his son's heart break by sending him into a place that won't even want him." Fear gripped her. She knew such areas; Paul did not. "God, some will hate him. They may even try to kill him."

The deepest flash of insight she had ever experienced planted words in her heart and mind. God had sent His Son to a place that didn't want Him. Some hated Him. Those who chose wickedness killed Him, the very ones He came to save.

All night Jonica struggled, alternating between an honest desire to know God for her own sake as well as Paul's and the feeling her prayers never got beyond the ceiling of her room.

Chapter 7

By morning, Jonica had gone from shock and disbelief to numbness and apathetic acceptance. Although it meant renouncing every promise she had made to herself, she had no choice. Nothing—even going back—could be worse than losing Paul. Yet little joy came with her decision. She dreaded seeing him and wondered if she were actress enough to convince him how much she'd changed overnight.

Unfortunately for her good intentions, Paul didn't appear. A brief note lay on her floor, evidently slipped beneath her door while she uneasily slept.

> *Darling,*
> *Dad and I are going out of town for a few days. I regret it, particularly at this time. On the other hand, you'll have some time to think.*
>
> *I love you.*
> *Paul*

"I'd be better off with time not to think," she said. She stuck the note under her pillow, comforted but more torn than ever. Paul deserved more than deceit and hiding her real feelings. Was it right to marry him and embark on a lifetime of keeping back resentment? In time, he would surely detect it. What then? She stubbornly set her mouth. It hadn't been right for God to let her meet Paul, then call him to chase off to the very place she had despised and escaped from.

Up and down, back and forth, her thoughts swung. At times she felt she must flee, simply disappear at least until she could sort things out. Yet the upcoming holiday season meant increased accidents and she'd be needed. How could she turn her back on those who desperately depended on good care?

Neither can Paul turn his back on those who need him, a little voice reminded. She ignored it and channeled her energy into working harder than ever. If her friends noticed she had grown quieter, they had little time to consider why. Christmas at Shepherd of Love meant added carol practices, decorating, and the cooperation of the staff so those who could not be home might still have a happy day.

Letters from Paul told that he and Peter had been detained in Portland. Contacts with persons who might be instrumental in helping establish the Sanctuary meant long hours. Yet, Paul wrote, more and more he realized the validity of the plan. God had obviously gone ahead of them and prepared hearts. There was talk that once the Seattle Sanctuary got going, concerned Christians with financial and spiritual resources wanted another built in Portland.

The news disturbed Jonica even more. In Paul's absence she had begun to feel it might not be so bad. As he said, she need not be personally involved. She could continue working in her cherished position until children arrived. Now it became clear that the Seattle Sanctuary would only be a beginning. A long procession of years in which Paul gave the majority of his time and life to the needy gnawed at the woman who loved him. Where did she fit in?

"I could handle being second, when God is first," she told herself. "But once Paul gets into this, where will I be on his totem pole of importance—third, or down below those who come for help?" The corroding bitterness she feared continually hounded her with such thoughts until she dreaded contact with Emily.

The gray-eyed, gray-haired woman's sturdy shoes still clung to the ground, but her heart floated. "To think I'll not only be Peter's wife but be able to work with him where we are most needed," she'd exclaimed the day after the fateful evening when she became engaged and Jonica did not. "Aren't you excited?"

"Ummm." Jonica didn't commit herself and Emily subsided. The younger nurse suspected her friend's keen eyes had seen something was amiss, but Emily never pried. She and Peter planned to be quietly married in the hospital chapel with only a few close friends present and a short honeymoon to the San Juan Islands. The new Mrs. Hamilton would continue in her job until the Sanctuary had been built.

Jonica thought she had made up her mind to tell Paul she couldn't marry him by the time he returned. Yet one evening when he strode into surgery, gowned, masked, and ready to operate as a special favor to the hospital director, her heart turned traitor. Outwardly steady, they worked as two blades on a pair of fine scissors. The poignant light in his eyes didn't detract one iota from the skill that saved the life of their patient, an elderly man with internal bleeding.

They finished their task, cleaned up, and Jonica knew no matter what the cost, she could never send him away.

"I'll be waiting when you get off," he told her quietly.

"I'm glad." She watched him go out, sighed, and turned back to her duties. A niggling little sense of emptiness accompanied her on her rounds. Like Ruth, she would follow. Unlike Ruth, it must be with reservations.

"The chapel will be empty at this hour," Paul told her when she stepped into the hall after giving her morning report to the next shift's charge nurse. He smiled down at her and she wondered, *Why does it all seem so right and easy when he's with me, so impossible when we're apart?*

The chapel shone with fresh wax, soft light, and red roses. They walked to the front and stood beneath a fine lithograph of Sallman's *Head of Christ*. "Well, Jonica?"

She looked up at him, knowing her heart shone through her eyes. " 'Whither thou goest,' Paul." She hastily averted her gaze from the humility she saw in his lean face. Something cold slipped onto her ring finger. She looked down. A plain gold band with the purest of diamonds glittered on her finger. It felt heavy and she suppressed a quiver, realizing the weight came not from the solitaire but from all it represented. The desire to be honest caused her to say, "I still have doubts."

"Not about our love." He looked shocked.

"No." Of that she could be sure.

"Then it will be all right, my darling." He drew her close, held her head next to his heart, and stroked her hair. The positive note in his voice stilled beating wings of uncertainty, and Jonica relaxed in his arms, silently pledging herself to become worthy of his love.

Jonica refused to formally announce their engagement until after Peter and Emily's wedding. She told Paul, "Let's keep our secret. I'll wear my ring on a chain under my uniform. I can't wear it during surgery, anyway."

"I'm ready to shout it from the hospital roof." Paul cocked a dark eyebrow at her. "I doubt that we'll have to announce it as far as Dad is concerned. He's pretty shrewd and commented that he has liked hearing me sing around the house for the past few weeks. Guess my feelings are like a barometer."

"My special nurse friends are just as bad. I catch sly knowing looks." Jonica sighed. She couldn't put into words how precious it felt to hug their engagement close to her for a time. Once it became public knowledge, a little of the special privacy she shared with Paul alone would be lost in congratulations and plans.

"How about announcing it on New Year's Eve—Dad and Emily will be back then—and we can get married as soon as we can get a license?" Paul suggested.

She hesitated, struggling with her feelings. "Would you think I'm too sentimental if I told you I'd like to be married on Valentine's Day?"

Paul's dark eyes smiled even before his lips curled into the heart-melting expression she loved. "I'd think you were just what I want, for always. Someone who isn't afraid to show honest sentiment and ask for what she wants." His laugh rang out. "Exactly what the doctor ordered."

The strength of his caring wove a protective web around Jonica and helped her laugh at her fears. Surely they could find happiness when their deep love combined with dedicated service to others. She resolutely put aside an inner awareness of the chasm between them concerning deep faith.

She still couldn't trust God for all things. Paul did. In an effort to be more like him, she spent time studying the Scriptures and ended up more confused than ever. Her heart leaped when she read 1 Corinthians 7:14:

> For the unbelieving husband is sanctified by the wife, and the
> unbelieving wife is sanctified by the husband.

Didn't that more than cover her situation? She certainly wasn't an un-believer; she just didn't know God the way Paul did.

Yet verses that talked about being unequally yoked and building a house on sand chilled her. Most of the time she could overcome fear and be happy, yet now and then, especially if she were overtired, she took it out and faced the fact that she needed to tell Paul exactly how she felt. Each time, she refused. How could anyone so strong understand the scars from childhood that left her weak and unable to give wholehearted devotion to a God she couldn't see?

◆━◆━╳╳━◆━◆

Emily became Mrs. Hamilton. Jonica wept at the candlelit service that was more a sacrament than a ceremony. Twin flames in Paul's eyes glowed in her heart, as did his low, "We're next."

Christmas passed with a minimum of patients and lots of special activities for those unable to go home. January found Paul deep in plans for Shepherd of Love Sanctuary. He had been asked to speak at several churches, not to raise money but to let people know why the combination clinic and shelter was being built. He closed with almost the identical statement Nicholas Fairchild had used years before—that no pleas for finances would be made. If some hearers felt God wanted them to be part of it, gifts would be gladly accepted, but no public credit given to any givers.

To both his and Jonica's amazement, Lacy Jones-Duncan sought them out after the service. She hadn't been around since her inglorious legal defeat. Every blond curl sparkled. So did her blue eyes. Toned-down makeup gave her a softer look. Instead of gushing, she said with a hint of wistfulness, Jonica couldn't decide whether real or fake, "I'd love to be part of your new venture." She glanced down so her lashes covered her eyes, then looked up appealingly. "I saw the announcement of your engagement in the paper, Paul. I'm terribly sorry I ever accused you. Forgive me, and let me help. My—husband left me a lot of money."

"You heard the condition," Paul reminded. A little frown drew his brows together.

"Thank you. You'll be hearing from me." She gave him a dazzling smile, then turned to Jonica. Safe from Paul's gaze, the smile froze. "Congratulations, Nurse. You have a fine man." She moved away to let others speak to them.

"Wonder what she's up to?" Paul looked after the trim figure. "She sounded sorry, but I still can't help being suspicious."

So was Jonica, although she wisely kept it to herself. But when Lacy presented Paul with a six-figure check and continued to enthusiastically spread the word about the new Sanctuary, it appeared she had really changed. She made a point of seeking out Jonica, prattling of hospital and clinic matters, though the beleaguered nurse wondered how she learned so much. In spite of Lacy's repeated protestations of repentance, Jonica didn't trust her and had a hard time not showing it. Lacy also became a thistle in the newly engaged nurse's little garden of Eden with her laughing reminder about the "childhood romance," as she called it, she and Paul had shared.

"Why, at one time, neither of us ever thought there could be anyone else," she confided once.

Stung, Jonica shot back, "Obviously there was and is."

Lacy laughed. "I'm sorry I offended you. I still consider Paul and his father among my dearest friends and I wouldn't want anything to ever come between us."

Jonica nobly bit her tongue and resisted the temptation to walk away and leave the "dear friend" standing there with her mouth open.

A two-day storm arrived at the end of January. The snow all but paralyzed the city. Shepherd of Love had its own backup system and suffered less than many, but stranded doctors and nurses doubled up with other staff members who lived at the hospital complex. Nancy Galbraith moved in with Jonica for overnight and insisted she would be perfectly comfortable on the couch. Patty and Lindsey made room for Shina and freed up another room. Off duty, Jonica enjoyed an evening with a large group of interns and nurses in the big living room, swapping stories and eating popcorn. But the time she shared with Nancy meant the most.

"I don't want to pry, but is everything all right with you and Paul?" Nancy hesitantly asked.

"Practically perfect."

"Just practically?" The warm brown eyes held reservations.

"You know how it is. We're both so busy we don't see as much of each other as I'd like and—"

"And Ms. Jones-Duncan hovers when you could." Nancy shook her head. "I may be unchristian, but sometimes I wonder how much the leopard really changes its spots."

"I do, too. Yet she acts so friendly I alternate between feeling guilty about my doubts and still having them."

Nancy stretched and yawned. "I wouldn't trust her a full hundred percent and I hope you won't, either." She yawned again. "On the other hand, I'm something of an alarmist at times." A smile showed beautiful white teeth. "Sorry, Jonica. I'm not bored, just dead on my feet. Mind if I turn in?"

"Not at all." Yet when her friend lay sleeping Jonica mulled over Nancy's comments. In the months at Shepherd of Love she had seldom heard the other nurse criticize anyone. The fact she evidently thought it necessary set off a warning signal in Jonica's mind. However, day followed day until Valentine's Day lay just a week ahead.

Exhausted by an unusually heavy schedule, all Jonica wanted was to peel off her uniform, soak in a tub, and sleep the clock around. She had the next two weeks off with plenty of time for wedding preparations and the short honeymoon that would nearly duplicate Peter and Emily's. She followed her program as far as the bath and wrapped herself in a fluffy aqua robe. She'd give herself a few minutes to unwind before going to bed. Once there, she had a feeling it would take Gabriel's horn to awaken her.

A staccato knock brought a groan. What now? Residents of staff quarters religiously observed the DO NOT DISTURB signs when posted on doors, and Jonica had put hers out.

The knock came again and a petulant voice called, "Jonica, answer the door. It's Lacy."

Muttering something more disgusted than elegant, the tired charge nurse reluctantly let her unwelcome visitor in but said, "I'm really tired. Could you come another time?"

"This won't take long and it can't wait." Lacy swished in on a wave of perfume, fairly radiating excitement. "All this time I've held back, but no longer. You can't marry Paul. He's mine, as I told you months ago." She closed the door behind her.

Indignation wiped out Jonica's fatigue. "I suggest you go." She started toward the door.

"Not until you read this." Lacy didn't budge while she waved a white envelope with heavy black writing on the outside. "It's from Paul."

Why would he write to her? A funny feeling planted an ice cube in Jonica's heart. She recognized the writing; it had adorned the only love letters she ever received.

"Really, Mrs. Duncan." She tried to laugh. "Are you trying to disrupt Paul and me just a week before our wedding?"

"There will be no wedding if you have the courage to read what Paul wrote to me."

Jonica flinched and saw the triumphant look in the watching blue eyes. She drew herself to her full five-foot, ten-inch dignity and stared at the slight woman. "I trust Paul Hamilton. Why should I read a letter he supposedly wrote? Can't you realize he stopped loving you years ago? If not, he would dump me and marry you, wouldn't he?"

"You little fool." Lacy's face mottled with anger. "Don't you want to know the truth? Can you marry him knowing he's still in love with another woman and always will be?"

The truth. Jonica though she knew it, yet if so, why hesitate? She took the letter, shook out the single page, and scanned the bold writing she knew so well.

Dear Lacy,

It's no use. The church would never go for it. Forget the whole idea; it won't work.

                                                Paul

"I tried to warn you," Lacy said. "Paul does love me but he's hesitating because he's afraid of what people will say." She preened. "I can make him come around, especially since there's no disgrace even among Christians in marrying a widow. I don't have a living husband and that's what held him back before. His father taught him to hate divorce." She laughed. "If you're as smart as everyone thinks you are, you won't stand in the way of Paul's happiness."

"You can never make him happy," Jonica cried, unwilling to accept the concrete evidence before her.

"Can you?" Lacy softly inquired. "In spite of professing to be a Christian, you're just a person from the other side of the tracks. I took the trouble to look you up. I have to hand it to you; you've come a long way from Slumville to Shepherd of Love, but not far enough, Jonica Carr."

"You are evil," the tortured nurse whispered. "Get out."

Lacy's blue eyes darkened. "I can't see that going after the man you love and always have is evil, but it doesn't make any difference now, does it?"

Jonica choked, feeling dirty all over, tainted with her past and smeared by this incredible, ugly scene. "Someday you'll be sorry." It sounded like an echo from childish threats at home. "You left your husband, came back here, and pursued Paul—"

"And got him." Lacy started toward the door.

The petite woman's move steeled Jonica's determination not to give up without a fight. "Just a minute!" Her voice rang and her head came up. "You won't leave until I call Paul."

A curious glint in Lacy's eyes made her look like a cat. "Good idea." She perched on the arm of the couch.

The telephone at the Hamiltons' rang three times. Four. Five. *Please, God, let me get Paul. If I can just hear his voice. . .*

"Hello?" A sleepy voice answered.

She sagged with relief. "Paul?" Her voice broke. "Did you write a note to Lacy Duncan?" She held her breath.

An eternity later Paul said, "Yes, but how did you know? It was supposed to be confidential—"

She cradled the telephone before replacing it on the receiver.

"Well?" Lacy's question cracked like rotting ice.

Jonica looked at Lacy and licked her parched lips. The phone rang in the stillness. Again. Both women stared at it and Jonica refused to answer. After ten rings it stopped—and the silence beat into her ears like a dinner gong. Somehow she got Lacy out, refusing to say another word. She must get away. Paul would surely come to see why she hung up on him. Soon. She snatched a weekend case, crammed whatever clothes and personal effects she could grab the quickest, and stuffed it full. She dressed, ran to her car, and put the case in the trunk, conscious of time passing with meteor-like speed. Chill air reminded her winter hadn't gone and she hurried back for her warm parka. Its down lining warmed her body but not her heart.

She experienced a moment of panic when the motor turned over but didn't catch. She hadn't used her car for several days. What if it didn't start? She tried again, it purred, and Jonica drove out of the parking lot, away from Paul and the only real love she had ever known.

Chapter 8

Jonica's headlights made twin streams that pierced the murky February morning. She aimlessly followed the flow of traffic to I-5, merged, and headed north. Fog and light rain grayed the day into nothingness. Exit after exit depleted the freeway as commuters headed toward work, but Jonica kept on. When she reached Everett, she hesitated. Canada lay to the north but she had no desire to go there now. Behind her lay—she gripped the wheel until her gloved fingers ached. It didn't matter where she went, just that she got away. Perhaps someday she could return and behave in a civilized manner, but not now. The healthy urge to wring Lacy Duncan's neck rose, then she remembered the hesitancy before Paul admitted his guilt.

"Forget it," she ordered. A large sign indicated a turnoff to Skykomish. She took it, crossed a long bridge, drove by the restored town, and headed east on Highway 2. Not the best time of year to go through Stevens Pass, but why not? Her all-weather tires were adequate unless a major storm came. "At least I have time off so I'm not letting the hospital down," she muttered, then a pang shot through her. What a far cry from the sleeping-in day she had promised herself to start her vacation and wedding preparations.

Sheer grit kept her alert for a time, but before she reached Skykomish the weather had worsened and exhaustion threatened. She found a simple but spotless motel, ordered a takeout meal, and forced herself to eat. To her utter amazement, she fell asleep the minute she crawled into the comfortable bed, and when she awakened, a feeling of physical rest made her decide to go on over the Pass. Storm predictions on TV gave her a few qualms, but she knew how to drive in bad road conditions, so she gassed up and continued.

Skykomish disappeared from her rearview mirror, a charming town lightly dusted with snow. Ahead lay—what?

"If I've heard once, I've heard countless times that when You slam doors, God, You open others." Jonica tried to keep the agony from her heart. "Well, now's the time to prove it. Except You didn't slam the door shut. Paul did."

Bittersweet memories rode with her away into the growing snowstorm that spatted wet patches on her windshield, but the runaway nurse didn't care. The wilder the evening, the better. It matched her reckless mood and challenged her driving skills until she had nothing left to waste in mourning an untrue fiancé.

◆◆◆

Dr. Paul Hamilton disbelievingly listened to the dial tone in his ear, shook the telephone, and pressed its redial button. The sound of angry bees buzzed. He hit the button again. This time he heard it ring. Three, five, ten times. "Impossible. Jonica couldn't have left her room between the time she hung up on me and I called back." Worry knitted his brows into a straight black line. "Why did she hang up in the first place?" He remembered the strain in her voice when she asked if he had written to Lacy, his own shock and stumbling answer. Disgust filled him. Why had he stuttered like an embarrassed school boy? No wonder she broke the connection. "I'd like to know what Lacy Jones-Duncan told her," he muttered, while dressing with quick movements. "On the other hand, what could she say? Why can't she get it into her head that anything I ever felt for her is deader than last year's fallen leaves?" Thankful that his father and Emily had risen early and gone for a walk, he changed, then scribbled a hasty note, *Gone to see Jonica,* slid into a jacket against the morning chill, and soon reached Shepherd of Love. Yet no amount of knocking roused Jonica. A sleepy Nancy Galbraith appeared a few minutes later, however, yawning and fastening a robe.

"Paul? Is something wrong?"

"I don't know. I got a strange call from Jonica, tried to call back and no one answered. Do you happen to know where she is? I doubt she could sleep through my knocking."

A little frown pencilled itself between Nancy's silky brows. "Come to think of it, I vaguely remember hearing her door close—twice—but I was too sleepy for it to register."

"Twice? Then someone was with her?" Paul's jaw set. "You don't happen to know if it was Lacy Duncan, do you?"

Nancy shook her head and her dark eyes looked trouble. "I don't know, but Lacy has been hanging around Jonica a lot lately."

"She's a spoiled troublemaker," Paul exclaimed. "Too bad someone doesn't teach her the lesson she should have had as a child." Satisfaction at the thought made him smile in spite of his nagging concern about Jonica.

"Maybe Jonica went over to the dining room," Nancy suggested. "Although she usually makes her own breakfast here."

"I'll look."

Paul sprinted down the hall, followed by Nancy's low call, "Good luck. I'll be praying."

He stopped and whirled back toward the watching nurse. "You think it's something serious?" he incredulously asked.

Nancy slowly shook her head but her eyes didn't brighten. "I just don't know. Usually Jonica is so tired when she gets off her shift she can't wait to shower and get to bed. It simply isn't like her to go out at this time of day." She glanced at her watch. "Better hurry if you mean to catch her. Breakfast is over in just a few moments."

One lightning glance at the deserted staff dining room sent Paul's heart plummeting. He forced himself to smile at one of the girls who was cleaning up and kept his voice casual. "Guess I missed Jonica."

"She didn't come in this morning, Doctor." The girl smiled. "You'll probably find her in her room if she isn't already asleep. Lindsey from Surgery said they had a rough night. I talked with her when she came in for breakfast."

"Thanks." Paul felt like a bloodhound sniffing out one clue one at a time. He curbed his first impulse—to rush to Lindsey Best's room and ask if she knew anything about Jonica. Her night would have been just as hectic. Besides, with Jonica off duty the next few weeks, Lindsey and Emily and the other surgical personnel were going to be swamped. Not even to appease his need to find and talk with Jonica could he disturb the tired nurses' rest. He walked to the doctors' lounge, wrote a brief note asking Lindsey to call him when she read it, and prepared to wait. Unease accompanied him on the duties he forced himself to accomplish, and when his pager summoned him late that afternoon, he could barely restrain his eagerness.

"Dr. Paul? You wanted me to contact you?"

He could visualize the puzzled look on the attractive redheaded nurse's face. He'd never before slipped a message under her door.

"Yes. I need to talk with you."

"I can meet you in our quarters' living room in a half-hour," Lindsey promised.

Rested-looking, freckles shining and face scrubbed, she appeared five minutes before her set time. "Is something wrong?"

He hesitated, unwilling to stir up anything, yet driven by an inner feeling that all was not well. He had periodically checked Jonica's room and the staff parking lot during the day and found no trace of her. "Did anything special go wrong on shift last night?"

"No—o. Busier than usual, but nothing extraordinary. Why?"

He matched her forthrightness with his own and gave her the same carefully thought-out story he'd told Nancy Galbraith. "Jonica called me maybe an hour after she got off duty. She sounded, well, strange."

A flood of angry color came to Lindsey's face and her brown eyes flashed. "I'll bet it was *her* doing."

"Who?"

"The witch." She flushed. "Sorry, that isn't a nice thing for a Christian to say, but she makes me so mad, coming around smoother than whipped cream and digging her painted claws into Jonica all the time. Never anything anyone can pounce on but little innuendoes and—"

"And reminders we were once engaged." Paul struggled with hatred for the albatross Lacy was around his neck. "By any chance, was she here this morning?"

"Was she!" Indignation raised Lindsey's voice and she mimicked the older woman to perfection. " 'Jonica, answer the door. It's Lacy.' A lot she cared that Jonica and I both had DO NOT DISTURB signs on our doors. I wasn't eavesdropping, either. Even our good acoustics didn't drown out Mrs. Duncan's knocking. I opened my door a crack, planning to tell her we'd had a really bad night." She broke off.

"Did you hear anything else?" Paul leaned forward. "I'm not asking because I'm curious. It's just that Jonica seems to have gone off somewhere and isn't back."

Concern erased Lindsey's natural aversion to gossip. "Lacy said in a kind of excited voice, 'This won't take long and it can't wait. All this time I've held back but. . .' I realized the conversation was going to be personal and shut my door. I must have drowsed because later I heard the door close—twice." She sighed. "I wish now I'd barged in and thrown Her Nibs out. Jonica is too special a person to be tormented."

"Yes, she is," the young doctor soberly agreed. "Lindsey, do you think she would resent it if you just stepped inside her room and looked around? She doesn't lock the inside door, does she?"

"No. None of us do. We all have keys to the door from the covered passage to this living room so leaving our own doors unlocked is perfectly safe." She shook her head. "If you think it's all right, I'll look."

They slowly walked down the long hall to the suite at the end. Lindsey turned the knob of Jonica's bed/sitting room and pushed the door inward. She gasped. "My goodness, she must have left in a hurry. Jonica never leaves her clothes strewn about like some of the rest of us."

Dismayed, Paul could only stare. The closed doors gaped open. A dress sagged from a hanger; a uniform lay crumpled in a corner. "Is anything gone?"

"Hmmm." Lindsey's observing gaze surveyed the disorder. "Her down-filled parka, heavy slacks, and shoes." She shrugged. "I can't tell what else."

"Check her dressing table, please."

Lindsey reported, after a cursory glance there and into the bathroom, "Toilet articles missing." She turned a sympathetic glance toward Paul. "She evidently plans to be gone for a few days."

Or more. But he wouldn't let his fear surface. "Lindsey, I want you to stay here long enough for me to make a call. I want a witness." He could see the shock in her face, although she nodded understandingly. It took but a moment to look up Lacy Jones-Duncan's number. "This is Dr. Hamilton. Please let me speak with Mrs. Duncan."

"Certainly." The well-trained servant added, "Just a moment, please," yet far more than moments passed before he returned. "I'm sorry but madam has left orders not to be disturbed."

Paul choked back anger and thanked the servant. He cradled the phone and told Lindsey, "She's going to be disturbed, all right. I still need a witness, though."

Lindsey looked stricken. "I'm sorry, but it's quite a distance to the Duncan mansion and I have to go on duty." She brightened. "Wait just a minute." Lindsey loped out the open door and knocked on the one next door. "Nancy?"

"Yes?" The off-duty nurse appeared. Her soft rose skirt and sweater highlighted her dark hair and eyes.

"Dr. Paul needs you," Lindsey said simply. "I can't get released from duty tonight and he has an errand to run that needs a witness. Can you go?"

"Of course." Not a moment's hesitation or demand for an explanation preceded her quick assent.

"Good. He will explain." Lindsey smiled and headed off down the hall.

In terse sentences Paul reported what Lindsey had seen and heard. "I have to find Jonica. I don't know what Mrs. Duncan has done, but it evidently sent Jonica into a spin. Lacy refused to accept my call. I'm going out there and get the truth. Are you game?"

"Absolutely. I'll just get a jacket." She vanished and reappeared clad in a warm jacket that matched her skirt and sweater. "Jonica is so vulnerable in spite of all her efficiency. Sometimes I see myself in her."

Paul saw the pain in Nancy's eyes and deliberated whether he should give her an opening to talk. She forestalled him by adding, "The wedding is so close, I hoped she could get through before anyone planted doubts in her mind."

"Doubts of my love? That's hard to believe." Paul helped her into his Accord, slid into the driver's seat, and fastened his seat belt. "I love her second only to our Lord."

Nancy slowly said, "I'm more concerned about Jonica doubting herself than you. She doesn't have a lot of self-esteem."

Again Paul felt the nurse hovered on the verge of saying more, but Nancy changed the subject.

"I won't be surprised to find that Mrs. Duncan isn't home."

"She'd better be," Paul grimly told her.

All his grimness availed nothing. A frankly surprised butler met them at the door when they reached the Duncan mansion with the news that Mrs. Jones-Duncan had suddenly decided to fly to California. "I'm sorry, Doctor." He shook his head. "I don't think she had planned to go, but shortly after you called, she summoned me and said she didn't know when she'd be back."

"Did she by any chance leave a message for me?" Paul held a faint hope that died when the butler shook his head. No. She had a maid pack and the chauffeur drove her to Sea-Tac International. An interview with the chauffeur elicited no further information. Yes, he had driven his employer to the airport. No, she had given no hint as to either her destination or when she would return.

"If I hear from her, would you want me to let you know?" the helpful butler asked.

"Very much." Paul turned away with a wide-eyed Nancy right behind him, concern written all over her smooth face.

"Now what?" he despairingly asked when they were back in the car. "Nancy, she is closer to you than to the others, although she likes them and I know they return the feeling. What is she likely to do?" He stared into the drizzle from massed dark clouds and made no move to start the motor.

Nancy didn't speak for a long time. At last she said, "Something has hurt her. Badly. We can be reasonably sure it came from her morning caller, who is incommunicado. She doesn't talk a lot about her childhood, but I know when things got too bad at home she fled. Perhaps she is doing the same now, seeking shelter and time to think." She stopped, then asked, "Do you know what Lacy Duncan might have said or done?"

"I suspect that she twisted the truth or lied outright in the hopes of doing mischief." A little bitterness crept into him. "I can't understand why Jonica didn't have more trust in me, no matter what Lacy said. She should know I would never do anything to hurt her."

"It is almost impossible to trust when life has hurt you deeply."

All through the silent drive back to the hospital and the next few days Paul remembered Nancy's comment. Why hadn't he been more sensitive? He'd thought his surrounding love could blot out Jonica's years of struggle, living in a false hope. What she needed was a deeper relationship with Christ. Until it came, Jonica Carr would continue to be prey to doubt of self and others.

"Perhaps she will find a place to hide and think," Nancy said several days later when no trace of the runaway nurse had been found. For Jonica's sake, her close friends had kept her absence downplayed. Paul surreptitiously consulted a friend on the police force and used a "case study" approach.

"It isn't a police matter, the way I see it," his friend advised. "There's no evidence of foul play. The woman you mention had time off coming. So it wasn't considerate of her to leave without letting someone know her destination. People don't always do what they should."

On the thirteenth of February, Paul, his father and Emily, Nancy and the minister who had been going to perform the wedding met for consultation. "Is there any chance she will come back and just be in the chapel at the time set?" the pastor wanted to know.

"I don't think so." Paul felt as haggard as his mirror showed he had grown. "I can't help believing she's in real trouble, but I don't know what it is. If only we knew where she is!" He gripped his fingers into fists.

"I think so, too," Nancy offered in her soft voice. "No matter how she felt, I don't think Jonica would allow the wedding to stand and not show up. Her sense of duty is so high it would be impossible for her to do such a thing."

The minister shook his head. "Then we'd better cancel the arrangements; just say they have been postponed."

Valentine's Day dawned overcast and murky. A little snow spitefully mingled with heavy rain. Weather forecasts told of exulting ski lodges that welcomed continuing falls of fresh snow on top of an already-good pack.

Paul stared out the living room window of his home, glad that Dad and Emily had insisted he continue to live with them for the present. The thought of rattling around in the tastefully furnished apartment he had leased until he and Jonica decided where to buy or build was more than he could handle. He had ordered the apartment repainted in her favorite colors: blues, greens, a vivid thrust of brighter colors here and there. When finished, he'd refused to let her see it, anticipating carrying her across the threshold in the time-honored tradition and dedicating their first home to God and each other.

Now—desolation. What had red hearts, foil-wrapped boxes of candy bearing enormous ribbons, and fat cupids to do with his loss? "God, where is she?" he prayed. "Please, wherever it may be, take care of her. Help her and heal her. If it be Your will, bring her back safely." He took a deep breath. "Most of all, fill her heart with Your Spirit that she may know even though others let her down, You never will."

Refreshed by the time with his Lord, Paul forced himself back to the plans for the Shepherd of Love Sanctuary. Even his personal travail couldn't slow the relentless progress of the project that would benefit so many. Yet again and again the sad-hearted doctor found his attention wandering. A wall clock ticked seconds into minutes, its cadence demanding, *Where is Jon-i-ca? Where is Jon-i-ca?* but Dr. Hamilton had no answer. Just a hundred disturbing questions. How could even a Lacy Jones-Duncan have made anything out of the only note Paul had written to her in more than ten years? Why had Jonica believed whatever she'd been told? And the final, hurtful question he couldn't overcome—if she had so little trust in him, could they ever have the kind of marriage he wanted? Or would their house be built on the sand of her uncertainty, only to crumble when life's storms pounded against it?

Chapter 9

"P aul." Peter Hamilton's troubled voice broke into his son's sea of turmoil. "It's time to file a missing persons report."

Paul shoved his chair back from the desk that overflowed with paperwork needing his attention. "I know. I've held off until today hoping she'd come back or call. Our wedding day. What a farce. I'm here worried sick and only God knows where she is, fighting battles we can only imagine!"

"Steady, boy." Love shone in the dark eyes that looked so like his son's. "God *does* know where she is and we can take comfort from that."

Paul stood, went to the window, and blindly stared across the sodden lawn. "Sometimes I wonder. There are so many crazies out there. What if one of them has her?" Fear hoarsened his voice.

Peter came to his son and put his arm around the sagging shoulders. "All we can do is trust God," he reminded. "There are a dozen reasons we haven't heard from her. Still, let's go file a report. Better get Nancy or Lindsey to give you as accurate a list as possible of what she wore and took."

It seemed pitifully sketchy when they presented it to a hardfaced officer whose kind eyes looked strange in such a time-worn setting. In a surprisingly soft voice, he took the information and promised to get it out immediately. He also suggested that TV and radio be alerted, with the request that if anyone had seen the missing nurse, they contact the police. "You'll get a lot of bad leads," he warned. "People who think any tall woman wearing a parka is your fiancée. On the other hand, we may get a decent clue or two."

Paul felt comforted by the man's efficiency, but when the predicted "sightings" began coming in, he wondered if the callers were making them up or if 90 percent of the women in Seattle were tall, attractive, and wearing parkas.

One caller insisted he had seen Jonica in deep conversation with a pilot at the airport who took off in his own plane. No, he didn't see the woman get in but she could have. He'd looked away, then back just in time to see the plane taxiing down the runway. He grew voluble about the plane. "Prettiest little bird I ever saw. Green as a shamrock and trimmed with the whitest white."

"Anything else?" Paul marveled at the patience of the officer who screened the calls and personally interviewed those that might be true, as in this case.

The eager man wrinkled his forehead. "Uh, yes. He had something painted on the side—a design. Kind of strange looking. A cloud, with a cross painted on it."

Paul's mouth fell open. Excitement quivered in him. "I know that plane. It belongs to Garry Sterling, a friend of mine."

Phone lines crackled. Paul clenched his hands. Had Jonica for some reason boarded Garry's plane? But why? She barely knew the pilot; he'd come to their table once when by chance they dined at the same restaurant.

The helpful officer grunted into the phone, listened, grunted again. He slowly replaced it. "Sorry, Dr. Hamilton. I have more bad news for you. Mr. Sterling's plane crashed over a week ago, in fact, the very day you say Miss Carr disappeared." His face worked. "Tough luck."

"Is Garry all right?" Paul prepared himself for the worst.

"He's in a coma at Harborview."

"So we have no way of knowing whether Jonica was on the plane?"

"Just a second." He dialed, waited, barked into the phone, "Any sign of a passenger in the Sterling wreck?"

Paul's nerves screamed in the silence.

"Plane too busted up to tell, huh. Okay. Thanks." He turned back to Paul. "The way I see it, Sterling's your best hope. You know the doctors at Harborview, don't you? Go see when Sterling's going to come out of the coma, if he is. He's the only one who can tell you if he had a passenger."

"If I didn't know God is in control of this world and not a capricious Fate, I'd swear there's a conspiracy against our finding Jonica," Paul told his father and Emily later that evening. A visit to Harborview had netted both encouraging and discouraging information. Garry Sterling had begun to show signs of consciousness. Perhaps in a day or two he would be able to answer questions. Yet his doctors made no promises.

"You know how it is," one told Paul. "The only predictable thing about comas is their unpredictable nature." With that, Paul had to be content. He requested that they let him know as soon as a change for the better occurred and dragged himself home, not knowing whether to be glad or sorry.

The worst news lay in the terrain where the plane had gone down, a rugged area in the North Cascades. If Jonica had been aboard, if she had been thrown clear and escaped harm, if she had survived the mountain storms, miles lay between her and help. Sterling had been off course. The rescue team who had helicoptered him out had no suspicion of a passenger's presence. When Garry failed to arrive at Bellingham on time, a reconnaissance flight spotted him from the air. He'd been rescued just before another storm swooped down.

Four days limped by. The hospital now knew the whole story. Compassion for Jonica and Dr. Hamilton shone in every face. Special prayer services were scheduled in the Chapel. Nancy, Lindsey, Patty, and Shina's natural gaiety surfaced only when working with patients who needed them. Nicholas Fairchild and the hospital director, all those involved in the Sanctuary project, Peter and Emily strove to lift Paul's dread. One night he cried out to God, "Please, if I could just know."

The next morning Harborview called. "Dr. Hamilton? Your friend Garry Sterling is awake. Give him a few hours and you can see him for just a minute, but don't disturb him."

Paul set his lips and obeyed. Long years of repression in the face of tragedy put a forced lilt in his voice when he wrung Garry's hand and said, "God sure was watching over you, old man. Say, good thing you didn't have a passenger, right?" He felt he'd suffocate before Garry smiled and nodded.

"Right. The passenger seat got it worse than I did." Garry stirred restlessly, eyes still dull.

"I'll come again when you get your sleep out," Paul told him and slipped away, relieved yet more puzzled than ever. The lead, like others, had proved false. Thank God for that! Yet, where was Jonica? How could the earth open up and swallow her so completely? Only the faith that God still held her in His capable hands gave Paul the strength to go on.

That night, the dedicated police officer called. "Dr. Hamilton? We have a real clue. A Jonica Carr that matches your description spent the night of February 7 at a motel in Skykomish. Well, sort of."

"What do you mean?" Paul gripped the phone.

"She checked in early, before noon. The motel owner said she normally didn't let anyone in that time of day, but Miss Carr looked so tired she made an exception. Something funny, though. She doesn't know when Miss Carr left. It could have even been in late afternoon or early evening. What with some snow and being busy, she didn't pay a lot of attention until about nine that night when she noticed the car was gone. She still didn't think much about it. People come and go at odd hours. The next morning she slept in, then found the unit empty when she went to clean."

"So she can't say for certain if Jonica went out to eat, came back and slept, or if she left the night before."

"That's right." The officer sounded sympathetic. "Nice enough woman. Didn't think much about it 'cause she gets all kinds. Then when Miss Carr's picture appeared in the newspaper she started wondering and called. I had her repeat the whole thing over again, but there wasn't anything else and she has no idea which way Miss Carr intended to travel. I'd guess over Stevens Pass, except the owner said a bad storm swept through that night. Think your nurse would take off over a mountain in the middle of a storm?"

"I honestly don't know. I hope not."

"So do I," the officer ponderously said. "Skykomish ended up with a foot of fresh snow and the pass is a whale of a lot higher."

New fear spurted in Paul's heart. "If there had been an accident, wouldn't someone know?"

"It's been known to happen that accidents sometimes happen when no other cars or trucks are around," the disembodied voice warned. "In a heavy snow, drivers are watching the road and not signs of tracks. Besides, there's always the danger of avalanches."

Oh, God, was Jonica buried somewhere under tons of fallen snow? Paul's hands, so steady when performing even the most delicate surgery, shook like aspen leaves in a storm.

"What do we do now?"

"I've already contacted Highway Patrol and the Leavenworth Police. Now we wait." The gruff voice stopped. "Uh, I understand you pray a lot. This is a good time. I just wish I had better news for you. This doesn't mean Miss Carr isn't all right. It does mean we have an idea of where she was and her probable destination. I'll keep in touch."

"Thank you," came through colorless lips. Paul buried his face in his hands and groaned. Instead of reassuring him, the detailed report had raised dozens of new fears, new visions of a terrified Jonica clinging to the wheel of her car; oceans of falling snow, enveloping, drowning. Death, instantaneous or slow. The lowering of body temperature. Oblivion. Paul clutched his trust in God and began to pray. . . .

❖

Jonica Carr left Skykomish behind and with it, some of her misery. Stevens Pass, especially in a growing storm, was no place for daydreaming. Scenic and beautiful, it didn't offer the wider highway that I-90 over Snoqualmie

Pass boasted. Neither did it have as much friendly traffic. Truckers chose the faster way when possible and tonight only a few vehicles came toward her, their lights ghostly in the softly falling snow.

"I hope that I don't get into a chains-required situation," she worried, anxiously watching the snowfall. "If I can reach the summit and start down the other side, I'll be okay." Gloved hands firm on the wheel, she expertly guided her car through slush. Not once did she consider turning back. She never had. Even at fifteen, when caring for herself looked impossible, when she felt at the end of her proverbial rope, she somehow tied a knot and hung on by sheer grit.

A long time later she breathed a sigh of relief and passed the summit, noticing the few cars and trucks sitting in the snow. Loneliness assailed her once she left the lights of the buildings behind. Traffic had all but disappeared. Still she kept on. If all went well, she could be in Leavenworth by midnight, even under the present road conditions.

With one of the strange quirks life holds in store, Jonica had just sighed with relief, knowing she had all but conquered the mountain when it happened. Above the keening storm a low rumble began. Northwest-trained, she recognized immediately what it was. She slowed, looked up. Above her a great ledge of snow shifted, gained momentum. Jonica slammed the gas pedal to the floor. Her car leaped ahead. Yet she knew she could not outrun the length of snow wall rushing down.

"God, if You're here, help me!" she screamed. She glanced to her right, away from the menace, and flicked her headlights to high beam. Instead of the steep drop from the highway most of the road had, a more gentle slope lay below her.

In the split second of decision, she knew her only hope lay in that slope. In seconds, the slide would cover the roadway and her car if she remained where she was. Going over the edge might prove fatal, but she had no choice. A slim possibility existed that the wall of snow would pile up and not spill over to bury her. Would the momentum of her car carry her far enough down for that to happen? She had to chance it. Setting her teeth in her bottom lip, she jerked the wheel to the right, glad for the speed she had gained. Down, down the car went with Jonica braced against the seat and relentlessly holding the gas pedal to the floor.

She sobbed as the snow-covered slope slowed her progress, wheels churning against the white peril. A gigantic fir loomed before her. She spun the wheel to the left. The snow-clogged wheels could not respond fast enough. In horror, Jonica saw the tree grow larger. In moments her car would crash into it head-on. "God, this is it." She flung open the door, released her seat belt, and jumped. . . .

"Cold. So cold." Jonica curled into a ball. Had the heating system in her room malfunctioned? She reached to pull her blankets higher and couldn't find them. Her eyes opened. Had she gone blind? Her room never got this dark. Even in the wee hours a little light filtered in from the illuminated hospital grounds.

She sat up and flung out both hands. Her dazed brain refused to comprehend until, in stretching, her parka sleeves pulled up and away from her gloves. The impact of snow on her bare wrists cleared her mind and everything came back—her flight, the slide, her wild plunge over the edge of the bank. She also grew aware of a weight of snow on her body and huge flakes beating down on her. "Thank You, God, that I'm alive," she whispered. "Now what?"

Jonica struggled to her feet and brushed away the snow. A glimpse at her watch told her she'd been unconscious for more than an hour. She shivered, remembering how she'd run back for her parka at the last minute when leaving Shepherd of Love. Where was the car? Could she find it in the storm? If only she could tell which direction she faced, but the snow made it impossible.

"I can't panic," she said and her voice came back to her, muffled by the storm. "All I have to do is climb up to the highway and keep walking down. A road crew will find me. Which way is up?" She stamped her feet until feeling came back into them, deeply grateful she had even awakened. Had God touched her shoulder or spirit that she might live?

She set out determinedly, but found that the ground soon sloped down. She reversed herself and rejoiced. Although snow swirled to her knees and made every step a chore, the exercise warmed her blood and made it race through her veins. Jonica laughed—and she thrilled to her height and weight. Suppose she were Lacy Duncan's size? She'd never make it through this ordeal. Somehow the malicious woman's importance faded when stacked up against the necessity of fighting for her life. Hands outstretched so she wouldn't walk smack into a tree, the runaway nurse stumbled into black night, not realizing she climbed a rise that led away from the road and not back to it.

Even her superb stamina faltered by the time her watch said four o'-clock. If she could only rest. "No!" she shouted. "That's how people die." She drove herself on until a little light behind the snow and her watch said morning crept near. Still she staggered through the deepening snow. Feet and legs had long since gone numb. Her medical training warned that hypothermia came closer all the time.

Jonica raised her foot to take a step, lost her balance, and tried to regain it. The heavy snow beneath her feet slid and she realized she had gained the top of something—a hill—a rise. The next instant she fell heavily, automatically throwing her arms in front of her face to protect it. Like a tobogganing child, she gathered speed. Her parka protected her chest and the snow hid sharp stones that could have ripped open her slacks and knees.

Heartbeats or an eternity later she slowed and stopped. A rapid check showed no broken bones, but one ankle had twisted and she knew it would swell. She strained her eyes—and saw nothing but more snow. Gloom surrounded her, a strange gray and white world that held no mercy. If only there were light she could cope. This terrible murk depressed her and prevented seeing what lay ahead, behind or to either side.

"God, are You here? I need You." Jonica stumbled to her feet and took a limping step forward. Pain sprayed through her right ankle. She gritted her teeth and took another step. What was the use of damaging herself further when she didn't even know which way to go? She closed her eyes and in spite of her best efforts, a single tear slipped out. She thought of Paul, the man she loved but hadn't trusted; of her friends at Shepherd of Love. Her mind wandered, back to the day she reported for duty. An electric current surged through her body, the knowledge she held a key in her mind that would unlock the answer to her dilemma. She concentrated, harder even than when she took the hardest tests to gain her coveted BS degree in nursing. If she could only remember. Forcing herself to go back to the moment she walked down the hall to the director's office, Jonica halted outside the door. "That's it." Words, engraved on the door, a strange inscription for a hospital director's office.

Thy word is a lamp unto my feet, and a light unto my path.

Chilled from the storm, miserable and aching, yet the words brought a ray of hope. "God," she cried. "Please, be my lamp in this awful darkness. I have to tell Paul—" What? For the first time she realized how her head pounded. She must have struck it when she hurled herself from the car. New fear gripped her. If she had a concussion and passed out, it meant death.

Jonica set her jaw and took another limping step, avoiding young snow-covered trees and low bushes that threatened to snatch her. She paused. Could she break a branch and use it for a crude crutch? It would take some of the weight from her injured ankle. She paused by a tree, shook snow from a branch, and gripped it with strong hands. It didn't budge. She tried again with the same results.

"You stubborn branch. I'm going to break you," she told the sturdy tree. Grabbing it with both hands, she pulled her feet up from the ground and let her full 150 pounds hang dead weight. The branch creaked ominously. Jonica put her good foot down, bent her knee, gave a little spring that sent her off the ground again. A splintering of wood warned her just in time. She quickly put her feet down again and tugged, hard. The branch broke close to the trunk of the tree and hung by a single strip of bark. Jonica yanked it free, struggled until she could get some of the bushy branches off, and triumphantly held up her homemade crutch. Now if she just knew which way to go.

Using the tree branch for support, she made it to the top of a nearby swell of ground and surveyed the vast, trackless scene that blurred with snow and low-hanging fog, turning in a complete circle, heart sinking. She froze and strained her eyes. Could that be the pale sun off to her right? If so, it meant she had been traveling in the wrong direction for hours. The light remained steady, smaller surely than sunlight, even if partially screened by the snow that no longer came so thickly but still fell. Did someone *live* out here?

"A light unto my path." The weary nurse turned her face toward the glow and set off again, grimacing when her right foot came down too heavily but never taking her gaze from the tiny beacon somewhere in the elusive distance.

Chapter 10

Paul Hamilton sometimes felt himself to be a classic case of dual personality. One side of him coolly executed the hundred and more details concerned with the establishment of the Shepherd of Love Sanctuary. The other half quivered and waited while minutes lagged into hours. The startling news that Jonica had stayed overnight in Skykomish had raised his hopes. Yet they dead-ended when no further trace of her could be found. Some clever research by the police did turn up an interesting fact. Highway 2 had suffered a slide across the road the same night Jonica supposedly traveled it, resulting in a closure for a full day while crews cleared it.

"Why so long?" Paul demanded. "I thought those graders were out all night in bad weather."

"That's the trouble. The snow kept coming down so hard it hampered getting the slide cleared," he was told.

"I suppose they checked to make sure no one got caught in it."

His policeman friend nodded. "Sure did. Found nothing out of the ordinary." He scratched his cheek thoughtfully. "Only trouble is—it snowed so hard they wouldn't have been able to learn much."

"Dr. Hamilton, now that we're pretty sure your fiancée took that road, and since Leavenworth reports no sign of her, Search and Rescue will be out there looking and they carry real fine-tooth combs."

Paul whirled. "Why didn't the motelkeeper know Jonica was missing sooner?"

The policeman shrugged. "She says she 'ain't much hand for TV and had been too busy to read the papers.' I guess she had them stacked in a pile and when she got around to reading them, called us."

"I think I'll go up there and see if I can find anything," Paul murmured.

"Don't. You'll get in the way. Search and Rescue know what they're doing. Let them do it."

The following day news came. Paul didn't know whether to let himself hope or sink in despair when he learned what the valiant crew had found—Jonica's car at the bottom of a slope, overturned and empty, hidden from the road above because of the heavy snow that had blanketed it and erased all sign of tracks over the edge.

"If she's wandering around out there they'll find her." The policeman's eyes showed disbelief that it would happen. He scratched at his cheek again. "If she wasn't too bad hurt, though, seems like she'd have walked out, 'cept the Weather Bureau reminded me how low fog and continuing snow kept visibility really poor the next day."

Paul turned to his only remaining source of comfort. "God, it looks hopeless. Yet You can move mountains. Now we need to find Jonica, regardless of what happened." He also decided that if no word came, he'd go look for her himself, regardless of disapproval. That afternoon when the phone rang, he raced to it, dreading possible bad news. Lacy Duncan's voice rang in his ear.

"I have to see you. I just got home from California and heard that Jonica Carr is missing."

"What can you possibly care?"

A little choking sound at the other end of the wire preceded a broken, "Please, Paul. I didn't mean for anything like this to happen."

Could it be a trap? Paul had to take the chance. An hour later he was ushered into Lacy's mansion. Red-eyed, without makeup, the small woman looked shriveled. She motioned Paul to a chair across from hers in front of the shining white fireplace. He hadn't seen her so messy since cheerleading days when she forgot her looks in the interest of leading yells. "Have they found her? Paul, she isn't dead, is she? I can't stand it. I never knew she would. . ." Her voice died.

He found himself repeating the question he had asked over the phone, voice harsh. "What can you possibly care?"

Lacy sobbed and dabbed at her eyes with a tissue. "I thought if she broke the engagement you'd come back to me, so I showed her the note you wrote to me."

"Note! How could you make her believe what I told you about the church never consenting to hold that benefit dance you wanted to sponsor had anything to do with us? Any of us?"

Shame sent dark red streaks into the fair skin. "I—I said you were holding back because I'd been divorced; that you were afraid of what the church would think."

He looked at her as if she were the serpent who once tempted Eve. "You told Jonica Carr that?" Fury raged. He wanted to grab her slender shoulders and shake the living daylights out of her. "Lacy Duncan, it would take a handwritten message from God to make me ever come back to you."

"Don't, oh, don't." She held out one hand as if to ward off his anger. "Paul, if she dies, will it be my fault? God, what have I done?" Fear made her voice tremble.

Her instinctive cry to her Maker stilled Paul's scathing denouncement. "You had better ask God for forgiveness, Lacy," he said in a dull voice. "Jonica is in His hands now. There's nothing either one of us can do." He started for the door then glanced back at the crumpled figure in the expensive room where luxury reigned and peace had no place.

"Can you ever forgive me?" She raised her mottled face and whispered the request.

"I'm not the one you have sinned against. Someday, I hope you have the opportunity to ask Jonica's forgiveness." His voice broke and he blindly walked to the door while Lacy's cries rang in his ears. . . .

Had she been walking forever? Jonica stumped through the snow, heartsick when she lost sight of the dim light somewhere ahead, encouraged when she saw it again. She no longer felt cold, but hot. Burning hot. *Left. Right. Left. Right.* Memory replaced her surroundings. She was the girl she had once been, stealing from a house that had never been a home, into the night, more frightened of what lay behind her than anything she might encounter. The look in her stepfather's eyes warned that even Jonica's mother couldn't protect the girl much longer. She shuddered in sympathy with the terrified teenager who escaped, but at great emotional cost. Physically unharmed, she knew she carried scars that affected her outlook on life. Those scars had made her distrust Paul when presented with what appeared undeniable evidence of his faithlessness.

Why hadn't she given him a chance to explain? If only she had answered the ringing telephone—was it only yesterday—she wouldn't be lost, alone, hurt.

Her guiding light flickered and she panicked. "God, please, don't let it go out before I get there!" she cried and tried to hurry. She knew she'd almost reached the end of her stamina. The rude crutch dug into her side when she leaned more and more heavily on it. It proved awkward and several times she fell in the deep snow. Finally she came to a clump of small trees, parted the branches, and rejoiced. The light shone brighter and through the gloom she could see the dark outline of a building—a cabin, maybe, or a hut. With the last of her strength she painfully made her way to the single step, limped across a covered porch, and beat on the door. "Please, let me in."

At first she received no answer. She pounded and called again. This time a feeble, "Come in," rewarded her efforts. Jonica pushed open the unlocked door. If she lived to be older than Methuselah she would never forget what she saw. First, a small wood heater, warmly glowing. She dropped her tree limb and dragged herself toward it, conscious that her former feeling of heat had changed to shaking chills. She stripped off her soaked gloves, stained with pitch, and held her hands out to the warmth. At the same time, the weak voice said, "Thank God you've come!" and she turned toward a bunk bed in the corner. Her shocked gaze took in the last thing one would imagine finding in a snowbound cabin: an elderly woman propped up in the bottom bunk bed, salt-and-pepper hair disarrayed, dull eyes enormous in a white face.

"Why, who are you? What are you doing here?" Jonica gasped.

"Sarah Milligan. I—"

Her visitor's legs gave way and she sank to the floor, barely conscious of her surroundings. "Tired. So tired."

"Can you get into the top bunk?" Sarah's voice penetrated the fog Jonica knew would soon claim her completely. She managed to shake her head no, the smothering grayness obliterated everything except the need for sleep.

Nightmares followed. Friends and enemies danced in and out of her feverish mind. Sometimes she threw off blankets that reminded her of the heavy snow pressing her down. At other times she curled into a ball and her teeth chattered, neither knowing nor caring where she was. Once she surfaced and asked, "Who are you?" to the strange woman who held a cold cloth to her forehead, but dropped back into oblivion before she learned the answer.

When Jonica at last regained consciousness, the warm room lay quiet and peaceful around her. She occupied the lower bunk bed. Nearby, the woman who had bid her come in nodded in a rocker. Gradually, the nurse's mind cleared. She surveyed the cabin's interior, noting how clean and cozy it was. Her eyes widened at a neat pile of blankets on the floor. Shame scorched her. Sarah Milligan must somehow have put her stranger guest in her own bed and slept on the floor.

"How long have I been here?" Jonica asked when the older woman opened her eyes and smiled.

"Three days." Sarah slowly stood, walked to the stove, filled a bowl, and brought the rich-smelling broth to Jonica.

She realized now she felt starved. No meal had ever tasted better than that bowl of broth and she drained it to the last drop.

"Good for you." Her wilderness hostess took the bowl. "Now, I know you want to know everything."

"Please." Jonica swung her legs over the edge of the bunk, sat up, and felt her head spin.

"Don't get up," the older woman ordered. Her voice sounded far stronger than when she first invited the visitor in.

"I can't take your bed any longer. I'll be all right after a moment." She forced a smile and waited, head down a bit so blood would rush to her brain and clear it. She glanced at her neatly bound right ankle, surprised at how little it pained but aware the swelling remained.

"Then let me help you to a chair." Sarah trotted over and gave Jonica a little help in getting out of the low bunk. She seated herself in another rocker and smiled. The nurse noticed with pleasure her sharp dark eyes that contrasted strangely with the dull look present when Jonica arrived.

"Now, do you want to tell me who you are and how you happened to find me?" Sarah asked. A look of reverence filled her face. "Although I believe God sent you."

"I do, too. I'm Jonica Carr, an RN, who foolishly got upset and ran away from Seattle instead of sticking it out and finding the truth. I thought I could get across Stevens Pass and into Leavenworth before the snow got too bad."

Sarah clucked her tongue. "Sounds like we're a real pair."

"Oh?"

"I ran away, too," Sarah confessed, then look shamefaced and chuckled.

It brought an answering smile to her guest's lips, who couldn't help exclaiming, "Really?"

"Cross my heart." She solemnly made the childish gesture pledging honesty.

"But why are you here in this awful storm?"

Sarah looked toward the window, shrouded with even more snow. "To prove I'm not a useless old woman." The pain in her voice made Jonica's heart ache.

"I'm sixty-nine years old and ever since I turned sixty-five my family has treated me like a Medicare casualty. They won't let me do this. They refuse to consider my doing that. 'Be your age, Mother' is their cry—which means sitting in a rocker of their choice, staring at TV, and waiting for them to visit when they have time." Twin spots of red marched to her cheeks. "Well, the good Lord's given me a strong, healthy body and my mind is still sound. I rebelled. I got tired of being tucked off in the basement apartment at my daughter's and watching life go on without me. The biggest mistake I ever made was retiring from teaching—although I'd planned to travel."

She sighed. "They convinced me to turn over my savings to remodel the basement, another bad decision on my part."

"Like King Lear?"

"No–o." Sarah looked heavenward as if praying for patience. "My children aren't wicked and they would never turn me out. They're just smothering me. Maybe I'm a rebellious old woman, but I'm so tired of being set on the shelf just because I've lived a long time."

"You're a perfect dear." Jonica leaned forward and put an impulsive hand over the ones lightly clasped in Sarah's lap. A little idea began in the back of her mind, but before she could formulate it, Sarah suddenly laughed ruefully.

"Caught in a net of my own making," she said. "I waited until they went away for a few days, climbed into a car they seldom use, and came up here."

"You can *drive* in to this cabin?" The news astonished Jonica.

"A dirt road from Leavenworth," Sarah told her. "I'd planned to sneak back and be in my usual spot when they returned." A frown creased her face. "Now I don't think I can. The first night I got here, I ended up deathly sick, feverish, aching bones, vile headache, and retching. It about did me in. Of course, there's no phone here. I could keep a fire going because my son wanted the cabin well-constructed; he uses it during hunting season. I got so weak it scared me, but by the next day I felt I could drive if I took it slow. Imagine my dismay when I couldn't get the car started! I suppose since it sits around so much the battery grew weak and standing out in a freezing night didn't help things."

"When was this?" A little twinge went through Jonica. No phone. No car. Continuing storms. At least they had a warm place, food, and each other. *Plus God,* she thought.

Sarah seemed to sense her guest's thought. "I came two days before you arrived. Even when I couldn't get the car going, I didn't worry. Someone would see the smoke from my fire and investigate, although the note I left for my daughter in case they unexpectedly came home sooner than planned just said I'd gone off for a few days." She sighed. "Now everything will be even worse. They'll consider me nothing but an irresponsible old woman who needs a keeper." Her face sagged, but the next minute she smiled. "Anyway, the storm swept down and I knew smoke wouldn't rise above the fog and snow, so I just told God, 'You've gotten me out of pickles before. Here I am again.' I knew no one in his right mind would be out here in such weather, but I had to do *something*, so I put the kerosene lamp in the window. That way I could pretend someone might come. Besides, if God planned to send help, wouldn't they need a light?"

The long strain, physical exertion, and mental turmoil Jonica had gone through exploded into laughter. Sarah's down-to-earth practical approach to God sent the runaway nurse into spasms that shook her body and left her with tear-wet eyes. The near-tragedy for them both had formed a bond more quickly than any other circumstance could do. Jonica finally settled down, wiped her eyes, and said, "Sarah Milligan, I know a place that would welcome you. You'd have your own apartment, the choice of cooking your own meals or eating in a dining room, freedom to come and go, and the chance for all the giving you want to people who need you."

"Hmmm, sounds like heaven and I'm not ready to go there." The sharp black eyes reflected unbelief.

"I mean it." Jonica felt her pulse race. "Listen, I have a story you'll love." She began to relate Nicholas Fairchild's experience and how the Shepherd of Love Hospital came to be built. Enthusiasm brought renewed energy and she realized more than ever how much she loved the institution dedicated to those who came. Sarah had heard part of the story but sat entranced at the full tale. Yet when Jonica finished, she shook her head.

"That's all very well, but where's the place for a rebellious old lady?"

"I saved the best for the last. The man who donated the land did so with the stipulation that a Retirement Center be built off to one side. It's the place I described. I've toured it and the suites are as attractive and homey as the ones in the staff quarters. In fact, the donor lives there. Permanently."

Sarah looked at her hands, head bowed. "I wouldn't be able to afford it," she confessed in a muffled voice. "All I have is my Social Security and a small teachers' retirement pension. Retirement centers cost money—pots of it. I know. My son and daughter looked at them."

Jonica saw the forlorn, beaten look of a woman who only wanted to be needed. How much she represented thousands of others, victims not of abuse but of over-concern and busy children who had their own lives and families to consider. "Sarah, Nicholas Fairchild built Shepherd of Love for all. Those who can, pay. Those who cannot are still welcome," she gently said.

Some of the fire that had accompanied her recitation about running away jerked the older woman's head erect. Again, red spots glowed in her cheeks. "How can they do it?"

"Requests for finances are made to God. He opens doors no one knows exist. Unsolicited contributions pour in. Why, right now, Mr. Fairchild and some of the doctors are working to establish a Shepherd of Love Sanctuary and Clinic in the heart of Seattle. It will be built and maintained the same way."

"He must be a wonderful man."

"He is, but so humble that the first time I saw him, I had no idea who he was."

"You said I'd be needed? How?"

"My best nurse friend, Nancy Galbraith, works in Pediatrics. Another, Shina Ito, is in Obstetrics. They tell how frightened children and babies sometimes are. Although the nurses cuddle when they can, their busy schedules simple don't permit time to read stories to and talk with the children and simply rock babies. I know the entire children's department would go wild if you appeared. Only thing is, they might just work you to death!"

"Better than rusting from disuse," Sarah retorted but her eyes shone with anticipation. "I suppose there's a waiting list a mile long for the Retirement Center."

"Probably, but if that's where God wants you, it won't matter, will it?"

"No, Jonica, it won't." Sarah sat up straight. "Now you need to get back in bed."

"Not I." She flexed her muscles. "People die in bed. If the storm keeps up, I'll need to have my stamina built up again."

That night after she carefully mounted the little ladder and settled in the top bunk over Sarah's protests, Jonica listened to the rising wind and snuggled into her warm blankets. By what strange paths God led people into each other's lives. What an asset Sarah would be to the hospital and how everyone would love her! Content in spite of the danger that still lurked, the night charge nurse fell asleep, lulled by the knowledge that Sarah—and God—were nearby.

Chapter 11

I f it weren't that folks must be worrying about us, I'd downright enjoy our visit," Sarah confessed two days later in the midst of another squall.

"I would, too. It's the first time I've had a chance to cook much." Jonica blinked back tears from the onions she had just chopped for a stew. "It's kind of an interlude, a chunk of time between two parts of our lives."

"Well, we have plenty of canned food when we run out of the fresh fruits and vegetables I pilfered from my daughter's refrigerator." She rummaged in a cupboard. "Here's a cake mix and canned frosting. Better than nothing, I s'pose, but you should taste some of my scratch cakes."

"I will when you come to Seattle."

"Am I coming to Seattle?" A hint of laughter in the question.

"You are. Just as soon as there's an opening for you." Jonica clamped down on what she started to add. Until she approached Dr. Peter Hamilton and Emily, she had no right to get Sarah's hopes up. They might prefer keeping their home to themselves while Sarah waited to get into the retirement center. On the other hand, Paul would soon be moving into the apartment. Her face warmed, then cooled. Could he ever understand why she had fled and caused all the heartache he must be experiencing?

"I'll make it up to him," she muttered while Sarah clattered pans and vented her regret in peeling carrots and potatoes.

"What smells better than chocolate cake?" she wondered aloud an hour later. "Isn't it cool enough to cut?"

"Of course." Sarah grinned and eyed the delicious dessert. "Now, I think the stew smells better. So does gingerbread. And pumpkin pie. And fresh hot rolls."

"If I live close to you, I'll look like a roll," Jonica said through a mouth filled with warm cake. "Mmmm. May I have another piece, please?"

Yet cooking didn't take all their time. Neither did tidying up the small space or stoking the fire. The storms continued day after day and with them, the conversational level between the two women deepened. Jonica told Sarah everything, starting with her miserable childhood straight through the moment she reached the cabin, guided by that light in the window that stabbed through darkness and beckoned her on when she wondered if she could continue. "If it hadn't shone for me, I would have died," she ended.

"That's how it is with the love of Christ. Millions die spiritually because they don't have His light. Jonica—there's something you need to hear. I probably wouldn't speak if we weren't stranded here waiting for help." She hesitated then went on in her forthright way, dark eyes soft and compassionate. "I've seen your faith increase in the time we've been together, but something is holding you back. Is it because you have never forgiven your stepfather—or your mother?"

Jonica flinched. The same thought had haunted her ever since God led her to safety in the middle of the storm. "I don't think I can do that."

"You must. Just as I must forgive my children, although not for the same reason."

"He doesn't deserve to be forgiven." Memory steeled her voice. "You can't imagine what it was like."

Sarah sat quietly for a long time before saying, "Have you never done anything you felt didn't deserve forgiveness?"

"No, I—" She broke off. "Sarah, that's not a fair question. You know I don't feel Paul should forgive me for doubting him, but I want him to. But that's different!"

"Is it, really?" Sarah looked sad, old. "Resentment gnaws away at the person who holds it until she becomes hard and bitter. That's why I ran away. So did you. I know I'm preaching, but think of Jesus hanging on a cross and asking God to forgive those who put Him there. He told us to forgive. Now, my dear, let's talk of happier things. It's been a long time since I visited Seattle. What places will I want to see?"

"Pike Place Market, Mount Rainier, the Ferry Terminal, the Arboretum, downtown." Jonica enumerated various points of interest.

When she went through the list, Sarah asked, "Tell me more about Shepherd of Love and your friends."

"I could talk about them for hours," she laughingly admitted. "Each of my special nurse friends is different and the difference makes them special. Shina is a combination of Japanese reserve and American fun. Lindsey Best, and she's one of the best surgical nurses I've seen, lives up to her red hair and freckles and big grin. Patty Thompson is an innocent-looking blond who could talk the birds out of the trees around the hospital, but she's also an efficient woman and her young patients adore her.

Nancy is—Nancy." Jonica stared into space.

"I have the feeling Nancy carries some childhood or teenage memory as painful as mine. I felt it the first time I met her and a few times have been on the brink of discovering what it is, but an interruption or simply Nancy's own reticence has closed the door."

"She's single?"

"Yes. Once I saw her gazing at a Dr. Damon Barton who is in private practice, a children's specialist we call in, attractive. I have a feeling that someday Nancy will share with me, although it's hard. I know." She sighed.

"What about Mrs. Jones-Duncan?" Jonica had long since told Sarah about the trouble the petite woman caused. "Have you forgiven her?"

"It's strange, but I think I have. In the storm she lost importance in my mind. Since then I keep remembering how she looked when she said, 'I can't see that going after the man you love and always have is evil.' I still hate the way she did it, for with the cushion of time and distance since she showed me that note I've come to realize something. If Paul Hamilton really wanted her, he would tell me point-blank. He wouldn't stick with me a minute and excuse himself to Lacy with a made-up alibi that the church wouldn't go for it."

"You are positive now that he loves you, aren't you?"

"I have never been surer of anything in my life except that God loves me even more. Sarah, why did it take me so long to accept it? God's love, then Paul's?" Her poignant cry sounded loud in the little cabin.

"Childhood chains can be strong. It takes time and courage to unlock and free ourselves from them."

Jonica rose and walked to the window she had stared from so many times. "I am really trying to forgive—my stepfather—and mother." Hot tears fell. "I want to be free."

"Desire is the first step." Sarah joined her and together they looked out into still another gray, obscuring day. "The seed is planted. Now God will nurture it."

"I've thought a lot, and when I get back to Seattle I'm going back. It's been almost eleven years. I've never heard anything or seen either of them. I'm afraid of what I'll find but it has to be done."

"Take your Dr. Paul with you," Sarah advised.

"To that hovel? Never!" Jonica's mouth set in a stubborn line.

"You think he hasn't seen worse? And won't see worse at his Shepherd of Love Sanctuary?" The words hit like ice pellets. "Jonica, your doctor is in the business of providing life and hope to those *exactly like your step-father*. Who could need it more?"

"That's one reason I've felt so unworthy. I—I don't know if I can work with those kind of people."

"They're created by God, even though they've chosen to follow the devil," Sarah reminded her, but a gentle pat on the shoulder softened the truth. "Besides, when a burden's shared, that burden is halved. I'll be surprised if Dr. Paul isn't overjoyed at the opportunity to take you back so you can begin your healing process, no matter what you find."

"Perhaps." But Jonica stayed at the window staring blindly past the storm and into her stormy future long after her newfound friend went back to her rocker. When she finally turned, she asked, "Sarah, you were still sick when I came. How could you take care of me?"

One of the sweetest smiles she'd ever seen rested on the other's face. "A body does what she has to. I just told the Lord that since I must be His hands, why, He'd have to increase my strength to be equal to the task. There's a lovely Old Testament blessing in Deuteronomy 33. Moses tells Asher, 'Your strength will equal your days.'"

Jonica felt her eyes sting. Would she ever gain the wisdom and peace this spirited woman possessed in abundance? Deep within, she realized these could only come with living. Perhaps going back and facing the past squarely was a beginning.

<hr />

Paul Hamilton stared at the charred remains of what had been Jonica's car, breathing heavily from the climb down to where it lay and weak with relief that his fiancée hadn't been inside. It must have caught fire on impact. A blackened snag, all that remained of a large tree, had crumpled the front end, and burned limbs lay on top.

"If it hadn't been for the storm and the road being closed because of the slide, someone would have seen it," said the Search and Rescue leader who grudgingly consented to let Paul come. "Rotten luck."

"It could be a lot worse."

"Yeah." He curiously looked at Paul's drawn face, started to speak, and refrained. "Okay, crew, we have work to do."

Paul walked away from the burned car and didn't look back. In the following hours he learned respect for the thorough team. They scoured every inch of snow-clad ground for clues, although the days and weather since that fateful night offered little to go on. Not until late afternoon did the leader stop.

"We'll take one more ridge, then knock off until morning." He grunted. "Wish this low ceiling would lift. We can't see far enough to catch anything moving."

"After all these days, it isn't likely she'll be moving, is it?" Paul faced the truth and a daggerlike thrust went through him.

"If she found shelter. . . Aw, Doc, you never can tell. Sometimes folks hole up and we find them." Yet the false cheerfulness didn't fool Paul. He wearily trudged after the crew to the top of the little ridge that overlooked a small valley, passionately praying the murk would rise.

It didn't. The Search and Rescue members silently stood and surveyed the limited landscape a long moment, then their leader said, "We'll try again tomorrow."

"Wait!" Paul's voice cracked and he speechlessly pointed. "I thought I saw a light." He forged ahead. Had wishful thinking created the tiny brightness? He sniffed. "Is that smoke?" he called over his shoulder, heart pounding. Light and smoke meant humans. Hampered by the snow, he broke trail, glad for the rough terrain he and his father had hiked over the years in their quest for good fishing spots. He could hear the others floundering behind him, their way made easier by his going. Ten minutes later he stepped onto the porch of an almost-buried cabin, whose single window held the yellow light he'd seen from afar. "Hello!" He pounded on the door, didn't wait for an answer, and lunged through it, snowy and dripping.

His heart sank. A gray-haired woman stared at him from a rocker by the stove. "Who are you?" he cried, hope dying. Oh, God, why hadn't Jonica found this haven?

"Paul."

He whirled toward the whisperer. Tall and pale, Jonica's eyes shone like blue stars. He started toward her, held out his arms, heedless of the snow melting onto the floor, too filled with gratitude to speak or pray. She ran straight into them, lifted her face. He saw regret, tears, and more love than he had dreamed possible. With a broken cry she clung to him. His cold lips touched her brown hair, then her lips. When he released her, a rosy blush had driven away her pallor.

"Welcome, Dr. Hamilton." Black eyes twinkled in the older woman's face. "About time you were coming for this girl of yours." She turned to the gaping Search and Rescue crew. "Come in, come in and shut the door.

You'll want coffee; Jonica made soup."

"I don't understand." Paul's gaze followed her as she trotted about. "What are you doing here? How long have *you* been here, Jonica? How did you find this cabin out in the middle of nowhere?" He hugged her to make sure he wasn't dreaming.

"Sarah's lamp in the window shone through the darkness. I followed it. She took care of me." What a few words to express all that had happened. Paul knew the whole story would come later. For now, it was enough to have found his lost fiancée. For the first time he realized a little of what Jesus must have felt when He found unharmed the sheep who had wandered from His fold. And what He felt every time a strayed sheep returned.

"Shuck off those wet coats," Sarah ordered. "Goodness, what a mess." She reached for a mop but the team leader beat her to it.

"Go back on the porch and shake off the snow," he ordered. "You, too, Doc. It won't do any good to find your nurse, then have her catch pneumonia from getting soaked."

Paul's laugh rang out. He obediently followed the others out, rid his jacket of most of the snow, then came back in, laughing to see how efficiently the leader attacked the puddles on the floor.

A half hour later, reasonably warm and dry, the Search and Rescue crew left. "We'll bring a new battery," they promised. "Sure you don't want to go with us, Doc?"

He coolly looked into their grinning countenances. "If you were in my shoes, would you?"

"Naw." They shrugged into their coats and went out, still laughing.

"Now." Paul looked first at Sarah Milligan, then at Jonica. "I want to hear the whole story."

It took a long time, with the women sometimes filling in for one another. Paul's relief knew no bounds. "Sarah, thank God you are just what you said—a rebellious woman." He eliminated the word *old*. No one with her spirit would ever be anything but ageless.

Jonica quickly told him of their plans for her rescuer's move to Seattle and he saw the eagerness in Sarah's lined face. He determined to do everything possible to get her into the Retirement Center as soon as possible. "In the meantime," he suggested, to Jonica's amazement and delight, "why don't you come stay with Dad and Emily? I know they'll love having you and you can get started loving those children who need you so much."

She seemed to grow taller. "Dr. Paul, you will never know until you're my age how much those words mean. Oh, to be needed again! It's just this side of heaven." Unashamed tears crept from her eyes.

"Will your son and daughter object?"

"Probably, but I'm still their mother, although the last few years they've tried to turn things around." Her lips set for battle and her black eyes flashed. "I know it's because they love me, but now I'll be free."

"Free," Jonica repeated wistfully when Sarah had considerately gone to the bottom bunk and turned with her face away from the two who sat with rockers close enough for them to whisper confidences without someone else listening. "Paul, if you knew how much I regret running away."

He took her hands in his and looked deep into her eyes. Flickering shadows from the turned-down lamp in the window couldn't hide their expression. "My darling, about the note—"

"I know it couldn't mean what she said." Perfect trust illumined her features.

The last unspoken question as to why she hadn't believed in him fled forever. To think she loved him that much, had the faith he would never betray her, after a life in which she had been subject to betrayal by those who should have cherished her. Humbled, he tightened his grip, hating to bring Lacy's name into the secure little cabin but knowing he must. "She wanted to have the church sponsor a benefit dance. My note told her how impossible the scheme was and to forget it."

"And I accepted that you—" The low, repentant cry tore from Jonica's throat. "Can you ever forgive me?"

"It's over. All of it." In whispers he told her of the blond woman's frantic call, her reception when he went to her empty mansion, his feeling that perhaps she had learned a lesson. He ended by saying, "Jonica, are you ready to leave the past? Will you marry me as soon as we can get home and arrange it?" The word *again* hung unspoken in the air. To his surprise, Jonica slowly shook her head. "Sarah—and God—have made me see I can't go into the future until the past is truly settled." She took a long, quivering breath, but her gaze never left his. "Paul, I've accepted God the way I should have done a long time ago when I went through the form but had little concept of His love. Before I marry you, I need to go see my mother and stepfather." She paused. "Will you go with me?"

The forlorn look that so reminded him of a hurt child cut him to the heart. He stood, pulled her up so he could put his arms around her, and whispered into her ear, "Nothing on earth can keep me from it. We'll go the minute we get home and cleaned up." He felt her tense body relax and heard the little sob, then turned her toward the bunk beds. "Get some sleep, Dear. Tomorrow's going to be a long day."

She climbed the little ladder and settled into the top bunk. Paul lay down on his bed on the floor, marveling that Sarah could have slept there. Or had she slept? Probably not. He'd just bet she spent most of the night caring for Jonica. Why hadn't the woman he loved been born to a mother like Sarah? Yet, who was he to question God's ways? Good would come out of evil every time. God had promised it. Paul fell asleep with a prayer on his lips, not only of thankfulness but that Jonica would receive strength for whatever appalling condition they might encounter when she retraced the painful steps to her childhood.

Chapter 12

The following morning help arrived, along with clear winter skies and a rise in temperature that set the eaves of the little cabin dripping. Search and Rescue personnel brought a new battery, installed it in Sarah's car, and overruled her insisting she could perfectly well drive back to Leavenworth. "Right on our way, Ma'am," they told her and grinned. By early afternoon she'd been delivered to a sputtering but relieved daughter and family after a whispered promise to come to Seattle if the older Hamiltons were willing.

Jonica hugged her and watched the car drive out of sight, feeling bereft, hating to see her staunch friend go.

"It won't be long." Paul promised. Yet she stayed quiet until they reached the spot where he had parked his car and joined the Search and Rescue crew. She noticed he pressed bills into the reluctant hands and she thanked each one individually.

"If the Doc here doesn't treat you right, you let us know," the leader told her. He chuckled. "Although there's no chance of that. If you could have seen his face when he looked at the burned car. . ." He shook his head, eyes sober. "That God you believe in sure took good care of you."

"He takes care of all who believe in Him," she told him. "If you don't believe me, try Him and find out for yourself."

"I will." He turned away. "Thanks."

She watched him go through a mist. How caring and giving Search and Rescue men and women were! They braved dangers on behalf of others and their jobs called for steady nerves. She offered a prayer on their behalf. If they added faith to their efforts—and perhaps many of them did—results might be even better.

With all her heart she wanted to stay awake on the drive home. She couldn't. Head pillowed against Paul's strong right arm and feeling that nothing could ever again harm her, she fell asleep just west of the summit and didn't awaken until they pulled into the hospital lot. "Why, where's the snow?" Eyes accustomed to everlasting white, the sun-washed February hospital grounds looked bare and unfamiliar.

"In the mountains where it belongs." Paul chuckled, unfastened his seat belt, and stepped out. A few moments later he unlocked her outside door, led her in, and said, "Take a warm bath and sleep. I'll let Nancy and the others know we're back, although Search and Rescue promised to notify Dad last night, so they probably already know. I also called on the car phone while you slept."

"I've slept enough." Jonica wouldn't put the inevitable off any longer. "Paul, if I bathe, can we eat and find Mother? I have a terrible feeling of urgency, as if she needs me."

Paul didn't discount it. They had both known of too many cases where an inner warning signal meant something important. "Can you be ready in an hour?"

"Yes." She caught a glimpse of herself in a mirror. Tousled, but rested-looking, eyes wide. Her parka smelled of smoke and needed a good cleaning. Her stained slacks would make good rags. "Goodness, what an awful looking person!"

He cocked one eyebrow in the way she found endearing, snatched a kiss, and went out the hall door. She heard him knock on Nancy's door and a moment later her beautiful friend entered.

"I'll run your bath. Get out of your soiled clothing and leave it in a pile."

How like Nancy not to insist on hearing the story when Jonica needed her ministering hands! Again came a feeling that one day she would learn what lay beneath the surface of Nancy Galbraith. She gratefully accepted the skilled nurse's help in shampooing her hair. "No wonder the children love you," she said. "You're so gentle."

Nancy rinsed her hair, toweled it, and waited until Jonica slipped into a robe before leading her to a low chair and blow-drying the brown hair. "Paul said you are going to find your mother. What do you want to wear?"

Jonica considered, remembering the slovenly area she'd grown up in. "Something cheerful but not too bright."

Nancy flipped through her wardrobe and held up a soft yellow sweater and dark blue slacks. She added a lined navy windbreaker, warm enough for the evening, and navy walking shoes. "How about these?"

"Fine." Jonica ran her tongue over lips dry from dread. "I—I don't know if I can do this but I have to," she confessed when she finished dressing.

"Would you like to pray about it?"

"I don't think any words will come out."

Nancy put her arm around the troubled nurse. "Then I'll pray." She hesitated and Jonica felt some of her friend's calm spirit enter her own heart.

"Our dear heavenly Father, we thank You for being with us wherever we go. We are grateful You brought Jonica safely home. Now we ask that You will go with her—no, go before her—in this hard task and that Your Holy Spirit will guard and guide her. In Jesus' precious name, amen."

"Amen," Jonica whispered.

The fragile moment of sharing ended when a rap at the door announced Paul's arrival. She ran to it, saw the way his dark eyes lighted when he saw her. Clean shaven and scrubbed, he'd chosen gray slacks and jacket with a pale blue shirt. "Ready?"

She looked from him to Nancy's encouraging brown eyes. Strength flowed into her body. She took Paul's hand. "I'm ready."

The street she used to know had grown even seedier. Broken windows in vacant houses showed that some residents had fled. A group of youths on a nearby corner stared in their direction, muttered something to one another, and laughed. Jonica felt her face scorch. Only too well did she know the kind of street humor such individuals chose to impress one another. Yet, as Sarah said, they were part of God's creation in spite of their sins. She felt sweat start and her hands grew clammy. Facing the past was even worse than she had expected. She longed to cry out, to plead with Paul to take her away. Yet if she did, it meant separation in their marriage forever. This area wasn't far from the Shepherd of Love Sanctuary already on its foundation and rising as rapidly as skilled crews could work.

"Turn here." She motioned to a short street that angled off to the right. The same desolation prevailed.

"Which house?" Sympathy colored Paul's voice and she caught the admiration mingled with uncertainty. This couldn't be easy for him, either.

"Last on the left."

He parked across the broken street and Jonica stared at the house. It looked smaller than she remembered, with an overgrown yard and sagging steps. She clutched Paul's hand when they walked to the door. Her mouth twisted. For one of the few times ever, no sound of cursing and quarreling greeted her. Perhaps they had moved away. No, Paul's knock brought the sound of shuffling feet. The door opened a crack. A voice Jonica had never forgotten demanded, "Who are you and what do you want?"

"Mother?" She strained to see the woman through the torn screen.

Silence greeted her, the silence of shock. The door opened wider. An emaciated replica of the woman Jonica remembered stood before her, shoulders bent, eyes surprisingly alive. "Jonica?"

"Yes, Mother." Like one in a daze she stepped inside and fearfully glanced around. Why, where were the alcohol and tobacco fumes that had permeated the house until her clothes reeked? Where was the blaring TV? Only a sagging daybed, a shabby refrigerator and stove, and one chair graced the cheerless room. Jonica gaped at their cleanliness.

"He's gone. He died of alcoholism years ago."

She turned back to her mother, a wave of relief threatening to overwhelm her.

"I tried to find you, after—" The too-old face worked. "No one knew where you were." Anguished tears made a steady stream. "Can you ever forgive me?" She held out trembling hands to the daughter she had tried to protect even in her own misery and weakness. "I never blamed you for going. I couldn't control him much longer." She tottered to the daybed and fell onto it. One hand went to her heart.

Paul sprang to her side. "I'm a doctor and your daughter is a nurse. We'll help you."

Jonica saw the involuntary brightening of her mother's wan face when Paul said *daughter*. Why hadn't she come back sooner? Why hadn't she faced her dragon, which now turned out to be in her own mind?

"Stay with her. I'll call an ambulance from the car phone." Paul sprinted out.

Jonica loosened her mother's clothing, found an old but clean towel, and wet it from the kitchen faucet. By the time the ambulance from Shepherd of Love arrived, her mother had rallied, but blue shadows beneath her eyes told their own story of poverty, malnutrition, and abuse of the fluttering heart. She clutched Jonica's hand all during the ride and tried to speak, but her daughter's firm hand and negative headshake caused her to subside.

"Will you do what's necessary?" Jonica asked Paul when they reached the hospital.

"I will." Yet when he finished an examination he came to her with a worried look. "She needs heart surgery. Shall we transfer her or shall I perform it? Or shall we call in another surgeon?" He placed both hands on her shoulders. "Jonica, she is a very sick woman. Would you be more comfortable knowing someone else performed the operation if she dies? Right now, she's in God's hands and needs everything we can do."

Jonica stared blindly at him, feeling his strong, capable fingers press into her shoulders. Yet she didn't hesitate. "If I can put my life in your hands, I can put my mother's there, too. Besides, as you say, it's really God's hands, isn't it?"

"Good girl." He kissed her and hurried to the operating theatre where Emily Davis Hamilton, Lindsey Best, and a full complement of medical personnel had assembled to prepare for the task ahead.

Part of Jonica wanted to remain with her mother. The more sensible side told her it wouldn't be wise. Already unnerved from the gamut of physical and emotional stress she had been subjected to in the last weeks, even her trained mind could play false. She must not take the chance of making the slightest sound that could distract the single-hearted team. So during the long hours, Jonica learned what waiting meant. How often her heart had gone out to those who helplessly sat by while a loved one hovered between life and death. Now she experienced it firsthand. A blessed numbness protected her from some of the pain, but it also prevented her from praying. Yet she took comfort knowing God could read her heart.

Paul found her huddled in a corner of the surgical suite staring blindly at the wall. "She came through, Darling."

The dam broke. Tears stored up since childhood cascaded. Paul held her close and let her cry. Tears brought healing.

"Is she really going to be all right?" Jonica finally asked.

"There is still risk. She's run down and in poor physical health. We still have a fight on our hands, but there's a good chance we can win." He stopped and held her away until he could look into her eyes. "I believe if she had gone through this surgery before she saw you, she wouldn't have survived."

Jonica sagged in his arms. "What do you mean?"

"You know as well as I how determination often makes all the difference." He swallowed hard. "You have given her something to live for. The last thing she said before receiving anesthesia was, 'I have to make it so my daughter will forgive me.' I told her, 'She already has.' I've never seen a more beautiful smile on a human face. Her body relaxed and made our job easier."

Emily continued her duties as night charge nurse so Jonica could be with her mother. She was there when first consciousness returned, using her skills to comfort. She prayed aloud beside her mother's bed and felt the blessing of a frail hand on her hair, as it had been so many years ago. She watched color come into the pale face and laughed when her mother finished everything on her tray and demanded more.

"We've wasted too much time," she said simply. A little frown crossed her forehead and she said half shyly, "Jonica, I can't go back."

"You never will. You'll be transferred to Intermediate Care when you're able and I promise, you'll never go back." Yet her mother's expression brought a little worry. Jonica discussed it with Paul. "I've just found her again. How can I leave her?" She felt pulled like a wishbone. "Paul, I want to marry you, but what about Mother?"

"We have to pray about it," Paul said soberly. A few days later, he pounded on her door and caught her around the waist when she let him in. "God is so good!"

"Of course He is, but what has He done now?"

"Nothing but to solve everything." Paul sounded like an eager boy. His mussed dark hair and glowing dark eyes made him look more like a high school senior than an eminent surgeon. "I've been haunting the director of our Retirement Center and just learned something ver–r–ry interesting." He laughed and freed her enough until they could sit down on the couch in her pretty blue and white room. "There is an opening and for one reason or another, everyone on the waiting list has turned it down; a few have moved and others decided to live with their families. This means Sarah has her suite ready and waiting."

"That's wonderful!" Jonica felt genuine gladness. "But—"

"It also means she won't be living with Dad and Emily. They're disappointed, after all the good things they heard about her. I think they've been planning ways to keep her and her good cooking, especially since Emily will be embroiled in the Sanctuary. Anyway, they'd like to have your mother come to them after she is well enough to care for herself; to rest and decide where she wants to be—hopefully, in the Retirement Center when another suite's available. She and Sarah will hit it off like ham and eggs."

"It's such a pat ending it sounds like a novel where the author works everything around so everyone has a 'happily ever after,'" Jonica said.

"My dear woman, if authors can do that in books, why should it surprise us that the Author of life itself keeps His promises? 'And we know that all things work together for good to them that love God, to them who are the called according to his purpose,' Paul tells the Romans. Notice how he doesn't just say *called*. He says *the called*. I've always felt that meant those who recognize and accept His calling." Paul's face glowed. "Don't you see? Everything that has happened, each step of our lives, has been part of His plan and built a foundation for the next step."

Jonica caught his train of thought. Her blue eyes opened wide. Her heart beat fast with new understanding. "If I hadn't come here and met you, if I hadn't run away and found Sarah—" She felt on the verge of great knowledge. "Why, Paul, I never would have gone back. Mother would have died alone without God and part of me would have stayed hard and dead. I could never have supported you or worked with you at the Sanctuary."

"Can you now, my darling?" The last barrier stood between them, waiting to be reinforced by her scars or torn down by unquestioning faith in God.

A hundred thoughts raced through Jonica's mind and heart. The way her mother had begun to listen to the Scriptures. Sullen faces of idle youth grouped on broken sidewalks. Sad-faced children, all with faces like her own, cringing from many kinds of abuse. Dirt. Poverty. Hopelessness. Alcoholism. Drugs. The lamp Sarah had placed in her window that shone into the darkness and helped save Jonica's life.

> Neither do men light a candle, and put it under a bushel, but on a candlestick; and it giveth light unto all that are in the house.
>
> Let your light so shine before men, that they may see your good works, and glorify your Father which is in heaven. Matthew 5:15–16.

Verses learned years ago because it was expected of her. Now Jonica realized the depth of their call, the responsibility they placed on every soul who enlisted in the Lord's service.

Many lit candles in sterile hospitals, clean surroundings, among hurting men, women, and children. The Scripture implied that when the candle had been lit and put in the candlestick, it must be carried to the darkest corners so that the entire house could glow with the light of the gospel. Kerosene lamps, candles, flashlights, torches, operating room lights. All gave their rays according to the power they possessed when lit or turned on. Jesus, the Light of the world, must be taken where most needed.

Jonica passed one hand over her eyes. She felt she had finished a long journey and could never again be the same person. Blackness of soul had been erased. She looked out her window. A single ray of sunlight bathed the grounds in rose before evening shadows fell. She turned to Paul. "With God at our side, I can."

Epilogue

Two weeks later a small group gathered in the hospital chapel. Hothouse roses delicately perfumed the air. Nicholas Fairchild and the hospital director, the Hamiltons, Lindsey, Patty, Shina, Nancy with her quiet smile, Sarah, and a few others, including Paul's friend Garry Sterling, filled the small area. Dr. Paul stood in front, tall and handsome next to the minister. A little rustle at the back turned heads. Jonica, lovely and gowned in the simplest of wedding dresses, gently helped her mother up the aisle, seated her next to Peter Hamilton, bent over, and kissed her. She straightened, wanting to memorize every detail of the ceremony in which God would join her life with Paul's forever. A tall white candle stood next to a polished, but old, kerosene lamp, surrounded by greenery and roses.

She smiled, saw the ardor in Paul's dark eyes, the love that beckoned and warmed her. Then she walked toward him and the circle of light in which he stood waiting.

FLICKERING FLAMES

Prologue

For a single moment, she saw his face—etched against the lurid light of flickering flames.

She never forgot.

Twenty years later, she saw his face again—outlined against a sun-glorified, stained-glass window.

She never forgot.

Chapter 1

*Thy word is a lamp unto my feet,
and a light unto my path.*
PSALM 119:105

Nancy Galbraith, RN, never passed the director's office at Seattle's Shepherd of Love Hospital without stopping to read the inscription neatly engraved on the door. Tall, dark-skinned, with warm dark eyes that glowed with love for her job and her Lord, she also always breathed a prayer of gratitude. Today, she glanced both ways, then ran a slim brown finger over the words. "This old world needs all the light You have to offer, Lord," she whispered. "Please, help me be able to give to others, as You have given to me."

The prayer steadied her. She smoothed her soft peach pantsuit over her waist and hips, drew herself to her full five feet, eight inches height, and smiled. Even after her years at the hospital conceived in response to God's leading, Nancy retained some of the training-school fear that always accompanied a summons to the director's office.

She raised one silky eyebrow and murmured, "A psychiatrist could have a field day with you," then determinedly shoved back unwelcome thoughts and tapped lightly on the open door. She received no answer, so she stepped inside. Her fetish for promptness exacted a price. Always early, she spent time waiting for others. Ten minutes remained before her scheduled appointment.

"I hope it doesn't take long," she fretted and stretched her 140-pound, streamlined body. Not an ounce of fat marred her strong muscles and graceful curves. The unstinting care and ministry she gave her small patients in the Pediatrics Department kept her trim. So did the mile-or-more daily walks she took faithfully.

Nancy wandered to the window that overlooked Puget Sound, white-capped with March waves and sparkling in the early spring sunlight. How simple and in keeping with the mood was the hospital director's office. Paneled walls and muted carpeting plus a serviceable desk and comfortable chairs provided a restful atmosphere with no trace of ostentation.

Just like the hospital itself, Nancy thought, with its white stone walls warmed to cream by the sun. She loved every inch of the sprawling two-story complex on the wooded slope above the Sound. It had become home when she had despaired of ever having a home again. Bible verses and land, sea, and mountain murals graced the walls, quiet reminders to patients, staff, and visitors of God's love and creation.

"How nice you look, Nancy." The hospital director came to stand beside her. Keen-eyed, modestly dressed, he kept his capable fingers on the pulse of the hospital without undue interference. His rare ability to make employees feel they worked *with* him, not *for* him, contributed much to the close bonds that inspired each individual to give excellent service.

"The children especially love the colored uniforms." She smiled at him. "And I'm glad we allow each nurse to choose the colors she likes best."

His eyes twinkled. "A suggestion of yours, if I remember correctly."

"Self-defense," she teased. Her eyes shone with fun. "Peach, pink, and yellow are my colors. If I had to wear lavender or green I'm not sure I could do my work well. They make my skin look muddy." He laughed appreciatively and she added, "I'm sure you didn't call me in to discuss uniforms, right?"

"Right." He motioned her to a chair and dropped into the swiveled one behind his desk. "I've—oh, here he is now. Dr. Barton, come in."

Nancy's usually reliable heart skipped a beat. In the time it took for the hospital director to shake hands with the white-coated newcomer, she sur-veyed Dr. Barton—and found him pleasing. Six feet tall, probably one hundred and eighty pounds, short black hair that was springy but not kinky, skin a shade darker than her own, and a white smile that relieved the look of sadness his face held when in repose. She knew he was thirty-three, and the quickly veiled look in his beautiful black eyes did nothing toward steadying her heartbeat.

I wonder why he isn't married. Or is he? Nancy glanced down at her ca-pable hands and willed the hot color she felt warm her face to recede.

The director's voice snapped her to professionalism. "I asked Dr. Barton to meet with us, along with Dr. and Mrs. Paul Hamilton," he explained.

Who? It took Nancy a moment to make the connection. Such a short time had passed since Jonica Carr, RN, Night Surgical Charge Nurse and Nancy's good friend, had become Mrs. Paul Hamilton that the hospital hadn't yet grown used to her new name. It actually didn't matter much; the staff's first-name basis added warmth to their association. Nancy remem-bered their simple but beautiful wedding in the hospital chapel, the pledges and lighted candle that signified both love and service to one another, God, and His children. Her eyes stung. Would she one day stand making such vows by candlelight? Or would the memory of flickering flames continue to burn hot and fierce, erupting into nightmares that awakened her with their intensity?

It took all her poise and self-control to slam shut the door of her past and greet the tall, brown-haired, blue-eyed Jonica and her dark-haired, dark-eyed surgeon husband when they entered. Minutes later, the hospital director turned to Dr. Paul. "It's all yours."

Dr. Paul's face shone with excitement. "Jonica and I have an announcement." The words tumbled out in his eagerness to share. "We've been talking with Dad, Nicholas Fairchild, and a few others and have decided we need to add to the downtown Shepherd of Love Sanctuary. The clinic is good; so is our shelter. Yet it isn't enough. What we need is a better program for the children, especially those under five. Single mothers are caught in the crunch of not being able to afford decent child care on their welfare checks, which means they can't work and get off welfare." His eyes flashed. "I know there are all kinds of so-called 'care centers.' Some are good. A lot aren't. What we visualize is a service that will include Bible teaching. Any parent who wants to enroll a child in the Shepherd of Love Care Center will agree to allow that child to be taught the truth of the gospel. In return, the Center will subsidize to whatever extent is needed."

"Won't a lot of people take advantage of free care?" Dr. Barton looked doubtful.

"It won't be free, Damon," Dr. Paul leaned forward. "We plan to offer counseling and will sit down with each parent and work out what they can reasonably afford. Otherwise, we'd be subject to misuse. This way, people who are willing to work can feel pride in knowing they're doing their best."

"Where do we come in?" Nancy inquired.

"Along with the care center, we want to do a children's clinic once a week. We're hoping we can get some help from the regular hospital personnel, plus those who come in on a consultant basis such as you, Damon."

Dr. Barton groaned. "Give me an eighth day every week and I'll be happy to oblige." He drew his brows together and looked troubled. "I already owe so much to Dr. Cranston for taking me into his private practice, I don't know how much more time I can honestly be away from it. He's been wonderful about the consulting I do for Shepherd of Love, but. . ." His voice trailed off.

Nancy understood his dilemma. Hospital personnel affectionately discussed one another and talk had it that Damon deserved everything he had in the way of prestige. She also caught his regret.

"We understand." Jonica's eyes looked like twin sapphires. "Once we get totally established, Nicholas says we'll hire more staff. We're not asking you to commit each week, Dr. Barton. Paul and I plan to screen. What we need from you is the knowledge we can refer specialty cases to you, many from those who won't be able to pay."

Relief brightened Damon's face. "I can promise you that," he quietly told them. "There's no reason such appointments can't be scheduled in my free time, is there?"

"Free time!" Nancy burst out, then bit her lip. No one knew better than she how much time the dedicated children's specialist spent in simply visiting Pediatrics and chatting with the small patients.

His eyes twinkled, although he solemnly said, "Really, Nurse Galbraith. I almost always am free between two and four A.M. Of course. . ." He stroked his smooth-shaven chin reflectively. "That might not be the most convenient time for the patients."

The room exploded in laughter and Nancy found herself caught up in it. A flood of joy that God had led her faltering steps to Shepherd of Love and coworkers such as these brought a bright mist to her long lashes and she quickly blinked it away.

"Nancy, what about you? Swamped, as usual?" Jonica asked.

"And how!" She spread her hands out in mock despair. "I sometimes think that every time I get a nurse trained the way I want her she immediately decides this is the time for her to marry. We've lost three in the last year." She grimaced. "I'm considering renaming Pediatrics—Galbraith Matrimonial."

"Hmmm. Might not be a bad idea." Dr. Barton's grin did strange things to Nancy. *What did he mean by that, anyway?* She didn't dare ask. Instead she sighed.

"Give me a few weeks to straighten out the schedule and I can probably work it so I can help at least sometimes." A thought gripped her. "I have an idea. Why not send advanced students from the training schools who do affiliation here down in relays as part of their training? They'll get a whole different perspective than what we offer here."

"Great!" Dr. Paul clasped his hands above his head in a prize-fight winning gesture. "By their final year, students will be more than able to handle most of the patients. Then if Jonica or one other registered nurse plus myself—Dad and Emily can help, too—are around, we're set." The informal meeting ended on a high note of hope, with joined hands and a prayer for guidance from their Chief, whose children they longed to serve.

Dr. Paul and Jonica vanished down the hall. The director ruefully confessed he had a "million, more or less" reports. Dr. Barton followed Nancy toward the stairs that led to the second story and Pediatrics.

"Nancy, are you losing weight?"

Astonishment stopped her in her tracks. "Why, no. Why do you ask?"

His searching gaze never left her face. "Your eyes are shadowed except when you laugh." Genuine concern underscored every word. "Is something bothering you?"

An unfamiliar warmth crept into her heart. Few of her associates, even Jonica or the other nurses, Patty, Lindsey, and Shina, saw beneath the cool mask she wore except when working with the children. To her horror, a large, hot drop fell and splashed on her hand. The price she paid for keeping an emotional distance from others also brought loneliness.

Damon's frank questions chipped away at her reserve. She looked down, hoping he hadn't noticed, but the action was in vain. The same trained eyes that never missed a child's woe could scarcely overlook Nancy's temporary letdown.

"Come." A strong hand guided her away from the staircase and across the large, skylighted central waiting area. They paused just inside the chapel door. "Good. It's empty." Dr. Barton seated her and dropped down beside her. "All right. What's the matter?"

If only she could tell him. If only she could put her head on his broad shoulder and spill out everything swarming in her mind and heart like angry bees. Instead, she shook her head.

"I've known for weeks that something inside is keeping you upset," he quietly told her. He made no effort to touch her but went on talking in his mellow voice. "It hasn't affected your work, yet. . ."

What he left unsaid struck her harder than a blow. "It mustn't," she whispered. "The children. They're my life."

She felt her lips tremble and pressed them together hard to steady herself. She heard the swift intake of breath before he said, "You're personally involved."

"Yes." The thing she had feared and dreaded came into the open. The single affirmative expressed her deepest doubts. She felt she must make him understand. "I know a nurse isn't supposed to take patients into her heart. I had it drummed into me all during training. *Be compassionate but dispassionate* is the motto. I've tried, Damon."

"And now?" He still didn't touch her, but she noticed how tightly his hands lay clenched on his knee.

"I just don't know." The words dragged out, dreary, foreboding. "During the past months I haven't been able to leave the children in the ward. They perch on my shoulder, sit on my bed, crying and pleading for my help with outstretched arms." The dam inside sprang a leak and a few more hot tears escaped. They didn't seem to matter. Nancy went on. "I'm so drained. I pray for strength and it comes, but just enough to complete my shift. I can't give up my work, but I can't go on like this, either."

"Are you sleeping?"

"Not very well," she confessed and wiped away the tears with a tissue from her pocket.

"Nightmares?"

"Yes."

"What about?"

She couldn't tell him. Only to God could she open up the past. She hedged. "Distorted images. Frightening things. Death and fire." She clamped her lips shut. Beyond that she would not, could not go, even to the doctor who had in the last few minutes become a person she instinctively felt she could trust with anything—except her secret.

He rested his hand on hers and his rich voice deepened. "Nancy, if you had a broken leg, would you trust me when I told you it had to be set?"

Odd that he would ask her that just when she had been thinking of trust. She mutely nodded, glad for the warm pressure of his hand.

"I am not a professional counselor, but I believe from what I see as changes in you and what you've said that you need to talk with someone who is."

She felt sick. Why had she confessed her problem? He wanted her to see a shrink. Did he think she was tottering on the edge of a nervous breakdown? The thought chilled her. She started to stand, to free her hand. He tightened his hold and firmly restrained her. She refused to struggle but froze when he told her, "Why is it that even medical personnel refuse to recognize the validity of emotional trauma when it comes to their own lives? Nancy Galbraith, you can't keep on the way you're going."

Rage flamed. She snatched her hand away and leaped to her feet. "You think I'm crazy! I was a fool to believe you." She bit back accusations and ran toward the other open end of the pew and freedom.

He caught her at the chapel door. Sadness gleamed in his black eyes when he looked down at her. "I don't think that at all. I just know you need help." His face turned to granite. "I've been there. I reacted the same way you did, except for a different reason. Only the grace of God saved me, Nancy."

Too filled with pain and mortification plus an appalling sense of loss, she refused to listen to either his unspoken or spoken message. "I have to get back to work, Dr. Barton."

He silently stepped aside and let her go. She proudly raised her head and marched away, stony faced, mask once more in place. Yet her traitorous heart longed to stay. . . .

Nancy worked on long beyond her shift, reading to the children, overseeing her staff, anything to delay going to her suite in the staff residence building. She got by with skipping dinner without anyone noticing. Tonight the soft green walls of the staff dining room would be prison walls.

Besides, for all she knew, Dr. Damon Barton might show up unexpectedly and she needed time. She thought of a tune from the musical *Camelot* in which the heroine realizes that before she sees the one she loves again there must be a time to weep, to forget.

Her lovely lips twisted. Guenevere and Lancelot's troubles were a myth; hers were real, raw, demanding. She reluctantly left Pediatrics, slowly walked down the curving staircase to Central Waiting, then made her way across the long, covered walk to the place she called home, praying she wouldn't run into her friends. Blond Patty from Outpatient; freckled, redheaded, efficient Lindsey from Surgery; and tiny Japanese Shina from Obstetrics all roomed at the far end of the first floor suites past the community living room, library, game room, and laundry. Any of them would be happy to talk with her, yet their more carefree upbringings made them seem years younger at twenty-three than Nancy at twenty-five. She toyed with the idea of calling Jonica, then shook her head. Her friend had also suffered an unpleasant childhood, but Dr. Paul's love had gradually brought her away from bad memories. Why inflict more on the woman as sensitive as Nancy herself?

She concentrated on good things: the way Jonica's mother had miraculously recuperated from malnutrition and open-heart surgery; how even now she was nearly ready to graduate from intermediate care to a place in Dr. Paul's father's home as housekeeper while Dr. Peter and his wife of a few months, Emily, continued their medical careers.

Nancy heaved a sigh of relief when she fled through the deserted living room and hall and reached the haven of her rose and white suite. A quick shower and a hasty soup-and-salad supper raised her spirits enough so she could evaluate the confrontation with Dr. Barton more objectively. Using a trick learned from Nicholas Fairchild, founder of Shepherd of Love, she spread the scene in her mind and replayed it with the roles reversed. Nicholas, who always found time to talk with anyone at the hospital available, had said, "It helps to pretend I'm the other person. I get a whole new look at things."

Now Nancy said aloud, "If I had been the doctor and he had told me what I told him, would I have reacted the same way?" The total honesty that characterized her brought a quiet "Yes."

"God, do I really need counseling? I thought I'd overcome all that garbage and tragedy." The low prayer only made her face the issue. "Is it really that I'm taking the children's problems too much to heart, or does it go a lot deeper? Do I need to face things again?" She felt her insides recoil at the thought. "Forgive me for anger and give me the courage to become whole."

Nancy gasped at the prayer. Never had she prayed in exactly that way. Had the Holy Spirit who guides into truth led her faltering tongue? She mulled it over while straightening up an already-immaculate room and laying out a soft yellow pantsuit uniform for the next morning. Heart pounding, she went into her tastefully decorated bedroom, thankful she roomed alone. She followed her nightly routine. A good face wash. Cream on her hands. A fluffy pink gown.

Yet tonight she varied. Instead of slipping into the nightgown, she took off the sports blouse she'd donned after her shower and deliberately turned her back to the large dresser mirror. For the first time in years she looked over her shoulder, braced herself, and swallowed hard. Faint scars crisscrossed the otherwise brown-velvet skin. Plastic surgery had done wonders but had failed to conceal the final evidence. Her practiced gaze noticed how much the scars had faded, but sweat popped out on her body from the memories they evoked. It took a second shower and a glass of warm milk to settle her down enough to sleep, and when she did, flames flickered around her and childish voices called.

Chapter 2

Nurse Nancy." Five-year-old Timmy clutched at her arm. "I'm thirsty." Feverish and bright-eyed, he lay spreadeagled in bedclothes tangled with his tossing.

"Good for you!" Nancy smiled, reached for his drinking glass with the bent straw, and handed it to him. "The more you drink, the quicker your temperature will go down."

"Then bring me the ocean, please." Timmy noisily gurgled down water through the straw.

Several children looked their way when their nurse laughed. Shepherd of Love preferred housing their young patients several to a room and reserved the semiprivates and a very few private rooms for those with contagious diseases or children needing special care.

"If you drank ocean water, you would really be thirsty," Nancy told her small friend. "You know how badly you want a drink after you eat salty popcorn and things like that? Well, the ocean is a lot saltier. Besides, the only way anyone can drink ocean water is if it goes through a process to remove the salt." She never talked down to those she served. Her healthy respect for children required endless explanations and answers to dozens of questions each shift. A typical workday could include, "Are there polar bears in heaven?" "Do grasshoppers sleep?" "Will Daddy come back to Mommy and me?" "Is God as big as the Seattle Center?" and "Do you have a little boy like me?"

Nancy conscientiously answered as best she could, and when she had no answer she frankly admitted, "I don't know but I'll look it up for you." At other times she simply held a little hand and quietly said, "No one knows that, Dear, but God. We can trust Him." If deep inside she winced at the memory of a time she had trusted God and He hadn't done what she asked, only her understanding Creator knew.

Now Timmy heaved a sigh of relief when her capable hands smoothed crumpled sheets, plumped his pillow, and bathed his hot face with cool water. "Nurse Nancy, when I go home, will you go with me?"

Her hands stilled. *Please, God, tell me what to say*. She waited, forced a smile. Timmy would be going home soon but not to his family. He was one of the chief reasons she had gone so far as to consider giving up Pediatric nursing. His wasted body grew more frail every day and all the staff could do was watch and give loving care to make him comfortable. Consultations with Dr. Barton and the mother had resulted in the decision to leave him in his familiar surroundings as long as possible.

"Will you? Please?"

Nancy marveled at the steadiness of her voice when she told him, "Timmy, you won't need me. You're going to be well. Although I'd love to be with you, what about all your friends here—the children who are still sick?"

Understanding crept into his intelligent face. It fought with his own needs. "Won't you ever come?"

"Someday," she said through stiff lips. To hide her emotion she bent over, carefully hugged him, then made a big show of fluffing his pillow again. "Enough questions, young man." She shook her finger at him. "It's time you took a nap. The same goes for you and you and you," she sternly told the others, who giggled into their pillows, even while settling down. Experience had taught that Nurse Nancy meant what she said, but the twinkle in her dark eyes showed how much she cared about them.

"Nurse Nancy, will you sing? It's easier to go to sleep." Timmy peered up at her, face a little less flushed. "Then when I wake up, Mother will be here."

The poignancy in the way he said "Mother" touched his nurse's heart. For the hundredth time she longed for a day when she would have children of her own and not just be a substitute mother to those who came, claimed part of her heart, and went away to forget her when released. Or those like Timmy, who carried part of her with them when God called. "Let's all sing a song together," she suggested. She patted Timmy's hand, made her rounds to check and hug each of her small patients, and began the song in her untrained but beautiful voice.

Jesus loves the little children,
All the children of the world;
Red and yellow, black and white,
They are precious in His sight.
Jesus loves the little children of the world.

Nancy thought as she sang, accompanied by her charges' clear, treble voices, *The anonymous author could well have stood in my shoes and written these words.* Her loving gaze rested on Hispanic, Asian, African, and American, and various shades of white-to-tan faces; innocent faces, precious in the sight of the Lord. Knowledge swelled within her. She belonged here. No matter how hard, how pulled she felt, her ministry lay in exactly what she now gave. God would grant her strength to endure, for the sake of these children—and Leila.

Helped by long practice, she jerked her attention back to the ward and away from deeply buried events that persisted in returning to haunt her. The song ended. The children obediently closed their eyes, even though, "We're not sleepy," Timmy loftily informed her.

"You don't have to sleep if you don't want to," she told him. "Just rest your eyes."

"Aw, that's what you said before, and the next thing I knew I woke up and Mother was here." Timmy eyed her distrustfully then stretched his mouth in a wide, gap-toothed smile.

It nearly proved to be her undoing. She managed an answering smile and figuratively bolted, although her smooth, graceful walk remained slow, as usual. Blinded by her fight to retain control, she walked toward the desk that served as a hub for surrounding rooms, staring at the floor. Her first awareness of another's presence came in the form of two highly polished black shoes just in front of her.

Nancy looked up. Gasped. "Dr. Barton. I didn't hear you come in." Why, oh why, had he caught her just now? All her hastily assembled poise wouldn't fool him. She read in his black eyes the same concern that had been there the previous day and dreaded what lay ahead.

Damon started to speak then stopped. She relaxed tense muscles when he grinned companionably and confessed, "I just wish I'd been here a few minutes sooner. I have a not-so-terrible bass voice and love to sing. Although you and the children certainly didn't appear to need my help."

She caught her breath and smiled at him, thankful for his teasing. "They really do fall asleep better if we sing."

"Sometimes I've heard you singing to them," he huskily said. The planes of his face softened and some of his perennial sadness fled for a moment. "It reminded me of my mother singing to my br— to me when I was a child. You are very like her, Nancy."

She could feel her pulse quicken. "Thank you." Without considering the consequences she added, "I sang to Leila."

His silent questioning glance brought realization of the door she'd opened and she hastily added, "My sister. She died, a long time ago." Tears clogged her throat.

"I'm sorry."

His genuine compassion unnerved her. "It happened twenty years ago. You'd think after all this time. . ." The rest of her explanation wouldn't come. She wordlessly thanked God when the telephone rang, and while she dealt with the caller, Damon lifted a hand in farewell and walked away. The rest of the day, with the admission of two new patients, kept Nancy so busy she had little time for either remembering or soul-searching, and her contact with Dr. Barton over the next few days related strictly to duty.

More than a week passed before she had time to speak with him seriously and it concerned Timmy. The little boy daily grew whiter and thinner. Most of the time he felt too tired to even laugh. As he failed, he clung even more closely to his beloved Nurse Nancy. One night long after her shift had ended, she returned to check on him, prompted by an inner sense that he needed her.

Timmy lay perfectly still but slow tears leaked from his wide-open eyes.

"Timmy, dearest, what is it?" Nancy knelt by his bedside and gathered his thin body in her strong arms, passionately wishing she could lend him the strength he needed.

"I–I don't want to be here," he whispered.

She sensed his carefulness not to disturb his sleeping friends. "Why not, Timmy?"

"They all—look at me." He huddled in her arms, a broken bird who soon would soar beyond his earthly troubles.

"Would you like to be in a private room?" she asked.

"If you're with me. Or Mother."

It cut to her heart, but why not? He couldn't last long, and it was better for him to request a transfer than to be arbitrarily moved. "I'll talk with Dr. Barton tomorrow and see what we can do. Okay? Until then, your night nurse will take care of you." She stood long enough to reach for his chart on the end of the bed and to note that Timmy had been given a sedative a short while before. Good. It would take effect and release him from his childish woes.

"I—drather—have—you," he slurred. Moments later his even breathing told her the medication had done its work well. She held him a few minutes longer, then gently arranged his body in a more comfortable position. When she looked up, Damon stood on the other side of the bed. She didn't even question why. It felt right for him to be there.

They silently went out and as on the day of their confrontation, Damon led the way to the chapel, softly lighted and welcoming. Seated, she looked up at him. "You heard?"

"Enough to know what we have to do. Nancy, if you can handle it, I want you to special Timmy in a private room; to be there any time his mother can't. It's going to take a whole lot of emotional stamina and the ability to be objective. Can you do it?"

She longed to shout yes, to firmly convince him. Instead she stared at her hands. "I don't know." Something tore inside of her. "Why? Why does a loving God allow a child to die? What's the use of it? Why was Timmy, and others, ever born if they're to be struck down while young?" All the secret resentment she'd struggled with for years came to a boil and erupted. "Why, Damon? If God is love and we know He is, how can He. . ." A sob interrupted her questions.

"Nancy, my dar—" He broke off and took her hands in his. She felt his strength and rock-solid faith flow into her aching heart.

"I just want Timmy to be healed," she brokenly told him.

"He will be. Soon. Is it any less a miracle that Timmy, and others, are healed through death rather than in life?"

"What are you saying?" She stared at him in disbelief.

"Every Christian, every follower should know that death is the ultimate healing," Damon said in his resonant voice. "We doctors and nurses and surgeons and specialists do what I like to consider as temporary patch-up jobs. Through medicine and surgery, we repair bodies and minds. God, through death, restores those bodies and minds into eternal perfection. Nancy, would you have Timmy go on as he is, impaired, weak?"

"No, but God could heal him. We've seen many cases where He has," she quickly responded.

"But not all. Jesus didn't heal every leper, every blind person, every paralyzed individual, *in this life.* His mission included physical healing, but primarily, He came to give His own life to ensure eternal healing, of the soul as well as the body and mind. When He said He came that people might have life and that more abundantly, He didn't put a timeline on it. We live in an imperfect world and are subject to what happens. Sometimes, God in His wisdom alters the natural course of events, but it doesn't lessen His majesty when He does not."

"I recognize that. It's just so hard to see children who will never grow up and see the beauty God has given to us."

Damon increased the pressure of his hands on hers. "Nancy, the most gorgeous thing on earth is nothing compared with what Timmy is going to see when he enters the presence of God."

She felt some of her turmoil drain at the picture Damon had painted in such a few well-chosen words.

"I want to ask you again. Can you give Timmy the kind of send-off he needs? It won't be any more than a week, probably less."

She closed her eyes to shut out his face. Timmy's face rose in its place, pleading for her love, skill, and comfort. His murmured "I-drather-have-you" could not be denied. Nancy opened her wet eyes. "With the help of God, I can. The Scripture is filled with promises that when our strength fails, He will supply. When shall I start?"

"Not tonight; Timmy will sleep. We'll talk with his mother tomorrow and arrange things. Instead of a private room, we'll use a semiprivate so if she wants to stay nights, she can." He released her hands, stood, and looked down at her. "You are quite a woman, Nurse Nancy." He turned and walked out without looking back.

She stayed in the deserted chapel for a long time, wondering if Damon's voice had broken on his parting words. She told herself his partially completed word could not have been "darling." In all the time they'd known one another, there had never been any spark between them except for their mutual dedication to their work.

Until now.

She shied at the thought that perched on her shoulder all the way to her suite. Sleep mercifully settled the question of further consideration, brought on by the exhaustion created by Timmy's need. Nine hours later she awakened to a sunny day, inner renewal, and the realization of how much her attitude had changed because of Damon sharing his faith and beliefs. If she could cling to what he had said the way Timmy clung to her, it could make all the difference.

Nancy's new assignment tested her mettle to the utmost. At Dr. Damon's insistence, Timmy was told how seriously ill he was. Nancy would never forget how the child's mother nodded then asked, "Would you tell him, Doctor?"

Damon hadn't hesitated. "Yes, but I want both of you there." Later that day, the three who loved Timmy so much had gathered around his bed.

"Hi." The little-boy grin looked too big for the white face. "All my fav'rit people, huh." He yawned and covered his mouth with a fist. "How come I'm so tired?" He yawned again. "Wish I could go to sleep and when I wake up, be all well."

Nancy truly believed the opening was an answer to all their prayers. She had agonized over it, so when Dr. Barton picked up on Timmy's wish and said, "Guess what, Buddy? That's just what's going to happen," she shot an unspoken prayer of thanks toward heaven.

"Really?" His eyes brightened.

"Really, Timmy. You're going to be able to run and play and holler like you used to. Just one thing. Your mother and Nurse Nancy and I don't get to be with you for awhile."

Fear flared in the bright eyes. "How come?"

Damon cocked his head to one side and his face glowed. "Remember when you played games and got to be first? How you'd run ahead of everyone and maybe hide around a bend of the trail and wait for your friends?"

"I remember." The fear faded. "I ran fast and got there before anyone else."

"Timmy, this time is kind of like that. You know someday we're all going to live in heaven with Jesus, don't you?"

"Yeah. Mother and me and you and Nurse Nancy and everybody who loves Him. Mother said so." A look of perfect trust shot from his eyes. The next minute he struggled into a sitting position. "You mean I'm going to heaven pretty soon?"

"Right, Buddy."

Timmy thought it over. "And you'll come and find me, Mother? Like you used to come when I hid?"

"Pretty soon, Son."

"Will you miss me 'til you get there?" he wanted to know.

"Very much." She blinked and Nancy wondered at her courage.

"And I won't be sick ever again?"

"Never!" Nancy found her voice, although she had felt not one word would come out. "You'll be strong and, oh, Timmy, best of all, you'll get to see Jesus, before any of us." She took his hand. "When you get there, would you do something for me?"

" 'Course." His face lit with the chance to please his beloved Nurse Nancy.

"My little sister Leila died when she was just your age. When you see her, and I'm sure you will, tell her I'll be coming soon." She hesitated. "Or maybe even before then, Jesus will come back to earth like He promised, and bring you and Leila with Him."

"Wow! That's neat." A spurt of energy sent a faint color into the thin cheeks. "Mother, you'll watch real good so you won't miss us, right?"

"Right," she promised.

He sank back on the pillow. "I wish all of us could go together, but if Jesus is there, I guess it'll be okay 'til you come." He fell silent and a speculative look crept into his eyes. "Nurse Nancy, sing that song. The one about the charyut coming. Maybe God'll send a charyut for me." His eyes closed with weakness.

How could she sing around the lump in her throat? How could she not sing? Gratitude poured through her when Damon began the time-honored words of the beloved Negro spiritual in his rich voice.

Swing low, sweet chariot,
Comin' for to carry me home. . .

A few lines later, Nancy joined in. Then Timmy's mother added a soft alto. Damon switched to bass and their voices blended into beauty.

I looked over Jordan and what did I see
Comin' for to carry me home,
A band of angels, comin' after me. . .

Timmy's eyes opened. An indescribable look lit his face. He stretched out his arms, but not to the singers. The next moment his eyes closed. He sighed softly and Nancy knew his spirit had gone. The sadness she had expected didn't come. Was it the far-seeing look in the child's eyes at the last? Had he been granted a vision to comfort him in the twinkling between life and life eternal? She didn't know. She only knew that of all the people she had seen die during her years of nursing, never had she witnessed the kind of glory that still hovered in the quiet room.

Timmy's mother gathered her son into her lap and sat crooning. Yet the same wonder in Nancy's heart reflected in her tear-dimmed eyes when she looked up and told them, "I can never thank either of you enough."

Damon's comforting hand dropped to her shoulder. "Don't thank us, but the Holy Spirit. The presence of God attended Timmy's passing. Now, we'll leave you with him as long as you want to stay. Just come to the desk when you're ready to go."

Ten minutes later, she came out of Timmy's room and closed the door behind her. Much of the spirit experienced still surrounded her like an aura.

In the time it took to get necessary information, she continued to hold up well, perhaps too well. Damon stayed while Nancy took down answers, but when the woman stood, he counseled her, "Right now what we shared is holding you up. It will continue to do so but only to a point. Do you have someone who can walk you through the grieving process in the next few months? No matter how strong our faith in God is, we still have to get beyond all the human emotions and find peace."

"The pastor of my church is also a trained counselor. He and his wife have already asked me to stay with them for a time," she responded. "I also have a widowed lady who will come be with me if I choose to remain at home." She paused. "And I know I can call on you."

"Day or night," Nancy promised and Damon nodded in agreement. After she left, Nancy spontaneously turned to him. "I wish I'd had someone like you, all those years ago."

His quiet answer revealed how deeply he had been moved by their shared experience. Deep lines etched into his face. "I do, too, Nancy." As if not trusting himself to say more, he turned and walked away, leaving her warmed, not only by his look of compassion but by the Spirit he carried in a heart made large through service and his abiding love for his heavenly Father.

Chapter 3

If only I could live on the mountaintops where I felt close to God all the time, how happy I'd be. Nancy shrugged off the thought. She'd once heard a minister say, "For every mountain, there's a valley." How true. And how easy to slide back into the valley of despondency after even the highest, most poignant experience. She had hoped Timmy's death would strengthen her. It had, until she went back on duty and saw his empty bed. She felt herself crumple inside. Doubts dimmed the memory of his passing and attacked with renewed vigor. Days fled into weeks and spring limped into early summer. Still the troubled nurse kept her own counsel, refusing to admit she couldn't handle her life the way she must in order to continue in Pediatrics.

Nancy knew Dr. Barton observed her struggles but steeled herself against his unspoken invitation to unburden herself.

"When I can get past losing Timmy, I'll think about other things," she promised herself. Yet more and more she allowed the thought of seeking professional counseling to seep into her reluctant heart.

She had gone to see Timmy's mother a few days after the memorial service, which she had also attended, being glad it stressed life rather than death. For the first time in her nursing career, she felt uncertain. How did one approach a grieving mother who shed tears yet wore the same radiance her son had donned in his hospital bed?

"I am so glad you came." Warm, welcoming hands drew her into the house and into a circle of love. "Would you like to see Timmy's room?" She led the way to a typical little-boy's room; airplanes strewn on the wallpaper; a matching bedspread, far smoother than when it had covered a small frame.

Nancy impulsively turned. "How can you be so, so. . ." She couldn't go on. All her training disappeared and left a small girl, grieving for her lost sister.

"I thank God for every day of Timmy's life," came the surprising answer. "For five wonderful years I had a son who brought joy and gladness. His memory still does." A diamond drop slipped down one cheek and a gentle smile showed the strength God had supplied. "Nurse Nancy, as soon as I feel ready I'm going to apply for a child to adopt. Or if I can't get one, I'll do foster parenting."

Nancy started to speak then bit her tongue.

"Perhaps you wonder how I can think of it so soon. Actually, it's for Timmy. He would never want me to be lonely." She took in a long, quivering breath before adding, "Another child will never take my son's place, but God has put many rooms in our hearts. I need to ready one for the child who needs me—the boy or girl God knows I need, as well."

Nancy left the house uplifted, knowing she would return again and again to the woman made strong through Christ Jesus.

"If his mother can react like that, why are you, a nurse, allowing the loss to tear you down?" she demanded of her mirrored image that night. The woman staring back at her had no answers, and the dark eyes hid secrets too painful to resurrect.

In late May, Damon did something about Nancy's problem. He waited for her at the end of her shift, casually mentioned various patients and their progress, complimented her on her continuing excellent work, and abruptly said, "There's a new Greek restaurant not far from here that has terrific food, even better than in the staff dining room. Would you like to try it?"

It caught her off balance. She rallied enough to nod, while her heartbeat quickened.

"Tonight?"

Goodness, but he didn't waste any time. "Why, yes. Give me an hour to change." She smiled at him.

"I'll do better than that. Let's make it seven so I can get to my apartment and check my answering service." A frown creased his forehead. "You know, of course, our date is subject to interruption; it goes with the job."

The corners of her lovely mouth tilted up and her laughter sounded like a chime of silver bells. "I do." It sounded too close to a wedding vow to leave her unmoved, especially when his dark gaze rested appreciatively on her. "Pagers and answering machines are part of my life, too," she added.

"My boss leaves messages on the machine unless an emergency comes up, then he uses the pager," Damon told her. He grinned and added irrelevantly, "If you have a yellow dress, would you wear it, please? It makes you look like sunlight in a forest." He turned sharply on his heels and strode away.

Of all things! Nancy thought. *Dr. Damon Barton noticing colors and spouting poetic phrases!* Nancy stifled a giggle, feeling like a teenager and chastising herself for her unruly emotions. Yet in spite of laying out first a coral dress, then a white one, she met her date gowned in soft yellow that turned her skin to gleaming bronze and made her hair and eyes look even darker.

Damon merely said, "Thank you; you're lovely," but the look in his eyes betrayed much more than Nancy dared to interpret.

Two hours later, she sat back, replete and contented. Her escort's open admiration, the perfectly cooked meal, and quiet background music provided an atmosphere of total relaxation.

"Now we can talk," Damon announced after paying the bill and tipping a hovering waiter, who murmured thanks and whisked away dishes and crumbs.

"Isn't that what we have been doing?" Nancy laughed. "I thought we'd settled problems of world, state, and nation." She traced the shining pattern in the damask cloth with a slim forefinger, wishing the evening could go on and on.

"I'm glad to discover we share so many similar views," Damon told her. The timbre of his voice sent excitement skittering through her veins. "Added to our love for children and God, we really have a lot in common, don't we?"

She murmured assent, again feeling as fluttery as a young girl on her first real date. Something stirred within her that had lain dormant for a long time, a feeling of being feminine, protected, cherished. The thought sent her lashes down to screen the expression she knew must be in her eyes. All the respect she had felt for the dedicated doctor mingled with wistful hope. *God, if someday I can marry a man as fine as Damon, I will find the security that was snatched away in my childhood.* The idea brought warmth to her smooth cheeks, and she scoffed at a grown woman pinning nebulous hopes on a casual first date.

If only she could get to know him better. To discover and alleviate the pain that often rested in his eyes when he wasn't laughing. The desire to give as well as receive help from this man leaped within her. Again, she scorned the idea. How could she give aid to another until she herself first became whole? "Physician, heal yourself," Jesus had said.

In a sudden about-face, Nancy took a giant stride toward freedom. Tomorrow she would begin the steps toward finding a qualified, Christian counselor. The decision brought a sense of incredible relief. She knew it showed in the snap of her voice, the quickened pace of her repartee.

At her door, Dr. Barton made no effort to detain her but clasped her hands in his, pressed them, and said, "Next time will it be Chinese, Mexican, soul food, a thick steak, or. . . ?"

"Any or all of the above," she told him airily. Yet after he'd left and she'd stepped inside her rose-and-white haven, she compared the shining-eyed vision in yellow with the sad-looking woman who too often had observed her from the mirror—and rejoiced.

It took a long time for Nancy to fall asleep. Her dates, rare from choice rather than lack of opportunity, seldom made more than a pleasant impression. Damon Barton's magnetic personality, slight tinge of mystery, and genuine concern had left their mark.

She also considered how to best find just the right counselor. Should she ask Damon? *No.* Her dark head moved on her pillow. She'd rather not tell him at this time. Nancy discarded several plans and finally decided to go straight to the hospital director, bypassing Dr. Paul, Jonica, and her other friends.

Glad that she had time off the next day, at last she slept, only to enter the nightmare world of her childhood. Leila, arms outstretched, crying for her year-older sister. Flames, dancing on the wall of the modest home that Nancy, her mother, and sister occupied. Shouting. Curses. Prayers. A collage of terror. A blanket of gray smoke; streams of shining water. Then, a pit of blackness so deep that the writhing woman felt she would smother.

Nancy awakened drenched with perspiration and stumbled to the shower. For a long time she stood under its cleansing stream, feeling horror sluice from her body and down the drain in a swirling motion. "God, I'm going to need all Your help," she whispered. Dried and clad in a fresh gown, she turned from her messy bed in distaste, snatched sheets and a blanket from her closet, and parked on the comfortable living room sofa, as she had done countless times before. The next thing she knew, sunlight outside her window and the morning songs of a hundred birds bent on praising God awakened her.

An hour later she faced her director friend. "I've come to realize I need professional counseling to resolve a lot of things hanging over from childhood," she stated bluntly. "Who is the best and most Christian psychiatrist you know?"

"Nancy, I admire your courage in facing whatever dragons from the past are gnawing at you," he told her. "I think that perhaps you need a counselor more than a regular psychiatrist." He paused and his keen eyes surveyed her. "Do you have a male or female preference?"

She started to shake her head no, then reconsidered. Would another woman be better able to relate to her needs? "Perhaps a woman," she said.

He picked up the phone, dialed a number, and spoke into the receiver. "Helen, I have a special young woman here who needs exactly what you have to offer. Can you see her today?"

Nancy sat erect. *So soon?* She had resigned herself to waiting weeks for an appointment.

"An hour from now? Good. Her name is Nancy Galbraith; she's one of our top nurses and her Pediatrics patients adore her. So does the rest of the hospital staff." He smiled at her. "Thanks. I owe you one." He cradled the phone. "You're set. And Nancy. . ." Compassion filled his face. "Don't be afraid to tell Helen anything and everything. She's a deep well into which you can safely drop your confidences. She's also had a rather difficult time, although you'd never know it by her attitude toward life." The director scribbled on a piece of paper. "Here's her address. The door will be unlocked when you get there. Just walk in. Oh, her name is Helen Markel."

"Dr. Markel?"

A curious look crept into his eyes. "No, just Helen." He laughed at her obvious confusion. "You'll understand when you meet her."

Nancy wondered at his expression all the way to what she found was a private residence about a half-hour's drive from Shepherd of Love. The ranch-style home hugged the ground, surrounded by blooming impatiens in every color imaginable. A few choice roses nodded a welcome and a soft breeze fluttered birch leaves and played tag among a grove of evergreen trees. Surprise followed surprise. Nancy's automatic ring of the doorbell brought an instant "Come in, Nancy" in a clear voice that stilled some of the tumult in her breast. She pushed open the door and stepped into the simplest, coziest home she had ever seen. Off-white walls served as a backdrop for soft pastel upholstered furniture. A woman slowly stood, reached for a cane, and even more slowly came toward Nancy, right hand extended. "I am so glad you've come."

The last shred of fear evaporated. Who could dread a medium height, slender woman whose clear gray eyes were enhanced by smile wrinkles, whose sunny brown hair held silver threads here and there? *About forty,* Nancy figured, *but doesn't look it, because of the smooth complexion that models of twenty would covet.*

"I—I think God sent me here." Nancy took Helen Markel's slim, capable hand. She noticed how strong a grip the other woman had and felt calluses that betrayed who did all the yardwork that made her home a place of beauty.

"I think so, too, although He sometimes has a way of using others to accomplish His purposes." Helen motioned her patient, who felt more like a guest, to a chair. Only then did Nancy realize the extent of Helen's lameness.

"A bad accident, ten years ago," she explained. "And in some ways the best thing that ever happened to me."

Nancy leaned forward, intrigued by the startling statement. "Really? I'd like to hear if you. . ."

"For every trial, there is a testimony." Helen leaned her head back against the soft rose of her chair and smiled. That smile curled into Nancy's heart like a coiled, purring cat. "To put it briefly, I'd pretty much lived for myself. After the car crash, it took months to put me back together. Doctors said I'd never walk again. I promised God that if He permitted me to do so, I'd turn my steps toward Him in all things. You see the results." She gestured at the cane. "I went back to school, got my master's in counseling. Yet the One I know is our Master Counselor is behind anything I can do. Actually, what I am best at is listening."

The last shred of apprehension melted. Nancy looked deep into the older woman's eyes and started at the result. Soul meeting soul; suffering meeting suffering. Hope stirred folded wings into a flutter. If anyone could help dispel the past, it would be Helen Markel.

"I don't quite know where to begin," she twisted her fingers together and confessed.

"With a cup of tea and a cookie, perhaps? Or would you prefer coffee or juice?"

"Juice if you have it. I'm a pushover for any kind. May I get it?"

Helen settled deeper into her comfortable chair. "Of course. I'll have apple juice, there's some open in the refrigerator, and the cookies are in the jar. Cups and plates in the cupboard above the sink; spoons in the drawers below."

Nancy grinned to herself while preparing the snack. "I suspect this is her way of making me relaxed and at home," she said, half under her breath. "Good psychology."

By the time they had finished the cold juice and Nancy refused her fourth oatmeal-raisin cookie, the two women had become friends. Yet Helen permitted no serious talk until Nancy took the tray back to the kitchen and, in spite of her hostess's protest, washed and put away the few dishes.

"All right, Nancy," she said when they were again seated across from one another. "Tell me about you. What's the earliest memory you have?"

Her visitor-patient thought for a moment. "The way my mother looked when Daddy left. Sad, yet with something in her eyes I couldn't understand—then. In later years, I identified the look as relief. I suppose it came with knowing that at least the terrible arguments went with him."

Helen's silent sympathy bolstered her courage.

"I must have been about four. My sister Leila was three." Her voice caught but she determinedly went on. "Mama must have gotten approved for low-income housing because a little later the three of us moved into a house. I remember how excited I felt to have a real home and not just an apartment. We didn't have a lot, but Mama always told us we must thank God and help the 'poor' people—those in the development who had less than we did." A bright drop sparkled on her lashes.

"She made things fun. Although Mama worked hard, we still walked in parks and put crumbs out for the birds. We played with other children, but Leila and I loved just being with Mama more than anything else." She paused, lost in memories. The off-white room faded from consciousness. Again she was four, then five, happy in her innocence with her little sister depending on her, until the night her world ended. . . .

<hr />

"Nancy. Leila. Wake up!" A strong hand rudely shook her.

"Mama?" Nancy rubbed her eyes. "I can't see you." She took in a deep breath. "Why is it so hard to breathe?" She coughed and her eyes smarted. "Mama, why—?"

"Run outside, Nancy. Now!" Her mother snatched her from the bed she and Leila shared. "Don't stop for anything, no matter what happens. Get outside, you hear me?"

"Yes, Mama." Trained to instant obedience, she never questioned. Twisting herself free from Mama's quick hug, Nancy obeyed. Instinct stopped her in the doorway and she turned to look back. Her mother had scooped Leila from the huddle against the far side of the bed where she always curled into a ball.

Nancy screamed. Fire leaped between them, a wall of flame so hot the child shrank back. "Mama, where are you?" she wailed.

"Run, Nancy!" The hoarse command rang in the five year old's ears, along with Leila's frightened cries. In the heartbeat before Nancy fled, the curtain of flames lifted just enough for a final glimpse of her mother's agonized face, Leila's outstretched arms. Then with a demonic shriek, the fire roared hotter and higher. Nancy stumbled backwards.

"Run, Darling. Mama loves you!" The beloved voice echoed in her ears. She turned, tried to escape the pursuing heat. Something heavy struck her and she fell, screaming from the searing fever that spread across her shoulders and back.

A loud shout, strong arms, a voice saying, "It's all right, Child; we'll get you out."

Nancy knew she was being carried, but she struggled in the unfamiliar arms, regardless of her pain. "Mama. Leila. Please, get them!"

"More inside," the man who held her bellowed. He ran from the house, laid her on the ground, and started back to the house.

"God, help us," someone sobbed. The next instant, Nancy's dimming senses saw the home she loved collapse like a cardboard model beneath a powerful hand. Crashing, roaring, the inferno drove back those who sought to come close.

Nancy struggled to a sitting position, in shock until some of her pain subsided. She stared at the end of what had been their home, her and Leila's bedroom. A dark figure dashed across her field of vision.

For a single moment she saw his face, etched against the lurid light of flickering flames.

She never forgot. . . .

❖⟨❖⟩❖

With a shudder, Nancy returned to the present and the quiet refuge of Helen Markel's peaceful home.

"My dear child, how you have suffered!"

The speaker seemed far away and Nancy bent her head down to let blood rush in and drive away her feeling of faintness. "I've never told anyone all of the story since I grew up," she said when she could speak. "The authorities tried to trace Daddy and failed. Fortunately, a kind neighbor took me in and kept me after I got out of the hospital until Child Placement found a foster home." A shadow swept over her heart. "The first of several, actually. The families were all kind but busy with their own children. As soon as I turned eighteen I was on my own. Good grades brought financial help. I took my nurses' training and at last came to Shepherd of Love, the first real home I'd known since the fire."

"You still carry scars."

"Yes. Plastic surgery took care of most of the physical scars."

"But not the inner ones." Helen leaned forward, bridged the space between the chairs, and took Nancy's hands in her strong ones. The distraught nurse felt strength flow into her body. It gave her the courage to continue.

"The nightmare didn't end with our home lying there, rubble and a pile of ashes. The fire had been set, either deliberately or accidentally. The dark figure I saw against the flames turned out to be a teenage boy who lived not far from the development." Her hands tightened on Helen's, seeking consolation. "I never knew his name, just that after they released me from the hospital, a big man in a plain suit brought a lot of pictures. The boy had been in trouble before. They showed me photograph after photograph and every time I picked out the one I'd seen. . ." Her voice broke and she took a deep breath. "I think they put him in a home for juvenile offenders."

"You have never gone back to find out?"

Nancy slowly shook her dark head. "I couldn't bear to have a name with a face. It took everything in me just to go on living."

Helen's eyes brimmed, their clear gray softened with a fog of mist. "You became a Pediatrics nurse because of Leila?"

She nodded, too tired to speak.

"Perhaps it is the best thing you could have done. On the other hand, each time you lose a patient, it's like losing your little sister all over again."

Nancy felt the blood drain from her face. "How do you know?"

"My dear, you are flesh and blood, not a saint," Helen told her. "Right now you are feeling torn, aren't you? You want to go on saving life but wonder if it's worth the pain."

"You are a very wise woman," Nancy whispered. She freed her hands and fumbled for a tissue in her purse.

"Wisdom comes from God," Helen reminded.

"What shall I do? I really feel that God wants me to work with children, yet I don't know if I can continue."

Chapter 4

Nancy restlessly stood and paced to the open window. The blooming flowers and their subtle perfume that drifted in cooled her hot cheeks. "What shall I do?" she asked.

"No one can tell you what to do but God. You must listen to your heart." Helen hesitated. "Nancy, have you forgiven the boy who set the fire?"

She turned, stared; red haze clogged her throat. "Forgiven?" She clenched her hands into fists; her nails bit into her palms. "He killed my mother and sister!" *How could this woman with the understanding eyes ask such a question?*

"Yet you are a Christian."

"I'm also human," Nancy flashed back. "Do you know what it's like, the nightmares, the—"

"I do." A world of sadness rested in the words.

"Forgive me, I'd forgotten." Nancy remorsefully crossed to Helen's chair and dropped to her knees beside it. "Helen, how could you forgive the driver who struck you?"

"By the grace of God."

Nancy flinched. She hadn't expected the direct answer. "I've tried to forget it," she whispered, "but I can't say I've forgiven."

"Perhaps you should." Helen flicked a tear off the kneeling woman's cheek. "Now, this is more than enough for today. Tell me, do you have lunch plans or can you stay with me?"

A little dazed by the abrupt change of subject, Nancy murmured, "Why, I can stay, if it's not an imposition." Helen patted her shoulder as if Nancy were still five. "I'll let you do the work."

A half hour later they sat down to a charming table sheltered from the bright sun by a large beach umbrella. A quickly mixed chicken salad, French bread buttered and warmed, a plate of richly red sliced tomatoes, and tall glasses of lemonade comprised their delicious meal. "I usually eat lunch out here and sometimes dinner," Helen said.

Nancy couldn't believe how hungry she felt. Or how empty of anything except this world within the world, so different from her daily routine. "I think heaven must be something like this." She breathed in the fragrance of roses and fought down the insane urge to put her head in Helen's lap and cry when the older woman bowed and asked God's blessing on the food, thanking Him for "the new friend He had sent." The feeling persisted and at first she found it difficult to swallow, but Helen's quiet manner, the way she pointed out birds and butterflies did what nothing else could, and her guest settled down and enjoyed the meal.

"When shall I come again?" she asked when she had no further excuse to linger. Again she had washed and dried the dishes and put them away.

"You may come any time of the day or night that you need me." Helen's keen eyes held compassion and sincerity. "Nancy, also know you will be in my prayers. Continuously. Give me your schedule for the next few days, and every morning when you arrive for duty, remember that at that exact moment I'll be upholding you before the throne of God."

"I can never thank you, or Him, enough." She clasped Helen's hands in parting.

"I think you can, when you're ready."

Nancy pondered the strange remark all the way back to the staff residence. She took a long walk that brought her home in the midst of a glorious sunset fading to dusk. Just before she fell asleep later, the conversation that played through her mind reduced itself to a few words. Her own voice, saying: *I've tried to forget. . .I can't say I've forgiven.*

Helen, loving, gentle. *Perhaps you should.*

No flames tonight. No smoke. No crying child's voice. No nightmares. Just a soft voice that in the dark night hours changed to a different tone, yet always with the same words: *Perhaps you should.*

Nancy had been given enough food for thought to need time to digest it before going to see Helen again. She didn't report the results of the meeting to the hospital director, either, and she suspected that Helen would say nothing. She marveled at the instant confidence the servant of God who had been tested and found acceptable inspired. Could she someday do the same? The desire to care for far more than the physical bodies of her patients increased a hundredfold. She had always considered her duty to include caring for her patients' mental, emotional, and spiritual well-being as well as their physical. Now she saw clearly how crippled she still was by the past. Her soul cried out for freedom and always those significant three words *perhaps you should* lay just below the surface of her mind, ready to spring up in quiet moments.

Nancy rejoiced that she had Sunday off. She loved attending church. Shepherd of Love held several Sunday services and arranged schedules so the staff could attend one of them, but occasionally Nancy also liked going to a nearby church away from her work atmosphere. For this particular Sunday she prepared far more than usual. She reluctantly turned down a date with Dr. Barton and frankly told him she needed to do some soul-searching. She'd never forget the quick flare of happiness that lighted his black eyes and his, "I certainly understand."

She also fasted, starting with the Saturday evening meal and continuing her fast until after Sunday worship. "Lord," she prayed in the solitude of her room. "I feel I'm right on the verge of something wonderful and healing. I long to be whole. Please, open my heart and let Your Spirit take control."

Her heart thumped inside her chest when she took a seat in an obscure corner of the church the next morning. She saw groups from the hospital but preferred not to join them. All through the first hymn, she let her voice blend with the others in a song of praise. The invocation followed and then came a call to worship. Disappointment filled her. She had hoped that in some miraculous way the text for the morning would be aimed directly at her. The next moment she mentally chastised herself. Others here probably needed direction even more than she. Yet she sighed and opened her hymnal to the next song. The title leaped out at her. *FORGIVE OUR SINS AS WE FORGIVE. God, is this my answer?* Nancy couldn't get one word out as verse succeeded verse. What had the author, Rosamond E. Herklots, experienced to pen such powerful, applicable words that hurled themselves at Nancy like battering rams, asking how God's pardon can reach a heart that refuses to forgive; a soul that broods on wrongs and clings to bitterness?

Shaken to the very core of her being, Nancy stared at the rapidly blurring page. She heard little of the sermon, although she sensed the rapt attention of those around her. Not until the congregation stood and repeated the Lord's Prayer together did she regain control. Yet when they came to the phrase, "forgive our trespasses as we forgive those who trespass against us," she broke. A terrible tumult left her nauseated, but through it her mute lips cried to her heavenly Father for help. Memory of the peace in Helen's face when Nancy had demanded how she could forgive crept into the nurse's soul and the quiet reply, *by the grace of God.* ·

"I'll try, Lord," she brokenly whispered under cover of the closing hymn. She slipped out a side door, thankful for being able to escape unobserved. Bright sunlight greeted her among blue skies and a view of the Sound with its small, white-capped waves. Perhaps later in the day she would go to Helen Markel's and tell her of the seeds of peace she felt had been planted in her heart. For now, all she longed to do was find a spot where she could overlook the Sound in all its beauty and thank God.

———◆◆◆◆———

Nancy hadn't escaped detection, as she thought. A few pews back and to one side of her, Dr. Damon Barton had surreptitiously watched her from the time she entered the sanctuary until the moment she left, every line of her body showing her wish to be alone. He could not intrude at such a time. He automatically smiled and greeted those about him, even while silently thanking God for the way he'd seen tension drain from Nancy's body during the service. Her frank explanation of turning down a date the evening before had shown she'd begun to come to terms with the things that loomed large and fearsome in her life.

If only he could share with her how Jesus longed to slay monsters, real and imaginary! Yet how many years had it taken for him to accept the fact and put the past where it belonged.

Damon wondered at how quickly the threads of respect and admiration he'd felt for Nancy Galbraith, RN, had woven themselves into a web of attraction and something deeper. He cared far too much for her and had since the evening they'd shared at the Greek restaurant. A dozen times he had told himself, "Break it off while you can, Barton. You know there's no place for love in your life. You have vows to keep. Besides, what can you offer a woman like her?"

God, must this sense of unworthiness persist for the rest of Curtis's time on earth? Why should it be so hard for him to forgive himself when he knew beyond a shadow of a doubt that You forgave him long before he existed?

Damon shook his head to clear the cobwebs from his brain, yet his heart plunged, thinking of the humiliation and invisible chains that still bound him. He tried to analyze them, to let go so God could finish His plan without interference from old hangups. He thought of the words of the song when he had observed Nancy's rigid stance. They applied to him, as well.

" 'Old bitterness,' what an apt phrase," he muttered. Well, most of the bitterness had drained out of him. Yet the scar tissue sometimes grew tender from memories.

Fortunately for his peace of mind, when he reached his apartment, his answering machine held a message that drove speculation away.

"Damon, sorry to cut into your Sunday, but we have an emergency," Dr. Cranston's voice informed him. Incredibly, his voice shook, something Damon had never heard in the years they'd worked together. "My granddaughter Amy has had some kind of seizure. She's in Virginia Mason Hospital. Come as soon as you can."

Damon shot a prayer skyward. Four-year-old Amy, petite and charming, Dr. Cranston's only granddaughter, and the darling of his heart. What could have brought on a seizure? Damon's boss never tired of boasting how healthy Amy was. All the way to Virginia Mason, Damon continued to pray, as he did for each child he encountered. He also petitioned heaven for the right words to say. His heart fell. The Cranstons were morally upright people and attended church, yet in his association with them, Damon had seen no evidence of the abiding faith and trust in Jesus Christ that offered solace in troubled times.

An ashen-faced family met him. Their eyes silently pleaded for help. "You're to go right on in," Amy's mother said.

"I will do everything in my power to help," he promised. "In the meantime, you can help, as well. Ask God to give all who work with Amy His wisdom in discovering what's causing the problem." He left them staring after him, but his heart felt light. He had said what he felt needed saying. Now they must choose.

Hours later he told a haggard Dr. Cranston the same thing. "Bob, we have to wait for the test results, but you already know what I suspect."

"Brain tumor, possibly malignant," came through white lips. "I just don't see why it suddenly showed up. Amy's never showed symptoms before."

"It happens that way sometimes." Damon squared his shoulders. "There's a rush on the lab work so it won't be long."

"Every minute's an eternity." Robert Cranston shook his head. "From now on I'm going to have even more compassion on those who wait. I never knew it could be so hard."

"That's because we're in the middle of things, doing our job," Damon soberly told him. He gripped Cranston's arm. "I'm praying for Amy and for all of you." Shackles of reticence dropped off in the face of impending tragedy.

"Do you think if I promise God I'll try to be a better person that He will spare her?"

The eternal question, always with the same answer. "Bob, we can't bargain with God. We simply have to trust Him and allow His Spirit to guide us into what He wants from us."

Some of the hope in Cranston's face dimmed, but he lifted his chin and in the remaining time before the X-rays came back, he comforted his family in a way Damon found beautiful.

"Just as we suspected. There's a small dark mass." Damon pointed to the film. "That's the culprit," he told the family who had gathered close to the lighted panel that held the X-rays.

"Take it out." Amy's mother never faltered.

"Right." Her father put an arm around his wife's shoulder. "Dad, do we need a specialist? I know you can't do it."

"Damon's as good as any in Seattle." The older doctor turned to his associate. "I'd rather trust Amy to him, and to his God, than anyone I know."

Dr. Barton blinked hard. Never in all his career had he felt more humble. "I'll be proud to operate as soon as we can arrange things," he told them. "Bob, you'll want to be there?"

"Yes, but I'd rather not assist. I'll just watch."

Damon thought he caught a faint "and pray" but couldn't be sure. His heart leaped at the thought and even while he discussed details, made arrangements, and scrubbed for surgery, a constant prayer rose up that out of all this fear good things would come.

Amy looked small and defenseless when they wheeled her in. Her naked, shaved head lay still, her eyes closed. Dr. Cranston stepped close. "Amy, dear, Dr. Barton is going to take care of you. You're going to go to sleep and when you wake up, everything will be fine."

Her eyelids fluttered but she didn't rouse.

"She is, you know, no matter what happens," Damon said.

"I know. 'Of such is the kingdom of heaven.' " A white line formed around Cranston's mouth. "I just pray she'll pull through and stay with us." He strode away and when he returned, gowned and masked, all trace of personal involvement had disappeared.

From the time Damon lifted the scalpel and made his first incision, his Gibraltar-steady hand never wavered. He also had the assurance that so often came when he literally held life and death in his hand that One far stronger than He stood beside him, guiding, inspiring, healing. Yet the tumor lay in a tricky area. One slip meant disaster. Sweat beaded Damon's forehead above his mask, and a nurse wiped it away time after time before the skilled surgeon carefully lifted the walnut-sized tumor out and dropped it into the waiting receptacle.

"No sign of spreading," he rejoiced, voice steadier than his heartbeat. "I believe it's benign." He began to close.

A barely discernible "Thank God" came from beneath Dr. Cranston's mask, and the lightning glance of the doctors above the body of the child reflected joy and wonder.

With the resilience of the young, Amy Cranston healed rapidly and Damon knew that in a few weeks she'd be back playing and bringing even greater joy to her family than ever before. He also noticed how his boss scrupulously gave credit where due, frankly telling colleagues and family he thanked God as well as Dr. Barton for Amy's life.

◆━◆✕◆━◆

One summer evening when Damon and Nancy had gone for a drive after a quiet dinner, he parked in a spot close to the edge of a hill that offered a view of a strawberry-ice-cream Mount Rainier on one side, the restless Sound on the other.

"I believe the Holy Spirit is working in Bob's life as never before," he exulted. In his excitement he captured Nancy's hands and held them in both of his own. "So often people turn to Him when tragedy strikes."

"Sometimes they turn away from Him," she reminded, her face aglow with the setting sun's rays.

"Yes. Churches lose hundreds of members after shattering experiences. Sometimes people don't know how to meet hurting persons' needs, no matter how well-intentioned they may be." He suddenly burst out in a very un-Dr. Barton-like manner, "Don't you sometimes long for a time when all the pain and hurt and sadness are done away with forever?"

"Oh, yes." Her sensitive mouth quivered.

"Forgive me, Nancy. I don't mean to pry, but I've been so engrossed with the Cranstons I haven't been able to keep track of you." He searched her face for signs of change. "You seem happier, more at ease, especially in the wards."

"I am, Damon." A little breeze snatched at a dark curl and worried it onto her cheek.

"I'm glad," he fervently told her.

"I didn't realize how much difference there was until some of the children commented," she confessed. "They've always been precious, but yesterday a chubby tot said, 'Nurth Nanthy, thankth for bein' tho thweet.'"

It took Damon a moment to translate her exact imitation of the lisper's remark. When he did, he threw back his head and laughed. "Well, Nurse Nancy, I'd also like to thank you." His laughter died and he drew her closer. Hands still clasped between them, he leaned forward and kissed her full on the mouth. The second his lips touched hers, Damon knew. Nancy Galbraith was the woman he'd always looked for, but had never been sure would come. More shaken at the revelation than he cared to consider, he drew back and made a pretense of looking at his watch. "We'd better go. It's getting late."

"Yes." Her monosyllable told him nothing. He longed to pull her into his arms and let her spill every trial on his broad shoulders, but he resisted. He might know exactly what he wanted but she couldn't, yet. He saw a look of hesitation in her eyes, a slight tremble of her lips. Rushing Nancy was the worst thing he could do. He steeled himself against her charm and when he walked her to her door, he forced himself to merely brush her cheek with his lips. "Dinner soon?"

"Soon." The door opened. She stepped inside and closed it. For some obscure reason, Damon felt like a foundling left on the steps of an orphanage, alone and lonely.

Whistling to rid himself of the idea, he slowly drove to his apartment. He scanned it with new awareness. If he married, someday, he didn't want an apartment, even this one. He wanted a house, a real home. It didn't have to be huge or ornate, although now that he'd finished paying off medical school debts, money had ceased to be a real concern. He wanted a kitchen big enough for a rocking chair, the way he remembered from his own childhood. All the time-saving appliances he could buy. Whoever he married would in all probability be a nurse or doctor. She'd want to keep on with her career, at least until they had children.

Damon found himself resenting the word "whoever." Unless his affections changed with the instability of a weathervane, only Nancy Galbraith could sit across the table he imagined in their dining room, look up at him from a deep chair by a living room fireplace, laugh until the sound of her voice gladdened both home and hearth.

"Have you so soon forgotten all your intentions never to marry?" the ticking clock clacked.

Damon proudly raised his head. "I have not forgotten. I will still keep my vows and she will help me. God, I know You don't want me to do penance forever."

Yet some of his joy faded. Long before she ever could become Mrs. Dr. Barton, Nancy must learn things Damon had thought were buried forever.

Anything else would be unthinkable.

"All these years. She'll understand. She's suffered, too." He threw himself down on a couch, stretched and yawned, but felt too keyed up to stay there. It hardly seemed possible happiness lay waiting around a turn or two in the rocky road life had been for him. Damon restlessly walked to the window. Far across the Sound, a thick fog had gathered. Its purple weight spread, lightened to gray where streetlights shone, remained black in the shadows. For some reason it depressed him. Perhaps because the evening had been so bright and beautiful and filled with promise.

Never one to allow weather to dominate his mood, he pulled the drapes and shut out the encroaching fog. An hour with a long-neglected medical journal, a chapter in his Bible, and his nightly talk with God left him more like himself. Still, just before falling asleep, Damon roused enough to wonder what the next day might bring.

Chapter 5

After a satisfying, busy day, Damon unlocked his apartment door, feeling on top of his own little world. Love for Nancy Galbraith, a career of helping others, and knowledge he was making a difference in the world combined into contentment.

" 'God's in His heaven, all's right with the world!' " he quoted from *Pippa Passes*. "Robert Browning, I salute you. It's summer, not spring, and evening rather than morning, but everything else. . ."

He abruptly stopped, raised his head, and sniffed. *Smoke!* Dropping the medical bag he always carried to the entryway hall, he dashed into the living area. A premonition of disaster caught at his throat and was replaced with a familiar sickness he had prayed never to feel again.

"Hello, Damon."

Dr. Barton's peace shattered, the same way fragile Christmas tree ornaments break into a hundred, irretrievable pieces when dropped.

The man lolling on the couch, cigarette in one hand, raised an eyebrow, twin to Damon's. His face, also like that of the slowly icing statue in front of him, contorted into a malicious smile. "Some welcome for your long-lost older brother." He took a final puff on his cigarette, stubbed it out in a cup evidently purloined from the kitchen, and sprang to his feet in a fluid motion.

"Better than you deserve." Dr. Barton stood absolutely still. "What are you doing here, Curtis?" Body rigid, he surveyed his brother. Twenty years hadn't changed him much, except the boy he had been now stood before him as a man, enough like Damon's mirror image to be a twin. Closer examination denied the likeness. Harsh lines, faint signs of dissipation marred what could have been an open, likable countenance. Curtis Barton looked years older than his brother, although barely twelve months separated them in age.

"Well?" Damon demanded.

"Things got hot in L.A." Curtis lifted his shoulders in a careless shrug. "I decided to, shall we say, move my scene of operations to Seattle." A mocking gleam lit the midnight-black eyes. "Figured I could bunk in with you until I see where the action is."

Anger Damon thought he had conquered when he'd turned his life over to God swept through him. "Get out."

"You don't mean that!" Shock erased the sardonic, taunting expression. Something flickered in Curtis's eyes.

"I never meant anything more in my life. Get out."

Curtis turned curiously pale beneath his dark skin. A curse ripped the tension between them. "You can't just throw me out." Another curse. "You're my brother."

Damon laughed in his face, a laugh so unlike his usual self even Curtis took a step backwards. "Watch me. I've spent most of my life feeling ashamed and guilty because of you. Don't think you can come waltzing in here and lay a guilt trip on me because you're in trouble. You are, aren't you?"

A look akin to fear came into the older man's face. "Big trouble."

"What did you do, rat on someone?"

Curtis licked his lips. He furtively glanced at the door. "Keep your voice down, will you? Yeah, I turned state's evidence in a murder trial and the gang's out to get me." Stark terror showed in the way his hands shook. "I knew everything was going down and saved my skin. Anything wrong with that?" Some of his defiance returned. "Would you rather have me be a TV headline?"

Damon, who had looked on incredible suffering, felt sick. It was the same way he'd felt years before when a neighborhood bully hit him in the stomach. All the anguish he had fought so long to overcome stood embodied in his brother. "How did you get in?" he hoarsely asked. "First, how'd you find me?"

"I can still read the phone directory." An unpleasant smile curved Curtis's lips upwards. "Have to admit, I didn't expect to find you a doctor. 'You've come a long way, baby,' as the ad says."

In that moment Damon thoroughly hated him. *God, why does this specter I buried and left behind rise from the past?*

"I remembered we used to pass for one another." Curtis laughed suggestively and Damon's hurting heart leaped. "Figured I'd trade on it. Came in, smiled at the manager, female, fortunately, and said for some reason I didn't have my key. She fell all over herself letting me in." He rolled his eyes and simpered, " 'Any time, Dr. Barton. We're all just so proud of the wonderful work you're doing. My friend works as a nurse and she says you're the best young children's specialist in Seattle.' " Curtis dropped his falsetto. "She also got off a lot of stuff about what a fine Christian example you are. I guess it doesn't stretch to your prodigal brother."

The sneer sent a wave of blood into Damon's face. "Give me one reason why it should."

Curtis dropped back to the couch and lit another cigarette.

"Put it out," Damon ordered. "I don't permit smoking in here. By anyone." For a moment he thought Curtis would argue and felt inward relief when he sullenly extinguished the burning cigarette, muttering a curse.

"That doesn't go here, either," Damon told him sharply. "This is my home and it's dedicated to God, the same way I am. Nothing is allowed here that will displease Him."

"Don't preach at me," Curtis flamed. "I got enough of that rot when I was a kid."

Damon relentlessly told him, "Just remember one thing. God is the head of this household. He isn't leaving. If you can't respect that, you are." He saw the flare of hope in his brother's eyes and quickly added, "I'm not saying you can stay here. Just that while you're here at all, you'll play by my rules."

"Tough talk for a Christian. I thought they were supposed to be meek and forgiving." Curtis never could resist the urge to heckle, to pin an opponent as mercilessly as a butterfly marked for mounting. He yawned and stretched. "What's in it for you, anyway? I get along fine without Sunday school stories and pious hymn-singing hypocrites."

"Oh? Then just why are you here?" Damon softly inquired. "If you're doing so great, why are you running scared and using me to hide behind?"

Curtis sat up straight. For a moment Damon thought he would leap off the couch and hit him. "Listen, punk, I don't hide behind anyone. All I need is a loan. Bread. Bucks. Don't tell me you haven't got them, a successful doc like you."

Damon shook his head, braced his feet, and prepared for battle. "Sorry, big brother. I told you five years ago when you called that I'd never bail you out again. I meant it then. I still mean it. You got yourself in this mess; it's up to you to get out of it any way you can."

"You won't like the way I do it," Curtis threatened. His eyes turned to obsidian.

"So what's new? I haven't liked any of what little I knew about your lifestyle in the last twenty years."

"Why, you. . ."

Damon saw the way Curtis bit back an obscenity and the effort it took. More than anything so far, it pointed out how desperate Curtis really was. He would never take anything off anyone. Again Damon felt sick. *How far did being a brother's keeper go?*

Did Curtis, with the same ability to catch his brother's wavelength he'd had since childhood, discern the thought? His lips curled, lips that could have been handsome if not twisted into cynicism most of the time. "The way I remember it, when the prodigal son came home, his father threw a party for him, killed the fatted calf, all that stuff."

Damon didn't give an inch. "The day you return to your heavenly Father, He will rejoice and welcome you. I'm not God, just the brother who. . ."

"Don't throw the past up to me. I won't have my little brother strutting around all holy and righteous before the poor, lost sinner!" He ground his teeth until it sounded loud in the quiet room. "Are you going to help me, or not?"

"As the old saying goes, 'There's good news and bad news.' "

Curtis looked wary.

"The bad news is, no loan. No bucks. No staying here with me."

For a single instant, Curtis looked like a pricked balloon. He recovered so quickly Damon couldn't be sure he had actually seen the look of despair and fear in his eyes. "And the good news?"

Years receded. A small Damon who adored his brother danced in Dr. Barton's mind. Love he had thought gone forever, even after forgiveness came, roughened his voice. "You have the right to know why I won't give you money or let you stay here." He took in a long breath, praying that somehow the Holy Spirit would penetrate the layers of murk that bound Curtis. "Five years ago I realized part of your problem was me."

"Wha–at. . ." Curtis's mouth hung open.

Damon nodded. "A long time ago when I became a Christian and asked God to forgive me for the way I hated what you'd done to me, I also put you in His hands."

Curtis squirmed, started to speak.

"Wait! If you've never listened to anything before, you'll listen now." The words rang. Damon felt a surge of power and the desire to make Curtis understand he stood on the brink of destruction. "Even though I told God I would accept whatever He chose to allow in your life in order to bring you to Him, when you called pleading for help, I couldn't stand the thought of you in prison, or sick or in trouble. Maybe some of it was pride, or the way I felt dirty that my own brother had chosen to involve himself in unspeakable things. I never knew all of what you'd done. I didn't want to know. It hurt too much. I guess a spark of what Mother taught us about being a family still lived. Anyway, in spite of promising God to accept His will, I stepped in." Damon stared blindly at his nemesis, the figure he had loved, hated, idolized, and seen fall.

"So, I sent money, whatever I could. A couple of times it meant borrowing from the bank and doing without necessities."

Curtis sent a significant look around the tastefully decorated apartment. "It sure looks like you're poverty-stricken," he sarcastically said.

Damon ignored him. "The bottom line is, I realized the last time I stepped in had to be just that: the last time. Otherwise, my rescuing you meant all God's allowing you to be in misery meant nothing. You'd simply go on believing no matter what happened, I'd be here to take care of it."

"So you'll let your own brother rot in jail or be killed." Disbelief erased every trace of swagger.

The hardest words Damon ever had to say fell slowly and quietly from pallid lips. "Curtis, I have no choice."

The man on the couch sagged. His lips pulled back like a beast at bay. "Tell this to that God of yours. Anyone, God or not, who turns brother against brother, is pretty rotten. When you get a call to come identify me in the morgue you can remember who put me there." He stood and lurched toward the door.

Damon longed to rush after him, to give in. What did a vow mean if, as Curtis said, his brother's life hung in the balance? Yet a little voice inside reminded, *If you give in now, then all the agony of leaving him in God's hands is for nothing. God, was any man ever so torn?* Damon found his voice just before his brother opened the door and vanished. "It isn't I who put you where you are. It's you."

The door slammed. Damon heard footsteps pound away then dwindle into nothingness, the way Curtis's life had dwindled into sin. Unashamed tears fell and the doctor, made strong to do what he believed God required, dropped to his knees, pouring his heart out until a measure of uneasy peace returned, but without a trace of his earlier joy.

Time after time in the next few days Damon found himself mired in doubt. It took every ounce of strength he possessed to continue with his duties and wear an outward calm for the sake of his little patients. He avoided Nancy. A dozen times he reached for the phone to call then let his hand drop. How could he even consider involving her in his life when that life carried the albatross of a brother gone wrong? What if those who surely would trace Curtis discovered his brother? They would have no scruples in using any person even vaguely associated with their prey in order to get to him. For her sake, at least until. . .until what? In any event, he could not expose her to possible harm.

The strain took its inevitable toll. Damon dreaded coming home after work. Not that he expected Curtis to be there. Their final confrontation had killed that fear. A man as proud as his brother, once he saw the truth, would never beg. The answering machine became a foe. Damon nerved himself to play his daily messages, always with the words, *When you get a call to come identify me. . .* lurking in his brain. He had replayed the scene again and again, coming up with items he hadn't realized had registered at the time. Such as the lack of street language in Curtis's speech. Other than the taboo profanity and smothered obscenities, he had spoken as easily and well as Damon. It brought up questions. Surely Curtis couldn't have been all these years in the gang scene and not picked up the way they talked.

Determined to discover exactly what had driven him from L.A. to Seattle, Damon arranged with Dr. Cranston for a few days off. He flew directly to L.A. and went straight to police headquarters.

"I'd like to find out about a murder," he told the officer who asked what he wanted.

"*A* murder? How about a dozen? A hundred?" The officer stared suspiciously at him. "Who are you, anyway?"

"Damon Barton, MD, Seattle." Damon handed over a business card and received a noncommittal grunt in return. "A man I know, also named Barton, recently turned state's evidence in a murder trial. I need to know what happened." He silently prayed for God to open the way.

A half-hour later he left the station, heart in his shoes. In spite of the wealth of evidence against him, Damon had hoped Curtis exaggerated his latest crime. He hadn't. He'd saved his skin by fingering two men in a drive-by shooting, one he witnessed (according to him) from a storefront window. The killers insisted Barton had been with them, but Curtis had miraculously slipped through the net and his police record contained small stuff only. The DA had willingly cut a deal, letting the little fish swim away while he went for the sharks and got a conviction plus a life sentence for the shooter and a prison term for the accomplice.

"Your friend," the officer raised a skeptical eyebrow, "was lucky. Tell him that from L.A.P.D. You might also tell him the two he informed on have friends. Lots of them."

"I will." Damon thanked the officer and headed outside. Even the L.A. smog smelled better than the atmosphere of sin and misery inside. He caught the earliest flight to Seattle he could book and considered all the way home how to warn Curtis, even though his brother was already fully aware of his perilous situation.

"Did you say something?" the flight attendant inquired.

Damon shook his head. He hadn't realized he'd quoted Romans 6:23 aloud. *"For the wages of sin is death. . . ."* He mentally finished, *"but the gift of God is eternal life through Jesus Christ our Lord."* Suddenly, he understood more fully how Jesus felt when He wept over Jerusalem. How could men, women, even children, rush heedlessly toward spiritual as well as physical death, laughing gaily and spurning the only One who offered hope? Many didn't have the excuse of not knowing. TV and billboards, churches with spires toward heaven that served to remind those who rushed past their open doors, persons like Dr. and Mrs. Paul Hamilton and the others at the Shepherd of Love Sanctuary in the inner city; all offered a clear message of the way to salvation.

Damon bowed his head and prayed again that no matter what it took, God would one day bring Curtis to his knees and soften a heart that appeared to be made of lead, like the bullets in the little man's gun.

A sense of the need to find his brother and talk with him again sent Dr. Barton to the streets of Seattle. Without any idea of where Curtis might be, Damon walked aimlessly but with a knowledge that God could help him find the one soul among thousands. His faith proved justified a week later. He came face-to-face with Curtis on Broadway.

"Hello, little brother."

"Hello." He scanned the other for signs of hunger, secretly wondering how he had managed to survive.

With uncanny insight, Curtis sneered. "I'm eating. Never fear. Doing just fine without help." He motioned significantly toward an obviously new custom suit and expensive shoes.

"Where did you get them?" Damon felt stretched to the breaking point.

"I have ways." Curtis flicked ashes from his cigarette and walked toward a crouching black limo purring at the curb.

"Wait." Damon reached a long arm, caught his brother's shoulder, and lowered his voice. "L.A.P.D. says to tell you. . ."

"You fool!" Curtis' voice went low and deadly. "What do you know?"

"Everything. I went down and found out."

Curtis backed off, a flicker in his eyes Damon couldn't read. "Keep away from me. Get it?" He raised his voice in a stream of profanity that turned the air blue, wheeled, and was swallowed by the limo that glided away like a great jungle cat with its prey.

"Drugs," Dr. Barton whispered. "The only way he could wear that suit. Wonder who owns the limo?" He strained his eyes to catch a license number but the distance stopped him. Besides, what good would it do to know? He could do nothing to save Curtis without further endangering him. Caught in a web woven by Satan and inhabited by his followers, Curtis must choose to extricate himself or remain trapped forever.

Damon reached his apartment, ignored the blinking answering machine, and headed for his shower. Oh, to let the hot water pour over him and make him clean. He thought of the day he was baptized and of the moment he came out of the water. He had felt clean, then. As if every dark and ugly thing in life washed from body and soul had left him. Yet no one could live in today's world and be totally free of its smirch. Some tried. Not for him, the way of withdrawal. The same world that repelled him needed his skills and his witness.

He stayed in the shower for a long time before toweling himself and donning fresh clothing from the skin out. A rueful smile came to his lips when he dropped his dirty clothes in the hamper and hung his wet towel to dry. "Too bad we can't send out hearts and souls to the laundry when they get stained," he muttered.

Nothing on his answering machine required his immediate attention, so Damon settled down with his Bible. He'd found it the sure way to relieve tension and bring back hope. Yet now the Scriptures blurred a little. The way he had chosen seemed hard and long. Was there really any danger to him or to Nancy, if he renewed their friendship? He knew from the quick way she glanced at him when he ran into her at Shepherd of Love that she wondered why he had stopped calling. "God," he prayed. "I love her so much. You know I will never do anything that might hurt her. Guide and direct us both. In Jesus' name, amen."

Peace came slowly, on soft, kitten feet that tucked themselves into a sense of all-rightness. An hour later, Damon looked at the ticking clock. Only ten. He dialed, waited. When Nancy answered he said, "It's Damon. If you have tomorrow off, will you go to church with me?" He gripped the phone, tense as the first time he had called a teenage girl and asked for a date. She responded. He cradled the phone and chided himself for the spurt of gladness that spread throughout his body at the thought of their worshipping together in the morning. "Go slowly," he warned himself. "Don't try to run before the Lord."

Yet the steady pound of his heart and the anticipation he felt were completely out of proportion to the fact that Nancy had only agreed to a date for church.

Chapter 6

When Damon kissed her for the first time, Nancy Galbraith longed to respond with her whole heart. She couldn't. Suppose it meant nothing more to him than a pleasant way to let her know he liked her? She shrank from the thought, especially when Dr. Barton huskily said, "We'd better go. It's getting late."

"Yes." Nancy sat quietly beside him on the drive home, outwardly calm, inwardly quivering like an aspen leaf in the presence of her sweetheart, the wind. A great feeling of longing assailed her, the desire to be more to Damon than a good friend and someone to date. *God, is this of You?*

"Dinner soon?" he asked, after brushing her cheek with his lips.

"Soon." She stepped inside, closed the door, and leaned against it. His sure footsteps faded and died, but the sense of his compassion did not. Nancy flung herself on the bed, heedless of crushing her dress. She flipped on her back, clasped her hands behind her head, and stared at the ceiling. Surely she was old and mature enough to discern between friendship and growing attraction. She remembered the look in Damon's dark eyes and attempted to analyze it. *Admiration? Yes. Caring? Obviously. Love?* She stopped short in her dissection. She must not read into the dedicated doctor's attentions more than existed.

"What do I really know about him?" she whispered. Her active brain presented the facts: is a noted physician and surgeon, loves children, appears to be a strong Christian.

Nancy's eyes widened. Why would she qualify Damon's Christianity by saying "appears to be"? Did she doubt his sincerity? He had no reason to pretend, did he? Her heart shouted the affirmation of his integrity while her mind tried to remain objective.

"Stop playing psychiatrist and get ready for bed," she ordered herself. Yet far into the night she restlessly shifted between waking and sleeping, more troubled about Dr. Barton and her growing feelings for him than she wanted to admit.

She awakened to a new day filled with bright hope. Her mirrored image's eyes sparkled and she laughed out loud. "Can't wait to see him, can you? You're worse than a teenager." The chastisement resulted in her by-passing the yellow uniform in favor of a soft pink that made her look like a blooming Queen Elizabeth rose.

Her small patients' chorus, "Nurse Nancy, you're all pink!" gladdened her heart, and when the time came for Dr. Barton to arrive, she took three deep breaths and anticipated the moment with both pleasure and a little fear.

"Nancy," a fellow nurse called to her, "Dr. Barton is going to change his visitation hours due to some things that have come up. He will be in during the evening shift for a time."

Nancy's spirits hit the ground with a heavy thud. She could feel her face burn. Humiliated, she averted her gaze to hide her agitation. So she had been right. Damon evidently didn't want to see her. The kiss had meant nothing. A new thought pounded at the door of her heart and no barring could keep it out. Evidently he feared she might take his spontaneous affection to mean more than he intended. What if, with his trained understanding, he had seen how much it meant to her? She tensed, forced herself to relax. No one, and that meant Dr. Barton above all others, must see her distress. With a quickly whispered prayer for strength, she forced hands, feet, mind, and heart to go about her duties. Perhaps her inner turmoil and suffering gentled her voice and added even more skill than usual to her ministrations. In any event, the most fractious children settled at the sound of her instructions.

Each day brought more assurance that Damon regretted his attentions to her. Nancy's phone rang often, but never with the voice she longed to hear. The few times she saw Dr. Barton he acted brusque and wore an abstracted manner. Once Nancy thought she caught a look in his eyes she could only describe as pleading, but his continued avoidance of her and his cold demeanor when they met quickly erased that impression.

On the other hand, her friendship with Helen Markel grew with every visit to the charming, flower-surrounded home. Nancy found herself dropping by at every opportunity. She and Helen sometimes just sat in the garden, quietly chatting or silently absorbing the peace. "You're one of the nicest gifts God has given me," she wistfully told her hostess.

A tinge of pleased pink touched the older woman's face and her clear gray eyes misted. "I've been thinking the same about you, my dear." The look that passed between them spoke volumes.

"You never push." Nancy watched a bee, tipsy from pollen, rise and fly in an uneven path to another flower. "You just allow me to share when I feel I can and otherwise remain still."

"One of my favorite Scriptures is, 'Be still, and know that I am God,'" Helen softly quoted.

"Psalm 46:10. It's one of mine, too." Yet Nancy shifted restlessly in her chair. "It's hard to find time or a place to be still in today's chaotic world."

"One of the lessons I learned from the accident was that stillness can be internal and not depend on where we are." She suddenly laughed and Nancy's mouth involuntarily tipped up at the cheerful sound. A squawking blue jay perched on the edge of the birdbath, cocked his head to one side, cast a beady glance at the two humans who dared invade his kingdom, and scolded them roundly.

"Despite what Mr. Jay says, it's true," Helen insisted. "The reason I laughed is because even though I believe we carry much of our peace with us, I also made sure this garden would be here whenever I, or others, need it."

"It is a balm to the eyes and soul," Nancy confirmed. She drew in a fragrant breath of flower-scented air. "I leave here feeling like I am a new woman." She paused and lowered her voice. "I–I haven't told you before— I wanted to make sure I could carry through—but the Sunday after I first came here, something happened." She sketched in her day of fasting, the way Helen's words about the need to forgive had haunted her. She brokenly repeated her prayer of petition to be whole. Awe in her voice and tears shining in her beautiful eyes, Nancy told how the words of a hymn had sunk deep in her soul with their cutting message of the need to forgive.

"I could only tell God I'd try to forgive the boy who set the fire," she whispered.

"And since then?" Loving concern robbed the question of impertinence.

"I have been more at peace, at least until. . ." She stopped. Not even to Helen could she confess her feelings for a doctor who daily made clear by his actions that he had no interest in her.

If Helen caught an underlying message she gave no sign. "The most wonderful thing about forgiveness is what it does for the wronged person," she said. Her face shone with certainty. "I felt so chained until I could freely forgive."

"I've experienced some of that," Nancy admitted. Her taut fingers, which had tightened on her chair arms during her recital, relaxed.

"If you will continue practicing what I believe is the healing art of forgiveness, you will discover freedom beyond verbal expression." The tranquillity in Helen's face spread into Nancy's heart, the way spilled oil stretches into an ever-widening pool, coating whatever it touches.

"Nancy, when have you had a vacation?"

The change of subject startled her. "Why, I took a few days off last fall."

"I don't mean a few days. I mean a real vacation. One where you got away from your daily routine and did something completely different." Helen raised an eyebrow and waited.

"Never." She tried to smooth over the bald remark by explaining, "What with training and work and special cases needing me, there just hasn't been a good time."

"There never is, for those who are dedicated to what they do. Yet you cannot go on and on giving without time to be refilled. It's like draining a glass of lemonade and expecting to keep on pouring out when everything is gone. I suggest you think seriously about setting a specific time for vacation, two weeks at the minimum. Experts who study fatigue problems among workers say one of the greatest mistakes persons make is taking only a one-week vacation at a time. It takes two, perhaps three, days to shove aside job-related stress and thoughts of what you left undone. Two to three days before you go back, your mind always fastens on getting back to work. That doesn't leave enough time in between." Helen leaned forward with a no-nonsense-about-being-indispensable glint in her eyes. "This isn't a suggestion, Nancy. It's an order. I'm speaking as your professional counselor rather than as your friend and I'm telling you to get away."

"I don't know where to go or what to do." The spurt of excitement over just walking away from her problems died. How could she leave her biggest problem—herself?

Helen threw up her hands and grimaced. "You remind me of the classic story about a famous man, I don't remember who, but the tale goes that he became exhausted from working. He told his wife he had to get away. Like you, he didn't know where to go or what to do."

Nancy listened to the story carefully. She had found that Helen followed Jesus' teaching pattern and used parables to make important points.

Helen went on. A twinkle rested in her eyes and a smile lurked at the corners of her mouth. "Being a wise woman, the wife gave a fine suggestion. She told her husband, 'I agree that you need time off. Now, you must think of the place where you'd rather be, more than any other place in the world. You must decide what you love most in life and that's what you should do.'"

"And?" Nancy held her breath.

The corners of Helen's mouth went down. "The famous man went back to work!"

Nancy stared, then a chuckle burst from her throat and changed to a full-scale laugh.

Helen kept a straight face although her eyes gave away her inner mirth. "I wouldn't want to say you resemble the man in the story. . . ." A quirked eyebrow and droll expression wordlessly completed her sentence. She rose, slowly walked to her guest, and patted her hand. "Think about it, Nancy. Being married to your work is good to a point, but not when you become so involved you have no other life."

The seed fell into fertile ground. A short time later, Nancy signed up for two weeks' vacation. The prompt way her request was granted made her wonder if Helen Markel had dropped a hint in the right place. She shrugged. It didn't matter. Now that she'd taken the first step, the idea of getting away for a time intrigued her. She considered and rejected the idea of asking Patty, Lindsey, or Shina to accompany her. Even their cheerful presence would remind her of Shepherd of Love, and for two wonderful weeks she intended to shelve both hospital and her own problems, including the elusive Dr. Barton who continued to act distant and inattentive when they met by chance.

"If it weren't that you need to get clean away, I'd offer you my home for your vacation," Helen told her. "There's a special conference and I'm flying to California to attend. I'll also visit various friends." She drew her brows together. "Nancy, I've had a key made for you. There's no reason to wait for me to let you in even when I'm home." She smiled at the younger woman. "You're as dear as a daughter. If I weren't afraid you would lean too much on me and not become the person God wants you to be, I'd invite you to live with me."

Nancy blinked and swallowed hard. "Thanks, but you're right. I would rely too much on you when what I need to do is continue learning to rely on God." A vague idea flitted through her brain. "I plan to go to either the beach or the mountains, maybe both, for the first part of my vacation. If I get rested and want to come back before the two weeks are up, may I stay here?"

"Absolutely." Helen put on a ferocious scowl that didn't deceive Nancy. "No cheating, though. I don't want to come back and find out you've been here all the time, on call if the hospital thinks it needs you."

"I won't even give them your phone number," Nancy promised, then shivered, not knowing why. Nothing could be less threatening in the entire world than Helen Markel's quiet home and garden.

With each passing day, Nancy realized how wise her friend and mentor had been to insist that she take time off. Her heart bounced at the thought of long hours walking the beach. The crashing waves would surely drown out the cries of children who pleaded for her help. The clear, blue ocean and matching sky would offer a chance for her to regain perspective by their very timelessness. Sandpipers, plovers with their short, hard-tipped bills and more compact build, screeching gulls, scuttling crabs, and sand dollars; all fringe benefits to encourage beach tramps in fresh, salty air that promoted appetite and healthful sleep.

For several days she didn't see Dr. Barton. A real pang shot through her. What had happened to their growing friendship? She had felt it so real. He didn't appear at all on the Saturday that marked her final work day before vacation. She sighed and left the ward in a saddened mood. Fourteen days from now when she returned, hopefully rested and ready to take up her numerous and taxing duties, Pediatrics wouldn't be the same. Some of her patients would have been released; one or two taken home to their heavenly Father. The rush of feeling that rose inside her again confirmed her need to get away. A nurse who became too attached to her patients harmed rather than helped them, as well as herself. She slowly walked to her suite. Should she change her plans and start for the coast tonight? Although the snug cabin she had rented through a travel agency was reserved starting Monday, she could certainly find somewhere to stay.

She shook her head. Maybe not. With the continuing good weather, people flocked to the beaches. Before she decided exactly when to leave, she'd learned from the travel agent how necessary it was to get firm reservations. "A lot of people end up sleeping in their cars or on the beach," he warned. Nancy had paid for the first week with the understanding that if she wished to stay longer, she'd let him know no later than Friday morning. He'd have no trouble getting someone else for the cabin, should she plan to leave on that Sunday.

Unwilling to cling to the hospital, she ordered in a small pizza and large salad rather than going to the staff dining hall. She munched and watched a game show, in itself a rare occurrence, and ended up bathed and in bed by ten o'clock, propped up against her pillows and anticipating the joy of reading herself to sleep. No alarm to set tonight! She'd get up when she pleased, go to church, and let the rest of the day take care of itself.

The sharp ring of the bedside phone jangled into her plans. For a moment she felt tempted to just let it ring. Duty won over desire and she picked it up.

"Hello?"

"Nancy, it's Damon. If you have tomorrow off, will you go to church with me?"

A hundred thoughts milled in her mind, a hundred feelings in her heart. Just when she had begun to accept his disinterest, Dr. Barton crashed back into her life. Her lip curled. She should give him a flat "No" and get on with her vacation.

She couldn't do it. After a brief pause she heard her voice, controlled and even, agreeing to accompany him to church. A quick agreement on the time and a click ended the conversation. It did not end Nancy's dilemma. "Why did you say yes?" she demanded out loud. "Fine way to start getting away from everything." She thought of the way he sounded, not at all like the reserved Dr. Barton who had shied away from her in Pediatrics except when necessity demanded that they discuss patients' care. He had sounded more like the Damon who had showed his concern and genuine liking for her, the Damon she realized she had grown to love.

Seeing into her own heart also explained why she had felt so hurt when he rejected her. Or had he? Could there be another reason for his coldness?

"Well, God," she said. "There's no better place to get things straightened out than in church." Happiness curled into her heart like a sunwarmed blanket. She put aside her unread book, switched off her bedlight, and closed her eyes. To her surprise, when she opened them again, an errant ray of sunlight had sneaked in around the curtain, heralding a new and special Sunday.

Damon arrived promptly. Nancy saw the quick look he gave her and her heart fluttered. She hadn't dared wear yellow, but knew her white suit, scarlet shoes, and matching scarf became her.

"I'm glad you are free," he told her. His gaze said much more.

She bit her tongue to keep from affirming her own gladness and contented herself with a smile.

"Nancy, would you mind going to a different church this morning?" A kind of urgency laced his simple question.

"Not at all. What do you have in mind?"

"You know Dr. Paul Hamilton, Jonica, and Paul's father have recently completed a chapel at the Shepherd of Love Sanctuary downtown?"

"I hadn't heard." A little quiver ran through her. She hadn't yet gone down to the inner city to serve. Not until she fought and vanquished her own childhood dragons would she be able to work with those who were less fortunate.

"Paul's going to speak this morning and several of those the Clinic serves have promised to come." Damon's fine hands tightened on the steering wheel. "I thought it would be nice to give him some moral support."

"Why, yes. I haven't seen Jonica for a time, what with. . ."

A speeding car cut in front of them and sliced across Nancy's explanation about her upcoming vacation. She braced herself and noticed how capably her escort swung their vehicle out of harm's way. The near accident successfully drove all else from mind and Damon's quick, "Hope the Seattle Police get that menace off the streets," further sidetracked her.

After they had parked in a lot next to the newly constructed chapel, Nancy said, "Maybe I'll be overdressed."

"You look fine to me," he assured her, but she shook her head and resolutely untied the bright scarf, then reached into her carryall bag and pulled out a pair of plain white pumps with flat heels. "I'll wear these. I didn't know what plans you might have for this afternoon so I tucked them in." She slipped them on and smiled at him. "Not so dramatic as red."

"You're a very special and considerate woman, Nancy Galbraith." He got out, locked his door, and came around to open hers. "I'm proud to know you."

His words stayed with her while they entered the plain building with its simple furnishings and white walls. The chapel's only claim to beauty lay in the richly colored window in the east wall. Damon ushered Nancy into a pew on the west side and seated himself beside her. About twenty others sat scattered in the room, clean, but showing signs of poverty. Nancy felt then a sudden brightening and glanced at the window beyond Damon. Sunlight poured through, making a living mosaic of the colors.

She turned her gaze to Damon, and saw his face, outlined against the sun-glorified, stained glass-window.

She never forgot the moment. Her heartbeat slowed. She felt blood drain from her face and sat as it turned to stone. Twenty years receded and a long-remembered face etched against the light of flickering flames rose in her mind. A boy's face.

Nancy closed her eyes against the swell of pain, and reopened them to confirm the truth. Allowing for the changes of boy to man, the same face contrasted sharply against the chapel window.

Chapter 7

No, no, Nancy's disbelieving heart silently screamed. It couldn't be. Damon, the boy who had ripped her life to shreds? Impossible! Yet the evidence condemned, tried, and convicted him. Dr. Barton's face against the window could be no other than the face she'd seen twenty years before on that fateful night.

At first, horror left her numb. All remembrance of the Sunday she had promised God she would try to forgive fled. She hastily rose, one hand over her mouth, and stumbled to the side aisle, thankful no one had chosen to sit in the row.

"Nancy?" A gentle hand fell on her shoulder. A concerned voice asked, "Are you all right?"

She wanted to shriek, to cry out in the quiet chapel that her world had just ended for the second time, again because of him. She did neither. Shaking her head, she slipped from beneath his strong fingers and bolted. Could she make it to the rest room in time? Sickness rose within her and she blindly felt her way down the endless corridor, made it inside, and locked the door. There. She'd be safe. Deep breathing settled her down and her stomach stopped churning enough for her to think clearly. She must escape, now. In moments, Damon would send Jonica Hamilton for her; she couldn't be here. The incident had wrenched open a half-closed door and brought back memories from the dim recesses of childhood. Not only of the fire, but of the terrible life afterwards.

"I can't talk about it. Not to Damon or Dr. Paul or Jonica. Not to anyone," she brokenly told the sick-looking woman in the mirror. "God, help me get out of here. Please." She straightened, unlocked the door, and made a run for it. Good, no one in sight yet. A hysterical laugh slipped from between her tightly compressed lips. She didn't even have her car. Gathering her courage, she headed down the street in search of a cab or phone booth.

Fate proved kind. A cruising cab picked her up just a block from the chapel. "Where to, Ma'am?"

"Shepherd of Love Hospital." She climbed inside.

"Right."

Before they got away from downtown, Nancy had regained the ability to think clearly. Damon would immediately go to the hospital looking for her. "Driver, it's such a nice day I think I won't go home yet." She bit her lip, wishing she hadn't given away that she lived at Shepherd of Love. If Damon tried to trace her through the cab driver, the fewer clues she left, the better. Too late now. As one in a dream she heard herself giving Helen Markel's address. At the same time, she felt in her purse. Her fingers tightened on the cool metal key that spelled security and a place to hide. A rush of gladness that she had never told Dr. Barton she'd taken his advice and sought counseling left her weak with relief. Someday she must face him but not until time had softened the terrible blow that life had dealt in the telltale moment she had seen his face highlighted by the sun through the stained glass.

She added a generous tip when she paid her taxi driver and smiled a little at his hearty, "Thank you, Ma'am!" Such a small thing to bring such a big grin. When he drove away, she had the strange feeling she'd lost a friend.

Nancy opened the door into quietness, peace, coolness, and a place to heal. "If I hadn't promised Helen to leave Seattle, I'd stay right here, God," she whispered. The off-white walls and pastel furniture held out loving arms of welcome. Her racing heartbeat slowed. She took off her suit jacket and hung it in a closet. Her fine eyebrows came together in a frown. It wouldn't be safe for her to risk going to her suite at the staff residence to get her packed bags and car. The smart thing was to hide out here overnight, or at least until sometime after midnight, before attempting to go back. She doubtfully peered into a mirror. Her suit skirt and shell weren't all that comfortable to lounge in.

"Helen won't mind," she reassured herself and walked into the master bedroom. Distaste filled her at the idea of rummaging through her friend's clothing, but she had no choice. A simple cotton housedress caught her attention, green-and-white-checked gingham, crisp and cool. It would do nicely and be easy to wash.

Nancy slipped into the dress. For some unknown reason, she thought of the day she had told the hospital director she didn't look good in blue or green. Her lips tightened. If the dress were yellow or even pink, she didn't know if she could have put it on.

Making sure the front door was locked, she went into the backyard and dragged a chaise lounge into the shade of a towering maple whose leaves rustled above her. She sat down, leaned back, and stared at the patches of blue visible through the branches. The time had come to consider what had happened and what she should do.

"God, is it possible I'm mistaken?" Her low cry expressed her desire to believe it. She slowly shook her head. There simply was no chance of mistaken identity with the boy's features etched into her mind.

Why hadn't Damon told her? He knew her history. . . .

Nancy sat bolt upright, trying to remember every detail. So still a resident squirrel ran down a tree trunk and eyed her with a sharp gaze, she stretched her mind to remember every word she had said to him about her past. "I told him I had nightmares about death and fire," she whispered. "And that I sang to Leila, who died a long time ago. Damon was there when I asked Timmy to tell Leila I'd be coming soon to be with her. Beyond that, he knows nothing." Relief filled her. At least Damon hadn't deliberately hidden his past from her because he knew the part he had played in it.

Suddenly she regretted not wanting to know the young boy's name. At the time and through the years, she'd felt it would merely add to her burden. Now it opened a way to discover if what she had learned really concerned Dr. Barton. Police records could tell her what she passionately longed to know. If Damon had spent time in a place for juvenile offenders, there must be records.

Her heart sank. Once a minor reached eighteen, his past was officially blotted out. Her great idea dead-ended. The law forgave and allowed offenders to start over.

Forgiveness. Bittersweet memories of her experience that Sunday morning washed over her. Nancy closed her eyes, trying to retrieve the feelings so strong they had swept away long-held resentment and hatred. They wouldn't come. All she could see was the boy's face, then Damon's, against a burning background. Her heart twisted with pain. She switched mental channels. Now she saw the strong doctor who comforted Timmy and his mother; whose sad eyes with the little lines around them carved by life brightened or grew tender with compassion. What if he had made terrible mistakes as a teenager? Must he pay for it forever?

"God, I truly want to forgive him," Nancy prayed. "But could I ever forget, even if he cares as I do?" The prayer and question pounded away until she fell asleep in the chaise from pure emotional and mental exhaustion.

Nancy awakened to the evening coolness that makes Seattle delightful on most hot days. Sleepy birds sang in a low, minor key. Flowers nodded, all except the evening primroses that snapped their chalice-like blossoms open with a little pop. More refreshed than she'd have believed possible, Nancy stretched and realized hunger pangs took precedence over all else. She foraged in the immaculate kitchen and smiled at the well-stocked refrigerator. Helen obviously had suspected Nancy would come. Now the nurse opened a can of chunk chicken, boiled and cooled an egg, washed greens, chopped tomatoes and onions. The resulting chef salad plus toast with some of Helen's wonderful homemade jam did a great deal in lifting her spirits.

"Thank You, God, for this food and that I'm on vacation," she murmured. She laid her plans. Early to bed with an alarm clock set for four o'clock would give her ample time for her surreptitious visit to the residence hall. She'd be in and out before the night shift got off and the day shift rose.

Like a child playing hookey, she tiptoed into her rooms from her outside entrance. She'd need two trips to get her bags. Nancy hadn't realized she had been holding her breath until she closed the door behind her, felt her way to the windows to make sure the drapes were tightly closed, and let a little sigh of relief escape. She flicked a light switch—and froze.

On the living room rug just inside the door from the hall lay a square white envelope with *NANCY* written on it in bold black ink.

Damon. She'd seen his writing on too many charts to fail to recognize the penmanship. Her purse slid to the floor from weak fingers and she crossed to the envelope, eyeing it as a mouse eyes a cat ready to spring. In one quick swoop she snatched it up and ripped it open.

What is it, Nancy? she read. *Is there any way I can help? Why did you run away from the chapel? Please call me as soon as you come in, no matter how late.*

His dear and familiar scrawled signature ended the note.

Tears she had stifled all day gushed, although a tiny warm spot created by his concern glowed within her. She saw the attractive rose-and-white room through a waterfall, blurred and a little out of focus. Her gaze rested on the phone. If only she could call him! What release it would be to frankly tell him the entire story and ask if he were that boy.

"No." Both tears and grasping at straws left her. Until she could decide what to do and how to handle it if her worst suspicions proved accurate, she must not approach Damon.

"I'll go away as planned," she said. "The beach will give me time."

A prayer in her heart, the note in her purse, Nancy successfully made her escape without detection. Her unconquerable sense of humor arose and sustained her, fed by the picture of Nurse Galbraith sneaking out in the middle of the night, weighed down by bags. "If this is what a criminal feels like I'd never make a good one," she murmured. "I haven't done anything wrong, but I feel like one pursued."

The feeling persisted all the way from Seattle to the small cabin she had rented a few miles north of Long Beach. It evaporated when she stepped inside the furnished cabin, and fled entirely while she grocery shopped. No eating in restaurants for her unless she got sick of her own company, which wasn't likely. The solitude of the cabin suited her. So did the friendly lights a little distance away that appeared at sundown. If she needed help, she could get it. If not, no one would bother her.

At first she found it satisfying enough just to explore the beach at different hours of the morning, afternoon, and evening. She loved it best when the great red sun paused on the ocean's edge and slipped out of sight after coloring the world purple, rose, and gold. Only then did her reluctant steps turn homeward. After the first evening, she always left a light in her window. Somehow it tied her to generations of those who had wended their ways to cottage and mansion, from field or market or business—all eager for the moment they could step into a home whose lighted windows beckoned them.

Nancy nodded to grown-ups, talked with children, patted friendly dogs who came to her. Yet she held back from forming friendships. She hiked and bravely swam, but not far. The cold Pacific waters turned her as blue as their depths when she stayed in too long. By the end of the week she felt the wisdom Helen Markel had used in insisting Nancy take a vacation. Her daily Bible study and prayer reinforced and strengthened her.

"Lord," she wistfully said one evening while staring into the glow of a small fire she'd built in her miniature fireplace, "can I take this peace home? Right now I feel I can go back to Pediatrics and do my job without it tearing me apart when I lose a child. Please, help me to keep close to You, for their sake—and mine." A snapping stick sounded loud in the quiet room. "I have to talk with Damon. You know this decision hasn't been easy, but You've told us to do to others as we want them to do to us. It's going to be hard and painful—for both of us. Yet it's what I'd want if our roles were reversed. I need Your help."

She sat until the fire flickered and died, not moving until the room grew chill. Could she confront Damon? An idea flared, along with a final, sizzling coal. *Why not write him a letter?* The idea appealed to her. She could start with the reason she had run from the chapel and him. He would have time to consider the letter before they talked face-to-face.

Nancy shook her dark head. Sadness crept into her heart. A letter would not allow either of them to see the other's expression or to answer in person.

"Maybe it's just too soon," she told God. "So many times in the Bible You've cautioned us to wait. Until the time comes when I feel right about it, I won't rush ahead."

The vow freed her and she slept dreamlessly. Yet when Friday came, she called the travel agent and arranged to extend her stay through Thursday of the following week. He genially agreed; another party wanted the cabin starting Friday, if possible.

Precious day after precious day went by. Nancy alternated between never wanting to leave the coast and the stirrings inside that left her homesick for her suite in the staff residence, for Pediatrics, and most of all, for a tall, handsome children's specialist who had captured her heart. On Friday morning, she left the cabin with mixed emotions, yet more confident about herself and the future than ever before in her life and closer to the God she loved and served. She resisted the temptation to go straight to the hospital and instead headed for Helen Markel's home. What luxury—another few days to make the transition from vacation back to work. She remembered Helen's comments and realized how true they were. A person really did need two weeks to get away from their routines. Nancy meant to see that in the future she took time off.

<hr />

Her high resolves to see Damon and tell him she needed to talk with him changed to a total fiasco. Monday morning when she reported for work, a furious, haggard doctor waylaid her before she reached the ward.

"Where have you been? Nancy Galbraith, what do you mean walking out on me and disappearing for two weeks?" he raged.

Resentment replaced the twinge of pity for his distress. "I went on vacation. Nurses do take time off," she flippantly replied, even though her heart raced like a diesel engine.

"Of all the inconsiderate. . ." He grabbed her shoulders and his expression warned he'd like to shake the living daylights out of her. "No one knew where you were. Don't you care that you've worried your friends? Dr.

Paul and Jonica and I have wracked our brains trying to figure out what sent you skylarking out of the chapel and off to heaven knows where!"

"I'm sorry that you troubled yourself, Dr. Barton." She became aware of a student nurse standing open-mouthed nearby. "Now if you will remove your hands from my shoulders, I'll get on with my work. As I'm sure you're aware, Monday mornings are no time for staff members to stand around airing personal grievances." Her voice shook.

Damon's hands dropped. A glacial look replaced some of the anger in his eyes. "Very well, Nurse Galbraith. Just don't think this settles anything between us." He executed a 180-degree about-face and marched off, indignation in every line of his stiff back and his head held high.

"Welcome back to the real world," Nancy muttered.

"D—did you say something?" the student stammered.

"Nothing worth repeating." She pasted a smile on her face to hide the ache in her heart and consoled herself by thinking, *At least he must care a little if he can get that upset just because I take off for a time.*

She made it through the day, alternating periods of gladness by reacquainting herself with patients and fellow nurses, with an inevitable letdown. In spite of herself, her irritation grew at the highhanded way Damon had verbally attacked her. Well, when they had their little talk, she had some things to tell him, too. He needn't think he could be colder than ice cubes for weeks then turn around and expect her to report in to His Highness.

"It didn't take long to lose the peace," she ruefully admitted at the end of her shift. "Oh well, the sooner we have it out, the better."

Alas for Nancy's dream. Her telephone remained busy with all the wrong voices. Her charges exacted full measure of devotion to their needs. Dr. Barton made no move to carry out his veiled threat of a day of reckoning. A miserable week passed, then another. Doubts crept in. Nancy remembered her vow to wait for the right time. It obviously hadn't yet come. Damon barely spoke to her in the ward, although she was surprised by a look she couldn't define in his dark gaze several times. Her patience wore thin. So did her body. Even the excellent food Shepherd of Love served to staff and patients alike held little interest for her. In vain she chided herself as a love-sick weakling. It did little good.

With each passing day, anger smoldered. Why should Damon treat her like an outcast? She had done nothing except leave an impossible situation.

He doesn't know that, her heart reminded.

Torn with conflict, she snapped back, "He will." The postponing of the inevitable meeting in which everything must pour out left her ragged-nerved. It had been easy at the beach to visualize a rational exchange that would end with the past buried forever. Now her lips set in a straight line and her eyes flashed. How could she ever have cared for such a pigheaded, over-bearing individual? She marvelled at how those traits never appeared in his dealings with others.

"Con man," she branded him, then shivered at what she had said. If all she now felt to be true were real, Damon *had* served time.

One evening when Nancy felt she could bear the suspense no longer, she dialed Damon's home number. The phone rang. Five times. Six. Seven. At last a voice said, "Hello." It came jerkily, as if the speaker had been running.

"Damon?"

"He isn't here." *Click.* The connection broke.

Face flaming, Nancy dropped her phone like a burning brand. How dare Dr. Damon Barton have the nerve to calmly lie to her and say he wasn't home? Fury stronger than any she had ever known set fire to her brain. She grabbed a light jacket, threw it over the uniform she hadn't bothered to change, dug car keys from her purse, and headed for the door. Maybe she was running before God. Right now she didn't care. No one could insult her like this and get away with it.

She reached for the doorknob and remembered she didn't have the address. A quick check of the phone directory took care of that. She scribbled down the address and slammed the door behind her, taking pleasure in its decided thud.

"Ready or not, here I come," she gritted between clenched teeth. "You and I have a lot of talking to do; no way am I going to wait any longer. Not after this."

She climbed into her car, revved the motor, and drove out of the staff residence lot like an avenging angel bent on annihilating a foe.

Chapter 8

A faint warning bell rang deep in Nancy Galbraith's brain when she lifted her hand to knock on Dr. Damon Barton's door, a gut-level feeling of something amiss. She ignored it, an action she'd been trained not to take during her years of nurses' training.

"Come in," Damon's voice sounded strained, muffled.

She turned the knob, pushed open the door, and stepped inside. The niggling little feeling pinched at her again. Dr. Barton sat draped over a chair. The scent of tobacco tainted the air. Dim light came from a single turned-on lamp that left Damon's face in shadow.

"You could at least have the courtesy to rise," she snapped. Disillusionment ran through her like a river in flood.

"Why?" His insolence poured gasoline on the fire of her anger. She stepped away from the door, leaving it ajar. Guessing at the probable location of a wall light switch, she reached to her left.

"Don't turn on the light!" The lounging figure leaped to his feet and crossed the room in two giant steps. "Who are you and what do you want, anyway?"

Nancy slowly iced. She backed away from him, flung the door wide, turned, and ran into the hall.

"Nancy, what on earth are you doing here?" a familiar voice demanded. Strong hands caught and held her shoulders in a vise-like grip. Black eyes blazed down at her.

"Damon?" She stood stock-still, trying to understand. She shook her head, closed her eyes, and looked at him again. In the subdued hall light that still outshone the feeble light streaming through the apartment door, he looked worried. "Then who—it wasn't you, after all—"

Steel undergirded his words when he said, "Come inside, Nancy." He dropped his hands but one took her arm. The touch left her weak with relief, or did it come from knowing he hadn't lied to her?

A lazy drawl from the unknown man brought her to her senses. "Well, Brother, aren't you going to introduce me?" Nancy watched the man she'd mistaken for Damon in the dim light saunter back to his chair.

"How did you get in here?" A deep line cut between Damon's brows and he ignored the question.

"I have ways. Don't turn on the light," he repeated when Damon reached for the switch.

Dr. Barton smothered an exclamation, strode across the room, and pulled the drapes shut. "Are you in trouble again?"

Nancy hated the way the man who called Damon brother looked her over. She'd encountered some seamy things in her work, including men with greedy eyes. The same expression in a slightly more refined way rested on the intruder's face.

"Since my dear brother won't introduce us, I will." He stood and made a mocking bow. "I'm Curtis Barton, Damon's older brother, and at your service. Very much at your service." He bowed low in a caricature of a knight kneeling before his lady.

"I asked why you were here." Damon's voice sliced the performance in half.

"If I had known you expected—a visitor—I wouldn't have come."

Nancy felt tarnished by her presence in the apartment, although it wasn't late. Why had she rushed here? She should have known Damon would never lie to her and hang up so rudely.

"You'll forgive my lack of manners earlier, won't you?" Curtis continued. His pretense of humility sickened her.

A strong hand shot out and grabbed his shirt front. "If you've done anything to her, you'll pay for it," Damon told him. His face set in harsh lines.

Curtis jerked free and his eyes half-closed. "I didn't touch her. She came waltzing in here, got off a bunch of stuff about my not getting up, and headed out when I asked who she was."

"Is that right, Nancy?"

"Yes." She marvelled that the word could get past the growing ball of disgust for herself and pity for Damon that formed in her throat.

"Did you need me?" His fierce glance softened to midnight velvet.

With all my heart, she wanted to cry out. Instead, she took a deep breath and substituted, "It's just that when I called you—Curtis—said you weren't here and I thought it was you and couldn't understand why you'd lie." She pressed her lips together and turned blindly toward the door. "I'll see you some other time, Dr. Barton." Perhaps the note of formality would remove some of the innuendo Curtis had injected into a perfectly innocent situation. She gallantly lifted her head, said, "Good night," and marched out with Damon right behind her. Not for a million dollars would she recognize the introduction or presence of Curtis with his open sneer. If she did, Nancy had the feeling Damon would give his brother a well-deserved punching out.

Damon closed the door behind them and laid a detaining hand on her sleeve. Anxiety clouded his fine eyes. "Why did you really come?"

How could she open a dialogue that reached twenty years into the past when he looked so haggard and upset? She mentally shook her head and quietly said, "Some time when it's right, we need to talk." A quick flare of agreement threatened her control when he nodded briefly, so she added, "Not now."

He walked her out to her car and she knew he watched her out of sight. Churned by emotion, she drove home in a half-daze, torn by the encounter but keeping a careful lookout for traffic lights and possible hazards. Why did the day of reckoning she knew must come loom even more ominous than before? Had the restrained violence in Damon's face when he had confronted his brother shown her a new and frightening side of the kindly doctor she'd fallen in love with, a side that could be a carryover from childhood wildness?

Nancy sighed, thinking of the sunny, halcyon days when she and Damon had shared dinners and drives. Where had they gone?

"I wish we'd never gone to the chapel," she passionately whispered. "Then I wouldn't have seen him in that stained-glass light that brought everything back. Better never to have known who the boy was than this terrible fighting and ache inside."

Nancy sighed, completed her drive, and dragged into her suite of rooms. Even their quietude failed to revive her sagging spirits.

"Dear God," she prayed, on her knees just before crawling into bed. "I can't handle any of this. Please, help me. Open a way so. . ." Her voice trailed and died. For a long time she remained in the kneeling position, until a whisper of peace and God's love reminded her He understood all the things she could not say.

Five minutes after she had reached Pediatrics the next morning, a summons from the hospital director came. Wondering, she crisply instructed the other nurses to carry on, smoothed her peach uniform, glanced in a mirror to make sure every shining hair lay in place, and went to answer the call.

Nancy's heart did an involuntary little skip when a tall, handsome doctor met her just outside the director's office.

"I'm sorry about last night." He looked as if he wanted to explain, but something held him back.

She shrugged. "I shouldn't have come."

"Wrong." A slow smile relaxed his tense expression. "You will always be welcome." He abruptly changed tone. "Nancy, I hope you'll consider carefully what you're going to hear."

Her eyes opened wide. *How could he know?* The wild notion that this summons had something to do with the interchange in Dr. Barton's apartment crossed her mind, only to be rejected. What could an obviously hostile brother have to do with her, especially anything that affected her work?

Damon had asked himself the same question the night before. His steps had lagged on the way back to his apartment after watching Nancy out of sight. He still couldn't figure out why she had come. His pulse quickened. Would the day ever come when he could tell her of his love? His mouth twisted. Not with Curtis hanging to him like an albatross, casting a dark shadow over his life. He hadn't seen his brother since the strange encounter downtown weeks earlier. Yet here he was, parked in Damon's apartment, filling it with smoke in spite of Damon's injunction against it. Had he charmed the manager again?

"No," Curtis said when asked. "I took an impression and had a key made. Thought it might come in handy." He lit a cigarette.

"Either put that out or get out," Damon roughly told him. "Where do you get off thinking you can break in here and make yourself at home?"

Curtis squashed the barely lighted cigarette in a cup already filled with butts. Evidently he'd been there quite some time before Nancy arrived. "Something's about to go down. I figured I'd be safe here."

"Great." Damon stared at his unwanted guest. "You get in over your head and come sneaking here looking for a hideout. Nothing doing."

"Forgotten about the slab and the morgue?" Curtis inquired. He laughed significantly when Damon winced. "How'd you like to get me out of your face for a long time? I met someone who says Vancouver, B.C., is really hopping. Maybe I'll try a new country and see if my luck changes."

For the first time Damon looked beneath the veneer of bravado and saw the change in Curtis. The expensive suit needed cleaning, the fancy shoes were scuffed, and he wore a general rundown air. "When are you going to get smart and get out of the rackets?" he demanded, hands on hips.

"I might just consider it if I had a—*friend*—like the one who just left.

What did you say her name was? Oh, yeah, Nancy. Nancy what?" His eyes slitted and he cocked his head to one side. "Not bad." He laughed again, a thoroughly unpleasant sound. "Since you aren't jumping at the chance to get rid of me, I don't see why family loyalty should keep me from dating her up."

"Family loyalty!" Damon drove the nails of his clenched fists into his palms to keep from attacking his brother. "When did you ever have any? If you remember correctly, I—"

"Sure, always the hero. Not such a bad idea, actually. You're so pure I can count on any promises you make being kept," Curtis taunted.

Damon ignored the thrust. "If you ever get near Nancy with your rotten lifestyle, I'll stop you if it means turning you over to the police myself."

"You wouldn't!" Curtis flinched as if struck.

Damon's steady gaze never left his face. "You just said how well I keep my promises. Have you ever known me to break one?"

"No."

"You above all people know what giving my word means. Don't forget it."

Curtis stood. "And you won't lend me money."

"No."

Despair mingled with recklessness and desperation in his watching gaze. "Then it's off my back and your responsibility what happens."

"What's that supposed to mean?" Damon raised a skeptical eyebrow, hating the conversation but unwilling to end it until he learned more.

Curtis recaptured his strutting. "Just what I said." He stretched, yawned. "You know I can find out who Nancy is. She had on a uniform; she knows you well; calls you Dr. Barton. Easy enough matter to check the hospitals and learn her last name." His arms fell to his sides and he added, "Of course, for certain considerations. . ." He let it hang.

"I told you what I'd do if you get near her. Neither will I be blackmailed. Now get out of here before I forget everything I believe and let you have it." Damon took a step nearer, almost hoping Curtis would make the final move and justify the licking of his life, one he should have been given years before.

"You're in love with her, aren't you? Good enough for me." He shrugged carelessly. "Plenty of women in my life already."

"Not like Nancy." Damon couldn't have held back the comment if his life had depended on it.

A strange look, so fleeting it couldn't be identified, swept over his brother's face. To Damon's amazement, Curtis made no attempt to answer.

He opened the door, stepped into the hall, and glanced both ways. "Good-bye, little brother." His mocking whisper barely reached Damon's ears. The door closed behind him.

Damon crossed to the windows and opened the drapes a crack. No car purred at the apartment complex's entrance. A few minutes later he saw Curtis emerge, again look both ways, then cross the street and vanish behind a clump of bushes. His furtive movements showed his fear of being observed, and Damon let the drapes swing back into place, feeling drained. A new concern piggybacked on his worries about his brother. What if Curtis in some way involved Nancy so that his sordid dealings touched her?

He licked suddenly dry lips at the horrible thought. Revenge took innocent lives here as well as elsewhere. "She must not be touched," he vowed aloud. "But how can I prevent it? Anything Curtis wants, he breaks every rule to get." A vision of Nancy, so lovely and sweet in her work uniform, came to mind. Even a hardened man like Curtis would admire her; any man would. He thought of that unexplainable look Curtis wore at the words, "Not like Nancy." Had his brother been contrasting her charm and integrity with those other women he bragged were in his life? The terrible chasm that lay between a Christian woman and those who chose Satan's way rose in Damon's consciousness. God's own Son had died for both. How did He feel when women—and men—deliberately refused Him? A great yearning for his brother's life and soul sent Damon to his knees. He stayed for a long time, unable to pray audibly. At last he stood, only to pace the apartment rug until morning, asking God how to protect Nancy from this new possible danger.

The answer didn't come until just after seven. Damon, the tormented, had showered, forced down some breakfast, and changed to Dr. Barton, physician and surgeon, when the phone rang.

"Yes? Mmm. Right. I'll see about it immediately." He cradled the phone, filled with awe and rejoicing. Before he had cried for help, God had already put in motion forces to answer that cry. "Thank You," he breathed, snatched up his bag, and ran out with a far lighter heart than he would have dreamed possible even a few moments earlier. A quick session with the hospital director, a summons to Pediatrics that meant Nurse Galbraith would come soon, and the deep joy of accomplishment stilled Damon's tumult, at least for a time.

Once Nancy and Dr. Barton seated themselves, the hospital director went directly to his reason for her interview. "Nancy, Damon has a rather unusual request. I've thought it over and believe it might be a good thing. I'll let him explain."

Damon silently thanked God for the wise man's discretion. Without naming names or giving specifics, he had alerted the director to the fact that through a series of circumstances, the Pediatrics nurse could be in danger. It might be wise for her to get away from Shepherd of Love for a time. Now he frankly met Nancy's questioning gaze, glad for the validity of his call from Dr. Robert Cranston earlier.

"My boss called this morning. He'd just received a plea for help from one of the leading Seattle families. Their six-year-old son Eric has for some reason withdrawn into himself. He's always been a healthy child, but since the death of his grandmother, Eric has had a terrible fear of anything to do with doctors or nurses or hospitals. The family has taken him to psychiatrists who say there's nothing wrong with him. To top it off, he needs to have some minor surgery, not immediately, but soon. He fell from a swing and broke a leg not long ago. It hasn't healed as straight as it should, and Dr. Cranston isn't satisfied."

Nancy sat silently, a puzzled look on her face.

Damon cleared his throat. "What Eric needs is to have a companion who can win his trust, give him confidence, and help him realize there's nothing to fear. Will you do it?"

"I? Why not a nurse from the register? I haven't had any psychological training since I graduated and got my RN."

A quick look passed between Damon and the hospital director. The older man quietly said, "We both feel you are the very one for this job. The way you relate to children, especially those who are frightened, should be exactly what Eric needs."

"I agree." Damon tensed, knowing Nancy could not suspect his reason for wanting to get her in new surroundings for the time it took not only to help Eric, but to put her beyond reach, should Curtis carry out his half-threat.

"You really want me to go?" she asked the director.

"I think it will be a fine thing for you both," he heartily agreed and again Damon felt thankful for the director's support.

"I suspect it won't be long, a week or so at the most," Damon explained. "You'll need to live in." He ignored the look of protest that crept into her eyes and blandly went on, "The Caxtons feel, and Dr. Cranston agrees, Eric needs the continuity of having you in the house, a friend more than just someone who comes in. You'll be given time off, of course, but if you don't mind including the child when you go to church—there's one nearby—or even shopping, you'll receive extra compensation."

"Doesn't the mother or father do those things?" she crisply inquired.

"The mother's a fluttery little woman who is totally useless in an emergency, and Mr. Caxton isn't much better. Eric is an only child, born long after they'd given up hope for an heir. Surprisingly, he isn't spoiled. They simply can't cope with the change in their adored son." Damon laughed, a clear, ringing sound that brought smiles to the others' faces. "It's your chance to see a whole new social strata, Nancy," he teased. "The Caxtons live in a mansion, surrounded by well-guarded grounds and high walls. You can have breakfast in bed, lunch on the terrace, and you'll need dinner clothes; the Caxtons made it clear you will be treated as one of the family. I'll say this for them, they aren't the silly rich who consider those they employ inferior. They also don't isolate Eric by relegating him to the nursery for meals but keep him with them except on rare occasions when business dinners require a later evening mealtime than is good for a six year old." A frown crossed his forehead. "Mrs. Caxton thoughtfully sent word that any special clothing you need is to be considered part of your expenses and will be reimbursed."

"You were that sure of getting me?"

Laughter sent sparkles into his dark eyes. "I used the word *you* strictly in the generic sense, meaning whatever nurse took the job." He watched her slim, capable hands twist in her lap while she hesitated and felt a pang of compunction. "We know you hate leaving the ward and your special charges, but Nancy, this little boy needs you desperately. He needs your special compassion, your insight into why a child creates monsters that only exist in his mind. You will be truly serving one of God's children if you take on Eric Caxton's case."

"I agree, my dear." The director fitted the fingers of his left hand to those of his right. "You may also have the opportunity to drop some seeds of Christ's teachings in the Caxton home. During stressful times like these, hearts are often more open and fertile than at others."

Nancy shook her head. "I can't imagine preaching to a family of millionaires."

"Preaching, no. Living His pattern, yes." The director smiled at her. "Many of the wealthiest persons on earth are spiritually poverty-stricken. We sometimes forget that."

"I'll do my best," she said simply.

Damon turned away to hide the relief he knew must be painted all over him. Thank God, Nancy would be safe. Perhaps by the time she finished with Eric, whatever dire happening Curtis had hinted at would be over. All he could do was pray and trust God to continue to protect her.

And Curtis.

Damon gritted his teeth. His heart felt raw. No matter what Curtis had done, as he'd said, he was still Damon's brother—and a man who needed God.

Chapter 9

Nancy fell wholeheartedly, unreservedly in love five minutes after she had reached the Caxton mansion. She had driven what felt like miles, once she identified herself at the great gate that kept intruders out. The smiling guard waved her on, and Nancy remembered the twinkle in Damon's eyes when he told her this case offered the chance to experience a whole new social strata. Only in movies had she seen such opulence. The lawns and towering rhododendrons, rose arbors, and brightly blooming beds of annuals and perennials looked as if they had been clipped with manicure scissors, so even and straight, she blinked.

The house itself stood two stories high and shortened into wings and ells smothered in creeping vines and ivy. Perfection reigned inside as well as out. Floors and banister rails gleamed with polish that reflected the rich colors of fine paintings and costly tapestries. Yet Nancy didn't feel intimidated. A master decorator had skillfully made sure a feeling of warmth and welcome hung over the blended furnishings, Oriental rugs carelessly scattered, and gleaming bowls of flowers delicately scenting the rooms.

In spite of Damon's description of the Caxtons, she hadn't been able to form a clear picture. First glance confirmed his "fluttery little woman" image of Eric's mother, but the depths of love and concern in the light blue eyes and the way she took both of Nancy's hands in her own and whispered, "We're praying you can help our son," and her husband's fervent, "Amen," told more.

A six-year-old tornado whipped into the room—and captured Nancy's heart. Fire-engine red curls topped a grinning face. Gentian-blue eyes opened wide. "Hey, you're pretty!" Eric's mouth stretched into a gap-toothed grin and melted any possible awkwardness. "Mama, who is she?"

Nancy saw the slight drag of his right leg that betrayed an improper healing after the break, but it didn't slow him down.

"This is N— Miss Galbraith, Eric." Mrs. Caxton put an arm around her son in the eternal gesture of mother-love. A wave of red touched her thin pale cheeks at the near slip. Damon had been adamant that Nancy not be introduced as a nurse. Neither would she wear any type of uniform. Friendship

186

must come before trust. "She's going to be your companion for a time."

"Perhaps you'd like to show her around since she'll be living with us," Mr. Caxton quietly said. Nancy caught the slight tension in his stance that relaxed when Eric looked her over, grinned again, and said, "Sure. Wanna see the pool? I can swim. Can you?"

"I sure can. How about our going together?"

"Okay." He trotted ahead of her and Nancy made a V-for-victory sign behind her back to assure his parents so far all had gone well.

By the time the tall nurse and small boy toured the Caxton grounds and home, they had become firm friends. Eric obviously liked the responsibility of his guide duties and Nancy listened to his chatter, responding with a smile most of the time and a few quiet words or genuine admiration of his home. She also said a silent *thank you* to the Caxtons for their generosity in insisting she accept reimbursement for the two evening gowns and a few other things she needed to feel comfortable in her new, luxurious surroundings. She had refused the offer of a complete new wardrobe; the white and soft yellow chiffon dinner dresses highlighted her dark beauty but hadn't cost the earth and a few stars. A new swimsuit, shoes to match her new gowns, and her own street clothes rounded out what she would need for the short time she'd be here if all went well.

"I don't know who is whose slave," she laughingly told Damon when she reported in to him that evening after Eric had gone to bed. "I'm 'Miss Nancy' now—it sounds strange after being Nurse Nancy for so long. I suggested Eric just call me Nancy but his parents insisted on adding the 'Miss.' "

"We're all hoping it won't be long before you can tell him you're a nurse." Damon's voice came clear over the phone in Nancy's lovely suite of rooms next to Eric's. "There's a danger in letting it go too long; he could feel you tricked him."

"I'll do my best," she promised. They finished their conversation without one personal note, yet Nancy felt warmed. She fell asleep as soon as her head touched the lacy pillows.

With the alertness to sounds in the night that had begun after the tragic fire so long ago, she roused from deep sleep and glanced at the digital clock. Two. She sat up and reached for a nylon robe, pulled it over her satin pajamas, and slid her feet into matching slippers. "Eric?" She stepped to the open connecting door to his room. A night light showed him tangled in his sheets, sleeping, but with tear stains on his face, innocent now of the harmless mischief that rested there during his waking hours. Before rousing him, she slipped into the adjoining bath, dampened a fluffy wash-cloth, and took it back to his bed.

"Wake up, Dear." She gently shook him.

"Gramma?"

His sleepy whisper told her volumes. "No, Dear. It's Nancy." She switched on the lamp on his nightstand.

"I–I thought Gramma had come back." He dug his fists in his eyes. "That's dumb, isn't it?"

Praying for wisdom, Nancy gently took his hands down and bathed his hot face. "I don't think so. After my little sister died I used to think I heard her calling." She had to swallow hard to prevent her own emotions from clouding his need.

"Really?" His eyes looked like glistening blue jewels under water and he crept closer to her.

"Really. The nurses in the hospital helped—"

His little figure stiffened. "I hate nurses and doctors and hospitals. They killed my Gramma." His face screwed into an ugly frown.

She rejoiced at learning the root of his problem so soon and at the trust he showed in telling her something she realized he must have held back in his psychiatric interviews. "I'm sorry you feel that way, Eric." She talked to him as she would to an adult. "If it hadn't been for the doctors and nurses and the hospital, I don't know what I'd have done."

She sensed a waiting, a suspended judgment in his stillness. "I was burned in a bad fire." She took a deep breath. "Tomorrow when we go swimming you'll see some lines on my back and shoulders, Eric. They would be ugly scars if doctors hadn't taken such good care of me."

"I wish Gramma had those doctors," he muttered. "They wouldn't have made her die." Eric buried his face in Nancy's lap. She felt his hot tears soaking her hand and impulsively pulled him into her arms, crooning and rocking him back and forth.

When he quieted, she asked, "Why do you think they made your Gramma die?"

A negative headshake told her nothing. Then a small voice said, "I heard Daddy and Mama talking. Mama said they never should have let Gramma go to the hospital."

"Did you ever tell anyone what you heard?"

Another headshake. "I was scared. And when I fell out of the swing and broke my leg I screamed and screamed so they wouldn't take me to the hospital. I knew I wouldn't come back."

"But you did go and you did come back," she gently reminded.

"That's 'cause I made Mama stay with me all the time," he croaked, hoarse from crying. "Daddy says I have to go back and get my leg fixed better but I won't." His voice rose sharply. "I won't, I won't, I won't!"

"Shhh, Eric." She held him close until, worn out with his fears of past and future, he fell into a troubled sleep. Nancy didn't leave him until his even breathing told her the loss of consciousness had relaxed his tired body and mind. She straightened his bedclothes and wearily slipped back to her own room. How would he greet her in the morning? Some children felt ashamed at having broken down.

"God," she prayed, eyes closed, "please bless this hurting little boy and his family. Please give me the right words to say to all of them. In Jesus' name, amen." She fell asleep with the same prayer echoing and re-echoing in her heart.

Nancy sensed Eric's quick glance at her when she went into his room the next morning. She had deliberately waited until she knew from the sound of his movements that he'd dressed himself.

"Need help tying your shoes?" she called from the doorway.

"Naw." His gap-tooth grin opened up. A look of relief spread over his face. "D'you?"

"Naw." She imitated him and laughed at the delight dancing in his eyes. "I don't have laces. See?" She held out her right foot, clad in a low-heeled white pump.

He giggled and told her, "C'mon. Since you're dressed you don't get breakfast in bed." He took her by one hand. "I'm hungry. Are you?"

"I'm absotively, posolutely starvationed," she solemnly replied.

"You're funny. I like you." He dropped her hand when they came to the top of the stairs leading downward. "Can you do this?" *Swish. Thump.* He slid down the banister rail and landed on both feet at the bottom.

Did she dare? Why not? Anything that brought Eric closer to his undercover nurse meant a step closer to his mental healing. She gathered the soft pink folds of her cotton dress around her, mounted the rail, and *whooshed* down.

"Perfect landing," an amused voice commented from an arched doorway nearby.

Nancy felt like a fool when she whipped around and saw Dr. Barton leaning against the side of the arch.

"Who're you?" Eric demanded, feet planted a foot apart and hands on his hips. His red curls shone in the sunlight and his lower lip stuck out.

Nancy smothered a pleased smile. So she had a new champion.

Damon grinned easily. "I'm Damon, a friend of Nancy's. I came to invite both of you to have breakfast with me and go to the Woodland Park Zoo. Anyone here want to do that?"

Eric's belligerence fled. "Me, me, me." He danced over to the visitor, grabbed both strong hands, and swung back and forth.

"Me, too, if it's all right with the Caxtons," Nancy ungrammatically agreed.

"Why don't you have breakfast here before you go?" Mrs. Caxton and her husband came down the staircase.

"Aw, Mom, I wanta go to McDonald's," Eric complained.

"Even though the cook made cinnamon rolls for breakfast?" Mr. Caxton tempted.

Nancy saw the struggle going on inside the little boy and blessed Damon for his insight when he offered, "Why not have breakfast here— we wouldn't want to hurt your cook's feelings by not eating those cinnamon rolls, would we—then we can have lunch at McDonald's."

"All right!" Eric's world turned right-side up again. His enchanting grin flashed and he tore ahead in the direction Nancy knew from her tour the night before led to the dining room.

"We thought it might be a good idea for Eric to get to know Dr. Barton," Mrs. Caxton murmured, pausing for a moment before following her excited son. "Dr. Cranston says Dr. Barton will be doing the corrective surgery."

Again Nancy had the feeling of unplumbed depths in her hostess. It gave her food for thought that accompanied the delicious rolls, freshly squeezed orange juice, crisp bacon, and iced melon.

"Hurry, Miss Nancy," Eric prodded. "I'm through already." He swiped his napkin across his mouth and bounced on his chair.

"Go brush your teeth, Dear." His mother smiled at him and a mist rose to the nurse's eyes. How like her own mother it sounded, when she had reminded her girls so long ago.

"Are your shoes good for walking?" Damon asked. "There's a lot of ground to cover at the zoo."

"I think I'll change to tennis shoes," Nancy told him. Surely sometime during the day she would have the chance to quiz Damon about the fire. The thought depressed her but she shoved it aside. If her suspicions were accurate, this might be the last day she and Damon would spend together. *Then let it be perfect,* she told herself. *Don't let anything spoil it.*

Nancy hadn't counted on Eric's boundless energy when she planned for a quiet time with Dr. Barton. One hand in each of theirs, he dashed here and there, pulling them along. At times he jerked free and ran ahead. "I haven't been here since I was a little kid," he told them. He didn't notice how Damon covered his mouth and Nancy turned away to hide her smile. Every new sight brought him closer to the adults. His high laugh made heads turn and brought a look of joyous understanding to those around him, as well.

What if she and Damon were married and had a little boy like Eric? Nancy wondered. Of course he wouldn't have red hair or blue eyes, but the velvet dark eyes of the imaginary child would hold the same wonder; his laugh would ring sweet and clear, just as Eric's did. *Please, God, I just have to talk with Damon,* Nancy wordlessly prayed.

Yet the day sped by on flying feet. McDonald's beckoned. The afternoon passed and when Damon drove Nancy and her charge to the Caxtons', Eric contentedly leaned against her arm. "This is the bestest day ever," he mumbled, " 'cept my old leg hurts—just a little," he hastily added, obviously loath to complain in case it meant missing out on future fun.

"When you get it fixed, we'll do some other neat stuff," Damon told him. Before Eric could pop up and deny all intentions of ever going to a hospital again, Dr. Barton went right on. "It takes good legs to play ball at the beach and chase chipmunks at Mount Rainier."

Eric said nothing—then. Not until Nancy tucked him in and told him a story did he obliquely refer to their middle-of-the-night conversation. "S'pose the doctors who fixed you could make my leg better?"

"Oh, there are hundreds of good doctors," Nancy breezily told him. "Good nurses, too, and hospitals." She felt the familiar stiffening of his body and quickly said, "Do you mind if I say my prayers with you? It's always nicer with someone else."

Eric relaxed and sagged against her arm. "How come God can hear everybody at once?"

"Because He's God." She hugged the little boy. "You know how your daddy's computer takes in all kinds of information? Well, God is stronger and smarter than all the computers."

"Then how come He let Gramma die? I told Him not to." The age-old question from the childish lips brought an ache to Nancy's heart.

"Your mama told me your grandma had been really sick. You didn't want her to keep being sick, did you?"

"No." A violent headshake.

"Neither did God." She smoothed the tousled red curls. "It's hard to understand but God loves each of us so much that sometimes He does things we don't like but what is best for those we care about."

"Like your sister?"

"Yes." She thought back weeks to another child whose fear of death needed addressing. "Just maybe your grandma and my sister are keeping each other company."

He lay so quiet against her, Nancy wondered if he'd fallen asleep. "Miss Nancy, if Gramma had stayed here with me, would she still be dead now?" He tensed.

"Yes, Eric. Her body was too sick to get well." She realized the question behind his spoken question. "The reason your mama said what she did wasn't because having your grandma stay here would have changed things, or that the hospital and nurses and doctors are bad. She knew it wouldn't have made any difference. I believe she just wished she could have kept your grandma a little longer."

"Me, too." The voice dropped to a whisper. "Will I see my gramma again? Will you see your sister?"

"Oh, yes." She hugged him. "That's the most wonderful part of God's plan. If we love Him and serve Him and ask His Son Jesus to live in our hearts, God promises that someday we will be together again. There won't be any sad times or sickness or good-byes. Everyone in heaven will be happy and well."

"Then. . .I. . .want. . .to. . ." Eric fell asleep before he could finish his sentence. Nancy gently laid him back on his pillows, humbled by the responsibility of those who chose nursing. Body, mind, spirit, and soul all needed loving care. Again she thanked God for her profession.

The next day cemented Nancy's and Eric's friendship even more. They swam in the pool in the morning, his eyes frankly curious when she showed him the faint scars, all that remained of her burns.

"They don't show much," he told her, then patted her arm. "I'm glad the doctors fixed you."

She hesitated. Words trembled on her lips, needing to be spoken but held back in case Eric wasn't ready for them.

He wasn't, in the bright sunlight. "C'mon." He jumped into the pool, attention turned away from doctors and hospitals and nurses and fear. But that night, in the dim light of his room, he asked, "If I–I get my leg fixed, will you be there?"

Her heart leaped with excitement. "I'll do better than that. If you decide to get your leg fixed, I'll take care of you afterwards."

"Promise?"

"Cross my heart." She shook hands on their pact.

His bright mind seized on a new thought that tumbled out. "What do you do when you aren't here with us? I mean, before you came to live with Mama and Daddy and me?"

With a quick prayer that his trust would stand the truth, Nancy told him, "I take care of little boys and girls like you, only usually they're sick or have had an operation."

He jerked free, sat up straight, and stared at her. "Are you a *nurse*?" Disbelief underlined each word.

"Yes, Eric. God has called me to take care of His children. He trusts me to do everything I can to help make them well. I love the children I care for, just as I've learned to love you."

He fell back on his pillows. "A nurse. But I'm not scared of you!"

"I'm not scared of you, either," she teased. Her training told her the light touch often made the necessary difference.

"You better be. I'm a tiger and if you don't be good I'll eat you up." He growled low in his throat. "Grrrr. I'm Errrrric the Tigerrrr." With the ability of children to change from serious to fantasy he threw aside everything except his growling.

"Okay, Eric the Tiger, I'll be good, good, good." She half-sang the words. "How about a *good*-night hug? It's been a long day and tomorrow we're going to the beach. Right?"

"Right, Miss—uh—" He paused and his forehead wrinkled. "Are you still Miss Nancy?"

"Of course, except my patients call me Nurse Nancy. I have one little girl who has lost some front teeth and she calls me 'Nurth Nanthy.' " She tucked him in again. "Goodnight, Mr. Tiger."

"Good night, Nurth Nanthy," he mimicked. "You won't forget?"

She almost made the fatal mistake of saying, "Forget what?" then she remembered her promise. "Nurse Nancy never forgets. When Mr. Tiger gets the knot taken out of his tail—oh, excuse me—the kink out of his leg, I'll be right there."

"Will Jesus be there, too?" the sleepy voice demanded.

Nancy blinked back tears. "I know a wonderful children's specialist who asks God and Jesus to be with him every time he operates."

Eric's eyelids drooped. He started to say something but fell asleep before words came out. Nancy knelt beside his bed, as she had done countless times before with children from every kind of home, thanking God for His goodness and asking Him to be with her patients. Tonight she added a special thanks for His calming Eric's fears.

A slight rustling sound from the doorway brought her to her feet. The Caxtons stood there, hands clasped, tears on both faces. They beckoned her into the hall and closed Eric's door behind him. "Nurse Galbraith," Mr. Caxton said. "Is the specialist you spoke of Dr. Barton?" She nodded and he continued, "My wife and I can never thank you enough for what you've done."

"It's our heavenly Father you should thank," she told him simply.

"We already have," Mrs. Caxton put in without a trace of her usual flutter. Nancy had a feeling more had been resolved in the parents' lives even than in their child's.

Chapter 10

L ong before Eric awakened the next morning, Nancy jubilantly reported the little boy's wavering fears about medical personnel and hospitals.

"Good for you," Damon told her, voice ringing through the phone. "Use your own judgment in telling him I'm a doctor, the doctor who will operate on his leg." When she didn't answer, he sharply asked, "Or do you think I should?"

Nancy thought quickly. "I believe it might be well for us to both be there." They set up a time when Damon could get there between appointments and alerted the Caxtons what they intended to do. If Eric suspected anything when his new friend appeared for lunch, it didn't show.

Afterwards his mother said, "Dear, we want to talk to you."

" 'Bout my leg?" He bit into a sandwich, washed it down with a big swallow of milk, and looked up from above a white mustache. "Nurse Nancy's gonna take care of it."

"How would you like me to fix that leg so we can do all those things we discussed?" Damon asked him.

Eric's eyes looked like sapphires in his face. "But you—are you a—a doctor?" A succession of expressions played tag across his face; doubt, disbelief, a little remaining fear. The next instant his smile reappeared. "Hey, are you the guy Nurse Nancy told me about last night? The one who asks God and Jesus to help you do what you're s'posed to?" he interrogated.

"I certainly am," Damon told him. "Why, I'd no more try and fix a leg or anything else without having God's help than you'd wave your arms and fly up to the ceiling!"

"Well," Eric said when he stopped laughing. "You can fix my leg if God and Jesus and Nurse Nancy's there."

"Deal." Damon shook hands with his brand new patient.

"You gonna do it today?" Eric demanded.

"It will take a few days to get things set up," Nancy told him. An idea struck her. "How would you like to go with me to the hospital and see the place you'll be? I'm sure we will want to keep you for a little while. Besides, my other patients are probably missing me. This will give you a chance to get acquainted and I can check on them."

"Sure." Eric finished his milk and beamed. "Let's go."

Nancy told him on the way to Shepherd of Love, "Everyone here asks God to help them, and we're trying to make a lot of people well." She explained that they must be very quiet in the halls; she had special permission to let him visit. Dr. Barton and the Caxtons trailed along behind the other two.

When they reached the ward with its bright colors, a chorus of "Nurse Nancy! We missed you" greeted them.

Eric clung to her, palm moist until a boy a little older who had his leg in a cast hollered, "Are you gonna be here? What for? I got a broken leg."

"Mine got broken, too," Eric said. "But it didn't get fixed right, so Dr. Barton's gonna make it do what it's s'posed to."

"He's neat," the older boy said. "He fixed my leg." He wiggled his toes, bare beyond the cast. "You get treated good here. Nurse Nancy's super and the food. . .mmmm." Before they left, he and Eric had formed the beginnings of friendship.

At the Caxtons' request, Nancy remained in their home for the short time it took to schedule Eric's surgery. He came through beautifully and his new friend was right there in the ward to greet him. Damon and Nancy had encouraged Eric's parents to let him stay a few days beyond the minimum, then Nancy would go home with him for another week. She found herself wet-eyed the day she finally left, knowing as long as she lived, the Caxton home would be open to her. She also hugged a wonderful secret. Mrs. Caxton had shared that she and her husband planned to adopt a child as near Eric's age as possible just as soon as they could find one and be approved. "We also plan to start setting some priorities and number one is to start giving something back to God for all He's done," she added. "Not just financially. My husband and I are talking about possibly volunteering somewhere we are really needed." New interest sparked in her eyes. "Perhaps at the wonderful Christian school we found for Eric. Or helping tutor those who are illiterate."

"Seattle has many needy in many ways," Nancy soberly said. "I know whatever you choose to do will be valuable."

Eric scrubbed at his eyes when he said good-bye then gave her what he called a "tiger hug" with both arms tight around her neck. "You won't forget me?" he pleaded.

"Not if I live to be twice as old as Methuselah," she promised. Nancy had been reading Bible stories to him while he recuperated, and Eric always laughed at the picture in his storybook of the old, old man.

"That's a long time," Eric said. "Good-bye, Nurse Nancy." He cocked his head to one side and gave her his best grin. "Tell my friends at the Ped-yat-rix hi and come see me. 'Member, I'm Errrric the Tigerrrr. You gotta be good or I'll come eat you up."

She left with the drop of sadness that always filled her overflowing cup of gratitude when a child no longer needed her. Perhaps by the next time she saw Eric, he'd have a sister or brother. "It's so hard knowing I won't mean as much to them," she brokenly whispered. "God, someday I want children I won't have to tell good-bye until they're grown."

One thing cheered her. Damon had asked her to reserve the evening for him. By the time she got resettled into her suite, showered, and dressed, he'd be there to pick her up. She went from warm to cold and back again. She could not put off telling Damon why she had run out of the chapel that Sunday morning several weeks before.

The leaves of autumn had replaced some of summer's glow. The smell of wood fires from homes that had no other means of heating put a tang in the air. Crisp nights and early morning gave way to sunny but subdued afternoons. Heavy dew sparkled and grass lay wet underfoot when she stepped outside.

Nancy held her breath when she walked into her apartment, half afraid her stay with the Caxtons might have spoiled her more modest surroundings. It hadn't. The rose and white had retained their charm, and even the lack of spaciousness to which she'd grown accustomed couldn't dim the feeling of coming home.

She dressed for her date with exceptional care. Once before she had felt it would be her last time with Damon; Eric's glee at the zoo had eliminated any chance of private conversation with him. Tonight nothing must stand in the way. Her hands trembled and she had to try twice to apply the touch of lipstick she wore. Unable to decide if she faced Paradise or the guillotine, she steadied herself with the deep breathing that always helped, and answered the firm knock at her door.

Damon had never looked more handsome than when she opened the door and he smiled at her. A pang shot through her. Why, of all the men on earth, did he have to be the one she'd learned to love? On the other hand, how could she even think of loving another? The mental questions kept her busy trying to concentrate on his hospital chitchat on the way to the restaurant that overlooked Puget Sound. He had reserved a quiet window table that offered a measure of privacy. Fresh flowers adorned the white table-cloth. Soft background music enhanced the atmosphere rather than over-whelmed patrons.

Somehow she managed to keep things light during the excellent meal: steak for him, delicious prawns for her, with the crispest of salads, baked potatoes bursting with goodness, and raspberry sorbet after the meal. Several times Nancy glanced out the window at the massed gray clouds over the Sound. Although the double glass drowned the cries of the seagulls winging in the dusk, she felt the sadness of a fall evening. Soon daylight saving time would end and darkness would come even earlier. Nancy shivered in spite of the restaurant's warmth. The dying day had lowered her spirits. Dread of what lay just ahead filled her.

"Nancy, there's something wrong between us. What is it?" Sharp as a surgeon's scalpel his question cut through her depression.

"I. . .we have to talk."

His warm hand covered hers where it rested on the white cloth. The expression in his eyes set her heart to pounding and regret rose to choke her. "Where would you like to go?" He paused. "I can't invite you to my apartment. Curtis has a way of popping in at unexpected and inconvenient times."

She thought of the living room at the staff residence building and shook her head. No, too much chance of interruption. Ditto for her small suite. The vision of off-white walls and pastel furniture hovered in her mind. "We can go to Helen Markel's. Her California friends insisted she stay a lot longer than she had planned. She also met someone who needed her and you know what that means to her!"

"I certainly do." After he paid their bill and they got back in his car, he casually added, "I didn't know you were acquainted with Helen."

She remembered she had never told him of her counseling sessions and quickly said, "Oh, yes. She's a darling, isn't she?" Their discussion of the valiant lady lasted all the way to the welcoming home and until Nancy seated herself in a comfortable chair with Damon across from her.

"Well, Nurse Nancy?" The light tone belied the concern she saw shining in his dark eyes. "It goes back to the Sunday at the chapel, doesn't it?"

She shot a prayer for help skyward and laced her fingers in her lap. "No, Damon. It goes back a lot farther." She looked at him, pleading for help. His quiet demeanor steadied her, although she sensed a tension in him like a mountain lion preparing to spring.

"You know I lost a sister a long time ago," she began. "It nearly destroyed me. Not the burns I received in the fire, but the searing memories." Gaze firmly fixed on her hands, she felt rather than saw his involuntary start. She hurried on, knowing if she hesitated she would never dredge up the past, no matter how vitally important it was to do so. In a monotone voice, to keep from breaking down, she relived for him how she had awakened coughing, a frightened five year old taught to instantly obey her mama. She described the flames, her mother's command to run, Leila's outstretched arms, the pain across her shoulders. Tears dripped onto her clenched hands when she breathlessly said, "The house crashed and roared. I watched my home with Mama and Leila collapse. Then. . ." Her voice failed her.

"Nancy, darling, don't go on!" Strong arms reached and held her. She had the feeling as long as she stayed where she was nothing on earth could ever again hurt her. Lips dry, she forced herself back from Damon's comfort. She must continue.

"Please. There's more." She heard his quick prayer, "Dear God!" but steeled herself against it. "Just before I fainted I saw a dark figure." She closed her eyes then opened them and risked a glance at Damon. He sat stony-faced as Mount Rainier when the snow melted and left sheer rock exposed to view. In all her work, Nancy had never seen such agony on a human face. She looked away and went on.

"Against the flickering flames, he stood out. A boy, dark-haired, frightened-looking. I've never forgotten."

An audible gasp told her Damon's suspicions roused earlier in the story had become fact. In a fluid motion he stood, then knelt before her.

"No! I have to finish." Fingers twisted, stomach cramped from tension, Nancy refused to look at the kneeling figure, so close, yet with a chasm between. "That Sunday at the chapel, the sunlight came through the stained-glass window. It backlighted your face. Oh, God." Her control broke on the prayer. "Why did I have to see you—like that?" She quivered like a cottonwood leaf, waiting, hoping he would take her in his arms and tell her she'd been mistaken, that no matter how accusing the evidence was, he hadn't set the fire.

"Then you believe I killed your family."

She looked at him then and saw the haggard expression. He'd aged ten years in the few minutes it had taken to tell her tragic story.

"I don't want to believe it," she brokenly told him.

Hope flared in his eyes, then died. So did Nancy's last shred of wishing the nightmare had ended. He didn't touch her and she felt glad. "Later, after I started to heal, the police came. They didn't wear uniforms; I've always been thankful for that. I doubt if I even knew they were policemen at the time. Anyway, they showed me pictures. I picked out the face of the boy I had seen at the fire. Sometime later I heard he had been sent to a correctional facility." She mustered her final ounce of courage and whispered, "Damon, was it you?" She searched his face, desperately hoping he would deny it.

"I served time for the setting of the fire."

Nancy shrank from the truth, bald and ugly on his lips. Yet her fascinated gaze never left his face.

"Yes, I served time. But I never committed arson," he quietly told her. A little muscle twitched in his cheek; his face remained somber.

"Then it was all an accident, a teenage prank." Her flat voice inched out from behind the world of crushed dreams in her heart.

"I can't explain. Darling, it's asking more than any woman should be expected to give, but can you trust me enough to believe I am innocent?"

"How—why—Damon, I want to believe you." She barely noticed he had called her darling for the second time. "How can I? I *saw* you. I identified you. Now you say you're innocent." She unclenched her aching fingers and spread her hands helplessly, torn between memories and the longing to trust him.

"If only I could tell you," he cried.

"Why can't you?" she demanded. A wave of love and the desire to protect and bring him healing assaulted her.

"The awful thing is, I cannot even explain why." He rose, walked away from her, and stood staring at a picture on the wall. She could see his shoulders shake from a powerful, unidentified emotion she sensed had nothing to do with her. He wheeled back toward her, his face gray ashes. "I'll take you home."

Stunned by the suddenness of his defeat, Nancy could not protest, even though the whole disjointed conversation beat on her soul like hammers on an anvil. She silently preceded him out the door, waited while he switched off the lights and locked up, then stepped into the car when he held the door for her.

Lights from a car parked a little way behind them flashed. In their light she saw the deep sadness in Damon's weary face. She wanted to put her hand over his on the wheel, but clasped her hands instead. Before they rounded the first corner, she glanced back. Helen's home lay serene, brightened by a nearby streetlight. Would she ever again feel the peace it offered? Or would she always associate the former haven with the raw and horrible feelings she'd experienced there tonight?

She fumbled for a tissue in her purse and wiped her eyes. The next moment Damon's voice, sharpened into command, stopped her hand midway back to her purse. "Don't panic, but I have a feeling we're being followed."

She gasped and automatically started to look behind them.

"Don't look back. I'm going to see if I can outmaneuver the driver." She saw the vertical lines form between his brows when he increased speed, cut a corner, sped another block, and turned again. The lights behind them faithfully followed.

"Who is it?"

"Probably some friends of my dear brother." He shut his lips hard and Nancy knew he would say no more. After several unsuccessful tries to ditch the car behind them, a blessed yellow light let them through and mercifully changed to red. The other car slammed to a stop then turned right before traffic from the other direction could get going.

"Now's our chance." Damon grimly speeded up.

"Can we outrun whoever it is?" Nancy inquired.

"I doubt it. Instead, we'll do something else." He slowed. Nancy saw him glance in the rearview mirror and quickly looked back. No lights. Damon heaved a sigh of obvious relief, swung into a nearby driveway, killed the motor, and shut off the lights. "Get down," he ordered. Nancy crouched forward. Damon leaned sideways in the seat. His head brushed her skirt and she blindly groped for the comfort of his hand. His fingers tightened over hers and strength flowed through her. Whatever he had been in the past, Dr. Damon Barton would guard her with his life. She shuddered. Where had that horrible thought come from? A speeding car thundered past, screeched its brakes, and tore across an intersection.

"Stay down," Damon warned. "He. . .they may come back." His admonition came none too soon. Less than a minute later the terrifying sound of a car driven by some kind of maniac bent on who-knew-what reached her ears. She crouched lower. Damon's fingers tightened. An eternity later he cautiously raised his head.

"It's all right now." He straightened, put the car in gear, and backed into the street, after freeing her hand.

"Damon, is Curtis in trouble?" she whispered, still frightened from the strange incident.

"Yes. I don't know what, this time." In the dim light his face looked lumpy. "He has a talent for getting into unpleasant situations. Until now, they—usually—haven't involved me." A forlorn note in his voice caught at her heartstrings. He sounded so like a small boy needing reassurance and unable to ask for it.

"I'll pray for him," she said.

"Thank you, Nancy." He slid his hand from the wheel long enough for a quick grip. "It's all anyone can do." The hopelessness in his words showed how much he cared. Before she could respond, he added in a far-from-casual tone, "If you don't mind, I'll swing by my apartment for just a moment before I take you home."

Her analytical mind screamed, *He doesn't want to endanger you, just in case the tail picks you up again.*

She managed to say, "All right," even though fear prickled her skin. Nancy felt her muscles knot when they turned down the street toward the apartment. A block before they arrived he saw it—a parked car, unlighted, but with motor running.

"They're here." Damon took the corner at a sedate, unsuspicious pace. Evidently the watchers didn't notice; perhaps they had counted on their quarry not expecting a tail at the apartment. Nancy peered out the window just before they got around the corner. The menacing car remained in its place just back of the entrance.

Caught in the web of intrigue surrounding them, Nancy didn't notice their route for several blocks. Then she exclaimed, "Why, this isn't the way to Shepherd of Love!"

"You aren't going back there tonight," Damon told her. "I doubt that whoever stalked us knows about you, but it's impossible to be sure. The Caxtons will be happy to have you as a guest for a few more days, I'm sure."

"What about you?"

"I'm going to get to the bottom of this mess as soon as I can get my hands on Curtis." His set jaw boded no good for his brother.

"You'll be careful?" This time her hand moved of its own volition and rested on his.

"Yes, but it's time to clear up a whole lot of things."

She shivered in the warm car, wondering if her world would ever stop its topsy-turvy turning and let her and Damon get on with their lives. Even if those lives could never be joined because of what had happened in the past, this new fear for his safety made other things pale by comparison.

Chapter 11

The Caxtons showed surprise at their unexpected visitors, but when Damon explained, "For some reason we were followed tonight and until I find out why, I'd just as soon have Nancy away from the hospital," they asked no questions and invited her to stay as long as necessary.

"Eric's asleep but how thrilled he will be to wake up and find his beloved Nurse Nancy here," Mrs. Caxton told them. "We also have some great news. Just this afternoon we got a call, and it looks like some red tape will be cut. We may get a sister for Eric very soon, at least on the mandatory trial basis before adoption becomes final."

"That's wonderful! What does Eric think?"

"I'll let him tell you that for himself." A ripple of laughter warmed Mrs. Caxton's face and her husband wore a broad grin.

"Dr. Barton, why don't you stay with us, too? You know we have plenty of room and would love to have you."

Nancy knew how genuine his sigh was, how regretful his "thanks, but no thanks." He added, "I have things to straighten out."

Nancy walked with him to the door. She repeated, "Be careful," and knew her love must shine through her eyes.

Damon rested both hands on her shoulders and looked deep into her heart. "Trust me, Nancy." The next moment he had gone, leaving her feeling more like a wishbone than ever.

The Caxtons tactfully had remained in the living room talking while Nancy told Damon good-bye. Now she took time to lean against the closed door until she could control herself.

Less than an hour later she again occupied the lovely guest suite next to Eric's rooms. Her hostess had provided gown, robe, slippers.

"There's a new toothbrush in your bathroom," she said, "as well as toothpaste, deodorant, everything you'll need. We haven't replaced you. We never will, in our hearts."

Nancy had to keep her eyes wide open to stop the tears from spilling out and distressing the woman she had come to love.

Her bedside phone rang. She eyed it the way she would a deadly snake if it had appeared on her dressing table before she picked up the receiver.

"Hello?"

"All clear," Damon's voice came. "I called the hospital director and explained you'll be gone for a little longer."

"Was the car still there?" She clutched the phone with sweaty fingers.

"No." He sounded guarded.

"Is Curtis there?"

"Not now. Good night." The phone clicked. A moment later the dial tone rang in her ear.

"Good night, Damon," she whispered into the dead phone, then cradled it. A million questions cascaded through her brain, but she found herself too tired to consider any of them. They'd still be around to bombard her tomorrow. Tonight she was safe, secure, and in no condition to even think.

"Nancy?" A light tap at her hall door brought her alive.

"Come in."

Mrs. Caxton entered, holding a tumbler. "Warm milk. Just what the doctor ordered." She smiled and handed it to her guest.

Nancy obediently drank it and watched through a haze as her hostess left. *Just what the doctor ordered.* There must have been a mild sedative in the milk. She felt herself floating with dark eyes shining at her, a quiet voice repeating again and again, "Trust me." *Trust me. How could two words hold a universe of impossibility?*

Damon's fine hands tightened on the wheel of his car. No man in his right mind could expect anyone to have that kind of faith when his only flimsy defense was a claim of innocence. Weighed against the skyscraper of evidence, especially Nancy's clear memory, how could it stand? Again his jaw set. The day of reckoning with Curtis would be postponed no longer.

"God, it's long past time," he prayed. "I don't want to completely alienate him or I'll never be able to bring him to You, but things can't go on like this. Tonight Nancy and I faced real danger. I could smell it. Please, help me. First of all, I have to find Curtis."

When he got to the apartment complex, Damon checked out the atmosphere. Not a glimmer of light came from his window. No car sat waiting by the curb. Still cautious, he drove to the back parking lot, into a stall marked *visitor,* and locked the car behind him, a gesture he recognized as useless. The caduceus symbol told the world a doctor owned the vehicle, normally a boon, tonight a curse. He shrugged. God could protect him just as well against gang members, if that's what they were, as in his own bed. Still, he used care in going upstairs. His key sounded loud in the lock and before he stepped inside the room, he gave it a shove open and ducked to one side.

"You act like the devil himself is after you," Curtis observed from the couch.

Damon hadn't realized the extent of his tension until it washed from his body. "He is. Was."

"And that means what?" Curtis turned rigid. His eyes narrowed to mere slits and he licked his lips.

"Tonight someone trailed Nancy and me. He or they must have picked me up here, followed when I went for her, waited outside the restaurant, and trailed us to—a private home." He bit back Helen Markel's name. "What are you doing, Curtis, using me for a decoy? It's you they're after, isn't it? Are you counting on our looking enough alike at a distance for whatever rats are after you to come for me?"

Curtis swore and leaped up so fast he looked like a man on a trampoline. "What exactly happened?"

"Nothing, except it scared Nancy and didn't make me happy." He scornfully related how they'd escaped. "I don't know what would have happened if they'd caught us. Do you?"

"I'm afraid to even consider it." Curtis sank back to the couch. "I never meant to get you in it."

"Then why did you?" Damon flung on his way to the bedroom. He showered and threw on a lounge coat. The upcoming session would be long and painful. He might as well start out physically comfortable.

Curtis looked wary when his brother came back to the living room.

"All right, what is it?" Damon's heart pounded at the desperation in his brother's face.

"Revenge. From the California deal."

"I thought so. What are you going to do?"

"I don't know." His shoulders slumped. "Running didn't work."

"And in the meantime I'm a sitting duck, as well as anyone who happens to be with me."

Curtis shriveled, bravado gone. "I'm scared."

"You should be."

"Don't preach." But the old domineering older-brother sneer was missing. "What can I do?"

Naked fear shone in the dark eyes that should have held compassion. Damon took a long, unsteady breath.

"You can release me from a promise I never should have made."

In a twinkling an ugly devil-mask fell over his brother's features. "Why should I?" He leaned forward.

"Because the woman and child who died in the fire were Nancy's mother and sister." Damon let him have it full blast. Curtis just stared at him.

"I'm in love with Nancy. She's the only woman I've ever wanted or ever will. I believe she loves me. She also knows I did time in juvenile detention for arson—and that arson scarred her in a whole lot more ways than physically." Damon felt he pleaded not only for his love and Nancy's but for his brother's soul. If Curtis had any remaining decency he would say the word to end the twenty-year nightmare in which Damon had lived.

"If she doesn't believe you, why would she believe me?" Some of the sneer had returned.

"You know I haven't told her." Damon clenched his hands into fists to keep from slamming them into Curtis's face.

"You must have told her something."

"Just that even though I paid for it, I didn't set the fire."

Curtis silently eyed him for a minute before commenting, "If she's in love with you, why isn't it enough? Why's she so hot for the idea you did it?"

Damon's words fell cold and hard as pearls from a broken string to a polished, hardwood floor. "She saw a boy running. The flames behind him made an orange curtain. Later she identified the face. After struggling against her own burned shoulders and back. After continuing nightmares of her mother ordering her to run. After having the memory of her four-year-old sister holding out her hands, imploring Nancy to save her."

"Dear God!" This time Curtis's response was not blasphemy. He raised a shaking hand, wiped sweat from his forehead.

"If it hadn't been for God, she wouldn't have survived. She did. She became a pediatrics nurse because of Leila, reasoning that she'd help save other children even though she hadn't been able to save her sister. Curtis, she still has nightmares of that awful time."

"I don't get it." He continued to stare at Damon. "How did she connect you with the fire?"

Damon felt his face twist. "We went to a chapel in the inner city, part of the Shepherd of Love Sanctuary ministry there. I sat on her right. Sunlight streamed through a vivid stained glass-window. Nancy saw me in the bright glow, the same way she saw the arsonist against the flickering flames twenty years ago."

"What did she do?" Curtis sat like someone frozen in time.

"Ran out. It took weeks and working together to save a little boy from fear and a permanently crooked leg before she would tell me why. Tonight I got the whole story."

"And you wouldn't lie about it, even to keep her." Curtis shook his head in disbelief. "Doesn't it get tiresome, being Saint Damon?"

"You'd better be thanking whatever gods you believe in that I have a code of honor, or you'd be picking yourself up off the hall floor," Damon told him. "Now, are you going to release me from my promise?"

"What's in it for me?" An avaricious gleam came into the dark, watching eyes. "I might just do that, if the price is high enough to make it worth it."

Damon felt the blood drain from his face. He shook his head to clear the anger, disillusionment, final hope for Curtis from his thoughts.

"I think you'd better go. But before you do, listen to me and listen hard. Don't come back. Ever. From the time you could toddle, you've been in trouble. How does it feel to have broken the hearts of everyone who ever cared about you? I'm through, Curtis. I hope I never see you again as long as I live. Oh, I'll continue to pray that someday God will snap you up short and make you realize what you are." His voice rang in the silent apartment. "Until that happens, I have no brother."

"And you're supposed to be such a great Christian." Red-hot fury filled Curtis's eyes. "I'll get out, all right, but don't count on my turning into a Bible-thumping, hymn-singing hypocrite like you. I don't claim to be anything, but I wouldn't throw you out. Remember that. I'm a better man than you are, Dr. Barton. I always have been and I always will be."

He rose, crossed the room, and went out. The door closed behind him with a solid thud that spelled finality. Damon had never felt worse in his life. His brother's accusations stood in solid formation to arraign him, grotesque, accusing. In spite of everything Curtis was or was not, he had spoken the truth. No matter the extent of Damon's transgressions, the strange loyalty that kept his brother crawling back—and Damon realized it was loyalty, not just the need for a safe place—went so deep Curtis would never give up on him.

"God, what have I done?" He stumbled to the couch where Curtis had sat indicting him. "How often have you told us to forgive? Seventy times seven. How often have you forgiven me? Ten times that number? A hundred?" He remembered the time he had spent in the juvenile detention center, hating every minute of it, feeling the injustice. He thought of how evil influences had brought pressure to him; how the young boy he once was had been miraculously delivered by a warden who believed in him—he held out the hope of parole when Damon would have sunk to the level of others who had been there before. He remembered the day of his release. His tortured spirit had gradually opened folded wings, and he had seen how terrible choices could be. Had God's Holy Spirit spoken to his troubled heart at that moment? He never knew. He simply knew that a succession of people came into his life, each at the right time, all with the words of life that had resulted in Damon's accepting the servanthood of God.

Slowly other thoughts intruded on his suffering. He must inform the hospital that Nancy wouldn't be there for a time. He dialed, gave the information. Unlike with the Caxtons, Damon held little back from his director friend. Next he contacted Dr. Cranston and arranged time off. Robert knew the situation up until tonight and instantly agreed.

"Keep trusting in that God of ours," Dr. Cranston advised. "I'll be praying."

A quick call to Nancy completed his preparations. Damon walked to the window, looked into the dark streets, and shuddered. Could the Lord have felt this way when He set forth in search of lost sheep in the Scriptures? Both Matthew and Luke had recorded the matchless parable of God's love for His children. Neither had given the details of the search, but Damon remembered the beloved hymn often sung in church, "The Ninety and Nine."

He'd always had to take a deep breath as the graphic interpretation told of the rough, steep road that tore the Shepherd's feet; the deep waters; the darkness and desert and mountains. Now his heart swelled within him at the final, glorious moment when the Shepherd hoisted his lost sheep on his shoulders and rejoiced. Determination slashed through him. In quick strides, Damon hastened across the living room, into the bedroom, and exchanged his lounging coat for dark slacks and a dark sweater. *Dark clothing for dark deeds,* he thought—and rejected the idea. He tried to become Curtis and decide what he would do. Turned from his brother's door, would he flee and be swallowed up in the shadows? Seek out companionship, no matter how unsavory? Mind sterile as instruments from the autoclave, he snatched a warm jacket then knelt by his bed.

"I don't know where he is. You do." After long moments, he rose and began his search for the brother who had set his feet on the wrong path long ago. For three days and nights Damon searched. Neither his desire to contact Nancy nor his duties on hold deterred him. He talked with bag ladies, push-cart people, those at Shepherd of Love Sanctuary and Clinic. The earth might as well have opened and swallowed Curtis for all the trace he found. No one had seen him. No one followed Damon, either, although his car boldly sat in its usual spot during his visits to shower and change and he took no special pains to hide it while visiting the inner city. The fourth night he dragged home. Either a lot of people were ignorant, lying, or didn't care. Damon hadn't dug up a single clue to his brother's whereabouts. Time and again he had put Curtis in God's hands, only to feel he himself must be doing something. The clock struck nine as he opened the door and stepped inside. Right on cue, the phone rang. "Let the answering machine get it," he mut-tered. He'd left his pager home during his search and, with one or two ex-ceptions, failed to return calls on the machine. Some inner sense rebuked him. Damon sighed and wearily lifted the receiver.

"Dr. Barton."

"Damon?" Paul Hamilton sounded far away. "Come over to Shepherd of Love, Surgery, if you will. Okay?"

A chill swept through him. "Of course, but why?" He felt the answer before it came.

"We have a badly beaten patient here who needs some of my best work. He won't let me go ahead until you come." Paul paused and Damon's world rocked. "He says he's your brother."

"I'm on my way." Damon put the phone down, ran out, and set a new record for fast but careful driving to the hospital. He burst into the emer-gency ward but slowed to a rapid walk. His long training in not alarming other patients and their families took over.

"Curtis Barton?"

"He's gone up to Surgery. Dr. Hamilton will meet you there. He wants to talk with you before you see the—your brother." Compassion rested in the nurse's face. Damon saw the same look in Lindsey Best's eyes when he reached Surgery. The competent, vivacious, redheaded nurse led him to where Paul Hamilton stood scrubbing, then began her own preparations.

"Want to be in on this?" Paul shot at him.

"Yes." Damon stripped off his jacket. "What happened?"

"Disturbance not far from here, four guys beating your brother. People standing there gawking or running back in shops. Some college girl evidently couldn't take it. She sure has guts. She ran out toward the middle of the street screaming at the gang members. Her courage galvanized others into action—a girlfriend who works at a small restaurant hollered at her and at the owner. He called the police. They got there stat. The college girl identified them; they're in the slammer. It won't surprise me if they turn out to be members of a gang the cops have been after for a long time." He turned his level gaze on Damon and held up his sterilized hands for gloves. "I'm not asking and I don't want to know what your brother's connection with them is. The police will. Right now, we've got a job to do. If you think there's a problem since you're related, say so. Otherwise, just be there."

"No problem, and I will." Damon signaled to a nurse for sterile gloves. "How bad is he?"

"Contusions, deep gashes on arms—he threw them up to protect his face—on legs. One knife wound in the abdomen. Doesn't appear to have struck the vitals. I wanted to go ahead but he said not until you came. The guy's got grit." A reluctant admiration shone through his grimness.

"Yes." Damon pushed through into the operating theatre. "I'm here, Curtis."

"End of the line?" His gaze demanded the truth.

"Sure hope not. They got the gang."

"I saw. Gutsy girl yelled." His eyelids twitched. "Been thinking. . .what you said."

"Let's get you patched up," Damon crisply ordered. "Plenty of time to talk later. The rest of our lives." Something cried out inside him that if the knife wound had gone too deep, Curtis might not have much life left.

"Another chance?" Suddenly the pallid figure changed to the wayward older brother Damon had adored, always in trouble, always pleading for another chance.

"Of course. We're brothers, aren't we?"

The surgical staff took their places. The anesthesiologist stepped forward but hesitated when Curtis slowly shook his head. "Tell the truth, Damon." One drop escaped when he closed his eyes.

Through a welter of feelings Damon observed the procedures, noting Paul Hamilton's skill in repairing the supine body on the table. He breathed a sigh of relief when Paul murmured, "No penetration of vitals," and later when he added, "Looks good."

After closing he stepped back, dropped his mask, and grinned at Damon. "Thanks be to God, I see no reason he won't be good as ever before long."

Dr. Barton thought of the way Curtis had looked when he said, "Tell the truth." Did he mean about his shady activities? Surely not. Curtis must have been releasing his brother from a twenty-year-old promise.

He saw Paul's puzzled look when he said, "Good as ever isn't enough. Pray that he will be better," but he didn't explain. Only time could show how the near brush with death would affect the lost sheep.

Chapter 12

Curtis Barton sent a weak smile to Damon when he stepped into his hospital room. The other bed lay empty, waiting for the next patient. Autumn leaves blew outside the long, sparkling window, and a hint of blue sky showed through a gathering cloud mass that hinted at rain.

"Well, here I am."

How like Curtis! Damon laughed, glad for the return of his cocky brother. He remembered the days following surgery, when a stubborn infection had developed. It had taken massive doses of antibiotics to knock it in the head.

"Hey, old man, feeling better today, huh?"

"Don't call me old man." Yet affection shone in the dark eyes so in contrast with the crisp pillowcase. "Uh, Damon, did I do much mumbling? My memory's kind of hazy."

"Some." *Now what?*

"Forget what I said. Okay?" Curtis grimaced.

His brother's spirits dropped to an all-time low. Then Curtis hadn't released him from his promise after all. Damon still couldn't tell Nancy the truth. He forced a grin. "Don't worry about it." Damon glanced at his watch. "Sorry, I have to run. I'll be back in later."

"See you."

"Right."

Damon walked out, wanting to beat his fist against the wall. Just when his hopes had been raised to the highest heaven, a few words had sent them plunging to the depths of despair.

"God, won't he ever change?" Damon whispered, then firmly sent his personal problems scooting out the back door of his mind. He had work to do. Still, he knew the moment he ended his rounds and had time alone, those same worries would slip in through the cracks and torment him again. How thrilled he had been, how free, when he anticipated the happiness in Nancy's face at his story. Even though a nagging little wish she had been able to trust him without concrete proof persisted, he wrote it off as asking too much.

"I wish I had called her and told her everything the minute Curtis got out of surgery," he passionately cried out in the privacy of his room that evening. It had been impossible. Dealing with the police, sticking by Curtis while he had fought his way back to health, and allowing himself only the few hours of sleep his body demanded had given no opportunity to do more than briefly call Nancy. At least he'd had good news for her. With the gang members safely incarcerated, she could return to Shepherd of Love without fear. It had turned out as Paul Hamilton predicted: The hit men were wanted on far more serious charges and unless justice failed, would receive heavy sentences for their crimes.

Deep regret filled the pacing doctor. Was it quixotic to bind himself to a childhood vow, given under duress? The courts of the land held such vows invalid. Damon shook his head. Through all the misery of growing up, the one thing he had never done was go back on his word.

"God, I didn't even know You when I promised," he prayed. "Yet until Curtis releases me, I cannot speak—even if it means losing Nancy." The thought appalled him. To find a woman who could complete his life, truly be his helpmate in their work together for the Master, then lose her? Unthinkable. The other side of the picture was loss of his own self-respect if he followed the dictates of his heart and broke his pledge of silence. Damon finally knelt, turned the whole thing over to God, and fell into bed. At least Curtis had been spared, been given time to change, if he would.

Damon watched for signs of softening in his brother each time he visited him. If they existed, they lay so deep under layers of living they couldn't be readily detected. A few times a quizzical expression came to the watching eyes and once the recuperating patient had asked, "What's with you, little brother? You act like your favorite dog died."

"Tired," Damon admitted and yawned mightily. He knew Curtis didn't believe him by the way one eyebrow shot up.

Another time his brother casually asked, "What's become of the nurse? You can't be spending much time with her, hanging around here all the time and getting in my hair."

In spite of his misery, Damon caught the rough appreciation behind the sting in the words. "No."

"Did she turn out like all the rest of them?"

"No. You should know why I'm not seeing her." Damon turned on his heels and marched out, back stiff as if he had a steel rod instead of a spine.

"Hey, wait a minute. . . ." Damon didn't halt. Wasn't it bad enough to be alienated from the woman he loved without Curtis airing and dissecting it like a beginning biology student?

The few glimpses he had of Nancy proved unsatisfying, and he again avoided her as much as possible except when their work threw them together. *How long could things go on this way?* he wondered. His lips set in a hard line. Only God could straighten things out and it didn't look like He was in any hurry.

◆━◆━◆

"How long will we go on like this, God?" Nancy Galbraith wearily dropped to the sofa in her pleasant living room after a taxing day's work. Two new patients, one of them so obstreperous it had taken more energy than she felt she possessed to settle him down, had disrupted the entire Pediatrics ward. A passing glimpse of a stone-faced Dr. Barton in the distance hadn't helped. Nancy's heart ached. She'd kept abreast of the hospital scuttlebutt concerning Curtis and his progress, as much through the expression on Damon's face as the medical reports. Shepherd of Love's family feeling stretched to include all who entered its doors—visiting physicians, family members, friends. Thank God Curtis lay alive and healing! Rumor had it he'd been exonerated of any blame in the incident; one of the hit men had confessed they'd been hired to do a job on Curtis for identifying the shooter in the L.A. incident. Whatever sins Curtis had committed since he had come to Seattle remained hidden—Nancy hoped forever, more for Damon's sake than his brother's. Seeing the knifed look in Dr. Barton's face, wounded pride, brought an ever-deepening love to Nancy.

"Why should I go on holding something he did as a child against him?" she asked the quiet room. A dozen faces rose to support her growing conclusion that Damon so little resembled the boy who set the fire that not a trace of him remained. *Timmy. Amy. Eric.* They trooped through her mind. Even if the worst were true, if his careless actions had taken life, hadn't he more than repaid it through giving life and hope and health to dozens, no, hundreds of patients? By offering peace and assurance of life eternal to others?

"I don't believe he set that fire, God." Nancy lifted her chin high. "He claims to be innocent. If I really love him, do I have to have documented proof he is telling the truth?"

Her hand strayed to her worn Bible. She opened it and turned to marked verses that had helped her in the past. Reading them aloud sent them deeper into her heart than ever.

" 'There is no fear in love; but perfect love casteth out fear' (1 John 4:18).

" 'Faith is the substance of things hoped for, the evidence of things not seen' (Hebrews 11:1).

" 'Jesus saith unto him, Thomas, because thou hast seen me, thou hast believed: blessed are they that have not seen, and yet have believed' " (John 20:29).

Nancy closed her Bible. *Blessed. . .have not seen. . .yet believed.* Her eyes brimmed. She stood, went into the bedroom, and reached for the phone. Her heart pounded until her ears rang along with the phone. Damon's answering machine came on. She shook her head and cradled the phone. A lifeless instrument could not convey the well of faith in Damon she realized filled her, a bottomless, flowing sea of trust. She bowed her head, heart overflowing until words would not come. Then she walked to her desk, found paper and pen, dated the page, and began to write. One page, two, drifted to the floor but her pen raced on. At the bottom of the third page she stopped, then with swift determination signed it, *All my love, Nancy,* even while rich blood pumped into her cheeks. Her high mood persisted. She addressed and stamped an envelope, put her letter inside, and sealed it. If she went back and reread what she had written, she might not have the courage to send it.

With a sense of freedom she hadn't experienced since that terrible sun-lit moment in the chapel, Nancy rapidly walked the long hall, crossed the staff residence living room, and posted her letter in the box outside. It would be picked up early and Damon should receive it by late afternoon or early the next day. That night Nancy slept soundly and without nightmares. She awakened to a sense of urgency, stretched, and thanked God for the new day. With an impish smile she showered and slipped into a soft yellow uniform, then fixed herself a substantial breakfast. The next time she saw Dr. Damon Barton, she wanted it to be after he had read her letter, not across the staff dining room, out of reach and far away.

All day she smiled at her work. Children reached out to her and received even warmer hugs than usual. One little girl asked, "Somepin' nice hap'nin', Nurse Nancy?"

"Very nice." She beamed on the child, who cuddled closer. Just before her shift ended, a call came to Nancy. One of the other nurses took it. When Nancy came out of the linen closet with a fresh pillowcase to replace one stained with orange juice by an unsteady hand, her coworker said,

"Curtis Barton would like you to stop by when you're through here."

"Curtis Barton!" Nancy froze. She hadn't seen him since that unpleasant night in the apartment.

The nurse didn't seem to notice her agitation and went to answer a call light. Nancy automatically finished her duties, ran a comb through her hair, repinned her cap, and made sure her uniform had stayed reasonably clean. Head high, with questions knocking at her mind's door, she left Pediatrics and made her way to Curtis's room.

The door stood open so she tapped on it and stepped inside.

"Nurse Galbraith?"

Could this thin-faced man be the sneering creature who had made her feel unclean? Nancy gasped and clutched at her slipping reins of poise. "You wanted to see me?"

"Yes." His eyes brightened. "Sit here, please, but close the door first."

She hesitated, wondering what he might be up to.

"You don't have to be afraid." His gaze, so like yet unlike Damon's, softened and she did as he asked.

His first question unnerved her. "Are you in love with my brother?"

"I don't see it's any of your concern," she icily told him to overcome the riotous *yes, yes, yes* bubbling inside her.

"You are more wrong than you imagine." Curtis regained some of his spirit. "He's convinced that you are the moon and stars and sun all rolled into one. Still, he's going around with his chin on the ground. You're a Christian, aren't you?"

"I am." Where this strange conversation was headed, she couldn't guess.

"You believe in forgiveness and all that?" His sharp prod found its mark. She glanced away, remembering how long it had taken for her to reach the point of Christlike forgiveness, but warmed by the letter so close to reaching Damon.

"I do." She even smiled at him.

"Then why in the name of everything you hold sacred haven't you forgiven him now that you know the truth?" Scorn turned his words to stinging bits of ice.

Nancy stared at him. When she found her voice she faltered, "What do you mean? I haven't seen Damon since you came here except in the ward." She leaned forward, hands clenched.

"You honestly mean he hasn't told you?" Incredulity and shock widened his eyes.

"Told me what?" An inkling, a suspicion too bizarre to be real crossed her mind. Curtis drew in a deep, ragged breath.

"Nancy Galbraith, you sit there and tell me you still don't know who really set the fire that killed your mother and sister?"

Dawning consciousness blended with such a kaleidoscope of emotions Nancy reeled. "Why, you?" Her strangled whisper sounded loud in the room. "All these years—how could you do it?"

"I wanted to know how much he loved me." Naked pain twisted his face.

Nancy's rising anger shattered. "How could you doubt it?" she cried. "Hasn't he stood by you through everything?" Curtis's tough-guy façade crumpled into a million pieces, leaving a vulnerable man who held out one hand.

She shrank from him, still unable to comprehend the load Damon had carried for his brother all these years. "Will you at least listen?" Taking silence for consent, Curtis told his story in broken, jerky sentences. A mother who had doted on the older son, often had ignored the younger. One bad boy, one good. "I resented his goodness and it made me even worse," he confessed. "I got in trouble again and again. The night of the fire I'd gone out with a gang of older boys. I didn't know what they'd planned. By the time I realized the terrible thing they'd done, the fire terrified me until I ran."

"And I saw you." Again Nancy saw the boy against the flames. "I thought it was Damon. Why did they show me pictures of him, not you?"

His voice hoarsened. "No one would have believed me if I had said I hadn't been in on starting the fire. I pleaded with Damon to let them think he was me. We looked even more alike then. Damon crossed his arms and said nothing when the cops came. Mama honestly believed him guilty. The real culprits had scattered. Damon never said one word in his defense except that he had set no fire. I hid out so they wouldn't see me and perhaps get suspicious. I'd already convinced Damon it would kill Mama if she learned the truth. I'll never forget my brother standing there, thirteen years old, with a face like an angel saying, " 'I vow never to tell you were there until the time you say I can.' "

Curtis threw one arm over his eyes and his muffled voice sounded hollow. "They took him away. By the time the warden got him paroled I'd moved on. I won't go into what happened. Seeing us both now pretty much tells the story." He dropped his arm and looked at Nancy with anguished eyes. "All these years I told myself, *so what?* I took Damon for what I could get out of him. That's how people in the world I chose survived."

She looked into his face, saw the realization that had come almost too late. "Why are you telling me this now?"

"For some reason, Damon's and your God spared me. It only seems square to make things right if I can."

The divine spark Nancy knew lives in even the most desperate and wicked persons struggled to burn, to become a flame of self-respect. She felt she sat witnessing a soul trying to be reborn.

"Can you forgive me?" he asked, yet she knew what he really meant was, *Will Damon forgive?*

The door opened. Dr. Barton stepped inside.

"What are you doing here, Nancy?" He didn't sound shocked or disapproving, merely tired.

"I asked her to come. You big jerk, why didn't you tell her the truth after I released you from your promise?" Curtis struggled to a more upright position, face blazing.

Damon's face hardened. "If you remember, you took it back."

"I what?" Curtis stared at the tall doctor looming above him. "When?"

"The day you started feeling better, you asked if you had done much mumbling, said your memory was hazy. I told you yes and you said to forget it."

"Of all the. . ." Curtis flopped back on his pillows. "I thought maybe I'd spilled my guts about some stuff while I was out." He looked at Damon, then at Nancy. "I guess it's not that important. I told her. Everything."

Damon stepped back as if hit. His expression changed from passive acceptance to hope.

"Nancy?" She could only nod. For the first time the love in his eyes shone unclouded by doubt or secrets. Yet even while she watched, they changed. A tiny flicker of—disappointment—crept in. The next instant it vanished but the shadow left its mark. Nancy silently prayed to understand. When Damon turned back to Curtis, she stifled the urge to wrap her arms around him. Had the revelation come too late? A flash of insight told her an even greater truth than Curtis had revealed earlier. Damon grieved over her lack of trust in the face of insurmountable evidence. She shrugged off her gloom and felt her eyes shine. Dr. Damon Barton had a precious and unique gift waiting when he received his mail.

They left the room together, the pair of dedicated persons who worked with the precision of perfectly matched gears.

"I never thought he would do it," Damon said softly. "I'm glad he did."

She peered into his face and once more caught the inscrutable gleam.

They walked on, and when they reached the chapel door, he stood aside. She walked in. He followed and closed the door.

"Nurse Nancy, is there any reason I shouldn't tell you I love you more than life itself?" He put his hands on her shoulders.

"Not now." She felt his fingers tighten, then relax. The faintest of sighs came to her ears.

With sudden resolve she said, "Damon, will you do something for me? Will you go home, read your mail, and then call me?" She thought rapidly. *What if the letter hasn't yet been delivered? It should have been,* her common sense argued. *It got picked up just after dawn.*

"I think instead I'd rather go with you," Nancy reconsidered. If the mail held no letter from her, she would tell him its contents and beg his forgiveness for not trusting him more.

※

The letter lay clean and white on the top of a stack of medical journals and junk mail. Nancy snatched it up and thrust it at him. "I'll fix lemonade while you read it." Puzzled-looking but obedient, Damon sat down on the couch. Nancy watched him from the corner of her eye while he read, knowing by the way his hand stilled that he had reached the heart of the letter. She hadn't realized how deeply her words had sunk into her soul in their writing.

> *Jesus often said even to those who loved Him most, "Oh ye of little faith." You have every right to say it to me, my darling. I should have trusted you, should have believed in your innocence against all odds. I will spend all our years together regretting that I did not. I realize now you could never have set the fire, even as a young boy. Please, forgive me.*
>
> > *All my love,*
> > *Nancy.*

Damon stared at the page. Nancy held her breath until she felt dizzy from lack of oxygen. At last he stood and came to her. "I have nothing to forgive. I understand it was too much to ask." Yet the same hint of sadness that had rested in his eyes earlier remained.

He hasn't really forgiven, Nancy knew. She clutched the back of a chair, using it as a barricade. Unless he did, how could they base their love on a strong foundation? Hot tears scalded behind her eyes, but she crowded them back into her hurting heart.

Damon straightened as if throwing off a heavy burden. "Come out from behind that chair, Nurse Nancy. I can't propose with you huddled there like a bird with a broken wing. Thank God Curtis finally told the truth, so—"

Joy began in her toes and crept upward in a surge. "Curtis! Oh, Damon, look at the date on the letter." She ran out of her hiding place, snatched the pages, and triumphantly held up page one. "Look."

His startled gaze followed her pointing finger. His mouth dropped open. "But—why—that's yesterday's date. You wrote this before. . . ? Oh, Nancy."

His poignant use of her name sent her to the shelter of his arms. Her flame of faith had destroyed the last flicker of doubt. Their love would be a steady, purified glow and light the paths of those they served.

Epilogue

Two weeks later, Nancy stood in the glow of a sun-glorified, stained-glass window and became Dr. Damon Barton's bride.
They never forgot.

A Kindled Spark

Chapter 1

Thy word is a lamp unto my feet,
and a light unto my path.
PSALM 119:105

Redheaded Lindsey Best, surgical nurse, slumped against the muraled wall outside the Shepherd of Love hospital director's office. Lindsey stared at the inscription engraved on the always-open door, but for the first time since she had come to the hospital to complete her final training before graduation, she wasn't really seeing it. No trace of her usual smile lurked on her soft lips, and her eyes had no sparkle. Even the freckles on her tip-tilted nose, the ones Lindsey's parents stoutly insisted were fairy dust, looked drab and dull.

"Why so pensive?" a laughing voice demanded.

"Oh, to live in a world of your own, far away from mundane hospital life," a second voice caroled.

Lindsey straightened her lanky body, crossed her arms over her pale-green uniform, and looked down at her tormentors. Tiny Japanese Shina Ito capably cared for mothers and babies in Obstetrics, and the mothers adored her. Blond, blue-eyed Patti Thompson stood four inches shorter than Lindsey; her deceptive fragility hid the endurance necessary to deal with the multitudes who swarmed to Outpatient.

A reluctant smile tugged at Lindsey's lips. "Have you no respect for your elders?"

Patti clutched Shina in mock fear. "Behold the wise one. Even though we're all twenty-four, we are required to bow before my roommate's extra month of life on this terrestrial ball."

"You should. It's time you showed deference to your betters."

Irrepressible Patti raised her eyebrows. Innocence crept into her face. "Since when is older better?" Before Lindsey could reply, Patti and Shina chorused in unison, "We know. You're not better, you're the Best." Patti added, "You've told us enough times."

Shina's trill of laughter brought a grin that chased away the last of their friend's reflective mood. "So what are you two doing lurking outside the director's office at this time of day?"

"That's gratitude for you. We came to get you for supper." Patti raised a haughty chin.

"And to see if you learned anything more about who will take the director's place while he is on sick leave," Shina added honestly. A little frown marred her smooth forehead and she looked affectionately at the murals of sea, forest, and mountain scenes that transformed corridor walls to restful beauty. "I can't imagine having someone new in charge."

"Neither can I." Patti turned serious. Her wide blue eyes darkened. "He's been here ever since the hospital opened. Why, he's as much a part of it as Nicholas Fairchild." Her walk lost some of its spring. "Lindsey, did you learn anything?"

"Just that several persons are under consideration." She matched her longer steps to those of her friends. "The problem is two-fold: first, finding a dedicated Christian who will uphold the standards of the hospital itself— second, someone who is a top administrator." Her heart warmed, remembering how wealthy Mr. Fairchild had carried out his vision of a hospital where medical and surgical skills went hand in hand with prayer, and served rich and poor alike. Shepherd of Love never turned a patient away for lack of funds, even when the patient needed long-term care. Neither did the hospital have fund drives or ask for money. Needs were presented to God—and they were met by those who were impressed by God to support the hospital's unique goals.

In the years since it opened, Shepherd of Love had worked closely with the other excellent Seattle hospitals, winning their respect and admiration. In turn, the hospital on the hill faithfully transferred patients to Harborview, Swedish, Children's, or whatever other facility offered more specialized care when it was needed.

"An acting director won't be the only new face around here," Patti observed. She hugged her arms across her chest.

"Really? Who's leaving?" Shina stopped and stared at her.

"The chaplain is going to retire." Patti blinked hard. "He said he would stay until we found a new man—or woman—but since his wife has grown frail, he needs to spend more time with her. Specialists feel confident she can regain her strength by wintering in the Southwest where it's warmer." The blond nurse sighed. "Why do things always have to change? Who would I go to if I ever had a problem?"

"Which you don't," Lindsey teased. "Except changing *Patty* to *Patti.*"

"It's classier—and I might have a problem sometime." Patti sniffed. "Anyway, it would be a lot easier to talk with our very own chaplain than having to spill out to a stranger."

"He—or she—won't be a stranger long at Shepherd of Love," Shina softly put in. Her dark eyes glowed and she flung her arms wide in an unaccustomed show of exuberance. "Look at us when we came. Three scared rabbits—"

"Not me," Patti interrupted.

"Not I," Lindsey corrected. Her eyes shone with fun and her voice rose to a treble pitch. " 'P–p–please, Nurse,' " she mimicked. " 'I–I've lost Outpatient.' "

Patti groaned. "I'll never live that one down! Of course, I remember things, too. Like a certain sleepy nurse after a long, hard night in Surgery who mistook hair dressing for toothpaste."

Lindsey made a horrible face. "Yecch. I can still taste that awful stuff." When Shina laughed, Lindsey scowled and twirled an imaginary mustache. "Why jeerest thou?

"Methinks small maiden has soon forgotten the solemn presentation of a step stool at our first Christmas here as full-fledged nurses."

"Me thinks if we don't get showered and to the dining room they'll be out of food," Shina reminded, refusing to dignify Lindsey's taunt by recognizing it.

When Shepherd of Love Hospital was built, one of the things Nicholas Fairchild had insisted on was cozy, attractive decor. As much as possible, the creamy white building, perched on its wooded Seattle hill, was designed to be homelike. A covered, connecting passage led to the staff residence hall—women downstairs, men up. Built in the form of a T, the crossbar offered library, living room, laundry facilities, and game room. The three nurses lived at the far end of the long corridor. For some time after coming to work at the hospital, Shina had remained with her parents, who held traditional views about her living at home until she married. Finally, concern over Shina commuting, especially in winter, overcame her father's reservations and she moved into the charming yellow apartment near her friends.

The mini-suites—tastefully decorated living rooms, bedrooms, kitchenettes, and baths—offered views of either mountain or Puget Sound. Patti and Lindsey's double was done in soft greens. The door to a nearby rose suite stood open. At the extreme end, a cream and blue apartment also invited passersby.

"This end of the corridor feels deserted since Jonica and Nancy married," Patti complained. "I'm almost tempted to move into one of their old rooms."

"What? You'd leave me?" Why should the jesting words stir a nameless fear in Lindsey's heart?

Patti spun from her contemplation of the two empty suites. Mischief danced in her eyes and she cocked her head to one side. "One never can tell," she said mysteriously. The next minute a rush of warmth chased away her teasing. "Of course I'm not going to leave you, even though you boss me."

"Not boss. Just train in the way you should go." Lindsey ducked from her roommate's pretend blow and headed into their apartment. "Want first shower?"

"Please. It takes me longer to dress."

"True." Lindsey snatched a simple cream skirt and blouse outfit from the closet and laid it on the bed. "That's because you have more clothes and can't decide which outfit will make you most fetching in the eyes of the interns."

"Fetching! You sound like a book." The rush of the shower drowned out the rest of Patti's good-natured grumble.

Thirty minutes later the three hungry nurses entered the cool, green-painted staff dining room with its spotless white curtains swaying in the breeze from open, screened windows. Tables for eight offered distance enough between to allow individual discussions. Food was served buffet style instead of cafeteria. Fresh flowers and candles on the tables gave the room the atmosphere of a fine restaurant.

The nurses arrived late enough that only a few staff members still idled over after-dinner coffee, yet contrary to Shina's earlier dour prediction, no food shortage existed. Patti complained, "I don't know why I keep eating here. One of these days I'll be this round." She reached for an iced butter ball and another hot roll.

"Which?" Lindsey teased.

Patti shrugged and ignored her. The next moment the blue eyes that matched her soft cotton dress widened. "My goodness, would you look at that?"

Shina, glowing like a peony in her pink blouse and matching printed skirt, glanced over her shoulder. "Who is he?"

"Who is who?" Used to Patti's making much of the ordinary, Lindsey finished cutting her meat before looking up. All three nurses had the chance to date as often as they wished, but Patti had a new rave on the average of once a month, so Lindsey took Patti's present excitement with a grain of salt.

Lindsey raised her head and looked past Shina. A shock wave ran down her spine. A tall stranger, handsome enough to be a movie star, stood just inside the dining room doorway. Thirtyish, straight as a javelin, he stared across at the nurses' table, an unreadable expression on his lean face.

"You don't suppose—" Shina began, but Patti interrupted her.

"Have you ever seen a handsomer man?"

"Not since Rhett Butler," Lindsey admitted, unable to tear her gaze from the newcomer even when she saw amusement in his midnight-black eyes.

"Just remember, I saw him first," Patti whispered. "Oh, dear, he's leaving!" The dismay in her voice made Shina giggle. "He might be a doctor."

"Probably a patient's husband," Lindsey callously told Patti and went back to her dinner as if the brief interlude had not left her strangely shaken.

"Just my luck. The most spectacular man who's come to Shepherd of Love since I've been here and—" She paused. Hope sprang into her face. "Maybe he's our replacement chaplain."

Lindsey shook her head until the shining fall of red hair bounced. "Too good-looking."

"What does that have to do with it?" Patti challenged. "Is there a law or commandment that chaplains have to be old as Methuselah?"

"No, just wiser than Solomon." Shina's white teeth flashed in a grin.

"Mark my words, that man is no chaplain!" The vehemence of Lindsey's tone startled even her. Why had she said such a thing?

It didn't faze Patti, who doggedly asked, "How do you know, great oracle?" She leaned forward as if her life depended on the reply.

"I just do." Lindsey couldn't explain. Something about the stranger had set her pulse quick-stepping, even while faintly repelling her.

"After we finish dinner we could walk through the hospital," Patti suggested blandly. She bit into the roll that had cooled while she checked out the man in the doorway.

"Whatever for?" Shina's fork dropped with a tiny clatter. "I know you love this place, but didn't you just come off eight hours of duty?"

Lindsey snorted in the unladylike way that always brought a frown from her roomie. "Patricia Thompson, are you actually suggesting a man-hunting expedition in Shepherd of Love? How old are you, anyway, twenty-four or fourteen?"

Patti put on her best injured, you-don't-understand expression. "How can you accuse me of such a thing?" She loftily turned her head and looked out the window. "Besides, it's too late. He just climbed into a black sports car and drove off." She sighed. "Well, at least I won't have to run competition with you two."

Laughing and joking, they finished dinner, relaxed for a time on the shaven deep green lawn near the staff residence, and watched a spectacular sunset over Puget Sound. Soon the death of summer would drive them indoors. The thought depressed Lindsey.

What's the matter with me? she wondered. *Seasons never bother me. I love each in turn. All day I've been jittery and I have no idea why.*

"Oh-oh. Looks like a storm's brewing." Patti jumped up and headed toward the back entrance to the residence hall. Shina followed, but Lindsey lingered. She secretly loved storms: lightning that danced above the city; the sonic boom of thunder; even the torrents of rain that made Seattle the Emerald City. Yet she found herself shivering when an enormous inky cloud blew in from the west and parked directly over the hospital. Like a portent of doom it spread its wings and cast a black shadow that made the watching nurse shudder with excitement—and something more.

Transfixed by the awe-inspiring sight, Lindsey stood with clenched hands until the first enormous raindrop splatted against her upturned face. Another. Then a downpour. She barely reached shelter before the full force of the unexpected summer squall broke. Inside, she shook herself like a water spaniel, pressed her face to the shining-paned window, and watched the storm rage.

"I may be younger and in need of guidance, but at least I know enough to get in out of the rain," Patti smugly remarked. Shina smiled at the byplay as familiar to her as the roommates.

Lindsey whirled from her observation point. "Do you ever have a feeling something is going to happen?"

"Like what?" Patti abandoned her teasing and began brushing her hair.

"I don't know." Lindsey bit her lip. She looked appealingly at Shina, but met a puzzled stare. She wanted to cry out her feeling that more than a storm cloud hovered over the hospital they loved. She could not. The fragility of what she could sense but not identify made it impossible.

"Lindsey?" Patti's voice came to her through the Turkish towel Lindsey had snatched up to dry her face.

"Yes?"

"Nothing. For a minute there you looked, I don't know—fey."

"Fey? Now who's using book language? Besides, I thought *fey* meant 'doomed.'" Her rich laugh pealed out.

230

For the first time, Patti didn't respond. "It also means 'visionary, other-worldly.' Sometimes it's uncanny how you sense things before they happen." She crossed her arms over her chest and shivered.

Lindsey dropped the towel in amazement. "This isn't like you, Patti." Her troubled gaze sought Shina but found no reassurance, just growing concern. "What do you think I am, a witch?"

"Don't be ridiculous!" She sounded more Patti-like. "It's just that once in awhile I wonder. Remember that time you were on swing shift and we went to church on your night off? In the middle of the service, you felt you should go to Surgery. Five minutes after you got there and into scrubs the ambulances started bringing people in from a bad accident."

"I remember, but what has that to do with being fey?"

"I just wonder if you've been given a special gift of insight." Patti rushed on, heedless of the exchange of glances between Lindsey and Shina. "Remember in Acts where Peter quoted the prophet Joel? God said in the last days He would pour out His Spirit; that their sons and daughters, His servants and handmaidens, would prophesy."

"Many Christians believe these are the last days, but we can't be sure this prophecy has fully come to pass," Shina objected.

"Even if it has, I'm no prophet." Lindsey crossed to the window and peered out. "The storm is lifting and we'd best get some sleep. I go back on nights tomorrow."

Patti continued to look troubled. "I wish I knew what you think is going to happen."

"I do, too," Lindsey soberly said. "All we can do is pray about it."

"Then let's do it right now." An odd intensity filled Patti's quiet voice. The nurses knelt, hands clasped in a friendship circle. Each asked God's blessing on the hospital and all who served or came there. It wasn't the first time they had joined in prayer, yet Lindsey had a curious feeling about it. All the scoffing and telling herself she was getting too imaginative couldn't erase the memory of Patti's words.

Shina murmured good night and slipped away. Lindsey and Patti went to their separate bedrooms, but the cheerful redheaded nurse lay sleepless in spite of a tired body. She relived the fateful night when something beyond herself compelled her to rise and go where she was desperately needed. If she had remained in church until the service ended. . . She shut down on the thought. No one would ever know how much, if any, difference she had made, but Lindsey would never forget Dr. Paul Hamilton's fervent, "Thank

God you are here!" when he found her there and ready.

Now she pondered. Neither he nor his wife, Jonica, night charge nurse at the time, questioned then or later how Lindsey happened to be on hand. She had felt shy of mentioning her experience, except to Patti and Shina. She remembered their questions. Had she heard a voice? Was it a premonition? Lindsey had no answers. She rejected Patti's explanation. She didn't have an ounce of mysticism in her. And yet. . .

She fell asleep hoping the following day would dawn bright and beautiful. Gray days could give people the gloomies.

Lindsey received her wish. Every leaf and blade of grass shone from the recent shower. Sunlight sent gold motes dancing in the bay, along with tiny whitecaps from a gentle, but mischievous breeze. How good to be alive and young in God's beautiful world!

"I don't think I could ever be happy living where I couldn't see the mountains," she told her friends at breakfast.

"What if you marry someone who lives elsewhere?" Patti could be extremely practical when she chose. This morning she looked like a ripe peach in her pants uniform of the same color. Shina's pale-daffodil outfit made her more flowerlike than ever. Both enviously eyed Lindsey's jeans and plaid shirt, designed to withstand the assault of her multitude of brothers and sisters whenever she visited her family.

Glad for the day off, Lindsey grinned. "I'm hoping God has a nice man from right here in Seattle all picked out for me." Why should the handsome face of the stranger in the dining doorway flash into her mind? Nonsense! She quickly stood. "Bye, slaves."

"Don't rub it in," Patti retorted, then relented enough to wish her a good day.

Humming the first line of "This Is My Father's World" half under her breath, Lindsey headed for the dining room exit in her usual long, ground-covering lope. Just inside the door she glanced over her shoulder to smirk at her friends. Shina's warning cry, "Watch out!" came too late.

The next instant Lindsey crashed to the floor, victim of a head-on collision with a man striding into the dining room at a pace even faster than her own.

Chapter 2

In the dazed moment after the crash, Lindsey heard a rich voice say, "I certainly didn't expect to have anyone fall for me on my first visit to the hospital. You aren't hurt, are you, Miss? Or is it nurse?"

The comment in an unfamiliar voice didn't even register. An awful thought attacked Lindsey. Was it—it couldn't be the striking stranger who had coolly surveyed the nurses, then driven away in a sports car! She felt hot blood swirl into her face before her overdeveloped sense of humor came to her rescue. Leave it to her. Patti might have seen the stranger first, but *she* had certainly made the first impression. Lindsey scrambled to her feet and looked up, fully expecting to meet the amused dark gaze that had stirred her at dinner the night before.

She gasped. Her mouth fell open. Had she struck her head when she fell? Midnight-black eyes and hair couldn't change to laughing gray-blue beneath wavy, polished mahogany hair, could they?

The wide-shouldered stranger, an inch or two taller than she, steadied Lindsey when she involuntarily stepped back. Laughter gave way to concern. "You are hurt. What a clumsy oaf I am, charging through doors as if pursued by howling banshees." He led her to the nearest table, pulled out a chair, and gently forced her to sit. "Would you like a glass of water?"

"No. You—I—it was someone else." Of all the inane remarks, that had to be the worst. A glimpse of Patti and Shina with hands over their mouths to cover their mirth didn't help one bit. "Perhaps I could use some water," Lindsey mumbled, more to get rid of him and give herself time to collect her wits than because she wanted a drink.

"Right." He strode away at the same breakneck pace he had just decried. Who was he, anyway? No one she'd ever seen before. Decidedly attractive in a rugged sort of way, unlike the taller movie star visitor of the night before, although she'd guess they were about the same age.

Penitence filled her caregiver's face when he returned with a brimming glass of ice water. "Forgive me for making light of your fall."

"It's all right. I shouldn't have been walking so fast." Her shaken nerves steadied. "I'm not hurt."

"Thanks be," he told her. The worry in his eyes fled. "You are—"

"Lindsey Best, surgical nurse." Patti and Shina had controlled themselves enough to come over and show belated concern, although Lindsey knew merriment still threatened to break through their deceptively calm exteriors. "This is Patti Thompson, Outpatient, and Shina Ito, Obstetrics."

Her rescuer stood. "It's a pleasure to meet you." He ducked his head in acknowledgment and his eyes glowed, bluer than before. "I'm Terence O'Shea, hoping to be the new chaplain here at your hospital."

The look of amazement on Patti's face repaid Lindsey, who wickedly said, "You aren't quite what we expected."

"No?" He raised questioning eyebrows.

"It's just that our former chaplain was much older," Lindsey hastened to explain when neither of her friends made an attempt to enter the conversation. Delighting in the chance to get even with them for laughing, she casually glanced at her watch, then at Shina and Patti. "I hate to break up this happy gathering, but do you know what time it is?"

"Mercy, we'll be late." Patti roused from her unusual silence and grabbed Shina's arm. "Nice meeting you." She dimpled. Shina murmured something similar, and they hurried out—but not before sending Lindsey a furtive glance that promised a reckoning later in the day.

"I must go, too," her companion told her. "Don't want to be late for my interview with the board. If it goes well, I'd like to tell you about it." He glanced at her shirt and jeans. "It looks like you're ready to go out and about."

"Yes. My family has a sprawling, old-timey house on Queen Anne Hill. I promised to spend the day with them. I go back on night duty this evening." She rose, in full control again, and impulsively held out her hand. "Good luck, Mr. O'Shea."

His strong hand engulfed hers. "It's Terence, and I thank you, Miss Best."

"Lindsey."

"A truly sturdy name," he approved. Twinkles danced in his eyes. He gave her a little bow that in anyone else would have seemed affected, but somehow it fit his personality and did nothing to detract from his manliness.

She watched him go out in the pell-mell manner she often tried to curb in herself. Although her heart and pulse remained steady, she felt warmed. "He has to have Irish ancestry," she told the now-empty room. "Wonder if he's as full of blarney as his name suggests?" Lindsey thought of the steady look in his strong face. "Patti or anyone else shouldn't have a problem taking troubles to him," she soliloquized. She remembered an expression her grandmother often used and smiled. Terence O'Shea really did warm the cockles of one's heart. *How do you know?* reason demanded. Lindsey just laughed. A face as honest as the new applicant's couldn't even conceal his feelings, let alone a deep, dark, indescribable past. So he thought she had a sturdy name. She would need time to decide if she liked that!

<hr />

The excellent Metro King County bus service to Queen Anne Hill from the hospital meant Lindsey didn't need a car, a fact for which she was profoundly grateful. She didn't go around advertising the fact, but she turned over part of her salary to help five younger brothers and sisters. They in turn adored their older sister and studied hard to make her proud of them.

Lindsey's keen gaze softened. Her parents' neighborhood delicatessen took in more than enough for the family's needs, but Ramsey and Linda Best gave away enough food to feed a regiment. Not one of their children protested. They had been raised in an if-we-have-it-God-expects-us-to-share-it atmosphere. When they wanted something out of the ordinary, they mowed lawns or baby-sat. Each had contributed something toward putting Lindsey through nursing school.

She reached the conclusion that no one had a better family and the bus stop a block from her home at the same time. She swung down the step, loped up the sidewalk, and paused. The old house was inviting, from the deep yard, grass worn in spots by countless ball games, to the welcoming front porch with its rockers and swing. Spotless in a fresh coat of white paint put on by the family, it reminded Lindsey of a Victorian chaperone who spreads her skirts and settles down, refusing to budge.

She laughed at her fancy, raced up the steps, and flung wide the screen door. "Mom? Dad?" One would be at the deli, along with a brother, sister, or two.

"In here."

Lindsey followed her nose and the sound of her mother's voice to a high-ceilinged kitchen, fragrant with the aroma of baking beans and yeasty rolls. A rocker sat conveniently nearby, occupied by an orange-and-white cat. Lindsey hugged the mother from whom she had inherited her looks, scooped up the cat, and dropped into the chair with her purring bundle. "Mmm. When's lunch?"

"Didn't you have breakfast?" her older edition asked.

"Hours ago. Well, one hour." Tension she didn't realize she'd carried melted like the butter Mom lavishly spread on a hot roll. She handed the roll to her daughter, and a second roll soon followed. "When I meet Mr. Right, if I do, I'll bring him here and show him you. It will clinch the deal," Lindsey irrelevantly said.

"What a nice thing to say!" Her mother pinkened beneath the sprinkling of freckles on clear skin so like her daughter's. She cocked one eyebrow, pulled down the corners of her mouth, and looked smug, a trait Lindsey unconsciously copied without being aware of it. "Any new prospects?"

Lindsey stuck her long legs straight out before her. "Maybe. Well, sort of, only I don't know for sure." Her capable hand with its long fingers moved rhythmically over the cat's back. He rumbled his appreciation.

"Which translates to—?" Mischief shone in Linda Best's eyes, green-tinted from the green-and-white-checked blouse she wore.

They were still talking when different shifts of the family arrived for lunch. Each new wave brought familiar banter and complaints that Lindsey didn't get home often enough. All thought of her day-before premonitions, if that's what they had been, dissolved. She decided to walk back to the deli with her father and visit between customers. The smell of good cheese and meats, a whiff of potpourri, the tang of onions and pickle, all brought back a thousand memories.

"I am so glad we live in Seattle," she told her father while lending a hand at making sandwiches.

"So am I. If that makes us provincial, who cares?" Her sandy-haired father brandished a slim spatula like a sword, then swiftly spread mayonnaise on a split French roll. "Someday when all the kids are grown, I want to take your mother traveling, but we'll always come back to the Pacific Northwest."

The afternoon sped by on runner's feet. Lindsey at last tore herself away. "Have to get back to the hospital and sleep a few hours." She gave her dad a hug and started toward the door with its merry, jingling bell that announced customers. "Don't work too hard."

"Or you." Blue eyes looked deep into hazel. "We're mighty proud of you, Lindsey. Not just for what you do, but for who you are."

For some unexplainable reason, she wanted to put her head on her father's shoulder and cry. Instead, she blinked long, wet lashes and saluted. "Thanks." He came out on the porch he had added to the deli when he took it over, a big, gentle man in an apron that showed signs of his trade.

Lindsey turned at the corner and waved. Something about him reminded her of Terence O'Shea.

In a heartbeat, she mentally left one world for her other. By the time she reached Shepherd of Love, Lindsey the daughter had submerged herself into Lindsey the nurse, anticipating a long night of serving others. She went straight to her apartment. Patti and Shina would be at supper, but they knew to expect her when they saw her. Lindsey closed her bedroom door, set her alarm, and fell into dreamless sleep. A little after ten she awakened. Long before her eleven o'clock shift began, Lindsey, acting night charge nurse pending the selection of a replacement for Jonica Carr Hamilton, stood checking the shining surgical instruments that must be ready and waiting when needed. She slipped away to attend the prayer service held at the beginning of each shift. Shepherd of Love employed only dedicated Christian personnel, and one way they gave their best service was through mingled prayer for the patients they served in Christ's stead.

Her first four hours proved uneventful. No accident cases came in. No surgical emergencies. Lindsey used the time to diminish a mountain of paperwork. Her staff did routine duties they might not have time for later. At three A.M. she strode the silent halls to the dining room. Others on night shift throughout the hospital joined her, giving thanks for the quiet night.

They rejoiced too soon. The scream of an ambulance taunted them and sent doctors and nurses flying back to their wards. A flurry of activity ensued. "Bus wreck," came the terse explanation from Emergency. "No fatalities. Abrasions and contusions, except for a gashed leg." The disembodied voice went on with vital statistics taken on the scene by well-qualified paramedics. Lindsey quickly briefed her staff, double-checked the instrument table, and stood at the doorway, ready to receive and reassure the pale-faced patient who weakly said he was okay.

"Will you call my wife, please, Nurse? And my boss? I was on my way to work. I work in a bakery and start at four each morning. The boss will have to get backup for me."

"Of course." Lindsey made two quick calls before the hastily summoned junior surgeon arrived. She returned to say the patient's wife would be there by the time her husband was ready to be released. She laid expert fingers on the pulse in his wrist, noting how he visibly relaxed at the assurance.

The gash in the leg proved to be fairly deep, but not serious. The surgeon capably sutured and bandaged it, then ordered the patient to go home and stay off his feet for a time.

Distress filled the man's face. "I can't. We're barely making it on what I earn. If I lose my job, I don't know what I'll do." He raised up on one elbow.

The surgeon gently pushed him down. "It's only for a day or two. I'm sure your boss will understand."

"What if he doesn't?" the anxious man retorted.

Lindsey intervened. "When I called, your boss said to tell you to take what time you need," she told the patient. "He said you hadn't taken a vacation since you started working for him and you deserved a few days off. With pay," she added when the man's expression remained heavy.

"Thank God!"

"That's what this hospital is all about," the surgeon said quietly. "Nurse Best, I believe this man's wife is here. I'll sign the release form."

A few minutes later doctor and nurses watched the sprightly little woman trot alongside her husband's wheelchair, holding his hand and fussing over him. "One of the most rewarding parts of medicine," the surgeon commented. He yawned. "I guess that does it for this shift. Want a cup of coffee after we get cleaned up?"

"Thanks, but I need to make my report to the day shift," Lindsey said. She stifled a yawn of her own, marveling. She never felt tired while on duty, but once her shift ended, weariness set in. She threw aside her stained scrubs, promised herself a shower when she got to the apartment, and slid into the pants and knit shirt she kept on hand. Her stomach growled just as she finished reporting to the day charge nurse. "Right on schedule." Lindsey laughed. "Patti and Shina will be at breakfast by the time I get there."

Her fast, gliding walk carried her down corridors, stairs, and into the dining room. She selected creamy oatmeal, fresh strawberries, a blueberry muffin, and an enormous glass of orange juice from the buffet.

"No eggs or bacon this morning?" the friendly attendant who kept fresh food supplies coming to the buffet table inquired.

"This is enough to at least get me started," Lindsey told him. She threaded her way across the room to the last seat at Shina and Patti's table. "I'll help even the odds," she teased. "Five males and two females is a bit lopsided."

"I don't know about that." Patti coolly helped herself to a strawberry threatening to topple off Lindsey's plate. Her pale lavender uniform and Shina's pink made their friend feel rumpled and worn by comparison.

Lindsey dug in, making giant inroads on her breakfast and listening to the usual hospital scuttlebutt.

"I heard there was a spot of excitement last night," one of the interns offered.

"Really?" "Where?" "When?" Questions flew.

Lindsey continued eating.

"Personnel." He grinned maddeningly.

"What happened?"

"Prowler, I guess, but no one can figure out why. Papers thrown all over the place but, at least so far, nothing significant seems to be missing."

"Nothing significant?" Lindsey's quick mind seized on the word. She put down her fork and leaned toward him. "What *is* missing?"

He looked surprised and a bit abashed. "Sorry. Slip of the tongue. As far as I know, nothing at all." His forehead wrinkled. "Funny. You'd think if someone broke into a hospital it would be after drugs." He glanced at a clock on the wall near the door. "Hi-ho. It's off to work I'd better go or this intern will never achieve resident status. What I'd give for one full, uninterrupted night's sleep."

"Appreciate what you do get, Sleepy," hard-hearted Patti said. "Dopey here needs to go to bed, too." She pointed the comment toward a yawning Lindsey.

"If I weren't refusing to play your silly little game I could say a few things about a certain Grumpy," Lindsey squelched her. "See you." A chorus of laughter followed her out the door, this time unhindered by tall, dark strangers and mahogany-haired men hoping to be chaplains.

One shower and eight full hours of sleep later, Lindsey awakened to the sound of the outer apartment door opening. "Patti?"

"Shina. May I come in?" She sounded hesitant. Shina never intruded on anyone's privacy.

"Of course." Lindsey sat up in bed. "Where's Patti?"

"Man-hunting." Shina parked herself on the foot of Lindsey's bed and stretched like a sleepy kitten. Despite a full shift, she looked rested. White teeth flashed in her lovely tan skin.

"Who is it this time?" Lindsey flopped back on her pillows, a resigned tone in her voice.

"T.D.M., I guess."

"Who?"

"Tall, dark, and mysterious. You know, now you see him, now you don't. Patti saw a black sports car in the parking lot and headed that way." Shina patted a yawn with dainty fingers.

239

The arrival of a childishly disappointed Patti broke into their conversation. "I couldn't see if it was our stranger."

"Our stranger? My, she's getting generous," Lindsey said sarcastically.

Shina chimed in, "Tsk, tsk, and after she clearly pointed out she saw him first." She put her elbows on her knees, crossed her hands, and used them to prop up her chin. "Know what, Lindsey? Patti reminds me of a little dog chasing a big car. Once she catches it, what on earth is she going to do? Sit up and beg?"

"No. She will look at T.D.M. and—"

"Who?" Patti looked at her suspiciously.

"Tall, dark, and mysterious," Shina put in.

Lindsey went on as if there had been no aside. "One look from her forget-me-not blue eyes and he will go down for the count."

"I'm not like that," Patti protested, but a slight smirk denied any offense taken. "Besides, how do we expect to get married if we aren't in the right place at the right time?"

"I believe when God wants us to marry, He will let us know," Shina said. "Look at Dr. Hamilton and Jonica. And Dr. Barton and Nancy. They went through hard times but now they're together and happy." She yawned and got off Lindsey's bed. "I have to clean up for supper. Be back soon."

When the door closed behind her, Patti turned her blue gaze directly on her roommate. "Do you believe what she just said?"

Lindsey started to make a wisecrack but an unspoken plea in Patti's face stilled it. "Yes, I do. Don't you?"

"I hope so." She took the spot Shina had just deserted, even the same pose, cupping her rounded chin in her propped-up hands. "It's just that there are so many nice men, especially here at Shepherd of Love. How can we ever know which ones we should marry?"

"You are totally hopeless, Patricia Thompson. First of all, why not wait until you're asked?" Lindsey heartlessly pushed her off the bed. "Go shower and forget it, will you?" Yet she frowned when she caught Patti's faint whisper, "I wish I could," and filed it away for future consideration.

Chapter 3

If Terence O'Shea hadn't been in a hospital, he would have whistled his way out of the dining room and down the hall to keep his appointment with the board of directors. Instead, he walked more or less circumspectly, although his heart did an Irish jig and a lilt crept into his voice when he said "good morning" to those he met.

The sight of a woman's face hadn't stirred him like this since his senior year in college. Ever since his roommate had eloped with Terence's girlfriend, he had kept women at a distance. How, in the twinkling moments following the collision, had a redheaded nurse with golden freckles and changeable hazel eyes made such an impression? Her friends had been attractive, too. Yet only Nurse Lindsey Best had kindled a spark in the wary heart he had doubted would ever love again. "Two moving objects meet with force," he muttered. Had they ever! He chuckled. It was a wonder he hadn't fallen as well. Arms swinging free, Terence mulled over the last few minutes. He had wanted the chaplain's job before he came; now, God willing, he intended to have it if it were in his power.

The thought firmed his lips and grayed his eyes. He forced his attention to the coming interview. A silent prayer winged its way upward. *According to Thy will.*

Outside the hospital director's office where the interview would be held, Terence read the inscription on the door. *Thy word is a lamp unto my feet, and a light unto my path.* The familiar verse brought back bittersweet memories of a small boy at his mother's knee, chin on his hand, adoring gaze turned toward the frail woman who smiled down at him. He tightened his lips. This was no time for reminiscing. Taking another deep breath and slowly exhaling, he stepped inside.

"Are you Mr. O'Shea?" a pleasant-faced woman asked.

"That I am." He smiled.

"I'm afraid I have disappointing news for you." She sounded genuinely regretful. "The board is eager to interview you, but they would like Nicholas Fairchild, the hospital founder, to be in on the selection. He was unexpectedly called out of town on business. The chairman would like to

reschedule you for tomorrow afternoon at two. Will that be convenient?"
She laughed. "There, don't I sound efficient? The hospital director never
uses a secretary as a buffer, preferring to be available to staff at any time,
but he isn't here just now."

"You do—and tomorrow will be fine." Terence's heart was heavy. Was
this a polite brush-off? Or a stall to give them more time to consider someone else? Insisting on the legendary Fairchild's presence was calling in the
big guns, but Terence could do nothing about it.

"They really do want to see you, Mr. O'Shea," the woman told him.

"I'm glad." He smiled and went out, wondering how he could wait another day and a half. The smile changed to a grimace. This could be another of the Lord's lessons in teaching him patience, which he knew he
sorely needed.

＊＋✕＋＊

The following afternoon when he entered the hospital director's office, the
secretary's desk was empty. This time Terence noted the simple but taste-
ful furnishings in the office. Paneled walls and muted carpeting paled into
insignificance next to the large open window's spectacular view of Puget
Sound and the snow-capped Olympics.

A keen-eyed man rose from a chair behind a practical desk. He held
out his hand. "Thanks for coming, Mr. O'Shea. Sorry we had to postpone
our meeting." He introduced the other four members: two men and two
women. All appeared alert and observant. Last of all, he turned to the
scholarly looking older man next to him. "Mr. Fairchild, Terence O'Shea."

So this was the man God had directed to build Shepherd of Love
Hospital! In spite of Fairchild's white-streaked hair, Terence felt he understood why God had picked him. Keen intelligence shone from the blue
eyes. Compassion and strength lined the austere face.

Terence found himself measured as never before in his entire life. He
bore the scrutiny with head up and fast-beating heart. Without being told,
he knew no matter what the rest of the board thought, Nicholas Fairchild
must be satisfied or he had no chance of being asked to take over as hospital chaplain.

"Sit down," the chairman invited. "We'll get right to our interview. We
are particularly eager to fill the chaplaincy because of an unusual circumstance at Shepherd of Love just now. Our hospital director recently suffered a stroke. Our specialists feel he will regain full health, but of course

it will take time." He rested his elbows on the desk and methodically fitted his fingers together. "We haven't yet selected an acting director, but that's another matter entirely, one that only affects you indirectly."

A barrage of questions followed, starting with, "What brought you to Shepherd of Love? You have been out of the country, haven't you?"

"Yes. I came home when my father's health worsened."

Compassion showed in the board members' faces. "Is it serious?"

"Enough that I don't want to be thousands of miles away." Terence felt a muscle twitch in his cheek. "In spite of a history of rheumatoid arthritis, Dad did fine living alone until just a few weeks ago. This time when it flared up, it brought complications."

"There are always care centers," Fairchild suggested.

"Not for Dad," Terence retorted, feeling like a pinned butterfly. "Mom died when I was a child. Dad became mother as well as father. Unless it comes to the point where I can no longer give him the quality of care he needs, Dad and I will remain a team."

"Don't you have siblings who could care for him?" the chairman asked. "It seems too bad you were called home from such a distance."

"Oh, I do have siblings." Terence laughed out loud. "Four older sisters, all married. I was the baby of the family, born after my sisters married and moved away. They are scattered from Albuquerque to Akron. Dad still lives on the family farm near Redmond. I'd like to keep him there as long as possible."

"Suppose you marry?" one of the women wanted to know.

What a strange interview! Terence couldn't tell if the questions were meant to needle or test him. He hesitated. If he'd been asked that a half-hour earlier his answer would have been a direct, "I'm fancy free." Now the vision of a red-haired nurse persisted in knocking at the door of his mind. He slammed it shut and shrugged. "I won't worry about it until the time comes, if it does."

The finality in his voice effectively closed the subject. Terence sent a lightning glance around the circle of watching faces. The approval in their expressions gave him the courage to plunge to the heart of things. "To reply to your first question, I believe my coming to Shepherd of Love may be an answer to prayer. I asked for a job within commuting distance of the farm. The next day an old friend who 'just happened' to know your present chaplain's wife 'just happened' to drop by. She 'just happened' to mention your chaplain's plans to retire." He felt again the thrill that had come when he first heard of the job.

"I'd be interested to know," Fairchild stated, "why you say it may be an answer to prayer rather than stating positively you believe it is."

Terence knew his astonishment at the astute question must show. "I don't have the audacity to presume to know the mind or will of God until it is revealed and confirmed," he said. "In this case, by your receiving the impression I am the right one for the job." For a moment he feared he had gone too far. If so, so be it. He would not sail under false colors even to get a job he more and more longed to have. Everything about the hospital had impressed him favorably so far, including these men and women who helped shape its policies and practices.

Fairchild just smiled. Terence had the feeling he hadn't struck out, but gained at least first base.

The chairman hemmed and hawed a bit, looking embarrassed. "Would you be willing to come on a trial basis? For a month or two, maybe more?"

Terence's spirits, which had steadily soared throughout the stiff examination, sank at the suggestion. The board members evidently did not yet feel sure of him or such an offer wouldn't have been made. In the little pool of silence that fell, he considered. Should he accept the half-loaf, when he had hoped for a whole? Doing so meant having time to prove himself. On the other hand, if he gave two to three months to Shepherd of Love and they decided in favor of another candidate, where did that leave Terence O'Shea? Right where he was now—jobless and waiting for a door to open.

The chairman cleared his throat for the second time and fidgeted in his chair. "Nicholas is at a disadvantage concerning your application, Mr. O'Shea." His face reddened. "It appeared fine when it came in so we sent it on to Personnel to be kept on hand with others." He laughed shame-facedly. "I've been known to misplace, even lose things."

"Wasn't everything in order?" Terence interrupted.

"Very much so." The chairman squirmed. "In fact, we felt good about you."

"I don't understand." A bewildered Terence shook his head.

"Neither do we," one of the other men solemnly said. He lowered his voice as if afraid of being overheard. "A break-in occurred in the personnel department between the time the office closed last night and when it re-opened this morning."

"What has that to do with me?"

"When we sent for your file this morning for Nicholas, it was missing."

"Missing?" Terence exploded from his chair, then sank back in response to the chairman's wave. "Why would anyone want my application?"

"It isn't just yours," the chairman explained. "Actually, it may still be somewhere in Personnel. Right now, the employees are attempting to clean up the mess left by the intruder or intruders. Employee information is normally computerized. However, Personnel has been shorthanded. Applications received in the past few weeks were temporarily dropped into file folders to be held pending action. The material from those folders was dumped in a jumble on the floor."

"Sounds more like a malicious prank than a planned theft," Terence observed. He frowned and his brows formed a straight line above his intense eyes. "Yet why would anyone take the risk of discovery just to play a trick?"

"Do you know of anyone who might want to learn more about you or the work you were doing?" Fairchild asked. "Do you have enemies?"

Terence shook his head. "No—not that I know of."

One of the women moved restlessly, as if reminding them they were there to select a chaplain, not solve a mystery. "Will you recap your experience for Nicholas, please?"

Terence obligingly began to relate the basic information his application contained. "Degree in engineering from the University of Washington."

The chairman stopped him. "You didn't actually pursue that profession."

"No. I worked at Boeing for a couple of years and found myself restless." Terence stared out the window, remembering the dissatisfaction with his job. "I felt like a cog that could be replaced by any number of qualified men or women. Dad and I made it a matter of prayer. Over a period of time, I realized I wanted to make a difference in people's lives beyond being part of making bigger and better airplanes." His voice turned husky. "I never heard angel voices or saw visions, but gradually I felt led to the ministry."

"You entered seminary?" Fairchild inquired, an unreadable expression on his intent face.

"Yes. I enjoyed preaching but, unlike my fellow students, had little desire for a church of my own. I longed to serve, yet found myself in a web of uncertainty, unable to discover what God had in mind for me. He didn't seem to be speaking. Or I may have been so engrossed in myself, I wasn't hearing." He sighed. "It was a distressing time."

"I can see it would be." The conversation narrowed into a dialogue between Terence and Nicholas Fairchild.

"I approached a professor who never hesitated to give himself to the seminary students, and I laid my dilemma before him. I'll never forget his piercing, wintry gaze when he asked, 'Are you willing to go anywhere, do anything, be anybody God asks?' I hesitated, examined my soul, and told him I thought so.

"His giant fist crashed to his scarred desk. 'Mr. O'Shea,' he said. 'Until you can come in here, stand before God and me, and shout *yes* at the top of your lungs, I have no time to waste on you.' "

Terence wiped at his eyes to rid himself of the blur the scene brought.

"What did you do?" the obviously enthralled listeners wanted to know.

His voice dropped to a whisper. "Fasted and prayed for three days and nights."

"And?" Fairchild barked, his voice far different from his usual quiet tone.

A great laugh escaped from Terence's constricted throat. "I charged into the professor's office like a raging tiger and bellowed *yes!*"

Sympathetic chuckles greeted the story of his outburst.

Terence went on. "The professor leaped from his chair with such exuberance it crashed to the floor behind him. His hand shot out, gripped mine, and he said, 'Now I can help you.' And he did."

"By finding you a chaplain's job on a medical mission ship to Haiti," the chairman put in.

"Right." Terence felt himself come alive. "I wouldn't trade the experience for anything. Just being there for a staff who gave one hundred and ten percent of their time, energy, and love meant everything. I saw them offer hope to men, women, and children who had none. Every patient meant a new challenge, a new opportunity. I learned rudimentary lay medical procedures and assisted in physical healing as well as spiritual. More than ever, I realized how the two must work hand in hand."

"Which is exactly our goal," Fairchild murmured.

"I know," Terence softly said. "That's why I want to be part of Shepherd of Love." He bowed his head, but not before he saw the flash of approval in the hospital founder's blue eyes.

After a moment of profound silence, the interview ended unexpectedly. Fairchild turned to the chairman. "I believe we have heard enough, unless you or the others have further questions?"

Terence could tell nothing from his noncommittal statement.

When the board indicated they had nothing more to ask, the chairman said, "We will be in touch, Mr. O'Shea. Thank you for coming." He casually added, "Be thinking about the temporary offer, will you?"

Standard dismissal, Terence thought. In a few days he would receive a polite letter thanking him again, perhaps even praising his qualifications, but stating another had been chosen. Sadness filled him. Even though he had prayed for God's will to be done, he found it hard to understand. The chaplaincy offered work he loved, the means by which he could care for Dad. A fresh pang went through him. His father's farseeing eyes would ferret out his only son's disappointment, but how could he tell Dad? Should he have accepted the temporary offer when it was first mentioned?

He stubbornly shook his head. No. He hadn't felt any leading to do so and until he did, he could not shackle himself to a position that might in the end be taken from him.

O'Shea pride forced Terence to shake hands all around, thank the men and women for their time, and start out. Just before he reached the door, Fairchild said, "Mr. O'Shea, close the door behind you and wait outside, please."

"Certainly." What now? He stepped through the doorway, into the hall, and pulled the door toward him. The last thing he intended was to eavesdrop, yet just before the door shut, he heard Fairchild's voice. Something told him the older man intended for him to hear.

"I recommend we hire that young man, with no reservations."

Terence tried to control the grin that started in his heart and curled his lips. He leaned against the corridor wall, absently staring at a wall clock a little distance away. A minute passed. Two. Three. Funny. He'd never before noticed how seconds limped into minutes, like patients favoring an injured leg.

"Mr. O'Shea, will you come in again, please?" Fairchild himself opened the door and waited for Terence to enter. "We'd like you to be our chaplain. No probationary period. I'll walk with you to Personnel so they can get the necessary information to put into the computer." His eyes twinkled. "We're taking no chances on losing you a second time."

"Congratulations, Chaplain O'Shea. We know you will be an asset to Shepherd of Love." The chairman beamed, as did the others. Another round of handshakes, and Terence silently accompanied his new friend down the hall.

Fairchild chuckled. "Go ahead and say it, Son. You'll burst if you don't."

"I was just wondering—"

"—what I said after the door closed." Another chuckle rumbled deep in his throat. "Terence, no one who talks with you for any length of time can fail to see what you are." Laughter died. "Let an old man give you a wee piece of advice. If ever you are in doubt as to what to say to someone in trouble, simply tell them God loves them. Then share what He has done for you. I've found in my three score and ten years those two witnesses to be the most effective way to lead folks to the Lord, comfort them, or make them know life is worth living."

"You remind me of my father," Terence choked out from behind an obstruction in his throat that felt bigger than the Rock of Gibraltar. "I hope he can meet you someday. You'd like him."

"I already like his son," Fairchild said. "Very much."

Terence couldn't answer.

When he finished the necessary paperwork and came out of Personnel, Terence was surprised to find his sponsor waiting for him in the hall. "Mr. Fairchild, I just don't know how to thank you," Terence blurted out, feeling more like a ten-year-old schoolboy in the presence of a favorite teacher than a thirty-year-old, full-fledged chaplain.

"Simply serve Shepherd of Love with all you have." A poignant light softened the keenness of his blue eyes. He shook Terence's hand once more, started off, then turned and wistfully said, "Terence, there is one other thing."

"Anything."

"Call me Nicholas. We're brothers in Him, you know." Fairchild smiled and walked away, leaving the new chaplain feeling he had just been blessed.

Chapter 4

A dark figure nervously walked the floor of a musty room in a deserted, falling-to-ruin warehouse. Barren except for a battered desk that held a telephone, the worn boards groaned in protest at being disturbed. Fear like a living thing gripped the pacer. Why didn't he call? The prearranged time had long since passed.

Seconds dragged into minutes. His nerves twanged. He felt sweat form and bead in great drops. At last the phone issued a low scream. The instrument's volume had been carefully turned down, but even the faint noise further jangled his frayed nerves, sounding hollow in the vacant building.

"Yes? Yes. It's about time." A furtive glance around the empty room assured the speaker he could not be overheard, except by a multitude of spiders spinning their death trap webs in the corners.

"It went as planned." A smile of triumph touched the speaker's face. One hand closed in a convulsive grip. A long list of instructions poured into his ear; he listened with a brain made keen by waiting, interrupting only occasionally with a few grunts.

"Got that?" the man on the other end of the line barked. His tone demanded total obedience and left no room for incompetence or failure.

"Got it."

A click, then a dial tone. The dark figure unplugged the phone and carelessly stuffed it in the bottom drawer of the old desk. Relief came like a shower. If everything went as well as it had so far. . . Again, one hand shut in a gesture of victory. It wouldn't be long now.

———◆◆◆———

Terence O'Shea sang all the way from Shepherd of Love Hospital in Seattle across the floating bridge that spanned Lake Washington, then north on Interstate 405 to the Redmond exit. Once off the freeway, he curbed his impatience to reach the farm and slowed his station wagon to accommodate the country roads. His heart swelled and he broke off singing as he thought, *I missed western Washington while I was gone—but I didn't realize how much until I came back.*

Although he'd been born in San Francisco, Terence's images of the steep hills, trolley cars, Fisherman's Wharf, and Chinatown came from adult visits rather than childhood memories. With the birth of their fifth child and only son, Shane and Moira O'Shea followed their hearts to Washington where they purchased the rundown farm near Redmond. Terence grew up surrounded by hills and forests, meadows and gardens. He fished in the stream that ran through their property, and flat on his back beneath pine and firs, he watched cloud pictures form between the green needles. He tolerated the cows and chickens he helped care for as part of his chores, but he genuinely loved the wild rabbits, squirrels, and occasional coyote or deer that visited the farm. Tragedy had touched him when he was ten and his mother died in a car accident—but Dad had always been there: father, confidant, his son's best friend outside of God.

Now Terence sighed. He carefully swung into the long driveway leading to the old white farmhouse. "Never thought I'd miss the moo of cows or the cackling of chickens," he admitted with a grin. It died when he braked to a stop in front of the house. How long could he and Dad stay here? In the short time since he returned from Haiti, he'd made giant inroads on the weeds threatening to choke out the gardens, but he couldn't keep it up, care for Dad, and still do a good job at the hospital. The thought of selling the place made him blink. Could they find another alternative?

"I know You will provide, God," he murmured. A few long strides took him across the porch and through the front door. "Dad?" He sniffed. "Hey, you're up and cooking."

"You bet I am!"

"That's not the voice of an invalid," Terence teased when he reached the spotless white kitchen with its colorful tile floor.

"So who's an invalid?" Dad set an enormous bowl of potato salad on the round table in the window corner. The blue-checked tablecloth already held two place settings, plus bread, butter, and condiments.

Pain had lined Shane O'Shea's face and streaked his mahogany hair with silver, but it had not dimmed the eyes that were even bluer than his son's. The rheumatoid arthritis that stiffened his joints could not touch his magnificent soul. Shane put a plate of sliced tomatoes on the table, then turned back to the stove and took up fresh green beans cooked with onion and thick slices of turkey ham. The gnarled hands were a little awkward, and Terence itched to help. He knew, though, that his father wanted and needed to be allowed to do all he could.

"Looks wonderful and I'm starved. Oh, Dad, I got the job." He headed for the kitchen sink to wash his hands.

Shane's laugh rumbled deep in his big chest. "As if I didn't know the moment you stepped onto the porch! No man has such a spring in his step if he's just been turned down or passed over." His eyes gleamed. "Let's have the blessing, Boy, and you can tell me about it. My turn, I think."

Terence nodded and bowed his head. As always, he was touched by the simple words of thankfulness his father expressed to the God who ruled their lives. "So what did you do today other than cook for your starving son?" he inquired. "You aren't overdoing, are you?"

"Not at all." Shane cut his meat and looked subdued. "I'm a lot better, so much so I feel ashamed at having interrupted your life by allowing you to come home and care for me."

Terence stopped a forkful of salad halfway to his mouth. "Are you joking? Why should I be off caring for someone else when I can be here eating your cooking and growing excited about this new opportunity?" He ate the bite of salad and grinned. "Your potato salad gets better every time. Dad, you can't believe how right I feel about the chaplaincy. It's as if everything in my life has been directing me to this point." He didn't add the feeling had begun with his chance encounter with Lindsey Best.

Shane visibly relaxed. "I never want to be a burden," he quietly said. "One of these days you'll be finding the right woman and settling down. Never let me stand in the way of your happiness."

A certain wistfulness in his father's voice caused Terence to say, "Suppose we worry about that when it happens." Funny, first the hospital board had been concerned over his love life, and now Dad. He laughed outright. "You aren't going to start sounding like the girls, are you?"

Shane roared and his eyes twinkled. He put on a rich Irish brogue and reminded, "Shure, and what would ye ixpict wi' four colleens, each more happily married than the ither, all longin' for their baby brother to wed?"

A rollicking time of "do you remembers" followed, based on the many and devious ways Terence had outwitted his matchmaking sisters.

"They mean well, Boy," Shane finally said.

"I know, but aren't marriages supposed to be made in heaven?"

"True, but they're lived out on earth and your sisters cannot resist putting a hand in. You'll have to admit, the girls they brought around were always nice."

"Who cares, if they're not the one for me?" Terence retorted. He shoved back from the table. "I'm stuffed."

"Too full for apple cobbler ready to come out of the oven?"

"Not I." Terence hastily reversed himself. "I'll fetch it. Getting up and down will furnish a little exercise and make more room for it." He brought the steaming cobbler, dished up generous portions, and added a dollop of butter to the spicy apples and crust. "Dad, I'm really glad to be home—and I thank God you've improved."

"You know there's no real cure, Terence."

"I know but that doesn't mean there won't be one day. In the meantime, we're going to do everything possible for you." His Irish chin set in a fighting line that boded ill for disease or danger threatening one he loved. He loaded the dishwasher, still talking. Like the Bests' kitchen, the O'Sheas had a rocker that symbolized how much wonderful comradeship took place in the big room, and now Shane sat and rocked, while he thanked God for the light he saw in his son's face and heard in his voice.

***

Hours later, Terence stood at the window of his upstairs bedroom, looking into a glorious night. The desire to be out in it overrode the more practical need to get a good night's sleep. He quietly went downstairs, across the porch, and into the moonlit meadow. The stream he loved gurgled with joy and reflected the countless, shimmering stars that made the night sky a thing of wonder. Distant, snow-capped mountains showed between slightly swaying evergreens, eternal, immutable. A sense of peace pervaded him. Where else on earth could anyone feel closer to his Creator? At least for this night, crime and sin in the world seemed far away; the farm stood strong, a haven of stability in a mad, sometimes senseless world.

Terence did not go inside until a low keening in the trees told him the night wind had risen, and it became too chilly for comfort to a man standing motionless, even though he gazed on incomparable beauty. He quietly made his way back across the porch and up the stairs. No sound came from his father's room until Terence inched his bedroom door open and stepped inside. Then the greeting came, the words he'd unconsciously waited for and heard thousands of times, no matter what time he got home.

"Good night, Boy."

"Good night, Dad." He closed the door. Dad had been keeping watch. All was well. "Just like You, Father," he whispered into the cool air of his room, glad to be back where he could sleep with the window wide open and gaze upwards at the moon and stars.

A few days later, all hospital personnel who could be spared from the wards and offices received a summons to a general staff meeting. Scuttlebutt had it both the new hospital chaplain and acting hospital director had been selected. Patti, Shina, Lindsey, and the rest of the hospital knew Terence O'Shea had been unanimously chosen to fill the chaplaincy, but speculation as to the new temporary director ran like spilled oil. For once, Dame Rumor failed to discover and pass on the news.

The three nurses filed into the auditorium-like room used for such gatherings and found seats together. "There's Nicholas Fairchild," Patti whispered. She dug her elbows into Lindsey and Shina, who flanked her on either side. "See, with the directors? Oh, there's Terence." She stood and waved. Before Lindsey could tell her to sit down and stop acting like a beauty queen waving to everyone from a parade float, Patti gulped and added in a loud whisper, "My goodness, girls, it's *him!*"

"I don't see anyone special," Shina said.

"Him, who? Besides, the correct grammar is *he*, not *him.*" Lindsey succeeded in getting Patti back into her seat.

"*He, him,* who cares." Patti clutched her friend's arms with unexpectedly strong fingers. "Him. You know. T.D.M."

"Tall, dark, and mysterious?" Shina craned her neck in a vain effort to see past much taller persons laughing and swarming into the seats in front of them.

"Really?" Lindsey straightened her tired spine out of its slump. "You don't think—"

Patti clasped her hands and gave a deep blissful sigh. "I don't think anything. I just know he's even more gorgeous than before. It's positively unfair for any one man to be so good-looking."

Lindsey silently echoed her friend's sentiments when Nicholas, the board of directors, Terence O'Shea, and the tall, dark stranger walked onto the platform at the front of the room. The same thrill she hadn't been able to identify the first time she saw the spectacularly handsome man fluttered her pulse and quickened her heartbeat. A second feeling, even more elusive, brushed gossamer wings against her mind. A disturbed feeling that something wasn't right haunted her.

Nicholas Fairchild stepped to the microphone. "Welcome and thank you for coming," he said simply. The overhead lights silvered his gray hair. "I won't keep you long. Many of you need to get back to our patients. I just want to introduce our new chaplain and acting director."

In a mental daze, Lindsey watched Terence O'Shea step forward when beckoned. She heard his solemn voice vowing to give his best to Shepherd of Love. Before he returned to his seat amidst thunderous applause, she noticed his eyes shone more blue than gray, but she quickly turned her attention back to Nicholas Fairchild.

"As you all know, our hospital director will need some months to re-cuperate. We have considered several candidates, all highly qualified. I'm happy to introduce to you Dr. Bartholomew Keppler, although he says he prefers to be called Bart." A ripple of laughter swept through the group and Lindsey sucked in her breath. T.D.M.—Dr. Keppler—stepped forward.

"Along with Mr. O'Shea, I pledge to faithfully carry out my duties. I will make sure Shepherd of Love Hospital is given the homage and loyalty I feel it deserves." He spread his hands deprecatingly. "Stepping into your beloved director's place won't be easy. I'll need all your cooperation." He smiled with a flash of teeth so white that he could, Lindsey thought, obtain work advertising toothpaste. She bit her lips at the irreverent thought.

After a few more remarks, he smiled again and sat down in a din that showed how impressed the staff had been.

"Isn't he won—der—ful?" Bright pink spots flared in Patti's clear skin.

"He hasn't done anything yet but talk," Lindsey said perversely.

Shina giggled but Patti glared. "Don't be horrid, Lindsey Best. Come on. Let's go wish him—them—well." She practically dragged her friends up the aisle. Shina rolled her eyes in exasperation and submitted. Lindsey hung back a few steps.

"We just want to welcome you both," Patti said when they reached her prey. She quickly introduced herself, Lindsey, and Shina to Dr. Keppler. "I suppose you've already met Terence—Chaplain O'Shea," she added.

"Actually, I haven't. I arrived just before the meeting started." Keppler held out his hand. "Welcome to my hospital, Chaplain."

My hospital. Not *the* hospital or Shepherd of Love. Lindsey caught a cu-rious terrier-brightness in the new chaplain's eyes when he said, "Thanks," and took the extended hand. It reminded her of the look in a dog's eyes just before he unearthed and pounced on a rat. Laughter like carbonated water bubbled inside her.

She managed to say hello, but her voice shook slightly from controlled mirth. Another minute and she'd laugh out loud. "I have to go, Patti," she said. "Are you coming?"

"Y—yes." The reluctant agreement sounded dragged out of her roommate and the minute they got out of earshot, she demanded, "Well?"

Lindsey hesitated, knowing Patti wanted a glowing response but not able to give it. "As I said earlier, he hasn't done anything yet but talk. I'll reserve judgment for awhile, if it's all right with you."

Shina glanced back over her shoulder. "Me, too." Her midnight-black eyes looked solemn. "I think I like Terence better."

"For goodness' sake, why?" Patti stared at the tiny nurse.

"I know it sounds silly, but I read a western novel once and the villain's name was Black Bart—"

"Shina Ito, that's positively unchristian! Taking a dislike to someone because of his name? I never heard of such a thing." Patti's face turned red.

"She didn't say she disliked him and neither did I." Lindsey poured oil on the troubled waters. "Why the instant defense, anyway?"

Quick tears moistened Patti's long lashes. "I'm sorry. It's just that the Shepherd of Love staff has always been united and I don't want it to change. It's bad enough losing our director and chaplain and having to get used to new people. I just want everyone to be happy and like each other."

Lindsey and Shina exchanged glances. What a child Patti was, in spite of being a terrific nurse and twenty-four years old! Yet that very trait made her lovable.

"You're right, Patti. I'm being unreasonable," Shina apologized. She slipped one arm under Patti's, the other through the crook made by Lindsey's elbow. "I have time for juice before going back on duty. How about you?"

Patti nodded. "Lindsey?"

She started to say she needed to sleep but then decided a few minutes less rest wouldn't kill her. "Sure." They sauntered down the hall, differences forgotten or at least shelved for a time.

"The Three Musketeers, as I live and breathe." Terence O'Shea greeted them at the dining room door. "May I have the pleasure of your company?"

"Of course." Patti never let her admiration for one eligible male rule out spending time with others. Yet Lindsey had to admit her blond friend was neither shallow nor a flirt. She simply liked people and they adored her. Patti's sunshiny personality warmed all those around her, although she always insisted Lindsey was the one who brought happiness to others.

Four tall lemonades before them, talk naturally turned to Dr. Keppler.

"What did you think of him?" Patti boldly asked the question Lindsey had secretly hoped she would.

Terence sipped his icy drink. "Evidently he is eminently qualified. Gossip has it Dr. Keppler's credentials are as impeccable as his clothing."

Why did a slight frown crease the new chaplain's broad forehead?

Patti played with a straw. "It will be interesting to meet his wife."

"I don't think he's married."

Again Lindsey sensed a certain hesitancy in Terence's voice. Perhaps he had also decided to reserve judgment on the new acting director. She finished her lemonade and stood. "I can hear my bed calling. See you all later." She started out, glad to be free of the incessant chattering about "Black Bart" that buzzed throughout the room.

Terence caught her at the door, looked both ways, and lowered his voice. "Lindsey, what do you think of him?" His steady gaze, more gray than blue, searched her. "I'll wager you're a good judge of people."

"Usually." She hesitated. "Let's see. He's tall. Dark. Mysterious. The answer to many a maiden's prayer," she flippantly admitted.

"Yours, too?" He stood curiously still.

She sensed more behind the question than idle chit-chat, and she opened her mouth in denial. Yet, truthfully, each time she saw Dr. Keppler her pulse beats increased. "I don't know," she confessed. "There's something about him. . ." Her voice faded.

A shadow swept the last of the blue from Terence O'Shea's watching eyes. Surprise? Disappointment? A combination of both? "I'd best let you go get your rest," he told her and turned away.

She wanted to call him back. *Don't be a fool,* she told herself. *He's just a nice man, nothing more. Why should you care what he thinks?* Yet Lindsey watched Terence walk down the corridor, feeling she had lost something precious, something she could not even name.

Chapter 5

What do you have to report?"

"Nothing. It's too soon." The speaker clutched the phone, hating the empty warehouse and the metallic taste of fear.

"Don't make excuses."

"You want me to risk blowing my cover?"

A curse shivered in the listener's ear.

"Give me time," the low voice protested.

"Time is what we don't have. Either get results or get out and we'll put someone in who will."

"Impossible!"

The only answer was the click of the phone and then the buzzing dial tone.

———◆◈◆———

For the first few months after the advent of the new chaplain and acting hospital director, life and healing continued as usual in the Shepherd of Love.

"Not true," Lindsey muttered. Terry O'Shea's broad grin when they met never failed to bring a smile, and Bart—she stopped short. Why had he singled her out, when not only Patti but practically every single, unmarried female employee in the hospital made no secret his attentions would be welcome?

"Why me?" she asked Shina one Friday morning when Patti was on duty. The nurses sat curled up on either end of Lindsey's sofa. Shina looked like a Japanese doll in the kimono outfit she liked to wear off duty. "It can't be because I don't fall at his feet and worship. Neither do you."

"Don't sell yourself short, Lindsey." Shina's dark eyes shone with fun.

"Short I am not, small, dark, and beautiful. How come he avoids you like the Bubonic plague?"

"He didn't at first." Mischief danced in Shina's face. "He asked if I'd like to take in a concert. I thanked him, said I was sorry, but I planned to be married."

"Shina Ito, that's an outright lie. You're no more engaged than I am!" Lindsey couldn't believe it. Like Lindsey, Shina stood for the truth, the whole truth, and nothing but the truth.

"I didn't say I was engaged." She smirked. "I said I planned to be married. I do, someday, when God sends the right man along." A trill of laughter showed how delighted she felt to put one over on observant Lindsey.

"Well, I never. All this time I didn't think you had a devious bone in your body." Lindsey stared. "Just for curiosity's sake, why did you turn him down?"

Shina's laughter died. "I don't know." Her silky eyebrows drew together in a straight line. "He's handsome, courteous, dedicated—Mr. Perfect, as far as anyone knows."

"Do you know differently?"

"No." She folded her hands into the wide kimono sleeves. "I guess I just can't forget the villain in that silly book. Until the last chapter, no one knew he was anything but respectable, but it turned out he led an outlaw gang that plundered and left havoc in their wake. I've even prayed about my aversion. Patti's right, you know. Distrusting someone because of his name is totally unchristian." She sighed. "You were out with him last night. What's he really like, other than attentive?" She sent a meaningful glance at the enormous bouquet of yellow, gold, and orange dahlias and mums on a nearby table.

"I don't know," Lindsey admitted. "He's asked me out so many times I finally ran out of excuses. Besides, yesterday he stopped me in the hall and wanted to know why I kept turning him down."

"Why did you?"

"Who knows? Maybe because I read the same western you did."

Shina's soft laugh rewarded her, but Lindsey grimaced. "It didn't help when he asked pointblank if I found him repulsive."

Shina sat up straight and her mouth dropped open. "What did you do?"

"What does any dumbfounded person do? I just shook my head." She paused, remembering the triumph that had showed on the handsome face.

"Don't stop now," Shina ordered.

"Dr. Keppler flashed his famous smile and said, 'Good. I'll pick you up at seven. Don't claim you have to work. I checked the schedule.'" Her friend gasped but Lindsey went on. "You haven't heard anything yet. He started away, turned on his heel, and said, 'You'll want to dress up. I have reservations at the Space Needle restaurant.'"

"Really? My goodness, I take a day off to visit my parents and look what happens. What did you wear?" A cloud came to her face. "Does Patti know?"

"I wore the turquoise sheath I bought for last year's staff Christmas party. Patti helped me get ready." Lindsey knew her troubled feelings reflected in her face. "I saw it bothered her, but she's a good sport. She kept telling me I'd have a wonderful time and she insisted on lending me that short fake fur jacket of hers. Good thing, too. These fall evenings are getting chillier every night."

After a long, silent moment she added, "The weird thing is, I did have a good time. Bart Keppler is everything an escort should be. He knows all the niceties, such as having me tell him what I wanted before he ordered for me, serving me bread, all the stuff Patti dotes on. He's sophisticated, charming, able to make even my tired pulse beat a little faster." She yawned and snuggled deeper into the sofa's welcoming depths.

"And today the gorgeous flowers came."

"I'm too comfortable to move but if you want gorgeous, look in the fridge."

Shina uncurled herself and ducked into the kitchenette. She reappeared a moment later carrying a clear florist's box, a delighted expression on her face. "Ooo, they are exquisite." She opened the box and gently withdrew a spray of dainty white orchids held with a knot of silver ribbon. "Lindsey, Dr. Keppler must really want to make an impression." She cocked her shining dark head to one side. "Did he ask you out again?"

"For tomorrow."

"Are you going?" Shina eyed her curiously.

"Yes, but I won't be alone with him." She grinned at Shina's mystified look. "At breakfast yesterday, Terence O'Shea put in a bid. He, Patti, and I had been talking about the outdoors. We told him how much we loved to hike. He promptly said the nights have been cold enough on Mount Rainier to make the leaves spectacular and would we go with him on Saturday. No glacier climbing, or anything like that. Just some of the forest and meadow trails. You're invited, too. Terence said, 'Don't forget to ask your pretty friend.' "

Shina blushed. "How did Dr. Keppler get in on it?" She made a wry face. "I just can't bring myself to call him Bart."

"A psychiatrist would have a field day with you," Lindsey callously told her. "Anyway, when I mentioned the trip, Bart promptly said he'd been wanting to hike the mountain and see the color. He added that if we didn't mind, he would join us. Want to come? If it will make you more comfortable, we'll ask one of your stag line to even the number."

"Thanks, but I'm on duty." Shina took the orchids back to the fridge and returned to her place on the sofa. "Lindsey, how do you think this is going to work out?" Uncertainty lurked in her dark eyes. "Dr. Keppler has dated Patti several times. I'm afraid she's infatuated, if not genuinely in love with him."

"I hope not, but I agree. With every other man she admired, Patti always chattered incessantly about how wonderful he was. Not this time. Except for when he first came, she hasn't mentioned him. If his name happens to come up, she changes the subject. It really concerns me."

Shina folded her arms back into her kimono sleeves. "On the other hand," she slowly said, "it might be the best thing in the world. If he has made her think she is special to him—and men like him usually do—the fact he took you to such an expensive place and sent flowers is bound to set her wondering. Those outsize blue eyes may appear candid and childlike, but they hide a keen brain and are a lot more observant than people who don't know her well ever guess. A whole day spent with him, you, and Terence may enlighten her a lot, especially if Dr. Keppler can't resist the opportunity to impress you."

"You may be right, but I wish he hadn't asked to go." Normally cheerful, Lindsey knew she sounded sullen, but she didn't care one bit.

"We may be doing him a grave injustice," Shina remarked. "Perhaps he simply likes women and is trying not to play favorites."

"Maybe he's just trying to date as many as he can in the time he's here."

"Any idea how long that might be?"

Lindsey remained quiet so long Shina repeated the question.

"I don't know. Bart said last night he heard the director wasn't doing quite so well as before. Evidently the board of directors indicated Bart might be needed here longer than they thought at first."

The sound of the door opening cut short their conversation. Patti, perky in an orchid pantsuit uniform, bounced in. Her smile-wreathed face successfully masked whatever troubles or hurt she might secretly carry. "No fair, Shina. I'll bet Lindsey's told you all about her date." She dropped into a recliner and tilted both her chin and the leg rest skyward. "Well, she can just start over."

"What are you doing off duty, anyway?" Lindsey wanted to know.

"For some strange reason Outpatient got really quiet. The charge nurse gave me the afternoon off. She said I deserved it, what with the extra shifts I worked when she had to be gone. Now give," she sternly ordered.

In a surprising few words Lindsey gave the gist of her evening, omitting the conversation in the hospital corridor. Shina brought out the florist's box. If Patti felt envious, she hid it well. "Whew, orchids even. He said it to me with gardenias." She giggled and her friends exchanged a glance of relief. This was more like the old Patti.

"Did Dr. Keppler tell you he'd be joining us tomorrow?" Lindsey cut to the heart of the situation and watched the blond nurse carefully.

"Uh-huh. Nice, huh?" She couldn't have sounded less caring than if she'd learned one of the stuffed animals from Pediatrics was accompanying them. "When do we leave? Shina, are you coming?"

"Early." "No, I'm working," they chorused. Shina rose. "Time for lunch."

"Not I." Lindsey yawned. "I had a huge breakfast. I traded for swing shift and need some beauty sleep before heading to Surgery, my home away from home."

"Think it will help?" Patti teased.

Again Shina and Lindsey's glances met. Shina gave a quick thumbs-up behind Patti's back before she went out. Nothing too serious could be weighing on their friend's mind when she joked like that.

Lindsey had no time to brood over undercurrents that evening. After a quiet afternoon, Surgery turned into a madhouse, one of those occasions the staff dreaded yet knew inevitably came. "Road construction, big events at the sports complex and Seattle Center, and impatient people don't mix," the chief surgeon announced when two more accident cases came up from Emergency. "Neither do driving, booze, and tailgating. We'll be lucky to save this one."

Lindsey blinked hard and took three deep breaths. Her righteous anger helped restore her control. The woman on the table whose life hung in precarious balance had not been drinking. Neither had her husband. Yet as so often happened, their compliance with every law of the road failed to protect them. The other driver's blood alcohol had tested far above the legal limit, accounting for his careening the wrong way onto a one-way street. His truck struck the older couple's subcompact head-on; he escaped unhurt. The husband ended up with minor injuries, but the wife had received serious head wounds.

Please, God, help us do our best. How many times had she offered the prayer? How many times had she privately agonized, even while keeping hands steady and mind alert to anticipate a surgeon's needs? They seldom had to ask for an instrument when Nurse Lindsey Best stood by the operating table. No thought of self or the passing of time intruded.

When the last patient had been cared for and sent to ward or ICU, Lindsey glanced at the clock. After midnight. Bone weary, still she rejoiced.

Thanks to God and a dedicated staff, no sheet-covered patient would go from Surgery to the morgue this night.

Lindsey shed her soiled scrubs, washed her hands, and climbed into clean clothes, feeling hollow from skipping supper. She stepped into the hall and found Terence O'Shea waiting for her. "You here? Is our hike off?"

"That's what I wanted to ask you. Will you be too tired?" He looked far older than his years, his jaw set in a grim line. "It's been quite a night."

"I'll be fine." She yawned. "What's it like in Emergency?"

"Bad. Two DOAs—teenagers on their way home from a victory bash." He sounded depressed. "This is the worst part of my new job, talking with parents whose hearts are breaking. It's so hard to know what to say that can make a difference."

Lindsey laid one hand on his arm. "Just being there to listen may be the best you can offer."

He gratefully covered her hand with his own. "I know. Just the way you're listening to me when I needed to spill out my feelings."

His eyes had gone from stormy gray to gentle blue; something she saw in them caught at her heart. Lindsey smiled. "If we're going hiking tomorrow, no, today, we'd better get some sleep."

"Right." He released her hand. A wary look crept into his steady gaze. "We want to be able to keep up with our acting hospital director." He sounded like a small, subdued boy.

Lindsey impulsively said, "I didn't invite him."

"You didn't?" Terence looked startled.

"He said he wanted to see the leaves and hoped we wouldn't mind if he joined us." She felt herself redden. Why on earth had she felt she needed to explain?

The radiance in the young chaplain's face more than repaid her confusion. "Thanks, Lindsey." He didn't say for what, but his hard grip on her hand made her fingers tingle. "May I see you home?"

She nodded and bit her tongue to keep from blurting out that he sounded like the olden days, when gentlemen quaintly asked permission to accompany young ladies to their dwelling places. Deep inside she liked it. The expression fit him, just like the courteous little bow he always gave women when he met them.

"I'm really looking forward to tomorrow," he told her when they reached her apartment. "It's been several years since I got to do any climbing on our mountain. It's one of the things I missed while I was in—"

"Lindsey, is that you?" Patti flung open the door. "Hi, Terence. We're still on for tomorrow, aren't we? You won't be too tired, Lindsey?" Concern for her roommate warred with eagerness for the outing.

"I'll be fine after a few hours sleep."

Terence laughed, the rollicking laugh that automatically made others smile in sympathy with his exuberance. "I'm out of here. Oh, I think Dr. Keppler said seven? He assumed you'd want to have breakfast here."

"Yes." Patti frowned. "Oh dear, I meant to pack a lunch."

"You don't have to. Dad volunteered. He's a great cook, so don't stuff down too much breakfast," Terence warned. Crinkles appeared at the corners of his sparkling eyes. "Although if you get as hungry as I do, we'll be more than ready for lunch no matter how much breakfast we eat."

Morning came clear and crisp, Seattle September at its best. Lindsey and Patti donned jeans, T-shirts, heavy socks, and walking shoes. "Which color?" Patti held up red and blue zip-front sweatshirts with hoods. "It's going to be cold this morning."

"Either. I'm wearing navy. It doesn't show the dirt." Lindsey slipped into the fleece-lined garment and caught her hair back into a short ponytail.

"Good idea. I will, too, if you don't mind us looking like the Bobbsey Twins."

"Sure, with me four inches taller and red-haired."

"Hey, you're speaking of the roommate I love." Patti came to the doorway, navy sweatshirt in one hand. "Did God ever make a more beautiful day?"

"It's great, all right." Lindsey ran a lipstick over her mouth and pronounced herself ready.

Terence arrived halfway through breakfast and repeated his warning about not overeating. "Dad outdid himself on lunch," he boasted.

Patti looked at the steaming cinnamon rolls on the buffet and plaintively asked, "You mean I have to turn down a second roll?"

"Third," Lindsey heartlessly reminded her.

"Only if you don't care for nut bread, fried chicken, ripe tomatoes and lettuce from our garden, and juicy peach turnovers that melt in your mouth," Terence solemnly told her. "Dad packed the chicken in ice and we fixed it so I can carry it in my backpack."

"Then I'll pass up seconds. Okay, thirds." Patti grimaced at Lindsey.

"So will I. That sounds wonderful, O'Shea." Dr. Keppler's hearty approval held nothing of patronage. "This is going to be a day to remember. I feel it in my bones." He laughed and his dark eyes shone. In his black sweatshirt and jeans he looked taller and more handsome than ever, but not at all mysterious.

By contrast, Terence's mahogany hair gleamed above a hunter green sweatshirt and khaki pants. He looked far more rested than at midnight the night before and his eyes glowed with anticipation.

Lindsey's heart gave the little lurch she'd experienced before. When Bart smiled that way, she could see why he dazzled Patti. She felt color come to her face and hastily said, "If my esteemed friend is through ogling the cinnamon rolls, we can go."

Terence forestalled a scathing remark from Patti by whispering, "You may have an extra turnover. Dad sent enough so that if we got caught out overnight we wouldn't starve."

A flash of something strangely akin to fear came to Bart's eyes. "There's no danger of such a thing, is there?"

Terence looked surprised. "Of course not. I've hiked the trails for years and we aren't climbing the mountain itself."

"I didn't think so. It's just that there have been some fatal accidents on Mount Rainier recently." The next moment Bart reverted to his usual, suave self, and the hiking party headed out toward Terence's station wagon.

Patti sniffed ecstatically when Terence unlocked the wagon. She announced, "I'm sitting right in front of the lunch. Coming, Bart?" Intent on getting into the rear seat, she didn't notice Keppler's almost imperceptible hesitation, his fleeting glance at Lindsey. The next instant he said, "Right, Patti," and stepped into the wagon, leaving a disturbed Lindsey to crawl into the front seat. In that split second, she determined to cling to Terence like a leech and give the flirtatious doctor no cause for soulful glances that both attracted and upset her.

Chapter 6

Terence O'Shea smiled to himself, inordinately pleased at the flicker of annoyance on Lindsey's expressive face. His keen eyes had seen Dr. Keppler's slight hesitation, his fleeting glance toward the surgical nurse, before he climbed into the rear seat of the station wagon next to Patti. A wave of actual dislike for his superior swept through Terence. Remorse followed. Fine thing, the chaplain of a hospital dedicated to Christlike service entertaining the insane and unfounded desire to punch out its hospital director.

He was humbled by the realization of how far short he fell of the man he longed to be. God had a big job on His hands, taming the legendary O'Shea temper that flared without warning, sometimes with disastrous results. There had been enough incidents during Terence's growing-up years to show the futility of settling things with his fists.

"Never refuse to fight when you are in the right," Dad had taught his son. "Just be mindful of three things. First, make sure you are in the right. Second, never allow your opponent the choice of weapons." His blue eyes grew serious. "Third and most important, don't waste your energy on little things. Save it to fight the real battles such as hunger, poverty, prejudice, injustice."

It took time for the hotheaded boy to realize his best defense was a good offense. When verbally attacked, he never backed down. Instead, he folded his arms across his chest, threw back his head—and laughed in his tormentor's face. Nine times out of ten, others around him took it up, to the dismay of the would-be bully. On a few occasions it didn't work and he ending up walloping someone.

His lips twitched at the memory. Each time, it had taken only one licking to convince his adversary not to cross the invisible line Terence set. He sighed. If only Satan, the greatest adversary, could be whipped once and for all!

Patti's charming voice recalled him to the present when she gave a little bounce on the backseat and said, "I can hardly wait to get to the mountain."

Terence could see her eager face in his rearview mirror. A moment later, he took his gaze from the road and glanced at Lindsey. Patti's anticipation was also reflected in her eyes. How changeable their color! He had seen them brilliant with laughter, darker when she wore yellow, hazel with deep thought. Today they shone green with tiny brown specks. Rich color flowed into her smooth cheeks and her tiny freckles looked golden against her clear skin. His heart thumped. *I like her*, he silently told himself. *I like her height, the way she walks as if she owns the world, her laughing voice, her compassion and caring.*

"You should enjoy the scenery along the way instead of wishing you were there," Lindsey softly said to Patti.

"Yes, Mother." Patti didn't sound at all reproved. "Oh, look!" She pointed out the window toward an eagle wheeling in the morning sky. "How free and unshackled. No wonder our country chose the eagle for our national bird." She spoiled the moment by giggling. "I read that they almost selected a turkey. Wouldn't that have been awful?"

A lazy discussion followed, ending when Terence asked, "Bart, have you ever been to Mount Rainier?"

"No. In fact, I'd never been in Washington until this summer."

"How did you happen to choose our state?" Patti wanted to know.

"Heard Shepherd of Love needed an acting director and figured I could do a great deal of good." He broke off and peered from the window. "Is that another eagle?"

Terence heard Lindsey's slight choking sound before Patti exclaimed, "You need a short course in bird-ology. That's not the word, but I can't remember the real one."

"Ornithology," Lindsey supplied.

"Right. Anyway, that's a crow, not an eagle," Patti said. "You have a real treat in store, Bart. Although Lindsey disagrees with me, the very first hike you take on Mount Rainier is the best."

"Why do you think otherwise?" Bart challenged Lindsey.

She stared through the window, and Terence shot her another lightning glance. Her mobile face had taken on a dreaming look. "I'm like my grandmother, I guess. Someone asked her why she bothered to read books a second or even third time. The questioner insisted there was no joy in reading a story when you knew what would happen." A gentle smile curved her lips.

"What did your grandmother say?" Terence inquired. He felt rather than saw her shift her body in the seat belt until she faced him more squarely.

"She said she always enjoyed a journey more when she knew the destination."

"Good for her!" Terence approved. His merry laugh rang out.

"I guess she does have a point," Patti conceded. "If we didn't know how great it was on Mount Rainier we probably wouldn't be going."

"We could take someone else's word," Bart told her. "As we have to do with the Almighty. I mean, none of us have seen or heard for ourselves."

Why should the simple statement make Terence's hackles rise? What the self-invited hiking guest said was often true. Or was it an undercurrent of amusement in the smooth voice that annoyed him more than what Bart said? Unwilling to comment for fear he would show his feelings, Terence remained silent and concentrated on his driving. Even this early, enough traffic surrounded them to require his attention. Others evidently had also chosen to take advantage of the lovely day.

Lindsey turned her head toward the backseat. "Don't forget—even the courts of law accept as truth whatever is sworn to by several eyewitnesses. People saw God through Jesus. Others through the ages heard Him speak. Those of us who haven't actually seen or heard can seek Him and receive a witness of the truth in our hearts and souls."

Terence held his breath, wondering how Keppler would reply.

"You're right, of course. It is, however, easier to believe in that which you can see, hear, or touch." He laughed. "How did we get so serious, anyway? This is too grand a day to get into a theological discussion. How long before we get to where we start climbing, Terence?"

"Not for awhile." Terence grinned at Lindsey, who raised one eyebrow and shrugged. "There's plenty to see along the way, however. This early in the morning we're likely to find deer out, especially once we get off the freeway and onto the back roads."

His prediction proved accurate. Twice before they actually entered Mount Rainier National Park and several times after, graceful deer stepped from the brush alongside the road. One doe bounded across in front of them, causing Patti to squeal for fear they would hit her. Others simply stopped chewing, observed the station wagon and its occupants, and resumed grazing or daintily walked back into the forest.

"What I'd give for a gun right now," Bart exclaimed.

"It wouldn't do you any good. It isn't hunting season and the deer in the park are protected, anyway," Terence told him.

"I can't imagine shooting such a beautiful creature." Patti sounded disappointed the doctor would make such a remark.

"You eat meat, don't you?"

"Domestic animals, not those from the wild."

"My dear child, there's no difference." He laughed at her. "They're just animals, created to provide food for humans."

"There's a difference," she insisted, to Terence's surprise. Patti treated the doctor with such awe, Terence would have surmised she wouldn't contradict anything he said. She went on. "I don't mind if a hunter uses the meat, the way the Native Americans did. But many don't. They kill a deer, take the head and horns, maybe a haunch, and leave the rest to rot. It's wicked."

"I agree. Besides, I can find enough meat right in the supermarket," Lindsey put in. "What does our chaplain have to say?"

He waited to make a right turn into a sun-dappled road. Branches interlaced above them, giving a tunnellike atmosphere. "I'm with you, girls. Dad and I've hunted and enjoyed it, but we feel its criminal to do so unless you plan to use the meat. Too many hungry people in the world for that. When I was in—"

"Stop!" Lindsey interrupted.

He slammed on the brakes, accompanied by backseat cries of "What's happening?"

"Something moved at the side of the road. An animal." Lindsey stared out the front window. "See, there it is."

Bart leaned forward, one arm draped over the back of the front seat where Lindsey sat. She promptly scooted forward, as if to see better. Terence grinned. "What is it? A dog?" the doctor wanted to know.

"A fox!" Patti whispered. "Isn't he beautiful?"

Terence felt a thrill go through him. "I've seen many coyotes but not many foxes." He gazed at the bushy-tailed animal. "Look at the protective coloration." The orange-red fox with white biblike fur on throat and front blended into the pile of fallen leaves in which it crouched. The fox's unblinking gray-green gaze never left the station wagon.

"Look at the sharp snout and large, pointed ears," Terence said. "Foxes have fantastic hearing and an incredible sense of smell. Would you believe red foxes can hear a mouse squeak over a hundred feet away?"

For several minutes, fox and humans observed each other. The appearance of a car coming toward the wagon disrupted the scene. In a flash, the lovely creature leaped, whirled, and tore off into the forest at the side of the road.

"They are so fast!" Patti gasped.

"Their speed makes them good hunters." Terence took his foot from the brake. "That and their ability to creep silently."

"Does that mean you hate foxes, Patti?" Bart removed his arm from the front seat and leaned back. Terence saw Lindsey relax back into place, and he grinned again.

———◆◆◆———

Two hours later they paused after a hard climb up switchbacks that had left them panting. "Either this trail is new, has grown steeper since the last time I came, or I'm a lot more out of shape than I realized," Lindsey confessed.

"Same here, but what's waiting for us will be worth it."

Patti said between panting, "I'm not sure if I can make it."

"Of course you can," Terence told her. "Don't look ahead at how far we have to go." He laid one hand on her shoulder and gently turned Patti so she faced the series of switchbacks they had just climbed. "Concentrate on how far we've come."

The others also turned. "I wouldn't have believed it." Bart mopped his sweaty forehead. "That's—it can't be the station wagon! It looks like a toy car."

"There's a sermon in what you just said, Terry." Patti grinned impishly. "The next time I get discouraged and feel I'm not getting anywhere on life's rocky road, I'll remember to turn around and see how far I am from where I started." Her face showed she meant every word and even Bart Keppler didn't comment.

Another half hour of walking and Terence announced they'd stop for lunch just ahead. "There's a certain meadow that offers what I consider one of the most awe-inspiring views in the world," he promised. Step after weary step they followed, Lindsey just behind him, Patti and Dr. Keppler following. The trail emerged from the forest and leveled onto a small plateau at the edge of a meadow that sloped upward toward a stand of dark, guarding trees.

Terence slipped out of his backpack, motioned his party to stop, and breathed a prayer of thankfulness when no one spoke. Stillness matched their surroundings. Never had he seen the mountainside more dramatic. The snowy glaciers and gray rock of majestic Mount Rainier stood etched against a blue, blue sky. The meadow preened itself in yellow, orange, and scarlet dress. Even the grass and ground cover flamed crimson and gold from frosty nights, as though determined to flaunt itself in a last, mad, autumn blaze before fading to nothingness beneath the winter snows. Spruce, alpine fir, and other evergreens proudly raised branches in shades of green.

At first Terence heard nothing but the pounding of his heart, the hard breathing of his companions. Gradually, they quieted, and he tuned in to the sounds and feel of creation: lazy air currents that cooled his hot face and made bushes rustle; the hum of insects; a warbling bird; the swish of falling leaves. Peace entered his heart.

He turned to survey his companions. Patti had chosen to sit and lean back against a downed log that had once been a mighty forest monarch. Her rapt, upturned face and blond hair captured the sunlight. Terence found himself silently praying she might ever walk in the light. The intensity of his petition shocked him. Why should he feel compelled to silently cry out on Patti's behalf, here in this place of peace and contentment?

Terence shifted his gaze toward Bart Keppler, sitting next to her. He tried to read the closed face, to peer deep inside the inscrutable dark eyes that gave no clue to his present thoughts, no betrayal of his feelings or reaction to the beauty before him. Sneaking admiration filled Terence. He had half expected Bart to complain or ask for special consideration during the climb. Bart did not, even though at times he panted like a fox running from hounds. Though he was hot and disheveled, with twigs in his hair from ducking his tall form beneath overhanging trees, he had merely set his lips and kept going. Had Terence misjudged him?

Saving the best for last, the young chaplain surveyed Lindsey. She had walked a few paces away from the others and stood with her hands behind her. He believed she had forgotten the others' presence. From his position a little to one side, Terence saw exaltation in her face, similar to the expression Patti wore, but more pronounced. He averted his gaze, feeling he had unconsciously intruded on a moment between Lindsey and her God.

He could not help looking again. Kinship he seldom felt with anyone except Dad sprang full blown within him when a single diamond drop hovered on her long lashes. How often he had experienced the same sense of wonder.

Did Lindsey feel his regard? Perhaps, for she slowly turned her head and gazed into his face. Terence trembled. Would she resent his intensity? Awareness crept into her watching eyes but no condemnation followed. Rather, he saw the bewildered look of an awakening soul that does not fully understand what has pierced its tranquillity.

He involuntarily took a step toward her. An amused voice stopped him. "Wonderful as this is, I must admit hunger pangs are rapidly depreciating my ability to admire the flora and fauna." Dr. Keppler laughed ruefully. "You were right, Terence. Memory of breakfast has vanished like a zephyr."

His remarks, although spoken in pleasant tones, clanged in Terence's ears like a cymbal. Was the acting director totally insensitive to the feelings of others? A gleam in the doctor's eyes roused suspicion. Was it just the opposite? While Terence had been watching Lindsey, Keppler could well have been observing both of them and decided to break in. *Don't get paranoid*, Terence told himself. His irrepressible sense of humor came to his rescue. *Maybe the guy's just a jerk. Or hungry, the way he said.*

Terence threw down a plastic tarp from his backpack and they sat cross-legged in a circle, the bounteous lunch in the middle. If Bart had designs on a certain redheaded surgical nurse, he didn't let them show. He kept up a rapid-fire line of questions about Shepherd of Love Hospital that triggered a lively discussion. "I need to learn everything I can before instituting changes," he said frankly.

"What kind of changes?" Patti asked, waving a drumstick like a baton. "We like things the way we are."

"Oh, there's always room for improvement. For instance, is it necessary to require staff members to attend the prayer services before each shift? Don't get me wrong," he hastily added. "I'm just wondering if we wouldn't attract a lot of excellent staff members—in addition to those we already have—" he nodded at each of them, "—if they could choose whether to attend. After all, a person's religion should be his or her own, not subject to direction in order to hold a job."

"The whole concept of Shepherd of Love, as I understand it, is to combine medical skills with spiritual support," Terence put in. "Isn't this right?"

Patti nodded and Lindsey soberly said, "It's what makes us different from other hospitals. Hiring only Christians is one of the foundations on which the hospital is built." A niggling worry crept into her eyes.

"Yet there are many other sincere persons who could complement our staff," Bart pointed out. "I'm speaking as something of an outsider, of course, but isn't there a danger of the hospital becoming ingrown, or intolerant of others who believe differently?"

"No one forces patients to accept Christianity," Patti protested. She dropped the drumstick and wiped her fingers on a napkin Shane O'Shea had thoughtfully provided. "No one makes them come or stay in Shepherd of Love, either." She stared reproachfully at Dr. Keppler.

He backtracked. "I'm sure I didn't mean to criticize." He bowed his head and when he glanced up he looked chastened. "I just want to do my very best to give the hospital what I believe it most deserves."

Terence couldn't determine whether Bart's expression was reminiscent of Uriah Heep—or whether the look of contrition stemmed from true humility. He forced himself to say, "That's what we all want. Now, who wants to do what?"

"I ate so much lunch, I need to climb some more." Bart stood and smiled his charming smile. "Which of you two young ladies is going with me? Terence, how about you?"

"I'll go." Patti jumped up, eager as a puppy waiting to be petted.

"Lindsey?" A curious glint came to his eyes.

"Thanks, but after last night in Surgery, all this fresh air, sunlight, and good food, I think I'll just sit on the tarp and use the log for a backrest."

"I'll stay and protect her from marauding bears," Terence said.

"Good heavens, there's no danger of that, is there?" Bart looked alarmed.

"Stay on the trail and you shouldn't have a problem." Terence glanced at his watch. "Don't be gone much more than an hour. We have a long hike down and it gets dark earlier than you might think, especially in the forest."

"Okay, Boss." Bart saluted smartly and brought his heels together in a quick snap. "Anything else?"

Terence couldn't help laughing at the tomfoolery. "Holler if you need us."

Bart sent a laughing glance toward Lindsey, then said, "Come on, Patti." Swinging hands, they started across the meadow and up the sloping hillside.

"He's a curious combination, isn't he?" Lindsey's statement so paralleled Terence's, he hesitated and she quickly added, "I shouldn't have said that. Forget it, please. How are your chaplain's duties going?" She stretched out on one side of the tarp, arms behind her head to pillow them against the log.

He began to tell her, but before long the elements she'd mentioned earlier did their work well. Lindsey's eyelids closed, fluttered, closed again. Terence smiled. She needed the rest. For a long time he savored the day, then his own short night caught up with him and he, too, fell asleep.

Chapter 7

Lindsey slowly opened her eyes. Terence O'Shea sat slumped against the far end of the fallen log, mahogany hair rumpled and face as innocent as that of a sleeping child. The sight brought a smile to Lindsey's lips. The young chaplain didn't set her heart to fluttering, but she felt good knowing she had such a friend.

For a few moments she remained still, remembering the look that passed between them earlier. Warmth stole into her face and her breath came a little quicker. She had seen something more than friendship in Terry's eyes.

Wide awake now, her nerves twanged. Something felt wrong. She cocked her head and listened. Nothing. Not even the sound of a bird. Where were Bart and Patti? She looked up, noted how low the sun had fallen in the rosy sky, and checked her watch. Alarm filled her.

A full two hours had gone by since Patti and Bart left.

She crawled to the other end of the log. "Terry, wake up! Patti and Bart haven't come back."

He opened sleepy eyes, yawned, and peered into the sky. "Good grief, what time is it?" He sat up and rubbed his eyes.

"More than an hour since you told them to be back. Something must have happened." She reached for the sweatshirt she'd tossed aside earlier in the day. Its fleecy warmth felt good to skin cooled by the dying day. If only she had a fleece to warm her heart.

The last of sleep fled from Terry's eyes and he hastily stood. "Come on. We'll go find them." Lindsey saw the way he glanced at the sun, perched like a giant red pompom on the crest of a distant ridge. Apprehension grayed his eyes, but he smiled at her. "They probably just aren't paying attention to the time. Remember, Keppler's a newcomer to this area."

Patti isn't. The unspoken words hung in the rapidly chilling air. Terence reached down a hand and Lindsey sprang to her feet. "At least we have plenty of food." Her voice sounded loud in the stillness, but thank goodness it didn't tremble. She wished she'd kept still, though; no need to remind Terence of his laughing statement earlier about being well fed in the unlikely event they got caught outside longer than they'd planned.

Terence sharply told her, "We aren't staying out overnight. We're going to locate the others and hightail it out of here as fast as we can. We should have enough time. Besides, Dad would never make up a pack without including a flashlight—and matches, of course." He dug in the backpack and triumphantly waved both items, then snatched up his sweatshirt along with the sweatshirts that belonged to the other two.

"We can't very well start a forest fire just to let people know we're here," Lindsey told him. She laughed in spite of herself and rejoiced when an answering smile curved Terence's lips.

"Ready?" he asked.

"Ready." Following just behind him, she swung into the trail that led through the meadow and grew into a slope. Bart and Patti had trampled down the tall grass and weeds on their climb, so the two searchers made good time. When they reached the top of the nearest rise, Terence cupped his hands around his mouth and shouted, "Bart. Patti."

Bart. Patti. The hills took up the cry. It echoed in the forest and valley below.

Lindsey joined her voice with his. On the third try, they got a response. Far above a faint call of "Here" floated downward to where they stood.

"Are you all right?" Lindsey screamed.

All right. First an echo, then a human cry.

Lindsey sagged with relief. Terence bounded upward. She scrambled after him but had to stop for rest. "Don't wait for me," she pleaded.

He gave her a measuring glance. "Sure you'll be all right?"

"Of course." She panted like a dog, something her father had taught her the very first time the family went for a long hike.

"Back soon," he promised and went on.

She watched him until the path beaten by the other two turned and he vanished from sight. When she had caught her breath, she hurried after him; ears made keen by concern caught Terence's intermittent shouts and their responses. They sounded much nearer now. "Thank You, God." Her strangled prayer came out sounding more like a sob and she quickened her pace.

Ten minutes later, Lindsey again stood on a small, level plateau between two folds of the hills. She gulped in breaths of air and prepared for another climb. Each hill got steeper than the one before. She would need all her energy to forge ahead. How had Bart and Patti managed these steep hills? "They had a lot longer to do it," she muttered. Setting her lips into a firm line that boded no good for the tardy members of the party, she squinted upward. Two gigantic rocks marked the crest of the next rise. Lindsey cast an imploring glance at the reluctant sun hanging onto the remnants of day, then fixed her gaze on the rocks and stepped forward.

The muscles in her legs tightened from exertion. She ignored them and went on, hoping by the time she reached the rocks the others would also be there. A quarter of the way up. Halfway. Three-quarters. She straightened, rubbed her aching leg muscles, and stretched her arms to relieve the cramp in her shoulders.

How still it was! She could be a million miles from another human being. Even though she knew better, the thought plagued her, and she took a step forward.

An awful groaning sound, as if the world felt pain too harsh to bear silently, screeched in her ears. The ground on which she stood shook. Every warning about the massive earthquake seismologists insisted would hit Seattle and the Cascades flashed into Lindsey's mind, faster than the speed of sound. The Big One—and she and her friends were caught in a place as dangerous as downtown Seattle would be should the skyscrapers begin to sway! The noise and shaking continued for what felt like hours but could only be milliseconds. "Please, God, no!" Paralyzing horror gave way to rigid training in how to cope with emergencies.

In one frenzied leap, Lindsey instinctively vaulted to the side of the path and wrapped her arms around a sturdy tree trunk. She burrowed into the needle-covered ground as best she could and buried her face in her arms. A fusillade of debris assaulted her body. Numb and unable to think, she clung to her frail shield against nature and waited.

The rumble became a roar. A mighty wind battered Lindsey's eardrums with its thunder. She felt the breath of it fan her exposed hands, stir her hair. An explosion so loud it forced a scream from her constricted throat told her death stood at her shoulder. She rocked from its impact, hands locked around the tree, knowing only a brief time lay between her and final destruction.

The noise lessened. Stopped. Afraid to move, Lindsey lay motionless. A minute. Two. She raised her head and experimentally twisted her neck. Nothing broken. She opened her eyes to meet a sympathetic ray of sunlight's gleam. Her dazed senses adjusted. The earthquake had passed.

Lindsey unclamped her hands, found them covered with oozing pitch, and literally tore them free. Ecstasy at simply being alive filled her, followed by the sickening knowledge the others might not have fared so well.

"Lindsey?"

The sound of her name overwhelmed her with relief. She tried to call out and discovered her mouth was filled with needles and dirt. She spit them out and managed a feeble, "Here."

Two strong arms circled her half-reclining body. "Thank God!"

"Don't move her," a sharp voice ordered. "She has to be checked for injuries."

For some absurd reason, Lindsey wanted to cry when the security of that pair of arms fell away. "I'm all right." She rolled over and looked first into Terence's chalky face, then Bart Keppler's. "Patti?" A fresh wave of fear surged through her. "Where is she?"

"I'm here," a weak voice whispered. A wet drop splashed on Lindsey's upturned face. "Oh, Lindsey, can you ever forgive me? You could have been killed and it would have been my fault!" A shower followed.

"If you don't stop bawling all over me, I'm going to die by drowning," Lindsey crossly said. "Let me up, will you?" Aware she must be a total mess, she brushed them aside. "For goodness' sake, stop crying, Patti. You may be responsible for a lot of things, but causing an earthquake isn't one of them."

Relief softened her voice. "I–I thought you were all dead."

"Dead?"

"Earthquake?"

"What are you talking about?"

Thoroughly disgusted, Lindsey glared at the three astonished faces. "What's wrong with you all? The Big One that's been predicted for decades comes and you act like you never heard the word earthquake?"

"There was no earthquake, Lindsey." Patti's mouth quivered above her trembling chin.

"Have you gone daft?" she gasped. "No earthquake! What do you call that little performance a few minutes ago?"

Terence lifted her to her feet. Not a trace of blue showed in his eyes. He gently turned her and pointed. "Down there."

She stared at him suspiciously, then shifted her gaze to a canyon far below. An enormous boulder lay amidst the wreckage of shattered small trees and an upheaval of earth. Dust still rose from where it landed. Lindsey whirled, looked above her. Only one prehistoric-looking stone rested where two had been just a few minutes earlier. The sight made her dizzy, and she clutched at Terence's arm for support. "I don't understand."

"Something caused it to fall. You were directly in its path." His nostrils quivered; the skin across his cheekbones looked tight-drawn, as if he were holding in deep emotion. "Bart, Patti, and I met beyond the first bend on the other side of the crest." He passed a hand over his face as if to blot out the shadow of memory.

"We saw the stone begin to move," Bart explained through bloodless lips. "We ran toward it but could do nothing. When I saw you were in its path, I—"

"Thank God you leaped out of the way," Terence said in a voice so hoarse Lindsey had trouble catching his words.

"If Bart and I hadn't gone so far, it wouldn't have happened," Patti brokenly said. More tears spilled and she flung her arms around Lindsey.

"I don't understand. Why would the boulder suddenly dislodge and hurl itself down the mountain?" Lindsey puzzled. "I've been here before, although not for some time. I've even sat on those stones. They were always sturdy as the Rock of Gibraltar."

"Erosion, perhaps, or the ground may have been softened by rain or snow." Bart's pallor didn't lift. "Terence, if Lindsey isn't hurt, hadn't we better go?" Lindsey's gaze followed his to the ever-lowering sun.

"Yes. If we hurry, we should just about make it. It won't take nearly as long going down as coming up." He led the way back to the lunch site. In short order, they silently folded the tarp, made sure they'd left no trash, and set out single-file in the order they came.

Not for anything would Lindsey admit how shaken she had been. "And it isn't all from the fall," she whispered to herself, so low no one could hear. "God, why did that rock really fall?" Suspicion reared its ugly head. "It–it couldn't have been loosened, could it?" An ice-water chill poured down her back and made her shudder. "If so, who?"

Patti? To believe she had either cause or physical strength to undermine a boulder—if it had been undermined—in hopes of killing her best friend was the worst kind of insanity.

Bart Keppler? What reason would Bart have for attempting to kill the nurse he obviously admired? Unless he were psychotic, the fact Lindsey had rejected his advances wouldn't trigger such a horrible act. Nothing in his demeanor hinted at mental instability. Besides, he wouldn't have had opportunity, unless he and Patti had been apart during the time they absented themselves from camp. How could she find out if they had separated for a time, especially near the rocks? Unless approached in the exact right way, Patti would be furious; in spite of her concern for Lindsey, Patti's eyes betrayed that the afternoon had strengthened her growing attraction for Dr. Keppler. She might also let slip her roommate's probing and alert the acting director.

Terence? Lindsey grinned at the thought of evil lurking behind his open face. On the other hand, of the three above her on the mountain, the young chaplain would have been the only one alone at the rocks. His comment rang in her brain. "Bart, Patti, and I met beyond the first bend on the other side of the crest." How far ahead of the last member of the party had he actually been? Would he have had time to dig around the boulder? He also was the only one of the three who knew Lindsey came along behind him.

A terrible thought occurred to Lindsey just as the weary party started down the last switchback. If the boulder had been loosened with murderous intent, only two answers were valid: Either Terence wanted to kill a certain redheaded surgical nurse, or he was the intended target, set up by Bart Keppler for some obscure reason.

Horror filled her. She choked back a cry of protest. Satan himself must be filling her heart and mind with his poison for her to allow these ghastly thoughts to linger. *Killer or victim? Killer or victim?* The words beat time to her footsteps, even though she tried to crowd them out. Intent on her battle with fear, guilt, and fatigue, she stumbled and slid a bit on the needle-covered ground before recovering herself.

"All right, Lindsey?" Terence stopped and turned toward her. Only a little light remained. Soon they would have to rely on the flashlight.

The steadiness in his eyes reassured her. She hadn't realized how deeply her doubts had entrenched themselves until she met Terry's gaze. "I'm all right."

"Good. It isn't far now. Patti, Bart, are you making it okay?"

"Uh-huh." Patti wiped her face with a tissue. "You don't happen to have some of those leftover turnovers handy enough to reach, do you?" She sounded so wistful the other three chortled, but Terence slipped the backpack off and rummaged in it.

"Patricia Thompson, you are the limit," Lindsey told her. "Can't you wait until we get to the bottom?"

"I suppose so. I just thought we could use the extra energy." Patti was obviously regaining her usual aplomb. She squealed with delight when Terry handed her a turnover. "Mmm. Even better than at lunch."

"Bart? Lindsey?"

"Sure." Keppler took the offering, but Lindsey shook her head.

"My hands are all pitchy." She hadn't realized until now how hungry she'd grown on the long hike down.

"I'll tip back the edge of the plastic wrapping and you can eat it like a taco in a napkin," Terence told her. She couldn't remember anything tasting better.

They stopped at a gas station on the way home. The understanding owner obligingly lent her a cleaner, "guaranteed to take everything off but the skin." She came from the women's room with hands spotless, although shriveled from scrubbing.

"Do you want to stop for dinner?" Terence asked.

Lindsey surveyed her filthy, disheveled clothing. "If you don't mind, I'd rather just polish off the picnic lunch and get home to a warm tub."

"I second the motion." Bart Keppler's strong, supporting voice mingled with Patti's, "Me, too—especially if there's another turnover."

"There is." Terence pulled the station wagon into a well-lighted spot not far from the gas station. "Let me see if they have hot coffee. We can use it." He walked back toward the station, cheerfully whistling, and returned with a large thermos and four thermal cups.

The liquid warmed Lindsey from the soles of her sturdily-shod feet to the crown of her filthy head. She'd combed out what debris she could in the light of the rest room mirror, but she needed a good shampoo. Once they finished the last delicious crumb, she felt sleep encroaching on her eyelids. "Will your father worry?" she mumbled.

"I called him from the station."

Terence's voice sounded like it came from a far distance. She vaguely heard Patti's soft laugh and Bart's low voice. They faded. The next thing she knew, something prodded her shoulder, and Patti ordered, "Wake up, Sleeping Beauty. We're home."

Somehow she stumbled from the station wagon. "Ugh. Every bone in my body hurts. I feel as if I slid down the mountain along with that boulder." She regretted her remark the minute it popped out. The last thing she needed was to start thinking morbid thoughts and lie awake half the night trying to solve a crime that probably had never been committed.

Dr. Keppler gallantly walked Patti to the apartment door, after a veiled glance at Lindsey, who followed with Terence. For some reason, the chaplain dawdled. His stride so little resembled his usual ground-covering pace that Lindsey wondered, *Does he have a reason? Or does he just want to give Bart the chance to kiss Patti good night?*

On impulse, she stopped, stood on tiptoe, and whispered, "Why do you think that boulder toppled and fell?"

"I don't know and there's no way to find out." He looked somber. "Perhaps it's as Keppler said. Erosion, or soft earth from rain."

"Do you really believe that?" she demanded.

"There's no reason to suspect it happened any other way." Terence faced her squarely. "I can't think of justification to believe it more than a freak accident, but—" His harsh voice sent shivers through her and he gripped her fingers until they hurt. "One thing, Lindsey. Patti and Bart are sure to mention what happened, but keep your questions to yourself. Don't mention them to anyone. Understand? Not to anyone."

He dropped her hand, turned on his heel, and walked away, a grim man, far removed from the whistling hospital chaplain whose familiar grin automatically brought cheer.

Chapter 8

Killer or victim? The words pounded in Lindsey's imagination through a long soak in the tub and far into the night, like a metronome set to eternally tick out its measured beat. What had Terence O'Shea meant by his cryptic warning? Lindsey's mind ran double track. If innocent, but suspicious, he'd certainly be concerned for her safety. If guilty, he would definitely want her to keep silent.

"He can't be a murderer," she protested into her pillow, body rigid as a soldier at attention. "Not with those eyes and that innocent face."

Not necessarily true, a little voice inside argued. *You've seen victims who trusted in persons with innocent faces that hid souls filled with evil.*

Killer or victim?

Dr. Keppler? "He couldn't have tried to kill me," Lindsey wearily whispered. She remembered the shock in his face, and a spark of hope touched her for a moment. The next instant an unpleasant truth hit her with battering ram force and suspicion flamed again.

Dr. Keppler's shock could have been to find her alive.

Or from learning the boulder had almost killed the wrong person.

Lindsey threw back her blankets and ran noiselessly to the bathroom, afraid she'd be sick. The faces of the two men danced before her: both new to Shepherd of Love Hospital; both Christians—or so it appeared. Did one of those faces hide slimy depths, an unseen motive strong enough to justify murder? If so, which one?

Her system revolted, but long, deep breaths followed by splashes of cold tap water to her face returned her stomach to normal. Clinging to a forlorn hope, she gazed into the bathroom mirror without seeing the troubled reflection staring back. Perhaps the whole thing had been from natural causes. If so, she was doing both men a grave injustice by harboring unfounded suspicion. She clutched the idea like drowning persons clutch anything that will support them until they reach safety

Lindsey reluctantly took a mild sedative from the medicine cabinet, hating the need for it but knowing she needed sleep to clear her mind. "Things always seem hopeless in the middle of the night," she whispered.

A faint grin at the Best family maxim brightened her mood. She followed with the rest of it: "And they always get better in the morning light." She tiptoed to the kitchen on silent nurse's feet and warmed a glass of milk. Usually that alone relaxed her. Tonight, the addition of the sedative sent her into a deep, restful sleep, the best healing possible for her tired body and battered mind.

A bright September morning proved the second part of the Best saying right. It seemed incredible anyone would want to harm either Terence or her. With a light heart, she chattered on the way to breakfast with Patti and Shina. Yet when the blond nurse regaled those at the table with the story of Lindsey's near escape, a blanket of depression fell over her again and she hastily rose. "Since I was there during the gruesome details, I'm sure you can spare me." She tempered the remark with a grin, hoping her voice didn't sound as thin to them as it did her.

Patti was too engrossed in the story to notice, but Lindsey saw Shina's quick look of dismay. Lindsey managed a smile, waved, and headed out of the dining room, glad to be off until the next day. The climbing, not to mention the strain of hanging on to the tree trunk while the world disintegrated around her, had taken a far greater toll than she'd realized until now. Maybe she should go back to bed. She shook her head emphatically. No. She'd only lie there and rehash yesterday.

Lindsey considered her options. Shepherd of Love attempted to schedule personnel so most could attend services in the chapel or a church of their choice. However, in the weeks since the new chaplain came, Lindsey had either been unable to get away or had gone home over Sunday. Should she go to chapel services or the nearby church she and her friends sometimes attended? She privately admitted to reluctance, a desire for more time before seeing Terence again. She must not let him know she secretly carried doubts about him. His blue eyes would darken to angry gray, the way they had yesterday when he found her pitchy and dirt-covered beside the trail.

Lindsey stopped short. *Don't be a ninny,* she ordered herself. *The best way in the world to establish his innocence or guilt is to go hear him preach.*

Lindsey unhurriedly walked back to her apartment, sunlight warm as a benediction on her head and arms. She turned her face toward Mount Rainier, dreading the moment for fear its snow-capped visage would repel her. She loved the mountain and had looked east every day as far back as she could remember. As she gazed at it she remembered her father's laughing comment, "In California, the cry is 'surf's up.' In Seattle, it's 'mountain's out.' "

She smiled, and her heart filled with relief. Yesterday's horror did not have the power to spoil the grandeur for her, the sense of awe at this particular facet of God's creation.

She remembered how her father had changed from joking to seriousness, the look of wonder in his face when he quoted from Psalm 121: "I will lift up mine eyes unto the hills, from whence cometh my help. My help cometh from the Lord, which made heaven and earth. He will not suffer thy foot to be moved; he that keepeth thee will not slumber."

Lindsey drew in a ragged breath. God certainly had not been slumbering when she needed help on that mountain trail. He had kept her safe from the worst danger she'd ever encountered. She bowed her head. Her heart swelled with thankfulness too deep for words, yet she knew He heard.

The song of a robin roused her from her reverie and she lightly ran inside. Time to change for worship. Fifteen minutes later, Lindsey surveyed her pale-green-clad self. Fall might be here, but her heart felt more like spring and she had dressed accordingly. She touched a light, flowerlike cologne to wrists and behind her ears, slid her feet into plain white pumps, and reached for her worn Bible, a gift from her father on her seventeenth birthday. Normally, gifts came from both parents, but Ramsey Best had broken tradition that year.

"We're going on a shopping trip," he told his daughter. If she lived to be a hundred, she'd never forget it. Although all family members had Bibles, they were of necessity inexpensive editions. Lindsey had been thrilled when her father took her to the largest Christian bookstore in the city and told her to pick out any Bible she wanted. She felt like a child set free in a candy store. Her father reminded her they had all the time they needed, so she browsed to her heart's content.

At last she selected a soft, clear print King James Version. "Lindsey Best" in gold letters adorned the black leather cover, and she seldom used another Bible.

"Mom and Dad taught us stories from the King James Version. I'm used to it," she explained when friends pointed out advantages of The Living Bible, The New International Version, and others. "Besides, I like the poetic rhythm of the traditional language."

Now she hugged the Book to her, caught up a white purse, and headed for the Chapel, wondering what Terence would choose for his morning text. Hospital gossip had it that he preached like an old-time revivalist, head thrown back, fearless in his proclamations.

Patti didn't make it to the worship service, but Dr. Keppler was already there when Lindsey arrived. She chose a seat across the aisle and back a row. It gave her a good view of his handsome profile. She examined his face carefully and heaved a sigh of relief. Not a trace of villain showed. Shina—charming in an apricot-colored pants uniform—slid in beside Lindsey during the rousing hymn, "All Hail the Power of Jesus' Name." Her clear soprano blended beautifully with Lindsey's alto and added harmony. The chaplain led the song in a resonant voice that made Lindsey think of mighty armies marching for God. She took a deep breath. Much as she loved the former chaplain, Terry O'Shea's approach blew through the chapel like a salty ocean breeze, changing worship from quiet meditation to active participation. Yet an underlying current of reverence shone in the young minister's face.

His sermon kept the nurses and other worshippers on the edge of their seats from the time he quoted in a voice filled with conviction Paul's crystal-clear statement, "For all have sinned, and come short of the glory of God." Terence neither ranted nor raved. He did not pound the desk or wave his arms. Instead, he left the platform, stepped to the middle of the center aisle, and talked to his flock, a shepherd called to minister. His open Bible lay in one hand.

"We hear a lot these days how God is unconditional love. This is true. We also hear Jesus accepts us just as we are. Wrong." His voice rang in the stillness of complete attention. "I believe this is the most dangerous teaching ever to come forth in the history of Christianity, an insidious doctrine fostered by Satan to deceive the world and God's children."

A murmur of surprise rippled through the listeners. Lindsey's mouth dropped open. She shot a surreptitious glance toward Bart Keppler. He sat with arms crossed, one dark eyebrow raised. In scorn? Skepticism? Lindsey tore her gaze free and concentrated on the sermon.

"Jesus loves us as we are. He died that we might live. But He cannot accept us as we are. To do so would negate everything He taught." He held up his Bible. "Each recorded incident concerning someone who met the Master face to face ends with a command to go forth and become a new person. Christ's message was simple, 'Go and sin no more.'"

Lindsey looked around her. A few people nodded. Some faces showed understanding. Others looked stunned. A muscle twitched in Bart Keppler's cheek, the only movement in his curiously still body.

Lindsey sat spellbound. Some of what Terence said reflected things she had pondered. The fine line between tolerance and permissiveness. The courage to take an unpopular stand among friends away from the hospital. She leaned forward, eager to hear every word.

Terence held his hands out, palms upward. "We cannot choose for others, but God help us if we do not make sure they know where we stand, and why." His face grew shadowed. "Never condemn a person, only those actions the Lord abhors. Learn to disagree without being disagreeable. In so doing, the Holy Spirit will guide you in what you say. The same Spirit can put a check on your lips and teach you when to be still."

He paused and the blue of Puget Sound on the brightest day filled his eyes when he looked from face to face. "The single most important thing you can do is this: Be a living example, a sermon in flesh, blood, and bones."

Lindsey fancied his gaze lingered on Bart Keppler's face a little longer than the rest, and she chided herself for what might be fancy. She met Terence's steady gaze when it rested on her, and she wondered what he would make of the relief she could not conceal. No man could preach as Terry O'Shea had done and still be a menace, unless he were the biggest hypocrite who ever lived. That she could not believe.

The remainder of the service took on a dream-like quality. Shina slipped out during the final hymn to go back on duty. Terence ended the worship, "May the peace of God be with you all, now and forever. Amen."

Lindsey got out of the chapel and part way down the corridor before Bart Keppler caught up with her. Her heart bounced out of all proportion to his commonplace question, "Feeling all right? I was surprised to see you here this morning."

She found herself unwillingly responding to his smile. "I'm fine." She paused in mid-stride, the eagerness in his dark eyes sounding off a warning bell in her brain. "At least so far. I'll probably take the rest of the day to laze around."

His smile vanished. "Too bad. I hoped you'd spend it with me." A curious glint showed that whatever he had done the day before to make Patti look so radiant didn't exclude his desire to date her roommate.

"I just wouldn't be good company," Lindsey said.

"Is that an excuse?" he wanted to know. "I thought you had a good time at the Space Needle with me."

Lindsey debated. Should she evade the question she felt would lead to a confrontation? If so, it would mean trying to avoid him and making herself look ridiculous in the process.

"Well?" His voice crackled like splintering crystal.

She looked straight into Bart's eyes and saw a flicker of actual dislike. With sudden clarity, she knew whatever reason he had for trying to date her didn't involve caring. Ego, maybe, or pride, but not actual admiration. It made her unpleasant task easier. "I don't intend to lose my best friend in order to date you, Dr. Keppler," she told him pointblank.

"Bart," he automatically corrected. "Suppose I tell you Patti means nothing to me, that I only dated her to learn more about you?"

The invincible male, Lindsey thought. Refusing to admit a female existed who didn't bow to his charm. The thought steadied her. She decided to see if he'd allow her to play it light. Mischief ran from her toes to her face and she deliberately twinkled her eyes, knowing they reflected the green of her dress. "I'd say you're a real con artist—"

Her plan backfired. Bart turned pale, grabbed her arm, and hissed, "Just what is that supposed to mean?"

She wrenched free and rubbed the red marks his fingers left. "My word, but you're jumpy! Don't you recognize the light touch when you hear it? If you had let me finish, I'd have said when it comes to flirting."

Color returned to his face. "Sorry. It's just that I really do like you."

Again she desperately tried to lighten the atmosphere. "In the words of the man whose wife told him he couldn't expect everyone to like him, 'What's not to like?' " It sounded fatuous in her ears but served to bring a half-smile to his lips. Lindsey pressed her advantage. "I'd better get to the dining room."

"May I come with you?" He sounded uncharacteristically humble.

"Of course." Her lips twitched. Once, after an influx of too many relatives who stayed entirely too long in the crowded Best home, one of Lindsey's brothers whispered, "Know what hospitality is? The art of making people feel at home when you wish they were." Now she knew exactly what he meant.

Patti and Shina were already at a table. The blond nurse's eyes lit up when they entered and Lindsey's heart plunged. Why must her friend be vulnerable to this false-hearted man who would carelessly dismiss her in favor of dating someone for whom he cared nothing? Didn't it point to a darker, more devious side than the smiling hospital director showed to the world at large?

"Room for one more?" Terence's cheerful voice broke into her brown study.

"Sure." She scooted closer to Shina, making space next to Bart, who promptly scowled and bent a black look toward her. After she assuaged the first pangs of hunger, she laid down her fork and remarked, "I appreciated your sermon."

"Thanks."

"So did I," Shina put in. "It made me realize my timidity in speaking out."

"Imposing your beliefs on someone else, you mean?" Dr. Keppler had evidently decided to play devil's advocate.

"Is that what you got out of my sermon?" Terence inquired.

Bart shrugged. "Pretty much. I've always felt it would be arrogant of me to be so sure I am right about something that I can tell the world how to live. Isn't that why God gave people agency? Who's to say only one way is the right way?"

"Isn't that strange talk for a Christian?" Terry quietly asked.

Bart looked startled, even a little alarmed. "Of course not. It's like traveling to New York. We can choose to fly, take a train, or drive." His smile reminded Lindsey of a white reef on a night-darkened shore. "We can even walk or ride horseback. It may take us longer to get there, but the destination's the same."

Patti looked thoughtful, but Shina objected, "Some may get sidetracked and never get there at all."

"Sorry, Shina, that's a stock answer."

He sounded so patronizing Lindsey wanted to hit him. To her amazement, Shina didn't back down as she expected her friend to do. She quietly replied, "So is your example."

Terence had a sudden coughing fit and buried his face in a napkin. Patti looked distressed. Lindsey bit back a laugh at the look on Bart's face. To her amazement, he laughed. "Touché. You're a worthy opponent, Miss Ito. Or should I make that Ms.?"

"Shina will do," she pertly told him.

He laughed again and rose. "See you later, everyone." He sauntered out with head high, not at all like one beaten at his own game by a nurse half his size.

"Why do you all pick on him?" Patti cried when he had gone, keeping her voice low enough so those around couldn't hear. "Bart's doing a wonderful job here. Everyone says so. Why don't you like him?"

Lindsey frantically searched her heart and said honestly, "There are a lot of things about Dr. Keppler to admire. It's just that some of his ideas are odd."

"They aren't odd at all." Patti's eyes flashed blue fire. "He explained to me yesterday his dream is for all the world to live in peace and he will do everything he can to make it happen."

A squiggle of disbelief played tag up and down Lindsey's spine. If Dr. Bart Keppler were so intent on peace, why did he keep trying to make trouble between two of the hospital's longest-term nurses and best friends?

Chapter 9

The empty warehouse repelled the dark figure, who had learned to loathe it. With winter coming on, there had to be a better contact place. When the phone finally rang, his irritation showed in the barked "Yes?"

"Well?"

"The problem is a lot more serious than I thought."

Ominous silence, then, "What are you going to do about it?"

"I don't know. Why can't we try elsewhere?"

"You fool! This is a prototype. If we pull off here what we must, the whole world will know and applaud. Others are prepared and waiting, ready to follow our lead. Here's what you're to do." A long list of instructions followed, ending with, "Strike now, I tell you, or take the consequences." The click of the disconnected call rang like a distant knell in the listener's ear.

Five minutes later a huddled figure slipped unobserved from the warehouse. It all sounded so simple, yet had the brain planning the operation failed to take in one crucial thing: the human factor? The success or failure of the whole project rested on raggedly clad shoulders. Not just the project, but the future direction of the world. A furtive glance into the brutish night did nothing to dispel his gloom. On dispirited feet, the figure melted into the night, burdened by the part he had to play. Had anyone other than God—if there were a God—ever faced such a monumental challenge?

On a dreary November morning, Dr. Keppler caught up with Lindsey just outside the hospital dining room. "I have tickets for Saturday night for the Seattle Opera House," he told her as blandly as if she hadn't consistently refused to go out with him. "Don't say you're on duty. I know you just got transferred to days for the next week."

"I wasn't going to." She gave him a measuring look. "Thank you for the invitation but I told you how I feel."

A flare of dislike marred the beauty of the watching, dark eyes.

Lindsey impulsively laid one hand on his well-tailored sleeve. "I don't mean to make you angry. After all, we have to work together. Please don't embarrass either of us by bringing this up again."

Mockery replaced the anger in his eyes. Bart waited until a group of laughing employees passed them and in a voice calculated to reach her ears alone, he said, "I never get angry. I get even." He closed one hand over hers.

You are furious right now, Lindsey wanted to retort. She snatched her hand away and felt her temper rise. "Just what do you mean by that cryptic remark?"

Laughing innocence banished the last of Dr. Keppler's annoyance. Chameleonlike, he became his usual, suave self. "My, my, Nurse Lindsey, are we so hostile this morning we can't recognize a joke when we hear one?" He glanced out the window at streaming rain. "Must be the weather is getting you down. Three days of downpour is enough to put anyone out of sorts."

His condescending manner infuriated the red-haired nurse. "I meant what I said." Lindsey turned her back on him and walked away, biting her lip to keep from hurling words at him she'd later regret. A piece of long-ago advice from her father steadied her emotions. "A rude comment brands the speaker, not the person to whom it is made," Ramsey Best had said to his tearful daughter after a teasing child poked fun at Lindsey's coppery hair.

Now she clenched her capable hands, wondering how the acting hospital director would like it if those same hands wrung his precious neck. The thought made her lips twitch, and she gave a little skip in the empty corridor.

When she reached the chapel, the door stood open. She glanced at her watch, noted a little time remained before she had to report to Surgery, and stepped inside. Terence O'Shea sat in the front pew, head bowed, shoulders slumped in either fatigue or discouragement. Strange. No one had said anything at breakfast about losing a patient. What else could bring that droop to the wide shoulders usually squared against the world and its adversities?

Shocked by seeing the young chaplain in an unguarded moment, the watching nurse blinked. A curious tenderness went through her, even though she felt like an intruder. Could she get away before she disturbed him?

Lindsey hadn't counted on the fact that Terence's ears had grow keen from months of light sleeping in case his father needed him in the night. He rose and turned toward her, one hand behind his back. His haggard face little resembled the laughing Terry she knew. An exclamation of dismay escaped her and she hurried forward. "What's wrong? Is it your father?"

"No." The mahogany-red head slowly moved back and forth. "Dad's actually a little better." Not a trace of a smile curved the straight lips.

"Then why—"

Terence wordlessly withdrew his right hand from behind his back, held it out, and unclenched his fingers.

Lindsey recoiled from the object resting on the chaplain's open palm. Her heart leaped to her throat in one giant bound. Her eyes burned. She felt color drain from her face and grabbed the end of a pew to steady herself. She took in great gulps of air. "What—it's not—it can't be—"

"It is." Terry's eyes glazed with shock. "A voodoo doll."

"At Shepherd of Love? Impossible!" Lindsey couldn't tear her fascinated gaze from the ghastly thing. A moment later, a fresh wave of horror assailed her. Her voice came out strangled, disbelieving. "Terry, the doll—it looks like you!"

"Complete with a pin through the heart. I saw this kind of thing in Haiti."

She barely heard him. "Wh–where did you find it?" Her stomach churned and she swallowed hard.

"Someone shoved it under the Bible on the altar."

From sanctuary and peace, the chapel instantly changed to a place fraught with fear and darkness. Lindsey's teeth chattered. "What does it mean? What shall we do?"

Rage darkened Terry's eyes to gray. He hurled the obscene symbol of evil across the chapel with all his might. "Don't do anything, Lindsey." He gripped her shoulders and lightly shook her for emphasis. "Until I find out who is responsible for this, the best way to baffle the guilty person is to remain silent." He looked at her appealingly. "I know it's asking a lot, but if you really want to help, go on to work and say nothing. Not to anyone, hear me?"

She nodded, realizing the wisdom of what he said. "I'll try."

His grip relaxed. The beginning of a smile returned blue to his eyes. "You can do it." His forehead wrinkled. "We need to meet. Are you free after work?"

"Yes."

"Good. I'll call for you at six." He considered. "Wear jeans, will you, please? I'd rather not discuss this here at the hospital. You know the warning about walls having ears."

She shuddered. "You can't think anyone from Shepherd of Love is responsible! That's preposterous." Yet even as she disclaimed the possibility, cold reason told her differently. Who had a better chance to plant such a gruesome thing than a member of the hospital staff? Besides, who outside the hospital hated Terence O'Shea enough to send such a bizarre warning?

All day, between patients, Lindsey found the same questions haunting her. Day shift was far different from night, when much of the surgical work was emergency or accident generated. Unexpected things did come up, but for the most part, surgery followed surgery on a more orderly, scheduled basis, with breaks in between. The calm exterior routine gave her interior thoughts the chance to spin in frantic circles.

By six o'clock, Lindsey had showered and donned light blue denims. She slid into a matching shirt enhanced by red, green, and blue embroidered flowers and leaves, then opted for a green head band that brought out the green in her eyes.

Terry's tired face brightened when she opened the apartment door for him. "You look like a farm girl."

"You said to wear jeans. I've been wondering why all day," she confessed.

"They'll allow you to sit on the rug in front of a fireplace and still be comfortable," he teased. "I'll get into mine as soon as we get home."

"Home—oh, you're taking me to meet your father?"

"I called and told him to throw an extra plate on the table. We can talk freely there." He glanced uneasily around the quiet apartment. "Where's Patti?"

"Out with Dr. Keppler." Lindsey didn't describe the ecstatic way her roommate had floated in and announced they were going to Ivar's Salmon House for dinner. *If he truly liked her, I wouldn't care,* Lindsey mentally reasoned. *I don't think he does. I suspect this is simply the opening gun in his get-even campaign.*

<hr/>

"You didn't tell her or Shina—"

Lindsey felt herself tense. "I told no one anything." She shivered. "I'd rather not think about it at all, but we can't just ignore it, can we?"

"No." A worried look crept into his face. "Shall we go?"

Lindsey caught up the warmly lined denim jacket that completed her outfit and followed Terry to the parking lot. Once inside the station wagon and headed away from Seattle, she wistfully asked, "It couldn't be just a childish prank? Someone trying to scare you or the hospital?"

"I wish." His hands tightened on the wheel. The somber note in his voice killed any hope Lindsey had that it was all a bad joke. "The way the voodoo doll was tucked under the Bible makes me think it's a direct and diabolical challenge to God and all He stands for from some occult, Satanic force." He paused. "If it's all right with you, let's wait and discuss it with Dad. He's more level-headed and less hot-headed than his son."

She laughed and some of the gloom vanished. For the rest of the drive, they chatted on lighter subjects. They speculated as to when the hospital director might return, touched on one subject then another.

Never self-conscious, Lindsey found herself eagerly anticipating meeting Shane O'Shea. She'd put together a fairly accurate picture of the older man as much from the love and respect in his son's voice as the vivid vignettes Terence wove of his childhood. "You love the farm, don't you?"

"Yes. With the hospital chaplaincy, I have the best of both worlds." Buoyancy filled his rich voice. "Especially now. One of God's most recent answers to prayer came in the form of a neighbor. He and Dad made an arrangement for him to farm and care for our land on shares. It means we can keep the place and the crops will generate enough interest for taxes and repairs." He laughed. "A chaplain's salary doesn't include owning a place that doesn't pull its own weight."

Shane O'Shea turned out to be everything Lindsey expected and more. His keen blue eyes so like his son's beamed welcome, yet Lindsey felt she'd been thoroughly examined in one lightning glance. The silver in his hair, deeply etched facial lines, and gnarled hands bore mute witness Shane was no stranger to pain, yet in repose, he wore peace like a banner.

Lindsey ate until she felt ashamed. "Mr. O'Shea, even my mother can't make a better pot roast! This is velvety as cheese." She cut another gravy-covered piece with her fork and raised it to her mouth. The accompanying carrots, potatoes, and onions, Shane said, had simmered all afternoon in an old-fashioned Dutch oven. They were followed by wild blackberry dumplings made from fruit grown on the O'Shea land.

Terence insisted on doing the dishes, leaving his father and Lindsey to get acquainted. True to his prediction, she curled up on an old-fashioned hooked rug that lay in front of the fireplace, warmed as much by Shane's personality as the merry little orange and red flames before her. He sat in a nearby recliner, a lap robe over his outstretched feet and legs. By the time

Terence joined them, Lindsey felt she'd known his father forever.

"May I bring my family here someday?" she asked. "They'd love it." *And you,* she added to herself.

"Of course. Any or all of them." Shane smiled at her. "They sound like our kind of people."

She realized he had learned a great deal about her from the few simple questions he'd asked.

Shane turned to Terence, who had dropped to the rug next to Lindsey and sat cross-legged beside her. "All right, Son. What's the trouble?"

Lindsey gasped. "Are you by any chance psychic?"

"No, Lass. I just know my boy and something is amiss."

She tucked the comment away to take out and dissect later, then inhaled sharply when Terence held up the grotesque voodoo doll he'd thrown aside so violently earlier that day.

Shane reared back in his chair and bellowed, "For the love of Mike, is that what I think it is?" The peace in his face fled before the same turmoil Lindsey had experienced hours before.

"Yes, it is, Dad." Terry laid it in his father's lap. "I found it today in the chapel."

"I wouldn't have believed it. Not in Shepherd of Love." Shane fixed his piercing blue gaze on his son. Lindsey had the feeling he had forgotten her presence. "Did you make enemies in Haiti?"

Terence looked surprised. "Of course. We weren't at all popular with the witch doctors, especially—"

Lindsey couldn't hold back her curiosity. "What on earth were you doing in Haiti, trafficking with witch doctors?" She clasped her hands and leaned forward, feeling on the edge of some fantastic mystery. The snapping of wood in the fireplace made a perfect setting for whatever story Terry might tell.

He looked astonished. "I thought I told you." He paused. "Actually, I guess I started to a couple of times and got interrupted. Anyway, I went to Haiti as chaplain on a medical mission ship. Learned enough medicine to help where I could, under supervision, of course. Our simplest antibiotics cured dozens of those who swarmed to us for all kinds of help." His face turned grim in the firelight. "The local witch doctors hated anyone who showed them up. They especially hated me because I offered spiritual as well as physical help whenever I got the chance. A few of the patients actually found the courage to break free from the black magic that's practiced freely in Haiti. Some moved to other areas to avoid being harmed." He broke off and faced Lindsey. "How much do you know about voodoo?"

"Not much." She tried to lighten the heavy mood. "I don't have more than one or two witch doctors among my friends." The shock in Terry's eyes made her ashamed of her levity. So did the involuntary sound of protest from Shane. "I'm sorry. I don't mean to treat this lightly. I guess my brain can't accept such a thing could enter Shepherd of Love."

"The serpent entered Eden," Shane reminded.

"I know," she choked. One hand flew to her throat. "It's just that the hospital stands for everything right and good."

"All the more reason for the forces of evil to attack it." Shane's quiet voice sent ice splinters through Lindsey. She shifted position and hugged her knees to her chest. "Satan concentrates on persons or institutions that pose a threat. Why should he waste time in areas not engaged in doing good?"

Lindsey hunched closer to the fire, wishing it would melt the rapidly growing glacier in her heart.

"If we're to stamp this out right now before it gets worse, I'll need your help," Terry said frankly. "I haven't been at Shepherd of Love long enough to know who can be trusted and who can't. How about it, Lindsey? Will you be my co-partner in fighting crime?" He laughed. "Maybe we can write a book when we solve our first case and call it *Secret at Shepherd of Love.*"

"Now who's being facetious?" Shane demanded.

"Crime? Do you really expect other incidents?" Lindsey's mind whirled. "I mean, this is only one."

Terence stretched out flat on his back, arms folded beneath his head. "I'm not so sure about that. Someone broke into Personnel, you know. I learned yesterday my file never did turn up."

"Is anyone else's missing?"

He looked disconcerted. "Yes, but it might be a red herring." Terry grimaced. "An amateur detective five minutes and already I'm beginning to sound like a sleuth. Anyway, Dr. Keppler's file is also gone, which makes sense. Personnel was so swamped when we applied, our information didn't get entered into the computer."

"Perhaps your file is the red herring." Shane fitted the fingers of one hand against those of the other. "Without those files, what does the hospital really know about either you or Dr. Keppler, except what you told them?"

His direct question left Lindsey gasping. "T.D.M.," she muttered.

"Excuse me?" Terry sat up and stared as if she'd gone mad.

Lindsey felt red crawl clear up to her hairline. "Tall, dark, and mysterious. That's what Shina nicknamed Dr. Keppler." She laughed nervously. "I know it's silly and Patti says it's unchristian—which it probably is." The sheer astonishment on the men's faces restored her equilibrium. "Oh, dear, I'm babbling. Besides, it's too silly to mention."

"Nothing can be considered silly that may have a bearing on this," Terry reminded her.

"It's just that Shina took an instant aversion to Dr. Keppler. She said she once read a western novel with a villain named Black Bart. Every time she saw Dr. Keppler, she thought of it because his name's Bartholomew. I read the book, too."

Terry's shout of laughter cleared the air. "So you read the book, too. What's your impression of our acting director?"

A note of eagerness beneath the seemingly casual question caused Lindsey to consider well before she replied. "I honestly don't know. He can be charming—when he gets his own way." She squirmed, not wanting to go into the details of her stormy relationship with the dark-haired doctor.

"And when he doesn't?" Shane dropped his hands to the voodoo doll in his lap and an unreadable expression crossed his face.

"Sometimes he wears a biding-my-time look. At other times, he mocks. Or shows quickly suppressed anger." She stopped, unable to add more.

"Same impressions I got the day we climbed on Mount Rainier," Terry put in.

A stick snapped in the fireplace, sounding overly loud in the hushed room. Lindsey jumped. Surely God wouldn't let anything destroy the work being done for Him at Shepherd of Love! She glanced at the menacing voodoo doll still in Shane O'Shea's lap. The danger could well be directed toward Terry, not the hospital. A spurt of fear went through her. In order to squelch it, she quickly said, "If I'm going to be your helper, I have to be informed. Tell me about voodoo, please." Yet even as she asked, her inner self longed to flee the feeling of evil that hung over her request like a floating shroud.

Chapter 10

Uncertainty crept into Terence O'Shea's face. "Are you sure you want to hear this?" he asked Lindsey, who sat wide-eyed on the rug in front of the fireplace. "It's dark and frightening. Things that go bump in the night don't even come close to the terror that voodoo creates—and not just in its followers."

"Really?" Shane O'Shea glanced down at the voodoo doll that had been made in a crude caricature of his son. With a motion of distaste, he flung it toward the dying flames.

"Don't!" Some instinct beyond herself caused Lindsey to intercept the flying missile in a catch spectacular enough to make even her football playing brothers proud. "Put the horrid thing away. Who knows? We may need it sometime for evidence." She dropped the doll and rubbed her fingers on her jeans, scouring them against the denim until they stung.

"If you'd like to wash your hands, we'll understand," Terry gruffly told her.

"I would." A good scrubbing in the large farmhouse bathroom took away the feeling that she'd been tainted by her brief contact with the hideous object. She returned to find the doll gone. "I'm ready to hear about voodoo." She smiled at each of the men. "It's not like I haven't seen unpleasant sights."

"You've never dealt with pure, unmitigated evil, have you?" Not the gleam of a smile touched Terence's face.

"No, but since it's threatening my hospital and people I care about, I have to learn. Never let it be said a Best walked away from a good fight." She blushed at the blaze of admiration in Terence's eyes, but he sobered when he began.

"Like you, I knew little about voodoo until I went to Haiti. If I thought about it at all, I suppose I felt smug, even disinterested. After all, Haiti's thousands of miles away. I had enough in my life to keep busy without conjuring up a bunch of mumbo-jumbo stuff.

"Within a week from the time the ship docked, I was one smarter and sadder guy. Voodoo in Haiti is a fact of life."

He paused and Lindsey asked, "What is it, exactly? I'm like you were

297

as far as having any real knowledge."

"It's insidious, terrifying, and practiced by a vast number of persons!" Terry slammed a fist into the open palm of his other hand. "From what I could determine, only a small percentage of the Haitians follow other religions—most among that minority are Roman Catholics."

Lindsey felt her heart race.

Terry continued. "Voodoo is a strange combination of Christian and African beliefs and superstitions. Initiation ceremonies include drumming, dancing, and animal sacrifices." His mouth turned grim. "Part of the appeal is that voodoo teaches believers can be possessed by gods during their rites. I'll never forget witnessing one such ceremony. A former voodoo follower who converted to Christianity sneaked a buddy and me close enough to get a good look." Terry took in a ragged breath.

Lindsey found herself clenching her hands in sympathy at the sorrow and disgust etched into his face. "Wh–what would have happened if you'd been caught?" she faltered.

"I don't even want to think about it. It's one of the most foolish, dangerous things I've ever done, but I needed to see for myself. Well, I did." He paused, obviously remembering. "Night in Haiti can be as black as voodoo itself. I'll skip the animal sacrifice part." His face showed revulsion and Lindsey bit her lip.

"The houngan—voodoo priest—drew designs on the ground, using flour. People began to dance. They believe they must do so until a god temporarily possesses at least some of them. They have a pagan god for everything: love, war, farming, rain, and so on. Before long, the frenzy grew until I wondered that God Himself didn't strike those involved down. I personally couldn't differentiate between those who supposedly became possessed and the rest of the howling horde, yet the horrible fascination of it all kept me from moving.

"At last my friend tugged at my arm and whispered, 'We must go. Now. They must not find us here and soon the ceremonies will fade and die.' We slipped away but I will never forget it."

"How can anyone practice such evil?" Lindsey cried out.

"Many of those who follow cannot read. They follow the teachings that have been handed down for generations. They're crammed into the country's overcrowded mountain valleys and coastal plains, living in one-room huts of sticks covered with dried mud, with thatched roofs. They exist on what yams, beans, corn, and rice they can raise. A few have pigs, or chickens, perhaps a goat."

Lindsey's heart ached for the faraway people. God had created them in His own image and loved them as much as He did her.

"There are always those who try to escape. That's why boatload after boatload sets out hoping to reach America and freedom from poverty, oppression, death. Many sink." The saddest look Lindsey had ever seen on a human face crept over Terence's countenance.

"Human life is less valuable than a farm animal. My converted Haitian friend told how an ill-clad man and woman jammed themselves into an already filled boat. She carried a squalling baby; he had a squealing pig over one shoulder. The man in charge curtly ordered them to get rid of excess baggage." He stopped to clear his hoarse throat.

Lindsey felt her fingernails dig into the palms of her hands. Her nerves screamed in protest against what she sensed would come.

"Well?" Shane O'Shea's voice cracked like a rifle shot.

"The man held the pig in a death grip, snatched the child, and threw it into the heaving waves."

"Oh, how could he do it?" Tears dripped, but Lindsey made no effort to wipe them away.

"That's what I asked my friend. He looked sad. 'The man knows he can have other children. He also knows he will probably never again have a pig.' "

The fire in the fireplace sullenly hissed. Lindsey shivered.

"It is a bleak picture," Shane said from the shadows.

"There is some hope," Terry quickly said. He stood, threw another log on the fire, and settled back on the rug next to Lindsey. "Christianity is nibbling away, often through schools and sponsorships, anything to improve the cycle of poverty and hopelessness. Medical personnel who dispense healing also cast doubt on the validity of witch doctors. These things are having an impact. There are those, more than you would believe, who learn about Jesus and turn to Him. Yet each step is hard won."

He flung his arms wide. "How do you combat centuries-old fear? Voodooists believe gods, demons, and spirits of the dead rule the world. Foremost among them is Baron Samedi, ruler of the graveyard spirits. I personally talked with those who swore they had seen him, complete with the black suit and bowler hat he is said to wear.

"Then there is the need to always be on the alert, to ward off magical hazards. Voodooists hate and fear noon, for people cast no shadow. Their belief is, when a person's shadow vanishes, one's soul has also left the body and opened the door to inhabitation by unwanted spirits. Casting spells and wearing charms are said to ward off enemy attack, such as dolls made in the victim's likeness. Other spells and charms are used to ensure good crops, cure illness, make a desired one love the wearer. The list is endless. Can you see how impossible it is for those drenched in those beliefs since childhood to break free? There is also the fear of reprisal to self or family if one disavows voodoo."

For the second time that evening, Lindsey felt contaminated. No wonder Terry had asked if she really wanted to know all this horrible stuff. "Now it has touched Shepherd of Love. Why? Is the hatred of those in Haiti who resented you so strong it can travel this far?" Excitement stirred within her. "Terry, first thing tomorrow there's something you should do."

"What?" He raised one eyebrow and the corners of his mouth turned down. "Call an assembly and announce someone has a vendetta against the new chaplain?" His sudden grin took any possible sting from his suggestion.

"No." She felt red spots leap to her face. "Call some of the people from the hospital mission ship and casually work the conversation around to voodoo. They will surely mention it if they have received similar—uh—gifts."

"Hey, great idea!" He beamed at her. "That way we may narrow it down. If they haven't, it means—"

"One of two things," his father interrupted. Firelight gleamed in his blue eyes as Shane ticked the possibilities off on his fingers. "One: you're being targeted because of the spiritual work you did rather than simply being part of the medical team. Two: it's a warning to the hospital instead of you."

"I'd hate to think that." Terry looked shocked.

"We can't rule it out." Shane glanced from Terry to Lindsey and grinned. "How am I doing as a silent partner in your co-detecting?"

"I'm not sure there's such a word, but you're doing fine," she told him.

Terry stood and extended a hand to help her up. "I'd better get you back to the hospital or you won't be fit for duty tomorrow." His eyes shadowed. "I know one thing. We have to find and stamp out this spark of evil before it kindles and becomes a conflagration." He fetched Lindsey's denim jacket and held it so she could slip into its cozy warmth.

"Come again, Lass. Any time."

As Lindsey followed Terence out to his car, Shane's invitation curled down into her heart like a tired child in her mother's lap. She wistfully glanced back at the old white farmhouse, wondering what it would be like to live there, secure and protected from the human misery she saw every day. Yet she knew if that same house could talk, what tales it would share of birth and death, family squalls and sunny stretches, hope and despair, sickness and health.

Terence and Lindsey didn't talk much for the first few miles on the way home but maintained a comfortable silence. She had a feeling part of him had returned to Haiti, a suspicion confirmed when he said, "I honestly hope this whole thing is aimed toward me. I'd hate to have Shepherd of Love hurt." He paused then added in a low voice, "If I decide there is any chance of my bringing trouble to the hospital, I'll resign immediately."

"Don't be an idiot!" Lindsey blurted out. "The voodoo doll was obviously left to drive you away." The thought crept into her active mind. "Suppose you walk, thinking it's the best thing for the hospital. That may be exactly what someone wants you to do." The idea grew like Jack's beanstalk. "Terry." She laid her hand on his right arm, careful not to disturb his control of the wheel. "How do we know who they might plant here in your place?"

"They? Plant? You make it sound like a conspiracy," he scoffed. "I can't believe such a thing could happen."

"Your father does, and he's one sharp person," she softly reminded.

"Yeah." Terence sighed. A thoughtful note replaced his Doubting Thomas attitude. "Like Dad said, Satan's biggest targets are those who serve God best. Shepherd of Love certainly qualifies in that department."

Lindsey's mind raced ahead of him. She took her hand from his sleeve and turned toward him within the confines of her seat belt. "Play devil's advocate for a few minutes, will you? Suppose, God forbid, you are Satan. You're pledged to doing everything you can to win souls to your cause. You will roll over anyone and everything in your way, a juggernaut relentlessly championing the cause of wickedness, heartbreak, and evil. You have eyed a certain Seattle hospital for a long time. The very name is abhorrent to you. Shepherd of Love, called for the Son of God. How you hate Him! Even though you've won some major battles, He's bested you through the ages. Bah, what good is winning battles when you know you are losing the war?"

She gave her imagination free reign. "Month after month, year after year, the hospital negates your most diabolical schemes. You are determined to smash its usefulness forever. How? By using the cunning that first brought sin into the world and has grown ever since. What will you do to rid yourself of Shepherd of Love, the albatross around your neck that causes you to grind your teeth each time you behold it?"

Terence waited so long to answer she wondered if he thought her mad to suggest such an exercise, even in the interest of solving the mystery. At last he spoke.

"I'd attempt to infiltrate one of my henchmen into the hospital itself and order him to do his best, no, worst." He glanced at her and back to the freeway. "How many new personnel have been hired in the past few months besides Dr. Keppler and me?"

Lindsey shook her head. "I have no idea, but we don't have a real high turnover." She tried to recall unfamiliar faces in the dining room, but her frequent change of shifts meant it took time before she noticed the newer employees.

"There's no real way of finding out without rousing suspicion," Terence grumbled.

"What else would you do?"

"Attack at the hospital's weakest point," he promptly told her.

"Which is?"

"The feeling of security and well-being that all is well simply because it's Shepherd of Love."

Lindsey sat up as though a pitcher of ice water had been dumped down her back. "You don't mean it!"

"Of course I do. Don't get me wrong. I don't think we have a bunch of naive doctors, nurses, and other workers at the hospital. But I do feel that because of the requirement that only dedicated Christians be hired, over a period of time an attitude has developed that could leave the hospital vulnerable. Remember how you felt when you first saw the voodoo doll? Partly because of what it was, of course, but remember your exact words? 'What—it's not—it can't be. . . At Shepherd of Love? Impossible!' "

His exact imitation sent more chills down his companion's spine. After a moment she found her voice and weakly explained, "It's just that I was stunned and unprepared."

"My point exactly. Lindsey, every decent person, Christian or not, like it or not, is in a war." His voice softened and he touched her hand lightly before returning his own to the wheel. "It's easy to forget that, when things are going along fine. Good people quote, 'Why look for evil? It will come soon enough.' There's merit to the thought; it's even supported by Scripture. On the other hand, terrible things happen when we let down our guard against them."

She had no reply. Neither could words have escaped her constricted throat. The truth of what he said burned into her, along with a great fear. Were the hospital and friends she loved playing ostrich, burying their heads in the sands of good works while unknown forces threatened?

At her outside apartment door, she raised a troubled gaze to the young chaplain. "Thank you," she whispered. "I can't honestly say I enjoyed all of the evening; some has been too disturbing. I did love meeting your father and having dinner with both of you."

Terence looked down the short distance to her upturned face. "What big eyes you have, Grandmother." A twinkle came to his own. "Someday after we solve our mystery I. . ." He bent his head. Just before his lips met hers, the sound of laughing voices came from the parking lot behind them. He stepped back, an exasperated look on his face.

"Lindsey, Terry. Where have you been? Have you heard the news?" Patti ran to them on frivolous, high-heeled blue shoes that matched the wool dress peeping from beneath an unbuttoned raincoat. "Isn't it awful?" An air of excitement radiated from the blond nurse, but Lindsey suspected it came as much from Bart Keppler's presence at Patti's side as from whatever world-shaking news she carried.

"News?" Terry's strong fingers surreptitiously squeezed Lindsey's. She caught a note of warning in the quick glance he shot toward her.

"Yes. Someone sent a death threat to Nicholas Fairchild." Patti's round blue eyes displayed shock and genuine affection. "It's on every TV station in Seattle and even the major networks have picked it up. How did you miss it?"

"I took Lindsey home with me for dinner and we didn't have the TV on," Terry explained. His fingers tightened on Lindsey's. "What did the note say?"

"The police aren't releasing the contents." Dr. Keppler looked furious. "Of all the stupid things to do, this is the worst. Fairchild's one of the most loved men in Seattle. Doesn't the jerk who did it know the entire city will be up in arms?"

Score one for Black Bart, Lindsey thought. *Either he belongs on stage receiving an Academy Award for Best All-time Actor, or he is genuinely distressed. I'd hate to be in the note-sender's shoes and have all that anger turned on me.*

Patti fell silent, a jolted expression on her pretty face. Lindsey suspected she'd never seen the handsome doctor in such a rage. Patti's eyes looked the size of the dinner plates in a doll's tea set.

Doll. Voodoo doll. The whole appalling day flashed through Lindsey's mind, leaving her suddenly tired. If only she didn't have to work tomorrow. She might be twenty-four years old, but right now she wished she were four or eight or fourteen, surrounded by the parental love that chased away monsters.

Things that go bump in the night don't even come close to the terror voodoo creates—and not just in its followers, Terry had said. Now she understood. A caricature doll with a pin through its heart. A death threat against one of the finest Christian men she'd ever known. Foreign, terrifying happenings in the formerly peaceful hospital that existed only to serve. She slumped against the door.

"Lindsey, are you all right?" Patti tore herself free of the arm Dr. Keppler had draped over her shoulders and shook her friend. "You look like the original Ice Maiden."

She forced herself to laugh. "I'm okay. Just shocked and angry, like Dr.—Bart. If you don't mind, I'll hit the shower."

"Good night, Lindsey. Try to get some sleep," Terence told her.

She wanted to ask just how she was supposed to do that, but decided against it. With this new crisis in what Terry had laughingly dubbed the *Secret at Shepherd of Love,* could she ever again sleep within the walls of the staff residence hall and not feel surrounded by nameless, encroaching evil?

Chapter 11

The next morning, Terry put in a series of random calls to those with whom he had served in Haiti. "An advantage to living on the West Coast," he remarked as he hung up the phone. "I can call when dawn's still in the eastern sky without rousing Eastern friends from their beds."

Shane grinned and flipped smoking hot griddle cakes onto his son's plate. Always an early riser, he persisted in getting breakfast—over Terry's protests. "People die in bed," he always retorted to Terry's protests. "You miss the best part of the day by sleeping in. Besides, I can take a nap later."

"You can but you probably won't," Terry would say.

And Shane's eyes would twinkle as he answered, "If I get tired enough, I will."

Once the routine had been established, Terry found it charged his batteries for the day. He knew his father also treasured their leisurely breakfast, quiet talk, brief Scripture reading, and prayer.

This particular morning Terry had made six calls before breakfast. All his former associates sounded delighted to hear from him, urged him to come visit when he could, and anxiously inquired about his father. Terry didn't mention the voodoo doll incident. He did casually ask during each conversation, "Any more trouble with the witch doctors after I left?" He figured that question would open the door in case someone else had been harassed since the mission ended and the participants returned home.

Every answer was the same: threats by disgruntled witch doctors, minor vandalism such as voodoo signs drawn on the ground near where the medics worked, but no actual attacks.

"Not even voodoo dolls?" Terence kept his voice light.

"No. Nothing to concern or stop us," came the reply each time.

Terry took a bite of griddle cake, little wiser than he had been before the calls. "So either it's the religion thing or the hospital that's being targeted, just as you suspected." He drew his brows into a straight line. "Last night Lindsey came up with a knockout." Between bites, he repeated the weird conversation they'd had on the way home, including her challenge that had led to their brainstorming session. He did not add that Dr. Keppler and Patti's arrival had

305

cheated him of a kiss he knew would have been far more than a casual good-night salute. With each passing day, the attraction and admiration he felt for Lindsey grew.

He grinned. Why bother telling his father anyway? Dad read him as well as he read the Scriptures. He probably knew more about a certain chaplain's heart murmurs at this point than his son did.

Keen blue eyes stared into Terry's. "Be careful, Son. Very careful. Warn her again not to mention the doll incident to even her most trusted friends."

"That's one of the problems." He quickly sketched in Patti's growing involvement with Dr. Keppler. His face took on a thoughtful expression. "Lindsey didn't say so, but I know he's been after her. Now it appears he's using Patti to get back at Lindsey for rejecting him."

"You don't like him, do you?"

"No." It came out flat and hung in the room. "I don't know why and it bothers me." He considered for a moment. "Maybe he's just too—"

"Just too what?" Shane patiently prodded.

"Too good-looking. Too seemingly all together. Too good to be true. Too in control." Terry laughed at his strange reasoning.

"Has he ever been in Haiti?"

Terry shrugged. "Who knows? And I don't see how I can find out."

His father gave him a shrewd gaze and a little grin. "Wait until he's at the same table in the dining room, then regale those there with stories of your mission. It's natural for you to want to share and I guarantee they will be interested. Some more than others." Shane leaned forward, a blood-hound look on his face. "Be sure to mention the persecution, any run-ins with voodooists, then watch the faces of those around you, but don't let anyone notice what you are doing."

He broke off to look at the clock. "Enough mystery. There's just enough time for devotions." They followed their Bible reading with fervent prayers enlisting God's help in extinguishing the spark of evil in the hospital and ended with a special prayer for Nicholas Fairchild's safety.

❖◆◗✦◖◆❖

Driving to work, Terence rehearsed several ways to introduce the subject of Haiti into table conversation. During the time he'd been at Shepherd of Love, he, Bart Keppler, Lindsey, and her two best friends had formed the habit of drifting to the same table whenever their shifts allowed. A variety of other employees occupied the other three seats, again depending on work schedules. His heart beat faster. He felt a smile curve his lips. Lindsey would be at both lunch and dinner since she was on day shift.

The next instant he frowned. Could he steal a minute with her ahead of time to warn her what he planned to do? If someone, anyone within hearing distance, had knowledge of yesterday's incident, the slightest stir on Lindsey's part might turn suspicion toward her. "God, am I wrong to let her become involved?" His hands tightened on the wheel and he changed lanes to let a merging car onto I-405. He shook his head. Now wasn't the time to be questioning. He hadn't been able to dissemble about finding the voodoo doll and once she saw it, Lindsey was involved—for better or worse.

His irrepressible sense of humor returned the laugh to his lips. "For better or worse? Strangely familiar, Lord." Daydreams dismissed worry. God willing, one day Terence O'Shea would echo the same changeless vows he had asked so many couples to repeat. Would Lindsey Best be the woman who responded to the charge, with unbreakable vows of her own? Her piquant face danced in his mind, strangely untouched by all the heartbreak she had seen in her nursing career. He was overwhelmed with the desire to protect her from every ugly thing, but he knew he could not. He must do what he could and leave Lindsey's safety and happiness in the hands of One who loved her better than life itself.

<hr>

To Terry's chagrin and disappointment, he failed to see Lindsey before lunch. A heavy surgery schedule kept her too busy for interruptions and just when he thought he might contact her, a grieving couple hesitantly came into the chapel with a story that never lost its pathos. A hit-and-run driver, apprehended a few miles down the highway, unsteady from booze, wild with fear and remorse. The crumpled form of a child beside a road. Screaming rescue vehicles with paramedics who shook their heads, unable to do anything except carry the lifeless body away and notify the parents.

How many times had he heard it before? When would it end, the senseless destruction of innocent life by those who bragged they could hold their liquor?

"We believe in God, but we can't understand," the child's mother sobbed.

"He was our only child," the young father brokenly added. He gathered his wife in his arms and they clung together.

Terence simply listened for a long time before he quietly said, "No one ever understands such things." He placed a hand on each bowed head, praying for the right words, the way he'd prayed dozens of times before. He started to tell them as he had many others that God understood their agony; He, too, lost an only Son. No, that should come later. Instead he prayed, "Father, I come to You seeking a blessing for these, Your children. Cover them with a blanket of peace. Give them strength in this time of tragedy. Fill them with assurance of Your love. Help them comfort one another. In Christ's name, amen."

A chaplain in the best sense of the word, Terence waited, encouraging them to cry, to find the natural release God had created to help dull pain. When they quieted, he helped them focus on making arrangements. Just having something to do often brought temporary relief. He promised to see them through this dark time, and he gave them his home number. "If you can't reach me here, don't hesitate to call," he urged. "Dad will always know how to contact me."

An hour later they wordlessly wrung his hands and walked away. He watched them go, arms around each other for support, shoulders bowed. Never again would life be the same. Terence sighed. Would their marriage last? Statistics, hard and uncaring, showed many marriages did not survive the death of a child. His fine lips tightened. This couple would not be split apart by their grief, if he could help it. He'd see they got the grief counseling anyone losing a loved one desperately needs.

His appetite gone, Terry avoided the dining room. Time enough later to institute his plan. Right now he must be refilled to meet whatever challenges this afternoon held. He went into the small office adjoining the chapel and closed the door except for a crack wide enough to alert him if someone entered the larger room. He knelt, letting God read his heart rather than trying to put thoughts and feelings into words. The accident had victims other than the stricken child, he realized now. The driver. His family. The young man must live with what he had done. Crippled by guilt, would he ever be able to accept God's forgiveness? Or his own? Terence lifted him up to God.

The afternoon hours remained mercifully free. After his time of renewal, Terry tackled his mountain of reports and sighed with satisfaction when he finished the last one. "Good! I can see my desktop again." He stretched, feeling hollow, and his stomach growled. No wonder. Almost twelve hours had passed since he had been stuffed on Dad's griddle cakes. He headed toward the dining room, unsure whether he wanted to broach the subject shoved out of his mind by more recent events.

He didn't have to decide. Conversation around the table was taken up with the death threat to the hospital founder. In addition, both Dr. Keppler and Patti were conspicuously absent. A nod from Lindsey in response to his lifted eyebrow confirmed his suspicions that they were together. Again. An uneasy feeling drifted into Terence's heart like wraiths of fog over Puget Sound. Even if Keppler were not what he seemed, it didn't necessarily mean he meant to harm Patti. So why did Terry feel cold inside, thinking of the pert blond nurse Lindsey considered an extra sister? He glanced at her and noted her expression betrayed the same concern he felt. He must see her alone—and soon.

Supper ended and Shina grinned impishly. "I think I'll run along. See you later, Lindsey." The others at the table also disappeared, leaving Terry exultant. He glanced around the nearly deserted dining room. No one was close enough to eavesdrop if they kept their voices low.

"I'm glad for the chance to talk with you," he began. "About last night—" He stopped abruptly when a tide of red color swept into her face. "No—I didn't mean—it's not what you think." She blushed again and Terry felt his pulse quicken. If he read the signs right, Lindsey Best was not indifferent to him.

"So what is my co-detective up to?" she wanted to know.

"I told Dad what we discussed. He suggested I casually bring Haiti into the table conversation one of these times. You know, spill over with enthusiasm about how much good the medical mission teams do, that kind of thing, then watch for reactions. He also said to warn you to be very careful. We may not even see more than the tip of the iceberg moving toward the hospital—and us."

"I've been thinking of that all day in between surgeries," Lindsey admitted. Her hazel eyes reminded Terry of the quiet pool beneath a maple where he had once lazed away summer days, dreaming of what he'd do when he grew up. He sighed. Never had his boyish imagination conjured up a brush with voodoo. A creeping chill caused him to say, "Lindsey, do you have vacation time coming?"

She blinked at the blunt change of subject. "At least a week."

"It might be well if you took it."

Understanding sprang to her face and a hint of contempt. "What do you think I am, a coward who turns and runs?" she demanded.

"Sorry," he mumbled. "I feel responsible for getting you into this mess. For a minute I thought—"

Her resentment died as quickly as it had been born and her eyes softened. "Thanks, Terry, but I'll stand and fight."

"I knew you would."

She cocked her head to one side and wrinkled her freckled nose at him. "Think I'm going to miss out on the chance of a lifetime to be an amateur detective? No way. I'll out-Nancy Nancy Drew and out-Hardy the Hardy Boys, if that's what it takes to solve our mystery!"

He found himself laughing in spite of his worry.

In the November darkness, he walked her through the covered passage from the hospital to the staff residence building. They slowly went down the long hall toward her apartment, absorbed in their low, continuing conversation. Terry fully intended to get the delayed good-night kiss when they reached her door.

Again his plans were rudely torn asunder, in a way neither could have predicted.

"What on earth?" Lindsey stared at the garment bags, suitcases, and other personal possessions littering the hallway. Her face whitened. Shina, arms crossed in a belligerent attitude, stood glaring at Patti, whose face reflected a mixture of guilt and unease.

Lindsey raced toward them. Terry's footsteps pounded close behind. "What's happening?" she panted.

Patti's rounded chin elevated but she didn't meet her roommate's gaze. "Shina's upset because I'm moving into the cream and blue apartment." She added defensively, "It will give us both more privacy."

Lindsey felt like she'd been hit in the stomach. Memory of a conversation weeks before replayed in her mind.

Herself: "You'd leave me?"

Patti's mysterious retort: "One never can tell," followed by a warm, "Of course not. . .even though you boss me."

The same nameless fear that flickered then burst into firestorm. "What brought this on? Why didn't you tell me?"

Bart Keppler loomed tall, dark, and triumphant in the doorway, arms filled with more of Patti's belongings. The malice in his dark eyes little resembled his honey tones. "Patti knew her changing suites would cause an argument. She also knew she couldn't hold out against your stronger personality," he smoothly explained. "Don't look so stricken, Lindsey. Having her live a few doors away doesn't change anything, does it?"

It changes everything, Lindsey wanted to shout. *Stronger personality?*

What about the influence you're *having on her right this minute?*

Patti looked anxious. "It's for the best. This way I won't disturb you when you're trying to sleep after night duty."

"You never did."

Her friend shot a pleading glance at Bart. He promptly came to her rescue. "It's nice of you to say so, but things will be better this way. Patti isn't a little girl who needs a nanny. She's a grown woman who wants to be more independent, that's all. Why act as if the world just ended?"

"It really won't make any difference, Lindsey." Patti rushed to her on flying feet and hugged her, but the other nurse knew all this came from Black Bart's desire to get even. That knowledge left her standing stick-straight, arms at her sides, until Patti loosened her hold and stepped back. Her lips trembled like those of a rejected child.

"You are crazy," Shina accused. Her midnight-black eyes flashed and she looked more than ever like a beautiful Japanese doll, miraculously brought to pulsing, protesting life.

Patti didn't say a word. She simply turned, picked up some of the clutter, and marched to the end of the hall. Load after load she and Bart moved. Patti remained silent. Bart kept up an endless patter of repeated explanations. At last Patti disappeared into the cream and blue suite, and Bart came back, gathered the last armful, and hurled the final insult.

"If you can't swing the cost of the apartment alone, Patti is prepared to pay the difference, at least until you can find a roommate," he condescendingly said. "She doesn't want to put you in a financial bind."

Could people explode from sheer fury? Lindsey tried to speak and failed.

Not so Terry. His voice slashed like a sword. "Whose idea is that?" The arm he had lightly laid over her shoulders tightened. Lindsey would wager that right now he longed to mop up the spotless hall with a certain hospital director.

"You're out of line, O'Shea." For a single moment, Keppler's facade slipped. The next, he laughed. "This is ridiculous. Patti wants and needs a change. Period. Why make a tragedy out of it?"

It is a tragedy, Lindsey wanted to say. Only Terry's warning squeeze of her shoulders kept her from raging. She managed a laugh. "Right. Why make a tragedy, when there are enough tragedies in the world—and hospital—already?"

"What's that supposed to mean?" Bart looked amused. "Oh, you mean the death threat to the director, I suppose." He shrugged. "There are always crazies out there. They'll do anything to get TV and newspaper coverage. Well, good night." He vanished inside the door of Patti's new apartment and firmly closed the door.

"I'll be happy to move in with you, if you like," Shina offered. The glisten of tears just beneath the surface made her lovely eyes darker than ever.

"Thanks." Lindsey took a deep breath. "That would be great, but let's just leave things for a time." She found it impossible to believe this was happening. Or that Patti wouldn't come to her senses and back where she belonged.

A look of understanding filled Shina's face. She held out her arms. Lindsey flew into them, towering over the tiny nurse but glad for the comfort.

Terence said good night and left. Shina trailed Lindsey into her apartment and silently stood by while the taller nurse opened the door to a room empty of everything except the furniture furnished by the hospital. The bed looked naked without the puffy comforter Lindsey had curled up on too many times to count. She turned on her heel, walked out, and closed the door behind her. Reality set in. Patti had actually gone, blinded by infatuation, manipulated by a master.

"He really is Black Bart, isn't he?" Shina observed from her perch on the end of the couch. Trouble underlined every word.

"He appears to be." Lindsey curled more firmly into the opposite end. The desire to tell Shina everything nearly overpowered her. She stifled the words but vowed to ask Terry at the first possible minute if they could make Shina part of the detective team. Small she might be, but Shina possessed one of the keenest minds in the hospital. She could be a real asset.

Chapter 12

W hen Patti moved to the end of the hall, she might as well have taken up residence on Mars," Lindsey bitterly complained to Shina one evening, just before going on duty. Still on swing, she caught only brief glimpses of her former roommate. The fleeting encounters were not reassuring. A certain reserve had fallen over the blond nurse and a wary expression had replaced the candid, trusting gaze that made Patti so attractive and loved.

"I see her more than you do, but we never really talk." Shina took a couple of extra steps to keep up with Lindsey's longer stride. "I'm trying not to rock the boat." She giggled. "I never thought I'd say this, but I miss her chatter. So do others. They even give her a bad time about it. She just smiles, as if she knows a wonderful secret but won't tell."

Lindsey stopped short. "You don't think she's engaged, do you?"

"I hope not. I get the feeling Dr. Keppler's using her, although I can't figure out how or why." She twisted her fingers. "There's something else. He cornered me the other day and said in that butter cream voice of his, 'I haven't seen you going out with anyone lately, Shina. I assume this means you're no longer engaged. How does dinner sound?' "

Lindsey gulped. "What did you say?"

Shina's eyes twinkled. "I was saved by the bell—actually, the intercom paging him. I've been avoiding him ever since."

"Maybe you shouldn't."

Her mouth opened wide. "Are you out of your mind?"

"No." Lindsey couldn't explain that the invitation might be the bolt of lightning needed to get her and Terry's investigation going again. There had been no opportunity so far to tell him she believed Shina should be taken into the sleuthing team. Terry had extended his duties into after-hours, spending time with the hit-and-run driver and the couple who had lost their child.

His one attempt at mentioning Haiti netted a big, fat zero. There had been interest and questions, but no particular reaction. Dr. Keppler frankly admitted, "You're more altruistic than I, O'Shea. I can't imagine even going to that hotbed of radicals and mumbo-jumbo, let alone infuriating the local witch doctors."

One of the interns at the table commented, "You don't have to go clear to Haiti to find mumbo-jumbo. New Orleans is lousy with it and if what I hear is true, it's creeping in a lot of other places."

"Such as?"

Keppler's patronizing question brought a flash of resentment to the intern's eyes. "Such as right here. There are some strange things going on in the hospital." He clamped his lips shut, and Lindsey got the feeling he wished he hadn't allowed Bart to goad him into speaking.

"Such as?" Keppler repeated, his eyes slitted in amusement.

"I'm not saying anything yet, but I'm sure keeping my eyes and ears open," the other retorted. He glanced around the circle of watching faces. "The rest of you should do the same."

Dr. Keppler's face grew mottled. Angry sparks shot from his dark eyes. "If there's any mumbo-jumbo going on in my hospital, it's from delirious patients." He shoved back his chair. The sound grated into the sudden pool of silence like fingernails on a chalkboard.

Lindsey didn't dare look at Terry. Instead, she sneaked a glance at Patti. A horrified expression rested on her friend's face, much like the one she'd seen the other time Bart showed his rage.

She's slipping away from her friends, perhaps even from God, Lindsey thought.

Her worst suspicions were confirmed the very next day.

For the first time in days, when the three nurses gathered around the breakfast table, no one joined them. "Where's your troupe of admiring interns, Patti?" Shina teased.

The blond nurse's face flamed. She raised her chin. "As if I care anything about those childish interns."

"Maybe you should." Lindsey wished she'd bitten her tongue.

Patti turned on her. Blue lightning blazed in her eyes, but she kept her voice low. "Just because you're jealous that Bart dumped you doesn't give you the right to put me down," she said furiously.

"Excuse me?" Lindsey couldn't believe her ears. Neither could she believe what her eyes saw. Patti had been hypnotized into believing every word he said.

"Don't deny it. Just because Bart believes differently than you do, you persecute him." Defiant red flags waved in her cheeks. "Let me tell you something. I agree with him. As long as a person is sincere, God will honor his or her beliefs."

"Wrong." Shina jumped into the discussion with both feet. "Adolf Hitler was one of the most sincere men who ever lived. So are all those who fight in the so-called 'holy wars.' You're trying to tell me God honors them?"

Patti sniffed but her expression showed doubt. "You would bring up exceptions. I'm talking about good people."

"Who are they?" Shina snapped, her manner so unlike her usual quiet, accommodating self that the others stared. "Remember, Jesus said that there are none good but one—God. What's happening to you, Patti?"

For the beat of a pulse, Lindsey thought their friend would crumble. She looked totally miserable, so much so Lindsey unwisely whispered, "Give it up, Patti. He isn't worth it."

Every trace of weakness fled. Patti's face turned rock-hard. "Bart Keppler is a fine, far-seeing doctor and man. I intend to marry him, if he asks me." She turned on Shina. "As far as your Bible quoting, everyone knows you can prove any point you want by picking and choosing Scripture. Jesus was speaking in parables, as He often did." She pushed back from the table and walked out, but not before a lone tear escaped.

"She may argue all she wants about people having the right to believe the way they choose, but she doesn't believe it," Shina observed. She slumped in her chair, face strangely colorless even above her apricot pants uniform. "World War II was a Sunday school picnic compared to the battle raging inside Patti."

"Early teachings warring with her feelings for Bart," Lindsey muttered. "I should have kept still."

"Yes, you should have," Shina frankly told her. "Right now, her mind's telling her you're a threat to her happiness. Her long friendship is shouting it isn't true. Don't you see? If she could simply write you off as jealous, all the nagging doubts about Black Bart would die. She can't. I pray she never will."

Lindsey stood. "I owe her an apology. Wonder if I can catch her before she gets to Outpatient?"

"Be careful how you approach her," Shina warned. Her smooth brow wrinkled with concern. "She's in love with the wonderful image she's created. Until she sees Dr. Keppler as he is, nothing will change that. One thing's in our favor. So long as he's asking other nurses out, he certainly won't marry Patti."

"See you later." Lindsey hurried out in search of Patti.

She didn't find her. When she got to Outpatient, she ran into Patti's supervisor. "What's chewing on Patti Thompson?" the exasperated charge nurse demanded. "She bursts in here, says she isn't feeling well and can't work. This isn't the first time. In the last few weeks, she's gone from my most dependable nurse to the least. As much as I'd hate to do it, if she doesn't pull herself together, I'll have to write her up." She shook her head, obviously concerned. "I hope it won't come to that. To my knowledge, she's never had a black mark on her record."

Lindsey's heart plummeted.

"Talk to her, will you?" The nurse swung away before Lindsey could say she was the last person in the world to talk with Patti Thompson right now.

Determined to see Terence, Lindsey headed for the Chapel. To her relief, the door of his study-office stood open. "Terry?"

"Here." He came toward her in long strides, obviously delighted to see her. "I miss you, Lindsey." He grinned and ruffled his mahogany-tinted hair. "I sound like my favorite nurse had been visiting Kalamazoo or points east, don't I? But you might as well have been for all I've seen you lately."

His open admiration soothed her troubled heart like mud on a bee sting. "Do you have time to talk?"

Terry's eyes turned poignant blue. "Of course. How about a drive?"

Wondering, Lindsey started to ask why they couldn't talk there in the chapel. A quick shake of Terry's head, a forefinger held in the air, warned her. She swallowed her questions and said, "I report for work at—"

A second warning signal set her heart to thumping. So did Terry's hearty "Good." He quickly put in a call to let the switchboard know he'd be away from the hospital for a time, caught up a jacket and his pager, and ushered her into the hall. To her amazement, he headed for the covered passageway leading to the staff residence building. "Get a warm coat," he told her. "You're being kidnapped."

Lindsey silently obeyed. Coat in hand, she glanced down the hall toward Patti's closed apartment door, tempted to knock.

Terence shook his head violently.

Sighing, Lindsey followed him out to the parking lot. A scowling sky filled with lowering clouds directly above Shepherd of Love promised a deluge. She shivered, remembering the ominous black clouds months before that had made her wonder if trouble for her beloved hospital lay ahead.

"Why the cloak-and-dagger act?" she demanded, once they were snugly belted into the station wagon and he started the motor. She longed for a reassuring grin.

It didn't come. Instead, Terry said, "What shift are you working?"

"Swing. Why?"

"Think your parents would give us space to hash out what's happening? The kids will be in school, won't they? Maybe your mother would even feed two starving hospital refugees lunch." He added irrelevantly, "Dad and I really want to meet your family. There just hasn't been time to invite them out to the farm."

"Of course, but I don't understand. Why now, today?"

He sent her a pitying look. "It's no longer safe to talk at the hospital, Lindsey. Not even in the chapel or my office." He took his right hand from the wheel, fished in his jacket pocket, and laid something in her palm.

The closest she'd ever been to a bugging device was watching detective shows. Now she stared at the small eavesdropping tool with fascination. "Where did you get this? Why, there's dirt on it."

"Found it in a pot of flowers that appeared on my desk this morning."

"You just stumbled on it by chance?" She handed it back.

"No." His gentle voice contrasted strangely with the intrigue swirling through the hospital. "For the last few weeks I've been expecting some such thing." He grinned crookedly. "At least it isn't another voodoo doll."

She felt the weight of the world drop to her shoulders. "So it's real."

"Yes, and I have the feeling we haven't begun to see or comprehend the extent of what's going on." He dropped his hand over hers and squeezed, then returned it to the wheel. She knew the effort it took for him to lightly add, "Time for a ways-and-means meeting of the detective duo."

Her hand tingled from his quick grasp. "That's what I wanted to talk with you about," she eagerly said. In terse sentences she told him of Patti's outburst and that Dr. Keppler had invited Shina on a date. "Since she's already so much a part of this, I think we should tell her the whole thing and ask her to play Mata Hari."

"Would she consent to go out with him?"

"I think so, for such a worthy cause." An ice worm squiggled down Lindsey's spine and she sat up straight. "We're not putting her in danger, are we?"

He considered for a moment. "No reason to believe that, or I wouldn't agree. The things so far have been more harassment than dangerous."

She mulled it over.

"Do you think it would do any good for me to talk with Patti?" he asked.

"Maybe later." She stared out the windshield, where gray drizzle and the monotonous swish-swish of the wipers had a mesmerizing effect. "Right now, she'd feel Shina and I had set her up." Lindsey sighed, spirits at an all-time low. "I don't know what to do about the two-bedroom apartment, either. It's costing more than I can afford." Strange how easy it was to discuss finances with the young chaplain and know he'd understand. "Shina promised she'd move in with me but she feels as I do. Once that happens, we've lost Patti. Although she left of her own accord, it's bound to make her feel the door has closed behind her and that there's no coming back, even if she wanted to."

"What do your folks say?" His rich, deep voice inspired confidences. No wonder he so successfully performed his chaplain duties.

"They're absolute angels. So are my brothers and sisters. I didn't tell them why Patti moved out, just that she did, but I hoped she'd be back. They immediately offered to help make up the difference." She blinked hard and a lump grew in her throat. "Every one of them said I was contributing entirely too much to the family coffers and the time had come for me to think more about myself. How can I, when they did so much to help me through nursing school?"

He countered with a question. "How much do you enjoy giving?"

She turned her gaze from the gloomy day and let it rest on his serious face. "What a strange question!"

"Not really," he disagreed. "They sacrificed for you because they loved doing it. In turn, you became a gracious giver. Don't turn into a grudging receiver, as so many do when faced with the need to accept rather than give. If you do, you rob your family—and others—of knowing the great joy of giving."

Lindsey felt hot color redden her cheeks. Grudging receiver. She'd never thought of it that way. On impulse she said, "You're right. Pride, I guess."

Terence smiled. "It usually is. I had to fight Dad every step of the way when I dropped out of the hospital ship mission and came home. If I remember right, I used the same terminology to him I just gave you in my mini-sermon." His grin widened into a hearty laugh. "All right, where do I turn?"

◆━◆✕◆━◆

Later that evening when Lindsey prepared for work, she faced her mirrored image and brushed her auburn hair. "If I live to be an old, white-haired lady I'll remember today. Not so much for what we did as the simple joy of being together. Dad and Mom adored Terry, and I. . ." Her fingers stilled. The eyes looking back at her opened wide. Tell-tale streaks of color surged into the freckled face. Recognition came on gossamer wings. "Lord, am I in love with Terence O'Shea?"

Yes, a little voice shouted inside her, so insistent it could not be denied.

When had it started, she wondered, this feeling that she wanted to spend the rest of her life with the young chaplain? To laugh and love, to weep and mourn; to bear his children and make a home; to work side by side with the man who had conquered her heart? Perhaps it began with the caring and tenderness he showed toward those he served. Or the evening at the farm, feeling at one with Terry and his father. Had her response lain dormant until this afternoon, when he kissed her in the warm privacy of the station wagon and circled her with strong, protecting arms she passionately wished would never let her go?

Love had not come with trumpet and drums, as her puppy-love fantasies once predicted. Instead, a tiny spark of friendship—fanned by trust and a shared love for the Master—had kindled in the fortress of her heart and sprung into a warm, enduring glow, to last a lifetime.

<hr>

Lindsey had little time to examine her love throughout the following arduous hours. Patient after patient came up from Emergency, a result of the stormy night that had worsened after Terry and Lindsey got back from her parents' home. She remained far beyond the end of her shift, moving from task to task with strength so incredible she knew her heavenly Father granted it to match the present need.

Two o'clock came and went. Three. At half-past, the surgeon in charge announced, "That's it. Thanks for staying, Lindsey. Now get out of here."

Stumbling with fatigue, the exhausted nurse didn't take time to shed her filthy scrubs but headed out the door. The corridor stretched silent and empty before her, eerie, frightening. "Don't be an idiot," she told herself. "You've walked this corridor a thousand times."

Not at this time of night, a horrid little voice reminded. *It's usually at the end of a shift, or when you're going for a break.* Nerves already strained near the breaking point by the excruciating previous hours, she morbidly whispered, "Perfect time and place for trouble." Great. That certainly didn't make her feel any better. She speeded her steps, unable to throw aside a suspicion of something sinister in the quiet building.

Lindsey's uneasiness increased when she neared a deserted nurses' station. It served as a hub for several ICU rooms spraying out like spokes in a wheel. A desk lamp cast a golden pool of light on a welter of papers cluttering the desk.

"Impossible!" Anger replaced Lindsey's debilitation. This particular station should not be unattended. From it, personnel monitored postoperative patients. Was she having a nightmare? She rubbed her eyes, but no genie appeared. Neither did hospital employees. She quickened her pace, reached the station, and quickly scanned the monitors, relieved to find nothing amiss.

Lindsey heard a low cry from one of the rooms. Heedless of her disheveled condition, she hurried inside. The night charge nurse, a kindly LPN, and a scared-looking student nurse stood by the bedside of a white-haired patient Lindsey recognized as Mrs. Landers, a recent gallbladder case.

"Get me out of here," the woman cried. Stark fear showed in her face.

"You're going to be all right, Mrs. Landers," the charge nurse told her.

"I'm not all right!" She struggled against the LPN's restraining hands. "How would you like to wake up and find a hooded figure hovering over your bed, mumbling incantations? Get me out of this hospital!"

"You must have had a nightmare," the LPN soothed.

"Why don't you believe me?" Mrs. Landers sobbed. "It really happened."

Lindsey's blood chilled. Post-op patients sometimes had bad dreams, but Mrs. Landers appeared more alert than one coming out of a nightmare. Then, too, why had the student nurse acted terrified? If only she could talk privately with her.

She had the chance when the girl emerged from the room and stumbled back to the desk at the nurses' station. "How is Mrs. Landers?" she asked.

"All right. They gave her something to help her sleep." The student dropped into a chair, glanced both ways, and confided in a whisper, "She wasn't dreaming. I saw it, too, on the monitor. A dark figure bending over the bed. I told the charge nurse. She thought I was crazy, but she went to investigate."

It explained the abandoned nurses' station. It did not explain the mystery.

Chapter 13

Back and forth. Back and forth. If the telephone didn't ring in the next three minutes, the pacer wouldn't be there to hear it; he wasn't waiting in the cold any longer.

Hunched and furious, the dark figure rubbed freezing hands, trying to restore circulation. When the phone rang at last, he fumbled with the receiver with numb fingers.

No exchange of pleasantries this night. Not that there ever had been many. Now even the veneer of civility had vanished in mutual contempt. "What do you think you're doing? Are you trying to ruin everything we've worked for?" The harsh whisper echoed to the worn, barren rafters.

"You were getting nowhere," the other retorted.

"How is frightening an old woman half out of her wits going to help the Cause?"

"It's just the beginning." A click followed the jeering laugh, then buzzing, like a swarm of enraged bees. The listener held the phone so long a tinny voice droned, "If you'd like to make a call, please hang up and try again."

The receiver dropped with a little crash. As usual, the disembodied voice on the other end of the line had gotten in the last word. It always would.

Heavy pounding on her door roused Lindsey from unfathomable depths of sleep into which she'd drifted after hours of tossing and turning. "Wake up!" The pounding increased in intensity. "Lindsey, open the door."

Lindsey lurched out of bed and through the living room. "Shina?" Her sleep-clouded eyes opened wide when she finally got the door unlocked. "Patti! What are you doing here?" She grabbed the door frame for support.

"There's terrible trouble." Patti's eyes were wide, her face pale. "Let us in, will you?"

Sleep fled before the terror in her friend's eyes. Lindsey helplessly sank to a chair. The other nurses, who looked as if they hadn't slept in a week, sat on the couch. "Tell her," Shina ordered.

Patti's eyes glazed. "There's a conspiracy to destroy Shepherd of Love."

Lindsey felt as if she'd been kicked in the stomach. "Conspiracy?" Even in her wildest imaginings, she hadn't dreamed anything of this magnitude.

Patti licked dry lips. "Yes."

"How do you know?" Lindsey leaned forward, shaking. Shina tossed her an afghan from the couch. Lindsey gratefully wrapped it around her shoulders and sat on her feet to warm them.

"Remember what the intern said at the table about strange things happening? I didn't think anything more about it until after our argument at breakfast yesterday. I just couldn't work." Misery filled her face, but her blue gaze didn't waver. "I didn't want to run into either of you, so I took a different route from Outpatient and detoured past Emergency. Mike, one of the ambulance drivers who often brings patients in, stopped me in the hall."

She paused for breath and Lindsey's nerves screamed.

"Tell her what he said." Shina patted the nurse's arm encouragingly.

"He wanted to know if I knew anything about an undercurrent here at the hospital." Patti licked her lips again. "In the past week, two different families refused to allow Mike to bring relatives to Shepherd of Love, even though it's the closest medical facility. He naturally asked why." Her voice dropped to a whisper. Her eyes looked enormous in her pinched face. "They told him they heard something strange was going on. Rumors about voodoo and patients being visited by hooded figures that make signs in the air and chant."

"What did you say?" Lindsey burst out.

Some of Patti's old spunk surfaced. "Told him it was absurd, of course. Mike promptly said voodoo dolls in the chapel were more than absurd. He said everyone in the hospital knew Terry found a doll made in his image, tucked beneath the Bible on the chapel altar. Is it true?" Her voice quivered.

No need for secrecy now. "Yes." How had word gotten around? Only she, Terence, and his father knew. Lindsey's world spun. What if her earlier suspicions hadn't been so far off, after all? The chaplain freely confessed he'd been in Haiti. Was his candor an excellent cover-up?

O ye of little faith, she flayed herself. She'd stake her life on Terence O'Shea being a man of God and incapable of duplicity. She must never let him know she had doubted him for one moment. His laughing blue eyes would change to fog-gray with hurt.

"Why didn't you tell us?" Shina asked Lindsey, but Lindsey only shook her head and remained silent.

Patti flushed and continued her story. "I was furious with you two and angry anyone would do such a thing. I needed time to think and was glad when I heard Lindsey leave with Terry. I skipped lunch, but by afternoon I couldn't stand myself. I decided to get away from the hospital. Bart—Dr. Keppler—had given me a spare key to his sports car. He said I might want to drive it." She stared at her fingers. "I never had, but yesterday I needed to get away."

She looked up, face haunted. "I'd used up all my tissues crying, so I checked the glove compartment. No luck. Some people toss things under the seat. I groped underneath it. I didn't find tissues but something else." She shivered.

Why must Patti be so maddeningly slow? Lindsey longed to shake her, even while her heart twisted with pity.

"Lindsey, he had a voodoo doll." She cast an imploring glance at Shina.

"The doll looked like you," the tiny nurse explained.

Lindsey couldn't speak.

"I put it in the exact spot I found it, made sure everything else was left undisturbed, came to my room, and tried to think. Later I heard Shina come in and told her. We knew you'd gone on duty and would be safe." Patti faltered. She stood and stumbled across to Lindsey. "Can you ever forgive me?"

"Of course." Lindsey hugged her friend. Their tears mingled.

"Even when I told myself you envied me because of Bart, I knew it wasn't true," Patti brokenly said. She wiped her eyes with the back of her hand. The childish gesture said more than words. "I also secretly felt glad Shina didn't move in with you, although I wouldn't admit it to myself. Lindsey, when I saw that doll with a pin through its heart I thought I'd die from pain." She sat up, took the tissue Shina sympathetically offered, and blew her nose.

"One good thing. It brought me to my senses. How could I swallow all that stuff Bart fed me? How could I believe he cared, or think I loved him?"

Shina softly repeated what she'd told Lindsey earlier. "You fell in love with what you thought he was."

Patti refused to be so easily excused. "I should have known better." She made a face before asking, "Now what?"

"Now I get a certain Terence O'Shea over here." Lindsey sprang for the phone, sent her SOS, asked for a half-hour to get cleaned up, and headed for the shower. Its fine spray washed away the last traces of exhaustion.

Shina busied herself in the kitchenette getting a late breakfast for

Lindsey. Patti perched on Lindsey's bed while her friend dried her hair. "Please, Mother, may I move back in now?" she meekly asked.

"I don't think you should," Lindsey said from behind the auburn curtain of hair that hung over her forehead. She didn't notice the curious stillness from the end of the bed until she shut off the blow dryer and tossed her mane out of her eyes.

"I don't blame you for not being able to forgive me." Patti's bowed blond head showed total defeat.

"It isn't that at all," Lindsey protested. "Stop and think. The minute you come back, the whole hospital will know."

"Including Bart Keppler." Patti's eyes showed understanding.

"Right." A fantastic idea crossed her mind. "Patti, would you and Shina mind giving me a few minutes with Terry before we talk?"

"Of course not." Patti tousled her hair and grinned in the old way. "I may be able to survive that long without being killed by curiosity."

Ten minutes later, Terry and Lindsey sat the other two nurses down and told them the entire story. Lindsey also reported the incident with Mrs. Landers and added, "It's interesting that outsiders knew about it before it happened."

"Maybe they didn't. I intend to have a talk with the intern who made the comments at the table. This may not be the first such happening." Terry looked grim. "Patti, did you ever want to be an actress? Ever take drama or participate in a school or church play?"

She looked at him warily. "A few times."

"How about you, Shina?"

"Ditto. Why?" She cocked her shining dark head to one side.

"If you're game, you might be of great help. I understand Dr. Keppler has asked you out?"

Shina slid an apologetic look at Patti. "Yes, but I didn't go."

Patti looked disgusted. "What a sheik! I must be the most gullible person who ever had the misfortune to cross his path. I hope I never see him again."

"Just be glad you found out now and not later," Terry told her. "Do you think you can keep from letting him know you suspect him?" He rumpled his hair.

"I don't think so." Patti sighed. "I'm not good at hiding my feelings."

"The other alternative would be for you to go on vacation. You mustn't take the chance of his finding out what you saw."

"You could ask for personal leave," Lindsey suggested. "Your supervisor would back you up. She's concerned about the quality of your work lately. I wasn't snooping," she quickly explained. "I went to Outpatient to apologize. . ."

"For my mistakes," Patti choked. "I know my work has slipped."

"I wanted to apologize to you for my mistake when I came on too strong at breakfast," Lindsey gently corrected. "But the charge nurse is genuinely concerned about you. So much that she dreaded having to write you up and spoil your record."

"I made a mess of things, didn't I?"

"Who doesn't from time to time? That's why forgiveness is so important," Terry counseled. Again Lindsey marveled at his ability to say the right thing at the right time. Would things ever settle down so they could spend time together, instead of being embroiled in unsavory doings?

"Do you think Black Bart is the hooded figure?" Shina inquired.

"I don't know," Terry confessed. "It will be interesting to see what he does about it. We won't have long to wait. The hospital's rocking with scuttlebutt about Mrs. Landers's nightmare visitor. Our acting hospital director has called a general staff meeting for this afternoon. We all have to go, especially you, Patti. Sit with Shina, if you like. Better yet, go with someone from Outpatient. It's crucial for you not to betray your change of heart toward either Lindsey or Dr. Keppler." He looked thoughtful. "You don't happen to have a sick or aged relative who could conveniently call you out of town, do you?"

"No." She took a long breath and expelled it slowly. "Am I in danger?"

"I honestly don't know." Terry looked somber and spread his hands in a gesture of helplessness. "We won't take any chances. So far, we aren't sure if Dr. Keppler is guilty of anything except producing voodoo dolls and that could be because—" He stopped abruptly.

"Don't try to spare my feelings," Patti cut in. She raised her chin, a mannerism as familiar to her friends as her blue eyes and blond hair. "I know he can't stand rejection, especially by the female sex. At least part of what's been happening may be a getting-even thing because Lindsey turned him down." Her pretty lips tightened and her friends silently exchanged glances of relief. Evidently Patti's pride had been far more wounded than her tender heart.

That afternoon, hospital personnel assembled in the auditorium-like meeting room like a gaggle of noisy geese. The summons for every person who could be spared from duty to attend, along with rumors of voodoo dolls and mysterious night visitors, generated speculation and even wilder rumors. Lindsey, seated next to Shina and a goodly distance away from an obedient Patti who came with Outpatient friends, felt sickened. Six months earlier, Shepherd of Love staff had good-naturedly discussed the latest engagement or how successful some new procedure had become. Now she saw dismay, even fear in the eyes of her coworkers.

Nicholas Fairchild stepped to the microphone. The last whispers died. Lindsey gasped. She'd expected to see the man bowed before the enormity of the calamity. Not so. Calm as a July morning, shoulders erect as a soldier, he faced the group that in all probability held at least one traitor. Lindsey had the feeling Nicholas had spent most of the day in prayer. Nothing else could account for his tranquillity.

"I am sorry to say hard times have come to us," he said simply. "Someone or ones appear bent on destroying the work we do here. We don't know who or why." He stepped away from the mike and his far-seeing blue eyes flashed. "I promise you this. We will find out!" His resonant voice filled the room.

A thrill of hope straightened slumped shoulders, lifted bowed heads, lightened heavy hearts. For a full minute, the hospital founder let his gaze roam from one side of the room to the other. It lingered on no one, yet Lindsey felt every person present must feel weighed. Who among them would be found wanting?

She stopped her mental woolgathering and disciplined a laugh when Nicholas said, "Bartholomew has a few words for us." How did the handsome acting hospital director like being addressed that way? She stared at the man striding forward, anticipating the moment when he turned to face those he supposedly served.

Shina's small, strong fingers dug into Lindsey's arm. "I can't believe it," she hissed.

Neither could Lindsey. Bart's face flamed with righteous indignation, eyes darker than obsidian in his white face. "Even the most Christian hospital cannot withstand evil forces if they are allowed to continue," he said, voice deadly. "Measures must be taken to discover and resolve any disturbing influence. I pledge to you to do my utmost to bring about the ultimate best for Shepherd of Love and all those who work and come here." He walked out, in a wild storm of applause.

Lindsey felt confused. Had the voodoo dolls only been a childish way of getting even? If not, how could Bart Keppler stand before them like an avenging angel bent on destroying evil? Lucifer himself couldn't have been more convincing. Lindsey had come to the meeting believing she'd see guilt in his eyes, a furtive flicker strong enough to confirm suspicion and expose Black Bart's masquerade. Instead, truth rang in his voice. Sincerity. He simply couldn't have been the hooded figure in Mrs. Landers's room.

Lindsey burned to get her codetectives' reactions, but she had no opportunity. Too many persons milled around her, praising Nicholas Fairchild and Dr. Keppler and expressing confidence that the whole thing would soon blow over. Even Shina could only lift one silky, questioning eyebrow. Lindsey had the feeling her small friend felt as muddled as she. A glimpse of Patti showed nothing but a bland mask. Good girl. The tight knot inside Lindsey loosened. At least Patti's eyes had been opened. No matter how innocent Bart was of frightening patients, Patti would neither forgive nor forget the hidden doll made in the likeness of her friend.

Terence O'Shea stood to one side, allowing the crowd to thin. Lindsey lingered as well. When everyone had gone, she started out, walking slowly enough for him to catch up.

"Are you headed for the dining hall?" he asked, voice loud enough to reach anyone who might be listening.

"Yes. I'm starved." Lindsey added in a whisper. "What do you think?"

"He's a clever man." Terry kept his voice low. "He also won the full support of almost everyone there. Did you notice the expression on faces around you?" She nodded and he continued. "Lindsey, everything he said is true. The catch is, it's all generalities." He ticked them off on strong, sensitive-looking fingers.

"One: Even the most Christian hospital *can't* withstand evil forces.

"Two: Measures certainly must be taken to discover and resolve this situation.

"Three: He pledged to do his utmost to bring about the ultimate best." Terry half-closed his eyes. "That gave me the creeps. Just what is Bart's utmost? What does he consider is the ultimate best?" He broke off at the dining room door.

They walked inside. Lindsey stopped short. Dr. Keppler sat between Patti and Shina at their usual table. She felt anger spurt. How dared he?

"Your feelings are showing," Terry warned. "Now is the time for all good detectives to put on their most guileless faces for the good of the mystery."

Laughing at his nonsense, she hastily adjusted her expression, chose food from the well-laden tables, and marched to the table. "Hello, everyone."

Bart and Shina responded. Patti studiously avoided eye contact and peppered her salad. Lindsey wanted to cheer. Transparent her friend might be, but Patti's loyalty would see her through a hard time.

"I've just been telling these charming ladies we need a break from this unpleasantness. I'd like to take you out for dinner as soon as we're all off at the same time." He cut into perfectly done roast beef. "Patti?"

She started to answer, raised her napkin, and sneezed. Lindsey suspected she'd deliberately taken the chunk of lettuce with the most pepper. Patti sneezed again.

"Doesn't sound like you'll be going out," Shina observed. "Better take a few days off and see if this develops into anything."

A third sneeze saved Patti the need to answer.

Lindsey hastily turned attention to herself. "I have tonight off, due to the extra hours I put in this morning. I am absolutely beat."

"Too bad." Bart laid his fork across his plate. "Were you by any chance in on the disturbance with Mrs. Landers?" He eyed her curiously.

"Uh-huh." Lindsey forced herself to sound disinterested. "I finished in surgery super late—well, early." She yawned. "Still feeling it, by the way."

"So, what happened?"

"I didn't see anything except an upset patient and concerned nurses." *Good going, Lindsey,* she complimented herself. *You're turning into a master of evasion. Every word is the truth and nothing but the truth, if not the whole truth.* She bit back a grin.

Patti sneezed once more and excused herself. Lindsey had the feeling she felt herself on thin ice. Evidently Terence noticed it, as well. He immediately went into an amusing incident that had happened on the farm.

"Combite, huh?" Bart forked up the last of his chocolate cake.

"Excuse me?" The chaplain's eyes took on a terrier brightness.

"Interesting that you combine fun with your farm duties." He glanced at the wall clock. "I have to run." Never had his smile been more charming. "See you."

"Not if we can help it," Terry mumbled the minute Bart got out of hearing.

"Terry!" Shina's shocked whisper echoed Lindsey's reaction.

"Keppler's a first class liar," Terry whispered in a fierce voice. "He pretended ignorance of Haiti, but he just used the word *combite*. It's a Haitian word that describes how neighbors move from farm to farm, singing, planting, and harvesting." The chaplain's eyes gleamed with triumph. "That little slip is going to cost Black Bart dearly."

328

Chapter 14

A feeling of waiting stole through the hospital halls and into the rooms. To everyone's relief, no more hooded figures or voodoo dolls appeared. However, a rash of small incidents took place, each seemingly insignificant, all undermining the hospital's credibility.

"It's insidious," Terence told his father at breakfast. "No one knows how or why. Nothing's happening that can't be explained in a logical manner or attributed to human failure. Still, I can't help wondering what all this is leading up to and when it will end."

"For example?"

"Two different patients—one of them Mrs. Landers—complained to the charge nurse on duty that I didn't bother to come when they sent for me." His eyes took on a brooding look. "I knew nothing about their requests until the nurses called me personally. What could I tell the patients? That I may well be the victim of a conspiracy to help destroy Shepherd of Love's credibility?" He laughed harshly.

"Do you hold to the conspiracy theory?" The older man leaned forward in his chair, gnarled hands on the table.

"It can't be ruled out."

"Have you been able to figure out if it's you or the hospital that's under attack?"

"Probably both." Terry shook his head. "Dad, this is getting me down. There's also another problem. I don't know what Keppler will do if he finds out Patti Thompson saw the voodoo doll in his car. She took yesterday off, after sneezing at dinner." Some of his gloom lifted and his fine teeth flashed in a winning smile.

"Lindsey told me Patti shoved a forkful of well-peppered salad under her nose to keep from accepting Bart's dinner invitation. Shina innocently commented she should take time off. I wish she had an out-of-town friend or relative who needed her, so she could leave the hospital altogether."

"She does." Intrigue darkened the blue of Shane O'Shea's eyes.

"Who? She's racked her brain and not come up with anyone."

"Me," Shane promptly told his son.

"You?" Terry exploded with laughter.

"The same. Faith and mercy me, Lad, no one qualifies more. I'm out of town. Any friend of yours is a friend of mine."

"You don't need her."

"Oh?" Shane refused to abandon his idea. "Since when did a handsome Irishman like me not need a pretty colleen around to cosset him a bit?"

"It might not be such a bad idea at that," Terry agreed. "This is the last place Keppler would think of looking. Patti didn't let on she and Lindsey had made up their differences. Bart must know I'd be in sympathy with Lindsey." He shoved back his chair. "Dad, you're a genius." He laughed again. "Or maybe a knight in shining armor."

"Nay. Just a man who cannot abide the idea of an innocent maiden being harmed. Go fetch your friend." A canny look crept into his keen eyes. "If you really feel there's danger for her, don't tell anyone where she's to be." He paused. "Does the hospital require employees going on vacation to account for their whereabouts?"

"No."

"Good. The fewer people who know, the better. She'll naturally want to inform her parents so they don't send out an alarm, but have her call from here."

Terry seized on the idea. "She can tell them she's trying to avoid someone and if anyone calls asking for her address, not to give it. They can simply say she's out of town and they aren't sure when she'll be back. All true." He looked rueful. "It seems ridiculous for Lindsey and Shina not to know she's here."

"It isn't. One of them might be surprised into disclosing her whereabouts," Shane warned.

<hr />

Feeling like the lead character in a swashbuckler novel, Terence smuggled Patti and a well-packed suitcase out of her apartment under cover of darkness and the dinner hour. She acted glad to go. The past few days had taken their toll. She maintained a dispirited silence until they reached the farmhouse. However, the same atmosphere that had made Lindsey feel so at home weeks earlier gradually brought her peace.

She ate every crumb of the simple meal Shane offered, then insisted on doing the dishes and making up the bed in the guest room. Some of her sparkle returned. Terry had the feeling Patti was slipping out of a bad dream and back to normalcy.

"While I'm here, I intend to cook and clean to my heart's content," she earnestly told her hosts. "I'm a secret homemaker at heart." She fell silent and stared into the flames in the fireplace as Lindsey had done, curled up on the same braided rug.

True to her word, she did everything she could to fit into the family. Terry found himself looking forward to coming home at night to a house that bore an unmistakable woman's touch. After polishing off two pieces of pumpkin pie the third night she was there, he told her, "Miss Patricia Thompson, if I were not already smitten with your red-haired friend, I'd fall in love with you on the spot."

Her laugh sounded like the chime of bells in the wind. "Alas, kind sir, I fear 'twould only be for my pumpkin pie."

"Not true," he indignantly told her. "I also like your apple dumplings, baked salmon with dressing, and bread pudding."

She threw a dish towel at him and announced that for that he could load the dishwasher while she put things away.

When they finished, he laid one hand on her arm and looked into her eyes. "I meant what I said, Patti. Any man except one irrevocably in love with another woman would be proud to win your love."

The shine of tears softened her blue eyes. "Thanks, Chaplain. I needed that right now. It's good to know." Her serious mood vanished. "Especially when you're robbing me of my best friend, if the wind's blowing the way I think."

He shamelessly decided to pump her for information. "You think I have a chance?" he anxiously asked.

"Maybe. Want me to put in a good word for you?" she teased.

"You repeat what I just said and you'll be in mega-trouble," Terry warned with a mock frown. "When the time comes, I'll tell her myself."

Patti giggled and ran into the living room. "Help, your son is threatening me," she told Shane who sat watching with a half-smile.

"You don't look frightened."

"As if anyone ever could—here." A shadow crossed her expressive face, dampening her lashes. She raised her chin. "Let's forget all that while we can."

The next evening, Terry came home from work heavy-hearted. If only he could keep the latest hospital news to himself! No use trying. If Patti didn't see through him, Dad would.

Patti did. The minute Shane asked the blessing she said, "You may as well tell us." Her lips set in a thin line.

Terry saw her brace herself for bad news. "Fine thing for a chaplain," he said glumly. "I reflect change like a weather-vane in a hurricane."

"What happened?" she demanded.

"Mike reported another person refused to be brought to the hospital."

"What else?" Her clear gaze pinned him down.

"Isn't that enough?"

The relentless head shake brought a sigh and Terry cleared his throat. "Lindsey had a bit of trouble in surgery late last night."

"Trouble! How?" Her eyes resembled twin mountain lakes reflecting a cloudless sky.

"It happened during an operation. An important instrument turned up missing. Thank God the surgeon could substitute another instrument. The patient came through fine."

"Someone didn't set up properly?" Patti clutched the table with white-nailed fingers.

"That's the problem. Lindsey set up the table." Anger flared. Terry felt his blood boil at the blatant attempt to discredit the woman he loved. "She told me she personally checked, then double-checked the instruments shortly before surgery. I believe her."

"So do I!" Patti cried. "The rest of us make mistakes, but not Lindsey. Even when she's exhausted, she's never selected the wrong instrument or slipped up in any way." Crimson flags waved in her cheeks. "Terry, I'm going back."

"You can't! Don't you see? The viciousness of the attacks is increasing."

Patti paled but stood her ground. "I know. A patient might have died." She managed a wan smile. "I won't be sheltered any longer. These few days have given me time to get myself together. I'm going back to the hospital. If it takes pretending to go along with Bart Keppler, even getting engaged to him, I'll do it. I won't have Lindsey, you, and the hospital destroyed."

Terry expected a torrent of tears and marveled when they didn't come. He looked into the sweet face. His admiration grew. Here was a friend worthy of the name. Patti's set lips were the lips of a woman, not a much-admired girl.

"You not only can, you must," Shane said. "Finish your dinner. We'll miss you, but it's time for you to go back."

Before she and Terence drove away, the older man bade her kneel on the rug where she loved to curl up. He placed his hands on her head and asked God's protection, guidance, and wisdom for the difficult task that lay ahead. He closed by putting her in God's care. Terry had the feeling Patti would remember the blessing as long as she lived. So would he.

———◆—❈—◆———

The days of Patti's absence had shown Lindsey a fuller view of her own heart when it came to Terence O'Shea. She knew he had spirited Patti away. She recognized the wisdom of no one knowing where. Yet a little ache came now and then despite her best efforts and Terry's plea, "Trust me, Lindsey." At last she admitted to a secret fear. The young chaplain's obvious admiration for her friend appeared to be growing like zucchini. Where did that leave Lindsey?

In vain she prayed, asking God to remove every hint of jealousy from her heart if Terry fell in love with Patti. She knew he spent every evening with the blond nurse. Perhaps she had placed too much significance on the single kiss that now seemed an eternity ago. What did a kiss mean in today's world?

"It meant something to me," Lindsey confessed. She thought how all through the years she'd either been too busy or cared too little to date a great deal. Boys and men who attempted to turn evenings into a wrestling match found her unavailable for future dates. She just laughed and went her untroubled way when they called her old-fashioned and a prude.

All that changed when Dr. Keppler and Terence O'Shea came to the hospital. The attraction she had felt for the dark-haired acting director had been short-lived. Her feelings for the chaplain had not. Tired of fighting, she finally whispered into her pillow, "If this is how You want it, Lord, okay." The next second honesty forced her to add, "But I can't say I'll like it." She fell asleep smiling, less troubled than she'd been since Patti had been whisked away to some unknown destination.

The incident with the missing instrument shook her to the core. So did the unaccustomed reprimand from the surgeon in charge. She stood dumbly before him, unwilling to defend herself for fear of repercussions. Shina wanted to go to Nicholas Fairchild. Lindsey refused. He had enough to contend with just now without taking up the cause of a nurse who could prove nothing. Yet she couldn't help worrying.

"If this kind of thing keeps up, Terry and I will both be dismissed from Shepherd of Love for incompetence," she told Shina the day after the operating theater incident.

"It won't happen."

"It might and there isn't a thing I can do about it. If I say the table was sabotaged, every person in Surgery will be questioned. I can't cast a slur on their integrity." She stared straight ahead, feeling caught on a treadmill that offered no escape.

A light tap sounded. The unlocked door swung open. Lindsey normally locked it only when she was out of the room, but at Shina's insistence, she'd started bolting it except when Shina visited.

A blond-haloed face peered in. "Looks like I've not even been missed."

"Patti!" Lindsey sprang from the couch and hugged the perky nurse. "You look wonderful."

"Why shouldn't I?" She blew a wispy curl off her forehead. "I've been milk, egg, and chicken fed. I've slept with the night breeze coming in my window—under a quilted comforter, of course," she hastily added.

A rich chuckle came from the doorway.

Lindsey whirled. "She's been at the farm!"

"Yes, and a right good farm wife she'll make some lucky man." Terry's smiling face radiated affection.

Lindsey's heart dropped to the soles of her feet.

Patti laughed joyously. "Talk about blarney. Terence, take my suitcase to my temporary abode." She looked around the charming green apartment. "I can't wait to get back."

Terry's merry whistle and excellent spirits depressed Lindsey even more. Try as she would, she just couldn't be glad for Patti.

The smaller nurse flopped into a chair. "Good to be home, even though the farm is wonderful. I could fall in love with Shane O'Shea if I were older or he were younger."

"There's always his son." Lindsey managed to say.

"Are you kidding? You don't fall in love with a guy who's so gone on another woman he tells you so pointblank." Mischief lurked in Patti's eyes. "When are you going to give him a break, Lindsey? By the way, if you ever let on I said anything, I'll—I'll—I know," she cried. "I'll refuse to be in your wedding and it won't be legal." She spun around the room like a happy top.

"Only you could come up with something like that," Shina said cuttingly.

"I know. I'm awful." She looked repentant. "It's just that I missed you."

"Why did you come back?" Shina wanted to know. "If anything, things are worse, not better." She glanced at Lindsey.

Patti's impromptu dance broke off mid-step. "That's why." A deep flush stained her smooth cheeks. "Think I'm going to hide out on the farm and let my best friends in the whole world face this horror alone? A week ago, maybe. Not now. I'll have you know I'm going to take on Bart Keppler single-handed, if necessary."

"She looks like she means it," Shina said.

"I think she does." Lindsey felt the world slide from her shoulders and a light go on in her heart. If Terry cared enough to confide in Patti. . . She couldn't finish the sentence. When he came back, she saw the steady look he gave her. Unless she were completely off track, the sparkle of love lurked in his blue, blue eyes.

"So what's been happening?" Patti wanted to know. "I wormed a few things out of Terry, but he's tighter than a clam when it comes to telling things. Well, sometimes," she tacked on.

Lindsey saw the black look he shot in Patti's direction. Delight filled her and a sense of well-being. Patti might exaggerate, but even her over-active imagination couldn't conjure up a story unless enough truth existed to serve as a foundation.

"Black Bart asked me out again," Shina put in. "I said I'd go." The corners of her mouth turned down. "You know how crazy I am about that." She brightened. "Now that Patti's back, maybe he'll renege.

"One thing. I'm going to make the most of this opportunity. I do not intend to go out with T.D.M. more than once," Shina declared.

Patti yawned ostentatiously. "All the country air and relaxation left me beat. It's bed for me."

"Same here." Shina gritted her teeth. "A girl should look her best on every date—even if she can't stand her escort." She followed Patti into the hall, closing the door behind her.

"I feel as if a typhoon swept through here." Lindsey motioned Terry to a chair.

"Patti has that effect," he agreed. Lights danced in his eyes. "Did she say anything, uh, special, while I was out of the room?"

Lindsey couldn't have kept from blushing if her life depended on it. "Well—"

"It's all right," Terry told her. "I wanted to give you more time, but. . ." He stopped and she had the feeling he fought a battle. If so, he lost. In a swift movement, he caught her in his arms. "I know this isn't romantic and it's not at all as I planned, but hang it all, Lindsey, I don't know when we'll have time alone again. This whole hospital thing is messing up everyone and everything. I probably shouldn't be telling you this. We don't know what lies ahead." Poignancy softened his gaze. "I love you. I have since we collided in the dining room doorway. Right now all I have to offer you is that and what may be the worse part of 'for better or worse.' "

She placed one hand over his lips. "As if that matters."

"You mean it?" Worry lines smoothed out and Terry regained the boyish charm eclipsed by trouble in the past few weeks. He gently cupped her face in his hands.

"I do."

He pulled her hand free with one of his own, lowered his head until his lips touched hers, and kissed her in a way guaranteed to send doubt packing and happiness surging through her.

Later, they sat side by side on the couch, Lindsey's auburn head cradled against Terry's broad shoulder. She sensed a hesitancy, a certain withdrawal, but could not identify it until he tentatively said, "About Dad—"

"He will be with us," she interrupted.

"Are you sure?" He held her away from him so he could look deep into her eyes. "Most brides don't want an in-law around, at least at first. We could make other arrangements. That is, if I still have a job."

She temporarily ignored the last sentence. "I'm not any bride and Shane O'Shea's certainly not any in-law. What better arrangement than for him to be with us?" She nestled closer to him. "Once we're married, I'll tell the powers that be: no more shift or nightwork. We'll come and go home together—to Dad."

"What did I ever do to have God give me such a wonderful companion?" Terry whispered.

She laughed, a tender, understanding laugh that showed the height and depth of a love that surpassed all but the love of God. "Funny. I was just thinking the same thing."

Chapter 15

A niggling worry about Shina accompanied Lindsey like a minor strain during her entire shift. Could the small nurse handle Dr. Keppler, if the need arose? Had they been wrong to encourage her to go out with him, even on a fishing-for-clues expedition?

Don't get paranoid, she told herself. *Bart wouldn't dare step out of line at this point. He's more apt to be charming and try to make a good impression. Wonder if Shina will learn anything? I can hardly wait to see her. Something has to break soon.* She sent up a quick prayer and went on with her work, grinning at the secret code the three nurses had set up. If Shina got home before Lindsey finished her shift, she'd slip a small piece of paper under Lindsey's door.

"What about me?" Patti had demanded, round blue eyes indignant.

"You'll hear me come in," Shina had reminded her. "Just make sure Black Bart drives away in his sports chariot before you come roaring down the hall to my room."

"Sports chariot! You're getting as fanciful with words as Lindsey."

"Who says you can't teach old dogs new tricks?" Shina had smirked. Her shining dark eyes showed her joy that the three of them were together and back on their old footing.

When her shift ended, Lindsey bundled up in the warm coat she'd taken the precaution to throw over her arm before going on duty. The afternoon had been sunny, but now the night was cold. Fresh, slightly salty air blew in from Puget Sound, snatching reluctant leaves from nearly bare branches and ruthlessly whirling them to the ground. Thanksgiving came late enough this year that they might get a skiff of snow. Despite the darkness around her, she brightened at the thought of the upcoming holiday. The entire Best family would be together, along with Terence O'Shea and his father.

Lindsey stepped into the covered passageway and gave a skip of pure happiness. Even the shroud of intrigue surrounding the hospital couldn't smother this precious time of loving and being loved.

She walked into the common gathering room of the residence hall and yawned. Bed certainly sounded good tonight. A slight stir in the dimly lit room set her heart shivering in her throat. "Who—?"

"Bart." His mouth smiled. His cold, dark eyes did not. "I never get to talk with you, Lindsey. Is it true you're going to marry O'Shea?"

The last thing she wanted was a confrontation in a deserted room at this time of night. Summoning her most freezing tones, she told him, "I can't see how that concerns you."

His hands shot out, gripping her arms above the elbow. "More than you know." An unpleasant smile turned his normally charming face into an ugly devil's mask. "I've been asked to stay on as hospital director, at least until next summer. Seems my predecessor needs extra time to recuperate." He casually added, "In the event something—unexpected—happens, I will be here permanently, with the power to hire and fire."

She tore free from his restraining hands. "Are you threatening me?"

"Let's just say if you value your position here, you'll be more tolerant of others' beliefs. I intend to make sweeping changes."

"The board of directors and Nicholas Fairchild will never permit that."

"Boards of directors, even hospital founders, can be replaced." The light of fanaticism in Dr. Keppler's dark eyes showed him to be dangerously close to the line between sanity and madness.

Lindsey's gasp acted like cold water in his face. In a chameleon-like shift, he again became the urbane doctor. "I hope I didn't frighten you, my dear." He laughed lightly. "I'm just so eager to do what's best for Shepherd of Love, to modernize it and make the hospital an example to the world, I sometimes get ahead of myself." His smile was full of charm. "Seriously, Lindsey, why can't we work together, rather than being at cross-purposes?" His expression grew tolerant. "You've even turned Shina against me. She refused a simple good-night kiss. Said she never kissed a first date."

"That's between Miss Ito and you, Dr. Keppler." Lindsey detoured around him, unlocked the door to the long corridor leading to her apartment, and stepped through. He started to follow. She forced a smile. "Sorry. I need to lock this behind me."

He held the door open and lowered his voice. "I was a fool to ever date Patti and turn you against me," he said. "Can't we go back to our first date? We were real friends then. I just tried to make you jealous. You're the woman I want for my wife. Can you forgive me?" His wistful penitence would have done credit to a martyr.

"Good night, Dr. Keppler."

He reluctantly released his hold on the door closing between them. "Good night, my darling."

The solid click of the lock had never been more welcome. Lindsey went limp against it for a moment before slowly walking down the hall. No need to check for Shina's piece of paper under her door. Her friend was safely in. Lindsey sighed with relief and tapped lightly.

Patti yanked the door open, blond hair ruffled above a turquoise robe. "Hurry in," she whispered. "Just wait until you hear. Bart brought Shina home, hurried around to my door, and asked me to marry him! Can you believe it?" She made a horrible face. "I remembered my new role just in time and said I'd think about it, instead of slamming the door in his conceited face."

"You, too?" Lindsey felt a paroxysm of laughter well up inside her. She dropped to a chair. "He must plan to be a bigamist. He just proposed to me."

"How come I got left out?" Shina demanded, arms tucked into the flowing sleeves of the colorful kimono she wore in her room. "All he told me was since I didn't kiss guys good night on the first date, we must be sure to have another date as soon as possible."

They laughed until healing tears poured. Mopping her face, Lindsey sobered. "He's showing symptoms of insanity." She repeated their extraordinary conversation. "Something in his voice when he talked about Nicholas and the board of directors being replaced terrified me." She caught her breath. "That could explain the death threat Nicholas received. We can't wait any longer. I'm going to Terry tomorrow. He has to tell someone what's going on."

"Who?" Patti wanted to know. "If there's really a conspiracy, the hospital could be crawling with sympathizers to whatever cause Bart's supporting."

Lindsey felt herself blanch.

"She's right," Shina said. "The only person we can totally trust is Nicholas Fairchild himself."

<hr />

At eleven o'clock the next morning, Lindsey and Terence sat facing the man God had given the vision for Shepherd of Love. Item by item they poured out every happening, significant or otherwise, then repeated snatches of conversation that pointed toward Bart Keppler's duplicity.

"I knew beyond a shadow of a doubt when he used the Haitian word *combite*," Terry explained to the listening man whose eyes were shadowed with pain at the thought of evil in his beloved hospital. "He quickly added it must be neat to *combine* fun and farm duties, but I knew he'd lied earlier when he said he'd never been in Haiti."

They omitted nothing, even though Lindsey squirmed when she reported

Bart's proposals, first to Patti, then to herself. "I honestly think he's almost over the edge," she added. "Voodoo dolls are one thing. Frightening patients and stealing instruments laid out for surgery is something else."

"I agree." Nicholas clapped his hands together in a decisive gesture. "First, let me say I know you're incapable of criminal carelessness in your work, Lindsey. I have full confidence in you." He turned to Terence and smiled warmly. "And in you. Each of you represents the highest ideals of Shepherd of Love."

Lindsey held her eyelids wide open to keep back tears of gratitude.

"You're right about the situation worsening." Nicholas reached into his shirt pocket and withdrew a newspaper clipping. "This came shortly before you did." He read aloud:

BIZARRE HAPPENINGS AT SHEPHERD OF LOVE?

According to Dr. Bartholomew Keppler, acting director, reports of unusual incidents at the highly respected Seattle hospital are grossly exaggerated. "Nightmares can easily be construed as reality," Dr. Keppler says. "As far as the presence of voodoo dolls, I have seen no such evidence. Shepherd of Love will continue to serve the community as it has since its inception. I am personally spearheading a complete investigation but expect to find nothing."

Dr. Keppler will continue at the helm of the hospital until the former director is fully recuperated and able to resume his duties.

"Clever move," Terry observed. "He comes off as a good guy while informing the entire city of Seattle something weird is going on at Shepherd of Love."

"How can anyone be so vile?" Lindsey burst out.

"I strongly suspect Dr. Keppler sincerely believes in what he's doing," Nicholas told them. His blue eyes shadowed. "I also suspect he's part of a satanic cult determined to infiltrate any institution dedicated to doing the Lord's work. I've known the time would come. Satan will not permit those who serve God to succeed, if he can possibly stop them. The important thing is, how are we going to stop him? If I tip off the board of directors and ask them to fire him, it also alerts Keppler's allies. There may be one on the board itself."

Terry thoughtfully fitted the fingertips of his hands together. "Right.

You know the best way to catch thieves is to set another thief after them? I have an idea." He proceeded to outline it.

"It's too dangerous," Lindsey protested. "If it doesn't work. . ." The rest of the sentence rattled in her throat.

"It has to work." Terry ground his teeth and his eyes changed to November gray. "Don't forget. We'll have the element of surprise." He hesitated. "It's going to be hard on Patti. Can she do it?"

"She will have to. Besides, she's grown up a lot recently," Lindsey said.

Nicholas Fairchild had the last word. "Terence, tell only those who absolutely must know. We can't be sure how many have been snared into this thing." He rose, shook hands warmly, and told them to keep him informed.

Terry agreed to talk with Patti when she got off work; Lindsey would be on duty.

"She readily agreed," he told Lindsey over coffee in a deserted staff lounge during her break. He'd done some visiting and ended up outside Surgery on the chance he might see her. "When Bart presses her for an answer about marrying him, she's going to say, 'If you really love me,' then let her voice trail off. No promises, but he'll be self-centered enough to feel she accepted him. It should allay suspicion. That's phase one of Operation Hospital Rescue."

"Phase two concerns me more."

"I know." He stood, pulled her up, and let her head rest on his shoulder. "Don't worry, Lindsey. God is going to see us through. He actually has more at stake than we do. He won't allow evil to overcome work dedicated to Him."

Lindsey clung to him, raised her face for his kiss, then reluctantly freed herself. "Back to work for me." She added in a whisper, "When are you—?"

"Shhh." He placed a hand over her mouth. "You need to be surprised. A lot of our success depends on how well you play your part."

"Some comfort," she flared, then followed up with a grin. He left her at the door with a bland comment concerning how nice a quiet night in Surgery must be and headed down the hall without looking back. Lindsey wished he'd turn at the junction of the corridors, perhaps give her a thumbs-up signal. He didn't. She sighed, realizing they couldn't be sure no prying eyes watched.

———◆◆◆◆◆———

Dr. Keppler announced his engagement to Patti Thompson at breakfast the next morning. Lindsey tore her gaze from her friend's uncommunicative face and saw the malicious flash in Bart's eyes. She parried and thrust, choosing her words carefully. "Well, if congratulations are in order, they certainly should be given." She almost came unglued when Shina dropped her napkin on the floor, evidently to hide her feelings at the ambiguous, meaningless sentence.

Engrossed with his own importance, Bart didn't seem to notice. "We'll be married at Christmas." He attacked his eggs with gusto. "Have to postpone our honeymoon for a time, but that's okay with you, isn't it, Patti?"

"I don't care a thing about a honeymoon right now," she obediently agreed. A flash of humor twinkled in her eyes, but by the time Bart looked up, Patti's long lashes rested on her flushed cheeks like little half-moons.

The door to the dining room opened. Nicholas Fairchild stepped inside. Something in his manner stilled table conversation. "I am sorry to interrupt your breakfasts," he quietly said. "Something has happened you need to know. Chaplain Terence O'Shea's father was admitted at six o'clock this morning."

"Shane?" "Oh, no!" Dismayed expressions came from every corner of the shocked room. Even those who hadn't met Shane knew how close Terry O'Shea was to his father. Lindsey felt sweat start on her forehead. Her heart twisted in sympathy for Patti, who looked as if she'd been hit.

Dr. Keppler sprang to his feet, face mud-colored. "Will he be all right?"

"We certainly hope so. O'Shea will receive the attention he needs. Fortunately, we had a private room vacant on the second floor so he won't be disturbed." Nicholas strode out, leaving a buzz behind him.

Bart sat back down, face gray. Again Lindsey marveled. Keppler hated Terry. Why, then, did he look so stricken because the young chaplain's father now lay ill in Shepherd of Love? Not sure she could play out her part in the drama begun with Nicholas's announcement, Lindsey excused herself from the others and beat a retreat. She made sure no one was paying any particular attention to her, took a circuitous route, and ended up in the chapel.

"So far, so good," Terry whispered into her ear once she got inside his study-office. He kept his lips close to her ear. "Dad's having the time of his life. Said he'd been feeling miffed at having to play silent partner in our sleuthing stunts. In addition, he's going to get his annual exam—by a doctor we've known for years. I had a little talk with Mallory, explained our plan, and got blasted." Terry laughed. "Once he came down from hitting the roof, he agreed to go along with it. Said something had to be done before human termites undermined Shepherd of Love internally and it collapsed around our heads."

"Do you think this will force Keppler to make his move?" Lindsey scarcely breathed, mindful of the bug Terry had found.

"No time like the present. Dad's all set up in his private room." Terry's grin didn't erase the anxiety in his eyes. "Says he feels like a piece of cheese in a rat trap. How did Nicholas do?"

"Great," Lindsey enthusiastically whispered. "He's almost as good with weasel words as I am. He appeared to say everything and really told nothing!"

Terry chuckled before longing filled his voice. "I just want this whole thing to end, so we can be together." He tilted her chin upwards and landed a kiss on her lips. "I have to go. Say a prayer."

"I will." She watched him go, shoulders squared against the upcoming ordeal. *God, grant a speedy end to this nightmare of evil.*

Chapter 16

Terence O'Shea fought drowsiness in the narrow confines of the small bath off the private room where his father lay peacefully sleeping. Anything that happened would be soon. Swing shift had long since given way to the influx of night workers. Now the hospital lay as silent as it ever became, the perfect time for enemy forces planning to strike. The bustle of Emergency, even Surgery, where angels of life and death observed no lull, felt far away.

Terry yawned and passionately wished for action. Better to get it over with, as he had told Lindsey. His lips curled in a smile. A warm glow filled him. During the long years of being too busy for love, of wondering if he would ever find the companionship Dad had shared with Mother, God had known the blessing that awaited him.

A slight scraping sound banished his pleasant thoughts. Terry noiselessly slid the bathroom door open a crack, enough to permit a full view of the dimly lit room. The partly raised window shade let in enough light for him to see anything that transpired. His heart skipped a beat when a dark, hooded figure inched through the door and crept toward the bed. It raised its arms. An almost inaudible mumbling began.

Terry felt cold sweat bead his forehead, even though he knew no supernatural being loomed over his father. His muscles tensed, preparing him to burst into the room and grapple with the figure. *Not yet,* an inner voice warned. He crouched, ready to spring, held back by his gut-level feeling.

One hand of the mysterious figure swept downward, disappeared into the capacious, enveloping black cloak, and withdrew an object. A voodoo doll? No. When held aloft, the object shone silver in the dim light.

Now!

Terry launched himself like a missile toward the hooded horror holding the hypodermic needle, tackled the figure around the waist, and seized the upheld arm.

For a moment the unexpected onslaught halted the murderous intruder. The hypodermic needle fell to the floor. Then with strength increased a hundredfold by fear, the figure writhed from Terry's grip, muttered a curse, and spun to face the young chaplain. Terry sucked in his breath. Instead of Dr. Keppler's face, a hideous painted mask stared at him.

A slight sound came from the bed. *Dear God, has Dad been harmed?* Terry whirled toward the bed, forgetting all else in a rush of terror.

The moment gave the intruder an advantage. It leaped for the doorway, pulled the door closed behind it.

"Go after him," Shane hissed.

"You're all right?"

"Fine. Now go!"

Terry sprinted for the door, into the hallway. Not even a muffled footstep betrayed the presence of anyone foreign to the hospital. He hurried to the nearest nurses' station. "Did you see anyone pass this way?" he asked the LPN at the desk in a low voice, mindful of weary, sleeping patients who must not be disturbed.

"Why, no." She looked astonished. "This is the quietest night we've had in ages."

Terry hid his disappointment. "May I use the phone?"

"Of course. As long as you're here, I'll grab a cup of coffee."

The minute she got out of earshot, he dialed a number. "We've had an intruder. Follow anyone who leaves the hospital. Got it?" He hung up, chatted a moment with the returning LPN, and went back down the hall. His nerves twanged at the close call. No more playing bait for Dad.

Terry reentered the private room, lighted now from the bed lamp Shane had switched on. He stared at his father.

Shane looked none the worse for the episode. He sat on the edge of his bed, one hand clutching something.

"What are you grinning about?" Terry demanded. "What if the backup plan fails? We won't have a shred of proof."

"Wrong." Shane's eyes gleamed with triumph. He slowly opened his clenched fingers and displayed a piece of paper. "Do you recognize these names?" he read them off.

Terry identified them as his father spoke. "Substitute ambulance driver. Surgery. Personnel. Maintenance. Member of the board of directors. Mostly women." Understanding came like a shaft of light. Was this why Bart dated every female employee at Shepherd of Love who would go out with him?

Excitement hoarsened his voice. "Dad, where did you get this?"

"I could say it was a gift from heaven. Actually, I found it on the floor when I turned on the light." His triumphant smile made him look more like Terry than ever. "Our night visitor dropped it in the scuffle. Wait until you hear what's on the back." He started reading. Every incident starting with the theft of the personnel records through the planned attack on Shane O'Shea had been documented. The single sheet of paper contained incontrovertible evidence to the existence of a conspiracy, enough to convict the writer beyond a shadow of a doubt. "Do you recognize the handwriting?"

"It has to be Keppler's." Terry sank to a chair. "Thank God." He reached for the phone, got an outside line. "Detain suspect at all costs. Call me at this extension when you do." He somberly added, "Why would anyone keep such an incriminating piece of evidence?"

"Megalomania. Feelings of invincibility. Call it what you will. The obsessive need to have something to take out and gloat over will put Keppler—and others—away for a long time."

◆◆◆

The phone rang. Five times. Ten. Twenty. "Answer!" the caller pleaded, long black garment over one arm. Hollow suspicion grew into certainty. The unlisted number, to be used only in the direst emergency, was not going to be answered, for the man on the other end had fled. Who had tipped him off? What difference did it make? He'd obviously skipped, leaving the slaves who did the dirty work to face retribution.

He remembered terse instructions. "If it goes down, you're on your own. Expect no help. It would jeopardize future operations." Deadly emphasis came with the final order. "Don't get ideas about making a deal with the DA. You can't run fast enough or far enough to escape."

Had it been worth it, the skulking and toadying to one obviously inferior, the harassment and attempted murder? A fanatic light burned in a heart seized and made prisoner to the cause of Satan.

"Yes, a thousand times yes!" The hoarse cry echoed to the worn rafters of the miserable warehouse. "Tonight changes nothing. Let them run, the sniveling cowards. I will become the leader. No one suspects me."

Delusions of grandeur raised emotions to fever pitch. Filled with the desire to be possessed by the gods of darkness, the lone occupant of the abandoned warehouse slid into the black cloak. Black-garbed arms shot skyward. Incantations rose, whispered, but deadly as the figure went into a frenzied dance surely created by Satan.

A long time later, the spent worshiper considered the next move.

"Must make contact." Fingers fumbled in the cloak, tore it off, shook it. Fear tasted metallic. It had to be there. Safety and the world's destiny depended on it! He seized the dark fabric, ripping it in his search.

———◆◆◆◆———

The warehouse door burst open. Beams of bright light caught and held the frantic figure like a fly in a spider's web. "Police. Freeze."

"Looking for something, Dr. Keppler?"

Bart started at the sound of his nemesis's voice. "O'Shea!" He tottered, regained his wits. "What is this? A belated Halloween joke?"

"No." An armed policewoman stepped forward. "What are you doing here?"

Some of his assurance returned. "I got a call saying if I wanted to learn who sent the death threats to Nicholas Fairchild, I should come here."

"Give it up, Keppler." Terry's slashing voice cut his excuse to ribbons. "A cloaked figure was followed by hospital security directly to this building. The cloak in your hands condemns you. So does this." He held up the list.

"You—" Bart hurled an epithet and lunged toward the chaplain. All the pent-up anger and frustration that had built up each time Terry bested him rose in a tidal wave of hatred.

"Enough of that." Two policemen sprang forward, pinned Keppler's arms behind him, and handcuffed him.

The policewoman raised her voice. "Bart Keppler, I am placing you under arrest on suspicion of the attempted murder of Shane O'Shea. You have the right to remain silent. Anything you say can be used against you." She finished reading his rights. "Do you understand?"

He cursed, glared at Terry, and lurched toward the closely guarded door.

"The force is picking up the others," the policewoman said.

Bart's laughter rose, magnified by the desolate room. "You won't get the leader. He's long gone." Fanaticism gleamed in his dark eyes. "That God of yours may have won this time. Who cares? Our people are in every walk of life. Government. Hospitals. Churches. There's nothing you can do about it."

"No," Terry agreed. "But God can. Just as He did this time."

The laughter died, leaving silence more eerie than ever.

———◆◆◆◆———

Bart's prediction proved true. The roundup of those involved in the conspiracy failed to catch the Dr. Jekyll-Mr. Hyde board member who preserved the image of righteousness while working for the hospital's downfall. A search of his home turned up the full extent of the diabolical plan. Once Shepherd of Love's credibility vanished, personnel who refused to accept orders from Keppler were to be discredited and dismissed, replaced by those involved in devil worship.

The Seattle newspapers bloomed with headlines: GOOD TRIUMPHS OVER EVIL. ACTING HOSPITAL DIRECTOR CHARGED WITH ATTEMPTED MURDER. STRYCHNINE-FILLED SYRINGE DISCOVERED. SATANIC RITES NO MATCH FOR SHEPHERD OF LOVE. However, a few days later, attention shifted to a sensational robbery and the hospital returned to normal.

Thanksgiving morning, Lindsey rose, donned warm clothing, and stepped into a glistening world. An inch of white blanketed trees and lawns. A blue jay scolded from a snow-clad branch. A gray squirrel ran across the parking lot, leaving tiny tracks in the whiteness. Her heart swelled, as it did each time she saw a season's first, undisturbed snow.

Soon Terry and his father would arrive to take her to her parents' home for a day filled with laughter, love, promise. Now Lindsey cherished her time alone. She slowly walked to the exact spot where months earlier she had seen portentous black clouds hovering above the hospital. How much had happened since that long-ago day. A spark of evil had kindled, raged, been stamped out. A spark of friendship had kindled between her and Terry, deepened into love, and become an enduring flame.

She tilted her head back until the winter sun shone full on her face and turned in a circle. Mount Rainier, south and east, stood no more majestic than the Olympic Range across Puget Sound. A few stubborn clouds lingered in the blue sky, reminders that other storms would come. Lindsey shivered. In spite of the purity of the freshly painted world, at this very moment those who chose wickedness plotted to destroy right, beauty, holiness.

The clouds above Shepherd of Love moved on, driven by a brisk wind sweeping the sky like a magic broom. "Oh, God, help me treasure this day," she murmured. "And help me be strong for all the tomorrows."

"Amen to that." Two strong arms circled her. A husky voice asked, "Ready, Dearest?"

Lindsey sent a final glance toward the hospital she loved. "Ready." With God beside them, she and Terence O'Shea could face whatever those unknown tomorrows might bring.

HEARTH
OF FIRE

Chapter 1

Thy word is a lamp unto my feet,
and a light unto my path.
PSALM 119:105

Patti Thompson leaned against the soft green corridor wall and stared at the inscription on the hospital director's open door. Comfort swept into her deeply troubled mind, the same comfort the words had brought so many times since she first saw the inscription. Fresh from nurses' training, heart beating with hope and anticipation at becoming part of Seattle's unique Shepherd of Love Hospital, the brand new RN promptly adopted the verse as her talisman. From that moment on, Patti never passed the open door without stopping to read and marvel.

How long ago that first day seemed! Patti closed her eyes. Had she really once been that naive, dreaming girl? A young nurse with stars in her eyes, out to change the world even if she had to do it alone? She mentally compared herself as she was now to the shadowy image. Traces of the girl remained, but the hesitant woman who lingered in the mural-lined corridor sometimes wondered where the eager young nurse had gone. Waves of weariness washed over Patti as she continued her comparison. Both girl and woman stood five-feet, five-inches tall, weighing approximately one hundred and twenty pounds. Both had soft blond hair and blue eyes that reflected every changing mood.

Patti's face twisted. The eyes that had gazed back at her from the staff rest room on the Outpatient floor a few minutes ago bore mute witness to what a few short years could do. So did the set lips of the nurse wearing a pale green pantsuit. Suffering and disillusionment had dimmed far too much of her sparkle and stolen her Count-of-Monte-Cristo "The world is mine!" feeling that formerly characterized Patti Thompson.

Should I go forward, or retreat? Patti wondered. For a terrifying moment she felt as though she stood on the brink of a precipice. Unseen hands clutched at her, pulling her back to safety while a hidden force she was too tired to fight beckoned. *Lord, what's wrong with me?* she frantically prayed.

Her terror slowly receded, leaving her drained.

"I'm in no condition to make a decision now," Patti murmured. Realization brought relief. She turned and took the first step of the long walk back to Outpatient. The second step came easier. So did the third. By the time Patti reached her destination, the discipline required during grueling training and magnified by several years of hard but satisfying work had kicked in. She had long since learned to lay aside her own concerns in the interest of those for whom she cared. Now that knowledge served her well. A quick prayer for strength squared Patti's shoulders and brought her head up. She forced a smile that should pass inspection and briskly approached the cluttered nursing station desk.

"Anything else I can do before going off duty?"

"Thanks, but everything's under control. I really appreciate your delaying your break until now," her supervisor said. "Oh, your cowboy admirer called. Said you usually stopped by to see him after you're through here. He wondered if you were coming today. I asked if you should call him. He said not to bother and added, 'I reckon she'll come if I wait a spell.'"

Patti's low spirits rose a notch. "Don't make fun of Mr. Davis. He's a real dear, the two-legged kind. I love hearing his stories about the western Montana cattle ranch he used to own." She blinked. "It just about broke his heart when his health began to fail and he had to sell out."

The supervisor looked thoughtful. "Doesn't Mr. Davis have a son or son-in-law or someone who could have taken over for him?"

Patti shook her head until her blond curls danced. "No. He and his wife were married almost fifty years, but they never had children." She thought of the first time she had seen the white-haired, weathered rancher. He had been on his way back to Montana from transacting some business in Portland when a sharp attack brought him to Shepherd of Love. He admitted he'd experienced similar bouts before, but didn't "pay much mind to them." After the usual range of pre-operative tests, the doctors advised removing his gallbladder. The patient's reaction became legendary among hospital personnel. Never before had anyone responded by agreeing doctors should "get rid of the ornery critter as soon as possible."

"The chances are also slim anyone will again," Patti had remarked after laughing.

Dan Davis bonded with his nurse at that first meeting. In spite of his pain, he whispered to Patti, "You look like my Sarah when you smile."

"I'm glad," she told him, immediately liking the uncomplaining old man.

The procedure went beautifully, but Mr. Davis had a bad reaction to the pain medication. Dizzy and vomiting, he was in no condition to be discharged that day. The hospital admitted him as a regular patient. When they learned he had no one to care for him after he was discharged, they moved him to Transitional Care. They planned to keep him until he regained enough strength to look after himself.

"Mighty nice of you folks to keep an old codger like me," Mr. Davis told Patti when she stopped by. "Some hospitals chomp at the bit, wantin' to throw a feller out soon as he can get outta bed. How come you don't?"

"Shepherd of Love isn't dependent on anyone but God for its financing," Patti quietly told him. "Because of that, we can make exceptions they can't."

"How's that?" His eyes opened wide with interest.

Patti quickly sketched in the story of wealthy Nicholas Fairchild, the strong Christian man who believed God wanted him to build a hospital different from all others in Seattle. Shepherd of Love, named for Christ—its real founder—did not rely on government grants, with their regulations and restrictions. Time normally consumed by fund-raisers and pleas for money was spent in prayer. When other dedicated Christians heard the story behind the hospital that leading Seattle residents predicted could never be built, they quietly furnished the necessary finances without fanfare or public recognition.

The combination of fine Christian medical personnel and prayer meetings before every shift brought results that soon earned the respect of other superb hospitals such as Harborview, Swedish, Providence, and the University of Washington's Medical Center. Shepherd of Love wisely shifted patients needing more specialized care than they could offer to the appropriate hospitals. This policy created excellent working relationships.

Now Patti told her supervisor, "Mr. Davis once asked me if I could use a log cabin near Kalispell. Evidently he still owns one. Don't look so shocked. It wasn't a proposal, although we get those, too."

"Grateful patient reaction." The older nurse sounded skeptical. "Don't start packing! Extravagant promises are typical, but they never come to anything."

Her laugh did wonders for her starchy personality. "If I'd collected all the property and money patients promised to leave me in their wills and the like, I wouldn't be here."

Patti allowed herself a moment to ask curiously, "Where would you be?"

"On a cruise, maybe? Or gloating in a mansion with a view of Puget Sound where I could just sit and stare." The supervisor laughed again. "Run along to your cowboy, Thompson. Or should I say, get along, little doggie?"

Patti giggled. "Not doggie. *Dogie,* as in a motherless calf in a range herd."

"How come you know so much about range herds?" the other nurse retorted.

"*I* was raised on Zane Grey and Louis L'Amour western novels," Patti loftily told her. "Sorry you were so educationally deprived."

"Scat!" The supervisor made a shooing motion, although the corners of her stern mouth twitched.

Patti left Outpatient, her heart lighter than it had been for days. Childhood memories kept time with her steady footsteps. Her father had been a Western history nut. He taught his daughter to appreciate an era they would never experience except through books or movies.

A small smile curled Patti's lips and warmed her heart. The bittersweet memory of her family's first long driving trip returned. Somewhere in Montana, they had swung over a hill late one afternoon. A solitary horse and rider stood etched against the spectacular Big Sky sunset.

Patti's childish heart had pounded until it felt like it would burst from her breast. All the hero figures she had only read of in books and seen in movies came alive.

"Oh, boy, a cowboy!" she had squealed.

The dark figure raised one arm, removed the wide hat Patti knew must be a Stetson, and waved toward the car's occupants. She waved back until their car rounded a bend and her first real, live cowboy vanished from her sight.

Patti's thoughts trooped ahead. Her feet unconsciously slowed. She had been so young and impressionable at age twelve! After devouring Zane Grey's novel *The Border Legion,* she had carefully packed a small bag. She kept it with her while reading in a favorite tree near their rural home. The comb and brush, toothbrush, red scarf, and other items matched those the heroine Joan had with her when kidnapped by bandits. Should Patti also be taken, she'd be prepared. She refused to consider the fact that bandits on horseback hadn't been seen in the vicinity for at least one hundred years!

"Thank God I never was kidnapped," she fervently whispered. Yet the old desire to one day live on a cattle ranch still lurked in a locked chamber of Patti's heart. Perhaps she could visit a dude ranch someday. She shook her head. *No. Far better to keep her childish illusions than attempt to fulfill a dream and end up disappointed.*

The corners of her mouth turned down. Depression returned with a vengeance. The discovery a few months earlier that handsome Dr. Bart Keppler was a phony and cared nothing for her was disappointment enough to last her for a long, long time. So were the changes that had come to the hospital.

Patti sighed. "Lord, I'm glad my special nurse friends all married such great guys, but when is my turn coming?" She ticked them off on her fingers. "Jonica Carr. Lindsey Best. Nancy Galbraith. Even Shina Ito just deserted me." She made a face. "Sorry, God. I don't really mean deserted. I still see my friends both off and on duty. It's just that I'm beginning to feel like the last leaf on the tree."

Patti thought of the newcomers to the hospital and the staff residence hall where she lived. Other nurses had moved into the rooms formerly occupied by her special friends. Patti felt old enough at times to be their grandmother. *At 25?* an inner voice scoffed. *Who are you trying to kid?*

She couldn't help grinning, but April and Allison Andrews did make her feel old. The ink on the identical twins' hard-won certification was barely dry. Their enthusiasm reminded Patti of her own transition from student to employee. Regret filled her. *How could she have let someone like the pseudo Dr. Keppler rob her of the excitement, the on-tiptoe thrill of challenge to her skills each new patient brought?*

"Forgive me, please, God," she repentantly whispered. Patti immediately felt better. A real smile replaced the forced one. She stepped into a large and pleasant room. Off to the side and away from the few other patients present, Mr. Davis sat gazing out the windows toward glistening, wave-topped Puget Sound. His gnarled hands lay idle in his lap. They reminded Patti of the story of the "Praying Hands" painting. Albrecht Dürer had immortalized the toil-worn hands of a friend who sacrificed his own dream of becoming a great painter for the sake of the younger artist Dürer.

What stories Mr. Davis's hands could tell if they could speak! Patti wondered. *How many newborn calves and foals had they helped into this world? How often had they stroked a beloved wife's hair as it turned from sunny gold to silver? Did the fingers itch to swing a lasso, to tighten the reins and curb a wild mustang? Did the farseeing eyes look beyond the distant horizon to a place where Sarah, the beloved, waited the coming of the man who lingered a few steps behind?*

Patti felt choked up. Seeing Dan Davis in this unguarded moment offered poignant insight into what love and marriage could and should be. Two, no, three against the world, for the old cowboy had shared how God had always been head of the Davis household. She swallowed the obstruction in her throat and said, "I hear you were asking whether I'd come see you. Oh, ye of little faith."

Mr. Davis gave a guilty start and turned his head. Faded blue eyes set deep in squint and laugh lines focused on her. Their faraway expression changed to a mischievous sparkle. A chuckle started at the toes of his slippers and rumbled through his deep chest, becoming a range-sized laugh.

"That's tellin' me." He cocked his head to one side. "I reckon anyone who looks so almighty fetchin' is worth waitin' for." Approval shone in his time-worn face. "That pale green color reminds me of the willows along the creek when spring starts openin' the leaf buds after a long, hard Montana winter."

"Thanks. You're quite a poet," Patti accused.

Innocence shone clear as a mountain lake on a cloudless day. "The good Lord gave me eyes to see, didn't He?" Dan Davis pointed at her barren ring finger. "How come no one's lassoed you yet?"

Patti gave a mock sigh and clasped her hands over her heart in the best fair maiden tradition. "Alas, my friend. The men I know can't even ride a horse, let alone throw a lasso."

His hearty laugh showed how much he appreciated her response. "Too bad you didn't live when and where I did. Every cowpoke for miles around would have cluttered up the front stoop."

"The way you did with your wife?" Patti teased.

The old cowboy snorted. "Not so you'd notice! I took me one look when Sarah McClelland came to teach school and she did the same. We didn't waste much time in gettin' hitched. Stayed in harness for nigh onto fifty years."

Patti pulled a chair close to his and wistfully said, "I took a look once and thought someone was right for me. He wasn't. He turned out to be horrible. Now I—" She stared at her capable fingers.

"Feelin' a bit gun-shy about tryin' again, ain't you? Sort of questionin' your own judgment?" Mr. Davis asked. "Not that it's my business, but I've got big, listenin' ears if you want to spill anything. I also am a good hand at keepin' my lip buttoned. Always was. Sarah used to say tellin' me secrets was safer than storin' gold in a bank vault." His beguiling smile displayed strong white teeth. "If I were a guessin' man, I'd say you've got someone who wants to come courtin'. We used to call it sparkin' when I was young."

Patti considered. She really did want to talk with someone, but not anyone from the hospital. That's why she had backed off instead of going into the director's office earlier. Dan Davis would go return to Montana soon. They would probably exchange a few letters, but as he said, confiding in him would be safe. The desire to share prompted her to say, "I want the kind of marriage you had, Mr. Davis." She looked appealingly into his eyes. "I'd like

356

to think that fifty or more years from now, someone would remember me and look the way you do when you speak about your Sarah."

"It's the only kind of marriage worth havin'," he told her. "She'd have done the same." He fell quiet, then fixed a stern gaze on Patti. "I ain't sayin' we never had our differences. Sarah and I were too spunky to always agree! It's just that we loved each other and God so much, it warmed our home and kept it from bein' a hearth of fire."

"Hearth of fire?" Patti looked at him in wonderment. "I don't understand."

"Most folks don't. Folks today don't pay much mind to the prophet Zechariah. They should. In chapter 12, verse 6, he brings the word of the Lord, sayin': 'In that day will I make the governors of Judah like an hearth of fire among the wood, and like a torch of fire in a sheaf; and they shall devour all the people round about, on the right hand and on the left: and Jerusalem shall be inhabited again in her own place, even in Jerusalem.' "

Puzzled, Patti asked, "What's that have to do with love and marriage?"

"Everything." Dan Davis glanced out the window again. When he spoke, Patti had the feeling his spirit had traveled far. "I've seen a heap of so-called love in my day. There's the demandin', self-seekin' kind that treats folks terrible and thinks sayin' 'I love you' will make everything right. It's a passionate, ragin' flame, destroyin' whatever's unlucky enough to be in its path, like wildfire on the prairie, or a forest fire in the mountains."

He turned back to his companion. "Don't be fooled into thinkin' this kind of love can be tamed," he warned. "It's excitin' while it lasts, but it won't last. When love thinks more about gettin' than givin', it's the wrong kind. It makes a hearth of fire that burns out and becomes nothin' but ashes."

Patti sat silent. What a store of wisdom this simple, range-dwelling man possessed! Her throat burned from unshed tears flowing from her still-bruised heart. Except for the grace of God, she could have married Dr. Bart Keppler and been sentenced to a hearth of fire, instead of a home filled with radiant, enduring love.

"Sarah and I loved each other 'bout as much as anyone could," her new-found friend shared. "I can't remember a day I didn't urge my horse a little faster on the way home, no matter how tired we both were. Seein' the light Sarah always put in the window, knowin' she'd meet me at the door, face all shiny and glad, kind of took away the tiredness." His tone altered. "The first night after the funeral, I came in off the range hatin' to face a cold, dark house."

Patti felt his pain. She instinctively reached out and clasped his worn hand.

Mr. Davis smiled. "Don't be feelin' sorry for me. Cookie had lit a fire and the lamp, then sneaked back to the cookhouse. We never talked about it, but Cookie kept it up until the ranch sold and he and the hands moved on."

"I'm so glad!" Patti cried.

"So was I." The quiet reply said it all. Presently Dan Davis continued. "A feller havin' trouble with his wife asked me once how Sarah and I kept lovin' each other after all those years. I told him through hard times and good, we just kept feelin' thankful the good Lord brought us together.

" 'What did you do to find happiness?' " he asked.

The joyous, rumbling laugh came. "I up and told the galoot Sarah and I were so busy makin' sure the other one was happy, it couldn't help spillin' over onto us. Love may make the world go round, but unselfishness and carin' more about a husband or wife than you do about yourself keeps a marriage strong and healthy." He leaned forward and looked Patti straight in the eye. "Don't you ever get hitched 'nless you feel that way *and so does he.*" Mr. Davis leaned back and looked sheepish. "See what happens when you get me started? I climb on a soapbox and start preachin' at you!"

"I loved your sermon," Patti reassured him.

"Good. Are you ready to tell me about the young buck who's trailin' you?" His eyes twinkled until he looked like an oversized elf.

She glanced at the clock. "Not now. My goodness, it's time for supper and I need to change out of my uniform. Thanks for letting me cry on your shoulder."

He chuckled. "Swappin' stories is always good for a body. See you tomorrow?"

Patti thought he sounded a little anxious. "Sure. Same time, same place, if you're still here. Did the doctor say when you were being discharged?"

"Naw. He knows I ain't in a hurry. Grub's not too bad, either." Dan Davis produced a hollow, obviously fake cough. "Maybe they'll let me stick around a little longer."

"Don't count on it." Patti gave his shoulders a quick hug. "Hospitals are for sick people, not frauds like you." She slipped away with his rowdy laugh ringing in her ears and his little sermon on marriage echoing in her heart.

Chapter 2

A few minutes after nurse Patti Thompson's heart-stirring talk with Dan Davis, the petite blond nurse surveyed her quarters in the staff residence hall from the depths of a pillowed couch. Off-white walls, a deep blue rug, and matching draperies highlighted the small, tastefully furnished suite. Located at the far end of the leg of the T-shaped building, a large window on the west offered a spectacular view of white-capped Puget Sound in all its capricious moods. Screened windows in the kitchenette and bath overlooked manicured lawns, bright with early summer flowers and a wealth of shrubs and evergreen trees.

"I'm glad I changed locations," Patti decided. "The green suite holds too many memories of rooming with Lindsey." A reminiscent smile touched her lips. Red-haired Lindsey Best had mothered, scolded, and corrected Patti's grammar before becoming Mrs. 'Chaplain Terence O'Shea,' as her friends now called her.

Lindsey still did in the limited time they had together. So did Shina Ito Hyde. Patti sighed. "I've always relied heavily on my friends," she told God in the informal way she often talked with Him. "Probably too much. No more. It's time to stop being a clinging vine. That kind of woman went out of style with bustles and hoop skirts. Wonder how I would have fitted in back then?" The mischievous part of her recently suppressed by troubles took wings and soared. Patti sprang from the couch. She spread wide the full skirt of the flower print dress she'd donned after her shower. Knees bent in a deep curtsy, she fluttered her lashes in a belle-of-the-ball imitation and simpered, "My goodness, are those flowers really for little ol' me?"

The ringing of the phone destroyed pose and mood. Patti raced to answer, remembering to drop her Southern accent just in time.

"Hello?" she caroled.

Charles Bradley's amused voice sounded in her ear. "Well, aren't you happy!"

Suddenly she was, gloriously so. She felt rich color pour into her cheeks. "Would you rather have me otherwise?" She almost added "kind sir" but thought better of it. Doing so meant having to explain her silliness, and she didn't know the handsome blond pilot well enough to risk having him think her foolish. *At least not yet,* her heart impudently added.

"I'll take you any way I can get you," he drawled.

His boldness snatched at her breath. "Careful," she said. "Breaches of promise have been started for less than that."

"So let's talk it over at dinner. You haven't eaten yet, have you?"

She hesitated. Last-minute dates never had appealed to her. On the other hand, Charles Bradley did.

Was the man a mind reader? Patti wondered when he said, "Sorry I couldn't call sooner. I just got in from a charter flight. I can pick you up in an hour, if you're free. How about Italian food? The restaurant Cucina! Cucina! is always good."

"Great. I'm starving." Patti loved his low laugh, although it held a note of smug satisfaction that brought a tiny frown when he told her he'd see her soon.

Her sense of fairness rushed to his defense. A man as attractive as Charles must have a hundred girls after him, yet from what she could see, he remained singularly unspoiled. Perhaps she had been mistaken.

"Wish I could talk it over with Lindsey or Shina," Patti wistfully said, then straightened her shoulders. "Good grief, Patti," she scolded herself. "You're leaning again, exactly what you vowed not to do! Forget it. Anyone would think you were a high school freshman waiting for her first date." Her no-nonsense reproach brought a rueful grin to her face, but did nothing toward slowing down the unruly heart turning somersaults beneath her colorful dress.

Few men of Patti's wide acquaintance topped Charles Bradley when it came to looks. The trim, five-feet, ten-inch pilot had a smile that didn't quit, blue eyes and blond hair so closely matched to Patti's they could have passed for brother and sister. Patti secretly felt glad they were not.

"What a handsome couple," a woman whispered when the hostess ushered them to the table Charles had managed to reserve. Patti smiled to herself. Her escort's dark blue shirt, matching pants, and carefully selected tie set off the tanned skin that showed signs of recent contact with soap, water, and a razor. Charles walked with head back and shoulders up, as if he owned the restaurant. "A glass of wine before dinner?" the waiter asked after seating them.

Patti shook her head. "Just water, please." Her heart plunged when Charles hesitated. Earlier dates hadn't required a stand concerning liquor.

Patti abhorred drinking of any kind. She knew what it could lead to only too well.

"I'll have coffee," Charles decided. "I think we're ready to order."As soon as their attendant left, the thirtyish pilot leaned back in his chair. "Will it surprise you to learn I couldn't wait to get in today, on the chance you might be free?"

Patti felt herself redden. She didn't answer.

He laughed. "I believe in the direct approach. If things go my way—and they usually do—someday you are going to put on a white dress, instead of that delectable one you're wearing tonight. I'll be waiting for you when you walk down the center aisle of a church, Miss Patricia Thompson."

It took all Patti's control to keep from gaping. She knew her eyes burned like headlights in a Seattle fog, but she finally managed to choke out, "My, my, we're taking a lot for granted, aren't we?"

"You sound like the nurse who took care of me when I had my tonsils out," he mocked. "Everything was 'we,' as in 'how are we feeling?' " A curious glint sent shivers down Patti's spine when he repeated, "I told you I believe in the direct approach. Relax. I wanted to give you fair warning, but I don't expect an answer." He laughed confidently. "Until at least our next date."

The waiter returned with Charles's coffee before Patti could reply, but his biding-my-time expression showed he meant every word of his unexpected proposal. *Not a proposal,* Patti hastily reminded herself. It was more a statement of the way *he* intended for things to happen. Scraps of Patti's conversation with Dan Davis insidiously crept into her mind. Which of the ex-cowboy's descriptions best fit the man seated across from her, candlelight gleaming on his fair hair? Someone more interested in getting than giving? A person who offered the flame of passion the old man said wouldn't last, but led to a hearth of fire? Or was Charles one whose chief aim would be to love and cherish her, and make her happy?

Patti wondered again when Charles took her home. Her escort's good-night kisses stirred her yet raised more questions. Curled up on her couch, she tried to pinpoint why she felt uneasy.

"It could be what Mr. Davis said," she admitted. "A burned child dreading the fire reaction. Maybe I'm just not ready to seriously consider someone right now. Anyone." She paused. "Lord, what if You've sent Charles into my life for a purpose?" Patti wrestled with her problem until her brain grew too weary to concentrate. At last she knelt, put herself, Charles, and the future into God's hands, and went to bed.

An extremely busy day in Outpatient kept Patti overtime the next day and made her late in getting to the Transitional Care Unit. Mr. Davis, bursting with impatience, barely waited until she seated herself before saying, "Doc says I'm doin' so well, he has to discharge me in a few days. I'm headin' for home. Why don't you come with me?"

"You want me to go to Montana?" Patti gasped.

"Sure. My log cabin's got two bedrooms. I'm also old enough to have a nurse stayin' with me for a spell without causin' talk." His blue eyes twinkled and his laugh rumbled out. "If I remember right, you said you ain't had a vacation for some time. Kalispell in early summer's like a bit of heaven. It has everything: mountains, lakes, valleys, hiking, horseback riding, boat and raft trips. Ever been to Glacier National Park? If you stick around until the sawbones says okay, I'll take you across the park on the Going-to-the-Sun Highway." He cackled. "You'll think you are, going to the sun, that is. It's mighty high."

Patti thrilled to the idea. "It sounds wonderful," she wistfully said. "I haven't been to Glacier since I was a kid. We stayed at Fish Creek and Two Medicine, but didn't take the Going-to-the-Sun Highway. It spit snow the early June day we started across from the western side. We were on the outside of the road and Mom grew really nervous. Dad turned and went back."

"Good idea. If you're a mite shaky in high places, you do better to travel from east to west. That way, you're on the inside of the road almost the whole way." Dan Davis's eyes brightened. "Will you come? The folks who bought the Running H said I was welcome to come stay a spell with them any time." His strong forefinger traced a slanting *H* on the arm of his chair. "I'm certain they'd make us welcome and you could see what ranching is all about. Nothin' fancy or duded up about the Hoffs. Just plain, hard-workin' folk like Sarah and me."

A rush of blood to her head made Patti feel dizzy. "You really mean it?"

"Never meant anything more in my life." A callused hand rested on hers. "Sometimes gettin' away from ourselves helps sort things out," he observed.

Patti caught his meaning in a flash. What a God-given opportunity for her to gain a fresh perspective toward the hospital and her restlessness. Most of all, toward Charles's proclamation. A few days away, especially on a working cattle ranch, would surely restore her badly-shaken confidence in her ability to make decisions. She turned her palm upward and squeezed the hard fingers. "If I can get a leave of absence, I'll go," she promised. Patti released Mr. Davis's hand and jumped up.

"Don't go away." She laughed at her absurdity. "As if you would! I mean, I'll be right back." She knew she babbled and didn't care. Who wouldn't, with the dream of a lifetime coming true? Now if she could arrange for leave, everything would be perfect.

The first roadblock was her supervisor. Luckily, the older nurse had stayed to confer with the next swing shift's charge nurse. Patti held in her excitement until the nurse moved away, then exploded, "I have a chance to go home to Montana with Mr. Davis and spend time on a cattle ranch. Please, may I take vacation time?"

The astonished supervisor raised her eyebrows. "You mean it? Of course you may go! How much time do you want, or need?"

"Two weeks? Mr. Davis has some plans for after his recuperation."

"No problem." A wide smile creased the caring face. "So dreams really do come true. Go for it, Thompson. You'll come back rested and of more use than ever. Not that you aren't and haven't been a good nurse," she added. "It's just that you haven't had a real vacation for so long, it will be a real shot in the arm."

Two days later, family and friends informed of her impending departure for wild and still woolly (according to Mr. Davis) western Montana, Patti faced her last obstacle before leaving. Packed bags littered the blue rug of her suite. Security had been notified of her absence. Her fellow nurses had clamored for postcards and ribbed her about her elderly boyfriend.

"Too bad he doesn't have a good-looking son," April Andrews sighed when the twins dropped in to say good-bye.

"Grandson would be more appropriate," her twin sister Allison pointed out. "Mr. Davis is at least seventy years old, even though he doesn't look it." She roguishly cocked her brown head. "If you need help handling all the handsome Kalispell cowboys, don't hesitate to send for us!"

Patti blushed. Her color deepened when April volunteered, "What does your handsome pilot think about being deserted? Want me to look after him while you're gone? He's better looking than any cowboy."

"He's been out of town," Patti told the grinning nurse. "I left a message on his answering machine. Thanks, but no thanks, April, for your obviously self-sacrificing offer. Charles Bradley doesn't need a nanny."

Allison shouted with laughter at her sister's expense. "That's telling her! Come on, April. Our room looks like a hurricane hit it. Have a great time,

Patti. You really deserve it."

Patti warmed to the genuine affection in the girl's face. "Thanks. See you when I get back." She closed the door that led into the corridor and their room.

Heavy pounding battered her outside door. "Who is it?" Patti called. Although security patrolled the hospital grounds, she knew better than to open the door that led to a parking lot without identifying her caller.

"Charles."

Patti flung it wide. "How nice! I didn't think I'd see you before—"

The young pilot strode into the room and furiously demanded, "What do you think you're doing?"

Patti had never seen him so upset. "Didn't you receive my message?"

"Of course I did," he shouted. Strong hands shot out and fastened on her slim shoulders. "Are you crazy, taking off with someone who could die at any minute? Why are you going to Kalispell, of all places? What am I supposed to do while you're gone, sit around and twiddle my thumbs?" The edge to his voice was jagged enough to cut steak.

Anger licked at Patti's veins. "You're hurting me." She wrenched free and rubbed her sore shoulders. "Why are you acting like this? It's my chance for an all-expense-paid vacation, one I couldn't have without Mr. Davis. I explained all that in the message I left on your answering machine."

Some of Charles's rage died. Patti saw his struggle to become the charming pilot who first attracted her.

"I'm sorry," he said heavily. "I never want to do anything to hurt you. The thought of coming home to Seattle without knowing you're here threw me off balance." He held out his arms and his face took on a pleading expression. "Forgive me, please, Patti. I hate the idea of anyone else doing things for you. I spend hours thinking of special places to take you and planning what we'll do after we're married. I love you so much."

The contrition in his voice touched Patti's tender heart. Yet a nagging feeling of something important she needed to remember kept her from responding the way she knew he expected.

"I think you'd better go, Charles," she told him.

"Are you still angry with me? I don't blame you if you are. I acted like a jerk." He took her hands and gently kissed each palm.

Patti withdrew her hands and stepped back. "I'm shocked and disappointed in you and need time to think. Good night, Charles. Good-bye, actually. I won't see you before we leave tomorrow."

"Try to think of me kindly," he begged. The misery in his eyes intensified. "I can't ask you to forget, but please forgive me. You're my whole world, Patti. Sun, moon, and stars." Strangely enough, the trite expression didn't sound ridiculous coming from him, as it would from other men. Charles bowed his head and walked toward the outside door.

She longed to reassure him, to erase the lost little boy look in his face. She couldn't. The haunting feeling that something vital lurked just beyond her recognition locked Patti's lips as firmly as she locked the door behind her no-longer-welcome guest. She sank to the couch, knowing she would never sleep unless she recalled whatever lay hidden.

It took Patti a long time. She replayed the ugly scene over and over in her mind without finding the trace of a clue. Nothing came until she switched her attention to Mr. Davis. Suddenly scattered phrases from her cowboy friend's little "sermon on marriage" knocked at the door of her mind and gained entrance. *A heap of so-called love. . .demandin'. . .self-seekin'. . .treats folks terrible. . .thinks sayin' 'I love you' will make everything right. . .a ragin' flame. . .a hearth of fire. . .burns out. . .becomes nothin' but ashes.*

Tonight a man she admired, even wondered if she could love, had exhibited all the traits Dan Davis decried. Charles Bradley had claimed his actions sprang from feelings so tremendous he couldn't stand the thought of being apart from her, or seeing others do things for her. Patti slowly shook her head. A few days earlier she had watched a small child in a store bellow to get his own way. Although Charles was close to thirty years old, he so dangerously resembled the child it made her shudder. *What might a man who left bruises on the woman he was trying to impress do to her, once he possessed her? What would marriage be with a man immature enough to fly into a rage over nothing?*

"I'm glad I'm going away," she whispered to her heavenly Father. "I'll have time to think. I truly need it. If Charles is really like I saw him tonight, I'll know You've prepared this way of escape."

Patti stood under the shower for a long time, allowing the warm water to sluice away some of her stress. She towel-dried her short hair and crawled into bed. In an amazingly short time, she fell asleep. Hours later she struggled back to consciousness, wide awake in the darkness of the room. A question hovered on her lips, and she said aloud, "Lord, when Charles grabbed me and began shouting, he asked why I was going to Kalispell, *of all places*. Why would he say something like that?"

The night offered no answers. Patti eventually fell asleep again. The next time she opened her eyes, a gorgeous early morning chased away the shadows, making her wonder if the unpleasant incident the night before had only been a bad dream. Fading footsteps outside her door that led to the parking lot set her pulse quick-stepping. She hurried into a robe and called, "Who is it?"

No one answered.

"Who's there?" she demanded.

The sound of a car motor starting hummed in her ears.

Heart beating furiously, Patti ran out her corridor door. She beat on April and Allison Andrews' door. "Quick. Let me in. It's Patti."

The thud of feet landing on the floor and a startled exclamation followed. Allison opened the door.

"Patti? What's wrong?" Sleep clouded her eyes.

She slid inside and raced toward a window with a view of the parking lot. She was too late. Nothing moved in the now-silent lot.

"Patti, what *is* it?" a fully awake Allison cried. April just stared.

The Outpatient nurse told them. "I have to call Security," she finished, starting back to her apartment.

Allison snatched her sleeve. "You aren't going back until someone checks it out," she insisted. April grabbed the phone and reported what had happened. Minutes later, a patrol car swung into the parking lot. A guard jumped out. Patti and the pajama-clad twins ran back to the other apartment. She unlocked the outside door, opened it, and gasped.

A gigantic florist's bouquet overflowed the guard's outstretched arms.

Patti sagged against the door frame. "What on earth—"

The guard grinned broadly. "Looks like someone didn't think you'd be up, so he left a present. Any reason to suspect it isn't legitimate?"

"N–no." Patti's gaze riveted on a small envelope with her name scrawled across the front. She ripped it open and felt streaks of color stain her face.

"Well?" April, the more impatient of the twins, asked.

"It's a false alarm," Patti replied in a small voice. "A–a friend who had to leave town early dropped them off."

Allison glanced at the size of the bouquet the guard courteously carried in and set on a table.

"Some friend." She yawned and glanced at her watch. "Now that the excitement's over, I may as well shower."

Patti hid the card in the pocket of her robe. "Sorry I bothered everyone."

"Hey, that's what friends and security guards are for," the irrepressible April told her before she trailed after her sister.

"She's right, you know," the guard said seriously. "Better a false alarm than to ignore anything the least bit suspicious." He nodded. "Have a great vacation, Nurse Thompson." He walked back to the patrol car and drove off. Patti stepped inside, locked her door, and reread the note.

I have an early flight. I hope this isn't too little, too late. Have a wonderful time, my darling, and try to forgive me. I'll be waiting.

All my love,
Charles

Chapter 3

When Patti appeared in the staff dining room clad in a denim jeans and jacket outfit with a red bandanna loosely circling her neck, loud sighs greeted her from her two best nurse friends. Red-haired Lindsey O'Shea wore the cotton dress she kept on hand and changed into after her night shift on Surgery. Tiny Japanese-American Shina Hyde's crisp rose-pink pants uniform showed she was ready to begin a day in Obstetrics.

"Wish I could show up this time of day dressed like a cowgirl," Lindsey complained. "Yippee-ki-oh-ki-ay. She's off into the wild blue yonder."

"Mixed metaphors," Patti retorted. "Don't be silly. The Air Force goes off into the wild blue yonder. *I'm* headin' for Big Sky country, pardner." Laughter spilled over like a waterfall. She touched the red rosebud pinned to her lapel. Taking Charles' preposterously large peace offering with her to Montana had been out of the question. Patti had filched the bud and donated the floral arrangement to the Information desk in the lobby.

"Get along, little dogie," tiny Shina sang out.

"I had a long little dogie once." Lindsey's warm brown eyes twinkled golden motes of mischief. "It came from Joe's hot dog stand and gave me indigestion."

"We certainly are jealous this morning," Patti told her friends sweetly. "I'll think of you slaving away here while I'm riding the range and chasing rustlers."

"Thanks a bunch, but didn't rustlers go out with Prohibition?" Lindsey hunched her shoulders and yawned without waiting for a reply. "I had a night to remember in Surgery. Actually, a night to forget. I could use a couple of weeks of R&R on a ranch—rest and recuperation to you uninformed nurses."

Shina's silky dark brows shot up. "We aren't uninformed. It's just been so long since Patti and I had any R&R we can't remember what it's like, let alone what it means."

"Right!" Lindsey stumbled to her feet. One hand dropped to Patti's shoulder. "Have a great vacation. Mind your manners and don't fall off a horse."

"Yes, Mother," Patti meekly replied.

Shina's laugh trilled out. After a hasty glance at her watch, she also stood. "Sorry to eat and run, but duty calls." She smiled at Patti. "I hope your vacation is perfect."

"It will be. Absotively, posilutely." *Especially since Charles did all he could to make things right,* she silently added. She touched the rosebud again, blushing when her friends eyed it curiously but mercifully refrained from asking questions.

It didn't take long to finish breakfast and walk to the Transitional Care Unit. Patti checked with the nurse at the desk and learned all the necessary paperwork had been completed for discharging Mr. Davis. Nothing remained except to put him in a wheelchair.

"There you are." His weathered face brightened when Patti walked into his room. Polished cowboy boots that nevertheless showed signs of hard wear replaced slippers. A well-used Stetson lay in his lap. A key ring dangled from his fingers. His blue eyes twinkled when he held it out to her. "Ever herd a bronco?"

"Excuse me?" Enlightenment came. "Oh, you mean a Ford Bronco."

"Yep. I got mine just before they quit makin' them in '96. It's been corralled in the parking garage since I came here."

She couldn't help teasing him. "Was that 1996 or 1896 when you bought it?"

The old cowboy's laugh boomed loud in the quiet room. "I may be old, but I ain't that old, young lady. Are you packed and ready to go?" He hopped out of his chair like a long-legged grasshopper escaping an enemy.

"Whoa, there. I have to get a wheelchair," she protested.

He bristled. "Naw. I walked in here on my own legs. I'll go out the same."

"Sorry, it's a hospital rule."

Mr. Davis looked doubtful. "Well, all right, but I don't need mollycoddlin'. Doc says I'm better than new. Want me to do a little jig to prove it?"

Patti grinned at his high spirits. "Naw," she parroted. "Let's get out of here before they decide you're getting too big for your britches and keep you."

"You mean ridin' too high in the saddle, but it's all the same thing." He dropped into the wheelchair she brought, grinned at the staff who gathered to tell him good-bye, and heaved a sigh of relief when she wheeled him down the corridor. "There's a mighty fine bunch of people here, but I can't wait to get outside and breathe some fresh air."

Patti silently echoed his wish. She left him close to an exit door and hurried to the parking garage. The prospect of two whole weeks spent mostly outdoors loomed brighter than the red Ford Bronco she drove out into the sunlight. Mr. Davis contentedly settled into the passenger seat, rolled down his window, and relaxed after asking, "Would you rather have the window shut? There's air conditioning."

"Not yet, at least. I like fresh air, too." Patti stopped in the lot by her apartment, tied the red bandanna gypsy fashion over her head, and ran in for her bags. It took only a short time to stow them away and thread city streets until they came to Interstate 90 and joined eastbound traffic.

"The prettiest way is through Stevens Pass," Mr. Davis told her. "But Snoqualmie is the fastest." Longing colored his voice and Patti quickly agreed they should go by way of Snoqualmie. Now he burst out, "Montana or bust!"

Patti had the feeling he wanted to bellow like one of the bulls on the Running H, but refrained to keep from distracting her while she drove. Sympathy rose like a high tide. How glad she was to be going with him!

"I'm curious. Why is the ranch called the Running H, when the Hoffs only bought it recently? Shouldn't it be the Running D, for Davis?"

He laughed with an exuberance that tilted the corners of her mouth upward. "It was the Running H when Sarah and I bought it. Names have a way of stickin' in those parts. We never even considered changin' it. Too much bother, with our critters wearing the *H* brand."

Patti impulsively said, "You'll never know how grateful I am, Mr. Davis."

"What for?" He looked genuinely surprised. "You're the one who took time for an old man." He shifted in his seat. "Since we're away from the hospital, how about callin' me Dan? Every time I hear Mr. Davis, I think folks are referrin' to my daddy, God rest his soul."

"I'll be glad to, if you will call me Patti. So far, you've either called me nurse, or young lady, or nothing at all," she reminded him.

"Patti it is," he told her heartily. "How do you like herdin' my bronc?"

"I love it. Living at the hospital, I haven't needed a car, although of course I have a license." She changed lanes, glorying in the open stretch of road before them. "It's been years since I went to eastern Washington. Everything's new to me. I can hardly wait to see what's over the next hill or around the bend."

"Patti Thompson, you're a thoroughbred," Dan told her. "You also ain't seen nothin' yet."

The capable nurse nodded. They soon swept over the pass and down the east side of the Cascade Mountain Range through impressive scenery. Timbered rolling hills gave way to sparsely treed slopes. The travelers stopped in Ellensburg for cool drinks, then headed northeast, still on I-90.

They reached Spokane in early afternoon, after traveling across desolate stretches that impressed neither of them. Patti found it hard to believe the barren desert only needed water to blossom until she saw the difference irrigation made.

With every mile, more color returned to the ex-rancher's lined face, more sparkle to his faded eyes. In Spokane, he directed Patti to a family restaurant not far from the freeway.

"Even beats the food at Shepherd of Love," he bragged.

The home-style meal more than lived up to his raves. At her host's urging, Patti finished with warm peach cobbler topped with whipped cream.

"I should have bought my jeans a size larger, if this is how we're going to eat," she groaned.

"I'm a pretty good hand at cookin' when I have to," Dan modestly told her. "Don't worry. You'll work it off at the Running H."

A few qualms attacked. "Are you sure the Hoffs will want to take in a stranger?" She fought down disappointment. "Don't worry if things don't work out. I'll still have a good vacation."

"No need to fret about the Hoffs. They never met a stranger. Besides, you ain't a stranger to me," he gruffly told her. "That's all that counts." He glanced at his watch. "Reckon it's about time to get goin'."

"We aren't driving clear to Kalispell today, are we?" A little frown creased Patti's forehead and darkened her eyes. "We've already come close to three hundred miles and are only about halfway there."

Dan shook his white head. "I've done it, but we ain't in that kind of hurry. Coeur d'Alene's a nice place, not far over the Idaho border. I know a good quiet motel. It has a swimmin' pool and a cafe next to it that serves the best flapjacks this side of the Running H."

"Coeur d'Alene sounds fine. Food doesn't right now," Patti told him. When they were back on the road she mused, "It would be fun to know where some of the places we'll be got their names."

"Folklore says the word Idaho may have come from the Shoshone Indian words *Ee dah how!* It means 'The sun comes down the mountains,' or 'It is morning,'" Dan informed her. "Idaho is also called The Gem of the Mountains. Coeur d'Alene was founded as a fort in the 1890s by General Sherman, and named after the Indian tribe. Loosely translated from French, it means *hard-hearted*. Don't let sparklin' Lake Coeur d'Alene and the peaceful area around it you see now fool you. Winter can be as hard-hearted as a greedy landlord."

Patti laughed at his analogy and continued her lesson. "How about Montana?"

Dan's craggy face softened. "Spanish for 'mountainous.' Early travelers took a good long gander at the sun glistenin' on our snow-capped peaks and named it 'Land of Shining Mountains.' It's also called Big Sky country and the Treasure State. Kalispell's an Indian word meaning 'land going to the sun.' That's where they got the name for Glacier Park's Going-to-the-Sun Highway."

"You are an absolute gold mine of information!" she marveled.

The cowboy sage snorted. "A feller who doesn't take time to know about his town and state ain't fit to live there." He settled back and gazed out the window.

Patti concentrated on her driving, enjoying every minute of it. The more space she put between herself and Shepherd of Love, the lighter her spirits became.

Time enough to deal with uncertainties and Charles Bradley when she flew home.

"I am so glad you had the Bronco in Seattle," she said. "You see so much more driving than flying."

Dan didn't respond for such a long time Patti glanced over at him, wondering if he were asleep. She quickly returned her gaze to the road. Dan's faraway expression showed he wasn't ignoring her. Far more likely he had forgotten his nurse's presence. The dreaming light in his eyes betrayed him. Mind and heart had outrun the Bronco in reaching the land he loved, the land of shining mountains where he met and married Sarah McClelland so long ago.

Envy settled on Patti, light as butterfly wings. She did not begrudge Dan Davis his memories. She yearned for such a love to one day enter the gates of her heart. She trembled. Love was not always instant recognition, as with Dan and Sarah. Some love came quietly, stealing through the strongest barricades on kitten feet.

Hands steady on the wheel, a passage of Scripture came to mind. Patti remembered her mother reading it to her again and again, in a voice hushed with the same wonder that touched the small girl's listening ears.

And he said, Go forth, and stand upon the mount before the
Lord. And, behold, the Lord passed by, and a great and strong

wind rent the mountains, and brake in pieces the rocks before the Lord; but the Lord was not in the wind: and after the wind an earthquake; but the Lord was not in the earthquake: And after the earthquake a fire; but the Lord was not in the fire: and after the fire a still small voice. 1 Kings 19:11–12.

How would love come to her? In wind, earthquake, or fire? Or through a still, small voice assuring her all was well? Tears welled. Patti impatiently shook them away. God had granted one of her most treasured dreams by allowing her this interlude to draw closer to Him and provide time to listen for His still small voice. How ungrateful of her to cry for more, demanding that He also provide a mate!

Dan Davis's voice recalled her to the present.

"Take the next exit," he advised.

"All right." Patti closed the door to her thoughts, swung off the freeway and into Coeur d'Alene, a tranquil town that belied the meaning of its name. The motel Dan recommended hadn't changed. Its owners welcomed the ex-cowboy and his nurse as if they were long lost friends. Later in the evening, the travelers drove partway around Lake Coeur d'Alene. Patti drank in the resinous, pine-scented air, marveled at the sky's deep blueness reflected in the lapping water, and felt even more of the tension that had plagued her seep away. She awakened from a night of untroubled, uninterrupted sleep when her stomach rumbled.

"Lead me to those flapjacks," she told Dan in the motel lobby. Patti's professional eye noted how rested he appeared, and the renewed sparkle in his faded blue eyes.

After an enormous breakfast, they headed the Bronco into the rising sun and began the mountainous drive across Idaho and through the Bitterroot Range to Missoula.

"Do you mind if I sing?" Patti asked. "I'm so bursting over with all this beauty, it's hard to hold it inside."

"Go ahead," Dan told her. "I'll grumble along." He did, adding a surprisingly mellow bass accompaniment to Patti's rendition of "This Is My Father's World."

The Bronco ran smoothly, eating up the miles as if they were inches. Patti couldn't remember enjoying a drive more.

They lunched in Missoula at another of Dan Davis's favorite haunts, although Patti had sworn after breakfast she couldn't eat another morsel until dinner. She simply wasn't able to resist the cafe's homemade vegetable soup. Or the cornbread that melted in her mouth. Before she climbed back in the Bronco to head north on U.S. 93, she loosened the leather belt around her trim waist and warned, "You'd better get me exercising soon or my clothes won't fit."

The white-haired ex-cowboy fastened his seat belt and turned so he faced her squarely.

"I did some thinkin' about that last night. What say we hang around Kalispell a few days, then head east? We'll follow the Middle Fork of the Flathead River from West to East Glacier and stay there or at Browning. Some folks make the circle in one day, but we want time for stoppin' and lookin'."

His eyes twinkled. "Goin' that way also fixes it so we come from east to west and hug the cliff side on most of the Going-to-the-Sun Highway, also called Going-to-the-Sun Road. Logan Pass is over 6600 feet. Lake McDonald's also well worth seein'. Once I saw that stretch of country, I never had a hankerin' to visit the Swiss Alps." He laughed sheepishly. "Sound like a tour guide, don't I? Anyway, you'll like it."

"Good," Patti enthusiastically replied. "I've liked almost everything so far."

White eyebrows raised in amusement. "Like I said before, you ain't seen nothin' yet. There's the National Bison Range a short piece up the road. We'll stop a spell, if you like. Flathead Lake's after that, then home."

The yearning in his voice made Patti blink. "A log cabin."

"Yes. And the Running H. I know it ain't mine, but it doesn't matter. The ranch will always be home to this stove-up, tired old cowpoke."

Patti's face must have shown signs of argument for Dan chuckled.

"Not so bad for an old-timer, actually." She felt his keen gaze rake her face. "I figure stayin' at the ranch will be the best part of your vacation, so we'll save it for last." He chuckled again. "If it was folks other than the Hoffs, I'd say go first, so they wouldn't fuss. Ma Hoff ain't that kind. Her floors are clean enough to eat from all the time and she won't start repaperin' just 'cause we're comin'. She'll throw a couple more beans in the pot, be glad if you help peel potatoes, and set us places at the table."

"I'm glad," Patti exclaimed. "I know you said we'd be welcome, but so many people feel they need to jump in and practically remodel if they know someone's coming! Knowing the Hoffs won't do that makes everything perfect." She broke off and squealed with excitement. "There's a buffalo!" She slowed to get a better view of the shaggy-shouldered beast that peered at the

Bronco from beneath wicked-looking horns, then switched its tail and went on grazing.

"There are more. Look! There are some babies." Patti pulled to the side of the road and gazed entranced. Seeing buffaloes in their native habitat was a far cry from viewing the species in a zoo. "That's funny. The little ones are yellowish-red, instead of brownish-black like the others."

"Calves always are," Dan explained. "Bison, that's the proper handle for these critters in the U.S. and Canada, have their young in May or June. Once in awhile, a bison lives as much as thirty to forty years. The bull that leads the herd watches out for the mother cows. He helps protect the calves from enemies."

"Better than some fathers," Patti mumbled. She found it hard to tear her fascinated gaze from the herd, but at last drove on. Many miles still lay between them and Kalispell, the "land going to the sun."

"Is your log cabin like the ones we've seen so far?" she asked a little later. "They're so homey looking."

"A mite bigger."

Patti wondered at the terse answer but decided the prospect of getting home was flooding Dan with memories. She searched her mind for a subject to get him talking and decided against it. Such a ploy would be an intrusion. A cardinal rule of nursing was to respect patients' privacy.

One instructor had drilled into Patti's class, "Never forget what Ecclesiastes 3 says: 'To every thing there is a season, and a time to every purpose under the heaven.' Add this to the list: 'a time to speak and a time to be still.' Simply being there for another human being is often the most effective way to aid healing. Words too often fail. Compassion flowing from your hearts never will."

How wise the teacher had been! Dozens of times Patti had heeded the advice burned into her soul as much by the look in her beloved mentor's face as the words themselves. A lightning glance toward Dan Davis disclosed his absorption in his own world. All he needed from her was to be driven home as safely and rapidly as her capabilities and Montana state law allowed.

Dan didn't speak again until they reached Kalispell. Then he turned shining eyes toward her and gave directions. Patti felt his curbed impatience. She recognized part of him wanted to leap forward like a mountain lion toward its prey. The vision of the cowboy he had been, hurrying himself and his tired horse home toward home and lighted windows, misted her eyes. *Thank You, Lord, for allowing me to be with Dan,* she silently prayed. *I'm glad this homecoming isn't at night. I couldn't bear having him return to a dark cabin.*

A few minutes later, Patti pulled into a gravel drive and realized how beautifully God had answered her prayer. *Dark cabin? Anything but!* Late afternoon sunlight mellowed the logs of Dan Davis's home. It turned each sparkling window to molten gold. Long and far larger than she had expected, the "cabin" nestled close to the ground like an infant cuddled against her mother's breast. A host of cottonwoods swayed in a slight breeze that cooled Patti's warm forehead. They dipped and fluttered their leaves, bowing before the guest.

Dan silently unlocked and opened the large front door circled by wild roses broadcasting their pink perfume.

"Welcome home, my dear," he said huskily.

Touched by his courtliness, Patti stepped across the threshold, into a room so soul-satisfying it eclipsed all her vague hopes and expectations.

Chapter 4

The inside of Dan Davis's log cabin home blazed with color, yet retained quietude and a sense of peace. Patti Thompson crooned with delight when she stepped into the living room. Deep green, plushy carpet made her feel she trod a forest floor. A few brightly woven Indian blankets hung like tapestries on the off-white walls. Sunlight shining through many windows laid a golden patina over the room. An enormous multicolored rock fireplace served as the focal point for the main room, which stretched at least twenty feet.

The portrait of a laughing girl in a fluffy white dress and hairstyle of the early forties hung above the fireplace mantel. Patti's first glance into the dark eyes gave her the curious sensation Sarah McClelland Davis quite approved her coming. It provided the final touch to make the upcoming vacation perfect.

Dan walked toward a door at the right side of the generous room. "Here's your home away from home, as they say. I'm on the opposite side. Both bedrooms have their own bathrooms. Kitchen and dinin' room are at the back." He threw wide the door. "How about we do some washin' up, then go out fer supper and do our grocery shoppin' on the way back?" His eyes twinkled. "Like I said, I'm quite a hand at cookin'."

"Sounds good to me." Patti walked through the open door and stopped short. Her first glimpse of her new abode made her wonder if she had died and gone to heaven. The charming bedroom faced west, as did the living room. The sun was putting on its best imitation of King Midas, painting the walls with gold overlay. A polished cross-section of pine with the motto "I will lift up mine eyes unto the hills, from whence cometh my help" burned into the wood hung on the wall. Patti dropped to her knees by the brightly blanketed bed, too filled with peace and gratitude for words, yet knowing God would understand. In the short time before she rose and did a lightning wash-up job, the western sky—and the off-white walls of her room—had changed to violet and strawberry pink.

"How do you like my shack?" Dan eagerly asked when she stepped back into the living room.

"Shack? More like a log mini-mansion! I could be happy here for the rest of my life, with—" She paused and felt a rich blush mount from her neck.

"With the right man," her host finished. "Of course, you wouldn't want to give up your nursin', but that could be arranged." After they got back in the Bronco, he asked, "How would you feel about leavin' Shepherd of Love?"

Patti kept her gaze on the road ahead. "I never even considered working anywhere else until lately." She told him how restless she had grown with her friends married, touched lightly on her bad experience with Bart Keppler. "I started to talk it over with the hospital director one day, then decided I was not ready," she confessed. "Your invitation was a God-send, in capitals. I knew I needed to get away, but not how much until we actually started."

"I thought you might. We take the next left," he directed. Nothing more was said about Patti's career for some time. The proprietors of the small but spotless restaurant greeted Dan as if he'd been gone a century and warmly welcomed Patti. After a delicious meal and a productive trip to a nearby supermarket, the ex-cowboy and nurse headed back to the log cabin in the cottonwoods.

Apprehension touched Patti when she turned into the gravel driveway. Light poured through the living room windows.

"That's funny. I don't remember you switching on a light," she told her companion.

"I didn't." He opened his door and smiled at her in the dim glow from the dome light. "I got me one of those newfangled devices that turns lights off and on at dawn and dusk. It's a lot better."

Better than coming home to a dark house and no Sarah, Patti thought. To cover the emotion welling up within her, she sprang out of the Bronco and began filling her arms with grocery sacks.

Dan immediately complained, "You modern gals make it downright hard for a feller to be a gentleman." He reached for a bulging bag.

"Oh, no, you don't," she said. "I do the heavy lifting around here for awhile."

He snorted. "Just what I expected. We ain't been here half a day and already you're gettin' mighty bossy." He took the sting out of his words by adding, "Just like my Sarah when she caught me doin' something I shouldn't."

"That's the nicest compliment you could give me," Patti called after him when he went ahead to unlock and open the front door.

Dan stopped and grinned. The light from the room silvered his hair to a halo.

"I reckon it is."

It didn't take long to stow their booty. Capacious knotty pine cupboards in both the pine-paneled kitchen and adjoining dining room added to the attractiveness of the rooms, as did ruffled white curtains at the windows.

"Everything's so clean," Patti tactlessly marveled.

Her host bristled. "I have never lived in a pigsty and I don't aim to start now."

She felt terrible. "I'm sorry. It just surprised me to find it spotless when you've been gone some time."

Dan relaxed. "I normally do my own cleanin'." He hesitated and looked sheepish. "When I'm away, a neighbor comes in and gives it a once-over just before I'm due home." He complacently looked around the rooms. "Livin' alone means there ain't that much housework. Now, let's settle down and talk."

"Isn't that what we have been doing?" Patti pertly asked.

Dan chuckled, strode back to the living room, and waited until she seated herself in a comfortable chair before dropping into its twin.

"I have a question for you. Is there something you've always wanted to do outside of nursin'?"

"You mean besides stay on a working cattle ranch for a time?" She curled deeper in the chair that held her like strong arms.

"A secret dream, maybe. One you never thought could come true."

Patti hesitated. She did have a dream, something she hadn't shared even with her best friends at Shepherd of Love. They knew nothing of the desire that periodically wakened, only to sigh and slumber again. Could she share her wish? Why not? Dan Davis had such insignificant contact with her normal world, her secret would be safe with him.

Patti laced her fingers together. Her voice sounded small in her own ears. "I've always wondered if I could draw or paint."

"Did you ever try?"

"I dabbled when I was a kid, but have been too busy since," she told him.

"Too much else to do. I studied hard in high school and college. Then came nursing training. Ever since, my job has kept me busy."

"Is lack of time the only reason?"

She gazed at him wide-eyed. "Are you trying to psychoanalyze me?"

Dan shook his head. "Naw. It's just that years of livin' sometimes help me see things in folks." She didn't reply and he added, "Most folks find time for what they really want to do, unless they're a wee bit afraid to try."

Patti felt as if he had sent an arrow bull's-eye into her vulnerable heart.

"You mean because I—people think they'll fail? Isn't that a good enough reason?"

"I reckon folks like Thomas Edison and that Alexander Graham Bell feller would disagree. They tried and failed a heap of times before succeedin'. Good thing they did. Otherwise, we'd be sittin' in the dark without telephones."

Patti digested what he said then glanced up from the fingers she had been intently observing and into sympathetic blue eyes. "I've always been a perfectionist," she explained. "I want to do things well, or not at all. Maybe I've used being busy as an excuse."

"The good Lord don't expect us to always be the best," Dan reminded her. "I didn't stay long on a buckin' bronc the first time I rode one! I up and climbed back on, though." He laughed, a delightful sound in the quiet room. "Some feller, I don't know who, hit the nail square on the head when he wrote:

Never a horse what couldn't be rode.
Never a cowpoke what couldn't be throwed.

"If you want to draw and paint, you owe it to yourself to try. You might find out it's a hidden talent. One that needs diggin' out and polishin' like a gold nugget." He grinned at her. "Remember Jesus tellin' about the slothful servant who brought down a good scoldin' on himself for hidin' his talent in the ground? I always felt it was a cryin' shame the galoot didn't have gumption enough to take his talent and make it grow."

Patti threw her hands into the air in mock surrender. "Will tomorrow be soon enough for me to purchase a sketch pad?" she meekly inquired. A mighty yawn followed. "Sorry. I don't think I could keep my eyes open enough tonight to draw anything more than my bath!"

The grumbling laugh Patti loved started at Dan's toes, worked up volume, and came out as a bellow. When he sobered, he suggested they read a Scripture and hit the sack. She nodded. Worn but agile fingers leafed through an equally worn Bible until they came to the parable of the talents. Patti couldn't remember ever taking it so personally. Heart thumping with determination, she privately vowed to use part of her vacation in finding out whether she had any artistic talent.

The next few days flew with the speed of light. Dan was fortunate in getting overnight reservations at East Glacier after someone canceled. If Patti lived to be older than the Rocky Mountains, she would never forget her trip across Glacier National Park. Words like spectacular, awe-inspiring, and sublime paled before reality. Coming home on the Going-to-the-Sun Road surpassed Patti's wildest expectations: jagged cliffs on her right; a rugged, seemingly bottomless canyon on her left. Although she'd never been squeamish about heights, she gave silent and fervent thanks they were on the inside most of the time.

Patti's newly awakened desire to draw increased. Dan graciously suggested they stop several times along the way.

"I'm content to lean against a pine tree and rusticate," he whimsically told her. "Take all the time you need. Walk. Drink it all in. Sketch, if you like. I'll be fine."

She couldn't resist giving him a big hug. In the relatively short time she'd known him, Patti had learned to love the former cowboy. He taught her untrained eyes to appreciate God's creation more than ever. The first time she laughed at an ungainly moose, Dan wryly reflected, "Either God sees beauty we're missin' or has a mighty good sense of humor most folks don't recognize!"

Patti reveled in every moment of the trip. "It's like my whole soul is expanding to match this vast country, God," she murmured, trying to capture a breathtaking view with inept strokes of a pencil. She scowled in exasperation.

The panorama before her needed far more skill than she possessed to capture it.

"When I get back to Seattle, I'm going to take an art class," she told Dan.

"Good idea," he heartily approved. "May I see your latest effort?"

She reluctantly handed it over. "This is how a mother must feel when she shows her baby to the world for the first time," she ruefully said.

Dan glanced from the sketch to the scene before them. "Not bad, Patti." He pointed to the pictured hint of peaks and a leafy branch thrust into the sky, then their living counterparts. "Your first impressions are bold, a lot better than where you've retouched. They show you have a keen eye and a grasp for what's there. Trainin' can help you learn how to make the most of your natural talent and add all the other stuff you need." He frowned. "I ain't an expert, but it seems you'd do better with color. Black and white's a mite stark."

Patti blushed with pleasure at his praise and quickly agreed. "I'll buy watercolors, or at least colored pencils, when I get back to Kalispell." She sighed and gathered up her paraphernalia. "I suppose we'd best go."

"We could stay longer, but it'd mean cuttin' into your time on the

Running H," her white-haired companion teased. His brown face crinkled.

"No way!" Patti promptly contradicted. "This may be my only chance to stay on a ranch. I can't give it up. Even for all this." She waved around her.

Dan took a long time to answer. When he cleared his throat and spoke, Patti felt her friend chose each word carefully. "The room in my home's yours as long as you want it. No charge for room and board. If you consider stayin' on for a time, we'll come back to Glacier. I can also take you a heap of other places."

Patti felt like a wishbone. The new and free part of her she'd discovered since coming to Montana longed to cut ties and accept. The other part clung to the security of Seattle and the hospital. How much did Charles Bradley have to do with her feelings? Patti shook her head. Right now, the handsome pilot seemed faraway, unreal. How would she feel when she saw him again?

Perhaps she only had a severe case of vacation madness, the affliction that often attacked travelers to different areas of the country. It sometimes led them into unwise, spur-of-the-moment decisions concerning relocation and career changes.

"I really appreciate the offer," she told Dan. "It's tempting, but it's also a long way from Seattle to Kalispell, and not just in miles."

"I know. I probably just have an old man's fancy. Don't fret about it. But remember, Patti, the door's wide open if you ever want to come."

"I will," she choked out. Tears spilled and an errant thought came. A short time ago she had told God she needed to be more independent and learn to make decisions without leaning on her friends, especially Lindsey and Shina. God certainly hadn't wasted any time putting her to the test.

The same thought recurred to Patti when she and Dan Davis took up residence at the Running H. They swiftly became part of the Hoff household. Ma and Pa, as they insisted on being called, stood on no ceremony with their guests.

"Dan says you want to be treated like one of the family," Ma announced. "Fine with Pa and me. We can always use more hands."

Patti thrilled to being considered a "hand" on the large ranch. Dan's grin showed his happiness at being back on the spread. Slouched in the saddle as if he were part of it, he spent hours teaching Patti to ride and filling her head with cowboy lore. He audibly regretted he wouldn't have time "on this trip" to teach her to shoot and rope.

She exchanged the mental fatigue that had disturbed her sleep in Seattle for physical weariness. It inevitably claimed her in sleep halfway through her nightly prayers. Resenting time away from the fascinating work of running a large ranch, Patti settled for a one-letter-will-have-to-do-for-all to her nurse friends. In it, she ecstatically announced,

> *I can't remember being this rested in ages. I recommend time on a ranch like the Running H to anyone who needs rejuvenating. We're up shortly after daylight, but that's okay, because we head for bed a little after dark. I'm eating so much I feel ashamed, yet ask for more. Ma Hoff says I'm the best kitchen "flunky" she's ever had and I enjoy every minute of it!*
>
> *I won't go into all the other stuff I do, but the Patti I've become since arriving in Montana is a far cry from the poor thing Bart Keppler deceived. I'd like to see him try it now! Even if he fooled me (and I don't think he could) nothing gets past Dan Davis. A cowhand from a neighboring ranch looked me over a little too boldly to suit Dan when we met on the range. Dan told the guy if he had to gawk, he should go stare in a store window.*
>
> *My heart leaped to my throat. I could just see the rowdy climbing down from his horse and pounding my protector. He did nothing of the sort. He took one look at Dan's stony face and steely eyes, mumbled an apology, and rode away (in the words of my white-haired hero) "like a whipped puppy."*

Patti yawned. The pressing need to let her friends know she still remained in the land of the living couldn't keep her awake. She hastily scrawled her name and shoved the letter into a stamped, addressed envelope.

"I'm not satisfied, but there is far too much to tell in a letter," she justified herself.

Although sleepy, Patti had trouble falling asleep for the first time since coming to Montana. She replayed the events of the past twenty-four hours. She could recall nothing unusual. A glorious sunrise. The discovery time in the saddle had changed from stubborn endurance to actual enjoyment. Marveling at the vast numbers of cattle, each branded with the familiar *H*. Riding home in a kaleidoscope of color no one but the Master Artist could ever achieve. The western sky reflected every shade of red, orange, and yellow, then subtly turned to amethyst and deep purple against the clear blue.

Wait. There had been something a little different today. She and Dan had reined in their horses on a mesa miles away from the ranch buildings. Patti felt the view stretched forever. Dan warned they needed to start back soon. Before she could touch heels to her horse, a noise in the sky drew Patti's gaze up. A helicopter flew over them and headed northwest. The pilot waved. Patti waved back and asked, "Why is a helicopter out here?"

Dan shaded his eyes against the sun. "That's Mike Parker's Rescue Service chopper. I can't tell whether he's pilotin' it."

"Rescue chopper?" Patti visually followed the path of the helicopter. It looked like nothing more on earth than a giant, awkward white grasshopper trimmed with red markings and a bright red cross.

"Patti, my dear, we have people livin' in out-of-the-way places where medical help ain't to be had just for the askin'. We also have folks with less sense than God gave a goose visit this area." Dan warmed to his subject. "They come out here from who knows where, determined to rough it. More than likely, they end up in hot water. Or snow and ice. Or at the bottom of a hill they shouldn't have been climbin' in the first place. Mike Parker sends out medical help. His pilots know first aid and a whole lot more. They take a nurse with them and do everything from transporting seriously injured folks back here to deliverin' babies on the spot. I know of at least three little guys named Michael in honor of Parker."

Dan's eyes gleamed. "If you were living' here, there's always a chance Mike could use you. How would you like bein' a flyin' rescue nurse?"

"I don't know. I haven't delivered any babies lately," she teased.

Now the thought of the odd conversation haunted Patti. *This Mike Parker must be a pretty special guy, one who really wanted to help others.* Her last waking thought was a pang of regret she wouldn't be around to meet him and the question, *Not that I'm going to stay, but I wonder what Mike Parker is like?* She fell asleep and dreamed a handsome pilot waved to her, then crawled inside a white helicopter marked in red and bearing a bright red cross. She watched with racing heart until pilot and helicopter became a mere speck against a flaming Big Sky sunset.

Morning did not lessen her curiosity concerning Mike Parker. At breakfast she said, "We saw a Rescue Service helicopter yesterday. What's the owner like?"

"Mike Parker?" Ma Hoff deftly slid a plate of hot biscuits onto the table. "About fifty, balding, a little on the paunchy side. You couldn't ask for nicer people or better Christians than Mike and his wife. I don't know what folks around here would do without the flying hospital. It's saved a peck of lives."

"The helicopter isn't really a hospital," Pa Hoff corrected. He helped himself to a biscuit. "More like a flying first aid station."

Patti smothered her mirth in her napkin. Leave it to her to have romantic dreams about a middle-aged, married Rescue Service owner! Her smile died. Good grief! Was she so desperate to find someone with whom to share her life that she viewed every man she saw or heard about as a candidate for the position?

Chapter 5

Dan Davis took Patti Thompson through Glacier National Park the first weekend after they reached Kalispell. The following Sunday, which would be her last in Montana, they climbed into the Running H station wagon with the Hoffs and drove to church in Kalispell. The plain but well-filled chapel glowed with morning sunlight and rang with enthusiastic singing. Patti's heart overflowed. There was no stuffy, formal religion here, only the gospel, alive and real.

The minister looked nothing like mahogany-haired Terence O'Shea who tended the spiritual needs at Shepherd of Love, yet a common spirit reminded Patti of the hospital chaplain. After some contemplation she decided it was the unmistakable fact both believed every word they preached from the depths of their souls.

The Kalispell pastor had chosen the theme "Leave all and follow."

Patti drank in every word. She hated for the sermon to end, although the entire congregation crowded around to meet and welcome her.

"I want you to know Mike Parker," Dan Davis said. "Mike, this is Nurse Patti Thompson. I'm tryin' to rope her into stayin' in Kalispell."

About fifty. Balding. Paunchy. Ma Hoff's description brought a smile to Patti's lips when Mike's huge hand engulfed hers.

"We can always use more nurses in this part of the country," he said in a surprisingly gentle voice. "Right, Scott?" he asked someone just behind Patti.

"Right."

She turned toward the amused voice and was struck by the stillness of the tall man's face. Her first impression was that he was in his early thirties, rugged, and dependable, a man to be trusted. Short black hair topped a lean, tanned face. Finely chiseled lips wore a small smile that didn't reach his brown eyes, so dark they looked black.

"Miss Thompson, meet Stone Face Sloan, senior pilot for my Rescue Service."

"Scott," the tall man corrected.

Stone Face is more appropriate, Patti thought. *I'll bet you are solid granite when you believe you're right.* She held out her hand.

Surprise chased some of the impassiveness from the pilot's face. "You have a strong grip."

Patti sighed. "At least you didn't add 'for a woman.' I get that all the time."

A slight smile hovered on his lips. "I'll bet you do."

"I never could stand dead fish handshakes," she impulsively told him.

The clear, ringing laugh turned faces in their direction and made a world of difference in Scott Sloan's face. It reminded Patti of the way spring green softened bare branches after a long winter.

"Are you serious about relocating to Kalispell?" Scott asked.

Patti couldn't tell whether his polite question expressed interest or merely served to fill the silence. She also didn't know how to answer.

Dan Davis came to her rescue. "I'm serious. She's thinkin' about it. At least, I hope she is." He grinned at Patti.

A somber expression dulled Scott's eyes. "It's a good place to live. Nice meeting you, Nurse Thompson." He nodded to Mike and Dan, turned on his heel, and walked down the aisle, spine rigid and head held high.

The abrupt departure left Patti staring after him. Few young men walked away from Patti Thompson.

"Did I say something wrong?" she asked Mike Parker.

"Naw. Stone Face is like that sometimes. A real private person, if you know what I mean. He's also an ace pilot, best of my crew. I'd never have been able to sign him on if it hadn't been—"

"Sorry, Mike, but we have an appointment and it's getting late," a soft voice reminded. Its plump, gray-haired owner smiled at Patti. "This husband of mine tends to be forgetful now and then. I'm so glad you could come, Dear." She hurried Mike away.

Patti experienced disappointment totally out of proportion to the situation. Of all the times to be interrupted, just when the conversation became interesting. Reason tapped at her shoulder. Why should she care why the ace pilot whose nickname Stone Face fit perfectly flew for Parker's Rescue Service? She'd be gone in a few days and never see the man again.

The thought brought a feeling Patti couldn't identify. Dismay filled her, even while she told herself not to be an idiot. Scott Sloan was nothing to her but a courteous stranger who admired her grip.

Patti's mental scolding didn't help a bit. She couldn't help comparing her present feelings with the little crushes she used to have at church camp. The excitement of meeting new boys who sometimes drifted in from other states had always held a note of sadness. Knowing she'd never see them again once camp ended brought bittersweet twinges that kept new friendships from being perfect.

Strange she should feel the same way about the sober-faced pilot. She thought she'd outgrown such childish behavior. *Probably my vanity,* she decided. Scott Sloan had been polite but not interested. Perhaps he had a wife. Patti tried to dismiss him from her thoughts, but her ears pricked up like a bird dog's on the trail when the Hoffs talked about Scott on the way home.

"Anyone know why they call him Stone Face?" The question sounded casual, but Patti held her breath waiting for the answer.

"Folks privately speculate. No one knows for sure unless it's Mike Parker," Dan said. "It's obvious the boy's had a bad experience at one time or another, but that's his business."

Although Patti knew her friend didn't refer to her, she felt like a kindergartner corrected and sent to a corner in shame. She hid her reaction by saying, "It's hard to believe in a few days I'll be back on duty in Outpatient. I wonder if all this will seem as dreamlike and other-worldlike as Seattle seems now."

"You can always come back." Dan's hasty laugh couldn't quite camouflage the pathos in his simple statement. His blue eyes gleamed. "Only thing is, you might have to stay in the log cabin alone."

An alarm bell rang in her brain. "Is there something you're not telling me?"

"Just that the Hoffs have gotten used to having a cantankerous old ex-cowboy around the Running H this last week. They want me to move back out here." A quiver in his voice betrayed how much the suggestion thrilled him.

Relief rolled through Patti. "That's wonderful! You're coming, aren't you?"

"I reckon I'll take them up on it," Dan drawled.

"Once a cowpoke, always a cowpoke," Pa Hoff put in. He chuckled. "It will be good to have Dan here, especially when winter comes. Ma'd rather crochet and watch TV than play checkers, so I don't have anyone to beat since the kids married and left home."

Dan's white head snapped up. "You ol' tumbleweed, you still ain't goin' to have anyone to beat."

"If I'm an ole tumbleweed, what's that make you?" Pa retorted. "You're older than I am by a long shot."

"That's just what my birth certificate says. Inside where it counts, I'm young and frisky as a colt," Dan loftily informed his soon-to-be checker rival. They wrangled all the way home, to Patti's amusement and delight.

The final few days rushed past like a herd of stampeding cattle. Patti found herself marking off what she called "lasts": the last batch of bread she helped Ma Hoff bake; the last time she tried to capture distant mountains with crayon and watercolors; the last ride to the mesa overlooking the peaceful valley. She came to the point where if Dan again asked her to stay, she knew she would weaken. How could she leave this busy, satisfying life? On the other hand, Shepherd of Love and countless patients needed her skills and training. Dan said no more. She knew his creed made it impossible to coerce. He had given the invitation. Now he would respect Patti's right to choose.

The day before Patti flew home, the Hoffs moved Dan to the ranch. Patti knew she would never forget the look in his eyes as long as she lived; a look of coming home to the Running H, where he belonged. Even the now-empty log cabin in Kalispell hadn't been able to replace the ranch in Dan's life.

Pa Hoff bluntly said, "You're welcome to stay with us, or you can have a cabin." He indicated one of several small log houses scattered a short distance from the ranch house. "You'll eat with us, of course."

Dan chose the cabin. Surrounded by memories and the opportunity for solitude when he needed it, he would also have the comfort of knowing friends who loved him were close by.

Patti clung to her cowboy friend when it came time to board the westbound plane. "I–I feel like I'm leaving part of me," she choked out. "It's been perfect."

His gnarled hand stroked her bright hair. "Steady, there. You'll be back."

The prophetic ring in his voice stiffened her backbone and she brushed the mist from her eyes. "I hope so."

A curious glint accompanied his, "You will. Mark my words. Now, get to gettin', young lady, or you'll be missin' that plane." Her last sight of Dan Davis was his standing ramrod straight, right hand flung high in a wave Patti felt was more a benediction than a farewell.

Montana receded behind the speeding plane. So did Idaho. Washington State appeared. By the time the plane touched down at SeaTac International Airport, Patti felt she had passed from one life to another.

"I wonder if going from earth to heaven is like this," she whispered. "Simply leaving one place and arriving at another and better one." Her analogy fell apart. At this point, she seriously questioned whether Seattle was the better place for her.

The question continued for a few days, then lost itself in a maze of work and Charles Bradley. After his noncommittal acceptance of her stay in Montana on their first date, he seemed singularly disinterested except concerning whom she had met in Kalispell.

"Dan Davis. The Hoffs and their hands. Mike Parker," Patti reported.

"Is that Parker's Rescue Service? Helicopter outfit?"

Her eyes opened wide. "You know him?"

Charles grunted. "I know of him. Started on a shoestring and has built up a pretty good business. Anyone else?"

She thought of Scott Sloan, but wrote him off as insignificant. Charles wouldn't care about a pilot who seldom smiled and excused himself as soon as possible after meeting the nurse Charles considered his. Neither did she mention the loutish rider Dan Davis had so effectively put in his place. Why risk an unpleasant show of temper?

You aren't being fair, a little voice inside chastised. *Charles is obviously doing everything he can to erase the memory of his temper fit.*

The young pilot continued on his best behavior. Patti gradually spent more and more time with him. She felt herself responding to his magnetic personality and genuine affection more intensely with every date.

"I think I'm falling in love," she announced to her shining-eyed reflection in the bathroom mirror late one evening after Charles brought her home. Yet unlike the times she had formerly shared with Lindsey and Shina, she hugged the new-found feelings close to her heart and bided her time. Love for a lifetime had to be more than thrilling to a man's nearness, listening for the ring of the phone. Even though Charles continued to plan for after they were married, Patti hesitated. "Why?" she asked her image. "He attends chapel with me as often as his flight schedule permits. My slightest wish really is his command, as the old cliché says. What more can I want?" The mirrored eyes darkened. The vivid lips drooped. Impatient with herself for allowing introspection to dim the memory of an exciting evening, she turned away and prepared for bed.

Dan Davis sent infrequent postcards. Ma Hoff supplemented them with brief scrawls that said everyone was well and happy and their new cowhand got younger every day. If Patti didn't believe it, Ma Hoff wrote, she should come see for herself, maybe spend Christmas at the ranch.

Patti's heart thumped. If things continued as smoothly as they were going now, she might be wearing a diamond long before Christmas. Charles made her feel so special, so loved, cherished, and protected.

"I wonder if the Hoffs and Dan would welcome a fiancé as warmly as they did me?" she pondered. The thought raised a blush Patti knew outshone a fiery Montana sunset, but when she answered the invitation, she only said her plans for Christmas were uncertain.

Summer in Seattle changed overnight to a herald of things ahead. Afternoon temperatures rarely reached eighty degrees. Nights ranged from forty-five to fifty degrees. One morning a hint of frost sparkled on the hospital lawn. Flowers still bloomed brightly, but here and there a branch showed brown or red. Patti took out her sadly neglected art materials and tried to recapture the log home in Kalispell. Instead of green, she chose a sunny yellow for the cottonwood leaves to see if she could create an autumn version of the scene that was never far from her mind.

The results stirred a slumbering desire. Regret flicked her conscience. Why hadn't she carried through with her plan to take lessons in drawing or painting? One word: Charles. He wanted her to be available when he flew in. Patti's lips curved upwards. Were people now really so different from earlier generations? For years, Dan Davis eagerly rode home to lighted windows and the woman who waited for him. Now Charles Bradley no less eagerly flew back to Seattle—and Patti—from wherever his flight orders carried him.

Patti felt a kinship with Sarah McClelland. Had her pulse quickened to the beat of hooves, the way Patti's did to Charles' quick knock at her door? Patti wondered. Did she fling wide the door to heart and house, as a certain nurse was learning to do? Did she stretch her arms out in welcome to the man she adored? Had Sarah experienced the same feeling all was well now that her man was home that meant so much to Patti?

Why wait longer to admit my love for Charles? Patti decided that when he came that night, she would tell him she longed to be his wife. If he wanted to be married soon, she'd suggest spending their honeymoon in the log cabin home in Kalispell. She could think of no place more perfect. A twinge of doubt assailed her. *Would Charles be equally content with a Kalispell honeymoon?* He certainly hadn't wanted her to go there in the first place.

"I'll go anywhere on earth *my wife* chooses for a honeymoon," he huskily told Patti when she faltered an acceptance of his longstanding proposal that night. "If it's Kalispell you want, it's Kalispell you'll get."

Tears of joy mingled with his kiss. They partially blurred the fierce gleam in his face, but after Charles left, she wondered. There had been far more in that look than the mere desire to please her. Patti quickly brushed the disturbing thought aside and concentrated on the many things she would have to do for the simple wedding she'd awaited for so long. Chaplain Terence O'Shea would perform the ceremony in the hospital chapel, of course. Lindsey would wear pale green and Shina yellow to set off their red and black hair, respectively. As for herself, she would be gowned in her mother's carefully preserved satin wedding gown.

She hugged her chest with her arms and ecstatically planned to telephone Dan Davis as soon as she and Charles set a date. She knew he'd made no attempt to rent the log cabin home. Had he hoped she would return?

"I am, God," she told her heavenly Father and Friend. "Only not as Dan and I discussed."

◆◈◆

Patti couldn't make that call for some time. An unexpected cross-country flight took Charles away from Seattle for the rest of August. When he finally came home and joyously burst into her apartment, he found everything changed.

A grave-eyed Patti met him at the door. Her tear-stained face showed suffering. She gave a little cry and ran into his arms.

They closed around her. "What's happened?" he hoarsely asked.

She stared at him with unseeing eyes. "Dan Davis died this afternoon."

He relaxed. "I'm sorry, Patti, but he was an old man. Was it a heart attack?"

Patti pulled back, shocked at Charles's lack of real interest. Even though he hadn't known Dan, he knew how much she loved the old cowboy.

"No. His heart is—was as sound as mine." She shook her head, trying to clear away the fog surrounding it ever since Ma Hoff's phone call came a few hours earlier.

"Bad news about Dan," Ma tersely said. "One of those freakish things that can happen to anyone. A cottontail sprang up out of nowhere and spooked Dan's horse. The ornery cuss threw him." She paused.

> *Never a horse what couldn't be rode.*
> *Never a cowpoke what couldn't be throwed.*

The idiotic rhyme from long ago mimicked Dan's voice in Patti's brain and clutched at her throat. "How bad is he?"

"He didn't make it." Gentle sympathy flowed over the miles. "He hit his head on a rock outcropping. By the time Pa got there, Dan was dead."

"Why?" Patti whispered. "How can God let this happen, just when Dan was home and happy?"

She heard a quick-drawn breath before Ma Hoff said, "Pa and I've been asking ourselves that, Child. The only thing we can think is that if Dan had been given a choice, he'd have wanted it this way. The doctor who came out from Kalispell said he died instantly." The lengthening wire faithfully reproduced her tear-clogged voice. "He loved you, Patti. Just last night he talked about how much you reminded him of Sarah and how powerful glad he was to know you. He looked forward to seeing you again."

Patti's hand trembled until she nearly dropped the phone. "Now he won't."

Some of the sass came back to Ma Hoff's voice. "If you don't know better than that, you ought to be ashamed, Patti Thompson! Not a verse in the Bible's any clearer than John 11:26: 'And whosoever liveth and believeth in me shall never die. . . .'" Her voice softened. "Honey, Pa and I are hanging onto that promise mighty hard. You need to do the same, if you want to get past this. It would please Dan. Pa's coming in, so I'd better go. I'll let you know about the services. I'm sure we'll find Dan left something to show his wishes."

Patti stared at the silent phone long after she hung it up. Snatches of the conversation returned. Ma Hoff's unshakable faith cushioned some of the shock, and warmth stole into the nurse's heart. She had seen death many times, even blessed it when it came as a release from pain. *Thank God Dan Davis had accepted Christ long ago!* The foolish cottontail and a spooked horse had not caught him unprepared. She could almost hear him drawl, "Sarah's been waitin' for quite a spell. I'll bet she's standin' as close to heaven's window as she can get. No need for her to light a lamp for me. God's glory will be chasin' away the shadows."

Healing tears came from the mental picture of the old cowboy whose homespun wisdom had enriched Patti's life and opened her eyes to many things.

Yet she longed for the comfort of human touch and counted off the minutes until Charles arrived.

❖

Now he had come, only to disappoint her. Where were the concern and comfort she craved? Patti searched the charming face. Admiration blazed like a forest fire in Charles's blue eyes, but they held no real understanding. Neither did his words, "I suppose this means we won't be able to spend our honeymoon in Kalispell." A curious shadow crept over his face, turning her fiancé into a stranger. A moment later his face cleared, but not before the damage had been done. It confirmed Patti's earlier suspicions. For some unknown reason, Charles Bradley had desperately wanted to honeymoon in Kalispell.

Patti felt chilled without knowing why. "I'm very tired, Charles. If you don't mind, I need to spend some time alone." How ironic. Sending him away after she'd waited hours for him to come!

"Of course. Perhaps you'll be more like yourself tomorrow." He brushed her lips with his and stiffly marched to the door. Patti knew she had angered him but was too numb to care. *How could he have been so insensitive, so unfeeling?* Charles obviously cared more about how Dan Davis's death affected his plans than about her grief. Patti sadly stumbled to bed, feeling she had sustained not one, but two great losses.

Chapter 6

The simple graveside service requested in Dan Davis's papers took place without Patti. She awakened feeling dizzy and nauseated the morning she planned to fly to Montana, with a fever well over 102 degrees.

"This is ridiculous," she complained to the doctor who came to check on her. "I take my flu shots as faithfully as I brush my teeth." She staggered back to bed after letting him in.

"Last year's shot would have pretty much worn off and it isn't time for this year's," he told her sympathetically.

"I know. Whatever happened to the good old days when people had the flu in winter instead of all year round?" She coughed and grimaced. "Ouch."

"You know the drill," the doctor told her. "Rest. Drink, drink, drink—as much water and juice as you can get down. I'll have the hospital pharmacy send you something for fever when it's over one hundred degrees. I'll also have someone check on you later today. Who's your nearest neighbor?"

"April and Allison Andrews, but don't bother." Patti scrunched down in her bed. "I just want to sleep."

The doctor's eyes twinkled. "My, my, nurses do make troublesome patients," he teased, then sheepishly admitted, "My wife says I'm the world's worst patient. Being on the other side of the sheets isn't much fun." He started away then stopped. "I'll leave your door to the corridor unlocked so you won't have to get up to answer it."

"All right," Patti croaked "If anyone bothers me, I'll breathe on them."

The doctor laughed. "No one will. The door at the far end that opens from the covered passage leading to Shepherd of Love is locked at all times."

It took too much effort to tell him she knew that. "Thanks." Something niggled at her tired brain. "Oh, could you please have someone call Mrs. Hoff in Kalispell? The number is by the phone. I was supposed to fly to Montana for a funeral service this afternoon."

"Of course."

Patti barely heard the click of the latch when he left. Pressure pushed down against the top of her head like a black cloud on a mountaintop.

When she put her left hand to her cheek, the diamond engagement ring Charles had placed on her third finger dug into her cheek. Patti removed it and put it under her pillow. She drank deeply from the carafe of ice water the doctor had thoughtfully left on a small table by her bed, slept, dreamed, slept again. The pharmacy messenger came and went. Patti gobbled down her medicine and slept some more.

Hours or what seemed like eons later, the Andrews twins came in. Patti was too tired to muddle out who gave her a sponge bath and who brought a fresh sleep shirt to replace her sweaty one, then fed her broth. Refreshed, she noticed how skillfully the girls used their training in how to change a bed with a patient in it. She and Shepherd of Love were in good, capable hands. After putting her engagement ring safely away in a jewel box that held mostly costume stuff, they quietly left her to sleep again.

Patti's first real bout with influenza since childhood eventually ran its course. Yet the listlessness that followed troubled her. Why was it taking so long to recuperate? she wondered. She had seen patients cling to illness to avoid facing life. Was she doing the same? It had been heavenly peaceful in her apartment with the excuse of being contagious to avoid work and its stress, even Charles.

Realization came the morning Patti planned to report for duty. By the time she showered and dressed, the dark cloud had again descended on her. She called the Outpatient supervisor and explained she just wasn't up to coming back. Patti sank to the couch and stared at the wall, wondering what was wrong with her, vaguely dreading Charles's visit that night. Influenza did strange things, but how could it have swallowed the eagerness she normally felt at his coming? Perhaps she subconsciously knew she couldn't deal with making plans just yet. He would want to talk about their future now that she was better.

"Am I really better?" Patti wondered aloud. She pressed her hands to her head. The foreboding sensation didn't budge.

An hour later, the hospital director knocked at her door. Patti gasped. "My goodness, what are you doing here?" She felt herself turn fiery red. "I mean, you're welcome, but this is a surprise."

The keen-eyed man waited until she seated herself then dropped to a nearby chair. "I came because I suspect one of my nurses may need me."

She shouldn't have been surprised. The caring director kept his finger on the pulse of every part of Shepherd of Love, especially his employees. Weakness and gratitude sent a rush of emotion through her.

"All right, Nurse Thompson. There's more here than influenza. I received a diagnosis from your doctor of flu and extreme fatigue. What have you been doing to yourself?" He leaned back in the chair as if he had all the time in the world.

"I don't know where to begin." Her voice sounded tight, even to herself. "Maybe with last year. It wasn't a very good one."

"Tell me about it." Bit by bit, the compassionate director extracted the ups and downs in Patti's life like nut meat from a shell. By the time she finished with the grief over losing Dan Davis, she felt she'd been turned inside out.

After a long, understanding silence, the director quietly asked, "Is there somewhere you can go to get away from everything and everyone for a time? What about your parents?"

Patti shook her head. "They're retired and away on a long trip."

"If it were possible, would you be able to handle going back to Montana? To the Hoffs and Running H? They sound like good medicine. What about the log cabin in Kalispell? Would it bring back too many painful memories?"

"I don't know." Patti closed her eyes. The peace she had known in both the log cabin and at the ranch enfolded her. "All my memories from actually being there are happy. Dan—Mr. Davis hoped I would come back. He said I could use his house, even though he was moving to the Running H."

"I want you to take an extended leave of absence. If you don't go to Montana, choose another place," the director told her. "Life has been hitting you with one blow after another recently. Your body and mind are clamoring for rest. God wants you to listen to them. If you refuse to ignore what they're telling you, it may result in serious damage to your health." He patted her shoulder and smiled. "Consider yourself on leave of absence, as of now. Let me know where you're going and when you're leaving the hospital."

"I will," she promised. With the decision out of her hands, the dark cloud oppressing her miraculously lifted. Patti felt like a fraud when she ushered the caring doctor out. "Good grief," she explained to the closed door. "All it took was knowing I needed to let down. That's the first step to recovery. Now to think things over." She curled up on her comfortable couch and closed her eyes. Instead of thinking, she promptly fell asleep!

The mentally exhausted nurse awakened feeling more rested than she had in weeks. Grief at losing Dan Davis remained, but she knew healing had begun. Instead of going to the staff dining room for lunch, Patti prepared an enormous sandwich and drank a large glass of milk.

"Flat out lazy, that's what I am," she admitted with a yawn. She quickly washed her few dishes, headed back to the couch, and picked up a new inspirational novel. Sleep claimed her before she finished the first page.

Patti roused from a dream of Montana. She tried to recapture it in the delicious interval between sleep and full consciousness. Much of it eluded her, yet she remembered riding the range with the sun and wind in her face. She rode alone, but the deep rumbling laughter she would always associate with her cowboy friend sang in the air, bringing her peace. The dream changed in a flash, putting Patti in the tranquil living room of the log cabin in Kalispell. The picture of Sarah McClelland Davis welcomed her, as she felt it had weeks earlier. Only now Sarah's face glowed with far more joy and her eyes shone with happiness.

Patti came fully awake. *What an odd dream!* She lay still and considered it. According to her beliefs, even now Dan and Sarah were reunited in the presence of the One they had loved and served so long and faithfully. Patti felt at peace.

"I know there will be times when a certain laugh, or song, or the way the wind blows will catch me off guard and I'll come unglued," she soberly told her heavenly Father. "I also know each time will be a little easier. Lord, is it Your will for me to go to Montana?"

She waited a long time. No thunder or lightning replied. God didn't speak in the mighty roar of a storm. Patti waited a little longer, then rose from the couch. She took out the painting of the cabin she had done using yellow for the cottonwood leaves and propped it up on a table. Nostalgia clutched at her heart. She could almost see Dan Davis opening the door and welcoming her home.

Her heartbeat increased. "Lord, is this my answer? This feeling of rightness?"

No still, small voice sounded. Yet the rest in Patti's soul gave answer enough. Eager to start the wheels of her going in motion, she reached for the phone. The Hoffs would either know about the log cabin's availability or be able to tell her whom to contact. To her dismay, the phone rang a dozen times. She started to cradle it, then heard the breathless, welcome voice of Ma Hoff.

"Hello?"

Memories overwhelmed Patti, leaving her weak. "Ma? It's Patti Thompson," she said in a small voice.

"My goodness, you sound faraway! I know you are, but it's not a very clear connection. Shall I call you back?"

Patti cleared her throat and raised her voice. "Can you hear me now?"

"I sure can. How are you feeling? We've been worried about you."

"That's why I'm calling. I'm over the flu, but the doctors say I need a long rest. Is there any chance I can rent Dan's Kalispell cabin?"

Ma Hoff sounded doubtful. "I really don't know. The lawyer who handles things told Pa things would be settled before long. For heaven's sake, don't wait until then, Child. Your room here's ready and waiting, just as you left it. You can stay as long as you like. Pa and I are rattling around this old ranchhouse like the last two beans in a stewpot since Dan moved on."

Moved on. What a typical, range-like way to describe death!

"You're sure I won't be in the way?"

"Land sakes, no! How soon can you come? We will pick you up at the airport."

"I'll have to let you know." Patti choked up again. "Thanks, Ma. Pa, too."

"Don't thank us. We miss our kitchen flunky something fierce." The warm-hearted rancher's wife quickly said good-bye and hung up.

For the first time in days, Patti's former enthusiasm sparked. A moment later, it went out, drowned by a flood of apprehension. *What would Charles say?* She glanced at her watch and turned the engagement ring she'd put back in its proper place around and around. She wouldn't have to wait long to find out. In a few hours, he'd swoop down on her the way hawks do on defenseless baby chicks.

"What's wrong with you, Patti Thompson?" she cried. "You've promised to marry Charles. How can you make such an odious comparison?" She pushed aside all thought of going to the dining room and stared at the four walls until she felt like climbing them. April and Allison Andrews ran in for a few minutes, but tactfully left when Charles arrived.

He had never looked more handsome than in his well-cut gray slacks and a soft blue shirt that matched his eyes.

"Darling!" Charles held out his arms the moment the twins disappeared. "I've missed you so much."

Patti relaxed in the security of his arms. How foolish she had been to let illness build up dread! This was Charles, the man she loved, the man with whom she planned to spend her life until death separated them.

For the first half hour, everything went well. Although Charles had kept in touch by phone and sent enough flowers to decorate a wedding chapel and reception, he acted as though they'd been out of touch for years. At last he said, "Now that you're feeling better, we can make plans. I've arranged to have the entire month of December off for our honeymoon. How about a wedding just after Thanksgiving?" He laughed a satisfied laugh. "I'll be the one giving thanks!"

Patti took a deep breath. "I–I'm not sure it will work out."

"Excuse me?" He drew back, looking as if he'd been slapped.

"The doctors are putting me on a leave of absence for an indefinite period of time. Would you believe the hospital director himself came to check on me?"

She managed a weak laugh. "Seems I've been getting myself so run down I'm not much good to either the hospital or myself. They're sending me away."

"Where? When?" His words cracked like a lightning-struck Ponderosa pine.

"To Montana, as soon as possible."

Charles's mouth set in a grim line. "Impossible! I can't get away now."

"You don't have to get away. The Hoffs want me to come stay with them, at least until Mr. Davis's estate is settled. After that, I want to rent the log cabin." She tried to overcome the fluttering in her throat and sound enthusiastic. "I'll have time for a long rest, which is the doctors' prescription. I can't imagine not being well enough to marry by the end of November, Charles, but I won't make a promise I may not be able to keep."

Rage contorted his handsome face. "Well, isn't this sweet. I go through the red tape of obtaining an entire month off of work and you tell me it's all in vain."

Some of Patti's spunk returned. "I didn't plan to get sick, you know."

"You probably wouldn't have, if you'd stayed here when I wanted you to, instead of gallivanting off to Montana with some broken-down ex-cowboy!"

"You call an all-expense-paid vacation and making an old man happy for a couple of weeks gallivanting?" Patti curbed her rising anger and tried for the light touch. "Them's fightin' words, pardner."

Wrong move. It touched off Charles Bradley like a match to tinder. "You are not going back to Kalispell. Period. Think I'll take the chance of—" He broke off. "I forbid it. You look fine to me except for being a little pale, which is to be expected. If you have to get away, go to the ocean or mountains, not Montana."

Patti made a desperate grab for the reins of her slipping control. She missed. "May I inquire what medical school issued your diploma, Dr. Bradley?" she asked in a tone that should have warned him. Instead, it pushed him farther over the edge.

"I hate sarcasm in women, so you may as well stop it right there," he ranted.

Patti had observed the miracle of cataract patients with their sight restored.

She had rejoiced with them, yet had never known the full measure of their clear vision until now. Charles's ultimatum was more effective than laser surgery. All Patti's nebulous doubts and fears sprang into full-fledged knowledge. They removed a far more dangerous blindness than not being able to physically see: blindness formed by her loneliness and mistaking attraction for lasting love. Life with Charles would be a hearth of fire.

"Well?" He gripped her shoulders, as he had done once before.

This time Patti did not wrench free. She simply said, "Take your hands off me, Charles. Get out and don't come back."

"You don't mean that." He attempted to draw her to him, but she stiffened.

"I never meant anything more in my life. I won't link my life with someone who tramples and doesn't respect me. You don't want a wife. You want a possession. I'm sorry I didn't recognize it sooner."

Charles freed her and crossed his arms. An ugly expression darkened his face.

"You may as well stop trying to get your own way. That's all it is, you know. I don't plan to fall for it. No woman is ever going to rule me. I'm leaving, but I'll be back when you've come to your senses."

Patti stripped off the engagement ring that had changed from a symbol of love to one of servitude and held it out.

"I meant what I said. Good-bye, Charles."

He laughed in her face and warded her off when she tried to drop it in his shirt pocket.

"Oh, no, you don't! I bought this for you and you're going to wear it. I never give up anything that's mine. Meaning you."

"Take it or leave it. I don't care. Once you go, I won't be responsible for the ring. I'm leaving soon." A burst of independence made her add, "Since I have no idea when or even if I'll be back, I'm giving up this place." It was a new idea, born of necessity, but it was a good one, she knew. "I'll store what I don't take with me. You probably won't want the ring left lying around in an empty apartment."

Charles sullenly accepted it but not an iota of defeat showed in his face.

"You'll be back." He raised an eyebrow. "I can't guarantee I'll still be available. I know a dozen women who'd be glad to accept me, with or without a ring. Sailors aren't the only ones with girls in every port, you know."

"Thank you," Patti quietly told him. "If I still had lingering doubts about you, that last despicable sentence erased them forever." She flung open the outside door. "Are you leaving, or must I call Security?"

He slouched out, head high. Anyone seeing him wouldn't guess in a million years the woman he professed to love had just dumped him. Patti watched him stride to his car, his "hail-the-conquering-hero" attitude intact. It made her feel better about the hideous scene. Her sharp rejection may have nicked Charles Bradley's pride, but it hadn't even come close to wounding his heart.

Would he accept her edict as final? Patti shook her head. Only the most conceited man on earth would believe any decent woman would take him back after that vile threat. Yet Charles' comment that he never gave up anything he wanted sent chills through her.

What would she do if she were him? "Stay away for a few days to teach me a lesson so I'd come crawling back," she decided. "Good! By the time he decides to honor me with his presence again, I'll be in Kalispell. Horrors! What if he follows me? He knows the Hoffs' names and the name of the ranch.

"Forget it and get busy," she commanded herself. "God can take care of you just as well in Montana as here." A wave of gratitude washed over her. "Thanks, Lord. You haven't showed me all of Your will in my life, but You certainly showed me just now Charles Bradley isn't part of it!"

Patti accomplished so much in such a short time, it amazed even her. She made plane reservations. A quick call to Chaplain and Lindsey O'Shea resulted in willing permission for Patti to store anything she liked at their farmhouse near Redmond. Lindsey had a day off, so she and Terence brought boxes and insisted on doing the packing while Patti supervised. Shina Ito Hyde and the Andrews twins came after day shift ended.

"You could at least have given us enough notice to throw a farewell party," Shina complained over the take-out chicken dinners her husband, Kevin, obligingly picked up and brought to the willing workers.

"We'll miss you, but you need a change, Pal. At least for now," Lindsey added. "Just don't forget us."

"Fat chance." Patti knew if she responded as seriously as her friends looked, the parting would be all sorrow and *not* sweet. She forced down a bite of potatoes and gravy wondering why it didn't stick on the lump in her throat.

"Okay," Terence said a little later. "You have what you're taking on the plane. We ship the boxes marked with an X and store the rest. Right?"

"Right." Patti secretly wished they would all just leave. One by one they did, with the frankly envious Andrews twins last. Patti avoided looking at the empty apartment. Doing so meant remembering how many years she had spent at Shepherd of Love. What did God have in mind for her? A leave of absence, or a whole new life?

Too weary to worry about it, Patti went to bed and didn't waken until her alarm sounded. An hour later, she stepped into the taxi she had insisted on taking to the airport. She simply couldn't handle lingering farewells at the airport.

"Good-bye, Mount Rainier, hello Montana," she saluted the snow-capped peak. Chin up, face forward, Patti Thompson flew into a future known only to God.

Chapter 7

Scott Sloan grabbed his denim jacket and stepped from the white Bell Jet-Ranger. *Another mission successfully accomplished,* he thought. Scott took off his black baseball cap and ruefully stared at the dirty helicopter. Dust streaks partially obscured its red markings and large red cross painted on the side.

"Not bad, considering where we've been." The nurse who had ridden beside him grinned. "Still identifiable, though."

"Yeah. Everyone in Kalispell knows the Parker Rescue Service choppers."

"As well as the miraculous feats Scott Sloan and his fellow pilots accomplish in getting expert help—such as mine—to those who need it," the nurse teased. She smirked at her double-sided compliment and headed for the hangar.

Scott paused long enough to give the chopper a surreptitious pat. The warm glow he always experienced after returning to Kalispell from a flight saturated him and a rare smile surfaced. Scott stretched his tall, lean body. Muscles rippled under the black turtleneck. It felt good to be home, even though home meant a strictly masculine apartment not far from the flying field. How different from the home he and the nurse who had accompanied him had left a short time ago! The rude cabin perched on a grassy knoll that overlooked an isolated, wooded draw. It shouted the fact it had been built with enthusiasm, furnished with love.

Mike Parker often raged at people who chose to live so far from towns where they had limited access to doctors, even while providing medical support. Scott admired their pluck. The young couple in the cabin reminded him of the countless intrepid pioneers who forged homes in the wilderness after crossing thousands of weary miles on foot or in covered wagons. If he married, perhaps he and his wife would be one of them.

Scott's smile faded. A mouth that shouted its owner had known tragedy and suffering tightened. Long, denim-clad legs carried him to the hangar. He found the flight service owner receiving an official report of the follow-up call. A few days earlier, Scott had flown a doctor to the cabin after a frantic call from the wife. Her husband had been felling a tree. In one of the hazardous twists of logging, it veered. A widow maker crashed down on the man.

"He's stunned, but conscious. He has a deep gash on his arm and something wrong with one ankle," the wife said. "I don't want to move him. I'm also afraid to bring him in our vehicle over all the rough miles between here and a doctor."

The hurry-up call resulted in a neat stitching job done on the spot. The man's leg proved to be sprained, not broken, and the victim showed no signs of concussion. The patient and the plucky girl-wife refused to be flown to Kalispell after the doctor admitted there was little need. Today's check-up showed husband and wife were both doing well.

"Anything to add?" the round-faced owner asked Scott when the nurse finished.

It amused Scott. His boss never failed to ask, even though all three knew the pilot wouldn't have anything more than what the nurse or doctor reported. Scott shook his head.

"Another happy ending."

"Also another happy landing," the nurse pertly told him.

Scott felt himself congeal. Nausea rose in him. He covered with a laugh, turned on his heel, and left the hangar as rapidly as possible, hoping to cover his reaction. It didn't work.

"What's wrong with Stone Face?" he heard the nurse ask. Scott knew she wasn't being sarcastic, just concerned. He flinched just the same. Gratitude replaced some of the sick feeling when Mike replied, "He gets that way when he's hungry. Speaking of which, my wife's going to have my head if I don't get out of here on time. I've kept supper waiting the last three nights."

"Ah, the life of a busy man."

Scott could hear them good-naturedly wrangling even after he climbed in his Jeep. He buried his throbbing head in his hands and waited for the feeling to subside. He refused to drive until it did. No one so churned up inside had the right to menace others by being on the highway.

His rapid heartbeat slowed perceptibly. Scott rejoiced. It took less time now than in former years and months. If only the thrusts from his past would give warning! They never did. He couldn't tell what might set him off. For a long time after the incident that changed him from laughing pilot to Stone Face, he had worried about what might happen if a flashback caught him in the sky. Only once had shattering memories attacked while on a flight. Intense prayer to the God he had known since childhood helped him overcome that particular fear.

Remembering that day sponged away the last of Scott's trauma, at least for this time. He had never told another living human being about the day cold sweat broke out on his forehead and threatened him with helplessness. He had been flying alone, sent back to base by a nurse who decided she needed a doctor for a patient she didn't want moved.

Exactly what triggered the flashbacks, Scott never knew. He only knew he cried for help at the moment fear began to engulf him. The answer came in a way he didn't expect. A way he knew the world would scorn. Even after all this time, Scott could almost feel the gentle pressure of hands covering his own wet and shaking ones. And the peace that had fallen over him like the diaphanous wedding veil on a bride.

Never again had he experienced the recall while flying. Episodes grew more and more infrequent, just as the rough but caring military doctor promised years ago. Today was the first in months.

"Thanks, God," Scott muttered. "Someday, I may be able to go back and thank the doctor, too. I wonder if he'd believe me?"

Confidence restored, he considered the idea on the way to his apartment. A quick check of the nearly empty refrigerator drew the corners of his mouth down. He'd eat out and shop on the way home. A pang of envy for the meal Mike Parker would find ready and waiting filled him. Scott shook his head. Until he could break chains from the past, he wouldn't inflict himself on any woman. Marriage was a tough proposition, especially in these days. Two broken people couldn't make one whole person.

A piquant face danced in the air before Scott while he showered and changed. Odd that he should think of the pretty blond nurse who had come from Seattle weeks ago. She must have a lot of the right stuff in her, or she wouldn't have taken time to drive Dan Davis home to Montana. Maybe she had an ulterior motive. Dan had to be pretty well off, after selling the Running H. Was Patti Thompson a gold-digger, out for what she could get from the lonely old ex-cowboy she'd cared for? She had certainly charmed Mike Parker, so much he offered her a job. God forbid. The last thing he needed was an opportunist worming her way into everyone's good graces in order to cash in on Dan's holdings.

The thought depressed Scott. He hastily pulled on his boots and strode out to the Jeep. Patti Thompson hadn't looked like a gold-digger. There had been something in her eyes. Scott couldn't exactly describe it, but it reminded him of the trapped look in the eyes of a wounded deer he'd once seen in the forest.

He snorted. "There's no guarantee I'd know a gold-digger if I saw one. I doubt they look like old-time dance hall floozies. At least the nurse doesn't." His comparison brought a grin. Yet after a substantial supper, the thoughtful pilot turned his Jeep toward Dan's log cabin home. The nurse would be long gone and it felt like a century since Scott had dropped in on Dan.

Disappointment far beyond finding no one home smote Scott when he reached the log cabin. Although light filtered through the drawn shades, a sense of emptiness surrounded the place. Repeated ringing of the doorbell brought no response.

"Dan's gone and lights are on a timer," Scott surmised. "Too bad."

He saw the old man for a few minutes after church the following Sunday. Scott learned the cowboy had "packed up his duds and hied himself out" to the Running H. "The Hoffs found out they needed my help in runnin' the ranch," Dan added. His faded blue eyes held more color than Scott had seen in some time. So did his tanned cheeks. The pilot congratulated him and promised to drop by as soon as he could find time. He started to ask about Patti Thompson but thought better of it. Long experience with well-meaning friends who leaped at the chance to play matchmaker silenced him. The most casual inquiry would be more than enough to bring a cackle from Dan Davis and a gleam into Ma Hoff's eye!

A busier than usual schedule for the next few weeks shoved everything out of Scott's mind except flying, eating, and sleeping. He missed church, something he hated doing. It couldn't be helped. A rash of incidents with tourists kept the entire staff of the Rescue Service on the go. Summer cooled into fall and Scott still hadn't made it out to the ranch.

One afternoon Mike Parker received a call. Scott lounged in a chair in the office. He saw Mike's usually jovial face sag.

"When? How bad?" He paused. "I'll send Scott and a doctor." He banged down the receiver, looking strangely shrunken. "Get ready for a trip out to the Running H."

Scott bounded from his chair. "Who's hurt?"

Mike shook his head and licked his lips. "Dan Davis. It's worse than hurt."

"Dead?"

"Hoff says so. We'll send a doctor, anyway." Parker dialed one of the doctors they called on for emergency trips and tersely explained the situation.

Scott shook his head to clear it.

"How'd it happen?" he demanded when Mike hung up. "I haven't seen

Dan for weeks, but he looked fine when I did."

"Horse spooked and pitched him headfirst onto a rock pile," Mike said heavily. "It happens." He leaned back until his chair squeaked. "At least, we know where he's gone. Dan Davis was not only a top hand and rancher, but a real Christian."

"Yeah." Scott reached for his baseball cap and shoved it down on his dark hair. "We'll miss him."

The doctor said the same thing when they reached the Running H.

"Died instantly," he confirmed. "Hard on those of us who liked and respected him, but quick and easy, the way Dan would choose to go." He gestured toward the rolling hills rising to distant tree-covered mountains.

"He also spent his last days out here where he belonged," Scott added. "We can be thankful for that." He smiled at the Hoffs. "I'm just sorry I didn't get to see him again."

"He understood. Dan never was one to put pleasure ahead of business. He knew you'd come when you could," Pa Hoff gruffly said.

Scott and the doctor climbed into the chopper and started back to Kalispell.

They reported in to Mike, who asked Scott if he had anything to add, as usual. Scott didn't, also as usual. Instead of leaving, he slumped back in the chair.

"Something eating you, Stone Face?" Mike wanted to know.

"No. Just thinking how much good Dan did during his life."

The round face beneath the balding head brightened. "He sure did. Half of Kalispell will show up for his funeral, or whatever kind of service he wanted."

"I'll bet the Bell Jet-Ranger it won't be fancy."

Mike chuckled. "No bets! Dan wouldn't stand for any such affair. Think that nurse, Patti Thompson isn't it, will show? It's a long way from Seattle, but she seemed to think a lot of Dan."

A funny little sensation ran through Scott. He'd been wondering the same thing.

"She might." He didn't add his earlier suspicions about her. Best not to judge. Time had a way of proving a person right or wrong.

"Dan really hoped she'd come back." Mike leaned forward and grew confidential. "He told her she could live in his log cabin home any time, even though he'd moved back to the Running H."

"He did!" Fresh suspicion poured over Scott like a deluge of ice water.

"How do you know?"

"He told me. Said he'd appreciate it if I'd give her a job if she took him up on it." Mike looked reflective. "Wouldn't be a bad idea. Some of our nurses are wanting to cut down on trips." He laughed. "I don't suppose she'll ever come. Not many gals are interested in giving up the city lights."

They might if they knew they would benefit financially. Scott kept the unpleasant thought to himself. Again, time would prove what kind of person a certain Patti Thompson really was.

———◆◆◆———

The simple graveside service Dan had left instructions to hold didn't attract quite half of Kalispell, as Mike Parker predicted. However, the large crowd included most of the churchgoers, ranch families, cowboys, and leading citizens of the area. The minister spoke simply and effectively. No one present would leave the service without knowing the way to salvation.

"It's what Dan wanted," Ma Hoff whispered to Scott, who stood beside her. "He said the last and best thing he could do for folks was make clear the path they'd have to ride if they aimed to get to heaven."

Scott nodded, wanting to ask why Patti Thompson hadn't come, but hesitant.

Mike Parker had no such qualms. When the service ended, he shook hands with the Hoffs and said, "I thought maybe Dan's nurse friend would be here."

"She planned to fly in this morning, but woke up so sick she had to have a doctor from Shepherd of Love Hospital where she works call and say she wasn't coming," Pa Hoff told them.

Scott skeptically wondered if she were really sick. She probably was, since a doctor had called. According to Dan Davis, Shepherd of Love hired only strong Christians, not personnel who would lie. He tried to shrug off a feeling of loss. If he never saw her again, so what?

"We're hoping Patti will come for Christmas," Ma Hoff put in. "She lost some of her forlorn look last summer when she stayed with us. Besides, her folks are retired and away on some kind of long trip."

Scott fought the instant change in his mood. He had no place for love in his life. Patti Thompson still might be a gold-digger. He shored up his defenses, but Ma Hoff's choice of the word "forlorn" wore away at them as water does on rock. Evidently he hadn't been the only one to sense trouble in the nurse's eyes.

"Pa and I are going to be a mite lonely." Ma laughed. "Well, as lonely as life on a cattle ranch lets us. Come see us when you can, Scott."

"I will." He took her hand in his, then shook her husband's. "Things should settle down soon. At least I hope they will." He drove his Jeep back to town determined to keep his promise soon. In the meantime, he vowed to keep in touch by phone. "If a person's too busy for their friends, then they're too busy, period," Scott's father used to say.

Scott winced. For the past several years, he had been guilty of doing just that. Something teased at his mind. It niggled until he reached his apartment and took down a dog-eared copy of the anthology *Poems That Touch the Heart*. He opened it to the first page and read "Around the Corner," the haunting words written by Charles Hanson Towne.

The poem spoke of one whose friend lived just around the corner. The narrator shared that his friend knew he thought as much of him as in the days before the busy world kept them apart. Again and again, the narrator planned to go see his friend. He didn't. One day a telegram came telling him his friend had died. He had put off visiting one day too many.

Scott closed the book. *Had Towne experienced what he wrote?* It would account for the poignancy of the poem. How fitting for Scott Sloan's life, as well. Because of work and regret, he had not only put off going to see friends, he had shut the door between them. No wonder he had earned the name Stone Face.

In the beginning, it had seemed the only thing to do. He couldn't bear the stumbling assurances of friendship, the shock in the faces of even his most trusted friends. He eagerly seized the opportunity to fly for Mike Parker and get away from everyone and everything he knew. In order to be fair, he told Mike as much of the story as his future boss needed to know.

Scott hadn't forgotten the paunchy man's response. First, a keen gaze bore into him, testing him. Then he asked, "Are you sure of what you've told me?"

Scott's stomach muscles twisted. "Before God, I wish I weren't!"

A long silence followed, broken by Mike's raspy voice. "The way I figure it, a man's past is past. I don't see that you did anything dishonorable." He held up his hand when Scott would have protested. "It all depends on where you're standing, Sloan. All I want to know is, can you do the job I need done?"

Back on secure ground, Scott squared his shoulders under his light-weight jacket. His head went up in the fearless manner that once character-ized him to those in his command. Flying, both fixed-wing and helicopter, was something he did and did well. "I can." He drew in a deep, troubled breath but met the watching gaze without flinching. "The only thing is, my references are checkered."

Mike shuffled the papers Scott had presented at the beginning of the interview. So far Parker had ignored them. "Why didn't you give me only the ones praising you?"

"It wouldn't be honest." Scott's jaw clenched. So much for securing the job.

He unzipped the tight line of his mouth enough to say, "Sir, I have to answer to God and live with myself. I can't withhold any information that will affect my job performance. It's all there. What isn't there is personal."

"Good enough. Are we ready do discuss salary, hours, that kind of thing?"

Scott felt as if he'd been hit with a lightning bolt. "You haven't read the reports."

"I've always been a good judge of men. I'll take you on trust."

Scott didn't waver by an iota. "I prefer you read my papers first."

A curious expression crossed the flight service owner's face. He scanned the pages so rapid-fire Scott knew Mike had either taken a speed-reading course or couldn't care less what they contained.

"Now if you'll slap a more cheerful expression on that stone face of yours, we'll talk about salary and hours. Right now you look like a cat that ate a sour mouse!" Parker's hand shot out.

Scott grabbed it with the desperation with which a cowboy bucked off into the middle of a stampede snatches for a partner's extended hand. The first real laugh he'd had in months burst forth. Along with the laugh came hope he had thought dead and buried. It also brought unbounded respect for a man who judged others by what was in himself, rather than words on a page. They had been friends ever since.

———◆◆◆◆◆———

True to his promise, Scott began to reach out. Instead of rushing from church, he stayed for potlucks or to visit unless he had to work. He had long since settled the question of working on the Lord's Day by following Jesus' example.

> And a man with a shriveled hand was there [in the synagogue].
> Looking for a reason to accuse Jesus, they asked him, "Is it lawful
> to heal on the Sabbath?"
>   He said to them, "If any of you has a sheep and it falls into

a pit on the Sabbath, will you not take hold of it and lift it out?

"How much more valuable is a man than a sheep! Therefore it is lawful to do good on the Sabbath."

Then he said to the man, "Stretch out your hand." So he stretched it out and it was completely restored, just as sound as the other. Matthew 12:10–13

Sickness, accidents, and folks in need couldn't schedule emergencies. Like Jesus, when a need arose on the Sabbath, the Rescue Service met it. The Master had not deferred help and left people to suffer. Neither would they.

Chapter 8

Every mile that transported Patti Thompson farther away from Seattle and closer to Kalispell brought the tired nurse a little more peace. She knew the first few moments seeing the Hoffs without Dan Davis and his broad smile in the background would be hard. However, the warmth of the ranch couple's welcome quickly dried her eyes. So did Ma Hoff's hearty hug and Pa's firm handshake.

"We're mighty proud to have you," he told her.

"We'll get you fattened up and back doing chores in the whisk of a lamb's tail," Ma promised, after a hasty examination of Patti's pale face.

"Lambs on a cattle ranch? My goodness, how the West has changed!"

Patti's temporary sadness fled in the laugh that followed. Her sense of loss returned when she glanced at the log cabin Dan had occupied the last weeks of his life. However, Ma wisely bustled her guest into the house, helped her unpack her clothes, and set her to peeling vegetables for stew.

"Best thing for a body is to keep busy," the kitchen philosopher said. "How is your drawing and painting coming? Dan told us you were quite a hand at it."

"I'm glad you mentioned Dan," Patti impulsively said. "So many people won't talk about those who—who have gone on."

"Land sakes, why not?" Ma's eyebrows shot up until they almost touched her graying hair. "Seems to me doing that makes it like they never lived." Her hands stilled from beating her biscuit dough and she waved a sticky spoon. "Far as Pa and I are concerned, Dan's more alive and a whole lot happier now than he ever was. It would be a pure shame to pack his memories away like my mother used to pack winter woolens in mothballs."

Patti laughed at the comparison. The Hoffs' homespun humor never failed to delight her. She looked around the spacious kitchen and inwardly purred with satisfaction. Except for Dan Davis's absence, it was as if the troubled time between her leaving and returning to the Running H never existed. Patti glanced at her ring finger. Not even the trace of a white mark showed the brief time Charles Bradley's diamond ring had circled it. She shivered. Thank God for her narrow escape! What if she had married Charles and been subject to his rages? Or worse? His boast about other women showed him incapable of fidelity.

Ma Hoff's keen eyes missed nothing. "Are you cold, Child?"

"No. I'm thanking God I'm here." Patti hesitated, then in a few well-chosen sentences informed the older woman what had happened in Seattle.

"My grandmother would say it's a good thing you're shut of him," Ma said.

"What if he follows me?" Another shiver chased up her spine. "Charles knows about the Running H. We talked about asking Dan if we could spend our honeymoon in his log cabin home." Patti made a face. "Ugh! How could I have been so mistaken about him?" She didn't add it was the second time her intuition had failed because of a handsome male face and charming manner.

"Most of us get taken in by a two-legged critter at one time or another," Ma dryly observed. "I hate to mention more practical things, but if you don't get back to your peeling, dinner will be a long time coming!"

Patti grinned. "Okay, Boss." Curiosity made her add, "Did you?"

"What? Get taken in? Oh, sure." Ma beat her dough more furiously than ever. "Long before I met Pa, I planned to marry someone else. He went off and found a new girl. Like to broke my heart." Her eyes twinkled. " 'Course the little rascal was only eight and I was six when we got engaged."

Patti gasped and laughed until her sides ached. Life on the Running H would never prove dull with Ma Hoff around to tell stories!

The next Sunday at church, folks greeted Patti like a long lost sister. The minister made a special point of welcoming her from the pulpit. Mike Parker beamed. Patti caught a glimpse of Scott Sloan across the church. He nodded and went back to turning pages in his songbook. Patti chastised herself for caring. She'd just run away from one man. The last thing she needed was another to complicate her life. She had to concentrate on regaining her usual excellent health so she could again be of service to others.

Patti turned her attention to Pastor Hill, the middle-aged shepherd of this particular flock of worshippers. He had a knack of enlivening his sermons with vivid stories. Today was no different.

"The Bible tells us in Mark 12:31 and several other places to love our neighbors as ourselves. What kind of world would it be if everyone loved those around them *more* than themselves?" He paused and scanned the congregation.

"A legend tells of two brothers who worked a large field together and planned to share the grain when harvested.

"One brother had a wife and children. One lived alone on the other side of a hill. At harvest, the single brother said, 'I have only myself to care for. My brother needs much more than I.' Each night he filled a large sack and smuggled it into his brother's barn.

"The married brother told himself, 'I have children to care for me when I am old. My brother does not.' He also secretly carried grain to his brother's barn.

" 'How strange,' both thought. 'I give away, yet my grain is abundant as ever!'

"One night on their pilgrimage, the brothers met each other. They shouted with laughter and embraced when they saw each other's sacks of grain.

"According to legend, God was pleased with the brothers. He said the place where they met was holy. There His temple should be built. Solomon's temple is said to stand on that spot."

What an example of selflessness! Patti opened her songbook and joined in singing, "Bringing in the Sheaves," rejoicing along with the writer of the beloved words. How lighthearted she felt! She sneaked a glance across at Scott Sloan. This time he gave her a faint smile. He also took time after church to say, "It's nice to have you here again. Great sermon, wasn't it?" Yet the look in his eyes warned Scott was reserving judgment of her for some unknown reason.

"It's wonderful to be here," she frankly told him.

Mike Parker pushed up to them. "How long are you staying? What's chances of your doing some work for me? My flying nurses are complaining they don't get enough time off." His Santa Claus stomach shook when he laughed.

"Miss Thompson's been sick. Give her time to rest before shoving her into a helicopter," Scott said sharply. He turned on his heel and strode down the church aisle the same way he'd done last summer when Patti first met him.

"Well, I never!" Ma Hoff stared after him then back at Mike. "He's right. This young lady isn't doing any flying until I get some meat on her bones."

"Sorry." The rescue service owner had the grace to look ashamed. However, his bouncy personality didn't keep him down long. He winked at Patti. "If you don't call me, I'll call you. You have a job when you're ready." He walked off.

Scott Sloan slammed into his Jeep feeling like a fool. *What possessed me to protest against Mike railroading Patti Thompson into a job? She could take care of herself, couldn't she?*

"I don't want or need some out-of-condition nurse who'll fold if we get in a tight situation," he muttered. The defense fell apart like a cardboard sword. Why not admit his concern over the nurse's pale face and obvious weight loss had little to do with her ability to perform rescue work? When Patti glanced across the church, the shadow in her eyes called forth a chivalrous desire to protect her.

"She may not need it," Scott reminded himself on his way home. "That clear, blue gaze of hers could be camouflage. Folks will find it hard to believe her motives are anything but sincere." *Were they?* Surface evidence pointed to the fact she had been sick and come to Montana to rest. Scott shrugged and told himself for the umpteenth time to forget about Patti Thompson. Her motives meant nothing in his scheme of life, did they? He had a good job. He helped people, not with sacks of grain, but through his flying. Why borrow trouble?

Leaves changed color and swirled into red and yellow blizzards. Nights crisped and spread frost. Scott returned from a visit to his parents in Salt Lake City and learned two pieces of news that rocked his world.

Mike Parker announced Patti Thompson was fit for duty and ready to fly.

And, Dan Davis's probated will disclosed he had left ten thousand dollars each to the Hoffs and the church. Everything else went to the nurse from Shepherd of Love.

All Scott's earlier suspicions came back. *No wonder she had been so eager to drive Dan home!* He tightened his lips and prayed he wouldn't have Patti in his chopper. He couldn't very well ask Mike to schedule her with one of the other pilots. Yet he rebelled at the thought of flying and working with a girl who had turned out to be a common gold-digger, taking advantage of her position as a nurse in order to inherit Dan's considerable estate. *Despicable!*

"I have to hand it to her," Scott bitterly admitted. "She's clever."

He was amazed to discover others felt differently. The Hoffs lamented the fact they'd be losing Patti to a home of her own, but loyally insisted they were glad.

Mike Parker thought only of his rescue service.

"Now she'll stay," he exulted. "Maybe that's why Dan did it. He hoped she'd come back and work with us. Said she was just the kind of nurse we and those we serve need."

Scott didn't have the heart to remind his boss and friend that Patti might well sell the log home, take Dan's money from the sale of the ranch, and vamoose. He also wondered why he felt so let down. Hadn't he suspected all along there was more behind the innocent face than others saw? He firmly determined to stay as far away from the scheming little double-crosser as possible.

Patti stared across the massive desk in the lawyer's office. Had she heard him right? Yes, for he patiently repeated she had just inherited a log cabin home, a Ford Bronco, and more money than she could accumulate in a lifetime of hard work as a nurse.

"Why me?" she demanded. "Surely Mr. Davis's holdings should go to someone closer. I'm just a nurse who happened to be on duty when he came to Shepherd of Love." She shook her head. "It's too much like a fairy tale. Or something out of a novel."

"It does happen in real life," the lawyer told her.

"What if I refuse it?"

Disapproval oozed from the stern man. "Why would you do that?"

"I don't know." Patti looked at him appealingly. "It just doesn't seem real."

He relaxed. "Mr. Davis made no provision for your turning down the bequest. He said this letter would explain everything." He handed her a white envelope. "Would you like to read it before signing the papers?" His laugh made him seem more human and less an efficient, remote machine. "Turning over property, including land and bank assets, requires a great deal of paperwork." He rose. "Perhaps you'd rather be alone when you read Dan's letter."

"Yes, please," Patti gratefully said.

He smiled and went out. The door closed behind him. The ticking of the wall clock ponderously counting off time sounded loud in the quiet office.

Patti slit the sealed envelope and took out a single sheet of paper. The strong writing she knew from Dan's rare communications between Kalispell and Seattle blurred her vision. She impatiently brushed mist from her eyes and focused on the letter. Dan had spelled the words correctly, yet the letter sounded so much like him, Patti could hear his drawl and dropping g's at the end of his words.

Dear Patti,

By the time you read this, whenever it may be, I'll have moved on to a bigger, better range. You already know I'm raring to go. Sarah's waiting. Don't waste a passel of time in tears. You probably have a long life ahead of you, but looking from God's view, it won't be long before we meet again.

There's a couple of things I have to say. You're one spunky gal. You may balk like a mule about accepting what I'm leaving you. Don't. I want to know what the Good Lord's blessed me with is left in capable hands. If you don't hanker to settle in Kalispell permanent-like, sell the log cabin to someone who won't be likely to cut down my cottonwoods and spoil the place. Scott Sloan, maybe. He's a fine man and he always liked it.

The other thing's been on my mind a lot since you left. Remember what I said about joining up your life with the wrong man. Better to ride lonesome than be in double-harness with a no-good who'll break your heart.

I sent one of the sketches you left behind to an artist feller I used to know. He wrote back all excited. He said you need training, which we both knew. He also said you have a certain something in your work that needs to be developed. It made me scratch my head, but I never did figure out exactly what he meant. At least it sounds promising. You'll have enough with what I left to take time off and find out.

Vaya con Dios, meaning "Go with God."

Your old cowboy friend,
Dan

Patti gently refolded the letter and put it in the envelope. She would treasure it forever, even more than all the material things she had inherited. The lawyer had been right. The message tore down barriers to accepting what had been given in friendship. No, in love, forged during the short time she had known Dan Davis.

Absorbed in her own thoughts, Patti didn't hear the door open.

"Miss Thompson?" The lawyer stepped back into the room. "I trust you found Dan's message satisfactory. Are you ready to sign the papers?" He sat down behind his desk in an attitude of waiting.

"It would be wrong not to accept what he left me," Patti humbly said.

"The way he put it, my inheritance is a sacred trust."

A gleam of satisfaction brightened the watching eyes. "That's how Dan hoped you'd see it. I didn't read your letter, of course, but my client and I talked about you. A lot."

Patti squirmed. "I always feel uncomfortable when someone tells me that."

"No need to, in this case," the lawyer brusquely told her. "Now about your signature. . ." He took the top page from a sheaf of documents.

By the time she finished signing, Patti's head spun. Dan Davis had chosen his legal representative well. The lawyer meticulously explained each paper and faithfully asked if she had questions before going on to the next. At last they finished. "It will take a little more time to get everything transferred into your name," he said. "I'll call you. You're still at the Running H?"

"Yes. I'm not sure Ma—Mrs. Hoff will let me move into the log home, even if it is mine!" Patti confided.

"She's a fine person. So is her husband. They're my clients." The lawyer stowed the signed documents in his briefcase and smartly snapped it shut. "I trust this takes care of everything except the actual turning over of keys, bank books, etc. If you think of anything else, please drop by or call."

The finality in his tone made Patti feel he had washed his hands of her and was ready to move on to new business. She told him good-bye, tucked her precious letter in her purse, and walked out into a perfect autumn afternoon.

When she slid behind the wheel of the ranch station wagon the Hoffs had graciously lent her, Patti hesitated. "I'm not ready to go back to the Running H, Lord." She started the motor and pulled into the street. "I think I'll visit Dan's cabin. Mine, actually."

A curious thing happened to her while she drove. The numbness and disbelief she'd felt in the lawyer's office dissolved in the clear air. Wonderment came, along with gladness and humility. As much as she loved nursing, Patti had found herself dreading the need to return to work after the holidays. Now the need no longer existed. Dan had bequeathed the means to support herself and follow her dream of drawing and painting. *Why not use it to the utmost?*

Joy shot through her. Shepherd of Love had put no time limit on her leave of absence. Why not push aside all thoughts of when she would return? Or if? Patti couldn't imagine a better place anywhere to pursue her second dream. Surely she could find an art teacher in Kalispell. If not, she would purchase books on technique and diligently study them. The blazing fall countryside offered unlimited inspiration. Her new log home provided the solitude and peace needed to set her own schedule.

She reached the cabin and turned into the gravel driveway. Patti killed the engine and simply sat. Before her lay the scene she had painted from memory. Her golden leaves adorned the cottonwoods and formed great heaps at their bases.

She bowed her head in thankfulness and humility. "So much for one person," she murmured. "Lord, help me be worthy of Dan's trust in me. And Yours."

Patti stepped from the station wagon and walked around her newly acquired property. She ached for the thrilling moment she would unlock the front door and take possession of the place that held so many happy memories. Scuffing through the downed leaves, she decided she wouldn't change a thing, at least for now. Patti tilted her head back and gazed at the slowly swaying cottonwoods. *No wonder Dan Davis feared having the property fall into uncaring hands! Cutting such magnificent trees would be nothing short of sinful.*

Patti stayed until the sun rested on a western hill like a balancing rock, then reluctantly started back to the Running H. Dan and the Hoffs had warned her many times about miscalculating daylight. After the Montana sun set, night quickly followed, especially this time of year. Once away from the lights of Kalispell, no glow such as from lights of Seattle guided a traveler's way. Besides, the Hoffs would grow anxious if the nurse they had unofficially adopted as another daughter lingered away from the ranch after dark.

Patti sang all the way home sheltering hymns, such as "Rock of Ages" and "God Is My Strong Salvation." How far away trouble seemed! The last words of a song died on her lips. Charles Bradley had warned he never gave up what was his. Suppose he came to Montana?

Patti's hands tightened on the wheel. "If he learns of my inheritance, he's bound to show up," she grimly said. Strange how accurately she read the handsome pilot since the betraying glimpse into his real personality. "Well, he won't learn it from me, and I hope no one else tells him."

"So much for anonymity," she complained to the Hoffs a few days later. An enterprising reporter had unearthed news of Dan Davis's will. His story was splashed all over the front page of a leading Montana paper under the caption:

WELL KNOWN COWBOY/RANCHER
LEAVES BULK OF ESTATE TO SEATTLE NURSE.

A basically accurate account followed, complete with photographs of Dan Davis and the Running H. It closed by saying the value of the estate was considerable but the exact amount unknown.

A few hours later, the Running H swarmed with TV camera crews and a flock of reporters.

"Better talk with them, Honey," Ma Hoff advised. "Just be careful."

Patti took the wise advice. She fended off personal questions and simply said, "Yes, I cared for Mr. Davis and drove him home at his request. He and the Hoffs gave me a wonderful vacation. His will surprised me, but I am grateful. I plan to stay in Kalispell for a time. Beyond that, I have no plans." She insisted the Hoffs pose with her when the camera crew wanted more pictures. Ma and Pa proved equally discreet and adept at saying little or nothing.

"If they had simply stuck to the interview, it wouldn't be so bad," Patti complained when she and the Hoffs watched the evening newscast. "It's bad enough being called an angel of mercy and kindness. The speculation that I'm a schemer who took advantage of Dan is worse."

"Folks who know you also know better," Ma reminded. "I wouldn't worry about the others too much. Remember, even Jesus was known for good and bad."

I wonder what Scott Sloan will believe. Patti blushed. *Who cares? You do,* a little voice accused. *Seeing doubt or contempt in his dark eyes would hurt.* She squelched the idea, then forgot it when the phone rang for her.

"Congratulations on your good fortune," Charles Bradley drawled. "No wonder you were so eager to leave the bright lights of Seattle and bury yourself in a Montana cow town."

Chapter 9

"Hello, Sloan."

Scott stopped halfway between his Bell Jet-Ranger and Mike Parker's Rescue Service hangar and spun around. A ghost from his past stood waiting.

"What are you doing here?"

That same sardonic smile flashed on the intruder's handsome, mocking face. It had always filled Scott with an uncontrollable urge to wipe it off. "What kind of welcome is that from your old flight buddy?"

Scott clenched his fists and took a warning step forward.

Charles Bradley raised an eyebrow and fell back. "I actually came to see my fiancée. Just thought I'd drop by and renew an old acquaintance."

"Fiancée?" Scott felt like a trained parrot.

"Patti Thompson. The nurse who wormed her way into old man Davis's affections and inherited half of Kalispell." Triumph flamed in Charles's blue eyes. "It's easy street for yours truly from now on." His fists shot up. "Yes!"

The Rescue Service pilot felt like he'd been kicked in the stomach. He had written Patti Thompson off just as Bradley described her. Yet hearing her treachery fall from this man's lips sickened him. *He could be lying,* Scott reasoned. The gate to his heart he had slammed shut creaked, then clanged back into a locked position. *Charles could be right. Renewing an old acquaintance?* Scott sneered. If he never saw Charles Bradley again, it would be too soon. What cruel fate had sent first Patti Thompson, then Charles Bradley back into his life?

"I fail to see that anything in your life concerns me."

Some of the tension went out of the blond pilot's face.

"It concerns you. I understand your boss wants Patti as a rescue flight nurse. I won't have it."

"Don't cry on my shoulder. I'm no more excited about the idea than you are." Scott regretted the words the second they came out, especially when an avid expression came over Charles's face. It galled him to ask, and he hated the conciliatory tone in his voice, but added, "Don't go shouting it to Nurse Thompson. Flying with an enemy can be dangerous, as you already know."

Charles turned a furious red at the hidden meaning. He started to speak, then fixed his gaze over Scott's left shoulder and drawled in an unnecessarily loud voice, "So you're not excited about flying with my fiancée. Interesting."

"Very. And I'm not your fiancée, Charles." Icicles hung on the words.

Scott whirled. Mike Parker and Patti Thompson stood not ten feet away. She looked downright fetching in a trim denim jeans and jacket outfit with a red turtleneck and a matching bandanna at her throat. The nurse shot an annihilating gaze toward Charles before turning to Scott. He felt shriveled by the scorching look in her blue eyes.

"Mr. Parker wants you to show me your helicopter," she told him in a level voice.

The dark-haired pilot couldn't have moved if his life depended on it. No such paralysis attacked Bradley.

"That won't be necessary." He stepped forward and draped a possessive arm over Patti's shoulders. "Sorry, Parker. She isn't going to fly for you. Especially with Sloan."

Red flags waved in Mike's round face.

"I say she is. She says she is. What you or anyone else thinks doesn't count." He leveled a glance at Scott.

Charles' face turned ugly. His fingers tightened. "Oh, yeah?"

"Yeah," Mike belligerently told him. "Now let her go and get off my property before I throw you off."

"You and who else?" Charles blustered.

"Better do what he says," Scott advised in a deadly voice.

"I suppose you're going to make me, the way you thought you'd make me—"

"Shut up and get going!" Mike bellowed. "If you come around again, I'll call the police and have you arrested for trespassing and causing trouble."

Patti jerked free from Charles's grasp and rubbed her shoulders. Scott saw her wince.

"That goes for me, too," she snapped.

Shock and a look akin to fear chased the smirk from Charles's face. "You can't mean that! What kind of lies have these guys cooked up? Don't let them turn you against me, Patti. I don't know what Parker's up to, but I know plenty about Sloan. More than any other man alive. I was there."

Pain shot through every part of Scott's body. All that kept his hands off the taunting man was the knowledge that if he once touched Charles, he might kill him. So much for all the years of trying to forgive his one enemy, to follow in Christ's footsteps and rise above hatred and the desire for revenge. Cold sweat sprang to his forehead. Scott pressed his arms close to his rigid body. In a few short minutes, the hard-won peace he'd felt gradually returning had deserted him.

Patti raised her chin and stared straight into Charles's face.

"Whatever is between you and Scott Sloan is your business. Your insisting I'm your fiancée is a lie. I told you we were through before I left Seattle. I also had no idea until after I came back to the Running H that Mr. Davis planned to leave me anything," she passionately went on. Scorn lashed like a quirt, leaving dull red streaks marring Charles's good looks. "I suspected you'd come running as soon as you learned about my inheritance. It didn't take you long to get here, did it?"

Scott wanted to shout "Bravo!" He wisely kept still, but began to revise his estimate of Patti. Her statements rang with truth. Maybe she hadn't known. Scott hid a smile. One thing for certain. Any love she may have felt for his old enemy no longer existed. Relief flowed through him, even while he mentally kicked himself for caring.

Charles groped for his obviously shaken self-confidence.

"I'm sorry, Darling." He turned on the charm Scott had seen create havoc so many times. "I can explain everything." He shot a glance of pure venom at Scott and Mike. "Just five minutes away from these louts, Patti," he wheedled. "You owe me that."

Sticks and stones will break my bones, but names and faces won't hurt me. The old nursery answer to challenges sang through Scott's mind and made him feel better. He grinned at Mike Parker, who loftily observed, "Sloan and I've been called a lot worse things than louts by a lot better persons than you, Bradley. Now make tracks, with the heel toward my hangar."

A ripple of mirth at Mike's sally escaped Patti's tightly closed lips. It grew into full-scale hilarity.

"I owe you nothing," she said when she stopped laughing.

Naked hatred sprang into Charles's eyes. Scott took an involuntary step toward the girl, fearing the rage he knew lurked inside the unwelcome visitor. Even all those years ago, Bradley never stood for anyone laughing at him. Now he clenched and unclenched his hands then turned his fury from Patti to Scott.

"Don't think this is over. You came between me and what I wanted once before, remember? I beat you then and I'll beat you now. My fiancée is suffering from overwork, on the verge of a nervous breakdown. I suggest you get her full medical reports before taking her on a mercy flight. Another accident would be inconvenient, to say the least."

God, help me let him walk away, Scott fervently prayed. Strength he hadn't believed possible came. Charles marched off after his cryptic threat like a soldier who loses a minor skirmish but knows the final victory is already his.

"Unpleasant cuss," Mike Parker announced. "Scott, if you'll show Patti the chopper, I'll get back to my paperwork." He hesitated. "Uh, you both might want to watch your step. Our departed guest reminds me of a rattlesnake, even down to rattling off a warning."

"Sorry you had to be let in for that," Scott said with regret when they walked to the waiting Bell Jet-Ranger.

"So am I." Her clipped tones showed she hadn't forgiven his comment about not wanting her to fly with him. All traces of former friendliness had vanished.

Scott felt he had lost something precious. "I only kept my hands off Bradley by the grace of God."

"I can fight my own battles. Now, about the helicopter?"

Scott had the sensation of being inexorably frozen. "One more thing. Don't underestimate Charles Bradley. He never gives up anything he considers his."

Patti's slim shoulders dropped. She suddenly looked small and vulnerable.

"Thanks for the warning, but he already told me that." A wobbly smile brought a rush of admiration for her valor. "By the way, I *am* capable of flying or I never would have consented. Being here has done wonders for me. A recent checkup proved it." Her defiant gaze met his. "One other thing. If you're still reluctant to fly with me after our first mission, I'll ask Mike to use me elsewhere."

"If you handle that mission as well as you handled Bradley, I'll have no objection to working with you," he told her. "Truce?" Scott held out his hand.

Patti looked surprised. Her lips twitched and she shook with him. "Truce."

By the time Scott finished his first teaching session, Patti knew more about helicopters than she ever dreamed she'd need to learn. The white Bell Jet-Ranger, with its red cross and trim, fully lived up to and beyond Pa Hoff's description of it as a flying First Aid station. Manned by an expert pilot and trained medical help, Patti realized it would be a godsend to those in isolated areas.

This particular model chopper had two front seats, for pilot and nurse or doctor, plus a rear bench that would hold three passengers. Standard equipment included a two-person survival pack. Patti marveled. *So much necessary material stowed in the orange backpack that weighed only six pounds and measured eleven inches wide, ten inches high, and four inches deep!*

"Everything to stay alive, including MRE: meal, ready to eat," Scott translated. He gave Patti a list of contents to study. "This will help you know how to pack your medical bag," he soberly told her. "We don't break into the survival pack unless it's an emergency."

She carefully tucked the list into her jacket pocket. A quiver went through her. "Have you ever needed one?"

"Yes." To her disappointment, Scott didn't elaborate.

"I have so much to learn," Patti admitted when he finished explaining the hazards of the job. She felt his keen gaze on her before he suggested,

"Would you like to go up today for a dry run? I don't want to discourage you, Nurse Thompson, but some people can't stand riding in a chopper. It's a lot different than flying fixed-wing. I've hauled a lot of folks who get sick, no matter how often they fly with me."

"My goodness, I never thought of that!" Patti gasped. "I hope I'm not one of them. By the way, Nurse Thompson sounds awfully formal if we're going to work together."

"Okay, Patti. How about a ride?"

She glanced at her jeans outfit. "Is this okay for flying?"

"Put the bandanna over your hair and it will be perfect. Of course, this winter you'll want a sheepskin coat, fleece-lined boots, insulated gloves, that kind of thing." He grinned at her and Patti felt her heart lift. Disapproval from others always depressed her. "That is, if you survive today's flight."

"All right." She trotted along beside him, to keep up with his long stride. Shoulder harness in place, Scott turned his full attention to her.

"For your own protection, I need to put the chopper through its full paces," he quietly said. "This isn't to scare you or a ploy to make you quit before starting. It's imperative for you to learn whether your system can take sudden drops caused by down drafts, that kind of thing."

Her heart flew to her throat and parked there. "I understand. Do your best. I mean your worst. Oh, dear, I'm babbling."

Scott's clear laugh rang out, a contagious sound that restored her to normal.

Too bad he didn't use it more often. It changed him from Stone Face to a living, breathing human being.

The thrill of Patti's first helicopter ride made a lasting impression. Despite Scott's warning, she hadn't realized how very different helicopter flights were from regular airplanes, or "fixed wing" as Scott called them. Here there was no taxiing down a runway, just a thrust up from the tarmac then flying thousands of feet lower than in commercial planes, feeling she could reach down and touch the tops of trees. Such maneuverability she wasn't prepared for even from watching popular TV shows that featured helicopters.

Patti knew her face glowed when they returned and landed.

"I love it!" she squealed, forgetting the man beside her hadn't really wanted her to fly with him. She clambered out of the chopper, knocking off her red scarf. Patti ran to a broadly grinning Mike Parker, who had deserted his paperwork and come out to meet the returning travelers.

"Well, how did she do?" He sounded impatient.

Scott dangled the bandanna from one hand. "She passed with flying colors." He waved the scarf back and forth like a banner.

Patti wanted to hug him. Instead, she grabbed the bandanna and did a little jig. "When can I go on a real mission? Soon, I hope." She felt herself redden. "I don't mean I want anyone to get sick or hurt. I'm just excited about flying."

"In the meantime, you may want to review everything you know about making do and nursing under primitive conditions," Mike suggested.

Patti touched her jacket pocket. "Yes, and I'll study the list of what's in the survival pack as if my life depends on it."

Scott frowned at her comment. "Do that. Sometime it may." He walked away before she could tell him she was serious, not being facetious.

"Oh dear, now he's upset with me again," Patti mourned.

Mike awkwardly patted her shoulder. "Don't worry about Stone Face. He carries heavier burdens than most men. Glad you'll be working with us." He walked her to the Bronco and courteously waited until she drove away.

That night, Patti settled down in the living room of her inherited log cabin. A fire crackled in the fireplace and cast rosy shadows on the off-white walls. The plushy dark green carpet stretched beneath her slippered feet like a forest floor. How she loved it all! Here she had found rest. Here the turmoil of many weeks and months seemed long ago and mercifully far away—until today.

Patti shifted position and grimaced. A twinge of pain reminded her of Charles's fingers biting into her shoulder. She thought of the faint blue marks she'd seen after she showered and slipped into a warm fleece robe. Again she gave thanks. Prayer gave way to speculation. *What shared experience had created the animosity between Scott Sloan and Charles Bradley?* she wondered.

"Something shattering enough to turn them into lifetime enemies," she murmured. Snatches of Charles's bitter accusations returned.

"I suppose you're going to make me, the way you thought you'd make me—"

"I know plenty about Sloan. More than any other man alive. I was there."

"You came between me and what I wanted once before, remember? I beat you then and I'll beat you now."

"Another accident would be inconvenient, to say the least."

"Worse than trying to put a jigsaw puzzle together," Patti decided aloud. One more conversation fragment returned. Both Scott Sloan's face and voice had definitely warned when he remarked, "One more thing. Don't underestimate Charles Bradley. He never gives up anything he considers his."

Patti shook off the apprehension the warning brought. What could Charles do but accept her ultimatum? And Mike Parker's, to keep away from the Rescue Service property? Why did the home in which she had felt so secure suddenly feel just a little too isolated?

"Lord, now that I have my own place, maybe I should get a dog." The idea grew more appealing with every moment. On impulse, she called the Hoffs.

When Ma answered, Patti breathlessly asked, "Where would a person go if he, in this case she, decided to get a dog? Besides in a pound, I mean. They don't always have the kind you want."

"Where you get a good dog depends on if you want a real dog, a rag mop, or a rat," Ma promptly told her. She laughed. "In other words, what breed?"

"One that will bark if anyone comes around, but won't make the closest neighbors wish I'd never moved in," Patti replied.

Ma's voice sharpened. "Is there something you aren't telling me?"

"Charles Bradley showed up today. He claimed me as his fiancée in front of Scott Sloan and Mike Parker. I told him off. Mike told him off. Scott and Charles threw a few verbal bombs and my ex—as in highly ex-fiancé—intimated I was on the verge of a nervous breakdown and unfit to fly. Mike ordered him to leave and not come back," Patti summed up.

"Is that all?" Ma sounded relieved. "I thought it might be something serious."

Patti had to cover the mouthpiece to keep from howling into her friend's ear.

"I'd say that was quite enough! By the way, Scott took me up in the helicopter and checked me out. I have a job. I mean, I'm officially cleared to fly."

"Good." Ma never wasted much time on unnecessary talk, especially on the telephone. "About the dog. I'll ask around and see if anyone has one they can't keep and that needs a good home. A Labrador would be good. They aren't mean like some dogs, but their bark will scare the sheet off a ghost!"

The excited nurse hung up, still laughing. *Leave it to Ma Hoff.* The capable woman would probably find the exact dog to best meet Patti's needs and deliver it to the log cabin before its new owner could lay in a supply of dog food!

Patti washed a juicy apple in the kitchen and brought it back to her seat in front of the fire. Now to study the list of survival pack contents. She found it arranged in six basic groups necessary for survival and rescue. She read aloud, "Medical and First Aid Group. First Aid and burn cream. Small and large butterfly closures. Gauze roll and surgical tape. Sheer strips, gauze pads, and elastic bandage. Wound compressors. Complete snake-bite kit. Cotton pellets and pain-relief drops. Metal tweezers, toothache kit, antiseptic towelettes. Ammonia inhalants, throat lozenges, and aspirin tablets. Salt tablets. Antihistamine, antacid, and anti-diarrhea tablets.

"Goodness, it really is complete," Patti exclaimed. "Let's see what's under the Food and Water group. Water/fuel storage container, canteens, tropical chocolate bar, water-purification tablets, tea bags, fruit drink packs, sugar bags, soup packs, granola bars, and chewing gum." She nodded approval.

"Signal and Light Group. Cyalume light sticks? I can ask Scott what they are. Whistle, aerial flares, orange smoke signal, signal flag, long burn candle, signal mirror. Emergency Devices Group. Utility knife, nylon rope, copper wire. Razor blade, safety pins, liquid-filled compass, toilet tissue, and survival manual."

More impressed with every item, Patti continued. "Shelter and Protection Group. Large, orange, two-person tent. Emergency space blankets. Sunglasses, insect repellent, and sunburn protection. Fire and Cooking Group. Waterproof matches, two fuel bars, one-quart metal pot, two pint containers."

She laid aside the list, heart pumping. "God forbid we ever need all this stuff, but I'm so thankful it will be on hand."

Patti rose and crossed to the window. She pulled aside the drapes enough to notice a high-riding, tipsy-looking moon. Suppose the worst happened? What if she and Scott Sloan were pitted against the wilderness of western Montana?

A glow that had nothing to do with the fire warming her hearth stole into her cheeks. How ironic that of all the men Patti had ever known, Stone Face would be her first choice as a companion with whom to be stranded in the wilds.

Would she be his?

"Don't be absurd," Patti said. "He doesn't even like me."

So change his mind, a little voice advised. *Scott Sloan is well worth knowing.*

Patti restlessly reached for sketchpad and pencil. A rough image of the pilot emerged. Disgusted with herself for acting like a lovestruck adolescent, she crumpled the page and threw it in the fire. It would take more chipping away than she felt capable of doing to make a dent in Stone Face's reserve.

Chapter 10

Two major events occurred in Patti Thompson's life almost simultaneously.

First, she acquired a housebroken, guaranteed-not-to-chew-the-furniture, half-grown black Labrador named Obsidian.

"What a strange name!" she commented to the Hoffs, who had taken her to a distant ranch to get acquainted with the dog. "Isn't that the natural glass made when hot lava cools quickly?"

"Obsidian is black. So is the dog." Pa Hoff's matter-of-fact explanation made Patti want to giggle. He obviously saw nothing odd about the name.

"Indians used obsidian to make arrowheads. Have you ever been to Yellowstone Park?" Ma put in.

"No, but I would like to go. Maybe next spring." Patti gave a happy little bounce.

"Take a look at Obsidian Cliff, an enormous mass of obsidian worth seeing."

Patti admitted the name fit when she saw the black Labrador lying on the ranch house porch beside his master's chair.

"You darling!" She plumped to her knees and held out one hand. Pa had primed her on how to approach a dog on their ride to the ranch. Obsidian needed to accept her before she took him home.

The dog's clear brown eyes looked trustingly into hers. He sniffed, licked her hand, and cocked his head.

"He's trying to decide about me," Patti said. "I hope I pass the test!"

She told the dog, "We're going to be friends, Obsidian."

He nosed her hand, crept closer, and pressed his well-shaped head against her jeans. Patti laid her hand on his head and stroked. A quick wriggle brought him even closer. She put both arms around his silky body and hugged him. Obsidian rewarded her with a face-washing and a bark that started from his toes. It really would scare the sheet off a ghost!

"May I take him with me?" Patti asked the rancher who owned him.

"No reason why not. He's sure taken to you," the weather-beaten man cleared his throat. "I hate to see him go, but my wife isn't well. In fact, she's already in Helena with our son. We've sold out so we can be closer to him. A city's no fit place for a big dog. He needs to roam. Same goes for his owner, but things don't always stay the way a man wants." His keen gaze bore into Patti. "I hear Dan Davis left you his log cabin. You'll have plenty of room for Obsidian there. He's an outdoor dog, so I'll send along his dog house. He's used to it, so don't be bringing him inside, especially to sleep, unless something scares you." He paused before saying, "My wife and I took Obsidian with us a few times when we dropped in on Dan. It won't be like he's going somewhere totally strange."

"Will he run away when I'm gone?" Patti asked, petting the sleek head. "I've heard of dogs that go back to their original owners' homes."

Pa Hoff spoke up. "Naw. The boys and I'll put up a fence this afternoon quicker than you can say scat."

"You won't have to cut down the cottonwoods, will you?" Patti worried. Her voice trembled. "One reason Dan left me his home was because he knew I loved it the way it was. He said if I ever decided to sell it, to make sure it wasn't to someone who's likely to rip out the cottonwoods."

She started to add Dan had also suggested she offer the home first to Scott Sloan. A sharp thrust of suspicion stopped her. *Was that the reason for the distrust in Stone Face's eyes? Had he hoped Dan would leave the log cabin to him?* Learning someone else had inherited the place he loved was bound to leave a sour taste in Scott's mouth. Especially when that someone was a nurse Dan Davis had never heard of until a few months before he changed his will.

"Miss?"

Patti jerked herself back to the present. "Yes?"

"Are you planning to sell? It could make a difference about Obsidian. I'd hate for him to just get settled and have you head off to Seattle," he told her bluntly.

She stared at the concerned rancher. Perhaps he was right. After a long, soul-searching moment she told him, "I have no plans to leave Kalispell. I love my new home and look forward to flying for Mike Parker." Patti drew in a long breath and slowly expelled it. "On the other hand, I can't promise to stay in Montana forever. I can promise one thing. If I ever leave, I'll take as much care in finding a good home for Obsidian as you are doing now."

"Shucks," Ma Hoff put in. "If Patti ever flies the coop, we'll take care of your dog. Same goes if she gets caught out overnight on a rescue flight. No trouble at all for one of us or a hand of ours to drive in and make sure he's okay."

The rancher visibly relaxed. "Good enough for me." He shook Patti's hand. She felt calluses born of hard work press into her palm. "I'd kinda like to say good-bye to Obsidian by my lonesome." He smiled at Patti. "My wife said on the phone that anyone Dan Davis trusted with his possessions would take good care of our dog." He snapped his fingers. The dog leaped from Patti's arms and followed the rancher off the porch and toward the Hoffs' station wagon.

"His heart's broken at having to leave this place," Ma Hoff observed.

Patti nodded, too filled with emotion to speak. She glanced at the rancher and his dog. Obsidian stood rigid as the Yellowstone cliff with the same name. A few minutes later, man and dog returned. Sadness lurked in the rancher's eyes, but he smiled and placed Patti's hand on Obsidian's back.

"Go with her, Boy." He walked onto the porch and into the house without looking back.

Obsidian stayed, but gazed after his owner. The puzzled expression in his eyes when he turned back to Patti nearly broke her heart. Again she knelt and put her arms around him.

"It's okay, Obsidian. He will be all right. So will you." She stood, one hand on his head. "Shouldn't we, I mean, don't I owe for the dog?"

"It would be an insult to offer him money," Pa Hoff quietly told her.

Patti flushed at her insensitivity. "Of course it would. Come, Obsidian." He followed her into the back seat of the station wagon, pressed his nose to the window, and watched until a bend of the road hid the ranch house. Then he sighed, lay down, and put his head on Patti's knee.

When they arrived at the log cabin, Obsidian perked up. He trotted around the property, sniffing and occasionally barking. Patti let him explore, but he looked so forlorn sitting on her porch, she didn't have the heart to leave him there alone. All afternoon she ran and played with him to the tune of pounding and men's voices. Before nightfall, a hastily constructed but serviceable fence enclosed her property. Obsidian's dog house settled beneath a large cottonwood as if it had been there since the land began.

"Thank you so much," she told the workers.

They doffed sombreros, Stetsons, and straw hats according to individual taste and grinned.

"A pleasure to be neighborly," one said.

Another, bolder than the rest, added, "It 'pears you're aimin' to stay a spell, what with gettin' a dawg and buildin' a fence, and all."

He sounded so much like Dan Davis, Patti had to blink back tears. "I am."

" 'Course she is," Pa Hoff defended. "That's why Dan left her this place." He pounded a final nail and laughed. "C'mon, boys. We're through here and it's almost supper time. Cookie means it when he yells 'come and git it or I'll throw it out the window.' "

The hands scrambled into the station wagon and a couple of other vehicles. A chorus of good-byes brought an answering bark from Obsidian. Patti waved until they were out of sight, then started inside. The dog's nails clicked on the porch floor behind her, but he made no attempt to follow her into the house. She fought against the desire to let him sleep inside for at least the first night and won. It simply meant postponing the inevitable. Tomorrow night wouldn't be any easier for Obsidian—or her.

Patti opened a can of dog food and broke it apart in one of the bowls she had purchased for her new pet's exclusive use. She poured fresh water into the second, praying Obsidian would eat. The Hoffs had warned he might take a few days to adjust. "Don't force him," they warned. "Let him decide."

To Patti's joy, he ate every morsel and licked the bowl. He lapped water and sat down on the doormat when she went back into the house. Twice before getting ready for bed, she went out and petted the dog. At last, she turned off the living room lights except for those on automatic timer and went to her bedroom. She heard the familiar scrabble of Obsidian's nails on the porch and glanced out the front window of her bedroom.

Her dog stood just outside looking in with intelligent eyes. Patti opened the window and said through the screen, "It's okay, Boy." A bright idea came. She left the window, ran to a closet, and unearthed the oldest of the blankets Dan Davis had left behind. She took it outside and spread it beneath her window. "Here's a bed for you, if you like it better than your dog house," she told Obsidian. "Lie down and try it out."

The dog turned in a circle, then settled on the blanket and licked her hand. Patti suspected the spot would become his permanent bed until cold weather forced him to seek better shelter. Icy winter winds would surely blow across the roofed, open-sided porch.

"I won't ask the Hoffs for any more favors," she told the dog. "But I think I'll inquire about carpenters. It wouldn't take much to enclose the porch. Just the ends. I won't do anything to shut out my view of the sunsets." She gave Obsidian a final pat and headed to bed. It had been a long and exciting day. Her last thought was of the dog on guard. No one could approach her window or the front of the house without disturbing her new barking machine. Patti fell asleep smiling at the ridiculous description.

The shrilling telephone tore Patti away from sketching late mid-morning of the next day.

"We need you," Mike Parker stated flatly. "Sloan's been notified. My other nurses are scheduled or down with the creeping awfuls."

Patti wondered what on earth the "creeping awfuls" were but bit back the remark that none of her medical texts described such a malady.

"Be there soon."

"Right." The call ended as abruptly as it began.

Thank goodness it wasn't too far from the log cabin to the flying field. Patti quickly dialed the Hoffs.

"On my way out," she said tersely. "Would you please call me this evening, just in case? If you get the answering machine, it means we had to stay overnight. I fed Obsidian this morning, but he is supposed to eat twice a day. The way he gobbled dinner last night, I'm afraid he will stuff himself and be miserable if I leave extra food out."

"Be glad to help. Happy flying, Honey."

Bless Ma Hoff. She conveyed more in a few words than many people did in hours of conversation! Patti scrambled into her jeans outfit, substituting a navy scarf and turtleneck for the red set. She slapped together a belated breakfast: a multi-grain peanut butter sandwich. She also gulped down a glass of orange juice and reminded herself to buy bananas. They made great quick-energy snacks. Halfway to the hangar, she let up on the gas pedal.

"Great! I forgot to ask Mike about a lunch. Am I supposed to keep one packed, just in case?" She shook her head and grinned at the gorgeous fall morning. "At least I won't starve. There are always the food supplies in the survival pack."

A short time later, Patti swung the red Bronco she loved driving into the parking lot next to the hangar. She locked it, stowed her keys in the medical bag she'd packed the day after getting approved for flight, and hurried into Mike Parker's office.

"Reporting for duty, Sir."

"It sure didn't take you long," Mike praised. His brows drew together in a frown. "I hope you had breakfast. Can't have you getting weak in the knees."

Patti nodded until her blond hair bounced beneath the navy bandanna tied gypsy-fashion. "Yes. Where are we going?"

Scott Sloan stepped through the door. "To bring in two hikers who shouldn't be allowed out of city limits." He shook his dark head. "They drove an ATV—that's an all-terrain vehicle—into the wilderness, parked it and started hiking. A few miles in, they tried to cross a steep gravel slope. Both fell. One thinks he may have fractured ribs. The other went back to the vehicle and sent out a call for help. A trucker picked it up and relayed it. I wish people would learn you don't tackle western Montana's mountains and canyons unless you're mighty sure of what you're doing. Even then, it's risky." A slight smile smoothed away his frown. "Ready?"

"Uh-huh." She nodded again and followed him to the waiting Bell Jet-Ranger. Once inside, Patti buckled up as Scott had taught her. She felt again the exhilaration when they lifted off.

"How far do we have to go?" she asked.

"Less than a hundred miles. Roughly forty-five minutes flying time." Scott expertly headed the helicopter north and west.

Patti marveled at the scene below them. Shining silver rivers threaded the land. Foothills sloped upward and became part of the Rockies. Their snowy caps warned winter lay just ahead. It lurked in shadowy glens, dying leaves, heavily-mossed boulders. Scott flew low enough to point out animals. A herd of powerful elk stood poised, then sprang away from the buzz of the helicopter. A fat bear batted fish from a glistening stream.

"I wish I'd brought my sketch pad." Patti sighed. "Not that I can ever do this justice." Memory of the sketch she'd made of the man beside her sent fire to her cheeks. *Good thing Scott didn't know about it.*

"No one but God can ever really do justice to what we see on these flights," Scott said soberly. "Have you always wanted to draw?"

Patti told him the same story she had shared with Dan Davis months earlier.

"This winter I plan to take classes, or study. For the first time in my life, I'll have time. I will, won't I? I suppose flights slow down in winter?"

Scott shrugged. "It can go either way, depending on weather. We get called on to help Search and Rescue teams, the Ski Patrol, that kind of thing. There are also calls from people who get snowed in and can't make it to a doctor." He laughed. "We get all kinds of calls. Last year I flew a nurse in to answer a frantic call for a female in labor. Turned out it was a cow trying to deliver a calf breech!" He chuckled reminiscently.

Patti tensed. "What did you do?"

"Followed orders from the nurse and helped Mother Nature along. Cow, calf, nurse, and pilot all survived." He laughed again. "I'll never forget the look on the nurse's face when the rancher announced he was naming the calf Sarah. I thought she'd split. Good sport, though. She told the grateful owner to take good care of her 'namesake.' However, when we got back, the nurse glared and said, 'Not one word from either of you, or I'm through.' " Scott shot Patti an amused glance. "How would you like to have a critter named after you?"

"I can't picture a calf called Patti," she demurely said. Thankfulness for the relaxed atmosphere between them sent a silent prayer upwards. Flying and working with an incompatible coworker would be miserable. She also gave thanks for Scott's outstanding flying skills. On reaching their destination, he hovered the chopper over a spot close to the two men frantically waving their arms. Patti swallowed hard and hid her shaking hands in her jacket pockets. *How could he land a helicopter on such a precarious-looking perch?*

Scott brought the chopper down. Blessed silence followed.

"Ready?"

"Ready." Patti grabbed her well-packed medical bag and stepped out to begin her first case. *What a far cry from Shepherd of Love, with all its modern equipment!* There was no array of sterilized instruments, no hum of muted voices as doctors and nurses reassured patients; only the mournful cry of a flock of wild geese getting a late start south gave an eerie mood to the scene. A mountain goat bleated down at them from a cliff above the narrow strip of level land where they'd set down. It made Patti wonder if she were really here, or dreaming.

A few questions brought the same story the trucker had relayed. Patti caught Scott's quick glance at the hikers' inadequate shoes. No wonder they had slipped and fallen.

"Better get the right kind of footgear before doing any more hiking in the mountains," he advised.

Patti forced her attention to her patients. A quick examination brought a sigh of relief. One hiker had suffered little more than abrasions and contusions. Scott administered first aid while Patti examined the second man.

"I wanted to walk out with my friend," he reported. "Couldn't make it. Climbing made me cough and brought excruciating pain." He winced when she touched his rib cage.

"You'll be fine, although you may have fractured a rib." Patti smiled, thankful he had no trouble breathing, a symptom of a punctured lung.

"What do you do for him?" the friend wanted to know. "Tape him?"

"Not anymore. It's best to simply get him to the hospital. They'll X-ray."

"Since I don't have much wrong with me, is it okay to drive out?"

Patti nodded and Scott said, "We'll take you back to your vehicle. You've probably had enough hiking for one day."

"Thanks." He looked embarrassed. "Uh, you're a private company, aren't you? What about charges?"

"You will receive a bill." Scott turned to the more badly injured hiker. "Ready?"

Patti heaved a sigh of relief after an uneventful flight back to Kalispell. Alerted by Scott, Mike had an ambulance waiting. Patti watched the medics load the accident victim and murmured, "Thus endeth the first flight. What next?"

"We report in. That is, you report, then Mike asks me if I have anything to add. I normally don't." He sent her an oblique, unreadable look.

Normally? Does that mean he has something to add today? Patti wondered. She tried to think. Had she done something wrong? Nothing came to mind.

"So how did it go?" Mike eagerly inquired when they entered the office. Patti briefed him.

"Anything to add?" the flight service owner asked Scott, as usual.

Stone Face didn't move a muscle. "Yeah."

Mike's mouth dropped open. Patti's heart dropped to her toes like an out-of-control elevator going down. *Uh-oh. That sounds like trouble.*

Scott flipped off the baseball cap he wore while flying.

"I don't want Thompson flying with me when she's not up with the other pilots."

What happened to calling me Patti? she wondered. Then she inwardly blazed, *You—you jerk!* The words wouldn't come out.

Mike's round face turned purple. He leaped from his chair and glowered at his pilot.

"Flight assignments are my call, not yours."

"Let me finish, okay? I'm requesting her on a permanent basis, any time she's willing to fly."

Parker dropped back into his chair. "Of all the—what's with you, Stone Face?"

Scott crossed his arms behind his head. A twinkle began in his eyes and he counted on strong, lean fingers.

"One, she knows her business. Two, she knows when to talk and when to keep still. She comments on the scenery but doesn't gush. Three, there wasn't a peep out of her when I landed in a tricky spot. I could tell she was nervous, but she didn't let on."

"Anything else?" Mike barked.

Scott hesitated and looked uncertain.

"I'll tell you later," he mumbled.

Patti roused from the roller-coaster swing she had ridden from the depths of anger to pride and amazement at the unexpected praise.

"Since it's obviously about me, I'd like to hear it," she said in a tight voice.

Was that an all-right-you-asked-for-it glint in Stone Face's watching eyes?

He raised an eyebrow, then turned and spoke to Mike as though Patti had remained at the rescue site.

"There's no place in my business for a flight nurse who calls attention to the fact she's a woman and I'm a man. Patti doesn't." He followed his succinct evaluation with a comradely grin.

Scarlet and tongue-tied, she watched him unhurriedly stride across the room and go out whistling.

"Well, I never!"

"Neither did I." Mike Parker agreed. A strange expression settled on his full moon face. "Never in all the time he's been flying for me has Stone Face requested one nurse over another. What did you do to him?"

Patti speechlessly shook her head. She wished she knew!

Chapter 11

Only one thing stood between Patti Thompson—homeowner and rescue flight nurse—and complete contentment: Charles Bradley, who kept popping up like a wicked jack-in-the-box. Following his first dramatic reappearance in Patti's life, he began a "now you see me, now you don't" game that kept her on edge.

"How can he take so much time off from his job?" she asked Obsidian one sunny afternoon while romping with him in her fenced yard. "Charles raged when I planned to come here early. He said he had to pull strings to get off for the month of December. Now I can't turn around without seeing him. Is he banking on winning me back, along with my inheritance? Has he gone so far as to quit his job in hopes of wearing me down?"

Obsidian obligingly gave a sympathetic bark and ran after the tennis ball Patti pitched into the air. He leaped and caught it before it fell to the ground.

"At least Charles can't follow me when I'm out on a rescue mission," she rejoiced. "I suspect Stone Face would welcome an excuse to boot my persistent ex-fiancé out of the chopper."

Annoyance with Charles transferred to Scott. Although Patti seldom admitted it even to herself, she had hoped his requesting her to fly with him meant the beginning of real friendship. It hadn't. At times she felt tempted to use feminine wiles and crash through the invisible barrier her coworker kept firmly in place. Each time she violently rejected the idea. The one thing Stone Face definitively admired about her was her lack of flirting. Why risk his contempt by showing she admired far more about him than his flying skills?

"He only wants a buddy, not a sweetheart," Patti admitted. "Now where did that gem of rhetoric come from?" She scanned her memory. "Oh, yes. Grandma Thompson used to sing a song with words that made a lot of sense." If Patti remembered correctly, it had been handed down from her great-grandmother and World War I times. "What's the rest of it?" she asked Obsidian.

His ears perked up and he brought her the ball to throw again.

Patti laughed. "Some help you are!" She hummed the tune. Words came back. She sang them, wondering if the writer had based the song on a sad experience.

> *I only want a buddy, not a sweetheart. Buddies never make you blue. Sweethearts make vows that are broken, broken like my heart is broken, too.*
> *Don't tell me that you love me, say you like me,*
> *No lover's quarrels, no honeymoon for two.*
> *Don't turn down lover's lane, but keep on just the same,*
> *I only want a buddy, not a gal.*

A hateful laugh followed the final note of her song. Patti turned toward the man lounging against her new fence.

"What are you doing here?"

"Watching you and our honeymoon cabin. Not a bad place."

A crimson tide washed into Patti's face. Charles's appraising look at the house and herself made her feel she'd been put on the auction block, to be sold to the highest bidder.

"Go away or I'm calling the police." The anger in her voice must have rung a warning bell in Obsidian's alert brain. He barked and raced toward the fence.

Patti followed. She'd never seen the black lab in action as a guard dog. She doubted he would clear the fence and take a chunk out of Charles, but didn't dare chance it.

"Down, Boy!" she called sharply. "Sit, Obsidian!"

The barking broke off mid-howl. The dog hesitated, then obeyed.

Charles sprang back from the fence, face contorted with rage.

"Better chain that mutt before he attacks someone who will sue you," he snarled.

"Don't get any ideas," Patti flung back at him. "Obsidian is on his property, protecting it—and me." Her steady gaze met Charles's and she added significantly, "He also sleeps just below my window, in case trespassers or unwanted visitors pay a night call. Now, are you going, or must I call the authorities and get a restraining order to keep you away from here?"

"Fat chance." Charles smirked. "You have no grounds. The police would laugh at you." He abruptly changed tactics. "Forgive me, Patti. My world fell apart when you walked out on me." He took a deep breath and looked from her to the log home. "Seeing all this and remembering how we planned to spend our honeymoon here is harder than you'll ever know." Misery clouded his eyes.

"That song also brings back memories. If you won't be my sweetheart, please, at least be my friend. I'm too weak to be the kind of person I know I should be. With you, I can make it. I haven't been worthy, yelling at you and everything, but I pray every day you'll give me another chance. My whole life's at stake."

Caught off guard by Charles's apparent sincerity, Patti felt herself weakening. He evidently saw it. Excitement over his impending victory flashed across his face and he overplayed his pretense of humility.

"I knew you couldn't turn me down," he exulted. "You're a Christian. That means you have to forgive me."

Patti stared at the man she had so nearly married. Fear replaced pity and she shivered. The man before her definitely showed classic symptoms of mental illness, berating her one moment, pleading with her the next.

Charles put a hand on the gate. Confidence shone in the jaunty step he took forward.

"Call off your dog, will you, Darling?"

Obsidian's warning growl loosened Patti's frozen tongue.

"If you want my forgiveness, you have it," she said. "I'm afraid anything else just isn't possible. Find a woman who really loves you, Charles. Someone you can be true to for the rest of your life." She took a deep breath. "I'm sorry, but it won't be me."

"It's Sloan, isn't it? Do you know you're in love with a murderer? He was cleared at a hearing, but it doesn't change the fact he was guilty as sin."

Why must blood rush to her face making her appear even more guilty? Patti furiously wondered. "You don't—you can't mean Stone Face!"

"So that's what they call him now. The families of the two persons he killed had other names for him." Charles laughed unpleasantly. "Chain the dog and I'll tell you a bedtime story that will curl your hair tighter than it is now. I've kept track of Sloan for years. I knew he was here. That's why I objected when you planned to come here without me to protect you. It was for your own good."

Patti's world spun like a Ferris wheel before her training on how to handle critical situations kicked in. A barrage of mental images of Scott Sloan came to her rescue. *Murderer? Never in a million years! Yet Charles Bradley's statements held the ring of truth.*

That's it, Patti decided. *Not truth, but clever deceit that fooled me before.*

The thought steadied her.

Charles ignored her silence and continued his harangue. "He tried to make me lie. Said I was the only one who could clear him. Even if it had been true, I wouldn't have done it. He came between me and a girl I tried to protect from nasty gossip. That's why he hates me." His lips curled back. "I hear he's posing as a Christian now, pillar of the community and all that. If the hearing board had listened to me the way they should have, Sloan would be in jail."

"He said you could clear him?" Suspicion popped into Patti's mind like crocuses through snow. She didn't dare add the question that burned in her soul: *Was Scott really responsible, or were you?*

"I told you I was there." His eyes turned mocking. "Sorry. If you want the rest of the story, as Paul Harvey says, you have to let me in."

With suspicion came freedom and the courage to say, "If I want the rest of the story, I'll ask Scott Sloan."

Patti wasn't prepared for the violent reaction that followed. Charles tensed. For a moment she thought he would burst through the gate and attack her.

"On guard, Obsidian!" she cried.

The black lab leaped toward the fence. Charles backed away.

"You win, this time. Just remember, your dog won't always be with you." He walked down the gravel drive and started up the road.

The fact Charles had taken the precaution to park some distance away from her home turned Patti's knees to quivering gelatin. Once before she had been in terrible danger because of misjudging a man. This time, she would be prepared. She ran into the house and dialed the police.

Charles had been wrong when he warned her the authorities would laugh. The officers who responded found nothing funny in the situation. Patti told them exactly what happened, only omitting the part about Scott. She felt guilty, but couldn't bring herself to reopen old wounds until after she talked with the sober-faced pilot. The fierce desire to protect him raised questions in her mind, ones she must face and answer later. Reporting Charles's threat must come first.

"Do you know where this Bradley is staying?" the female officer asked.

"No. I assume his employer, possibly former employer now, would."

"I want you to seriously consider this before answering, Miss Thompson. As a nurse who has dealt with unstable patients, has Charles Bradley's rage, his level of violence, escalated since the first time you saw that side of him?"

"Definitely."

The officers exchanged meaningful looks. "We'll be in touch," the policewoman said. "In the meantime, don't fall for any phony attempts that can result in making you vulnerable. Let's face it. Bradley sounds unscrupulous. You're an attractive woman. You're also desirable because of your inheritance."

She looked regretful. "I'm not trying to terrify you. Just be careful."

"What kind of thing do you mean by phony attempts?" Patti asked above the chilly feeling surrounding her throat like clutching fingers.

"Hoaxes," the policeman warned. "Phone messages at night calling you to the hospital because a friend has been hurt. Anything designed to get you away from home. If you absolutely must go out at night, take the dog."

"I'll be careful. Thank you for coming." Patti ushered them out and beckoned to Obsidian. He might be used to sleeping outdoors, but she needed his comforting presence inside tonight. She spread a clean blanket over the rug next to her bed and fell asleep with one hand on the dog's silky head.

◆◆◆◆◆

Two days passed. Then three. Then five. Patti made a couple of routine flights. No opportunity arose for her to confront Scott with Charles's accusations. However, she used the time to observe him more closely than ever. Her heart insisted he must be innocent. Her head acknowledged there had to be some truth in the story. What had changed Scott from the laughing pilot she suspected he had once been to Stone Face Sloan, a man who maintained a certain distance even from Mike Parker, his closest friend?

An manila envelope with no return address left Patti more confused and torn than ever. It contained photocopies of newspaper clippings about a hearing several years earlier. Someone had painstakingly put them in chronological order, making a continued story. Patti curled up in front of a warm fire and started reading.

A chilling picture emerged. Scott, Charles Bradley, and two friends took off from Salt Lake City in a chartered plane for post-Christmas skiing in Colorado. A freak storm roared out of nowhere and caught them. According to the news stories, Scott had also committed a cardinal sin. He failed to file a flight plan. In any event, the plane went down in the mountains. Only Scott and Charles survived. Scott remained unconscious until after the rescue crew arrived. Charles reported the other two died in the interim. He hinted that Scott's carelessness in not filing a flight plan had made the difference between life and death.

Scott testified Charles had been the one at the controls, but admitted he couldn't be sure. Neither could he account for the fact a flight plan hadn't been filed. A blow to the head followed by the unconsciousness had erased his memory of everything from before takeoff until the actual rescue.

Charles swore Scott lied, trying to weasel out of responsibility by attempting to shift blame. The hearing board found itself in a quandary. They had the word of one pilot against another, one a self-confessed amnesiac. They also wondered. How much difference did it make who piloted the plane? It was doubtful even the most skillful pilot could have successfully flown through such a storm.

Patti held her breath and picked up the last clipping. The headline read:

AIRPLANE CRASH KILLING TWO
RULED TRAGIC ACCIDENT.

A capsulized account of the hearing followed as well as the statement neither of the surviving pilots was being held responsible.

No wonder the shadow of Scott's past lurked in his eyes. Patti's heart went out to him and she blinked back tears. Regardless of actual circumstances, a caring man like Stone Face would blame himself.

"I don't believe he'd overlook filing a flight plan," Patti murmured. She stared into the flames leaping high in the soot-blackened fireplace. "He was younger then, but Scott doesn't seem the type to be careless. What if he thought Charles filed the report, Lord?" Her heart pounded. "Suppose he left it to Charles, who overlooked it? Scott can't remember, but he must suspect. What about the girl and the nasty gossip?"

These were all knotty questions demanding answers. But no real answers came, only the throbbing of a fiercely partisan heart. *Scott Sloan might be grossly negligent,* but with every breath she took, Patti Thompson prayed for him to be innocent.

◆◆✕◆◆

A few hours before Patti received her anonymous package, Stone Face sorted through his mail: mostly junk, a few bills, and a large manila envelope on the bottom of the stack. He opened it. A sheaf of papers cascaded out, like the ills of the world released when Pandora of mythical fame opened the forbidden box. A typed note on top read, "An identical set has been sent to Patti Thompson."

Scott grunted. "What on earth. . ." He tossed the note aside and froze. Spread out before him were photocopies: a complete collection of newspaper clippings recounting the tragedy he still hadn't been able to put in the past. He waited for the sick feeling that always accompanied memories of that terrible time. It came. So did the same assurance and peace he felt in the Bell Jet-Ranger that day long ago.

"Thank You, God," he fervently prayed. "For the first time in years, I feel free." Buoyed with strength he knew came from the Holy Spirit, Scott did something he had vowed never to do. He began at the earliest dated newspaper report and read straight through. When he finished the final clipping, he allowed it to fall to the floor, marveling. Tragedy remained in the happenings, yet from his present viewpoint, it felt as if it had happened to another man.

" 'Therefore if any man be in Christ, he is a new creature: old things are passed away; behold, all things are become new,' " Scott softly quoted. "Second Corinthians 5:17, King James."

Verse 18 swept into his mind. "And all things are of God, who hath reconciled us to himself by Jesus Christ, and hath given to us the ministry of reconciliation." Scott squirmed, wanting to savor his newfound freedom. Yet the words "ministry of reconciliation" refused to be sponged from his mind. Until he could forgive Charles for lying, if indeed the other pilot had sworn falsely, how could he expect to maintain the feeling of chains broken in his own life?

Scott had struggled to put the past behind, including his hatred of Charles. Yet no one on earth except Bradley would have reason to send a full account of the hearing to Patti Thompson. Had he done it in retaliation for the scene at the flying field? How would the nurse who won more of Scott's admiration with every shared flight receive the news her pilot had been accused of negligence?

Only one way to find out. He dialed Patti's number.

"It's Scott. If you haven't had dinner, are you free to go out?" He felt awkward and grinned to himself. Too many years had limped by since he had invited a female out for dinner.

"Why, yes. I am." She added in a troubled voice, "I need to talk with you."

"Concerning a packet you received from an anonymous donor?"

The telephone line faithfully reproduced her gasp. "How did you know?"

"Our mutual friend, question mark, included me in his information shower, along with a note informing me you were also a recipient of his generosity."

Patti didn't reply for a moment. When she did, her voice sounded brisk. Had she used the silence to recover from the shock of his invitation?

"Why don't I fix something here? It will be quieter than a restaurant and a better place to talk."

Scott made a counter offer. "Why don't I bring take-out? What do you like, Chinese? Ribs? There's a place here that serves lip-smacking ribs along with cornbread and coleslaw. Just one thing. You'll need a bib."

Some of the strain left her voice. "I don't have a bib, but I have several rolls of paper towels."

"Good enough. I'll be there in about forty-five minutes."

"All right."

Scott put down the phone and headed for his closet. Why was the prospect of a business dinner with a fellow employee sending pleasurable anticipation through him? That's all it was, a business dinner. Nothing more. *Right,* a little voice mocked. "Then why are you reaching for your new western shirt?"

Scott laughed. "Why not?" he demanded while shaving, as much of God as of himself. "Once I have closure on the past, is there any reason why I shouldn't start looking for a life companion?"

"No reason at all," he told the man in the mirror. Strange how different his reverse image looked from the unsmiling reflection he usually saw while shaving or brushing his short, dark hair. This man looked alive, eager, ready to move on. The other had not.

All dressed up in the new navy shirt and gray slacks, Scott toyed with the idea of taking Patti some flowers. The corners of his mouth immediately turned down and he rejected the idea. Flowers went with courtship. He certainly wasn't courting his flight nurse. He ignored the skeptical "oh, yeah?" his little voice sneaked in before he could shut it down, and headed for the rib place. Their spicy aroma filled the Jeep on his way to the log cabin home.

When Scott rang the doorbell, Patti flung it wide. She looked downright delectable in a fluffy white sweater and dark slacks. One hand lay on a half-grown black lab's back.

"Quiet, Obsidian. Scott is a friend."

Scott stepped inside and waited while the dog sniffed and checked him out. "Don't you know better than to open the door without identifying callers?"

"Believe it or not, I could smell those ribs from the time you reached the bottom step," she told him. "Do you mind eating on trays? I never had a fireplace before, so I usually eat my meals in front of it."

"Sounds good to me. I spent a lot of time here with Dan. Not enough, though. Too busy, or thought I was." He looked around the colorful living room then followed her to the pine-paneled kitchen. "I see you haven't changed things. Don't most women rearrange the furniture? Seems I've heard they do." He laid the large package of food on a counter.

"I'm not most women," she told him pertly. "I like it the way it is. Good grief, you brought enough food to feed a bunkhouse filled with cowboys!"

"Not quite. Did you ever see a cowboy eat? Or a pilot?" he teased.

By unspoken consent, neither brought up the subject uppermost on their minds until a great many crunchy brown ribs and most of the other food vanished. Scott trailed Patti to the kitchen again. He insisted on helping her wash and dry their few dishes.

"No need dirtying the dishwasher for them," he cheerfully told her. "It's kind of nice, being in a kitchen. I don't spend much time in the one in my apartment." He caught both the wistfulness in his voice and her quick glance. "Not that I can't cook," he hastily amended. "It just doesn't seem worthwhile when I'm alone."

"I know what you mean." Blue eyes soft, she smiled and hung her dishtowel to dry. When they settled back down in the living room, she went straight to the point. "What I read today shocked me."

Scott's hopes for Patti's trust in spite of the evidence died unborn. He leaped from his chair and stared down at her. Pain and disappointment harshened his voice.

"And knowing what I am, you don't want to fly with me."

Chapter 12

Knowing what I am, you don't want to fly with me.

Scott's words hit Patti like pieces of granite chipped from his stony face. Before she could answer, he turned on his heel and headed for the door. The rigid set of his shoulders betrayed the suffering she had inflicted by stating she'd been shocked at the newspaper accounts.

Don't let him go like this.

The little voice whispering in her soul freed Patti from the paralyzing impact of Scott's misinterpretation. She sprang from her seat, ran across the moss-like carpet, and clutched his arm.

"How can you think such a thing?" she choked out. "Scott Sloan, I'd trust you with my life!"

His gaze raked her face. Never had she been subject to such scrutiny. The dullness in his eyes gave way to disbelief. He shook off her hold and placed his hands on her shoulders.

"Do you mean that?" he grated.

She forced herself to meet his look squarely. "I don't lie."

Patti had seen many sunrises since coming to Montana. She remembered well the dawn hush, followed by a gentle hint of radiance in the sky then the eager sun bursting over a distant hill in all its glory. Scott Sloan's slow acceptance of her trust dawned the same way. She felt she had glimpsed the very soul of the man before her. The next instant, he gathered her into his arms and held her close. Not fiercely, or passionately, but as a shepherd cradles a lost lamb plucked from danger.

Twice in her life Patti had experienced what she believed was love. Never had she known the feeling of rightness, of coming home to the shelter where she belonged. She wanted to stay in Scott Sloan's arms forever. All too soon he released her. His forefinger tilted her chin upward. His lips sought and found hers in a tender kiss that ended almost before it began. Scott's arms dropped. If Patti lived to be a hundred, she knew she would never forget the expression in his eyes when he said, "Thank you, Patti," and walked out.

Blinded by the rush of tears she could not stop, she stood where she was. Someday they would talk again. Someday they would discuss blame, regret, all the things that must be cleared away in order for perfect healing to take place—just as wounds required the removal of dirt and foreign matter to avoid infection. For now, the gentle memory of Scott's kiss was all that mattered.

Scott Sloan drove away from the log cabin as if pursued by a Montana northern storm. He laughed mirthlessly. Neither his Jeep, nor the Bell Jet-Ranger could escape his love for Patti Thompson. He'd crash-landed permanently when she looked up at him with clear eyes and proclaimed her unbounded trust in him.

"Trust is a long way from love," Scott grimly reminded himself. "Patti is only a few weeks past an engagement with Charles Bradley, Lord. The last thing she needs is pressure from me. Help me keep calm and steady." His mood lightened. "I'm not sorry I kissed her, though." Scott grinned and his pulse quickened. "A pilot needs to file his flight plan!"

The lyrics from one of the songs from *South Pacific* bubbled up and spilled out. Scott changed the words from "I'm in Love with a Wonderful Guy" to "wonderful girl" and sang all the words he could remember. A laugh of sheer exuberance escaped when he finished. *Rodgers and Hammerstein were right. A person in love really did feel high as a Fourth of July flag waving in the sky.*

Scott grinned at his flight of fancy. The soar from despair to the heights had certainly turned him poetic! How would Patti greet him the next time they met? Had she sensed his iron control when he kissed and released her? It hadn't been easy. In that precious moment, he had longed to wrap her in his arms and never let her go.

Scott's state of euphoria lasted all through the next week. He forced himself to act natural, but found it impossible to overlook the knowing expression on Mike Parker's face. Every time Scott carried on a conversation with their flight nurse, the Rescue Service owner fatuously grinned until his pilot wanted to punch him.

"Sorry," Scott apologized to God. "I'm just afraid he'll give me away before Patti is ready." His heart thumped at the thought. *What would it be like to come home to lighted windows, the log cabin—and Patti? Or with her?* Blood quickened in his veins at the thought. *Had God ever created a sweeter, truer woman?* Scott burned with remorse at his earlier suspicions of her.

Fresh doubt pressed hard on the heels of regret. He had saved a tidy sum, with the idea of buying a place of his own if he decided to remain in Kalispell. It paled in comparison with what Dan Davis had left Patti. Scott thought of Charles, pursuing Patti's inheritance as intently as the nurse. God forbid he should follow in Bradley's crooked trail by considering possessions!

Scott's mouth set in a grim line. "If she ever cares, Lord, there will have to be some kind of understanding between us. I can't see allowing her to provide for me, except maybe in sickness. I want to take care of her 'for better, for worse,' and all that." He laughed sheepishly. Why fly over mountain peaks before he reached their base? A single kiss, too brief for him to tell whether she responded, was a long way from discussing financial arrangements and wedding vows.

Along with Mike's curiosity and unspoken approval, Scott's heightened awareness also registered Patti Thompson's warm blush and her sidewise glances at him when she thought him absorbed in flying. Neither had mentioned the incriminating newspaper articles. Doing so meant raising the need to discuss what followed. Scott wasn't ready for that. Apparently, Patti wasn't, either.

They also didn't discuss the invisible something between them. Scott's promise to himself to remain calm and steady wavered again and again. The discipline of years and sense of fair play held him to his self-appointed course. He didn't want a wife—even Patti—on the rebound. If she showed signs of restlessness or mentioned leaving Montana, he would speak. Otherwise, his sense of fair play must keep him on his friendly, undemanding path.

It didn't keep him from dreaming. Or searching for telltale signs Patti might be learning to care. He failed miserably. Just when a look convinced him of Patti's fondness, her quick and natural interest in the country through which they flew robbed the moment of sentiment. Scott wished he knew more about women. He had thought himself in love a few times, but it always proved short-lived.

"There's a certain amount of glamour attached to the fact we fly missions of mercy," he reminded himself. He frowned. Once or twice a flight nurse had garbed him with hero-worship because of his job. He wanted no such adulation and had adroitly warded them off.

"At least Patti won't be influenced by my so-called uniform," Scott mused one evening after crawling into bed. "Denims and a baseball cap are a far cry from spit and polish, plus brass buttons. No relying on 'the fancy wrapper sells the goods.' I don't want Patti's love to be based on anything except who I am."

He yawned, turned off the light, and thanked God for another safe day of flying.

A few miles away, the object of Scott's soliloquy lay staring into the darkness. Why should she care that the tall pilot hadn't followed up on the kiss? Thank goodness he no longer maintained the glacial aloofness she had secretly battled early in their acquaintanceship. Now he treated her as a friend; no more, no less. *An improvement, but unsatisfactory,* Patti reluctantly admitted.

Had the kiss merely been an expression of gratitude for her spontaneous announcement of faith in him? She blushed from toes to hairline. Until or unless Scott pursued it, she must never let on how badly his touch had shaken her. Or that his gentle touch lingered in her mind and heart, erasing all others who had come before.

"You'd think you'd never been kissed before," she flouted. Honesty made her add, "I haven't like that, Lord. What shall I do? I'm terribly afraid this is for real. Will he ever care?" She fluffed her pillows in an attempt to sleep. Although her health had improved tremendously, she needed full strength to match the sometimes arduous demands of her job. *Too bad someone didn't invent a key to turn off the mind and all its worries at night.*

One glass of warm milk, two crackers, and a prayer later, Patti fell into a heavy sleep. The ringing of the phone awakened her. The large red numerals on her digital clock showed six-thirty in the morning. She shook her head to clear away the caterpillar-like fuzz in her brain.

"Hello?"

"Miss Thompson?"

"Yes."

"This is Dr. McArdle calling from. . ." The muffled voice named a local hospital. "Pilot Scott Sloan's Jeep collided with a pickup truck a short time ago. He was lucky and came out of it with some abrasions and a broken leg. He gave me your number and asked for you to come."

Patti's brain spun like a tumbleweed in high winds.

"Of course. Tell him I'll be there as soon as I can."

She hung up and grabbed the first clothing her hand touched when she opened the closet. She gave her teeth and short, blond hair a quick brush. No time to bother with lipstick. Once the shock of the call began to wear off, her heart sang a melody of joy: "He asked for me. Scott Sloan asked *me* to come."

Patti ran down the hall toward the front door. She unfastened the safety chain and stepped onto the porch. Obsidian, who again slept under her window now that no more had been heard of Charles Bradley, barked once and raced toward her. A morning chill struck her face and cleared most of the lingering shreds of sleep from her system. She rubbed her hands, wishing she had taken time to grab mittens. What difference did it make? Who cared about freezing fingers when Scott had asked her to come to the hospital?

She flew down the steps. Across the wide front yard toward the Bronco, ready and waiting for her ride to the hospital.

"No, you can't go with me," she told Obsidian when he joyously bounded after her.

The next instant, her foot hit a frosty patch and halted her wild rush. She sprawled on the ground with a solid thump to her left hip. It jolted her fully awake and mentally alert. Something lurked just outside her range of consciousness, something important, clamoring to be recognized and heeded.

Patti got up, rubbed her sore hip, and looked at the dog, a dark shadow in the pre-dawn. Snatches of a half-forgotten conversation returned, chilling, warning.

The police officer: "Don't fall for any phony attempts that can result in making you vulnerable. I'm not trying to terrify you. Just be careful."

Her own voice: "What kind of thing do you mean by phony attempts?" The chilly feeling surrounded her throat like clutching fingers.

The officer: "Hoaxes. Phone messages at night calling you to the hospital because a friend has been hurt. Anything designed to get you away from home. If you absolutely must go out at night, take the dog."

Patti turned and fled, backtracking like a fugitive trying to cover his trail. The heavy thud of footsteps beat behind her. She knew they only hammered in her mind. Otherwise, Obsidian would be barking his head off in pursuit instead of racing back up the steps and across the porch with her.

She blew on her icy fingers and warmed them enough to unlock the door. She almost fell inside, commanding Obsidian to follow. The tranquillity of the room itself did more to settle her down than the relocked, rechained door when she sagged against its reassuring solidness. Doubt assailed her. There really was a Dr. McArdle at the hospital. She had met him briefly at the flight field. What if Scott really had been hurt and wanted her to come? Was she allowing foolish fear and cowardice to hold her back from answering his request?

Patti hurried to the phone and dialed.

"This is Nurse Thompson," she asked in her crispest, most businesslike voice. "I'd like to speak with either Dr. McArdle or Scott Sloan, a patient. I understand he was admitted a short time ago."

"Of course." An eternity later, a puzzled voice told her, "I'm sorry, but Dr. McArdle is at a medical convention in Helena and Scott Sloan isn't here.

Actually, we haven't admitted anyone at all this morning."

Patti clutched the phone in a death grip. "Could he still be in emergency?"

"I'll check. Hold, please."

Another eternity crawled by before the nurse came back on the line.

"ER says no. Perhaps you have the wrong hospital." She sounded sympathetic.

I doubt it, Patti thought.

"Perhaps," she said. "Thanks, anyway." She hung up.

Obsidian whined and rubbed his nose against her slacks. Patti had learned long ago how quickly he sensed her moods.

"It's all right, Boy," she reassured, knowing when she said it things were *not* all right. Someone wanted to frighten her badly enough to impersonate a doctor. Did the muffled voice that successfully masked the identity of the caller belong to Charles? She'd heard covering the mouthpiece of a phone with a handkerchief altered voices. Discovering Dr. McArdle's name and connection with the hospital would be child's play for a man as dedicated to trickery as Charles Bradley. Was he parked just up the road from her place as he had been that other time, waiting like a vengeful spider for her to fly into his web of deceit?

Fed up with the blond pilot and his ruses, Patti came to a quick decision. The tempo of her heartbeat increased, but she determinedly punched in Scott Sloan's phone number for the very first time. He answered on the third ring.

Her hand felt sweaty on the phone.

"This is Patti. I hope I didn't wake you."

"You didn't."

How could he sound so casual when every nerve in her body twanged?

"I hate to bother you, but I had to check. Are you all right?"

"Of course I'm all right. Why?"

Good grief, does he think I'm some on-his-trail female inventing excuses to call him at home? The thought steadied Patti.

"Someone posing as Dr. McArdle called me from the hospital. He said you had been hurt, and—"

He cut her off. "I'm on my way."

Patti put down the phone and stared at Obsidian.

"Well! He doesn't waste any more words than Ma Hoff." She took off her jacket and went to hang it up. A glimpse of the disheveled nurse in her bedroom mirror made her groan. She changed to clean pants and put the others to soak, then bathed her face and hands before brushing her hair again.

By the time Scott arrived, Patti's singing teakettle performed its merriest tune.

"Sorry I don't have coffee," she apologized. "It always smells so good and tastes so bad. I have boiling water, chocolate and herbal tea."

"Chocolate's fine. I'm not that much into coffee," Scott told her.

Patti sensed his impatience, curbed for the sake of courtesy until she prepared the hot drinks and they sat facing each other across the table in the pine-paneled dining room. Obsidian lay close to her chair.

"The call awakened me. I was really out of it, since it took me a long time last night to get to sleep."

"Why?" Scott barked. His dark gaze demanded the truth, the whole truth, and nothing but the truth; exactly what she couldn't tell him! Patti relaxed when he added, "Has Bradley been up to something? I mean, before now. It sounds like one of his tricks."

"Not that I know of." Patti heaved a secret sigh of relief. She had no intention of telling Stone Face he, not Charles, was the source of her sleeplessness. She rushed on, failing to exercise caution because of her narrow escape. "The bogus Dr. McArdle said you were asking for me. I tossed on clothes, got halfway to the Bronco, and—"

"You rushed out before daylight because I supposedly sent for you?"

"Yes."

The word hung in the air.

Scott drew a shaken breath. Patti risked a look directly into his eyes. The softest light she had ever seen in the dark depths shone like a beacon before he collected himself and gruffly ordered, "Go on."

"I slipped on frosty grass." She ruefully rubbed her sore hip. "The fall and Obsidian brought me to my senses." She repeated the police officer's warning she had remembered and finished by saying, "I came back inside and called the hospital. Dr. McArdle wasn't there. Neither were you."

"Thank God you didn't fall for the hoax." Scott reached across the table and grabbed her hand in his long, supple fingers. "Have you called the police?"

"Not yet. I don't see what they can do about it," Patti reflected.

He glanced at the window.

"It will be light enough soon for them to do some checking. Patti, are you holding anything back?"

She shook her head. "No. I already told the police the way Charles behaved that time he came here and Obsidian acted so unfriendly."

"What time?" Scott's voice cracked like a pistol. "Why didn't you tell me?"

She sat very still. How could she admit Charles's threat had grown out of her reaction to his maligning Scott? A long moment followed while reluctance and honesty fought. Honesty won. Patti chose her words carefully. "Charles didn't want me to fly with you. He talked about you—" She stopped and steadied her voice. "He asked me to let him in so he could tell me the rest of the story. I told him if I wanted to hear it, I'd ask you."

The same light Patti had seen in Scott's eyes when she cried out her faith in him returned. He reached across the table and took her cold hands in his. Patti saw a tiny pulse beating in his temple. She tightened her grip on his strong hands and swayed toward him. To her amazement, the light went out in his eyes. Scott dropped her hands and leaned back.

"Not now, Patti."

She scorched with shame. How could she have allowed herself to betray the newly awakened love that longed for his protecting arms? She had been right. Stone Face cared nothing for her as a woman. His kiss had been nothing more than gratitude for her trust.

She jerked back. The quick movement brought Obsidian's ears up and he whined.

"It's all right," Patti told him. She patted his head and hesitated. Should she open the wound inflicted by Charles Bradley that had been festering inside her? Yes. Exposing it was the only way to start the healing process. "Sorry. You must think me as brazen as the woman Charles mentioned."

Scott's face went deathly white. "Woman?" he asked in a ragged voice.

"He said you came between him and a girl he was trying to protect from nasty gossip," Patti faltered. Why had she ever brought it up?

"And you believed him."

His gaze burned into her like a red-hot branding iron. Patti felt she had been seared to the soul. She closed her eyes, shot up a desperate prayer for guidance, then forced herself to look Scott full in the face.

"Not if you tell me differently."

The glacial ice encasing Stone Face gradually melted and trickled away. Warmth flowed into his face once more.

"Thank you," he quietly said. "Yes, there was a girl. Thank God it's not a bedtime story. Bradley was wild about her. She loved one of the men who died in the crash." He paused. "It didn't matter to Bradley that she cared nothing for him. He hounded her, while pretending to be her fiancé's friend." Scott's steady gaze never left Patti's face. "The same kind of thing he is doing to you."

She shivered and crossed her arms over her chest.

"She came to me, afraid of what her fiancé might do when he learned Bradley was persecuting her. I warned Charles to back off or the girl would bring him up on harassment charges. I had observed enough to testify against him. Bradley retaliated by starting some pretty ugly rumors about us." A faint smile crossed his lips. "Fortunately, people knew me. They also knew Bradley."

Suspicion attacked like the enemy at dawn. Patti leaned forward, Scott's withdrawal from her forgotten. A question hovered on her lips, the way the Bell Jet-Ranger hovered before setting down. Instinct shouted a piece of the puzzle crucial to finding the truth about the tragic plane crash lay in Scott's answer.

Chapter 13

Scott." Patti caught her lower lip between her teeth. "Did you threaten to testify about Charles Bradley's harassment before or after the plane crash?"

"Before." His unreadable expression told her nothing.

"That's it!" She shoved her chair back from the dining room table and stood. "He must have set you up so if it ever came to trial, you'd be discredited."

"I've always believed that but I can't prove it." Scott also rose, dark eyes appealing. "Until I do, and until we can get Charles Bradley and his evil schemes out of our lives, much as I'd like to, we can't move on."

Patti felt blood rush into her face until she felt she might suffocate. He hadn't rejected her!

"Then that's why you. . ." She bit her tongue instead of speaking the rest of the sentence: "didn't respond when I betrayed myself."

"Yes." He reverted from Scott Sloan to Stone Face, except his lips twitched and spoiled the effect. "Now I suggest we notify the police."

The same officers came but had no way to trace the phone call.

"We know where Charles Bradley is staying," they assured Patti when she told them she believed he had impersonated Dr. McArdle. "He has also accepted a temporary job with a charter service, flying hunting and hiking parties into the mountains."

"I hope we never run into him." Scott gave a short laugh. "I'd be tempted to flatten the guy."

"Don't. We've been doing some checking into his past."

"And?" Patti's nerves screamed.

"Let's just say he isn't a pleasant guy when he doesn't get his own way," the second officer warned. "Keep us informed if anything else unusual happens, and don't tangle with Bradley. His smooth, All-American-boy image is only a thin crust over a boiling volcano. We have the feeling it's only a matter of time until he explodes. You don't want to be around if or when it happens."

His counterpart sighed. "It's too bad we can't haul him in, but we don't have proof Bradley has broken any laws so far. Until he does, we're stuck."

A wave of helplessness threatened to swamp Patti. "I understand, but it doesn't make me feel any better."

The officers looked around the comfortable room, then at Obsidian.

"You might consider checking into a motel, although you're probably safe enough here with the dog."

"The Hoffs would be glad to have you at the Running H, but driving in takes too much time if we're on a hurry-up call," Scott reminded. "So does coming to get you in the chopper."

Iron entered Patti's backbone. She set her lips in a stubborn line. "I refuse to be intimidated and driven from my home. Besides, the danger isn't here. It's somewhere out there." She waved toward the window.

The officers warned her to be careful and departed. She and Scott walked to the road and watched the police car stop a short distance from Patti's driveway.

"Looking for tire tracks," she murmured.

To her disappointment, they gave no indication of their findings. When they completed their leisurely examination, they simply nodded to the watching couple and drove away.

"Well, that's that." Scott smiled at Patti. Her heart beat fast at the look in his eyes. "I'm heading home to shower and change." He rubbed one hand over the dark shadow on chin and cheeks. "Shave, too. At least I hope I have time before Mike calls us. See you later."

"See you," she called when he crawled in the Jeep and left. Then, "Come on, Obsidian. I need a bath, too. I hope things stay quiet for a time. A long time."

For a few days, it appeared Patti's wish had been granted. She flew two routine missions with Scott and faithfully reported all remained calm. Charles Bradley had neither turned up nor attempted another fright tactic.

October 30 came, clear and bright. The next day, the colorful month exited in a rainstorm as gray as steam from a fairy-tale witch's cauldron. The short glimpses of blue sky and clearing showed fresh snow on distant peaks.

November 1 dawned with overcast skies. Lowering clouds warned of rain. The chill in the air hinted of possible snow at Kalispell, as well as in the mountains.

Mike Parker's call caught Patti at her easel. True to her vow, she used much of her free time drawing and painting. She could see the improvement in her work with every completed project. Mike's sober voice effectively changed her from would-be artist to competent rescue nurse.

"We need you. There's a small plane down in the mountains. Probably an inexperienced pilot who got caught in a down draft. Or one who had been drinking." He sighed. "No sense wasting time talking about it. Wear warm clothes, boots, and don't forget your sheepskin-lined jacket. You may need it."

Patti put on thermal underwear under her favorite denim outfit and red turtleneck. She donned thick socks, her boots, and caught up her red bandanna, heavy lined gloves, and warm jacket.

"I feel ten pounds heavier," she told Scott at the hangar. She took in his garb similar to her own. "We look like the Bobbsey Twins, except for your black turtleneck and baseball cap."

"Thanks, but I have something in mind other than being your twin," he teased.

The ready-to-fly nurse felt red flags wave in her face. Although Scott couldn't always control the expression in his eyes, he seldom let himself off the leash enough for such a remark. It set butterflies quivering in her rib cage.

The next instant, he became all business.

"We're not sure what we'll find. The radio message was garbled. Thank God it didn't fade out until we learned the location." He glanced at her medical bag. Hard wear and contact with rough ground gave it a worn look. "Do you have everything you need?"

"Yes." She trotted with him to the waiting Bell Jet-Ranger and climbed inside. She noticed Scott's furtive glance at the horizon. "Is it going to storm?"

"Probably. Don't worry. If all goes well, we'll get to the downed plane, collect pilot and passengers, and be back before it amounts to anything. Piece of cake." He sent her a reassuring smile and lifted off.

They had no trouble finding the downed plane. A little over an hour later, they discovered the small charter plane sprawled like a broken toy near the bottom of a wide canyon. A stream tumbled by a few yards from the wreckage. Patti marveled again at the expert way Scott found and landed on a spot of level ground she hadn't believed large enough to hold them.

He slipped from his harness.

"Let's get them and get out of here."

Patti followed his gaze to the threatening sky. It looked worse than when they had left Kalispell. She grabbed her medical bag and headed for the wrecked plane.

One look at the scene before her exploded Scott's piece-of-cake theory. Four men in various states of shock and injury had managed to crawl a little distance from the wreckage. Four men plus Patti and Scott equaled six. The Bell Jet-Ranger only held five.

"We'll have to double up, somehow cram four into the back," she whispered to herself. A hasty examination of the first crash victim crumbled her hope. His terribly twisted knee required an inflatable cast to immobilize it for the flight back. Patti tried to ignore the all-gone feeling that settled in her stomach. She checked the other two passengers and sighed with relief. They showed signs of shock, but had sustained no serious injuries.

An exclamation from Scott sent her hurrying to the pilot, doubled over in the grotesque position on the ground where he had evidently fallen when he crawled from the plane. Semi-conscious, his breathing tainted the wintry mountain air with the smell of liquor. Blood stained his face, oozing from a cut on one cheek.

Patti's heart leap-frogged to her throat. "Charles?"

"Yes." Scott moved aside to allow Patti better access. "How is he?"

"Stunned." She ran expert hands over the injured man's limbs. "No sign of broken bones. You need to get him and the others to a hospital right away."

Patti set her lips. "I have to put an inflatable cast on one man's leg. It's not going to be easy to get all of them into the chopper."

Scott didn't pretend to misunderstand her use of the word "them." His face twisted and he suddenly looked old.

"If only you could fly the bird! You can't." Color drained from his cheeks until they resembled dirty snow. "Patti, our first duty and loyalty is to those we serve."

"I know." She fought fear of what lay ahead and forced herself to raise her chin. "The sooner you leave, the quicker you'll be back." She resolutely ignored the darkening sky and managed a strangled laugh. "I always wondered whether I'd get any use out of the survival pack. I guess this is when I find out."

"I'll put up the tent and start a fire while you do first aid," he told her.

What felt like an eternity later, but was actually an incredibly short period of time, Scott led Patti into the assembled tent away from possible curious stares.

"It tears me apart to leave," he whispered. "I promise before God to come back for you. Three hours should do it." He pointed to a pile of wood he'd stacked inside the tent. "It's damp from yesterday's downpour, so keep piling it on the fire I built. The heat will dry it enough to burn. Except when you're feeding the fire, stay in the tent. Use the space blankets if you can't keep warm enough from the fire. There's food if you get hungry." He paused. "Here's something to think about until I come back." He gathered her into his strong arms, tilted her chin, and kissed her.

Patti felt the same feeling of all-rightness she had before. Only this time Scott did not pull away so soon. She sensed his reluctance to release her even when he raised his head and said, "Ironic, isn't it? Of all the pilots flying in Montana, it would be Bradley. Maybe God is trying to tell us something."

Patti thought of his words long after the whir of the chopper echoed from mountain to canyon and died. Did things really just happen? What were the odds against Scott and her being sent to rescue Charles Bradley? The call for help could easily have gone elsewhere. Even if it came to Mike Parker, he had other pilot/nurse teams. Was Scott right? Did God have a lesson in all this?

"If you do, I sure don't know what it is, Lord." Patti hastily added more branches to the fire. With Scott's departure, it had turned sullen and smoldered instead of burning brightly. She waited to make sure it continued burning and went back into the tent.

"At least Scott won't have any trouble finding me again." Patti giggled. It sounded loud in the silence, but she felt better. "Here I sit like the wife in Peter Pumpkin Eater's pumpkin shell."

She checked her watch. Her eyes widened in disbelief. Had it stopped? Surely more than fifteen minutes had passed since Scott tucked her in the pumpkin orange tent and flew away! Patti held the watch to her ear. Its rhythmic ticking faithfully counted off the seconds. Each felt like an hour.

"Lord, how am I going to stand being alone in the mountains for nearly three more hours?"

She began to repeat favorite Scriptures, ending with "God is our refuge and strength, a very present help in trouble." Of course! Hadn't God created the very mountains in which He permitted her to be left behind? He must have had a reason. Her part was to simply trust him and wait for Scott.

An hour limped by. Wisps of fog united and wove a gray flannel blanket Patti's keen vision found hard to penetrate. Fear turned her mouth metallic. Her prayers for Scott's return changed to a frantic plea he wouldn't attempt to come back until the weather lifted.

"He knows I'm all right, Lord," she prayed. Yet memory of Scott saying "I promise before God to come back for you" robbed her of even that comfort.

A second hour passed. The murk danced and swirled with occasional breaks. Patti faithfully fed the sulky fire. What would she do when the wood ran out? It would surely do so if Scott were delayed or she had to stay over-night. Was the utility knife in the survival pack strong enough for her to cut more? Could she find downed branches and brush? She forced herself to leave the security of her makeshift camp. Triumph sprang to her eyes when she found storm-broken trees. A great pile of branches lay at the foot of a stark, lightning-scarred snag. Her heavily gloved hands tore at them. She gathered an enormous pile, encircled it with her arms, and staggered back to her haven. Load after load she carried, until the treacherous fog threatened to lure her into losing her direction if she strayed farther.

Patti tingled with the exercise and discovered she was ravenous. Trips to the bubbling stream nearby resulted in a goodly supply of water. She longed to throw herself down on the bank of the stream and drink her fill, but re-membered the need to purify it before drinking. She used a water purifica-tion tablet according to directions in the survival manual, then prepared a cup of hot tea. Never had anything tasted better than it and the tropical chocolate bar she wolfed down. That and the tea would be her lunch. She must hoard her provisions against the possibility fog kept Scott from mak-ing it back. Lonesome, more frightened for Scott than herself, Patti repeated every comforting Scripture she could remember. It was her only shield against terror until the pilot she loved safely returned.

※

Scott Sloan gritted his teeth. Never had a trip to home base flown on such leaden wings. At first, the three injured plane passengers said little. Charles Bradley more than made up for it. He had regained consciousness enough to recognize Scott for a moment, but not enough to differentiate between the recent plane crash and the one long ago. He babbled about getting re-venge by failing to file a flight plan and swearing Sloan had been at the con-trols instead of him.

Although the day had darkened even more, Scott felt the sun rise in his soul. He hadn't been responsible for the death of those two men. *Thank God!*

The youngest-looking passenger caught part of Charles's mumbling. "This jerk didn't file a plan? What is he, crazy? If we hadn't sent a message before the radio conked out, we'd still be back there with a downed plane!"

"He's talking about another flight," Scott explained. "Remember what he says, will you? I took the heat for him failing to follow orders."

"I'll remember all right," the man grimly said. "Bradley's going to lose his pilot's license over this. None of us realized he'd been drinking until he took off. We insisted he turn back. He refused. Said one drink made him more alert. It's a wonder we didn't all die in the crash."

"What exactly happened?" Scott wanted to know. "Did a down draft pull you into the canyon?"

"Are you kidding?" The passenger sounded incredulous. "Bradley's judgment must have been impaired by booze. He veered right. The wing evidently hit the rock wall. Next thing I knew, we were going down." He soberly added, "Hard to believe any of us are alive. Lucky, I guess, or someone watching out for us."

"You'd better believe it," Scott agreed.

"Leaving the nurse behind was rotten," the man observed. "We should have left Bradley, but she wouldn't stand for it. Or for any of us staying. I volunteered. What a woman! Is she married?"

"No, but she's going to be." Scott couldn't keep a broad grin from stretching across his face. "To me." *I hope,* he mentally added.

"Some guys have all the luck! Say, are you going to be able to go back for her? It's getting pretty ugly out there."

"I'm going." Scott folded his lips shut and concentrated on his flying. The talkative passenger took the silent hint and subsided.

An hour later, Scott and Mike Parker watched the ambulance take the crash victims away.

"Thank God they aren't all dead," Mike fervently breathed. Scott had filled him in while unloading his passengers. He squinted at the blackening sky. "Maybe you'd better hold off and see if this stuff lifts."

"Not on your life. Patti's waiting. I vowed before God to come for her."

"She'll wait a lot longer if you don't make it," Mike retorted. He folded his arms across his paunch. "I can order you not to go, for your own good. I won't."

His pudgy hand shot out and gripped Scott's with surprising strength. "I knew Patti Thompson would be like this."

Scott squeezed Mike's hand until the other man winced, then climbed back into the Bell Jet-Ranger and began the most important mercy mission of his life.

Weather worsened and snarled warnings to the unwary on that endless flight. "Turn back. Turn back." Scott ignored the voice and flew on. Patches of fog appeared. A light wind followed, tossing the fog into writhing, snakelike banners. When he entered the canyon a few miles from his destination, the fog thickened into gray globs, decreasing visibility. Scott peered between them, gauging distance. He had to set down where he had before.

A vivid thrust of red he recognized as an aerial flare cut through the fog and brought an approving grunt. Patti must have heard the chopper and set off the flare.

"Smart girl. Okay, Sloan. Time to take this bird down." A fog patch moved, making a hole in the murk. Scott loosened his shoulder harness, leaned forward to see better, and began his descent. He wouldn't make the same spot, but could hover and see exactly where he was.

A heartbeat later, the stark, lightning-scarred snag where Patti had gathered fuel for her fire appeared in the gloom. The capricious wind chose the worst moment possible to show its power. It picked up, gusted, and blew the Bell Jet-Ranger straight toward the snag. The main rotor blade hit the dead tree with a resounding smack. The impact flipped the chopper on its side.

Scott's loosened shoulder harness couldn't restrain him enough to keep him from pitching forward when the blade slammed into the snag. His head made contact with something hard, leaving him dazed, unable to think clearly.

A short time earlier, Patti Thompson had roused from her study of the survival manual. She hadn't realized how tense she'd been until her muscles and nerves began to unknot at the distant sound of a chopper. Yet fear did not retreat. The wavering fog spelled danger. Patti grabbed a red aerial flare and ran outside. Long experience with the helicopter's deafening "clackety-clack" told her the best moment to set off the flare. Its welcome glow when it shot skyward calmed her.

Patti caught a glimpse of the familiar white chopper through the fog. She longed to race toward it but knew better. Until it settled down like a broody hen over her chicks, people on the ground needed to keep a safe distance. Down, down—Patti gasped in horror when the descending chopper swayed in the wind. Her cry of protest mingled with the heart-stopping sound of the rotor blade striking the snag. The next instant, the chopper flipped on its side.

"No, God!" Patti screamed. She rushed forward. The smell of leaking fuel sent a fresh wave of terror through her. *Would the chopper catch fire? Explode?* The gruesome thought lent the strength she needed to wrench open the helicopter door, help Scott out, and yell, "We have to get away from the chopper." Inch by inch, foot by foot, she led him past the fire she had faithfully kept going and into the tent.

"I have to check you over. Standard operating procedure," she ordered.

It brought a grin. "I'm okay except for this." He touched his forehead.

"I'll decide that." She peered into his eyes. "Good. No signs of concussion. Did you lose consciousness at all?"

"No." He caught her hands. "Thanks for hauling me out. I was pretty dazed."

A crackling sound caught Patti's attention. She freed one hand and pointed through the open tent flap at the helicopter. Tongues of flame grew higher every minute.

"I was afraid it would explode before I could get you out."

Scott shook his head. "Choppers are powered by jet kerosene. A fuel line breaks and puts gas on the hot engine. Fire starts in the back part of the fuselage, just behind the back seat." A worry line made an inverted V between his dark eyebrows. "We're in a spot," he told her. "We have no radio contact. Our ELT—Emergency Locator Transmitter—would have sent a signal the chopper has crashed, but we can't expect help as long as the fog holds."

Dread of what lay ahead caught Patti's throat in a death grip. Yet when she looked into Scott's shadowed face, she felt a renewal of courage.

"We're alive and together, aren't we? Nothing else matters." The expression in his eyes before he opened his arms and she flew into them echoed her words.

Chapter 14

I need to level with you," Scott told Patti after a meager meal of hot soup and granola bars. "You aren't a child. You have the right to know what we're up against. Normally, staying put is the best thing for crash survivors. We may not have that option. It all depends on the weather." A muscle twitched in Scott's cheek and he looked deep into her blue eyes. "You once said you would trust me with your life. Does it still hold?"

Patti answered the pleading in his voice rather than the question. "Yes."

A dark red tide swept into the pilot's strained face. "That's all I need to know. Actually, there is one thing more." He paused and measured her with his dark gaze. He grinned and asked, "Are you a romantic?"

She blinked at the sudden change of subject. "A romantic?"

Sparkles danced in his eyes. "Is there an echo in here? You know what I mean. Are you the kind of girl who dreams of receiving marriage proposals in a rose garden, or while watching a spectacular sunset?"

Unable to believe her own ears, Patti eyed him suspiciously. She tried to control the red tide she felt sweep up from the collar of her sheepskin-lined jacket. She put her hands on her hips.

"Why do you care, especially now?"

Scott's grin faded. He sounded strangely humble when he said in a low voice, "I just wondered how you'd feel about a guy who loves you so much he would propose in an orange survival tent."

He briefed her on Charles's semi-conscious ramblings and closed by saying, "I'm finally free from guilt and ready to move on. I want you to know you're the only woman in the world for me, just in case."

His last foreboding words couldn't drown the happiness Patti's heart radiated to every part of her body.

"Pumpkin shell," she muttered.

"What?!" Scott gaped as if she had gone stark, staring mad.

Patti felt like a fool. How could she have answered him that way?

"I—I'm sorry. It's just that when you left I kept thinking of the nursery rhyme about Peter who put his wife in a pumpkin shell and 'kept her very well.' " She put one hand to her burning face and fervently wished he'd do something other than stand there looking like the Stone Face she first met!

A full minute passed before laughter spilled from Scott like a waterfall cascading over a rocky cliff to the bottom of a ravine.

"Never in *my* wildest dreams did I suspect the girl I'm asking to share my life would answer like this!" he said when he caught his breath enough to speak. "I can't promise you a pumpkin shell. Just a pretty good pilot who loves you second only to God. Will you, Patricia, take this man. . ."

"I will," she whispered. Patti wrapped her arms around Scott and raised her face for his kiss. Someday after they fought the elements and won, she would repeat that promise in the presence of family and friends. Yet Patti's heart pumped with secret knowledge. White lace and wedding vows could never be more precious or binding than the pledge made in a pumpkin shell tent with only God and a worsening storm as witnesses. It accepted all the rest: better and worse; richer and poorer; sickness and health; as long as they both should live.

"I'm sorry I don't have a ring for you," Scott told her when he finally released her and stepped back. "We'll take care of it first thing when we get back."

Patti's glow of happiness dimmed. Contrary to the old cliché, people did not live on love, especially in the treacherous Big Sky Country with winter lurking around the corners of the tent.

"If the weather forces us to leave, where can we go?" she asked. "Thank God you know this country better than I."

Scott nodded. "There's a ramshackle cabin about ten miles from here. I've flown over it. We follow the stream up the canyon until we can find a good place to climb out. It's beyond me why anyone would build his perch partway up a canyon wall instead of closer to water. Afraid of flooding, maybe. Anyway, we won't have trouble finding it. We also have the survival pack compass."

"How will the rescue chopper know where to find us?"

Scott grinned, tore a blank sheet from the back of the survival manual, and wrote in large letters: GONE TO CHARLEY'S FOLLY.

"I'll post it on the remains of the Bell Jet-Ranger. Mike or any pilot he sends will know exactly where to find us. All of us who fly this region make it a point to know where we can find shelter in case we need it."

"Why is the shack called Charley's Folly?" Patti wanted to know.

"It happened before I came to Kalispell, but according to the story, a crazy old coot named Charley built the shack. Said he was going to find gold. Charley claimed to be over a hundred years old, and looked it! Folks only saw him when he stumbled into nearby towns for staples: salt, flour, sugar, coffee. Otherwise, he pretty much lived off the land." Scott smiled. "Game wardens left him alone. They weren't as careful in those days. Besides, just getting to his place meant a long, hard trek."

"What a strange story. Like something from the Old West," Patti burst out.

Scott lowered his voice to a mysterious whisper. "You haven't heard the beginning of strange! All of a sudden, Charley stopped coming in for grub."

Patti clasped her hands together and leaned forward.

"Did he die?"

"No one knows. He simply vanished. Disappeared. Vamoosed." Patti could tell Scott was enjoying her full attention. He continued, "A couple of smart guys from Kalispell figured Charley might have found gold; maybe hid it in his cabin and then fell over a cliff. Or died of old age somewhere out in the woods. They searched the place. Everything looked like the owner had just up and walked away. Dishes on the table. Clothing on hooks. An open Bible with pages falling apart next to a rickety cot. The get-rich-quick guys called the place Charley's Folly. The name stuck."

"It's sad to think the man died alone in the wilderness," Patti murmured.

"Why?" Scott sounded genuinely surprised. "That's how he lived. What more fitting place for him to die?" His gaze softened. "The Bible by the cot shows Charley wasn't as crazy as folks thought. It had seen a lot of hard use to be in the condition the men found it. They left it where it was. It may be there yet."

"I hope so." The thought of a Bible, worn and aged as it might be, offered one bright spot of welcome to what Patti knew must surely be a hovel.

"Enough stories," Scott told her. "Try and get some sleep."

"I've never been more wide awake," she protested.

He dropped a kiss on her forehead. "Obey the pilot in command. He's going to replenish the fire. Good thing you dragged in all those tree limbs for fuel." He reached for an armful and hauled them to the fire.

To Patti's utter amazement, she fell asleep before he returned. She roused twice in the night, saw Scott's comforting dark bulk, and went back to sleep. She awoke to a demanding hand on her shoulder and a white-shrouded world.

"Wake up, Patti. We have to get out of here. Now, while we still can."

The urgency in his voice chased away tatters of sleep. Stiff and sore from her unaccustomed bed, she stretched and rubbed kinks from her arms and legs. She tried to lighten the tension emanating from Scott.

"What? No breakfast in bed?"

He didn't take time to respond to her sally. "It snowed three inches last night. If the sky's any indication, we're in for more. I only pray it will hold off until we reach Charley's Folly." He handed her a cup of hot, sweetened tea and half of a chocolate bar. "Sorry, but we need to hoard our rations."

"It's all right. Thanks." The tea warmed Patti's stomach. She stepped from the tent. Snow had mercifully shrouded part of the Bell Jet-Ranger's remains. After one quick glance, Patti avoided looking in its direction. So many happy, serving hours and memories were connected with the chopper!

Stop standing here like a ninny and get busy, she sharply ordered herself. *The last thing Scott needs on this expedition is a helpless female moping around and shedding tears over a downed helicopter.*

Scott expertly repacked the survival pack. He made no attempt to include the wet tent, but folded it into a compact package. Patti admired the way his deft hands cleverly roped pack, tent, filled water container, and the two canteens together in a yoke-like arrangement he could carry on his back.

"Can you manage your medical bag?" he asked.

"Yes. It's like an extension of my arm." Patti wiggled her fingers more firmly into her gloves, adjusted her bandanna, and picked up the lifesaving medical bag. Its familiar weight comforted her. At least she and Scott were well equipped.

Before they started out, they joined hands. Scott's prayer was simple, terse. "Lord, we need Your help. Guide us to Charley's Folly and help us overcome obstacles on the way. We thank and praise You in Jesus' name, amen."

"Amen," Patti whispered. She refused to allow herself to conjure up those obstacles Scott knew lay ahead but kept to himself.

They found the going fairly easy for the first mile. After that, it became a nightmare. Gully-washers since Scott flew over the area had changed the course of the stream, leaving debris and boulders to surmount. At first, Patti clambered over them as nimbly as the mountain goat that surveyed her on her very first rescue mission. Yet each succeeding barrier drained her of a little more energy. She laughed to hide the growling of a stomach in need of food. Oh, for a plate of those crunchy brown ribs Scott had brought to her log cabin!

"Concentrate on something else," she muttered, making sure he didn't hear her. "Wishing for the moon—or crunchy ribs—won't get us to Charley's Folly any sooner." Patti grinned to herself. Thinking about food had one advantage: It made her mouth water and relieved its dryness.

Minutes struggled into an hour. Then two. Then three. If they had been on flat ground, the travelers would have already reached their destination. The waiting snow allowed them no leeway, no time extension. A few lazy flakes warned them to take cover. There was none.

They plodded ahead. Patti felt as if she had been ascending and descending log jams and piles of boulders forever. A slight bend in the trail brought the hikers right up against the highest jam yet. Mustering strength, Patti painstakingly followed Scott over it, only to find the space between stream and canyon wall had narrowed to less than two feet! A little farther, it dwindled even more. When its width became less than eight inches, Scott called a halt.

"It's not the best place to climb, but we don't have a choice." He pointed to a structure above them and a little to the left. A steep and tipsy trail zigzagged up to it from the stream. Patti strained to see through the increasing snowflakes.

Scott laid down his burdens and untied the rope from his hastily assembled carrying contraption. He rooted matches from the survival pack and stuffed them in his jacket pocket.

"The trail is steep and may be slippery from the snow." He sounded as casual as though reciting a poem. "We won't take any chances." He tied the rope around her waist, then his own. "Leave the medical bag here. I'll come back for it and the other stuff. Keep the rope slack, in case I slip. If you start to fall, dig in fingers, toes, and hang on. I won't let you drop."

Patti couldn't have held back her giggle if her life depended on it.

"All this and a course in mountain climbing, too," she told him.

Scott flashed her an appreciative grin. "All this and the Charley's Folly Hilton waiting on top. May I show Madame Thompson to her room?"

Laughter released a fresh thrust of energy. Patti started up the crooked trail, leaving the rope slack between them as ordered. Once her boot hit a concealed patch of ice and she lost her footing. The rope tightened. She dug fingers and toes into the earth. Scott held her steady and a moment later, she scrambled forward.

They successfully navigated the final turns in the crazily tilted path. Patti stopped to catch her breath and gazed at her temporary home away from home.

Scott grinned. "We won't spend our honeymoon here, but it's shelter."

"Barely." Patti looked at the precariously perched hut that looked as if it had started out as a log cabin a century or two before. Various and sundry nailed-on pieces of wood patched it. Rough boards over frayed canvas outlined window openings. She giggled. "It resembles a crazy quilt my great-grandmother made. Why hasn't it blown away?"

Scott examined the structure more closely. "No danger of that. Charley built his Folly to withstand Montana blizzards and northers. Care to step inside?"

"Not really." She laughed again, this time to cover the quaver in her voice. Entering this squalid shack wouldn't be easy. "You go first. A critter or two may be occupying the bridal suite."

Scott gave two hard jerks and opened the creaking, weather-swollen door. He lit a match and grunted.

"Good. There are a few ancient candle stubs." He lighted one and made a face at Patti, who hesitated in the open doorway. "Whew! It's musty in here. I'd say we need to do some housecleaning."

She forced herself to step inside and look around. Housecleaning? Where should they start? With the dusty, web-covered ceiling and walls? The rickety looking sheet-iron stove, leaning table and two tipsy chairs? The floor, inches deep with dirt? The falling-down cot, whose filthy blankets partially covered boughs that had long since lost their needles? Charley's Bible still lay by the cot.

Don't let Scott know how appalled you are. He has enough to worry about without your failing to be a good sport. So God didn't provide a Hilton. As Scott said, it's shelter.

Patti squared her slim shoulders. Her chin raised. She forced snap into her voice and a sparkle into her eyes.

"Well! The sooner we start, the sooner we'll be through." She firmly squashed the sardonic little whisper in her heart, *"Oh, yeah?"*

"Fire first." Scott examined the stove, shook the stovepipe to make sure it hadn't rusted into a falling-down state, and grunted again. "Thank God it's serviceable."

A quick search of the cabin disclosed a crumpled newspaper. Scott crumpled it, stopped long enough to kiss Patti's upturned nose, and went back outside. Before despair over the condition of Charley's Folly had time to clutch her again, Scott returned, carrying an armload of bark-covered tree limbs. He stripped off the bark, placed it on the paper, lighted and blew it into a small flame. Patience and the addition of small, then larger branches resulted in enough heat so Patti could shrug out of her jacket.

She found a decrepit broom, gritted her teeth, and began brushing cobwebs and spider webs from the ceiling and walls.

"Spiders, start packin'. This place ain't big enough for both of us, and I ain't leavin'," she announced in a passable imitation of John Wayne's drawl. She was delighted at Scott's hearty laugh. Her spirits rose a notch. This interlude in an isolated mountain cabin would be something to tell their children and grandchildren. Patti pounced on an aged water bucket, then a large shallow pan perfect for heating water. She felt she had struck gold.

"If you'll bring me some water, I can heat it and start scrubbing this place while you bring in more wood," she suggested.

"Right. You're the best sport in the world, Patti," he praised.

She caught the admiration in his face and bit her tongue. Even though she didn't deserve his approval, telling him otherwise wouldn't help their situation. She peered out the narrow crack where Scott had left the door open to air out the place. "Maybe I should come with you. It's starting to snow harder."

"I'll be better off without you."

"Thanks a lot," Patti retorted, although she knew he was right. "Run along then, water boy. You're holding up progress." Again his laughter raised her spirits. It also gave her a foretaste of the strength Scott would show throughout their life together. Anyone who could laugh while stranded miles from civilization would certainly wear well. Patti whispered a little prayer to be worthy of his love and went back to her cleaning.

By nightfall, the inside of Charley's Folly had been relieved of as many layers of grime as they could manage. After a meager meal, Patti and Scott gratefully seated themselves on the chairs, taking care not to make any sudden moves. She rubbed her aching back and looked around in satisfaction. The Folly even smelled clean. She and Scott had disposed of grimy blankets and dead boughs. Repeated sweepings, then mopping with stream water heated on the iron stove, had cleansed the floor enough so Scott could sleep there. Best of all, no spider could possibly have withstood the cleaning onslaught.

"Still a far cry from a Hilton," she said. "But a whole lot better than before."

"You're a pioneer in denim," Scott teased. The love in his dark eyes warmed Patti. Nothing in his lean face warranted the nickname Stone Face now.

"Pioneer in Denim would make a good book title," Patti mused. Her eyes half closed, then popped open. Her fingers itched for pencil or brush. "Scott, I want to paint pictures of this place when I get back. I'll call them 'Before and After.' "

He squeezed her hand, then dropped it. "I've seen some of your work, Patti. You can do it. If not now, later." He abruptly broke off.

Patti felt his spirit had retreated to a place where she could not follow. Surely he didn't regret telling her he cared! Yet what else would darken his eyes and bring the old brooding look back?

"What is it?" she whispered.

"I'm trying to figure out the right way to deal with Charles Bradley."

She straightened. The prehistoric chair creaked a warning and she gingerly sagged back against it.

"Do? Force him to admit the truth, of course. Isn't it what you've waited for all these years?" Patti's indignant words tumbled into the room like kittens at play chasing one another.

"Yes." He stared at his clenched hands, then looked at her beseechingly. "When I heard Bradley mumbling, I could barely wait to use his confession to set the record straight. I asked the passenger who overheard to remember, so he could be my witness. Yet ever since the crash, it doesn't seem important. I keep thinking how Jesus preached forgiveness and practiced it even on the cross."

Scott's troubled gaze never left Patti's face.

"Charles Bradley is washed up as a pilot. Why kick him when he's down? Rehashing the past will also bring everything back to the families of the men who died. It just isn't worth it."

Patti took his strong hands in her smaller ones, rough from scrubbing.

"If I hadn't already loved you more than anything in this world except God, I'd fall in love with you now," she fiercely told him. "Scott Sloan, I'm so proud of you I could cry, but I won't!" She blinked back the flood just behind her eyes.

"Do you really mean it?" Scott whispered. He stood and put his arms around her. "What about the way Bradley treated you? Are you sure you won't always secretly feel I let you down by not retaliating?"

Patti buried her face against his chest and shook her head. "I will always feel you did what Jesus would do," she whispered. She felt the tempo of his steady heartbeat quicken. Her own unpleasantness with Charles seemed long ago and far away, as if it had happened to a totally different person. Perhaps it had. The last two days' ordeal had irrevocably changed both Scott and her. Because of God's great mercy, turning the other cheek had become a privilege, not a chore.

◆━◆━◆

A day of light snow followed that adventurous day, then another day of fog. Food supplies ran low.

"Why couldn't we have ended up in this predicament when there were berries for food?" Patti privately asked God. "Our rations won't carry us much longer. We need Your help, Lord." She knew Scott felt the same by his set expression. He had tried to catch a fish, but the venture proved unsuccessful.

Late in the afternoon of the third day at the Charley's Folly Hilton, Scott hiked down to the stream for fresh water. Patti watched him fill the canteens and sling them over his shoulders. He filled the bucket and started back. Two-thirds of the way up the trail, he stumbled over a hidden rock and knocked it loose. The snow-softened earth loosened and moved beneath his boots.

"Look out!" Patti screamed. She raced down the upper part of the trail, heedless of her own safety.

"*Go back!*" Scott yelled. The bucket of water went flying. The canteens jounced against his body. A mighty leap forward landed him on solid ground. He grabbed Patti's arm and raced with her to safety. A horrid rumbling sounded.

They whipped around. The place where Scott had stood moments before no longer existed. A ragged break in the earth a few feet below them marked where the trail had been before Scott inadvertently triggered the avalanche.

Patti clung to his arm. "You could be down there!" she choked.

"I'm not, but the water is." He shut his lips tightly.

Patti sensed he regretted pointing out the obvious.

"We can always melt and purify snow," she reminded. "Besides, it's starting to clear." She pointed west.

"So it is." He relaxed. "If it stays like this, help will come tomorrow."

Patti rejoiced and followed him back to the shack. When they got inside Scott said, "When the chopper arrives, you're going to have another new experience."

"Is that a promise or a threat?" she asked, hoping to make him smile.

He didn't respond to her teasing. "A little of both. There's no place up

475

here by the shack for a chopper to set down. We can't climb back down to the crash site. After what happened today, no way are we climbing on up to the top of the canyon. That means we'll have to be airlifted out of here."

Patti felt as if the wind had been knocked from her. "You mean like on TV?"

"Exactly." A teasing expression came into his face. "I'll stay on the ground and catch you if you fall."

Bang! Patti's attempts to be a good sport popped like a taught balloon. "That isn't funny, Scott."

"I'm sorry. It was a fool thing to say. You'll be perfectly safe." He wrapped his arms around her and held her until most of her fear evaporated. Scott would never lie to her. If he said being airlifted from the ground to a helicopter was safe, she had no need to worry.

The next morning, Patti licked dry lips and tried to smile while Scott got her into the harness that had been lowered from the Bell Jet-Ranger. Mike Parker was at the controls. Patti realized he must have checked out their situation, for he hovered a safe distance above them while a second man worked the airlift. Patti followed Scott's advice, "Don't look down if it bothers you," until he called, "Take her up." She felt herself lifted from the ground. Heart in throat, she risked a quick glance then concentrated on being drawn up and up, and into the chopper.

"Fancy meeting you here," she managed to get out between her clenched teeth.

Both pilots roared at her inane remark. "Now for Stone Face," Mike said. Down went the harness. Up came Scott, carrying her medical bag and the badly depleted survival pack. No use in leaving its contents. The avalanche had made access to Charley's Folly next to impossible.

"Thanks for rescuing me and my fiancée," he said easily. His broad grin set Patti's pulses racing.

"About time," Mike Parker chortled. "Let's go home. There's a couple of surprises waiting for you in Kalispell. Want to hear them now or later?"

"Later," Scott replied. "We've had enough surprises."

"Okay. Just remember. I tried to warn you." Mike chuckled.

Patti wondered what he meant by the cryptic remark. She was too tired to care. Out of danger, all she wanted to do was sleep and. . .

"You don't happen to have a steak up your sleeve, do you?" she mumbled.

"No, but we brought sandwiches and hot soup." The copilot passed them back. Patti hadn't known ham and cheese on sourdough bread could taste so good. By the time she finished eating, Charley's Folly, even the helicopter crash, seemed a lifetime ago. She fell asleep with her head on Scott's shoulder.

"Reporters. Great. Just what we don't need."

Scott's disgusted comment awakened Patti. Mike had set the helicopter down at the flying field. Camera crews and reporters raced across the tarmac.

"Hey, Sloan, how does it feel to be a hero?" one shrilled. Other questions followed.

Mike Parker leaped from the chopper. His bellow cut off the babble. "Pilot and nurse are fine, but it's been rough out there. Go ahead and take your pictures, but I'll do the talking. Otherwise, I'll have you thrown in the hoosegow for trespassing on private property." His grin didn't hide that he meant it.

<hr />

Patti didn't learn what had happened in her absence until the next day. The Hoffs returned Obsidian from the Running H. They had taken him home with them the first night Patti spent on the mountain.

"Land sakes, but we were worried," Ma confessed. "Then the paper came out and—"

"The paper?" Patti's brain still felt tired after hours and hours of sleep.

"Yes." Satisfaction oozed from her voice. "I cut out the story."

Patti stared at the headlines.

PILOT SCOTT SLOAN CLEARED OF OLD CHARGES
AFTER RESCUING INJURED PLANE CRASH SURVIVORS.

The well-written story played up the bizarre twist to the rescue of Charles Bradley and his three passengers. Evidently the youngest passenger had wasted no time in exposing Charles's inexcusable conduct in flying after drinking, along with the facts that came out on the helicopter flight back to Kalispell.

That evening, Scott, Patti, and Obsidian sat in front of a blazing fire— a family, soon to be together forever with God as head of the household.

"The Lord was in control all the time I agonized about Charles," Scott said.

"It doesn't lessen the worth of your decision," Patti reminded him. "You had no way of knowing what God had planned for the future."

"I know." Scott's fingers strayed to his shirt pocket. He slowly took out a sealed envelope. "Neither did Dan Davis, but he gave this to Mike Parker shortly after you brought him home from Seattle, with specific orders about delivery."

Patti stared at her and Scott's scrawled names, followed by the words: "To be opened together."

"I don't understand."

"I don't either, Darling. Open it."

Why should her fingers tremble? Had Dan changed his mind at the last minute and made a will in favor of Scott? Was her inheritance to be snatched away? Patti hated herself for the selfish thought. Scott's or hers, it didn't matter.

She spread out the single page and read it aloud.

If you receive this letter, it means God has seen fit to grant an old man's wish. Patti, you're the daughter I never had. Only one man I know is good enough for you: Scott Sloan. That's part of the reason I'm leaving you my property. If you're here for a time, perhaps you will learn to know and love my friend Scott. If not, you'll never be troubled by an old man's foolishness. God bless and keep you, second Sarah.

Patti's heart overflowed. She slipped into her beloved's arms and silently thanked God for His love and Scott's: warm, lasting, and radiant enough to surpass even the orange and scarlet reflection of glowing promises dancing on the hearth of her log cabin home.

A Letter to Our Readers

Dear Readers:

In order that we might better contribute to your reading enjoyment, we would appreciate you taking a few minutes to respond to the following questions. When completed, please return to the following: Fiction Editor, Barbour Publishing, Inc., P.O. Box 719, Uhrichsville, OH 44683.

1. Did you enjoy reading *Seattle?*
   □ Very much. I would like to see more books like this.
   □ Moderately. I would have enjoyed it more if _____
   _____
   _____

2. What influenced your decision to purchase this book?
   (Check those that apply.)
   □ Cover   □ Back cover copy   □ Title   □ Price
   □ Friends   □ Publicity   □ Other

3. Which story was your favorite?
   □ *Lamp in Darkness*   □ *A Kindled Spark*
   □ *Flickering Flames*   □ *Hearth of Fire*

4. Please check your age range:
   □ Under 18   □ 18–24   □ 25–34
   □ 35–45   □ 46–55   □ Over 55

5. How many hours per week do you read? _____

Name _____

Occupation _____

Address _____

City _____ State _____ Zip _____